MW01254083

Quests of Doom

Authors: Casey W. Christofferson, J. Collura, Michael Curtis, Matt Finch, Scott Greene, Ed Greenwood, Clark Peterson, James M. Ward, Bill Webb, Skip Williams, Steven Winter
Developer: Greg A. Vaughan, Bill Webb
Editors: Jeff Harkness, Erica Balsley, Skeeter Green, Greg A. Vaughan
Layout ,Typesetting, Cover Design: Charles A. Wright

Cover Art: Rowena Aitken
Cartography: Robert Altbauer, Ed Bourelle, Conan Venus
Interior Art: Chris McFann, Andrew DeFlice, Brian LeBlanc

FROG GOD GAMES IS

CEO
Bill Webb

Creative Director: Swords & Wizardry
Matthew J. Finch

Creative Director: Pathfinder
Greg A. Vaughan

Art Director
Charles A. Wright

Mr. Wolf
Skeeter Green

Shadow Frog
James Redmon

FROG GOD GAMES

Table of Contents

Bugs & Blobs

The Noble Rot

By J. Collura

Introduction

The Noble Rot is a location-based adventure for 4–6 characters of levels 5–8. This adventure may be played in one or two sessions of reasonable length. It is a straightforward haunted house style adventure that is ready for exploration and adventure.

The adventure revolves around Le Chateau Gluant, a vineyard and winery of repute. Vintages of its famous white (chardonnay) and red blend (cabernet sauvignon) are sought throughout the land and beyond. Some vintages can cost up to 200 gp per bottle. A case (12 bottles) of the wine in pristine condition can fetch up to 1,500 gp. Unfortunately, the winery fell upon dark days and the wine has not flowed from its prized cellars for a few years.

Approximately five years ago, the head winemaker Malcolm Roth hired Tobias Suey to be an apprentice. Unfortunately for Roth, Suey was a member of the Cultus Limus (Cult of the Ooze). The Cultus Limus makes sacrifices to their demonic master Lumastzu in her faceless form. Lumastzu, or "she who erases," is an ancient demoness who once served Jubilex the Faceless Lord before his disappearance and rumored imprisonment millennia ago. Lumastzu rose from Jubilex's shadow as a nascent demon lord in her own right, a demoness who preys upon travelers by drinking their blood, the cause of nightmares, pestilence, infestation of pure water, and a bringer of disease, sickness and death. Her worshipped form in Cultus Limus is a gigantic, vaguely anthropomorphic ooze. The Cult of Jubilex (such as it is) despises worshippers of Lumastzu and considers them traitors and their patroness a faithless betrayer, but the Masters of the Ooze are so few and far between that they are not capable of mounting any organized resistance against the ooze cult usurping much of their lord's station.

Suey turned the field hands that tended the vines against the winemaker. Then the new cult turned their attention to the Gluant family. Later, the Cultus Limus members turned upon each other. With each sacrifice to the ooze, Suey's power grew. That is until no one but Suey was left.

The whim of demons is fickle. As a result, Suey was blighted and corrupted for his work. He now lurks deep in the cellars under the chateau as an ooze demon. However, his handiwork remains. The chateau is now the abode of the undead former residents and workers. Also slimes, molds, fungi and other foulness rot in the fields, buildings and cellars. The riches of the Gluant family remain undisturbed as many would-be thieves and robbers found a quick end at the hands of the current residents. Also, cases of wine remain undisturbed and awaiting plunder.

The *Noble Rot* refers to a few factors in this adventure. The first is the rot that befell the Gluant family in the form of the Cultus Limus. Another is an actual *noble rot* disease that may aid the PCs in overcoming the challenges posed. However, the phrase noble rot *also* refers to the real world helpful/harmful gray fungus *Boytris cinerea.* This helpful fungus in the right conditions creates world-class dessert wines such as French sauternes. In the wrong conditions, however, it destroys the grapes and is known as *gray rot*.

Notes for the GM

This adventure requires the *Pathfinder Roleplaying Game Core Rulebook*. It is a straightforward, location-based adventure. Each location operates fairly independently of the others. The reason is that the slime in one area is not going to trigger the zombies in another to attack. In essence, this is a good adventure for a new GM as the encounters lack interdependence.

However, that is not to say that the adventure is not FUN! The GM is strongly recommended to make this adventure his or her own. For example, a number of rooms in the upper Chateau are available for the GM to script. Also a bit of knowledge of vinification is recommended but also highly encouraged! For those of legal age, sampling some of the types of wines discussed may bring a better sense to the adventure. Also, you may never look at certain wines the same way after the Crushing Room encounter.

The largest recommendation is to make this adventure your own. Since the 1970s, GMs have been told to read the entire adventure and make it your own. However, for almost 40 years, GMs have failed to do that very thing. So before you start rolling d20s, put the dice down, grab a goblet of wine (or grape juice as appropriate) and read this adventure. Thereafter, make notes, change names and take ownership. It may be that instead of a winery, the chateau specialized in producing herbalist concoctions or poisons for an assassin's guild. Whichever way you play it, there are no wrong choices.

One final note is that the author would caution against making this a brewery. A particularly vile and wretched brewmaster that may be found in a future **Necromancer Games** book that would take an exception to making a winery into a brewery.

Adventure Background

This adventure begins when the PCs enter the vicinity of Le Chateau Gluant. The Chateau can be placed in any remote area. Obviously, a small estate full of ooze and undead is unlikely to be right down the river from a legally minded society. Thus a remote area is necessary.

The climate and geography can be any temperate clime in the GM's home campaign. It would not be logical to place a vineyard in an icy fjord or on a tropical island. A remote hillside location may be ideal. In the ***Lost Lands*** campaign setting, Le Chateau Gluant lies at the western edge of the County of Coutaine, just outside the Elderwood and near the southern slopes of the Broken Mountains.

In some campaigns, the PCs may desperately be seeking money (all PCs are always seeking money, please note the use of the word "desperately"). The liquid treasure in the cellars may be the type of treasure the GM would like. What the author means by this is that sometimes it is good to have goods that are not fungible so the GM has more control over the cash flow of a party.

The adventure has three areas. The first area is a low wall and the former vineyard itself. This includes a few outer buildings where the former workers used to live and work. The second area is the chateau itself. This is a fairly large estate with three levels. The first level is the main level. The front entrance enters into the main level. An upstairs level is where the Gluant family used to live. The rear entrance is where the grapes would be brought into the building. This leads to the cellars, which are a cave system that expands into the bedrock below the chateau. Deep in the caves is the lair of Suey, the ooze demon.

Corruption and evil permeate the entire area. As a result any detection spells or devices always show evil. Thus, such mechanisms are worthless within the walls of the chateau unless the detection is maintained for more than 1 round in any given location. A single round of *detect evil* reveals the presence of evil, and evil is ever-present here.

The weather is up to the GM. However, it would be very appropriate for the chateau to be experiencing a mild storm with random lightning strikes. Visiting the chateau in the evening or at night would also work to increase the ambiance of this haunted house.

Local knowledge of the chateau is fairly sparse. It is well known that for some time the chateau has not been producing its famous vintages. It is also rumored that something vile befell the chateau. The sidebar Rumor Table functions as an ability check with the more difficult pieces of information to find higher in the table. The number on the rumor table is the DC for relevant skill checks to learn that rumor. Skills such as Diplomacy to gather information, Knowledge (history), Knowledge (local), Knowledge (nobility), and Profession (vintner) may be applicable. This may be used in a number of ways. One way is that the PCs know about the chateau before traveling to it. They may ask local barmaids or even do research in a local guild. For example, if a merchant's guild hired the PCs, a savvy PC may want to see the accounting records for the chateau to determine when it fell. Doing so may cause a conversation with the clerk who may have further information.

Encounter Listing

Each encounter is listed with a GM description. This is not to be read aloud to the players. It lists the bare essentials for running the adventure with a few items of flavor. It is highly recommended that the GM make the adventure his own with his own style and choices.

Certain encounters note additional items that may be found by searching and exploration. The term "*search*" is used for items that require some action by the PCs. Finding some items might require opening a box, whiles others might be hidden behind a bookcase (just be sure to put the candle back). "*Fine*" are very hard-to-find items or descriptions noticed only by the most observant PCs. These do not require Sherlock Holmes, but they do require more than a basic search. These descriptions may be used with a difficulty class or other game mechanic. It is suggested that they be used with intelligent playing or inquisitive PCs instead of a dice roll. However, that is the GM's choice. Not every encounter has these further descriptions, only those that require them. There is not a DC listed for every such "*search*" or "*fine*" item. It is up to the GM to determine how difficult it is to find these items.

Following the description is the section on monsters. This section includes the statistics for the encounter.

Adventure Hooks

The most obvious way to begin the adventure is also the easiest: The PCs happen to find the chateau. Perhaps it is a respite during a storm. Maybe the PCs are familiar with the wines of Chateau Gluant and want to explore the ruins for a bottle. However, this may not work for every campaign. Thus, a few hooks are provided to get the PCs into the area where the GM has placed the chateau.

The first is that someone hires the PCs to recover a case of Chateau Gluant. This could be a merchant guild looking to make a small pile of gold. It could also be a benefactor whom the PCs have worked with in the past and owe a favor.

Another hook is that the PCs hear a tragic story of someone who visited the chateau and was never seen again. This could be a farmer's wife who makes it to a walled town and is pleading passers-by for assistance from whatever befell her husband. Another option is that a princeling and his retainers are missing. Maybe a distant relative of one of the PCs goes missing and they must undertake a quest to assist their friend.

A third hook is that the PCs are on the run from the law, a local band of thugs, the assassin's guild or some other underworld element and decide to lie low in a remote area. This hook is particularly promising for unsavory parties. The chateau with its reputation for being haunted is a good diversion.

Rumors

DC	Result
9	The chateau has been abandoned for at least 3 years.
10	The chateau produced wines for more than 200 years.
11	The red and white wines the chateau produced are equally prized.
12	The chateau sourced its oak barrels from a cooper who lived on property.
13	The chateau is the hangout of a gang of highwaymen (False).
14	Beware the vines around the chateau. Some of them move like a snake.
15	The family that owned the chateau was very wealthy.
16	The Gluant family that owned the chateau was demon worshippers (False).
17	The undead walk the night around the chateau.
18	Under no circumstance do you open the old crushing tank.
19	Bring fire and oil with you. The dead and muck are alive but fear fire.
20	Sulfur (brimstone) is a good way to kill rot.
21	Some winemakers used sulfur to kill rot and preserve wine.
22	If you go to the chateau take a priest who can turn away the unliving.
23	Deep beneath the chateau are the cellars where the most prized wines are stored.
24	A cult of demon worshippers caused the downfall of the chateau.
25	The Gluant family collected silverwork and kept it hidden in their quarters.
26	A cult of demon worshippers worshipped in the caves below the chateau.
27	The Gluant family kept a djinn in a wine bottle (False).
28	A secret entrance to the caverns is accessible from the upper level. It is a ladder built into the walls.
29	If you find sulfur, be sure to not mix it with water. That makes a witch's brew that can melt anything.
30	A cult called the Cultus Limus once existed. The fall of the chateau appears to be their handiwork. (This result grants the PCs a bonus at the GM's discretion for any lore of knowledge checks while at the chateau).

A final hook is a divine inspiration. Perhaps the PCs' cleric or similar holy person has a vision of abject horror with an inkling of where to look. Another option is that a priest at a local temple has the vision but lacks the courage, stamina or ability to do something about it.

Whatever the hook, be mindful of what motivates your players. Some

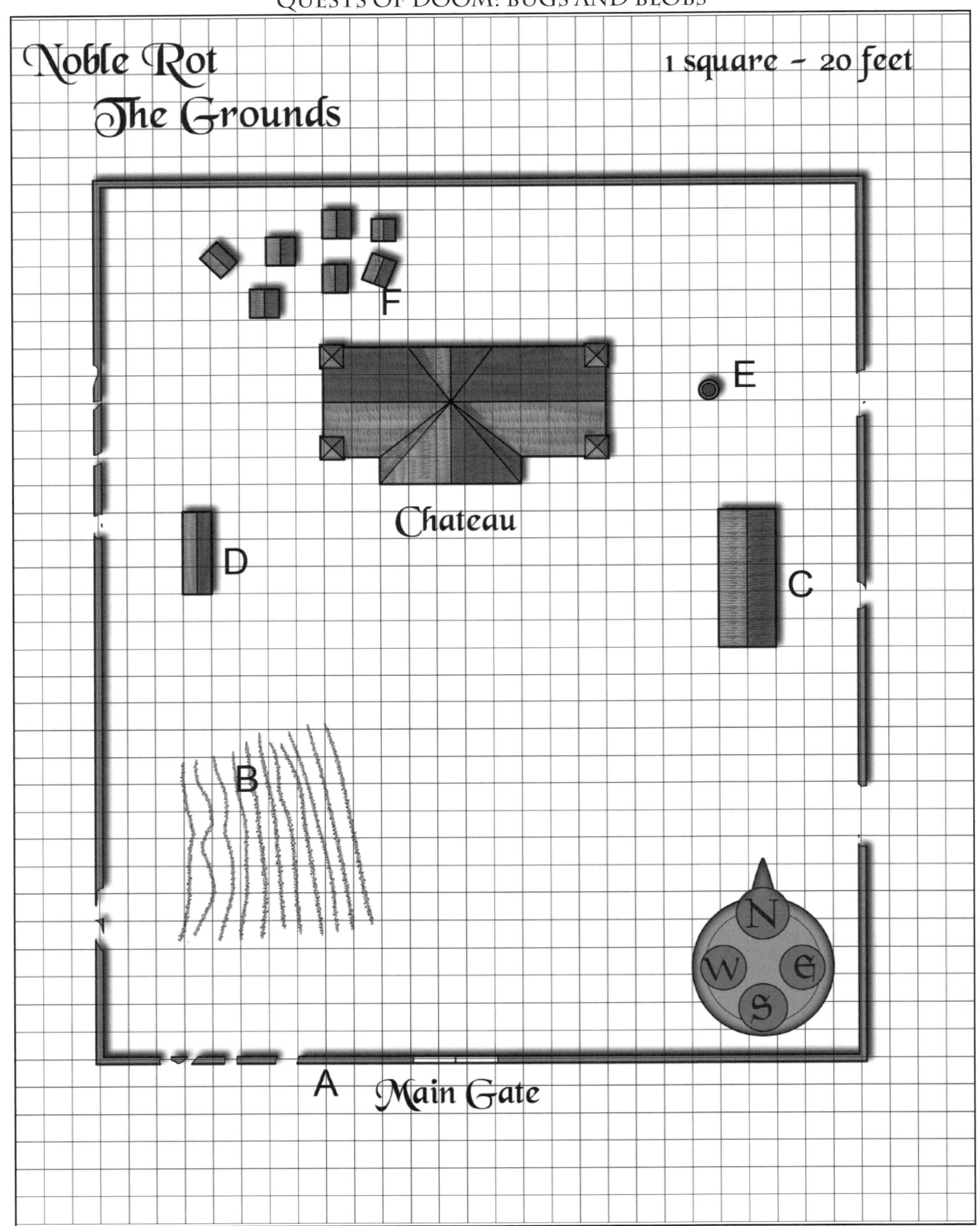
Noble Rot
The Grounds
1 square – 20 feet
F
E
Chateau
D
C
B
N
W
E
S
A
Main Gate

The Noble Rot Disease

Throughout the adventure, the PCs come into contact with various forms of winemaking. This includes the vines, the barn, the crushing facility, the wine itself, etc. All of these areas and indeed the entire chateau are overrun with the gray fungus that causes the disease *noble rot*. The GM is encouraged to use the *noble rot* disease as a plot device and perhaps a "white knight" to assist the PCs if necessary. There are no descriptions provided in the adventure of where or when the PCs should check for succumbing to the disease. However, a good rule of thumb would be each hour or two the PCs remain within the walls around the chateau. The check is a simple DC 12 Fortitude save. If the GM feels that the PCs need a boost, then add one to the Constitution check each time until the PC succumbs.

Once a PC succumbs to the disease, he suffers 1d3 points of Constitution damage for 12+2d6 hours. However the PC gains a bonus of +1d6 points to a prime attribute of their class (other than Constitution) for the same period of time.

The signs of the disease are a gray pallor to the skin, profuse sweating and terrible body odor. Also, everything the PC tastes, including water, is exceedingly sweet for the duration of the disease. Fortunately for the PCs, few, if any, of the encounters include monsters that can "smell them coming." The disease is not contagious from person to person. It can be acquired only by being in contact with the gray fungus.

There is no mundane cure other than to let the disease run its course. Magical cures work as normal. Once the disease is ended by magical means or by the passage of time, the PCs cannot reacquire the disease. Hence, intuitive and enterprising PCs cannot expect to make a *noble rot* farm or to bottle the disease.

players enjoy the promise of roleplay, some the promise of combat and frankly some the loot. Use those desires to your advantage and sell the promise of an adventure. Follow up with the surprises of ***The Noble Rot***.

The Vineyard

Area A: Outer Wall and Entrance

The outer wall is a simple cobblestone wall that surrounds the entire estate and vineyard. It is a mere four feet high and easily climbable at any location. The wall has fallen into disrepair, and loose stones can be found throughout the wall. In a few locations, the wall has collapsed completely. A main entrance has a rusted signpost that proclaims "Chateau du Gluant — Vin Superior." Many of the letters in the sign have fallen to the ground or are missing. A former side entrance has a wooden gate. The gate is long gone and all that remains are two rusty hinges. If anyone attempts to climb the wall, there is a chance (1–2 on a 1d6) that the wall falls on the climber for 1d4 points of damage.

Upon a reasonable search (DC 15 Perception check), a small rune marking can be found. Someone familiar with dwarven runes (anyone who speaks Dwarf) or who has an adequate knowledge (a DC 15 Linguistics check) notes that it signifies safe passage. This is a 20-foot section of the wall that won't fall over.

Area B: The Living Vines (CR 6)

The area within the low wall originally held orderly rows of vines. To the west were vines with different varieties of red (or black berries in the parlance of winemakers). This included cabernet sauvignon, merlot, cabernet franc and petite verdot. To the east were vines with different varieties of white. These vines were exclusively chardonnay.

Today, the vineyard is one amorphous mass of twisted vines. What once was hand-pruned vines and cleared gravelly rows is now a mass of twisted vines. The vines themselves no longer produce the noble varietals. Instead, the berries are putrid green. Some are shriveled while others are overlarge. Instead of the sweet juice of what Galileo called captured or trapped sunshine, the berries now have whitish pus.

The chateau and its few surrounding buildings cannot be accessed except through the mass of vines. The low wall contains the vines within the property. However, the vines rise up to 15 feet in the air.

To bypass the vines requires either magic or traditional hacking. A sickly slimy residue coats most of the vines, so clearing them with traditional fire does not work. Instead, hacking through the vines is proportional to the Strength of the character. The ratio is one foot per one Strength per five minutes. Thus, a Strength 10 character may hack through 10 feet in five minutes. The width of such an endeavor is the width of the character.

Magical means such as a *fireball* or another similar spell also clear the vines. How this affects the vineyard is up to the GM. It should be remembered though that with the residue it should be virtually impossible to burn down the vineyard. Plus, it would likely burn down the chateau and spell a quick end to the adventure

Exceptional eyes (DC 25 Perception check) may find the remains of former adventurers who attempted to traverse the vineyard. Rusty weapons or the odd dented helm may be found within the vineyard, but a sack of gems worth 115 gp and an *amulet of natural armor +1* can also be discovered.

At varying points throughout the vineyard are **3 living vines**. This monster is unique to the adventure and is described below. The vines attempt to constrict the first PC to make contact with it. Thereafter, it drags the PC toward its maw to consume him. If the PCs are so inclined, beneath the maw is a large digestive sac of the living vines. Within this sac are the skeletal remains of a number of humanoids. Also within are 10 pp and a *+1 longsword*.

LIVING VINES (3) **CR 3**
XP 800
hp 27 (see New Monsters at the end of this adventure**)**

Area C: The Barn (CR 8)

The barn is a rickety two-story wooden structure with no windows. The roof of the barn is thick with a sickly green moss. The moss is actually a mass of **green slime**. The green slime does not move to attack the PCs — unless the barn itself collapses.

A single set of sliding doors on the barn are chained together with a fairly simple lock (DC 20 Disable Device). Written in Common in blood (which may be difficult to see at night [DC 15 Perception unless the viewer has darkvision]) are the words "*DO NOT OPEN*."

The inside of the barn housed the tools and carts used in the vineyard. During the chateau's fall, some of the fortunate field hands who escaped used the tools to fend off attack and carted away what they could. Thus, the barn was left empty except for two draft horses. The Cultus Limus found that undead wandering about were a nuisance, so they rounded up the **8 human slime zombies** and caged them within the barn.

The slime zombies are mostly human, but include the **2 draft horse slime zombies**. The zombies have not fed in years and are fairly lethargic at first. However, the prospect of fresh meat quickly rouses them.

If the inevitable fight takes place in a cleared area outside the barn, it is unlikely that a miss damages the barn. However, inside the barn is a different story. Each miss with a weapon has a chance of collapsing the barn. The GM should count any roll of 5 or below on a to-hit roll as striking the barn. A roll of 1 is counted as a critical strike on the barn. The barn is made of wood and has hardness 5. It collapses once it takes 20 points of damage, doing 3d6 points of damage to those inside (a successful DC 15 Reflex save avoids the worst of the debris and does half damage). This also allows the **green slime** to fall onto the combatants (1–in–6 chance). The GM should alternate between the zombies and the PCs on who is hit. Once it hits a combatant, the slime is located at that position as the combatant is covered in the quick-dissolving slime. Thereafter, the green slime engages whoever is closest.

A search of the barn (DC 15 Perception check) finds a small crate in the corner of a former stall. In the crate are three vintages of the Chateau Gluant red blend. The bottles have the famous red wax seal emblazoned with the Gluant crest (the head of an eagle). Unfortunately, two are spoiled. One is obviously spoiled with a large crack down the side of the neck. One is not noticeably spoiled as the crack is near the red seal. To the right buyer in a nearby city such as Cantelburgh or Tourse, the unspoiled wine is worth up to 125 gp. Each bottle found in this adventure is an opportunity for the GM to make a side adventure. Perhaps the PCs sell the spoiled wine to an unsavory wine merchant. When the wine merchant discovers his error, he sends some ruffians to take back his money (or worse). The author suggests having the ruffians appear at the worst possible time, such as when the PCs feel safe in an inn, when meeting with an important contact or in the early part of a dungeon campaign. It is also recommended that in certain circumstances the wine merchant (perhaps a wererat wine merchant) accompany his (wererat) retainers. The zombies and green slime do not have any treasure. One of the humanoid zombies has the key to the lock for the Cooper house and workshop (**Area D**).

HUMAN SLIME ZOMBIES (8) **CR 1/2**
XP 200
Pathfinder Roleplaying Game Bestiary, "Zombie"
NE Medium undead
Init +0; **Senses** darkvision 60 ft.; **Perception** +0

AC 12, touch 10, flat-footed 12 (+2 natural)
hp 12 (2d8+3)
Fort +0; **Ref** +0; **Will** +3
DR 5/slashing; **Immune** undead traits

Speed 30 ft.
Melee slam +4 (1d6+4 plus slime)
Special Attack slime

Str 17, **Dex** 10, **Con** —, **Int** —, **Wis** 10, **Cha** 10
Base Atk +1; **CMB** +4; **CMD** 14
Feats Toughness[B]
Special Qualities staggered

Slime (Ex) Any successful hit by a slime zombie does additional 1d6 points of acid damage. The target takes 1 point of acid damage each round on the start of its turn. The slime may be scraped off or damaged by doing 3 points of damage from weapons, cold or fire. This slime has no effects on objects (like a green slime). No matter how many of a slime zombie's attacks hit, the target only takes 1d6 acid damage and 1 point of acid damage per round after that.

SLIME ZOMBIE HORSES (2) **CR 2**
XP 600
Pathfinder Roleplaying Game Bestiary, "Zombie"
NE Large undead
Init +1; **Senses** darkvision 60 ft.; **Perception** +0

AC 13, touch 10, flat-footed 12 (+1 Dex, +3 natural, –1 size)
hp 22 (4d8+4)
Fort +1; **Ref** +2; **Will** +4
DR 5/slashing; **Immune** undead traits

Speed 50 ft.
Melee 2 hooves +1 (1d4+2 plus slime), slam +6 (1d8+6 plus slime)
Space 10 ft.; **Reach** 5 ft.
Special Attack slime

Str 18, **Dex** 12, **Con** —, **Int** —, **Wis** 10, **Cha** 10
Base Atk +3; **CMB** +8; **CMD** 19 (23 vs. trip)
Feats Toughness
Skills Acrobatics +1 (+9 to jump)
SQ staggered

Slime (Ex) Any successful hit by a slime zombie does additional 1d6 points of acid damage. The target takes 1 point of acid damage each round on the start of its turn. The slime may be scraped off or damaged by doing 3 points of damage from weapons, cold or fire. This slime has no effects on objects (like a green slime). No matter how many of a slime zombie's attacks hit, the target only takes 1d6 acid damage and 1 point of acid damage per round after that.

Slime zombies are created using the normal zombie template and have the Slime special attack.

GREEN SLIME **CR 4**
XP 1,200
(*Pathfinder Roleplaying Game Core Rulebook* "Green Slime")

Area D: The Cooper House and Workshop (CR 4)

This modest three-room house and workshop is near the stable. It was the former home of the Gluant family cooper. This was an important position in the running of the winery. The Gluants used fine oak from the nearby Elderwood to make nearly perfect oak barrels to age their wines. While most wines in the area or country would not be aged, the Gluants learned techniques to control oxidation that would normally ruin the wine. A key component of these techniques involved the master cooper and his protégés. In fact, some scholars would argue that the key to the wine was not just the *terroir* of the Gluant winery, but the fine oak that aged the wine for one (white wine) to three (red wine) years.

But all that is in the past as the master cooper was one of the first sacrificed to the demon after an apprentice named Rall betrayed him. This deceit led to the deaths of the master cooper and his family. Rall was richly rewarded for his treachery; Suey slit his throat and practiced his powers by raising Rall as a **ghoul**.

Like the zombies in **Area C**, Rall was locked in the cooper's house and workshop. However, unlike the zombies located there, no grim warning is found outside the house.

The house has a double-door entrance with a normal lock (DC 25 Disable Device). The key for this lock is on one of the workers who was slain and rose as a zombie in **Area C**. The door is below an overhang that functions as a porch. Shuttered windows are adjacent to the door. The shutters are effectively glued shut and stuck. It takes a DC 17 Strength check to open.

The door opens into the cooper's workshop. The workshop was ransacked before Rall was locked up, but a few metal tools, an anvil and a brazier remain. Hanging from the ceiling are many loops of metal that the master cooper used to form his barrels. In one end is a debris pile of dust and old wood. Making their home in the debris pile is a **rat swarm** afflicted with filth fever.

Adjacent to the cooper's workshop is the family room where the cooper lived. All of the furniture is smashed to bits and pieces. Rall in his undead rage broke it apart when he realized he was trapped. A single set of drawers propped against one of the walls has survived.

A half open door at the back of the building leads into the family room. In this room is a moldy down mattress and a single chair. A misshapen lump on the bed lies below a torn blanket. This is the rotting corpse of one of the cooper's adult sons. Rall is actually beneath the bed (assume he took 10 to hide for a total Stealth check result of 17). Unless the PCs are impressively stealthy (Stealth checks opposed by Rall's Perception), he hears their approach and hides beneath the bed. When the PCs are within a few feet of the bed, Rall springs from beneath it and unceremoniously dumps the mattress and corpse on the unsuspecting PCs.

Beneath the refuse pile in the workshop is a small sack of copper coins (20 cp). However, a wise PC may deduce (DC 20 Appraisal or DC 15 Knowledge [history] check) that these are actually very rare coins that may be sold to the right buyer for 100 gp each! In the set of drawers in the family room are a silver mirror and a leaky flask of oil.

The cooper was stingy man in life and hoarded his earnings. He ritually stuffed his earnings in a secret alcove (DC 20 Perception) in the wall between his bedroom and the workshop. A very large sack containing 196 gp is between the boards.

RALL THE GHOUL **CR 1**
XP 400
hp 13 (*Pathfinder Roleplaying Game Bestiary* "Ghoul")

RAT SWARM **CR 2**
XP 600
hp 16 (*Pathfinder Roleplaying Game Bestiary* "Rat Swarm")

Area E: The Well

Outside the chateau is a circular stone well. It has no bucket or pulley system. Like every adventure that mentions a well, this well is not what it seems. A faint residue of transmutation magic around the well is easily detected by a *detect magic* spell. The magic is identifiable as *purify food and drink* with a successful DC 20 Knowledge (arcana) check. The well is approximately 40 feet deep and ends in a pool of crystalline water. If magical or other light is used, something can be seen twinkling at the bottom of the well. The well itself is very slippery, as a clear slimy residue coats the walls. This makes any climb very difficult (DC 20 Climb if not using a rope). Of course a fall into shallow water is perilous (1d6 points of damage per 10 feet fallen, with the last 1d6 being nonlethal damage for falling into water).

If the PCs make it to the bottom, they find that a natural spring feeds the well. At the bottom is a tin cup with no discernable value that was dropped some time ago. A former group of adventurers cleansed the well with magic so it provides fresh water.

This encounter is a type of overeager PC trap. These are fun to place so that PCs are not encouraged to seek and destroy their entire way through your adventure!

Area F: The Huts

Farther from the chateau are a series of huts where the field workers and chateau staff lived. Originally, these were little plots with an area for domesticated animals and gardens. The vines have taken over the entire area, leaving just a few huts still standing.

Within the huts are meager possessions that are unlikely to interest any PC. However, it is within the GM's discretion to flesh out these areas and include additional monsters and traps.

Level One — Chateau Main Floor

Area 1-A: Entry (CR 4)

The chateau itself looks like a replica of a castle. It is two stories tall and has small arrow slit-like windows on all sides. Metal bars in each window make entry nearly impossible for all but the smallest PC. Small minarets and faux stone towers stand at each end. These towers do not serve any purpose other than decoration.

A **gargoyle** oversees the chateau's entrance. It is particularly hard to spot (DC 27 Perception, assuming it took 10 on its Stealth check) as a number of crude gothic gargoyles stand along the roofline. The gargoyle occasionally flies off during the night to stalk prey in the nearby forest. However, it spends most of its time waiting for tasty gnomes. If the party includes a gnome, the gargoyle directs nearly all of its attacks against the gnome, even attempting to fly off with such a tasty morsel. The gargoyle has no treasure; thus, a jaunt up to the roof is an exercise in futility.

The main entrance into the chateau is up a set of wide stone stairs. A broken statue of a griffon stands on each side of the stairs. Filth and muck adorn the defaced statues. The double oaken doors are open but one is stuck, requiring a DC 12 Strength check to pry open. The other door swings out easily. The GM is encouraged to play this where the PC first

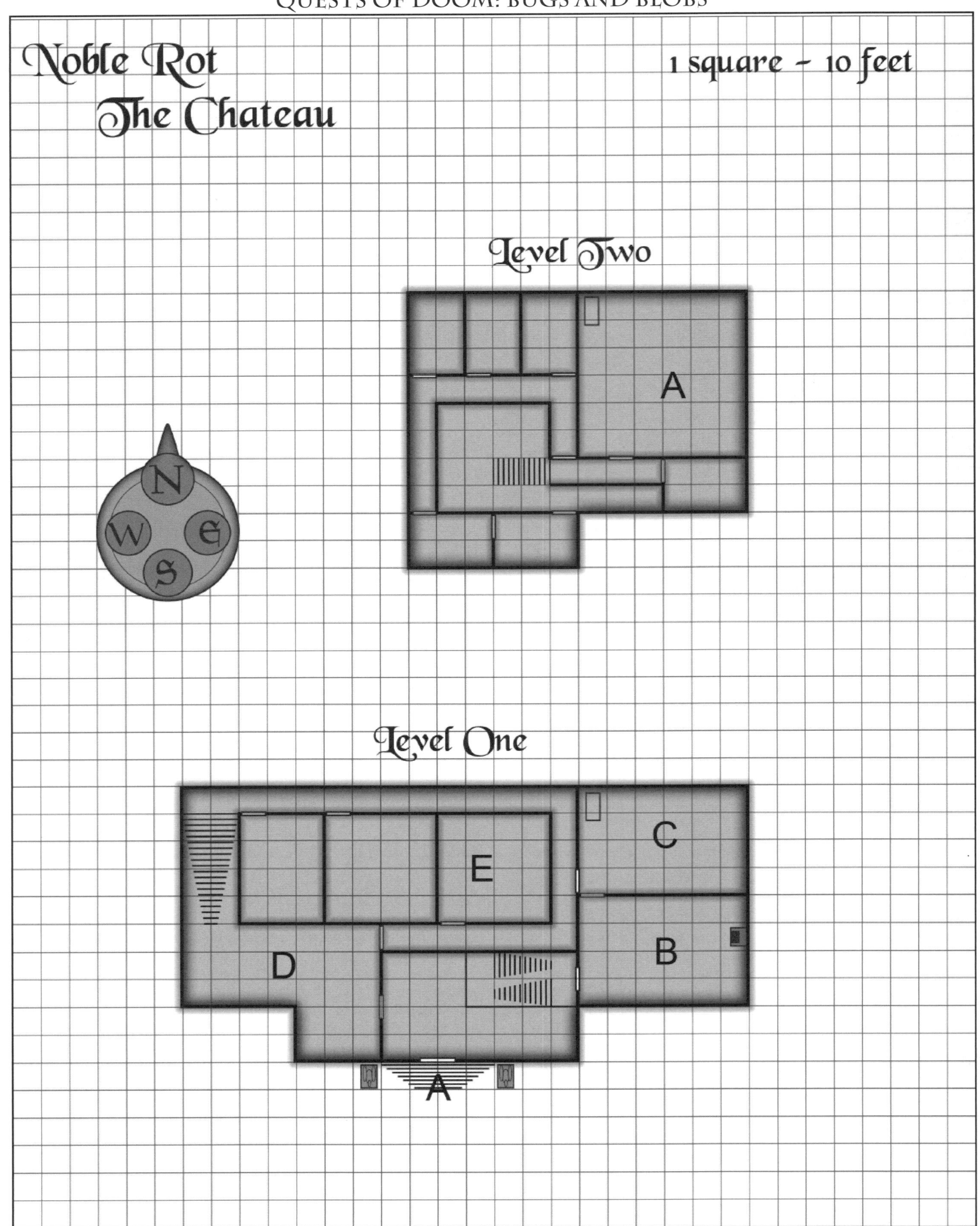
Noble Rot
The Chateau
1 square = 10 feet
Level Two
A
N
W
E
S
Level One
C
E
B
D
A

tries to open the stuck door.

Beyond the door is a two-story foyer with a curved staircase leading to the upper level. The staircase is rotten. Any PC weighing more than 200 pounds has a 1–in–4 chance of crashing through the staircase to the ground below for 1d4 points of damage. If three or more PCs (or the same one three times) fall through the staircase, the entire thing collapses, causing 2d6 points of damage to the PC and anyone else on the stairs.

Broken arrows, an axe handle and scorch marks can be found, evidence of combat that occurred here. Master Gluant made his last stand here before being dragged off to the sacrificial pit. On either side of the entrance are double doors. One leads to the parlor (**Area 1-B**) and the other to the Ballroom (**Area 1-D**).

Beneath the stairs (or at least until the stairs collapse), is a small alcove where the porter made his home. The porter pilfered two bottles of the white Chateau Gluant wine. Both are in good condition (65 gp each to the right buyer).

GARGOYLE **CR 4**
XP 1,200
hp 42 (*Pathfinder Roleplaying Game Bestiary* "Ghoul")

Area 1-B: Parlor (CR 4)

Adjacent to the foyer, the parlor is in fairly good shape. The room contains long couches, a large marble bar area and numerous stuffed animals including a buffalo head, a moose head, a full brown bear, rabbits, a woodchuck and a beaver. This was a tasting room of sorts for the Gluants. They would entertain merchants and passing aristocracy here. The object of Gluant's hunts would be the usual and boring conversation pieces.

A fireplace is along one wall. The fireplace is sooty from where one of the less intelligent cult members attempted to burn a stuffed lynx for heat, which resulted in a quick pile of lynx ash.

Within this ash is a **gray ooze**. The ooze quivers slightly when the PCs enter the room. This causes the ash pile to obviously move. Of course, woe to any PC who thinks sticking his weapon in the ash is a good idea.

Within the stuffed bear's head cavity (DC 25 Perception) are a couple of large rubies (75 gp each) that Master Gluant kept in case of emergency.

GRAY OOZE **CR 4**
XP 1,200
hp 50 (*Pathfinder Roleplaying Game Bestiary* "Gray Ooze")

Area 1-C: Kitchen (CR 3)

Unlike most of the chateau, the kitchen saw service for many months after the fall of the Gaunt family. The Cultus Limus used the kitchen as a commissary and meeting place. A number of outdoor wooden tables and benches are wedged into the room. The oven itself is fairly clean. The room was cleared of any cleavers, knives or means of making fire.

On one end of the kitchen is a crude dumbwaiter. It is rather large with a 5-foot-by-2-foot opening. In front of the opening is a loose door on a hinge. Next to the door is another opening with the rudimentary pulley system. The pulley is currently mucked over, and the rope is slick with slime. The shaft goes up a floor to the master's quarters (**Area 2-A**). The platform is currently between floors. It takes either a DC 15 Strength check or a DC 12 Disable Device check to make the dumbwaiter operational.

If the PCs dislodge the platform, it quickly comes crashing down and unloads a **gelatinous cube** that was trapped in the shaft by the cult. The cube presses through the opening like a gelatin mold forced through a small rectangular frame before bouncing back to its larger shape. To the untrained eye, it appears as a floating kobold skeleton and a small brass crown (10 gp).

GELATINOUS CUBE **CR 3**
XP 800
hp 50 (*Pathfinder Roleplaying Game Bestiary* "Gelatinous Cube")

Area 1-D: Ballroom (CR 2)

The ballroom was once an astounding architectural marvel. The entirely wooden structure from the floorboards to the tall ceiling was made without the use of a single nail, touch of cement or use of stone. It was appropriately made of fine oak and stained in a rich dark brown hue. A cutting of the Gluants still stands proudly over a large marble fireplace. The entire ballroom cost the Gluants a small fortune.

The ballroom has of course seen better days. The arrow slit windows to the outside are boarded up with piles of refuse to keep the boards from falling over. The remains of the furniture are thrown about the room. Like most of the chateau, a fine patina of dust is everywhere. In the center of the room, some cultist thought it would be a good idea to burn the furniture as a bonfire.

Disturbing the large bonfire also disturbs a nest of **6 rats** that make the pile their home.

A silver locket (20 gp) is under an overturned table (DC 15 Perception). The locket has a silhouette of the winemaker and his wife.

RATS (6) **CR 1/4**
XP 100
hp 4 (*Pathfinder Roleplaying Game Bestiary* "Familiar, Rat")

Area 1-E: Winemaker's Quarters (CR 1)

Near the stairs to the cellar level are the winemaker's quarters. The door is locked (DC 25 Disable Device) and the key dissolved in Suey the Ooze Demon long ago. The room is relatively untouched except for cobwebs and dust. A double-sized feather down bed, a desk and a rickety wooden chair are in the room. The chair breaks if anyone sits on it (1–5 on 1d6).

Suey used the room of his former master to amass his followers, take the chateau and then later cause chaos in the surrounding countryside. On the table is crude map of the surrounding area.

The desk is also locked (DC 20 Disable Device) and is trapped with a poison needle trap. The poison is black adder venom. Inside the desk is a diary written in the Abyssal language. The journal details how Suey tricked the winemaker; how he gained Gluant's confidence; turned most of the field hands to his cause; and how his cult flourished. The journal ends with Suey turning on each of the cult members until he was the only one remaining.

POISONED NEEDLE TRAP **CR 1**
XP 400
Type mechanical; **Perception** DC 20; **Disable Device** DC 20

Trigger touch; **Reset** none
Effect Atk +10 melee (1d3 plus black adder venom)

A large jug of Chateau Gluant wine is under a floorboard (DC 20 Perception). It is in pristine condition and worth 200 gp to the right buyer.

Level Two — The Upper Floor

Area 2-A: Master's Quarters

The master's quarters were looted after his demise. Most of the furniture was shredded or torn apart. A large bed sits in the middle of the floor at an off angle where it was pulled to the center of the room and forgotten. The sheets are missing, as are three of the four bannisters. A small desk and a stool are in the far corner.

Sitting on the stool is a skeletal form with long slimy gray hair. The woman's back is to the entry. The form is the former Lady Gluant. The corpse looks rotted and frozen, and holds a large silver brush as if she was brushing her hair. Lady Gluant is very much dead. The cultists brought her here after her demise. Suey placed her doing what he thought was her favorite pastime. If the PCs attack, the body likely falls over. A closer inspection (DC 10 Perception) reveals bits of twine propping the body in position.

The dumbwaiter from **Area 1-C** terminates here behind two shutters that swing wide on one wall. If the PCs open the shutters, the **gelatinous cube** as described in **Area 1-C** does nothing as it is a few feet below the PCs. Anyone foolish enough to jump into the dark shaft gets what is coming to them. The dumbwaiter cannot be raised from this room.

The silver brush Lady Gluant holds has some value (70 gp). On the back of the desk is a hidden compartment (DC 20 Perception) that contains a large sapphire (50 gp) and a key to the dumbwaiter.

Level Three — The Cellar

Area 3-A: The Gathering Room

The rear entrance to the chateau is down an earthen ramp. The entry is two large barn doors that easily slide open. The fieldworkers would bring carts of grapes for sorting to the cobblestone room. Ironically, the fieldworkers and their wives would spend hours removing any grapes with the faintest taint or rot. Once sorted into large wooden baskets, the grapes would be taken through an archway to the crushing room (**Area 3-B**).

Currently, a number of overturned carts and smashed baskets are in this room. The smell of mold and must is more prevalent here than in the upper parts of the chateau or outside. Four skeletal remains are in the corner of the room. This is a party of failed adventurers. A few torches, some moldy clothes and a few rusty weapons sit by their bodies.

One of the dead adventurers is a halfling with a large satchel. Within the satchel are three bottles of white Chateau Gluant that are in fairly good shape (75 gp each).

Area 3-B: The Crushing Room (CR 3)

This long and narrow room slopes downward almost 15 feet. Near the archway entrance are two large wine presses. The presses are wooden buckets that are 5 feet wide and 4 feet tall. Above one bucket is a large metal plate. The other metal plate is currently on top of the other bucket. Between the buckets is a large capstan large enough for four men to turn. A system of ropes and pulleys high above hold each of the plates. When in operation, one of the presses would be in use and connected to the windlass. The plate would be lowered and pressure exerted with ropes along the floor that attach to the capstan. The pomace would be pressed and a barrel would be filled at the top of the slope through a large brass spigot that sits at the bottom of the barrel. Since there is a slight slope, the barrel is raised high enough off the slope to be level and to provide room to fill. Thereafter, the barrel would be rolled down the slope to the barrel room (**Area 3-C**).

The metal plate hanging in the air does not move unless a rudimentary rope brake is loosened. The capstan then spins and the plate unceremoniously falls, doing 5d6 points of damage to anyone standing in the bucket.

The unengaged metal plate sits atop the other bucket. If the spigot is turned, the barrel is damaged or the plate is re-engaged, then the **wine slime** lurking in the barrel bursts out of the bucket and attacks the nearest PC. This white Zinfandel wine slime is pinkish in hue and attacks with pseudopods.

WINE SLIME **CR 3**
XP 800
hp 38 (**see New Monsters** at the end of this adventure)

Area 3-C: The Barrel Room

At the end of the long ramp in the crushing room (**Area 3-B**) is another stone archway that leads into the barrel room. At one time, dozens of barrels sat for years gently adding oak to the wine.

Unfortunately, with the cult drinking most of the wine and the damp conditions introduced by their activities, the barrels in the room have almost all spoiled into terribly acidic-tasting vinegar. While the vinegar is not acidic enough to be classified as a weapon, it is still very unpleasant.

If the PCs search the barrels for the "right stuff," they have a 1–in–20 chance of finding a barrel of acceptable wine. Only 2 barrels out of 50 are still acceptable. These barrels contain 300 bottles of wine worth more than 30,000 gp to the right buyer! The GM is encouraged to adjust this to her campaign. It is possible that in the process of opening and tasting the barrels that the PCs allow too much oxygen in, which fully oxidizes the wine by the time they find a buyer.

Area 3-D: The Bottling Room

Adjacent to the barrel room (**Area 3-C**) is this bottling room. Barrels would be placed on a wooden platform here and wine would be bottled by hand. While the bottles were sealed with wax in this room, the winemaker would later seal the bottles with the Gluant insignia.

A few cases of smashed bottles sit next to a couple of empty barrels on the platform. Bags of cheap red candles also are nearby. However, the most important part of the room is the pile of yellow powdery sulfur or brimstone in the corner.

The Gluants' winemaking secret was the slight addition of sulfur to the wines. The addition of sulfur preserved the wines and acted as an antioxidant to prevent the ruining effects of oxygen. To those astute enough to deduce it on a DC 15 Knowledge (dungeoneering) or similar check, the sulfur is an exceptional tool against the oozes and slimes infecting the chateau.

Sulfur is toxic and does 1d4 points of damage per 10 minutes if handled carelessly. Properly handled, the sulfur does 2d6 points of damage per round *per handful* to all slimes and oozes found in this chapter. A wheel barrel full of sulfur is dumped in the corner of the raised platform. It is up to the GM how many handfuls the PCs may appropriately take with them.

Area 3-E: Natural Cavern Entrance (CR 6)

Beyond the barrel room is a rusty metal gate. The gate is ooze-encrusted and rusted in place. It takes a DC 15 Strength check to open it.

Beyond the gate is a natural cavern that goes deeper into the bedrock below the chateau. The cavern is only 10 feet tall and has a worn path down the middle of the cave. A foul, rancid stench emanates from the cavern. If the PCs open the gate, **10 slime zombies** that are hidden (DC 12 Perception to spot) drop down on the PCs and attack. If successful, this maneuver gives the slime zombies a +2 to their initiative check.

HUMAN SLIME ZOMBIES (10) **CR 1/2**
XP 200
hp 12 (see **Area C, The Barn**)

Area 3-F: Temple of Lumastzu (CR 7)

The temple is roughhewn from a natural domed cavern that stretches 40 feet above the floor. Stalactites remain dripping with ooze. The sludge from the stalactites forms slippery pools around the floor. While some of the dripping does evaporate, much remains. Movement at normal speed is unimpeded. However, quick movement or combat requires a DC 10 Acrobatics check to avoid slipping and falling prone.

A secret door (DC 20 Perception) on one cavern wall leads to the hidden alcove (**Area 3-G**). The door is weighted to spring closed behind whoever enters. It takes someone to divine or reason a solution (DC 12 Intelligence check) to the crude sandbag and ropes on the other side to pry the door open once through. In other words, if the entire party goes through the door, there is not a way back to **Area 3-F**.

The floor is roughly cut into a round theatre. Three concentric circles surround a center stage. Each circle is five feet lower than the cavern floor and mark where parishioners of this foul place would congregate to observe the obscene rites. A stone stage stands 5 feet higher than the lowest circle.

The stone stage is square with 50 feet to a side. The stage is covered with arcane symbols and Abyssal script written in blood. Much of the script has been worn off over the past few years, while the dripping sludge from above has also erased some of the foul text. Rising from the stage is a large stone bowl. The bowl is just over 60 feet in diameter and nearly 5 feet tall. The bowl has no markings and appears to be hewn from the same stone as the blockish stage. The bowl fills most of the stage with only a few feet to a side.

Above the bowl are yards of rusty chains. The chains are connected to a pulley high above the bowl. On the highest circle is a rusted winch. The winch is rusted, crusted and inoperable. It is easy to deduce that the cult lowered their sacrifices into the bowl.

Within the bowl are the remains of the winemaker, the Gluants, the workers, a few adventurers and the Cultus Limus. Lurking within the bowl is a **yellow ooze** that grew larger with each sacrifice. Now it is almost

Noble Rot
The Cellar
1 square - 10 feet
G
S
F
E
Storage
C
D
B
A
N
W
E
S

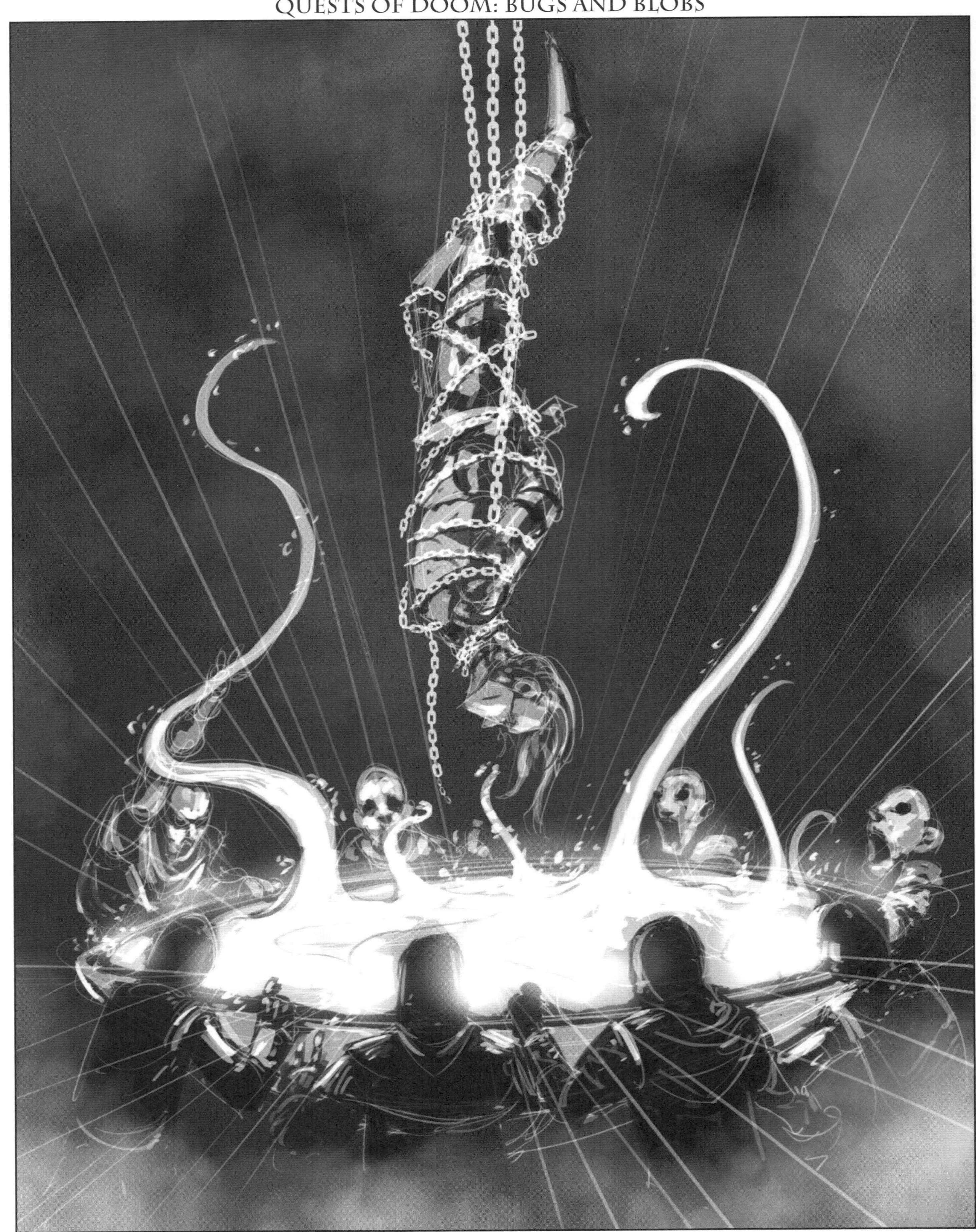

impossibly large. The yellow ooze is a variant black pudding.

The yellow ooze thrusts out a pseudopod and attacks whenever PCs are within 20 feet of the bowl. As discussed in **Area 3-D**, brimstone or sulfur is a good way to dispatch the ooze. The bowl provides protection to the ooze and functions as improved cover (+4 to AC). If the PCs attempt to simply move to range and attack the ooze, the ooze "spills" out of the bowl and lumbers toward the party. While this means that it must leave its protective "shell," it also won't simply wait for the PCs to dispatch it.

A search of the area (DC 12 Perception) finds tracks leading to the secret door to the hidden alcove (**Area 3-G**).

YELLOW OOZE (VARIANT BLACK PUDDING) **CR 7**
XP 3,200
hp 105 (*Pathfinder Roleplaying Game Bestiary* "Black Pudding")

Split (Ex) A yellow ooze is immune to slashing and fire damage. Instead, the creature splits into two identical oozes, each with half of the original's current hit points (round down). A yellow ooze with 10 hit points or less cannot be further split and dies if reduced to 0 hit points.

Area 3-G: Hidden Alcove

Beyond the secret door as described in **Area 3-F** is a very narrow natural hallway. Stalactites and stalagmites are throughout the area. A narrow, 3- to 4-foot-wide passage leaving the room curves slightly to keep **Area 3-H** out of view. This entire room is coated with thick yellow mucus that decreases speed by half unless a PC makes a DC 15 Acrobatics check. If the PC fails, he falls prone and is covered in the relatively harmless ooze.

Hidden (DC 25 Perception) under a foot of hardened mucus next to a wall is a bag of jewels. Inside the bag are various gemstones worth 1,500 gp.

Area 3-H: The Ooze Demon (CR 6)

The narrow corridor from **Area 3-G** ends in this cavern and marks the end of this adventure as well. This chamber is a circular room 50 feet across. The ground is level and the natural features of the cavern are hewn away. At the entrance is a step down into a pool of calm yellow slime. A small stone platform is in the middle of the floor. An idol made of gold, rubies and ivory is on top of the platform and is sculpted like a woman with a lioness head, donkey ears, nail-like fingers and bird talons. It is worth 5,000 gp to the right buyer. Beyond the area of the chateau, the idol radiates evil. Also, anyone possessing the idol is plagued by horrible nightmares. Additionally, any diseases or poisons that afflict a PC while it is in their possession last twice as long.

At the feet of the idol are a number of offerings. From the dust present, these offering were made long ago. The offerings include a skull with a large ruby (150 gp) inside it, sacks of coins (750 gp), a *+1 dagger*, two tomes ("*Fine Wines and Winemaking*" by Robin Peeker worth 115 gp and "*Fungi and I*" by Jay Suchling), a large golden wine goblet encrusted with lesser precious stones (500 gp), and a spellbook. The contents of the spellbook are up to the GM.

Anything touching the ooze causes it to retract. For 30 seconds it retracts and forms an anthropomorphic shape next to the treasure. Damage may be done to the ooze during this time at AC 10. However, the ooze fast healing 10 during this dramatic entrance. After 30 seconds, **Suey the ooze demon** attacks.

SUEY THE OOZE DEMON **CR 6**
XP 2,400
Advanced ooze demon (The Tome of Horrors Complete 171)
CE Large outsider (chaotic, demon, evil, extraplanar)
Init –1; **Senses** darkvision 60 ft.; **Perception** +17

AC 16, touch 8, flat-footed 16 (–1 Dex, +8 natural, –1 size)
hp 69 (3d10+36)
Fort +10; **Ref** +1; **Will** +5
DR 5/good or cold iron; **Immune** acid, critical hits, electricity, paralysis, poison, polymorph, sleep, stunning; **Resist** cold 10, fire 10; **SR** 14

Speed 30 ft.
Melee bite +12 (1d8+7), 2 claws +12 (1d6+7), slam +12 (1d8+7)
Space 10 ft.; **Reach** 10 ft.
Spell-Like Abilities (CL 5th; concentration +5)
1/day—*summon demon* (level 3, 1d2 lesser ooze demons 35%)

Str 24, **Dex** 8, **Con** 20, **Int** 10, **Wis** 10, **Cha** 10
Base Atk +6; **CMB** +14 (+18 grapple); **CMD** 23
Feats Blind-fight, Power Attack, Toughness
Skills Climb +16, Escape Artist +8, Intimidate +9, Perception +17, Stealth +4, Survival +9
Languages Abyssal; telepathy 100 ft.
SQ acid

New Monsters

LIVING VINE **CR 3**
XP 800
N Large plant
Init +2; **Senses** low-light vision; **Perception** +0

AC 12, touch 11, flat-footed 10 (+2 Dex, +1 natural, –1 size)
hp 27 (6d8)
Fort +5; **Ref** +4; **Will** +2
Immune plant traits

Speed 0 ft.
Melee slam +7 (1d6+6 plus grab)
Space 10 ft.; **Reach** 15 ft.
Special Attacks constrict (1d6+6), pull (slam, 5 feet)

Str 19, **Dex** 14, **Con** 10, **Int** —, **Wis** 10, **Cha** 3
Base Atk +4; **CMB** +9 (+13 grapple); **CMD** 21

WINE SLIME **CR 3**
XP 800
N Huge ooze
Init –2; **Senses** blindsight 60 ft.; **Perception** –2

AC 6, touch 6, flat-footed 6 (–2 Dex, –2 size)
hp 38 (7d8+14)
Fort +4; **Ref** +0; **Will** +0
Defensive Abilities split; **Immune** fire, ooze traits, slashing

---

Speed 10 ft., climb 10 ft.
Melee 2 slams +5 (1d8+2 plus intoxication)
Space 15 ft.; **Reach** 15 ft.
Special Attacks intoxication (DC 15, sickened 1 hour)

Str 14, **Dex** 6, **Con** 15, **Int** —, **Wis** 6, **Cha** 1
Base Atk +5; **CMB** +5; **CMD** +3
Intoxication (Ex) A creature struck by a wine slime's slam attack must succeed on a DC 15 Fortitude save or suffer alcohol intoxication. An intoxicated creature is sickened for 1 hour. This is a poison effect, so resistances and immunities to poison apply. A *neutralize poison* removes the sickened condition from an affected creature.
Split (Ex) Slashing weapons and fire deal no damage to a wine slime. Instead, the creature splits into two identical slimes, each with half of the original's current hit points (round down). A wine slime with 10 hit points or less cannot be further split and dies if reduced to 0 hit points.

Of Ants and Men

By Bill Webb

Sometimes bugs are just bugs, and sometimes they are organized into a hive mind that is just as smart as humans. Ants are just that. In battle, the ant creates a horde of raging combatants that form a blur on all sides. While typically peaceful unless threatened, should the nest be threatened, ants create a scale of violence almost impossible to imagine as they sweep ahead with a suicidal single-mindedness. Utterly devoted to duty, ants never retreat from a confrontation — even in the face of certain death. The engagements are brief and brutal. Working in teams, ants grab enemies, holding them in place until one of the warriors advances and rips into the captive's body, leaving it smashed and bleeding.

The adventure begins as a quest to recover (i.e.. steal) giant ant eggs for a wizard from a giant anthill located near the town of Endhome. The real treasure is the *two-edged sword,* a sword made of a rare and strange metal that has amazingly powerful anti-magical properties.

This adventure is designed for up to 6 characters of levels 4–8. The adventure can also be played (perhaps more effectively) by smaller groups. In response to many requests from our fans, I designed the main encounter mechanic to work well with groups of 2–3 characters of levels 6–8 — even a solo adventure would work well in cases where the individual character has very good climbing, trap-finding and stealth skills. Druids, barbarians and rogues will fare best in cases where the groups are limited in size.

This adventure is best played as a thinking adventure; hacking one's way through it is likely to result in death.

Starting the Adventure

If the GM is using the ***Lost Lands*** setting by **Frog God Games**, the anthill is located just south of the Penprie Forest near the city of Endhome and along the banks of the Oldrock River. GMs using another setting could place this adventure anywhere with virtually no modification. This could require minor re-tweaking of the "finding the body" portion of the adventure, but otherwise is playable anywhere.

The GM can use a number of hooks to get the players involved with this adventure. Rumors of a giant anthill "filled with treasure" could be presented in the local watering hole, or perhaps a more direct method could be employed. Bug-hunts such as this often lack treasure (as does this one), so if incentive is lacking, several methods can be employed. Potential **Adventure Hooks** include:

• Player characters are hired to get giant ant eggs. A kindly old wizard, perhaps a friend characters, needs these eggs for magical research. He pays them 500 gp if they retrieve eggs for him.

• Player characters are *geased* by a not-so-kindly wizard to gather eggs from the anthill. While not a very nice way to treat player characters, this is about as truly old-school as you get. In fact, in the original white box version of the game, virtually all wizards and clerics encountered used *geas* and *quest* on player characters regularly. Alas, this is a different day and age.

• Legends speak of a powerful lord lost in battle with gnolls on the fields of south of the Penprie Forest, very near where the giant anthill is located. When reinforcements arrived to recover the dead, they found the bodies being taken by giant ants. His family offers a reward of 1,000 gp for recovery of his body (impossible, he was eaten) or 500 gp for recovery of his plate armor. The armor is inscribed with his family crest — a pair of unicorn heads entwined by vines and facing one another.

• Herdsmen have complained about sheep going missing in the area. They beg the player characters to investigate the cause and stop the loss of livestock.

Whatever the method used, the GM can find some way to encourage the party to head toward the location of the anthill. Once there, they find a dead body of a man wearing leather armor lying a few hundred yards from the anthill. The man is on a small island of rock in the center of the Oldrock River. His body is bloated and red, and his armor shows significant signs of being "melted," as if by some form of acid.

A partially melted short sword lies in his hand, and he wears a belt pouch. Within the belt pouch is a journal.

Speak with dead or perusing the journal details that a wizard hired the man and his friends to retrieve giant ant eggs — in fact, they were offered 500 gp, with a 500 gp bonus should they get a royal queen egg. They fought their way into the nest, soon realizing they could never win a battle with all the ants. Eventually, their druid used his magic to make them invisible to the ants, and while working their way down into the egg chambers, they discovered a series of cut caverns and worked stone tunnels and chambers. In it, they found a strange vault of carved stone covered with ancient, mystic writings. For some reason, the druid's magic failed, as did that of their wizard and their priest, and the ants returned with a vengeance and attacked.

They tried to run out, dropping most of their equipment in an attempt to run faster. The man was stung several times by the warriors, but made it out and sought refuge in the river where the ants would not follow. His last entry states that he is in great pain, and hopes that a short rest will allow him to recover. He died of the poison.

The journal also notes that the workers seemed docile enough at first, and that the warriors, while quite aggressive, were fairly slow moving. It also contains a rough map, indicating that the entrance leading to **Area 2** is the one used by him and his comrades.

The anthill itself rises up 40 feet above the plain. Multiple entrances can be seen, some with ants moving in and out of them. Careful inspection reveals that the ants are not active outside at night. The area around the anthill is heavily defoliated for approximately a mile around. If approached during daylight hours, intruders are investigated by a party consisting of **3d6 workers, 1d6 warriors** and **1 bomber ant**.

Giant Ants and the Hive Mentality

Before I go into the adventure itself, the GM should understand certain general information that governs the whole of the ant lair. Members operate without a power hierarchy or permanent leader. Colonies are decentralized, with workers that individually know little making combat decisions that nonetheless prove effective at the group level without oversight — a process called swarm intelligence. Different varieties of ants are described, and different conditions exist depending on player character (or random event) actions that occur, as well as the type of terrain (e.g. the portion of the hive) that encounters with ants could occur in all play a factor in their behavior.

During the course of the adventure, the player characters can encounter 5 different kinds of ants. A successful DC 10 Knowledge (nature) check means a character is familiar with ant behavior and is aware of the following information.

Most of these ant stat blocks can be found in the *Pathfinder Roleplaying Game Bestiary*, but since they are encountered so frequently in this adventure their full stat blocks are replicated here for convenience. The ant kinds are:

Workers: These are sterile females which do the bulk of the heavy lifting, hive construction, and expansion and food gathering for the colony. The workers present in this colony are not particularly aggressive, and, absent pheromones being released indicating that "the hive is in trouble," generally won't attack a creature that enters the hive, *unless it is another ant*. Lacking a poison sting, these ants typically approach any intruders and "smell them" using their antennae. While it may seem at first that a player character is being attacked, these ants do not aggressively bite anything moving about unless attacked first. In combat, these ants typically grab a leg or an arm and hold on with grapple checks while the warriors attack the held opponent. There are 900 workers in this hive. Each week, 10d6 more join the hive to replace slain comrades.

GIANT WORKER ANT **CR 1**
XP 400
Pathfinder Roleplaying Game Bestiary, "Ant, Giant"
N Medium vermin
Init +0; **Senses** darkvision 60 ft., scent; **Perception** +5

AC 15, touch 10, flat-footed 15 (+5 natural)
hp 18 (2d8+6 plus 3)
Fort +6; **Ref** +0; **Will** +1
Immune mind-affecting effects

Speed 50 ft., climb 20 ft.
Melee bite +3 (1d6+2)

Str 14, **Dex** 10, **Con** 17, **Int** —, **Wis** 13, **Cha** 11
Base Atk +1; **CMB** +3; **CMD** 13 (21 vs. trip)
Feats Toughness[B]
Skills Climb +10, Perception +5, Survival +5; **Racial Modifiers** +4 Perception, +4 Survival

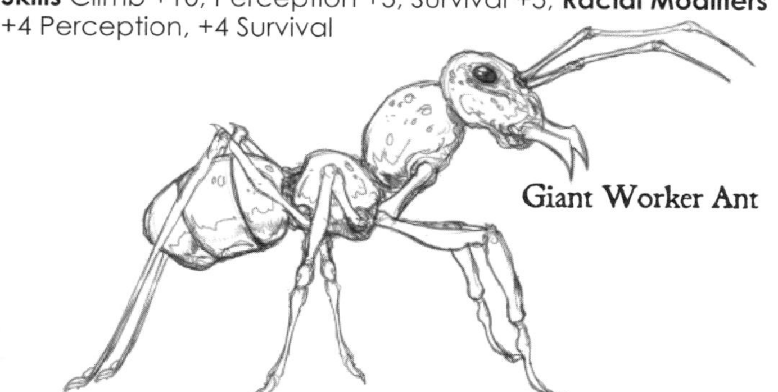
Giant Worker Ant

Warriors: These ants are 5–6 feet long and much more aggressive than their worker sisters. In addition to a nasty bite, these ants have a poison sting. Also sterile females, these ants are the organizers of colony-wide resistance and attack. Attack groups typically are organized into groups of 1 warrior with 6 workers that attack single opponents as a group. The probability of attack depends on several factors if a warrior ant is approached within 50 feet. There are 120 warriors in this hive. Each week, 4d6 more join the hive to replace slain comrades.

GIANT ANT **CR 2**
XP 600
Pathfinder Roleplaying Game Bestiary, "Ant, Giant"
N Medium vermin
Init +0; **Senses** darkvision 60 ft., scent; **Perception** +5

AC 15, touch 10, flat-footed 15 (+5 natural)
hp 18 (2d8+6 plus 3)
Fort +6; **Ref** +0; **Will** +1
Immune mind-affecting effects

Speed 50 ft., climb 20 ft.
Melee bite +3 (1d6+2 plus grab), sting +3 (1d4+2 plus poison)

Str 14, **Dex** 10, **Con** 17, **Int** —, **Wis** 13, **Cha** 11
Base Atk +1; **CMB** +3 (+7 grapple); **CMD** 13 (21 vs. trip)
Feats Toughness[B]
Skills Climb +10, Perception +5, Survival +5; **Racial Modifiers** +4 Perception, +4 Survival

---

Poison (Ex) Sting—injury; *save* Fort DC 14; *frequency* 1/round for 4 rounds; *effect* 1d2 Str; *cure* 1 save

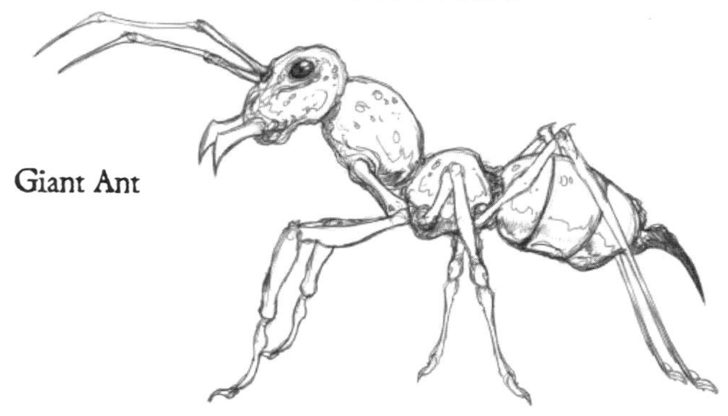
Giant Ant

Drones: These winged male ants are fairly rare outside of the queen's chamber, and quite short-lived (she eats them). They exist only to procreate, only mobilizing to fight if the hive is attacked. They are quite large, but lack the poison sting of the warriors. There are 16 drones in this hive. Each week, 1d6 more join the hive to replace slain comrades.

DRONE ANT **CR 3**
XP 800
Pathfinder Roleplaying Game Bestiary, "Ant, Giant"
N Medium vermin
Init +2; **Senses** darkvision 60 ft., scent; **Perception** +7

AC 19, touch 12, flat-footed 17 (+2 Dex, +7 natural)
hp 25 (2d8+10 plus 3)
Fort +8; **Ref** +2; **Will** +3
Immune mind-affecting effects

Speed 50 ft., climb 20 ft., fly 30 ft. (average)
Melee bite +5 (1d6+4 plus grab), sting +5 (1d4+4)
Special Attacks poison

Str 18, **Dex** 14, **Con** 21, **Int** —, **Wis** 17, **Cha** 15
Base Atk +1; **CMB** +5 (+9 grapple); **CMD** 17 (25 vs. trip)
Feats Toughness[B]
Skills Acrobatics +2 (+10 to jump), Climb +12, Perception +7, Survival +7; **Racial Modifiers** +4 Perception, +4 Survival

---

Poison (Ex) Sting—injury; *save* Fort DC 16; *frequency* 1/round for 4 rounds; *effect* 1d2 Str; *cure* 1 save

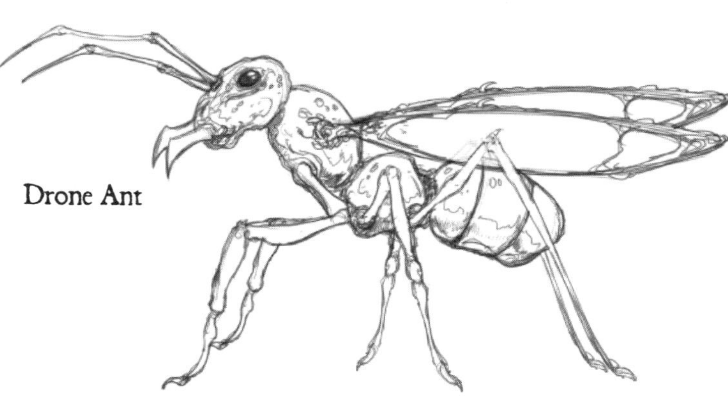
Drone Ant

Bombers: These ants look like workers with large hind ends. Really large hind ends. These Sir Mix-A-Lot inspired critters have a terrible special attack. They are basically suicide bombers that unleash a caustic poison in a 10-foot radius, covering everything near them in the same poison as if one were stung by a warrior. These creatures are also fairly rare in the hive, and are non-aggressive unless directed by a warrior to attack or if they sense the hive is threatened through release of pheromones. There are 60 bombers in this hive. Each week, 2d6 more join the hive to replace slain comrades.

GIANT BOMBER ANT CR 2
XP 600
Pathfinder Roleplaying Game Bestiary, "Ant, Giant"
N Medium vermin
Init +0; **Senses** darkvision 60 ft., scent; **Perception** +5

AC 15, touch 10, flat-footed 15 (+5 natural)
hp 18 (2d8+6 plus 3)
Fort +6; **Ref** +0; **Will** +1
Immune mind-affecting effects

Speed 50 ft., climb 20 ft.
Melee bite +3 (1d6+2)
Special Attacks death throes (10 ft. radius, poison)

Str 14, **Dex** 10, **Con** 17, **Int** —, **Wis** 13, **Cha** 11
Base Atk +1; **CMB** +3; **CMD** 13 (21 vs. trip)
Feats Toughness[B]
Skills Climb +10, Perception +5, Survival +5; **Racial Modifiers** +4 Perception, +4 Survival

Poison (Ex) Death throes—contact; *save* Fort DC 14; *frequency* 1/round for 4 rounds; *effect* 1d2 Str; *cure* 1 save

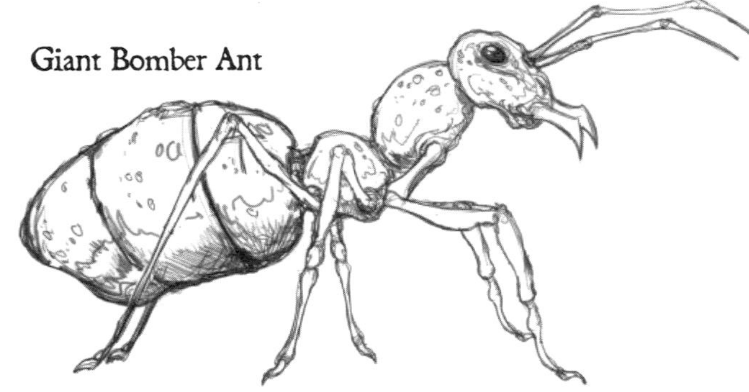
Giant Bomber Ant

The Queen: Her Majesty resides in her throne chamber, and basically sits there, mating with drones and making eggs. The queens are the center of colony life because they reproduce. They do not lead troops or organize labor. Several queen eggs are always hidden in other chambers at any given time in case she is slain or dies. While she lives, queen-bearing eggs are brought to her and devoured. The queen is always accompanied by 3d10 workers and 2d6 warriors. Only one queen exists. If she is slain, another is born within 1d2 days, growing to full size in 6 weeks.

This queen ant is unusual in that she is intelligent, and is treated as if she were the recipient of an *awaken* spell. Thus, she is counted as being a magical beast, and, not being mindless, she has skills and feats. These extra abilities make her CR 5.

QUEEN ANT CR 5
XP 1,600
hp 50 (see **New Monster** at the end of the adventure)

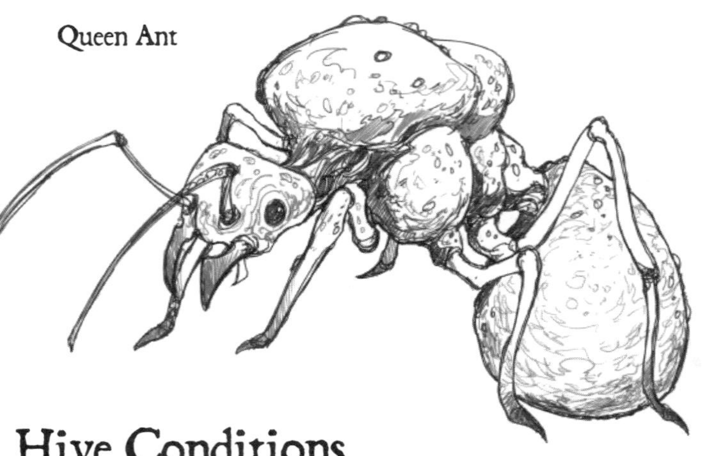
Queen Ant

Hive Conditions

Certain conditions determine how the hive reacts to intrusion by outsiders such as the player characters. These include:

The Hive is at Peace

This is the standard condition of the hive. Normal attack chances occur if any intruders are present. The worker ants touch and sniff anything within reach, but do not physically attack unless attacked or directed by a warrior. Drones and bombers just ignore intruders unless a warrior is present and hostile. The warriors' base chance of immediate attack on anything within 50 feet is 20%, modified as follows:

Circumstance	Modifier
Player Character within 20 feet	+05%
2–3 player characters within 20 feet	+20%
4–5 player characters within 20 feet	+40%
6+ player characters within 20 feet	+60%
Hive in trouble! (One or more ants is killed within 500 feet of the hive)	+90%
Another giant ant (e.g. *polymorphed* character)	+100%
Within 200 feet of queen's chamber	+30%
Within queen's chamber	+100%
Silence spell on character	–40%
Invisibility spell on character	–40%
Character in stealth mode	–30%
Character tosses sweet food (e.g. honey, sugar or aphid jelly)	–30%
Character is coated in giant beetle guts	–50%*
Character slays an ankheg or bulette	–75%**
*There is a 50% chance if not attacked that the warrior sprays the player character with pheromones, making it "one of the gang" unless they attack an ant or enter the queen's chamber. **There is a 50% chance if not attacked that the warrior sprays the player character with pheromones, making it "one of the gang" unless they attack an ant or enter the queen's chamber.	

The Hive is in Trouble!

This occurs if one or more ants is slain within 500 feet of the hive. This causes the slain ant to release pheromones that indicate the hive is under attack. Note that instant kills, such as by *cloudkill*, *fireball*, etc. do not allow the ant to release this warning. Should this occur, all outsiders are treated as hostile, and the ants organize and attack. While some of the workers that first reach the attacking force try to delay or subdue the intruders, another group does not join the fight immediately, but instead returns home, leaving an odor trail behind. When they arrive home, they warn their nest mates by moving their bodies back and forth, and touching the antennae of the other ants with their own antennae. This gathers **6d6 workers**, **3d6 warriors** and **1d6 bombers** as reinforcements to join the fight. If they are slain or losing, another batch of the same numbers arrives every 10 minutes thereafter. Another cause of war is one colony (basically anything that is or resembles a giant ant) entering the territory of another.

Famine!

This situation occurs if the aphid nest or the fungus garden is destroyed after a 1-week delay. In this case, workers attack at the same probability as warriors. All the remaining ants remain unchanged.

A Note on Using Area of Effect or "Kill the Hive" Spells

Use of spells such as *fireball* and *lightning bolt* in dirt tunnels can be very dangerous. Any use of large destructive spells within a tunnel or chamber has a chance of causing a collapse within its area of effect equal to the points of damage done by the spell (assuming no save). This area has a 25% chance to expand 50% in all directions. Hence, if an 8-die *fireball* is cast in a 40-foot chamber doing 32 points of damage before saves are calculated, the 20-foot area centered on the burst area collapses 32% of the time, with the area expanding to a 30-foot-diameter area on a second roll of 25% or less.

"Kill the hive" spells such as *cloudkill* can certainly wipe out a large number of ants. Keep in mind the area of effect and duration of the spell, as the vast size of this place would only allow a small portion of the hive to be killed. One nice effect of spells that cause instant death is that they prevent ants from releasing "The Hive is in Trouble" pheromones.

Four Areas — One Hive

Nearly all of the hive area is un-numbered areas. These tunnels and chambers are full of random ants, and little else. Numbered locations are described specifically at the end of this section. Movement through the hive absent the map in **Area 2** is rather random, as it is a huge, trackless maze. Each minute, roll 1d20 on the following chart to determine what the player characters find. Encounters are dictated in each level description. Following the map (or using a *find the path* spell or equivalent) uses 60 of these features (as selected by the GM), but always encounters **Areas 3**, **5** and **6**, and terminates in **Area 8**.

1	Pathway up to the surface, requires crawling (1–9) or can be walked (10) out of (into keyed **Areas 1** or **2**). Applies only in the Upper Hive; otherwise, it moves the party up one level.
2–4	Tunnel continues 100 feet at a flat slope.
5–6	Tunnel continues, but reduces in size (anything larger than a halfling must crawl).
7–8	Opens into a chamber of 10d10 feet in diameter with 1d3 exits.
9–10	Opens into a chamber of 5d10 feet in diameter with 1d3–1 exits.
11–12	Dead-ends.
13–14	Opens into a numbered area (determine randomly) from the keyed area.
15–16	Tunnel slopes up or down at a steep slope for 100 feet.
17	Obstacle blocks path: deep deadfall (01–25); sheer cliff of 10–60 feet (26–50); partial blockage requiring crawling (51–75); or collapsed tunnel (76–00). This requires the GM to improvise to some degree, and allows player characters to use climb or other skills
18–19	Tunnel leads down to the next level
20	Tunnel leads deep into the earth (GM's choice of where this leads)

Entrance and Upper Hive

The entrance and upper levels of the hive consist of dirt tunnels and chambers dug out by the tireless labor of the workers. These tunnels typically are 6–10 feet in diameter and are composed of hard packed earth. Eleven surface entrances lead down into the hive, and these lead into chambers full of workers and the occasional other ant. Only the entrances leading to **Areas 1** and **2** are passable by anything larger than a halfling unless one crawls inside. If using the map, this area requires 20 minutes to traverse.

In this area, wandering monsters check must be made once per minute by rolling on the following table.

1–9	**1d3 worker ants**
10–11	**1 warrior** and **1d6 worker ants**
12	**1 drone**
13	**1d6 warriors**, **1 bomber** and **2d6 worker ants**
14–19	No encounter
20	Intruder!

Worker Ants: These ignore all beyond 20 feet (roll 6d6 for distance); otherwise, they behave as described above. They typically carry leaves and sticks or other food items.

Warrior Ants: These behave as described above.

Drones: These ignore intruders unless commanded to attack by a warrior.

Intruder: This is **1d6 ankhegs** (50% chance), **1d6 giant boring beetles** (see **Area 6**) (35% chance) or a **bulette** (15% chance) here to eat ants (and anything else). They attack anything they encounter. Note that covering oneself in beetle guts, or defending the ants against the larger predators can have positive consequences. Any intruder encounter automatically draws an encounter as if 13 was rolled after 5 rounds of combat.

Keyed Areas in the Upper Hive

Area 1. Are Those Big Grasshoppers? (CR 8+ . . . but with help if the PCs leave the ants alone!)

The tunnel entrance at this location seems devoid of ants. The walls and ceiling of this 20-foot-diameter hole are made of the same compacted earth as the rest of the entrances, but the floor seems freshly dug and soft. Carefully inspecting the floor reveals that various bits and pieces of ants (legs, a thorax or two) are mixed in with the soft dirt piles. The odd leg or antennae sticks out of the piles.

The tunnel leads to a chamber 60 feet across with large piles of rock and earth blocking all other exits. Four rounds after the chamber is entered, **6 ankhegs** break through the floor and attack anything within the chamber (unless it was entered by someone under magical *silence*). This in turn draws 1 battle group of ants every minute, starting on the 5th round of combat. A battle group consists of **3d6 workers, 1d6 warrior** and **1 bomber ant**.

The ants have largely abandoned this entrance, blocking access from below after deciding that losses were too high to defeat the ankheg nest. That being said, should sounds of battle emanate from here, the ants join in the fray. Player characters who are carefully observant notice that while the ants attack the ankhegs, none attacks the player characters. If any player character attacks an ant, they are sprayed with a pheromone indicating they are hostile — and all ants automatically attack them for 1 hour.

ANKHEGS (6) **CR 3**
XP 800
hp 28 (*Pathfinder Roleplaying Game Bestiary* "Ankeg")

GIANT WORKER ANTS (3d6) **CR 1**
XP 400
hp 18 (see **Giant Ants and the Hive Mentality**)

GIANT ANTS (1d6) **CR 2**
XP 600
hp 18 (see **Giant Ants and the Hive Mentality**)

GIANT BOMBER ANT **CR 2**
XP 600
hp 18 (see **Giant Ants and the Hive Mentality**)

Ankheg Tactics: Ankhegs gain automatic surprise on the first round of combat except against someone with mining skills or a dwarf. They burst through the ground and attack using their bite immediately. Each round thereafter, an ankheg has a 25% chance of spitting acid and a 75% chance of attacking physically. If wounded over 50%, an individual ankheg retreats underground and burrows away.

Ant Tactics: The ants attack individual ankhegs in groups of 6 worker and 1 warrior, with extra workers aiding their "allies" (the player characters) until a total of 7 creatures are on a single ankheg. The bomber ant heads toward the farthest away ankheg and explodes on it. To help run this combat, you might want to let your players each run a worker ant or two (or three) in addition to their character. Of course, if the PCs attack the ants, this option is off the table…

Development: Should the player characters help the ants defeat the ankhegs, any surviving warriors (roll for each) has a 50% chance of approaching one individual player character (it seems aggressive, but is not) rear end first and spraying a pheromone on them. This spray lasts 1 hour, and prevents the individual player character from being attacked by any ants unless the queen's chamber is entered or the player characters is within 10 feet of an ant killed (releases a counter pheromone that labels the individual an enemy) by the player characters or an ally.

Area 2. Dead Dudes (CR 4–10)

This large tunnel entrance (8 feet in diameter) leads 40 feet down at a 10% slope and opens into a 40-foot-diameter chamber. During daylight hours, it contains **3d6 worker ants**. It is abandoned during the night. The far wall is spattered with blood and bits and parts of nonedible adventuring equipment. Present in the chamber are the following:

A spear head, 2 daggers (one is bent and corroded and has the broken condition), a mace head, a completely destroyed suit of plate armor, a shredded (and very bloody) suit of chain armor (also broken), a metal shield (missing its leather straps)

An iron box containing two potion bottles (*potion of flying* and *potion of levitation*)

An ivory scroll tube containing a map of the best path through the middle levels leading to the worked stone area and the sword vault. Travel using the map takes 1 hour to reach the stone tunnel area. Ants and other creatures encountered on the map path include wandering monsters as well as **Areas 3**, **5** and **6**.

No organic or body parts are here, as everything edible was picked clean by worker ants.

GIANT WORKER ANTS (3d6) **CR 1**
XP 400
hp 18 (see **Giant Ants and the Hive Mentality**)

The Middle Hive

Dozens of tunnels and chambers fill this area, most full of workers. This creates a maze that makes it almost impossible to follow without a map or spell indicating the correct way to go. This area contains the "cow farms" of giant aphids. Random wandering through this area likely leads to certain doom, as eventually the player characters are attacked by a warrior, forced to defend themselves, and are either killed or kill an ant (creating a "Hive is in Trouble" situation). If using the map, this area requires 30 minutes to traverse.

In this area, wandering monsters check must be made once per minute by rolling on the following table.

1–9	1d3 worker ants
10	1 bomber
11	1 drone, 1d2 warriors, 1 bomber and 1d6 worker ants
12–19	No encounter
20	Intruder!

Worker Ants: These ignore all beyond 20 feet (roll 8d6 for distance for all encounters [in feet]); otherwise, they behave as described above. They typically carry chunks of dirt or rocks, aphid jelly or other food items.

Warrior Ants: These behave as described above.

Drones: These ignore intruders unless commanded to attack by a warrior.

Intruder: This is either **1d4 ankhegs** (35% chance), **2d6 giant boring beetles** (see **Area 6**) (50% chance) or a **bulette** (15% chance) here to eat ants (and anything else). They attack any they encounter. Note that covering oneself in beetle guts, or defending the ants against the larger predators can have positive consequences. Any intruder encountered automatically draws an encounter as if 11 was rolled after 5 rounds of combat.

Keyed Areas in the Middle Hive

Area 3. The Aphid Nest (CR 4–10)

This chamber is 200 feet in diameter and is filled in the center with torn up bits of plants and branches covered in leaves. At any given time, **3d6 worker ants** are present here, running aphid puke out of the chamber to warriors and the queen at regular intervals. This area represents the primary delivery area for outside vegetation brought in by the workers each day. In addition to all the greenery, approximately **200 giant aphids** rove about the chamber munching way on the leaves and branches. The aphids ignore intruders unless touched (or attacked), in which case they regurgitate a sticky, sweet substance on the ground (gallons) and squeak and retreat from the one contacting them. The aphids are harmless. If attacked, they do not defend themselves. A giant aphid has AC 12, touch 10, flat-footed 12 (+2 natural) and has 11 hp.

These giant aphids are used as cows by the ants. The aphids secrete a sweet substance called honeydew that ants prize as food. This substance consists of partially digested, highly concentrated plant sap and other wastes, and is excreted by the aphids. These aphids have a symbiotic relationship with the ants that resembles the relationship of domestic cattle to humans, hence the name "ant cows" for aphids. The ants tend the aphids, transporting them to their food plants at the appropriate stages of the aphids' life cycle and sheltering the aphids. The aphids, in turn, provide honeydew for the ants.

Should all the aphids be slain, the ants go into "famine" mode as described above. Note that the aphids do not release ant pheromones, nor do the worker ants present react to aphids being killed.

GIANT WORKER ANTS (3d6) **CR 1**
XP 400
hp 18 (see **Giant Ants and the Hive Mentality**)

Treasure: Careful digging around in the dirt piles reveals a few pieces of plate armor. One of these (a breastplate) is inscribed with the family crest of the dead noble slain in battle (see adventure hooks). One could also obtain a bunch of honeydew and use it to pacify warrior ants (1 gallon pacifies an ant if offered before it attacks) if containers are available.

Area 4. Bombs Away! (CR 8–13)

This is the nesting area for the hive's bomber ants. At all times, **6d6 bomber ants** are present here. They are generally nonaggressive and slow moving. The ants segregate them to avoid "accidents" should

The Hive

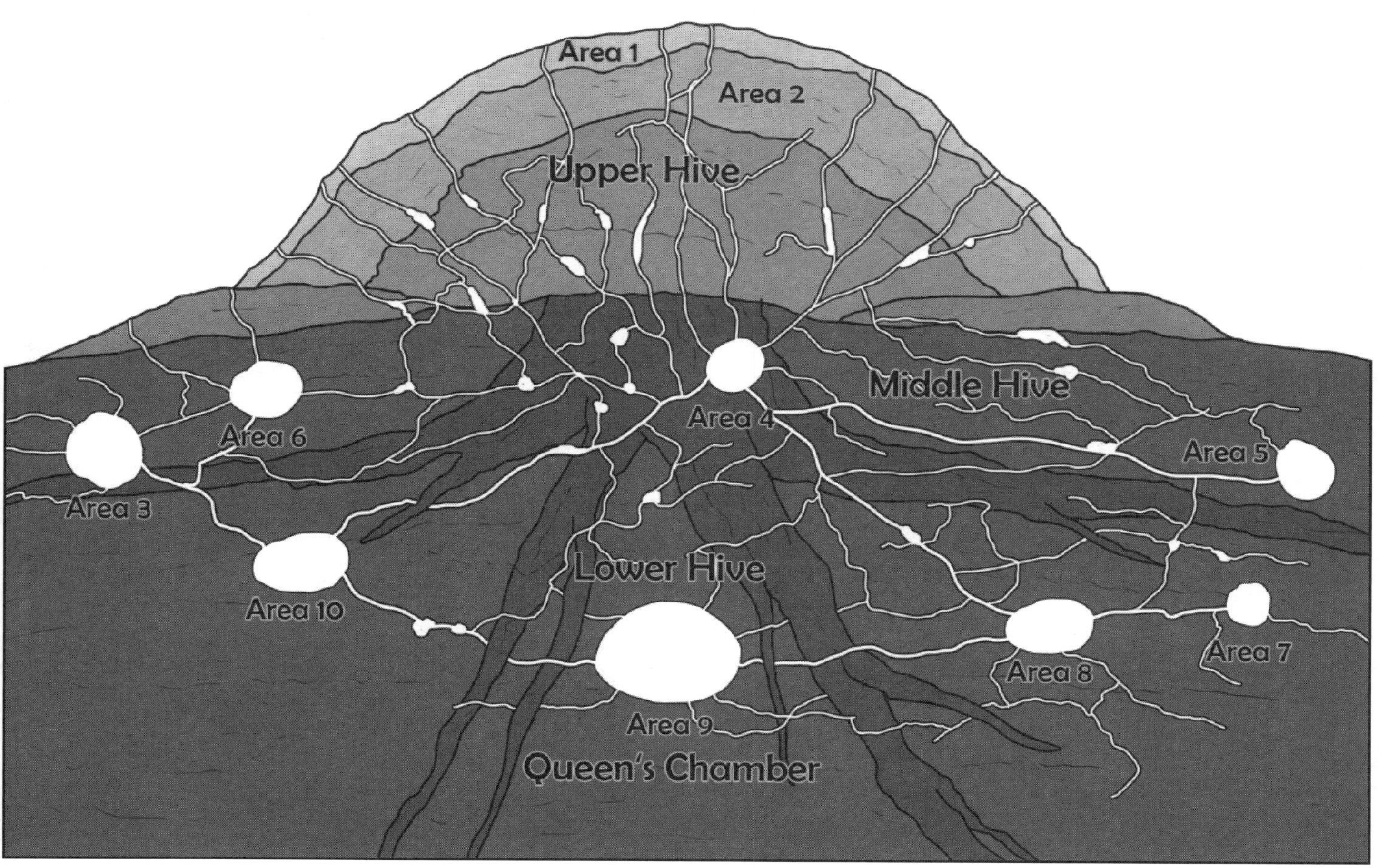

they accidentally pop. The ants only bother intruders if attacked or if the hive is on alert due to famine or war pheromones. If any player character bears hostility pheromones, this area is very dangerous. Otherwise, the bomber ants just sit still, resting, and do not even sniff or investigate intruders (its tiring carrying around that big butt!).

GIANT BOMBER ANTS (6d6) **CR 2**
XP 600
hp 18 (see **Giant Ants and the Hive Mentality**)

Area 5. Eeek! It's a Mushroom (CR 9–11)

This chamber is made of packed dirt and spans an area of roughly 100 feet in diameter. It is completely covered with hundreds of mushroom growths the ants use as food. Some of the growths are as small as a few inches high and some are as large as a man. There are always **3d6 worker ants** here. Several species of very large fungus are in the center of the cave. Two of these are of note:

Large grayish, 4-foot-tall brown mushrooms are present in a 10 foot area. Careful inspection from afar reveals that the dead and rotted bodies of several worker ants are present in a decaying state near their base. These **6 mushrooms** are a form of **violet fungus**. They move and attack anything that comes within 10 feet. The ants are oblivious to the danger they pose.

Two large silver-and-red mushrooms stand in a small wet area near the center of the cavern. These are **2 shriekers**. If anyone approaches within 10 feet, they sound off, causing a wandering monster check with +12 on the roll (ants are used to the noise, but other creatures see this as a dinner bell!).

Should the fungus all be destroyed, the famine condition described above applies to the colony.

GIANT WORKER ANTS (3d6) **CR 1**
XP 400
hp 18 (see **Giant Ants and the Hive Mentality**)

VIOLET FUNGI (6) **CR 3**
XP 800
hp 30 (*Pathfinder Roleplaying Game Bestiary*, "Violet Fungus")

Area 6. Raid! (CR 9)

This is more of a fixed encounter than it is a room. At some point in the exploration, the player characters encounter a mass melee between giant boring beetles and ants. When the player characters enter the room, **12 workers**, **7 warrior ants**, and **2 bombers** are fighting **7 giant boring beetles**. These beetles have developed a taste for giant ant and burrowed here to get a meal. Similar to the ankheg encounter, this encounter provides an opportunity for the player characters to become "one of the gang" with the ants for a short period of time and facilitate passage through the hive. Once again, the ants do not attack the player characters unless attacked and treat them as allies in this fight.

GIANT BORING BEETLES (7) **CR 3**
XP 800
The Tome of Horrors Complete p. 56
N Large vermin
Init +0; **Senses** darkvision 60 ft.; **Perception** +0

AC 15, touch 9, flat-footed 15 (+6 natural, -1 size)
hp 30 (4d8+12)
Fort +7; **Ref** +1; **Will** +1
Defensive Abilities hive mind; **Immune** mind-affecting effects

---

Speed 20 ft.
Melee bite +6 (2d6+6)
Space 10 ft.; **Reach** 5 ft.

Str 18, **Dex** 10, **Con** 16, **Int** —, **Wis** 10, **Cha** 9
Base Atk +3; **CMB** +8; **CMD** 18 (26 vs. trip)

Environment temperate forests
Organization cluster (2–5), swarm (6—1), or hive (12–19 plus 2–8 shriekers)
Treasure none

Hive Mind (Ex) All boring beetles within 1 mile of each other are in constant communication. If one is aware of a particular danger, they all are. If one in the group is not flat-footed, then none of them are. No boring beetle in a group is considered flanked unless all of them are.

GIANT WORKER ANTS (12) **CR 1**
XP 400
hp 18 (see **Giant Ants and the Hive Mentality**)

GIANT ANTS (7) **CR 2**
XP 600
hp 18 (see **Giant Ants and the Hive Mentality**)

GIANT BOMBER ANTS (2) **CR 2**
XP 600
hp 18 (see **Giant Ants and the Hive Mentality**)

Beetle Tactics: Being far larger than the ants, the beetles try to quickly kill anything non-beetle that they can and move onto the next victim. If the beetles win the combat, they take anything killed to devour.

Ant Tactics: The ants attack individual beetles in groups of 6 workers and 1 warrior, with extra warriors or workers aiding their player character "allies," until a total of 7 creatures are on a single beetle. The bomber ant heads toward the ankheg that is farthest away and explodes. As before, you can let your players run some of the ants in this encounter.

Afterword: Should the player characters help the ants defeat the beetles, any surviving warriors (roll for each) has a 50% chance of approaching one individual player character (it seems aggressive, but is not) rear end first and spraying a pheromone on them. This spray lasts for 1 hour and prevents that player character from being attacked by any ants unless the queen's chamber is entered or if the player character is within 10 feet of an ant when it is killed (the counter pheromones released with the ant's death labels the individual an enemy). Anyone smeared with beetle guts is treated as if he had the friendly pheromone for 1 hour as well.

The Lower Hive and Queen's Chambers

This area features more aggressive warrior ants as well as several areas central to the adventure. The warrior and drone ants here are always aggressive (+30%), and usually attack anyone not coated in beetle guts or friendly pheromones. One ant always runs immediately to the queen's chambers to warn the ants of intruders, even if the intruders have the correct smell. If using the map, this area requires 10 minutes to traverse.

In this area, wandering monster checks must be made once per minute by rolling on the following table:

1–7	1d6 worker ants
8–10	1d6 solder ants
11–15	1d6 warriors and 2d6 worker ants
16–19	No encounter
20	Intruder!

Worker Ants: These ants ignore all beyond 20 feet (roll 8d6 for distance for all encounters [in feet]), otherwise they behave as described above. They typically carry aphid jelly.

Warrior Ants: These behave as described above.

Drones: These ignore intruders unless commanded to attack by a warrior.

Intruder: This encounter is with **1d4 ankhegs** (15% chance), **2d6 giant boring beetles** (see **Area 6**) (35% chance) or a **bulette** (50% chance) here to eat ants (and anything else). They attack anything they encounter. Note that covering oneself beetle guts or defending the ants against the larger predators can have positive consequences. Any intruder encounter automatically draws an encounter as if 11–15 was rolled after 5 rounds of combat.

Keyed Areas in the Lower Hive

Area 7. The Queen's Chamber (CR 9+ if the players feel like fighting lots and lots of ants!)

This 200-foot-by-200-foot square chamber is constructed of cut stone and has been commandeered by the ant queen as her throne chamber. Nine exits lead out of the room at various places, none of which is big enough for anything larger than a halfling to crawl, except the stone passageway that leads to **Area 8**. The ceiling is 20 feet high and also made of cut and mortared stone. The room is filled with thousands of eggs, as well as pools of honeydew and choice tidbits of animal flesh, plant matter and fungus. There are always **2d6 warriors**, **1d6 drones** and **3d10 worker ants** here, as well as the hive's unusually intelligent **queen**. Note that all warriors here are elite and have maximum hit points.

As the center of intelligence for the any colony, the queen directs the warriors to position themselves in front of her and on her sides. She does not order them to immediately attack, preferring to wait until she sees how PCs react. During this time, **2d6 workers** scurry off to gather reinforcements. A total of **1d3 battle groups** (**3d6 workers** and **2d6 warrior ants**) arrive each minute after the first. No bombers come to this chamber.

GIANT WORKER ANTS (3d10) CR 1
XP 400
hp 18 (see **Giant Ants and the Hive Mentality**)

GIANT ANTS (2d6) CR 2
XP 600
hp 25 (max hp) (see **Giant Ants and the Hive Mentality**)

DRONE ANTS (1d6) CR 3
XP 800
hp 25 (see **Giant Ants and the Hive Mentality**)

QUEEN ANT CR 5
XP 1,600
hp 50 (see **Giant Ants and the Hive Mentality**)

Development: This room can either be a boon or a deathtrap. Note that pheromone spray of any kind does not fool the queen. She recognizes intruders for what they are. Tactics that can be employed here are to either 1) present an offering of sweet food to the queen, then back off slowly and leave, or 2) converse with the queen. Although she cannot speak any language, she understands Common and can communicate with gestures and body language. Understanding the queen requires a successful DC 15 Sense Motive check. Any other tactics or actions result in the entire hive coming down and attacking intruders. The queen is suspicious, but should the player characters have beetle guts or pheromones indicating they have helped the hive, she likely lets them pass, assuming they are suitably deferent.

As long as the player characters persuade her that a) they mean no harm and b) are not stealing eggs, they are either left to wander (if they have fought the ankhegs, beetles or bulette) or are attacked and eaten. It is possible that the queen would send them (under threat of death) to deal with the bulette in **Area 10**, as she has lost too many warriors attempting to rid her hive of it. If asked for eggs, she indicates that if the bulette is killed, she will grant a boon of 10 royal eggs (she would have just eaten them anyway, as a new queen is a potential rival and not tolerated). If this is the case, she sends a warrior ant to guide the player characters to **Area 9** and allows them to take 10 eggs. Roleplaying with the queen and the player characters can be a fun experience and is largely left to the individual GM. She is haughty and highly intelligent. She knows nothing of the sword vault and directs her minions to avoid the area as many were killed while examining it.

The queen has no treasure.

Area 8. Tunnels of Stone

Eventually, either by luck or by using the map from **Area 2**, the player characters find this area. The dirt-and-mud tunnels suddenly change to a mud-brick, mortared stone complex. This area is obviously constructed by men, not ants. The entrance to these tunnels is where the ants dug to, and the room here is 30 feet square, with exits straight ahead (to **Area 7**) and the left (to the **Dungeon of the Sword**). The left tunnel runs 60 feet straight and ends in a staircase going down.

Area 9. Royal Eggs (CR 7)

This chamber is made of dirt like the rest of the ant hive. The chamber itself is 40 feet in diameter and has no other exits. There are always **6 warrior ants** here. Only warrior ants are allowed to transport royal eggs, and these stand guard in case the queen is killed, in which case a drone is summoned to fertilize three of them. The eggs are allowed to hatch, and the infant queens then fight a three-way duel to the death with the survivor becoming the new queen. Thirty royal eggs are here.

GIANT ANTS (6) CR 2
XP 600
hp 25 (max hp) (see **Giant Ants and the Hive Mentality**)

Area 10. Bite the Bulette (CR 7)

The solid stone tunnel leading to this area is nearly devoid of ants, with only a half dozen workers at 30-foot intervals along its 180-foot length. The workers stand motionless, not even bothering to sniff intruders unless the **bulette** makes an appearance. The end of the tunnel opens into a stone-and-dirt walled chamber 100 feet in diameter. Unlike the other chambers in this place, this one has a stone ceiling covered with stalactites, although its floor is dirt. Bits of the fallen limestone cover the floor in small piles, and water drips down, making the floor somewhat muddy and slippery.

There is a 20% chance that the bulette is asleep here, a 40% chance it is out hunting, and a 40 % chance it is awake and waiting in the ground. The bulette has reached an uneasy truce with the ants, neither wanting to give up its lair nor wishing to continuously fight these nasty-tasting, acid-filled insects. Unlike the ankhegs and beetles, the bulette does not particularly enjoy ant as a meal. Likewise, the ants, after initially trying to drive the beast off, quickly realized that his thick armor and devastating attacks were more than a match for them, and decided to leave guards posted and well enough alone.

BULETTE **CR 7**
XP 3,200
hp 84 (*Pathfinder Roleplaying Game Bestiary* "Bulette")

Tactics: The bulette seeks meals elsewhere, but due to his ability to track prey by vibrations, quickly realizes something tastier than ants is coming down the tunnel. His favorite tactic is to keep his nose just above the ground (it looks like a rock) and attack by crawling up and out of the ground to surprise opponents. The bulette attacks any within the chamber, ignoring dwarves and pursuing halflings throughout the corridors leading to this chamber.

At the first sign the bulette is active, the worker ants retreat to get help. Unlike combat with the ankhegs and beetles, the ants stand back from this fight, scattering away from the bulette unless he approaches the queen's chamber. A battle group of **3d6 workers** and **2d6 warrior ants** arrives each minute to fight the creature.

Development: Should the player characters defeat the bulette, any surviving character is approached by an ant warrior (it seems aggressive, but is not) rear end first and sprayed with pheromones. This spray lasts for 1 hour and prevents the individual player character from being attacked by any ants unless the queen's chamber is entered or the player character is within 10 feet of an ant when it is killed (the counter pheromones released with the ant's death labels the individual an enemy).

The Dungeon of the Sword

The ant colony found a very easy way to expand its hive recently. While tunneling, they came across a long-buried, worked stone dungeon. Defeating everything residing there, they used the worked stone corridors and rooms as new space without having to dig. This uncovered a strange vault area that killed many of them. They now give that place a wide berth. This area begins where the stairs connect down from **Area 8**. The downstairs area is off-limits to the ants, and none come here. No wandering monsters are encountered on this level.

Keyed Areas within the Dungeon of the Sword

Area 11. Ants Don't Build Traps! (CR 2+)

At the base of the stairs, the corridor continues 60 feet and turns to the left. The floor is filled with desiccated and crushed remains of ants,

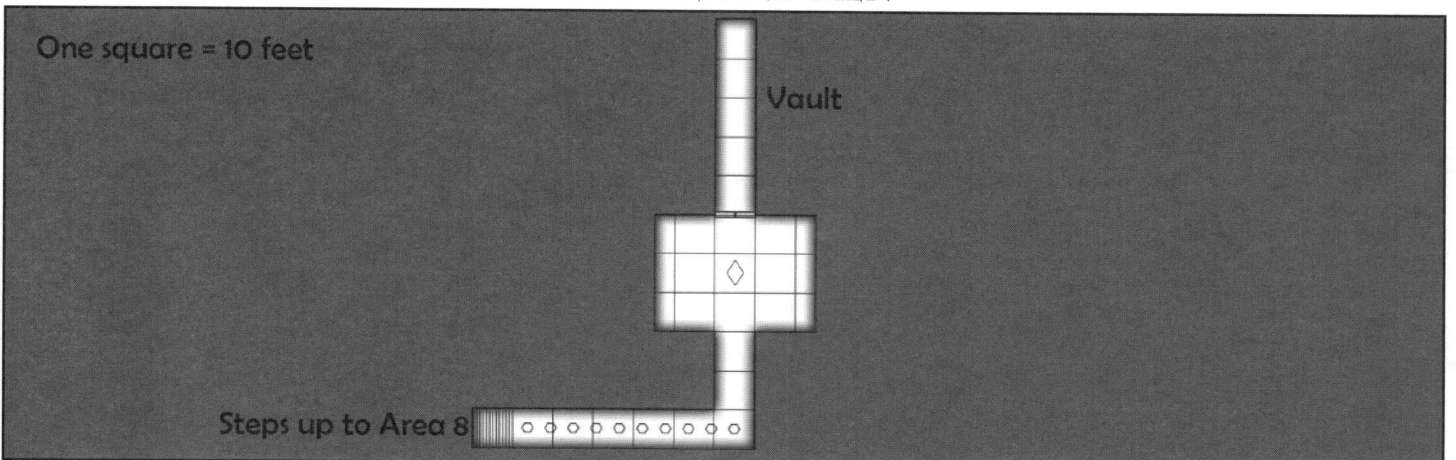

perhaps a dozen or so. Bits and pieces of these are smashed flat in places, while other parts seem basically intact. Careful inspection reveals the floor to be composed of 1-foot-by-6-inch rectangular bricks surrounding 2-foot-wide hexagonal bricks spaced 3 feet apart. The hexagonal bricks are all pressure plates — each triggers a release mechanism that unleashes a heavy spring that thrusts the 2-foot-wide hexagonal columns into the ceiling. Anyone in contact with a hexagonal section of the floor is thrust up into the ceiling and smashed flat. Moving around the hexagonal bricks requires a DC 5 Acrobatics check if one is specifically trying to avoid the hexagonal plates. Triggering these causes 6d6 points of damage; a successful DC 20 Reflex save negates the damage. There are 20 such sections in the 60-foot hallway, but the characters only get XP for the ones they actually disable, avoid with an Acrobatics check, or set off. Once the corridor turns, the hexagonal plates are not present.

CRUSHING COLUMN TRAP(S) **CR 2**
XP 600
Type mechanical; **Perception** DC 20; **Disable Device** DC 20

Trigger touch; **Reset** none; **Bypass** DC 5 Acrobatics check
Effect 6d6 damage (DC 20 Ref negates)

Area 12. Something Wicked This Way Comes

The corridor continues another 30 feet and opens into a 30-foot-by-40-foot room. A large, stone double door is present on the far side, opposite the corridor. In the center of the room is a 5-foot-per-side, diamond-shaped stone of pure blue marble, sharply contrasting against the other reddish-brown mud brick of the place.

The Door (CR 6)

In the center of the door is a large keyhole with a cup-shaped depression 3 inches deep encircling the actual keyhole. The cup is surrounded by a series of small quarter-inch holes. The door is carved with mysterious runes and hieroglyphs. No magic of any kind functions within 10 feet of the door. The GM should read the description of the new magic item below before proceeding, as magic items fail within 10 feet of the door and may in fact be permanently destroyed.

Read magic (if cast 10 feet or more away from the door) deciphers the runes as an inactive *curse* spell, powerless and drained of its former magic. *Comprehend languages* (if cast more than 10 feet from the door) can be used to read the hieroglyphs. They pronounce a general curse in an ancient tongue against all wizards and priests, calling them "deceivers and villains," and stating that "all of them will die in lakes of fire and blood." A successful DC 30 Linguistics check also reveals this information. The door is locked with an extremely intricate lock and requires three consecutive DC 20 Disable Device checks with any single failed check requiring a restart of the three checks. Further, failure triggers breakage of a hidden vial and release of a poison acid-gas trap that fills the entire room in 3 rounds. Anyone within 5 feet is automatically affected. The glass vial can be detected with a DC 20 Perception check but cannot be removed, as it is 3 inches inside the door frame. If the player characters ask exactly how far in they saw the glass object, be very clear on the distance, as this may come into play when they use the key-scepter found in the coffin as described below. The gas dissipates in 1 day. Anyone affected by the gas must succeed on a DC 20 Fortitude save each round they are in it or take 8d6 points of damage on each failed save (half damage on a save). The gas triggers only once.

LETHAL GAS TRAP **CR 6**
XP 2,400
Type mechanical; **Perception** DC 20; **Disable Device** DC 20 (3 consecutive successes)

Trigger touch; **Reset** none
Effect lethal gas (8d6 damage, DC 20 Fort negates); multiple targets (all within 5 ft. of the door)

The Blue Diamond (CR 3)

The blue diamond in the center of the floor is a stone slab. It is not set with mortar as are the other bricks in this room. Prying it up requires a crowbar or other lever and can easily be accomplished by someone with such an implement (DC 15 Strength check).

Beneath the stone is a 5-foot-deep, 3-foot-wide and 5-foot-long vault that contains what appears to be a mummy case-like coffin. Contrary to popular opinion, no undead is within the coffin. What is contains, however, is a terrible menace known as a **scarab beetle swarm**. The swarm bursts out of the coffin 1d3 rounds after the diamond plate is removed or immediately if the coffin is opened. It attacks the nearest opponent then moves randomly toward the next closest target.

SCARAB BEETLE SWARM **CR 3**
XP 800
Dunes of Desolation 60
N Diminutive vermin (swarm)
Init +2; **Senses** darkvision 60 ft., tremorsense 30 ft.; **Perception** +4

AC 16, touch 16, flat-footed 14 (+2 Dex, +4 size)
hp 28 (8d8–8)
Fort +5; **Ref** +4; **Will** +2
Defensive Abilities swarm traits; **Immune** weapon damage

Speed 40 ft.
Melee swarm (2d6)
Space 10 ft.; **Reach** 0 ft.

New Special Item

The Two-Edged Sword

Aura none
Slot none; **Weight** 6 lbs.

DESCRIPTION

This longsword is a non-magical sword made of osmium, one of the rarest metals in the world. Osmium is a hard, brittle, bluish-white metal in the platinum group that is found as a trace element in alloys, mostly in platinum ores. This is probably the largest piece of pure osmium in the world. Osmium is the densest naturally occurring element, and the sword is so heavy it is treated as one size category larger for Medium and Small creatures.

The *two-edged sword* radiates magic drain in a 60-foot radius (similar to an *antimagic field*). The magic drain creates a field of anti-magic that prevents all spells and spell-like abilities from functioning within its area of affect, including those generated outside and brought inside. This affects all spells cast by player characters regardless of class. The wildshape class ability is not affected.

Unlike an *antimagic field*, spells are automatically dispelled within its range and magic items can be affected beyond suppression. Magic items brought within the area must make a save once per day (as per *disjunction*) or be permanently destroyed. Artifacts are suppressed but not destroyed.

DESTRUCTION

The *two-edged sword* is not a magic item, and can be destroyed in any way which would completely destroy a normal sword. Since the magic-canceling properties of the *sword* are in the metal itself and are not a magical property, breaking the sword simply creates 1d4+1 osmium fragments, each with a magic-cancelling aura with a radius in feet equal to 60 divided by the number of fragments. The metal of the *sword* must be completely destroyed; melting it in non-magical fire at 3,300 degrees kelvin (5,480 degrees Fahrenheit) is one way of achieving that.

Special Attacks daze (DC 10), distraction (DC 13)

Str 1, **Dex** 15, **Con** 8, **Int** —, **Wis** 10, **Cha** 2
Base Atk +6; **CMB** —; **CMD** —
Skills Perception +4; **Racial Modifier** +4 Perception

Environment desert or underground
Organization solitary, or scourge (2–5 swarms)
Treasure none

Daze (Ex) Any living creature that begins its turn with a beetle swarm in its space must succeed on a DC 10 Will save or be dazed. This is a mind-affecting fear effect. The save DC is Charisma-based.

Treasure: Inside the coffin are a golden rod worth 2,500 gp and the bones of a man. The scepter is 3 feet long and has a large knob on one end and a large knob with a 4-inch key-like protrusion of the other. It is carved with entwined snakes with large fangs, their heads facing the end with the extended key. If used to open the door, the end with just the knob works like a key and simply opens the door. The end with the key protrusion does likewise, but also triggers the gas trap as described above as it shatters the vial containing the acid-gas. If anyone asks, be clear that the key would hit the glass object (if detected) inside the keyhole.

Area 13. The Sword Vault

Once the door is opened, a corridor leads back 50 feet and ends in a blank wall. No magic of any kind functions in this corridor. Careful searching locates a single brick that is not mortared along the base of the floor in the center of the back wall. If this brick is pried loose, a keyhole is found. Not surprisingly, the key-like protrusion on the golden rod fits it perfectly.

It is possible to open the lock without the rod, but highly difficult (a DC 30 Disable Device check).

In any case, once the lock is opened, a rumbling is heard, and the bricks and mortar start to crack and fall apart. At this point, have the party roll initiative; the floor's initiative is +0. The floor and vault below rapidly rise up toward the ceiling. In two rounds, the floor rises up completely until it is flush with the roof and squashes to jelly anything trapped within (5d100 points of damage per round, no save, no XP for this "trap" as the characters have 2 rounds to jump to safety and their death by inaction is their own fault…). The key to escaping this trap is running rapidly back into **Area 12**. Anyone foolish enough to stay in this corridor is dead.

The vault itself is composed of the same blue marble as the diamond in **Area 12**. In its center lies a sword wrapped in dusty red cloth. The cloth falls apart if touched. This is the *two-edged sword*.

Escape!

The obvious problem with getting back outside with the sword is that no magic or magical abilities can be used. Hence, even if the party is able to become invisible or use some other means such as druidic shape change to find and enter this place, none of that works on the way out. If the player characters befriend, or at least have not offended, the ant hive, this should not be impossible. In any case, it requires the full 60-minute run of the gauntlet (assuming the map was used) to escape this place. That means that going out is just as difficult as coming in. Half the difficulty of this adventure is getting out intact. Remember: Possession of the sword is "two-edged."

New Monster

QUEEN ANT **CR 5**
XP 1,600
N Large magical beast
Init +1; **Senses** darkvision 60 ft., scent; **Perception** +7

AC 20, touch 10, flat-footed 19 (+1 Dex, +10 natural, –1 size)
hp 50 (4d8+28 plus 4)
Fort +11, **Ref** +2, **Will** +4

Speed 10 ft.
Melee bite +8 (1d8+6 plus grab), sting +8 (1d6+6)
Space 10 ft.; **Reach** 5 ft.
Special Attacks poison

Str 22, **Dex** 12, **Con** 25, **Int** 13, **Wis** 17, **Cha** 15
Base Atk +3; **CMB** +10 (+14 grapple); **CMD** 21 (29 vs. trip)
Feats Power Attack, Skill Focus (Sense Motive), Toughness[B]
Skills Acrobatics +1 (–7 to jump), Climb +6, Diplomacy +7, Intimidate +7, Perception +7, Sense Motive +10, Survival +7; **Racial Modifiers** +4 Perception, +4 Survival
Languages Common (cannot speak)

Hidden Oasis - Temple of Thoth

By Matt Finch and Bill Webb

Introduction

The *Hidden Oasis-Temple of Thoth* brings the characters to a hidden temple of Thoth, god of knowledge, magic, and travel, where they are confronted with a force of invading dimensional locust-creatures and the chance to get their hands on an ancient artifact. What band of heroes could resist the challenge? The adventure is designed for 4-6 characters of levels 7-9.

Background

Deep in the desert sands lie the ruined remnants of the hidden Oasis-Temple of Thoth, once a thriving center of trade and magic, now abandoned and forgotten. If you are playing this adventure in the **Frog God Games *Lost Lands*** world setting, the temple is found in the Maighib Desert, 300 miles west of the Gorge of Osiris. This sand-swept region is far from the more familiar environs of Bard's Gate and the Stoneheart Valley, but the characters are brought here (and might even return from here) by magical means. Since the entrance to the adventure is a magical portal, the module can be used in any campaign without difficulty.

The Wax Plague

In centuries gone by, the Oasis-Temple of Thoth was a gateway between worlds, used by the priests of Thoth to travel between various strongholds and libraries of the god, even on different planes of existence and in strange, foreign worlds. Calamity struck, though, in the form of a deadly curse brought down on the temple by a desert-cult known as the Sickness Dancers. Their curse infected the entire oasis with the "Wax Plague," a body-melting disease so called because the features and bodies of the afflicted began to run like melted wax as time passed. The priests of Thoth, dissolving into formlessness, cast mighty wards upon the temple to ensure that the plague would not spread through the planar portals and dimensional gates contained in the complex. A great dome formed over the oasis, coalescing from the very air as the dying priests chanted the mystic words of their final, greatest spell.

The Changing of the Priests

The creation of the quarter-mile dome over the entire temple complex prevented the Wax Plague from spreading across the sand and through the portals of many dimensions, but it could not save the priests of Thoth from the curse. Utterly changed in mind and body, they fought to maintain the temple, preventing it from being used by dark forces as a way to move from one plane of existence to another, from one world to another, from one dimension to another. Only the high priest of Thoth retained his mind, for he was not human; the others of the priesthood could only follow his orders as best their broken minds could manage.

The Final Battle Looming

Now, after centuries, the last resources of the High Priest Thoth-Antef are failing. Thus far he has kept the ceaseless crawling of evil from traveling through the sacred gates he protects. The magic items are spent or worn out, however, and many of his priests have been killed in the frequent incursions by those who travel in the far dimensions, intending malice and harm. Now, an ancient peril, the sinister beings known as Planehoppers, have broached the arcane wards of the Oasis-Temple from one of their own planes of existence. The Planehoppers are an insectlike species with a bizarre caste system that are exploring outward to find new colonies and slaves for the hive.

The Cry for Help

The high priest used his last of three commands to a genie and ordered it to deliver a letter to suitable adventurers. Several adventuring parties have already rejected the genie's letter, and it is getting desperate. On a whim, it selected the characters as the next attempt to recruit help for the priests of the Oasis-Temple. As its own petty bit of vengeance for its long servitude, the genie does not offer a piece of information the high priest forgot to order it to say. As a result, the characters most likely won't know that Thoth-Antef, the high priest of Thoth in the Oasis-Temple, is a massive, transparent slug the size of a horse with a brain suspended in the middle of its body. Or that the living priests of Thoth are now nothing more than barely intelligent gelatinous cubes.

So it Begins (CR 5)

> A tall man dressed in desert robes approaches you and hands you a letter. He holds up three long, thin fingers, and says, "Ask three questions, and then you must give one answer."

The letter is a papyrus scroll, which (if seen using *detect magic*) has a faint abjuration aura and nothing indicating evil. It has eight strange markings scribed across the top, almost like a decoration. The symbols are in order:

- A sun
- A moon
- A circle
- A diamond
- A book
- A sphinx
- A pyramid
- An ankh

The rest of the letter, after the markings, reads as follows:

> *"I, Thoth-Antef, once the High Priest of the Great Oasis-Temple of Thoth, beseech your help.*
> *"The Oasis-Temple of Thoth was once a thriving gateway to many worlds and dimensions, a place of study and rest, where travelers could exchange knowledge and trade.*
> *"Then came the Sickness Dancers. They brought the tallow plague, melting flesh and changing those it did not kill. The plague would most certainly spread into more planes of existence, peeling diseased new realities into the multiverse. So we sealed the temple, calling on great forces to create a massive dome of spells and stone, woven into a net that the tallow plague could not sneak through. And so the plague died alongside us, leaving only the changed ones.*
> *"We have worked to protect the sealed sanctuary of Thoth, as the wards and protections have worn down through the years. The portals are constantly being tested by those who would venture through them looking for prey, or for new lands to conquer. Since the days of the temple's greatness, the worlds outside the gates have changed. Some are new and unmapped, some have gone bad. It would not be good for the portals to reopen all at once, as they once were.*
> *"The Planehoppers of the Kharn Drauk are at the portals. My resources are spent. Aid me in keeping them back, and I will give you a great gift in the name of Thoth — the Scorpion of Sekhmet. Go to the arch and speak the words, 'Orthanu, Thoth, Orhaptu.'*
> *"Thoth-Antef"*

The djinni's name is **Periaptes**, and he is anxious to fulfill this last mission and be free. Nevertheless, he fairly and scrupulously answers the first three questions he is asked. After this, he simply asks the characters if they accept or decline. If they decline, he holds out his hand to take the letter back, since he cannot be free until he finds rescuers for Thoth-Antef. Unless he is specifically asked a question about the shape, form, condition or appearance of the priests, he does not mention that the high priest is a giant slug, and the ordinary priests are reduced to semi-intelligent skeletons whose flesh has swelled into gelatinous cubes.

The characters may have some knowledge of Sekhmet, Thoth with a successful DC 20 Knowledge (religion) check, and even the artifact *Scorpion of Sekhmet* with a successful DC 25 Knowledge (arcana) check, but if they do not, they might ask the genie about these.

PERIAPTES THE GENIE **CR 5**
XP 1,600
hp 52 (*Pathfinder Roleplaying Game Bestiary* "Genie, Djinni")

Sekhmet

Sekhmet is the healer of the gods, a woman with the head of a lioness. Her symbol is a sun disc with a serpent twined around it, and she is worshipped by healers. However, the goddess has a darker side as well. She came into being as part of a great vengeance of the gods upon humanity, and it was she who slaughtered the humans and drank their blood. In addition to her healing side, she is a goddess of retribution, pestilence, and searing heat. Her breath is the hot desert wind, and she slays her enemies with arrows of fire. In fact, it was Sekhmet who sent the Sickness Dancers to Thoth's temple in retribution for taking two Scorpions.

Thoth

Thoth is, as stated in the letter, a god of magic, travel, and knowledge. He has a human body with the long neck and head of an ibis (a bird similar to a crane or stork). In addition to being the messenger and record-keeper of the gods, Thoth is the creator of magic and of speech. His temples usually contain libraries, and are rumored to contain portals from one plane of existence to another.

The Scorpion of Sekhmet

The *Scorpion of Sekhmet* was thought to be legend, but the letter of Thoth-Antef certainly indicates that it might be a real artifact. It is said to be a hollow iron shell in the shape of a Scorpion, large enough for several people to enter within. PCs succeeding a DC 30 Knowledge (arcana) check know that from inside, the Scorpion follows the orders it is given, walking and even attacking things as directed by the controller. As the characters discover, two of the Scorpions are in the Oasis-Temple.

Development: If the characters speak the words, "*Orthanu, Thoth, Orhaptu*," they are immediately drawn into the Plane of Shadows (see below).

Realm of Shadows

> You feel a sudden, powerful twist, and find that you are standing 6 foot away from a ghostly image of yourself. It glows with what looks like reflected light, but this place is dark, with no visible source of light to reflect. It is the darkness of shadows, not the dark of night, but the sun seems to have disappeared. The only sign of it is the light that somehow reflects on these bright shadows of yourselves.

These "bright shadows" are the characters' actual bodies [DC 15 Knowledge (planes)], as seen from the shadow plane they have entered. They can see the reflected sun on the bodies because sunlight is indeed shining on them — but in the Material Plane, not here. If they want to return to the Material Plane, all they need to do is step into the images, and they return [DC 20 Knowledge (planes)]. If they step into the wrong image, they switch bodies. The physical characteristics of the new body remain, but the mental characteristics are those of the body's new inhabitant.

The genie does not follow them into the Plane of Shadows. Once the characters say the magic words, the genie is freed from servitude and disappears.

Once they survey what is around them:

> Everything appears in shades of gray rather than colors, and you can see vast, forbidding pyramids in the distance, black silhouettes against a dark gray horizon. Clouds roll like octopus ink in the strangely low sky of this place. Directly in front of you stands an archway.

The characters might be discussing various possibilities at this point. Exploring the Plane of Shadow is a bad idea, although not impossible. This particular area is infested with **shadows, greater shadows** and other creatures of the dark, and explorers begin encountering them with some frequency if they set out from the archway in a random direction. The ***Sword of Air*** adventure by **Frog God Games** has a significant level of detail on the Plane of Shadow. Most likely, even a determined expedition turns back at this point. If not, then you're running an adventure in the Shadow Plane and we at **Frog God Games** salute you as the type of Referee that isn't afraid to wing it!

SHADOW **CR 3**
XP 800
hp 19 (*Pathfinder Roleplaying Game Bestiary* "Shadow")

GREATER SHADOW **CR 8**
XP 4,800
hp 58 (*Pathfinder Roleplaying Game Bestiary* "Shadow, Greater")

Eventually the characters get to the point where they are ready to inspect the archway.

> This is a strange, 10-foot-tall metal archway. It is smooth to the touch and feels slightly warmer than the ambient air. There is enough room in it for two men to stand abreast. The metal itself has an odd-looking bluish tint and is covered in dozens of crisp, un-weathered hieroglyphs and runes of a strange and ancient make. No rust or other damage appears to have affected the metal, although you somehow feel that it has been here for a long time.

Any attempt to damage the archway fails, short of cutting away at it with a +4 or better magical weapon. Doing so creates a large, magical explosion, teleporting all within 20-foot radius to a random plane. The whole archway radiates strong conjuration, and the structure also seems immune to any magic cast upon it.

This archway is in fact a *gate* to the Oasis-Temple of Thoth, PCs can determine this with a successful DC 20 Knowledge (arcana) check. Careful inspection (DC 20 Perception) of the runes reveals that eight of the symbols match those present on the letter the player characters received from the djinn messenger. A creature desiring to use the *gate* must first touch each symbol inscribed on the archway as noted in the letter. Once touched with bare flesh, the runes glow a deep red color. If touched out of order, the runes (all of them thus far touched) cease to glow. Once all eight runes are touched (in order), the *teleport* effects of the gate are activated. Speaking the activation words in the letter causes

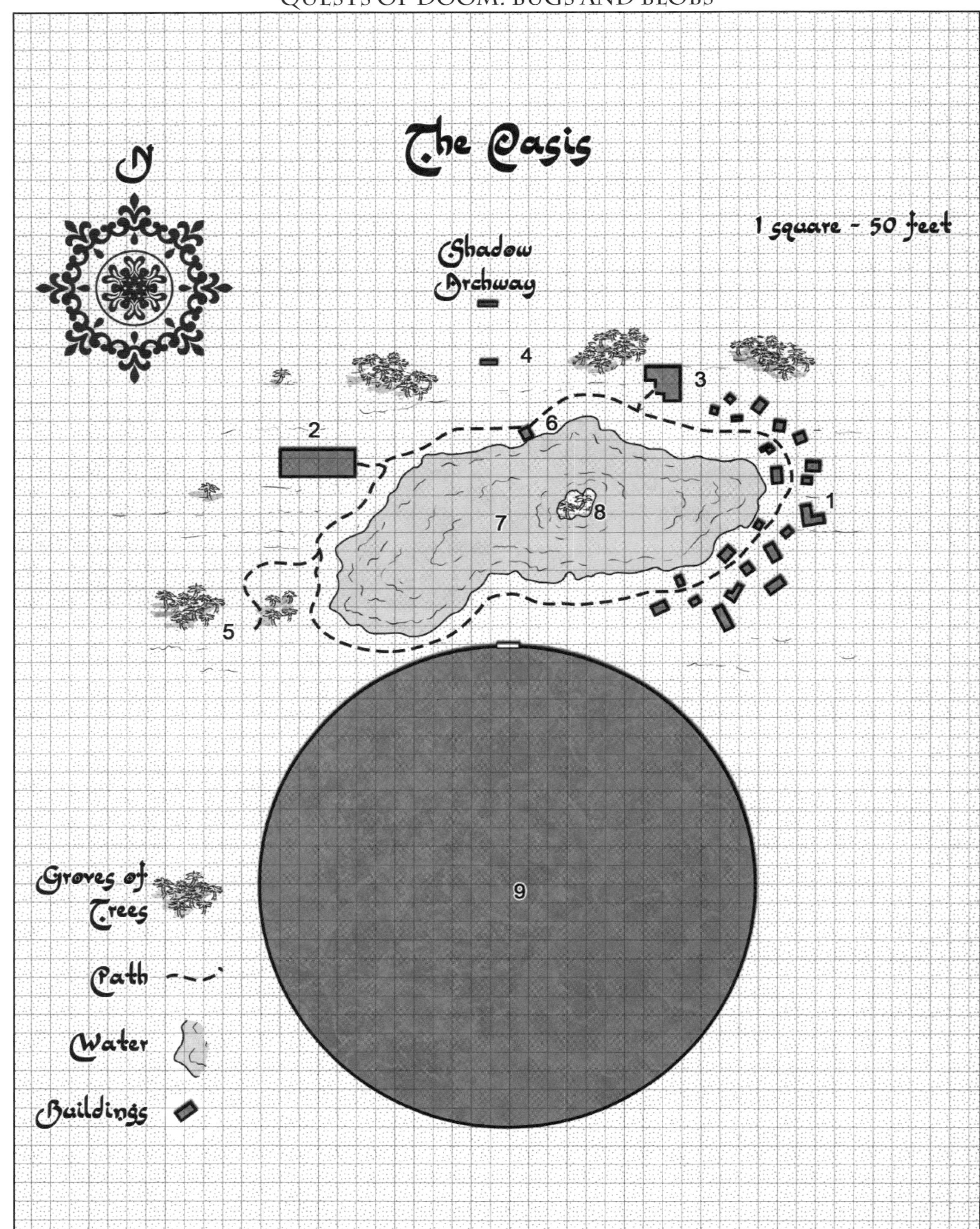
The Oasis
N
1 square - 50 feet
Shadow Archway
4
3
2
6
1
8
7
5
9
Groves of Trees
Path
Water
Buildings

the interior of the archway to glimmer with an opaque, silvery sheen. The sheen remains active for 3 minutes. Anyone stepping through the archway while the sheen is present is teleported to the Oasis *gate*.

The Oasis (CR 1/4 or 1)

After stepping through the archway, the player characters find themselves in an entirely different place, having been teleported into a large oasis in the desert. A successful DC 20 Knowledge (planes) check reveals to the PCs they are in fact on the Material plane. Behind them is a gate identical to the one that brought them here. The method of use for this gate is to touch the letters inscribed on the letter in the exact reverse order that brought them here. The glow effects of the runes and the activation words remain the same.

A large expanse of hot, green space now surrounds them. The area is covered with a myriad of palm, date and olive trees, as well as a sundry of large grasses around its edge. Beyond the greenery, a vast, expansive brown and tan, sandy desert can be seen in all directions. In the center of the oasis is a quarter-mile-long, 300-foot-wide pool of living water. The lake here is clean and clear, and quite safe, although it does contain a wide diversity of small invertebrates, insects and fish. The lake is spring-fed, and the water is fairly cold (60 degrees Fahrenheit).

The temperature ranges from the high 80s at night to more than 120 degrees Fahrenheit during the day, making it uncomfortable for anyone wearing heavy armor, see "Heat Dangers" in Chapter 13 of the Pathfinder Roleplaying Game.

Dotting the area are the remains of what appears to once have been a village of perhaps 100 souls, although the fallen and ruined nature of the structures is evident. The buildings are constructed of mud-brick and mortar, most are missing roofs (palm fronds were used for most) and have portions of the original structures collapsed. It appears no one has lived here for centuries.

Tiny jerboa (desert mice) hop around the fallen bricks and through the grass and the occasional dung beetle can be seen, rolling its load toward the north. A brick path leads in a circle around the lake, and anyone traveling through the brush off the path has a 10% chance per minute of encountering a **horned viper** or **deathstalker scorpion** (equal chances for either). Both of these nasty vermin live here in some numbers, and are potentially lethal. If they achieve surprise, they attack a random character (surprise indicates that a player character stepped on one of these creatures, causing it to attack).

HORNED VIPER **CR 1**
XP 400
hp 13 (*Pathfinder Roleplaying Game Bestiary* "Snake, Venomous")

DEATHSTALKER SCORPION **CR 1/4**
XP 100
hp 4 (*Pathfinder Roleplaying Game Bestiary 4* "Scorpion, Greensting")

Those following the path can easily avoid (or crush) any vermin they encounter. A number of interesting areas are detailed below.

Area 1. Random Houses

Several old, ruined buildings appear to have once been houses. Most have 1–2 rooms and are made of mud-brick, with no roofs. Within the perimeter of the oasis are 22 such buildings. None of these is of particular interest, although each contains 1d3 of the following:

1d12	Result
1	A **horned viper**
2	Pottery shards
3	A grave
4	Intact glassware or pottery
5	Old, rotted and brittle tools with copper fittings
6	Bone fragments and skeletal remains
7	A strange idol of a slug-like being/god (once only)
8	A cameo of gold (once only)
9	A large necklace of beads
10	A copper knife (once only)
11	A stone or fired-clay amulet
12	A gemstone amulet or small statue (twice only)

Horned Viper: These creatures attack if they gain surprise, else they retreat away from anything that notices them or spots them first, slinking off into the brush.

HORNED VIPER **CR 1**
XP 400
hp 13 (*Pathfinder Roleplaying Game Bestiary* "Snake, Venomous")

Pottery Shards: These are worthless, but could at the GM's convenience be used to convey clues or other relevant details about the slug (see below) or invaders.

Graves: These usually (90% chance) contain the mummified remains of: a human (01–80%), a cat (81–90%) or some other animal (91–00%) of the GM's choice buried under 4–6 feet of sand, and marked by a stone marker. If a human corpse is indicated, it wears mummy beads and jewelry worth 1d6x100 gp. Cats are typically covered in beaten gold (worth 4d6 gp). If a cat grave is defiled, the desecrator has a 10% chance of being subjected to a curse from Bast, the cat goddess.

CURSE OF BAST
Type curse; **Save** Will DC 20 negates, no save to avoid effects
Frequency –
Effect target takes a –2 penalty to all saving throws for 2 weeks.

Intact Glassware or Pottery: These containers occasionally (10%) are sealed and contain either grain (01–50%), wine (51–80%), oil (81–90%), internal organs (yuck!, 91–99%) or gold dust (00%, worth 1d6x100 gp). The vessel itself is worth 1d6x1d100 gp, and double that to a sage or collector.

Old Tools: Nothing of interest here

Bone Fragments: See old tools

Strange Idol of a Slug-like Being: This idol is 3 inches long and made of polished quartz, with a strange reddish-white inclusion in its head. If divination spells are cast upon it, it radiates good and magic as well. The idol acts as a *stone of good luck* (grants +1 luck bonus on saving throws, ability checks, and skill checks) as long as it is carried. The item attunes to its bearer.

Cameo of Gold: This cameo can be of any relevant Khemitian god or goddess, or it could be a scarab beetle or cat at the GM's choice. It is worth 300 gp.

Large Beaded Necklace: This necklace is composed of copper, gold, shells and semi-precious stones. It is worth 1d6x10 gp.

Copper Knife: This knife, while made of copper, seems sharp and durable. The knife radiates moderate conjuration if *detect magic* is cast upon it. The knife counts as a *+1 evil outsider-bane dagger*, as it is focused against all evil outsiders. Its bone handle is engraved with an image of Ptah, the creator god, as well as stars, moons and other symbols.

Stone or Clay Amulet: Cute but worthless.

Gemstone Amulet: Two of these can be found, with an equal chance of finding either. The first is in the shape of a scarab beetle and is carved out of pure rose quartz (worth 50 gp). The second is a perfect sphere of a strange red substance and feels slightly warm to the touch, although it does not radiate magic. These are *power-crystals* and can be used to power a *Scorpion of Sekhmet*. They are fully charged. The Scorpions are found in the temple.

Area 2. The Granary (CR 10)

This large building is almost completely intact except for its door, which has long-since rotted away. This building and the temple alone have roofs of stone slabs. The building stands 20 feet high, and measures 80 feet by 200 feet. It is composed of the same mud-brick as the others, but is considerably more solid. The doorway stands on one of the 80-foot sections, directly in the center of the wall. Unlike most of the other buildings here, this one is inhabited. Upon approaching within 30 feet of the structure's entrance, the player characters must make a surprise check. Success indicates that they notice movement within. Failure indicates that what is within notices them, and comes out to attack.

The building contains a nest of scorpions of unusual size, along with hundreds of smaller centipedes. These creatures lurk here to keep out of the hot sun, going out at night to hunt in the open desert. A total of **10 giant scorpions** and **2 centipede swarms** are here. They attack anything they perceive as food. They have no tactics, per se, and just attack the closest opponent.

GIANT SCORPIONS (10) **CR 3**
XP 800
hp 37 (*Pathfinder Roleplaying Game Bestiary* "Scorpion, Giant")

CENTIPEDE SWARMS (2) **CR 4**
XP 1,200
hp 31 (*Pathfinder Roleplaying Game Bestiary* "Centipede Swarm")

Area 3. Lugal House

The lugal (chieftain) of the village once lived here. From the nature of the building, it is apparent that it was something of an important structure, as it is far larger and contains six rooms. The building itself, while still made of mud-brick and roofless, has 10-foot-tall walls. The structure contains a grand entry hall (60 feet by 40 feet), as well as five attached smaller rooms (four sleeping chambers and a kitchen with a fireplace/oven), two each on the sides and one on the back. These rooms are all 20 feet square.

The entry chamber itself has a carved stone chair sitting at the far end opposite the entrance. The chair is plain, without any carvings or paint. It is solid granite and weighs about 500 pounds. If the chair could be transported, its fine workmanship makes it worth 700 gp.

The walls of the entry chamber are painted and carved with numerous hieroglyphs and pictograms. Careful inspection or translation, DC 20 Knowledge (religion) or DC 15 Linguistics check of the writings reveals that most of the writings are prayers to various deities (Ptah, Ra, Horus), complete with curses and pleas for protection against the evil god Set. One prayer praises the god Thoth for sending a guardian being to defend the village against the evils of the night god and his servants, and references the "guardian of the temple."

The pictograms associated with this prayer show a large, whitish-gray circle within an oval — but strangely, only the inner circle resembles a brain. This is, of course, a reference to the slug-being in the temple. Other pictograms show the god Thoth teaching the people about a sundry of things — clearly their ascent from being cavemen came from this deity, and he was the teacher, or bringer of knowledge.

If the chair is moved, it can be noted on a successful DC 20 Perception check that the bricks on the floor are of a slightly different color than those covering the rest of the chamber. They also lack the mortar present in the rest of the room. If the bricks are pried loose (DC 15 Strength check), a sarcophagus is found buried in a 7-foot-by-4-foot hole beneath.

The coffin itself measures 6-1/2 feet by 3-1/2 feet, and is carved in bas-relief of a kingly-looking individual. The coffin lid is sealed with a strange waxy, fragrant material with a successful DC 15 Craft (alchemy) check or DC 20 Knowledge (arcana) check to correctly identify the substance as myrrh. If the sarcophagus is removed from the pit, it can be opened. In ancient writing (a successful DC 30 Linguistic check or by *comprehend language* spell) on the lid of the coffin are the words:

"Disturb not the rest of the Lugal, lest you join the dust of the desert forever"

The Sarcophagus

If the myrrh is removed and the seal broken, any within 20 feet must make a DC 20 Fortitude save or be affected by *mummy rot*. Inside the sarcophagus are the mummified remains of the lugal. He wears a bone-and-lapis necklace under a baked clay death mask. The lugal has been dead for more than 600 years, likely preventing *speak with dead* attempts. The death mask is painted with his image (worth 20 gp), and the necklace

The Mummy's Mace

MACE OF ROT GRUBS
Aura strong conjuration; **CL** 13th
Slot none; **Price** 37,440 gp; **Weight** 8 lbs.

DESCRIPTION

This long rod of meteoric-iron is topped with a large piece of orange amber embedded with a strange insect-like creature. It functions at all times as a *+1 heavy mace*. After a full week of wielding, the mace (actually the rot grub that grows within the mace) becomes attuned with the user. This allows the wielder to use its command word to discharge a rot grub from the mace once per day on a successful melee attack.

On the successful strike a rot grub bursts forth from the amber casing and instantly burrows itself into the victim (this by passes armor, but any amount of damage reduction is enough to provide immunity to the infestation).

Once a rot grub has infested a victim, it burrows towards the host's heart, brain or other key internal organs causing 1d2 Constitution damage per round. Unless removed the rot grub continues to deal this damage until the host eventually dies, at which point the rot grub also dies.

On the first round of infestation, applying flame to the point of entry can kill the grub and save the host, but this inflicts 1d6 points of fire damage to the victim.

Cutting the grub out also works, but the longer the grub remains in a host, the more damage this method does. Cutting them out requires a slashing weapon and a DC 20 Heal check, and inflicts 1d6 points of damage per round that the host has been infested. If the Heal check is successful, the grub is removed. *Remove disease* kills the rot grubs in or on a host.

CONSTRUCTION

Requirements Craft Magic Arms and Armor, *bestow curse;* **Cost** 18,720 gp is woven with gold thread and is quite valuable (300 gp). Wrapped inside the mummy is a long rod of meteoric iron topped with a large piece of amber embedded with a strange insect-like creature. The rod serves as a *mace of rot grubs*. Its command word can be gained only by magic as it is lost in time.

Area 4. The Alabaster Wall

Unlike the other structures present in the oasis, this 30-foot-long, 4-foot-high wall is made of alabaster blocks. The wall is intricately painted and carved, with hundreds of inscriptions and pictograms. Trying to decipher all of them would take weeks, unless one knew what they were looking for. Should the player characters inquire about the runes present on the letter, or if they look for any references from the lugal's house associated with a "temple guardian" or "Thoth," they locate (DC 20 Perception check) several inscriptions of a large sluglike creature providing food, teaching them how to craft and grow grain, and fighting a battle against insectlike minions of the evil god, Set.

Area 5. The Sphinx

This statue stands 10 feet high and is inscribed on both sides with ancient writing (a successful DC 25 Linguistic check or by *comprehend language* spell). At its base are the words: "*Those who seek the gods must show the wisdom to see them first.*" Translating the writing on the sides of the sphinx reveals two riddles that allow the player characters to select the correct icons to activate the gate present on the island and gain egress into the collapsed temple.

On one side, the writing reads:

"I am what all men seek, yet many will never gain
"I serve the wise, and punish the foolish
"I make men strong, yet strengthen only their minds
"Without me all things that wither to dust are forgotten"

The answer is knowledge — associated with Thoth, the god of knowledge.

The riddle on the second side reads:

"I protect the wise, and slay the evil
"I am not a god, yet protect them and their house
"I serve the teacher and teach the servants"

The answer is the guardian — the sluglike creature depicted in the lugal's house and on the alabaster wall.

Armed with these bits of knowledge, the player characters should be able to enter the Temple of Thoth from there.

Area 6. The Boathouse

This rickety wooden structure sits on stone piles near the edge of the lake. The wood is old and brittle, and cannot support the weight of any Small creature or larger. Anything stepping on the remaining portions of the wooden, overwater deck in excess of 30 pounds crashes through the structure and lands in 1d6+2 feet of water after a 6-foot fall (no damage). It also creates a great deal of noise, alerting the beasts in the lake that dinner has arrived.

Adjacent to the structure, an ancient boat still floats, wedged between two of the support columns that hold up the structure. The boat holds up to 8 man-sized creatures and, while old and dry, it was treated with lacquer and oils, and retains its ability as a (albeit fragile) boat. The boat is 20 feet long and 4 feet wide.

Area 7. The Lake (CR 13)

The lake is more than 300 feet across and a quarter-mile long. Its edges are overgrown with bulrushes and other aquatic plants. Frogs, crawfish and insects are present everywhere, creating a great deal of noise at night. Several species of small fish are present in the lake. These fish are extremely colorful and create darting patterns as small schools react to stimulus (such as splashing or swimming).

The lake itself is spring fed and is cooler by far than the surrounding air. It is more than 100 feet deep in the center, with its edges dropping off rapidly in a clifflike manner. The water is clear to about 20 feet, and rocks can be seen dotting the shallows.

Living deep in the lake is a family of a **dragon turtle** and **5 juvenile dragon turtles**. These creatures have adapted to life in the desert, having everything they need here (food, heat and water). Being amphibious, they survived over the years by self-reproducing (adults can fertilize their own eggs). When the lake becomes too big for them, the largest either kills or drives off the rest, sending them off into the desert (usually to die), and thus maintaining the fragile ecological balance of this small ecosystem.

Currently living here are a female and her brood of 5 juveniles. They breathe air but remain submerged most of the time, hunting gazelle and camels in the desert at night. They attack only if the water is disturbed (e.g. by splashing and other noisy activity). Skilled, unarmored swimmers have a 50% chance of attracting 1d3 random turtles. Boating across gives them only a 10% chance of being attracted. The GM should use his judgment about how much noise the party makes and have the turtles react accordingly.

DRAGON TURTLE **CR 9**
XP 6,400
hp 126 (*Pathfinder Roleplaying Game Bestiary* "Dragon Turtle")

JUNVENILE DRAGON TURTLES (5) **CR 8**
XP 4800
Young dragon turntle (*Pathfinder Roleplaying Game Bestiary* "Dragon Turtle")
N Large dragon (aquatic)
Init +5; **Senses** low-light vision, darkvision 60 ft., scent; **Perception** +16

AC 22, **touch** 10, **flat-footed** 22 (+13 natural, –1 size, +1 Dex)
hp 102 (12d12+24)
Fort +10; **Ref** +9; **Will** +9
Immune fire, sleep, paralysis

Speed 20 ft., swim 30 ft.
Melee bite +15 (2d6+4), 2 claws +15 (1d8+4)
Space 10 ft. **Reach** 5 ft.
Special Attacks breath weapon, capsize

Str 19, **Dex** 12, **Con** 15, **Int** 12, **Wis** 13, **Cha** 12
Base Atk 12; **CMB** 19; **CMD** 31
Feats Awesome Blow, Blind-Fight, Cleave, Improved Bull Rush, Improved Initiative, Power Attack
Skills Diplomacy +16, Intimidate +16, Perception +16, Sense Motive +16, Stealth +13, Survival +16, Swim +29; **Racial Modifiers** +8 Stealth in water
Languages Aquan, Common, Draconic

Breath Weapon (Su) Cloud of steam 20 feet high, 25 feet wide, and 50 feet long, once every 1d4 rounds, damage 12d6 fire, Reflex DC 18 half; effective both on the surface and underwater. The save DC is Constitution-based.
Capsize (Ex) A dragon turtle can attempt to capsize a boat or ship by ramming it as a charge attack and making a CMB check. The DC of this check is 25, or the result of the boat

captain's Profession (sailor) check, whichever is higher. For each size category larger than the dragon turtle's size, it takes a cumulative –10 penalty on this CMB check.

If they notice the party, the turtles attack anything attempting to cross the lake. They are immediately aware of the presence of "food" if the boathouse platform is damaged and something or someone falls into the lake.

Area 8. The Island

This 60-foot-diameter island sits near the center of the lake, and rises up out of it about 4 feet above the water. The island is heavily vegetated, as is the rest of this place, and a large grove of olive trees stands near its center, completely obscuring vision beyond a few feet in. Access to the center of the island requires moving through this heavy vegetation (half movement) although the scorpions and snakes present in the rest of the oasis are absent here (there were no frogs to carry them across on their backs). In the center of the tree stand is an archway quite similar to the one that brought the PCs to the oasis in the first place. The area is so overgrown that the dragon turtles ignore anyone on the island unless they make a major ruckus.

The archway is a gate to inside of the temple of Thoth. Activating it requires speaking the same words as the prior two archways; however, the runes present on the initial two archways are not present here. Only by touching the symbol of Thoth and the symbol of the guardian (two symbols among hundreds inscribed on this archway) and then only by speaking the activation words from the letter, can this gate be activated. Once activated, its surface shimmers, as do the previous gates, and anyone stepping through is teleported into the Old Temple.

Area 9. The Old Temple

> This building is a vast dome, at least a quarter of a mile across, made of monolithic blocks of stone. The dome appears to be metal of some kind, an impossible feat of architecture without the use of tremendous magical forces. As you draw closer, you can see that the entire building shimmers with some kind of energy. It almost seems to ripple like slow-moving water. Enormous double doors twenty feet tall stand open, and you can see two desiccated corpses just inside the dome, people who apparently died while trying to push the doors closed.

The entire domed temple is protected by the field of magical force, as *wall of force*, the priests invoked more than a century in the past. Although the characters can see into the temple through the open gates, they cannot get in. Touching the force field is unpleasant, and it is an impenetrable wall. The PCs cannot touch the doors, the bodies inside, or even the wall, since the field is placed about 1 foot to the outside of the temple's structure. Walking around the temple tells the characters that there are no entrances other than this one. There are no breaks in the walls, although some of the stones look a bit crumbled.

The PCs will likely try peering into the temple to see as far as they can, and the force field does not prevent this. They can see 300 foot into the unlit shadows, but beyond that all is darkness. What they see is a broad hall leading in, 100 foot wide, the walls on the sides painted with pictures from top to bottom. After 150 foot or so, the walls of the hallway widen out, and the characters are looking into what looks like an open area. A double row of columns, rising high to the dome above, begins not far beyond the point where the hallway opens to the wide chamber. The double line of pillars goes farther than they can see into the building, disappearing into the shadows.

Oasis-Temple of Thoth Map Key

Area T-1. Portal to the Outside World

When the first of the adventurers comes through the portal into the Oasis-Temple, this is where the PC arrives. The PC is looking southward, and the first, immediate items of interest are those statues of the ibis-headed priests:

> You reappear in a dimly lit place with a vast, open space in front of you and some sort of large figures looming behind you. Suddenly one of them moves. Roll initiative.

Just kidding. It's actually just a statue, and part of it just clicks back into its normal position after the portal functioned.

The figures looming over the character are 3 statues of ibis-headed priests of Thoth. This is the first Lotus-Portal of Thoth the characters encounter. The movement was one of the ibis heads moving from the "on" position into the "off" position. Until the heads are reset to the right positions, the gate does not function.

The characters encounter this portal-statue arrangement — three ibis-priests standing behind a lotus platform — in several places throughout the Oasis-Temple. See the Sidebox for general information about their function and construction.

Once the PCs look at the surroundings, after dealing with the shock of the statue, the following is a description of what is seen looking south from the Lotus-Portal:

> Somewhere overhead is a ceiling, although it is barely visible and is probably a hundred feet high. A hundred feet or so ahead of you are two massive statues that have their backs turned to you. Beyond them, you can make out two parallel lines of incredibly tall columns that seem to reach all the way to the high ceiling of this bizarre, epically proportioned place. To your left and right are curving walls 150 foot or so away, massive structures that apparently rise all the way to the top of the chamber.

At this point, the character make first contact with the mind of the High Priest Thoth-Antef, but it is a very weak nudging at the PCs' consciousness. He begs them to hurry to **Area T-2**.

Area T-2. Statues of Thoth and Sekhmet

> These two south-facing statues are 50 foot tall with a diameter of 10 foot or so. One is of a man with the head of an ibis holding a scroll in one hand and a quill pen in the other hand. The other statue is of a lioness-headed woman wearing a red dress and holding 4 scorpions in her clasped hands. Between the two statues is a massive, 20-foot-long translucent slug. It is reared upward so that its front half is upright, and you can see a brain pulsing in the almost-transparent flesh of its chest.

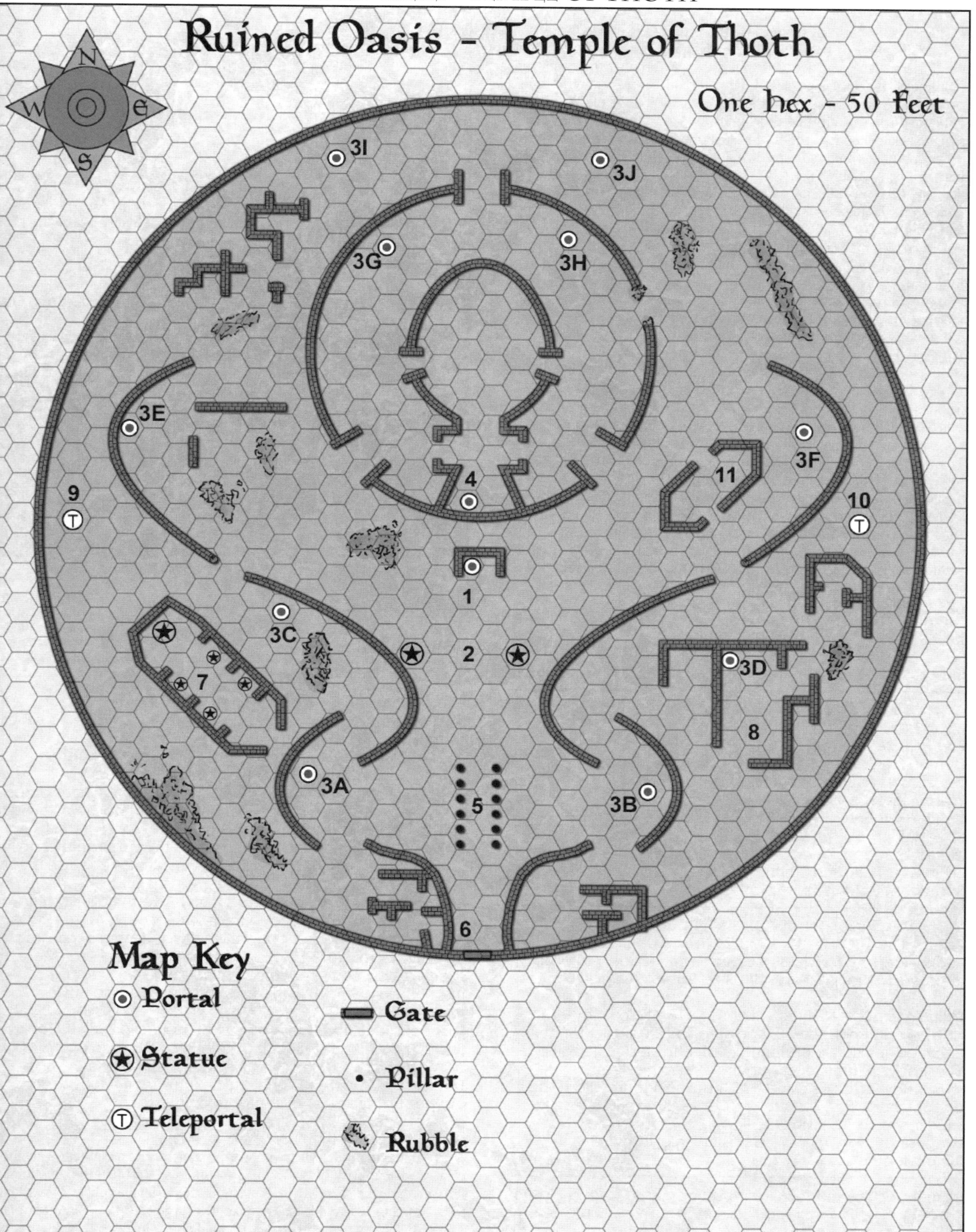

Ruined Oasis - Temple of Thoth
One hex - 50 Feet
N
W
E
S
3I
3J
3G
3H
3E
3F
4
11
9
10
1
3C
2
3D
7
8
3A
3B
5
6
Map Key
Portal
Statue
Teleportal
Gate
Pillar
Rubble

The translucent slug is **Thoth-Antef**, high priest of Thoth. He is one of the **giant slugs of P'Nakh**, although he has no knowledge of the place whose name he bears. He was hatched in a forgotten basement under a temple of Set in a long-destroyed city, and has no knowledge of his forebears. If the PCs kill him, they face the assault of the Planehoppers without assistance from the changed priests, and they may have trouble getting back to their point of origin. Nevertheless, it is a definite possibility.

Thoth-Antef communicates telepathically with the PCs, informing them that he is the high priest of Thoth. He thanks them for answering his plea, and begs them to stay and help him fight off an invasion of the evil Planehoppers. He explains that he will reward them with a great artifact held in the temple should they assist, and above all that he means no harm. Now then, any player worth his salt likely won't trust a giant slug with a pulsing red brain, so the creature allows himself to be enspelled with divination spells if the party wishes to do so. If they attack him, he tries to use his insanity and adoration blasts to quiet some of them so he can persuade the others that he means no harm. Thoth-Antef detects as Lawful and good if the appropriate spells are cast, and he truly does wish the party's assistance.

He explains that his power is weakened, and that he is near death from holding back the invasion. He further explains that the PCs can use two artifacts — *Scorpions of Sekhmet* — to assist in the battle. Finally, he tells them that not only can he instruct them on the use of the Scorpions, but that should they succeed in fending off the Planehoppers, as a reward they may take one of the machines with them, along with a fully charged *power-crystal* (the fuel for the Scorpions).

Should they persist in attacking him, he fights to the best of his ability. If slain, it takes the player characters one month to figure out how to effectively use the Scorpions — and thus they must fight the Planehoppers without the aid of the gelatinous cubes and the slug to gain the treasure.

Should all else fail, he offers the party the temple treasure as well, a total of five small chests of iron.

THOTH-ANTEF, GIANT P'NAKH SLUG **CR 10**
XP 9,600
LG Large aberration
Init +1; **Senses** blindsight 60 ft., lifesense 60 ft.; **Perception** +17

AC 24, touch 6, flat-footed 24 (–3 Dex, +18 natural, –1 size)
hp 152 (currently 45) (16d8+80)
Fort +12; **Ref** +2; **Will** +15
Defensive Abilities translucent body; **DR** 10/slashing or piercing; **Immune** acid; **SR** 27
Weaknesses susceptible to salt

Speed 20 ft.
Melee tongue +18 (2d8+9 plus 1d6 acid)
Space 10 ft.; **Reach** 10 ft.
Special Attacks insanity blast

Str 23, **Dex** 5, **Con** 20, **Int** 21, **Wis** 16, **Cha** 15
Base Atk +12; **CMB** +19; **CMD** 26 (can't be tripped)
Feats Alertness, Blind-fight, Endurance, Great Fortitude, Improved Initiative, Iron Will, Strike Back, Weapon Focus (tongue)
Skills Appraise +15, Bluff +5, Climb +15, Diplomacy +10, Heal +15, Intimidate +10, Knowledge (arcana) +15, Knowledge (dungeoneering) +15, Knowledge (engineering) +10, Knowledge (geography) +10, Knowledge (history) +15, Knowledge (planes) +15, Knowledge (religion) +15, Linguistics +9, Perception +17, Sense Motive +19, Spellcraft +15, Survival +12, Swim +15
Languages Aklo, Aquan, Celestial; telepathy 60 ft.
SQ malleable

Insanity Blast A giant P'Nahki slug can issue forth a blast of psychic insanity in a 60 foot cone. The save DC is Charisma-based. Anyone within the area of the blast must make a DC 20 Will saving throw or be affected as follows:

01–25: *frozen-by-fear* for 1d4+1 rounds; the character will fight back against a direct assault but can take no other action;
26–50: *insane rage* for 1d4+1 rounds; the character attacks any former allies in a frenzy of hatred;
51–75: *self-hatred* for 1d4+1 rounds; the character drops any held items and claws at his/her own body, inflicting 1hp of damage per round;
76–00: *adoration* for 1d4+1 rounds; the character drops all held items, falls to the floor, and grovels in worship of the slug.

Malleable (Ex) A P'Nahki slug's body is very malleable, allowing it to fit into narrow areas with ease. It takes no penalty to its speed or checks when squeezing in an area that is one size category smaller than its actual size (Medium space). It can only move half speed when squeezing through an area two size categories smaller than its actual size (Small space).
Susceptible to Salt (Ex) A handful of salt can burn P'Nahki slug skin as if it were a flask of acid, causing 1d6 points of damage per use.
Translucent Body (Ex) The bodies of P'Nahki slug is nearly translucent and in low-light conditions grant the slugs concealment.

P'Nahki slugs are massive, nearly translucent creatures. The most clearly visible part of the slug's anatomy is the disturbingly human-looking brain suspended in the slug's body, appearing at first glance to be floating in the air. These creatures originated in a forgotten place called P'Nahk; whether this was a ruined city, a lost world, or an entirely different dimension is not known.

The giant slugs of P'Nahk are highly intelligent, although this intellect is seldom put to use in a way that can be related to human motivation or logic.

Treasure: Chest #1: This chest holds a green linen sack with a carved ivory comb (32 sp) and an elegant silver-and-pink necklace. The necklace has lengths of delicate silver chain connecting clusters of pink gems — pink pearls set between pairs of rose quartz beads. Nine such groups of gems are on this necklace (1,335 gp).

Chest #2: The second chest holds a polished oak box (8 sp). Inside the box lie two pieces of jewelry. A shimmering necklace with a triple strand of silver holds a sparkling rose quartz oval set in a silver frame. From this hangs a lustrous gray pearl (necklace, 189 gp). Beside this, a faceted stone of deep burgundy (garnet) is held in a plain silvery frame (platinum). The stone, an oval the size of a lady's thumbnail, hangs on a double chain of platinum (necklace, 1,530 gp).

Chest #3: The third chest has a small black wooden box. Inside, on linen padding, rests a silver pendant strung on a set of five thin silk cords. The pendant is roughly diamond shaped but its frame is made of swooping lines rather than straight. In the center of the frame dangles another diamond-shaped piece of silver, in which is set a gleaming black opal the size of a man's thumbnail (necklace, 1,790 gp).

Chest #4: In the next chest lies a polished flat box with a reddish hue (2 gp). Inside the box, a small piece of pink silk (1 gp) is wrapped around a multi-strand necklace of hundreds of tiny freshwater pearls with accents of color provided by small, faceted garnets and rose quartz (necklace, 2,522 gp).

Chest #5: The final chest holds a blue silk pouch (2 gp) with a double-strand necklace made of small matching garnet beads (necklace, 2,246 gp). Instead of a pendant, the necklace is accented with a cylindrical silver filigree slide.

The Planehopper Assault

The main event of this adventure is a battle to keep the Planehopper horde (their scouts, anyway) from taking control of the Oasis-Temple of Thoth so they can repair and use the temple's portals. If the Planehoppers conquer the temple (the PCs refuse to stay, flee the battle, or are slain) they fortify it and use it as a staging area for the imperialistic expansion of their hive.

Time

From the point when the characters arrive, the Planehoppers arrive in 72 hours (3 days). If Thoth-Antef survives meeting the characters, he predicts that the time frame is 30–80 hours. Thus, the first phase of the adventure inside the temple is in preparation for the assault. It may be that the characters want to root around in the wreckage, build traps, and make complicated plans. If not, and they just want to let the battle roll, let it roll. Don't force the pace to slow down if the players want to jump straight into the fight.

If they want to prepare, emphasize that they don't know exactly how long they have, give them the player map, and let them plan. Experienced GMs know that whenever players are given a map and a lot of stuff to work with, no final plan ever emerges until you, as the referee, announce that they have (for example) 2 minutes before everything begins, ready or not. An hour of real time is probably enough time to give them, or even 30 minutes if the group has time constraints.

Where the Planehoppers Emerge

Once 72 in-game hours pass, roll 1d10 to see which portal the Planehoppers break open: 1=A, 2=B, 3=C, 4=D, 5=E, 6=F, 7=G, 8=H, 9=I, 10=J. The portal initially used by the characters to enter the Oasis-Temple has no letter because it does not lead to a dimension the Planehoppers can tunnel through.

Timetable and Psychic Shockwave

As Thoth-Antef may have warned the characters, the first effect when a Planehopper tunnel breaks through into reality is a blast of magical and psychic energy. This is the outward explosion of the planar residue being pushed in front of the psychic tunneling, like rubble in front of a drill bit. The drill bit itself packs quite a wallop when it suddenly breaks through into the Material Plane. Any physical material within a 50 foot radius of the portal disintegrates.

Round 1: Randomly determined portal (Breach #1) explodes with the force of psychic tunneling.
Round 2: **1 laborer**, **1 overseer** and **1 channeler** emerge from Breach #1.
Round 3: **2 laborers** emerge from Breach #1.
Round 4: **3 warriors** emerge from Breach #1.
Round 5: Randomly determined portal (Breach #2) explodes with the force of psychic tunneling. **2 laborers** and **1 warrior** emerge from Breach #1.
Round 6: 1 overseer and **1 channeler** emerge from Breach #1; **2 warriors**, **1 overseer** and **1 channeler** emerge from Breach #2.
Round 7: **1 warrior** emerges from Breach #1; **1 warrior** emerges from Breach #2.
Rounds 9-17: Nothing emerges.
Round 18: Randomly determined portal (Breach #3) explodes with the force of psychic tunneling.
Round 19: **1 overseer** and **1 channeler** emerge from Breach #3.
Round 20: **3 warriors** emerge from Breach #3.
Round 21: **3 warriors** emerge from Breach #3.
Round 22: **1 governor** emerges from one of the three breaches (roll 1d3) carried by **4 laborers**.

Battle Roster of the Planehoppers (CR 15)

These Planehoppers are a reconnaissance-in-force, led by a **governor** in charge of **3 overseers**, **10 warriors**, **6 channelers**, and **9 laborers**. Since they are exploring, no investigation follows their disappearance, or at least, not for some time.

PLANEHOPPER GOVERNOR **CR 9**
XP 6,400
hp 102 (See **Appendix**)

PLANEHOPPER OVERSEERS (3) **CR 7**
XP 6,400
hp 102 (See **Appendix**)

PLANEHOPPER CHANNELERS (6) **CR 6**
XP 2,400
hp 68 (See **Appendix**)

PLANEHOPPER WARRIORS (10) **CR 5**
XP 1,600
hp 51 (See **Appendix**)

PLANEHOPPER LABORERS (9) **CR 3**
XP 800
hp 30 (See **Appendix**)

Planehopper Attackers at Breach No. 1 (CR 12)

PLANEHOPPER OVERSEERS (2) **CR 7**
XP 6,400
hp 102 (See **Appendix**)

PLANEHOPPER CHANNELERS (2) **CR 6**
XP 2,400
hp 68 (See **Appendix**)

PLANEHOPPER WARRIORS (4) **CR 5**
XP 1,600
hp 51 (See **Appendix**)

PLANEHOPPER LABORERS (4) **CR 3**
XP 800
hp 30 (See **Appendix**)

Planehopper Attackers at Breach No. 2 (CR 11):

PLANEHOPPER OVERSEERS (2) **CR 7**
XP 3,200
hp 85 (See **Appendix**)

PLANEHOPPER CHANNELERS (2) **CR 6**
XP 2,400
hp 68 (See **Appendix**)

PLANEHOPPER WARRIORS (3) **CR 5**
XP 1,600
hp 51 (See **Appendix**)

Planehopper Attackers at Breach No. 3 (CR 11):

PLANEHOPPER OVERSEER **CR 7**
XP 3,200
hp 85 (See **Appendix**)

PLANEHOPPER CHANNELER **CR 6**
XP 2,400
hp 68 (See **Appendix**)

PLANEHOPPER WARRIORS (6) **CR 5**
XP 1,600
hp 51 (See **Appendix**)

Planehopper Command Group (CR 10):

PLANEHOPPER GOVERNOR **CR 9**
XP 6,400
hp 102 (See **Appendix**)

PLANEHOPPER LABORERS (4) **CR 3**
XP 800
hp 30 (See **Appendix**)

Thoth-Antef's Briefing

Provided that the characters don't slay him as a monster, Thoth-Antef briefs the characters on the following points:

Thoth-Antef is the last high priest of Thoth in this Temple. He quickly explains that a plague struck the temple and that the priests closed it off magically to keep the plague from spreading through the temple's magic portals into other dimensions. The plague killed many and turned the rest into gelatinous cubes, never dying of old age. He himself has not reached the natural end of his lifetime and was not affected by the plague. If the characters inquire further, he can tell them about the Sickness Dancers and that this was centuries ago, and other details from the background, but these details are of little interest to most players.

The attackers are a species known as "Planehoppers" because they resemble locusts and behave like locusts too, ravaging the worlds they invade and enslaving entire populations. Their word for themselves is unpronounceable. They have been psychically drilling through the substance of the planes of existence, and they are at the verge of breaking through one of the portals of the Oasis-Temple. He doesn't know which one of the portals. Unless the characters use some divinatory powers of their own, they won't know that the Planehoppers are working through 3 portals at once — until the drilling breaks through.

Thoth-Antef himself is already so stricken by his efforts to hold back the Planehoppers that he can no longer do much more than broadcast the characters' instructions to the changed priests. He can still bite but cannot manage a psychic blast anymore (he would need a week's rest, at least). He can't move very fast, either.

The "Changed Priests" in the temple, the lucky (or perhaps unlucky) servants of Thoth who were changed into **4 gelatinous cubes** by the Wax Plague instead of being killed by it. As long as the characters have Thoth-Antef to speak mentally to the cubes, they can communicate instructions. The original skeletons of the changed priests are visible in the gelatin of the cubes, and they are wearing holy symbols of Thoth. Without the holy symbols, they cannot "hear" Thoth-Antef's mental commands.

GELATINOUS CUBES (4) **CR 3**
XP 800
hp 50 (*Pathfinder Roleplaying Game Bestiary* "Gelatinous Cube")
Gear necklace of Thoth (holy symbol)

The PCs can decide where Thoth-Antef and the changed priests start the battle (e.g. the players decide where all the allied pieces start).

Changed Priests of Thoth

When the Wax Plague infected all the priests of the Oasis-Temple of Thoth, the first infected were the priests most vulnerable to the plague. These died before the true horror of the Wax Plague showed itself in them. The priests who were not killed by the disease were the unlucky ones, for they were irrevocably and horribly changed.

The changed priests are now immortal gelatinous cubes, the final stage of the curse brought to Thoth's temple by the Sickness Dancers. The priests' skeletons still hang motionless inside the translucent flesh of the cube: flesh that was once their own. Around the neck of each skeleton shines the necklace of Thoth's priesthood, the symbol of an ibis.

For all intents and purposes, the changed priests are treated as gelatinous cubes, with a single exception: the priests can "hear" the voice of Thoth-Antef through the necklace and follow his orders to the best of their limited abilities. They can be told to go places in the temple, and they understand and obey. They can be told to attack, and they can be told to wait in a particular place. Their reduced mental abilities cannot handle anything more complex.

If the characters attack the priest, it tries to retreat rather than attack, heading toward **Area T-2**.

Area T-3. Broken Portals

A white marble lotus-flower rests on the floor like a petaled bowl five feet across. Three statues of ibis-headed men stand behind the lotus, holding hands.

These portals are deactivated or in some cases physically broken by the priests of Thoth to prevent the Wax Plague from spreading through them into other realities or planes of existence.

Lotus-Portals of Thoth

Several of these portals are found throughout the Oasis-Temple of Thoth. They all look the same, and they are all portals to different dimensions, realities, and planes of existence.

An unbroken Lotus-Portal is a single marble statue of a large, flat lotus blossom on the ground, with a 5 foot diameter. Three priests with ibis heads stand behind the lotus, looking up or down. The heads are mounted on a metal armature, allowing them to be pivoted on the neck to look up or down. The center head moves directly up-down, and the ones at the sides are either looking in and down at the lotus, or up and sideways at the sky.

The correct placement of the statue heads, in order to make the *gate* function, is to have the central priest looking down at the lotus, and the two priests at his sides looking up/sideways.

When the heads are pointed in the correct directions, a blue haze forms in the bowl of the lotus flower. Anyone stepping into the flower and remaining there for a full minute emerges from some sort of portal on the far side — not all of the destination portals resemble the Lotus-Portals.

Once the gate has been used, the armature inside the statues moves the heads back into one of the "off" positions.

At the present time, all but two of the Lotus-Portals are broken, either by invaders or by the priests of Thoth themselves, before the Oasis-Temple fell to the Wax Plague of the Sickness Dancers. The gates could conceivably be repaired, but the details of such repair would lie with the Game Master. It would certainly require assistance from powerful priests of Thoth, possibly all the way from the city of Hermopolis.

Area T-4. The Gate of Hermopolis

A white marble lotus-flower rests on the floor like a petaled bowl five feet across. Three statues of ibis-headed men stand behind the lotus, holding hands. The one in the center looks into the sky, and the other two look down at the lotus.

This gate leads to the city of Hermopolis, a major city in the Material Plane. More importantly, as far as Thoth-Antef is concerned, Hermopolis is the seat of the temple of Thoth. If the Planehoppers get through this portal in force, the entire presence of Thoth's priestly hierarchy on this world is threatened. Defending this gate has been Thoth-Antef's main priority during his centuries of defending the ruined temple from those who manage to get through the gates from the outside.

City of Hermopolis

The city of Hermopolis is a major city of Lower Khemit. With a population of 115,000, the seat of the High Temple of Thoth, a major library called the Thocaenum, and a major university at the temple, Hermopolis is a center of learning and sophistication known throughout the Kingdom of Khemit. Its university produces scholars highly sought after by the Royal Court of Khemit and by administrators throughout the kingdom, and its library rivals the one at Pharos, though its content is more religiously oriented. The city is located at a confluence of the River Stygian and the seasonal Bakhari tributary. During flood season, the river is a muddy expanse more than 2 miles wide in which tens of thousands of storks and flamingoes cavort and feed, creating a cacophony heard more than a mile from the banks.

Area T-5. Columns

A double colonnade, six pillars long, proceeds from south to north. The pillars are massive, 10 foot in diameter, spaced 40 foot apart, and rise more than a hundred feet to the domed ceiling. They are painted with scenes of fabulous beasts and people with animal heads. The paint is quite faded, and you cannot make out details without stepping closer.

Most of the scenes feature the ibis-headed god Thoth, to whom this temple belongs. He is shown sitting in front of souls in the underworld, apparently asking questions and writing down the answers on a scroll in his lap. He is also shown stepping through portals that apparently have one world on one side, and another world on the other.

If the characters spend 10 minutes checking the pillars for details (DC 20 Perception), or almost immediately if they are specifically looking for pictures of lotus flowers, they find an interesting picture. It shows Thoth on a white lotus flower, with three other ibis-headed people — possibly priests or priestesses — standing behind him. The central priest is looking down at the lotus as the others look upward and to the sides.

Area T-6. The Gate

Two dried-out human bodies lie next to a huge pair of doors that the dead men were apparently trying to close when they died. Thousands of pictograms and runes cover the doors, but many of the images are hacked and damaged.

The two bodies are priests of Thoth who died in the early days of the plague. Investigation finds that their flesh was starting to melt and change when they died (DC 10 Perception). What they were melting into cannot be guessed from the corpses. A DC 15 Heal check can tell that the melting was fatal, and that the edges of the melted areas seem to be a bit translucent. It is also possible for character makes a successful DC 25 Heal check can discern that the melting of the flesh resulted from a disease.

The symbols on the door are all focused upon the god Thoth, who is shown in many of his different functions as a god of Khemit. In particular, though, he is shown in his capacity as a traveler and as one who teaches. A successful DC 20 Perception check allows the PCs to find a series of pictures that show the same scene, one on top of the other, all the way down one part of the door. The scene is simple: Thoth stands in front of a person wearing an ibis medallion, holding his hand over the person's head. The last of these pictures is strange, because instead of a person wearing the ibis medallion, it is some sort of formless shape with a circle in the center. It does have the ibis medallion draped around it, though.

The figure being blessed by Thoth is of course the High Priest Thoth-Antef, whose species is far from human.

Area T-7. Chapel of the Other Gods

This is an enclosed area the size of a cathedral. A statue at the very back of the long chamber holds aloft a disc of bright white light, which illuminates the entire area. The statue is almost too bright to make out the details, but from the shape of it, it looks like a statue of the god Ra, since it is a hawk-headed man. The 60 foot wide aisle leading to the statue of Ra also has 4 side-chambers, 20 foot or so deep. These also contain statues, although the shadows from Ra's blinding sun disc make them hard to see from the entrance of the room.

This temple contains statues of several gods other than Thoth. The statues here allowed visiting priests and dignitaries to give offerings and blessings to their own patron deities and be correctly identified with a DC 20 Knowledge (religion) check. The large statue at the back of the temple is, of course, Ra. Four other statues in alcoves along the side walls of this temple are Isis, Osiris, Sekhmet, and Set.

Statue of Isis: This statue shows a woman holding an ankh, her hair arranged on her head in a shape that looks like a chair, or perhaps a throne.

Statue of Osiris: This statue shows a man holding a shepherd's crook and a flail, wearing a tall crown with two ostrich feathers. His skin is painted green.

Statue of Sekhmet: This statue depicts a woman with the head of a lioness. The entire statue is painted red, as if with blood.

Statue of Set: This statue is an enormous, coiled, black snake.

Area T-8. Storehouse

> A few large support walls remain from what must once have been a warren of smaller rooms and chambers. There are remnants of a fallen staircase, and some toppled statues.

Treasure: In this area, in addition to the broken portal of Thoth, there is a great deal of potentially usable material. If the characters are willing to scavenge, they can find the following with a successful DC 15 Perception check:

- Huge quantities of clay bricks and wall fragments.
- Smaller quantities, but still several tons, of cut stone (1 foot x 1 foot x 2 foot).
- 30 wooden beams (sound and not rotten)
- 200 wooden beams in various stages of rot
- 30 covered, sealed clay drums of water (40-gallon containers with 20 gallons of water remaining)
- 30 covered, sealed clay drums of flammable oil (40-gallon containers with 5 gallons remaining un-evaporated). NOTE: The oil will catch fire, but not as fast as alchemist's fire.
- 30 covered, sealed clay drums of olive oil (40-gallon containers with 30 gallons un-evaporated).
- 1 ton of cloth, fairly rotted (too weak to make a torsion-powered ballista)
- 16 dried-out human bodies (priests of Thoth or temple guests)

No rope has survived in usable condition.

Area T-9. Teleportal

> A pattern of colorful, bird-shaped tiles is set into the floor to create a huge circle, 50ft in diameter.

This circle of tiles is a *teleportal*. Anything stepping on it (including one of the *Scorpions of Sekhmet*) is instantly teleported as per *teleport* spell to **Area T-10.**

Area T-10. Teleportal

> This is a circle of fish-shaped tiles, 50 foot across.

This circle of tiles is a *teleportal*. As with the *teleportal* at **Area T-7**, anything stepping on it (including one of the *Scorpions of Sekhmet*) is instantly teleported to **Area T-9**.

Area T-11. Garage

> Inside this long chamber, you see two giant scorpions made of metal. Each is 15 foot long, and they have bodies that are taller and wider thant the proportions of a real scorpion.

The *Scorpions of Sekhmet* are the artifacts guarded by the temple.

Scorpions of Sekhmet

They are vehicles created by the goddess Sekhmet, granted to six of her most devoted warrior-servants in the distant past. Two of these artifacts have, over the centuries, fallen into the hands of the priests of Thoth, who stored them away in Thoth's great Temple-Oasis.

SCORPION OF SEKHMET (MAJOR ARTIFACT)
Aura overwhelming evocation and transmutation; **CL** 30th
Slot none; **Weight** 11,000 lbs.

DESCRIPTION

A *Scorpion of Sekhmet* is a magical iron vehicle shaped in the image of a Huge scorpion, 15 feet long, with an unusually fat body and a proportionally short tail.

Close examination, and a DC 20 Perception check, reveals a secret catch that opens a hatch on one side. The hatch can be locked from the inside (treat as *arcane lock* spell if anything tries to force it open when locked). It takes a move action for a Medium or smaller person to enter or leave the hatch. Anyone who crawls inside finds seating for four Medium occupants.

All seats have small periscopes serving as windows (treat as arrow slits) that provide improved cover to the crew within, but allow each crewmate to see what is happening outside. Each seat has controls to different functions with seat for the driver, seat 2 can assist the driver, seats 2-3 control the claw weapons, and seat 4 controls the tail stinger. When a Scorpion has four operators, it is able to make 2 move actions each round as well as a standard action with each of its armaments.

Operating a lever is a full-round action and requires a check (see "Movement and Turning"). The Scorpion has physical limitations on what it can do, and the more the operators push the limits, the harder it is to make the device do exactly what is wanted. The operator in charge of driving must move the Scorpion one move action at a time, and the other operators (turning, clawing, firing) can interrupt at any time to turn the Scorpion 45-degrees as its second move action (which prevents the driver from making a second move action), make an attack with the claws, or fire a sun-ray from the tail. An assistant driver cannot attempt a turn move and make an attack with a claw in the same round.

When active, a Scorpion of Sekhmet has the following characteristics:

Init the Scorpion acts on the initiative of the individual operators; **hp** — (impervious to all mortal damage); **speed** 50 ft.; **AC** 5 (crew's AC see below); **melee** 2 claws +20 (4d10/19–20 plus grab) see "Attacking" below and tail stinger ray attack, +10 ranged touch (10d6 fire and holy) see "Vengeance of Sekhmet" below; **CMB** +24; **CMD** 34 (42 vs. trip).

Immunities: Anyone inside the Scorpion is immune to fire, cold, and electricity attacks. Sonic attacks (such as the song and the chirp abilities of Planehopper channelers) affect those inside the Scorpion normally although the carapace grants a +2 bonus to all saves.

Special Inside the artifact, the crew has improved cover, granting them a +8 bonus to their AC and a +4 bonus on Reflex saves if they should be attacked through the seams in the machine's carapace. These seams allow air to freely flow, and keep the artifact from being waterproof or gas-proof.

Switching seats: It takes a move round to get into an empty seat, and a full-round action for two seat occupants to switch seats.

Movement and Turning (Seats 1–2)

The Scorpion can move at its base speed for 24 hours as long as an operator is in the driver's seat and actively guiding the machine. It moves at 5 miles per hour, and therefore has an overland movement of 120 miles per day if it travels at this speed for 24 hours. Every 24 hours of movement uses 1 charge from the artifact's *power-crystal*.

The Scorpion can only move forward. A single driver can move the Scorpion forward in a straight line, but an assistant driver is required in order to turn the Scorpion. At the end of its turn, the Scorpion automatically comes to a stop unless the driver continues its course forward on the next turn. If the driver does not wish to move the Scorpion forward in a round, the assistant driver can attempt two move action turns if he chooses.

Tactical movement in combat at the Scorpion's base speed for a single move requires a base DC 5 Intelligence check (a driver with Knowledge [engineering] can substitute a skill check in place of the Intelligence check). In addition, if a driver wishes, he can push the Scorpion to greater tactical speeds by applying penalties to the check. A Critical Success occurs when the operator rolls a natural 20 on a check; a critical failure occurs with the operator rolls a natural 1 on a check (Movement Problem tables below). The movements require checks as follows:

Normal Movement, Single Move Action (Speed 50 ft.): DC 5

Success: Single move succeeds.

Failure: The move fails; the driver can attempt another move action in this round if he chooses.

Critical success: Treat as normal success.

Critical failure: Treat as normal failure and roll on the **Movement Failure Table**.

Double Move Action (Speed 50 ft.): DC 10

Success: Double move succeeds, and the driver can keep trying to push the movement, if desired. No turn may be attempted by the assistant driver in this round. Nor can this this be attempted if the assistant driver has already made a turn with a move action.

Failure: The move fails and the Scorpion can make only a single move action this round.

Critical success: May make a run movement at triple speed as a full-round action (move 150 feet, no turn possible in this round).

Critical failure: Treat as normal failure and roll on the **Movement Failure Table**.

Greater Than Double Move: DC 15 +1 per 10 feet of travel attempted beyond the distance of a double move (this cannot be performed in conjunction with a run action as described under Double Move Action—Critical success above), with the check for each additional 10 feet resolved separately. As with the double move action, no attempt to turn the Scorpion can be made in the round when this is attempted.

Success: The Scorpion moves 10 additional feet and the driver can keep trying to push the movement, if desired.

Critical success: The Scorpion moves that 10 additional feet and a bonus 10 feet beyond that with no check, if desired. Checks for further movement in this round are made as if the bonus 10 feet did not occur (i.e. the bonus 10 feet does not add to the DC for additional checks).

Failure: Roll on the **Movement Problem Table**.
Critical failure: Roll on the **Critical Movement Failure Table**.

Turn 45-Degrees, Single Move Action: DC 10
Success: The Scorpion turns 45-degrees and can proceed in that direction on its next move action.
Failure: The Scorpion does not turn and is unable to make any further move actions until next round.
Critical success: The Scorpion can turn up to 90-degrees if the assistant driver wishes.
Critical failure: Treat as normal failure and roll on the Movement Failure Table.

Turn 90-Degrees, Single Move Action: DC 20
Success: The Scorpion turns 90-degrees and can proceed in that direction on its next move action.
Failure: Roll on the Movement Problem Table.
Critical success: The Scorpion turns 90-degrees as a swift action and can still make two move actions in the round.
Critical failure: Roll on the **Critical Movement Failure Table**.

Claw Attacks (Seats 2–3)

Claw attacks do 4d10 points of bludgeoning and slashing damage. If a successful melee hit initiates a grab on the target. Held targets can be automatically hit by the second claw if that claw's operator has not yet acted and wishes to do so (assuming there's no fail on the roll to use the claw). The holding claw automatically deals normal damage until the held opponent manages to break free. Claw attacks do not use up charge crystals. Use of the claws requires checks as follows (this check is made before the attack roll):

First claw attack while stationary for the entire round: DC 5
Success: Make normal claw attack.
Failure: The claw attack fails.
Critical Success: In addition to a possible critical hit (with a +4 a bonus to confirm), any additional claw attacks in this round gain a +4 attack bonus.
Critical failure: No attack with this claw is possible for 2 rounds as the claw gets out of position or stuck.

Second claw attack while stationary for the entire round DC 10
Success: Make normal claw attack.
Failure: The claw attack fails.
Critical Success: In addition to a possible critical hit (with a +4 a bonus to confirm), any additional claw attacks on the following round gain a +4 attack bonus.
Critical failure: No attack with either claw is possible for 2 rounds as the claws get out of position or stuck.

First claw attack if there is movement during the round: DC 15
Success: Make normal claw attack.
Failure: The claw attack fails.
Critical Success: In addition to a possible critical hit (with a +4 a bonus to confirm), any additional claw attacks on the following round gain a +4 attack bonus.
Critical failure: Roll on the Critical Claw Attack Problem table.

Second claw attack if there is movement during the round: DC 20
Success: Make normal claw attack.
Failure: The claw attack fails.
Critical Success: In addition to a possible critical hit (with a +4 a bonus to confirm), any additional claw attacks on the following round gain a +4 attack bonus.
Critical failure: Roll on the Critical Claw Attack Problem table.

Vengeance of Sekhmet (Seat 4)

The stinger tail fires a ray of true sunlight in a 250-foot line dealing 10d6 points of damage (half fire, half holy) to all non-good targets (DC 25 Reflex, half). The tail can fire in a 270-degree arc forward. It cannot fire to the rear or flanks. It can be fired every other round, and uses 1 charge of a *power-crystal* per shot whether the check is successful or not. Use of the tail requires checks as follows:

Aim Stinger Tail and Fire While Stationary: DC 10
Success: Make normal ranged touch attack.
Failure: The ray attack fails.
Critical Success: Possible critical hit (with a +4 a bonus to confirm).
Critical failure: The ray attack fails. The stinger ray cannot be used for an additional 1d4 rounds as it recharges.

Aim Stinger Tail and Fire While Stationary: DC 20
Success: Make normal ranged touch attack at –4 penalty to the attack roll.
Failure: The ray attack fails.
Critical Success: Possible critical hit (with a +4 a bonus to confirm).
Critical failure: The ray attack fails spectacularly. The stinger backfires dealing 4d6 fire damage to the operator (DC 20 Reflex save, half), and the stinger ray cannot be used for an additional 1d4 rounds as it recharges.

Movement Problem Table

Roll 1d10	Result
1–4	No problem, keep going
7–8	Scorpion stalls and moves no farther this round
9	Scorpion flips over. Getting it righted requires a successful DC 20 check by the driver.
10	Scorpion skids out of control, and moves 1d8 x 10-ft. in a random (1d8) direction. Make a DC 15 check to control the skid by choosing the direction it travels.

Critical Movement Problem Table

Roll 1d10	Result
1–2	No problem
3–4	Scorpion stalls and moves no farther in this round
5–6	Scorpion flips over. Getting it righted requires a successful DC 20 check by the driver.
7–8	Scorpion skids out of control, and moves 1d8 x 10-ft. in a random (1d8) direction. Make a DC 15 check to control the skid by choosing the direction it travels.
9	Fire. Someone has to get out and spend 1d3 rounds outside the Scorpion to put out the fire. Otherwise, the heat inside begins rising after 2 rounds, with everyone taking 1d6 fire damage plus 1d6 fire damage per additional round after the third to a maximum of 6d6 fire per round (i.e. 0 damage in rounds 1 and 2, 1d6 in round 3, 2d6 in round 4, 3d6 in round 5, etc.). The Scorpion can continue all activities as normal; it's just on fire while doing so.
10	Scorpion flips over and rolls. Each character inside takes 3d6 bludgeoning damage and must make a DC 15 Fortitude save or be knocked unconscious for 1d6 rounds. The Scorpion has only a 50% chance to end the roll upright; otherwise, it requires a successful DC 20 check by an operator in the driver seat (which may require the removal of an unconscious driver) to get it flipped back onto its legs.

Critical Claw Attack Problem Table

Roll 1d10	Result
1–2	No problem
3–4	Lose 2 rounds of attacks as the claws are jammed/tangled.
5–6	One claw disabled (determine randomly); fixing it requires a successful DC 15 check.
7–8	One claw is disabled; fixing it requires DC 15 checks in consecutive rounds.
9	One claw is broken and permanently destroyed, chopped in half by the other claw.
10	Both claws are permanently destroyed (they cut each other in half, basically).

DESTRUCTION

A *Scorpion of Sekhmet* cannot be destroyed by any mortal means, but it can run out of power and become inert until a new *power-crystal* is obtained.

Power-Crystals

Power-crystals power these artifacts, acting as a fuel source for the Scorpions, and appear as perfectly cut rose-quartz crystals that glow slightly in the dark and are pleasantly warm to the touch. Currently, one Scorpion has 26 charges left and the other has 55 charges left. The crystals found in the oasis (the gemstone amulets) are charge crystals and are fully charged (1,000 charges each). When a charge crystal reaches 0 charges, the Scorpion fails to function. They cannot be recharged by any known (mortal) means.

Area T-12. Planehopper Gate

> A white marble lotus-flower rests on the floor like a petaled bowl, five feet across. Three statues of ibis-headed men stand behind the lotus, holding hands. The one in the center looks into the sky, and the other two look down at the lotus.

New Monsters

Planehopper

The Planehoppers are an intelligent insect-like species with a bizarre caste system: They are rapacious conquerors relentlessly expanding their strange empires across many dimensions and planes of existence. Their sprawling cities, with high spires, curving ramps, and countless thousands of inhabitants, can cover entire worlds and moons in the realities and dimensions that the Planehoppers have seized.

The basic form of a Planehopper resembles a locust without wings, but with an upright "torso" section. Thus, they are similar to centaurs in shape: a large, grasshopperlike, horizontal segment with 4 legs supporting an upright "torso" segment with 2 arms, with a head-segment atop the torso. All the castes of a Planehopper hive share this body form.

Planehopper eggs are either male eggs or queen eggs laid in a ratio of at least 100-to-1. Originally, perhaps, there was no more differentiation between the males than this, but a caste called the "vivisecters" developed at some distant point in Planehopper history to adapt young Planehoppers to the hive's needs. The vivisecters use surgical procedures — a combination of their innate magic, instinct, learning, and tools — to shape young Planehoppers into members of the various male castes. The vivisecters do not hesitate to practice their arts upon other species conquered by the Planehoppers — with varying degrees of success.

PLANEHOPPER CHANNELER CR 6
XP 2,400
CE Medium monstrous humanoid
Init +1; **Senses** blindsense 30 ft., darkvision 60 ft.; **Perception** +10

AC 19, touch 13, flat-footed 16 (+2 Dex, +1 dodge, +6 natural)
hp 68 (8d10+24)
Fort +5; **Ref** +8; **Will** +8; +4 profane bonus vs. mind-affecting effects
Defensive Abilities telepath defense

Speed 30 ft.
Melee short sword +9/+4 (1d6/19-20), short sword +9 (1d6/19-20) or 2 claws +10 (1d4)
Special Attacks psychic chirp, psychic song

Str 11, **Dex** 15, **Con** 16, **Int** 11, **Wis** 14, **Cha** 18
Base Atk +8; **CMB** +8; **CMD** 21 (25 vs. trip)
Feats Dodge, Two-weapon Fighting, Weapon Finesse, Weapon Focus (short sword)
Skills Climb +5, Knowledge (geography) +6, Knowledge (planes) +8, Perception +8, Profession (miner) +5, Sense Motive +4, Stealth +8, Survival +8
Languages telepathy 60 ft.
SQ planar excavation
Gear 2 short swords

Project Psychic Force (Su) The overseer's mental power alone is not focused enough to attack without the help of a channeler. As long as the overseer is not more than 500

feet from the channeler, it can project one of four different mental powers through the channeler (see the channeler for descriptions of these powers) every other round, up to twice per day.

- **Psychic Chirp (Su)** This psychic projection is a needle-thin ray. On a successful touch attack the psychic chirp causes 3d6 points of damage (DC 18 Will save for half damage). This save DC is Charisma based.
- **Planar Excavation (Su)** This psychic emanation "digs" through the fabric of different planes of existence or dimensions. The psychic power of the digging cannot be used as a weapon, although when it breaks through on the far side of a planar tunnel it explodes in a blast of psychic energy to any physical material within a 50 foot radius of the portal. This blast acts as the spell *disintegrate* cast at the originating caster level (typical overseer CL 12). A channeler can emit this psychic frequency whenever the originating creature — its overseer or governor — wishes, as long as the originating creature maintains concentration on the task.
- **Psychic Song (Su)** A channeler's song is actually a psychic frequency rather than a sound, but unless the targets are also psychic they think they "hear" the actually soundless ripples of the song. The song extends in a cone 60 foot. Anyone within this area must make a DC 18 Will saving throw or suffer 1d6 hit points of psychic damage and suffers *stunned* condition for 1d2 rounds. This save DC is Charisma based.
- **Repulsion (Su)** This psychic emanation is a cone of force 60 foot long that repulses (DC 18 Will save to not be affected) all living beings 60 foot away with no range increment. This ability can affect anything up to 2,000 pounds. If the creature hits a solid object, the impact causes 1d6 hit points of damage for each 10 foot that the target had *not* already been moved. For example, if the target was pushed back only 10 foot and hit a wall, the damage would be 5d6 because 50 foot of the 60 foot had not been traveled.

Telepath Defense (Su) As telepaths, the Planehoppers receive a +4 to saves vs. mind-affecting effects from mental training.

Planehopper channelers look like warriors but with much larger heads and longer antennae. They are able to receive mental waves from an overseer and focus it into a much more powerful projection.

The number of times a channeler can emit this cone of psychic repulsion depends upon the originating creature, not on the channeler. The channeler itself is not exhausted or depleted by focusing mental powers, but the originating creature has limited stamina. More than one originating creature can focus mental power through a channeler, but the channeler can only emit one power per round, regardless of how many originating creatures are ready to use it as a focus.

There are 4 different mental emanations that an overseer or governor Planehopper can project through the mind of a channeler. Their major role as a channeler is to use its planar excavation to create tunnels from one reality into the next. It is through these tunnels that the Planehoppers spread their rapacious empires to conquer and enslave the civilizations they find on the far sides of their constant tunneling.

Dual-wielding of short swords is seen as a social badge of honor amongst channelers and are worn ceremonially even out of combat situations.

PLANEHOPPER GOVERNOR **CR 9**
XP 6,400
CE Medium monstrous humanoid
Init +0; **Senses** blindsense 30 ft., darkvision 60 ft.; **Perception** +12

AC 21, touch 10, flat-footed 21 (+11 natural)
hp 102 (12d10+36)

Fort +6; **Ref** +8; **Will** +13; +4 profane bonus vs. mind-affecting effects
Defensive Abilities telepath defense

Speed 0 ft., levitate 30 ft. vertical
Special Attacks psychic flash

Str 8, **Dex** –, **Con** 15, **Int** 19, **Wis** 17, **Cha** 22
Base Atk +12; **CMB** +11; **CMD** 21 (25 vs. trip)
Feats Alertness, Blind-fight, Deceitful, Improved Iron Will, Iron Will, Toughness
Skills Appraise +10, Bluff +10, Diplomacy +15, Heal +8, Knowledge (arcana) +10, Knowledge (dungeoneering) +8, Knowledge (engineering) +10, Knowledge (geography) +10, Knowledge (history) +10, Knowledge (planes) +16, Knowledge (religion) +8, Linguistics +9, Perception +12, Sense Motive +11, Spellcraft +10, Stealth +7, Survival +10
Languages Abyssal, Aklo, Aquan, Auran, Celestial, Draconic, Infernal, Sylvan, Terran; telepathy 1 mile (limited to Planehopper overseers only) or 60 ft. for all other creatures
SQ channeler broadcast, telepathic hive-bond

Psychic levitation (Su) Governor Planehoppers can float as per *levitate* spell, rising up to a height of 30 foot, but they cannot move forward without help. They are usually assisted by 2–4 Planehopper laborers that push the governor where

it directs.
Psychic Flash (Su) Governors are able to build up psychic energy and release it in a 30 ft. cone once every other round that causes 12d6 psychic damage (DC 22 Will save for half damage). They are able to use this power 4 times per day. This power is very draining and if a governor uses this after the daily allotment, the governor must make a Fortitude save DC 15 +2 for each additional use until a full day of rest or become fatigued.
Telepathic hive-bond (Su) The governor may hive-bond with all Planehoppers up to a mile in every direction. Once a Planehopper has acted in a combat, the governor can alert all within its area. These Planehoppers will no longer be considered flat-footed. This hive-bond also allows the governor and its Planehoppers a +4 to perception as they gain a wider range of perceiving their environments.
Telepath defense (Su) As telepaths, the Planehoppers receive a +4 to saves vs. mind-affecting effects from mental training.

Planehopper governors are mostly brain. They look like a giant 5 foot diameter locust head floating in the air, with spindly legs and a rudimentary body dangling beneath it. The head's carapace is too small to contain the massive brain, so the back is split open like flower petals, leaving the pulsing yellow brain open to the air. Six whip-like antennae emerge from the brain and undulate slowly in the air.

Governors are the higher officers of a Planehopper horde. They can communicate telepathically with overseers over a distance of 1 mile, and can communicate telepathically with other castes of Planehoppers and other creatures at a range of 60 foot.

Planehopper governors cannot melee attack as they have no natural weapons. They can, however, focus a mental blast through a Planehopper channeler as an overseer does (see the description of the channelers for details) or build up psychic energy and release it in a flash. The link between the governor and the channeler can be blocked by metallic lead.

PLANEHOPPER LABORER **CR 3**
XP 800
CE Medium monstrous humanoid
Init +1; **Senses** blindsense 30 ft., darkvision 60 ft.; **Perception** +4

AC 15, touch 11, flat-footed 14 (+1 Dex, +4 natural)
hp 30 (4d10+8)
Fort +2; **Ref** +5; **Will** +4; +4 profane bonus vs. mind-affecting effects
Defensive Abilities telepath defense

Speed 30 ft.
Melee 2 claws +8 (1d4+4)

Str 18, **Dex** 12, **Con** 13, **Int** 7, **Wis** 10, **Cha** 9
Base Atk +4; **CMB** +8; **CMD** 19 (23 vs. trip)
Feats Endurance, Toughness
Skills Climb +8, Knowledge (engineering) +1, Perception +4, Profession (laborer) +2, Stealth +5
Languages telepathy 60 ft. (limited to Planehopper species only)
SQ spring-loaded, steady worker

Spring-loaded (Ex) Laborers legs are able to build tremendous pressure and can make incredible jumps. They receive a +4 to acrobatics when jumping.
Steady Worker (Ex) Laborers are able to move about with tremendous loads. Their movement rate is 30 ft. and is never modified by encumbrance.
Telepath defense (Su) As telepaths, the Planehoppers receive a +4 to saves vs. mind-affecting effects from mental training.

A Planehopper laborer is the basic, fundamental form of male Planehoppers. They resemble a locust without wings, but with an upright "torso" section. They are similar to centaurs in shape: a large, grasshopperlike, horizontal segment with 4 legs supporting an upright "torso" segment with 2 arms, with a head-segment atop the torso.

Planehopper laborers are the bottom rung of the hierarchy. They are sentient, but dull-witted, easily fooled if not mentally linked with a member of one of the higher castes. Left to themselves, they happily drink and gamble away their money, psychologically incapable of seeing themselves as oppressed. The uncontrolled celebrations of worker Planehoppers have leveled entire blocks of captured cities.

Workers communicate telepathically with other Planehoppers, but not with members of other species. Although they have organs that can vocalize words, most worker Planehoppers never learn a spoken language at all since they have no contacts beyond their own hives. Planehopper workers are not combatants; their most effective attack is to drop any tools and fling themselves at an enemy, scratching with their short claws. In some cases, they might be ordered to do exactly this, simply to delay or block the enemy. Actual fighting, though, is left to the warriors and the channelers.

PLANEHOPPER OVERSEER **CR 7**
XP 3,200
CE Medium monstrous humanoid
Init +5; **Senses** blindsense 30 ft., darkvision 60 ft.; **Perception** +8

AC 21, touch 11, flat-footed 20 (+4 armor, +1 Dex, +6 natural)
hp 85 (9d10+36)
Fort +7; **Ref** +7; **Will** +6; +4 profane bonus vs. mind-affecting effects
Defensive Abilities telepath defense

Speed 30 ft.
Melee *+1 obsidian longsword* +14/+9 (1d8+4/19-20) or 2 claws +12 (1d4+3)

Special Attack hyperactive, resonating chirp

Str 17, **Dex** 13, **Con** 18, **Int** 15, **Wis** 10, **Cha** 16
Base Atk +9; **CMB** +12; **CMD** 23 (27 vs. trip)
Feats Alertness, Improved Initiative, Lunge, Power Attack, Weapon Focus (longsword)
Skills Acrobatics +3, Appraise +6, Bluff +4, Climb +8, Diplomacy +10, Heal +5, Intimidate +10, Knowledge (engineering) +5, Knowledge (planes) +5, Perception +8, Sense Motive +8, Stealth +5, Survival +10
Languages Aklo, Infernal; telepathy 60 ft.
SQ channeler broadcast, telepathic hive-bond
Gear chain shirt, *+1 obsidian longsword*

Channeler broadcast (Su) An overseer has a psychic ability to receive, focus, and re-broadcast the mental attacks. The overseer's mental power alone is not focused enough to attack without the help of a channeler. The channeler (whether nearby or distant) thus serves as the overseer's proxy for mental assaults. As long as the overseer is no more than 500 feet from the channeler, it can project one of four different mental powers through the channeler (see the channeler for descriptions of these powers) every other round, up to twice per day.
Hyperactive (Su) Two times per day as a swift action, an overseer can draw on its psychic reserves for a boost of speed, allowing it to take an additional move action in that round.
Telepath defense (Su) As telepaths, the Planehoppers receive a +4 to saves vs. mind-affecting effects from mental training.
Telepathic hive-bond (Su) Once a warrior or an overseer has acted in a combat, all Planehopper warriors within the controlled group are no longer considered flat-footed. This hive-bond also allows the controller and its warriors a +4 to perception as they gain a wider range of perceiving their environments.
Resonant chirp (Su) As a standard action every 1d4 rounds, an overseer can release a damaging resonance by rubbing its hind legs, dealing 9d8 points of sonic damage to creatures in a 60-foot cone (Fortitude DC 17 for half). The save DC is Charisma-based.

Overseers are essentially the squad-and-platoon level officers of a Planehopper fighting force. They have a mental link with all the warrior Planehoppers under their command; each warrior can thus see what the overseer sees, and what all the other warriors see. This hive-bond between overseers and their warriors is what makes the Planehoppers such a terrifying threat to civilization whenever they appear through their planar gates. Fortunately, the link is not unlimited: An overseer cannot bond with more than 4 warriors at a time, and warriors cannot switch in and out of different overseers' control. The link is to the death. New warriors can be added to replace casualties, but none can leave once bonded to a particular overseer. The only way to separate a warrior from its overseer is to kill the overseer. In addition to the 4 warriors, an overseer can control a single channeler.

They typically carry their weapon of station, an obsidian longsword. These are somewhat brittle as compared to a normal metal forged weapon, but they are psychically enhanced and given as gifts by governors to an overseer once it reaches maturity.

PLANEHOPPER WARRIOR **CR 5**
XP 1,600
CE Medium monstrous humanoid
Init +5; **Senses** blindsense 30 ft., darkvision 60 ft.; **Perception** +8 (+12 hive-bond)

AC 19, touch 11, flat-footed 18 (+4 armor, +1 Dex, +4 natural)
hp 51 (6d10+18)
Fort +5; **Ref** +6; **Will** +5; +4 profane bonus vs. mind-affecting effects
Defensive Abilities telepath defense

Speed 30 ft.
Melee lance +10/+5 (1d8+4/×3) or longsword +9/+4 (1d8+3/19-20) or 2 claws +9 (1d4+3)
Special Attacks leap-to-attack

Str 16, **Dex** 12, **Con** 16, **Int** 10, **Wis** 11, **Cha** 9
Base Atk +6; **CMB** +9; **CMD** 20 (24 vs. trip)
Feats Improved Initiative, Power Attack, Weapon Focus (lance)
Skills Acrobatocs +4, Climb +5, Intimidate +4, Knowledge (dungeon) +4, Perception +8, Profession (soldier) +4, Stealth +4, Survival +4
Languages telepathy 60 ft.
SQ spring-loaded, telepathic hive-bond
Gear chain shirt, lance, longsword

Leap-to-attack (Ex) A warrior is able to build enough power in their hind legs to be able to leap up to 60 foot as a charge attack. If the leap is over 30 feet, the warrior gains a +2 to hit and double damage with a successful attack.
Spring-loaded (Ex) Warriors legs are able to build tremendous pressure and can make incredible jumps. They receive a +4 to acrobatics when jumping.
Telepathic hive-bond (Su) Once a warrior or an overseer has acted in a combat, all Planehopper warriors within the controlled group are no longer considered flat-footed. This hive-bond also allows the controller and its warriors a +4 to

perception as they gain a wider range of perceiving their environments.

Telepath defense (Su) As telepaths, the Planehoppers receive a +4 to saves vs. mind-affecting effects from mental training.

Planehopper warriors are more intelligent than the workers. Their thought processes are quite alien, however, but they are approximately as intelligent as the average human being. Warriors are telepathically tied to an overseer in the same way that the workers are connected to a governor. Each shares perception through the overseer with all the other warriors he commands.

Planehopper warriors wear torso armor and plumed helmets into battle, and they fight with weapons, favoring lances and longswords. Warriors tend to specialize in leaping into combat with their lances.

Demons & Devils

Present in these pages are three relatively short but very difficult dungeons: **The Sorcerer's Citadel**, **"Ra's Evil Grin"** and **The Pit of Despair**. Each dungeon presents a perfect place to hide an item for which your party may be questing — whether a powerful magic weapon or some famous artifact. Each dungeon contains such an item as its final treasure: a *sphere of annihilation*, the *globe of Arden* and the *Sword of Karith* (a *holy avenger longsword)*, respectively.

The three adventures can be run independently or can be linked together as part of a larger quest, possibly to retrieve some multipart item. Or, to reward a party with one item of even greater power, the GM can replace each item found at the conclusion of the three adventures with a piece of a triune key. When fully assembled, the key could permit access to a final location where the party can find this greater item. Ultimately, the final use of these insidious dungeons is up to the GM.

As the name of this module implies, each of these three dungeons culminates in an encounter with either a demon or devil. In **The Sorcerer's Citadel,** the party must fight both an intoxicating lilin and, in the final encounter, a group of devils. In **"Ra's Evil Grin,"** the party comes face-to-face with possibly the greatest physical threat presented in any of these three dungeons — a vicious dark daughter, named Dendorandra. In **The Pit of Despair,** the party (unknowingly at first) encounters a demon of a different type — a wicked nalfeshnee of super-genius-level intellect who is the agent behind a grand evil deception.

Designed for characters of 9th and higher levels, the dungeons in this module progress in difficulty to challenge characters up to 13th level. **The Sorcerer's Citadel** is the easiest (yet by no means easy), and **The Pit of Despair** the most challenging. In addition to requiring high-level characters, each scenario is designed to challenge PCs of all classes. Rogues and clerics will not sit idly by while their party's wizards and paladins quest for their proverbial grails. Each quest must be a team effort to be successful; a less-diverse party will have a difficult — if not impossible — time achieving the final goal.

All of the adventures presented in this module should be the culmination of important quests. Such quests require lengthy travel and triumph over great peril. Resist the urge to allow PCs to conveniently *teleport* to a dungeon's location. Instead, set these dungeons in remote and inaccessible areas of the game world.

This approach is appealing for several reasons. First, it lets your players run high-level adventures without spending the years required to build characters up to that level through multiple campaigns. Second, using pre-generated characters allows players to experience the fun and danger of these perilous dungeons without risking the lives of characters that they have been playing for years and to whom they've developed attachments. Having no ties to pre-generated characters, players may also exercise less restraint when roleplaying such characters, which can lead to interesting choices. For example, in **The Pit of Despair,** demonic influences tempt a paladin, who retrieves a magic sword, to become an antipaladin and slay his good-aligned compatriots. The chances that a player, who has been roleplaying her heroic paladin for years, would be tempted by such an offer are slim indeed. But playing a pre-generated paladin in a one-shot adventure… that's another story.

In any case, we at **Frog God Games** hope that your players find these adventures as challenging and exciting as all the players and playtesters who have attempted them over the years. Their experience, summed up as follows, may be helpful to your PCs: "You can run if you want, but you'll just die tired."

Sorcerer's Citadel

By Clark Peterson and Bill Webb

Introduction

Designed for a party of at least 9th level, this adventure will challenge players seeking a powerful magic item of the GM's choosing. A *sphere of annihilation* has been provided, but any appropriately powerful item can be substituted as the final objective, as suits the GM's campaign. Though the adventure is designed to test every type of character class, a rogue with a high Disable Device skill is essential, as is a wizard or sorcerer able to cast 5th-level spells. This adventure culminates in an encounter with devils and a *forcecage* behind which is secured the *sphere of annihilation*.

The *sphere of annihilation* is hidden deep within the tower-and-dungeon complex of Crane the Sorcerer. Originally set atop a high mountain in a secluded and wild part of the world, the tower and dungeon can be relocated to meet the GM's requirements. Crane, an introvert, stayed as far away from civilization as possible, as is detailed below. GM's will notice that the tower and dungeon (excluding the central chamber) do not present many difficulties for a high-level party — thus lulling PCs into a false sense of security before the final encounter. The central chamber, however, is very, very nasty and will test even the most stalwart group's mettle.

The Legend of Crane the Sorcerer

Crane, a lawful-neutral sorcerer of great power was obsessed with all things lawful. He paid homage to the gods of law, whether evil or good. He was a great scientist and created numerous constructs, such as golems and homunculi. His other interests ran to the diabolic. Crane studied the use of extraplanar creatures as servants and messengers. He also developed a firm knowledge of trap building and alchemy. He acquired and learned to control a *sphere of annihilation*, with which he carved a dungeon beneath his mountaintop tower.

About 100 years ago, Crane set off to do battle with a group of chaotic-evil sorcerers, known as the Violet Brotherhood, whose black arts were linked to the foul demon frog-god, Tsathogga. Though mightier than any individual evil sorcerer, Crane could not prevail against all of them working in concert. Overcome by his foes, he cursed his own arrogance with his final breath. Yet he had taken a great precaution: fearing that, in magical combat, his foes might seize control of his *sphere* and turn it against him, Crane had decided not to use his magical globe of blackness against the Violet Brotherhood. Instead, he sealed his *sphere* within his tower and protected it with powerful magic. It awaits discovery there today, its former master now long dead.

Sages consulted by the PCs offer the following cryptic warning:

> Far up in distant mountains lies the Tower of Crane — master of darkness, lord of nothingness. Long is the path, and dangerous. Beware, adventurer, for peril lies both inside and out, both in between and beyond.

Reaching the Tower

Crane the Sorcerer's tower rises above the mist-shrouded summit of a distant mountain embedded within a faraway mountain range. The surrounding area is wild, and finding the tower is an arduous undertaking; just reaching this desolate part of the world should require a night or more of roleplaying. In the **Lost Lands** campaign setting by **Frog God Games**, Crane's Tower is located among the mysterious Lost Mountains, far across the Haunted Steppe and standing above thrice-cursed Lake Hali.

The Tower of Crane the Sorcerer

The Tower of Crane the Sorcerer is shrouded in a chilling, damp mist. The cylindrical tower, made of a smooth, dark stone, tapers gradually from the base to its peak, where it is crowned with three sharp spires of uneven height. There are no openings of any kind in the dark walls of the tower.

Some 100 or more feet from the tower is a depression of worked stone, set into the surrounding earth and accessed by a downward-sloping ramp. Inside the depression is what appears to be an archway which leads to the tower's interior.

The black stone of which the exterior of the tower is constructed is not native to this plane, but was imported by Crane's infernal servants. The tower itself measures over 160 feet tall at the tip of its tallest spire. The walls are unnaturally smooth and extraordinarily difficult to scale (DC 40 Climb check), as there are no available handholds. The walls of the tower and the floors between each level are some five feet thick and have been enhanced with immunity to spells of any type, except those spells specifically cast by Crane himself. The stone also proves impervious to any physical weapon or tool with an enhancement bonus of less than +5 (the result of a *wish*). Nonmagical weapons or tools striking the stone shatter immediately, and their wielder suffers damage equal to that which would have been inflicted against the tower. Magical weapons and tools of less than +5 enhancement suffer the same fate, though they are allowed a DC 20 Fortitude save. A successful save means the magical weapon or tool does not shatter, but the wielder still takes damage as noted above.

An unknown magical ward (again, the result of a *wish*) prevents magical ingress or egress of any kind; that option is reserved for Crane and those to whom he gave permission (which, because of his death, can no longer be obtained). Anyone attempting magical entry into the tower is stricken as per a *maze* spell (courtesy of a *permanent contingent maze* spell cast by Crane). When freed from the *maze*, the person reappears on this plane in the middle of the Poisoned Corridor (see below).

Five levels comprise the tower's interior — four above ground, the fifth below. The upper levels contain various living spaces appointed with the requisite creature comforts. Everything within the tower's interior lies shrouded beneath a thick layer of dust. All doors and trapdoors within the tower are locked and of average make and, unless otherwise noted, have the same surprisingly pedestrian characteristics detailed below.

Locked Wooden Oak Door or Trapdoor: 2 in. thick; Hardness 5; hp 20; Break DC 23, Disable Device DC 25.

Wandering Monsters

The tower contains no wandering monsters, because creatures that have tried to enter died in the poisoned corridor. Local monsters have learned of the poisoned corridor by hard experience and do not venture near the tower. Thus, the party can camp within 100 yards of the tower in relative safety. But don't tell the PCs that. Stress the darkness and lack of vision caused by the cold mists of the mountain top and the eerie shadow cast by the spires of the tower.

The only threats to a party camped outside the tower are **2 flesh golems,** created long ago by Crane to guard the archway leading to the poisonous corridor. With Crane's death, the golems went berserk. They now wander the surrounding wilderness, though they never stray more than five miles from the tower. They attack any creatures they see.

Random Encounters

Roll for wandering monsters every three hours while the PCs camp outside the tower on 1d20 with the following results:

Roll d20	Encounter
1–2	**1d2 flesh golems.** Since there are only two of these creatures, no more than two can be encountered. Once both are killed, treat this result as "No encounter."
3–7	**Strange grunts, shouts and shrieks off in the distance.** The berserk flesh golems utter these fearsome noises, and the sounds should unnerve the PCs. Once both golems are killed, treat this result as "No encounter."
8–20	No encounter.

BERSERK FLESH GOLEMS (2) CR 7
XP 3,200
hp 79 (*Pathfinder Roleplaying Game Bestiary* "Golem, Flesh")
Gear Each golem wears a strange amulet bearing the rune of Crane the Sorcerer. PCs can use these amulets to prevent the invisible door's *cloudkill* trap from triggering (see below). The amulet is otherwise not magical. Woven into the flesh of the golems, the amulets must be "surgically" removed after the golems have been killed.

The Entrance Passage

The stone-lined ramp descends some 12 feet to a flat-bottomed depression. Set into the far wall of this depression is a simple, unadorned archway approximately five feet wide and eight feet high. The cold, swirling mists seem to collect at the bottom of this depression. From the top of the slope, shapes can be seen lying just inside the archway, on the floor of the corridor beyond. Just inside the archway lie several animal and humanoid skeletons of all sizes. Debris surrounds them, some of which appears to be equipment that has long since rotted or rusted. The passageway beyond seems to be constructed entirely of seamless white stone. The sides of the walls appear perfectly smooth and show no chips or tool marks. The corridor stretches on, beyond the range of normal vision, sloping slightly downward.

Crane created this corridor using his *sphere of annihilation.* The corridor extends 180 feet, but the skeletal remains of birds, animals, monsters and humans litter the first 60 feet — creatures slain by the poison of the corridor, as described below. All mundane equipment has long since rotted or rusted beyond usefulness.

The Poisoned Corridor (CR 8)

The citadel's entrance is the most deadly element of the fortress' defense system, which Crane set up to protect his treasures. The floor, walls and ceiling of the corridor comprise a **magically poisonous trap**. Anyone touching these surfaces is exposed to a powerful poison.

Any material contacting an individual's skin, including boots and gloves, magically transmits the poison. Double-layering clothing or walking across stones, blankets or other items strewn along the floor does not prevent contact with the magical poison; such objects magically "conduct" the poison to any living being in the corridor. To successfully negotiate the corridor, PCs must avoid contacting any part of it. When Crane occupied the tower, guests forbidden magical entrance were carried down the corridor by the flesh golems who are immune to poison. Magical flight or *levitation* provides the most obvious way down the poisoned corridor, though a character doing so will most likely crash into the *invisible wall of iron* (see **Area 3**, below).

MAGICALLY POISONOUS CORRIDOR TRAP CR 8
XP 4,800
Type magical; **Perception** DC 29; **Disable Device** not possible

Trigger touch; **Reset** automatic

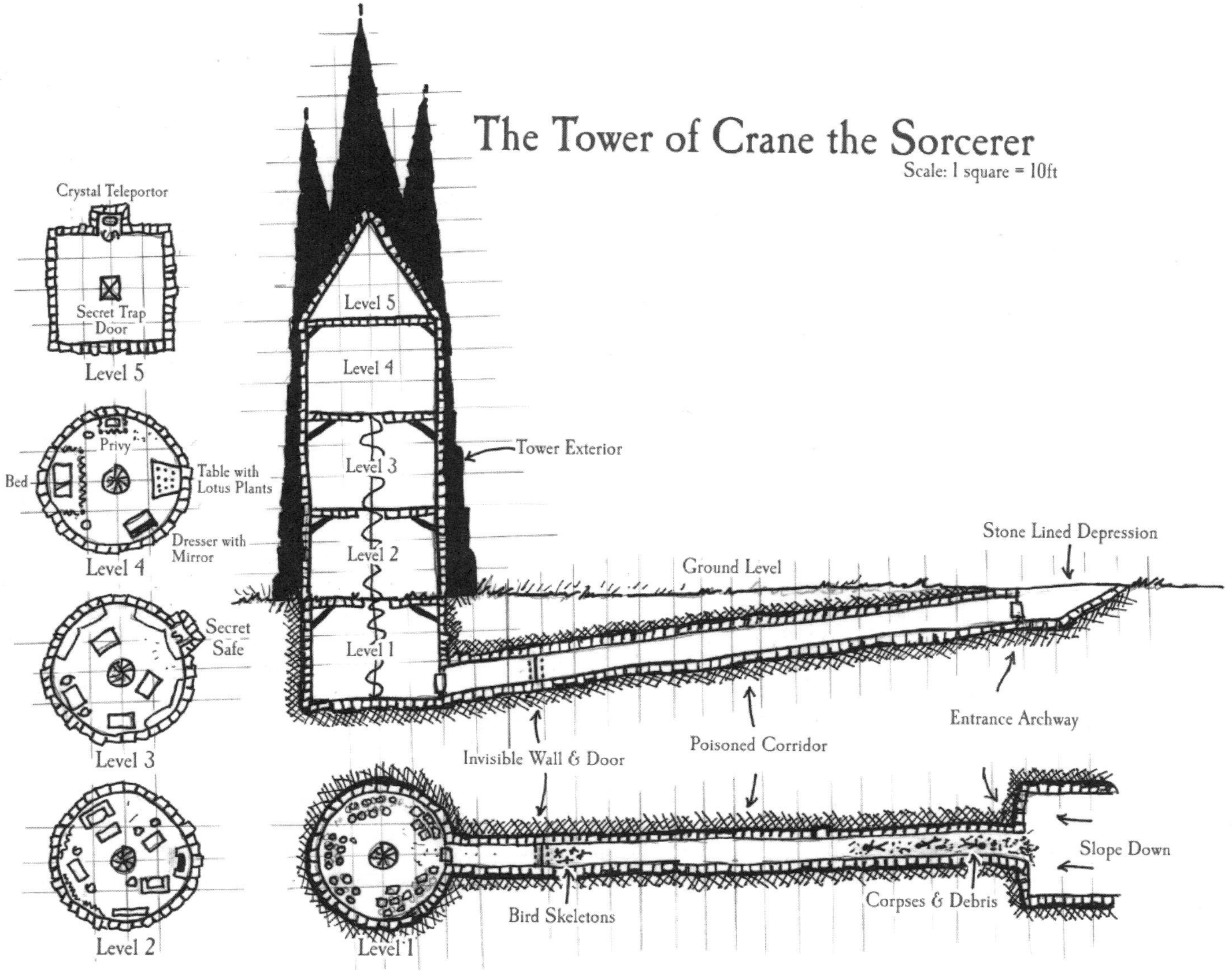

Effect spell effect (*poison*, DC 16 Fort save, CL 7th); multiple targets (all targets in the corridor).

A careful search of the debris and a successful DC 20 Perception check turns up a few interesting items of treasure. Touching the items requires a Fortitude save against the magical poison, as described above. These items lose their toxicity when removed from the corridor.

Treasure: The skeletal debris has three items worth noting: a *scroll of shades* and *hold monster*, a *potion of heroism* and a *luckstone*.

The Invisible Wall and Door (CR 7)

As the PCs hasten down the corridor they notice in the distance the end of the passage: a mundane-looking wooden door with iron bindings, set into the far wall. What they do not see, unless they succeed on a DC 25 Perception check, is the **invisible wall of iron** with its **invisible *arcane-locked* iron door**, which completely blocks their access to the door they see at the end of the corridor.

Located 150 feet down the passage (30 feet before its end) is an *invisible arcane locked* door (the *arcane lock* cast at 18th level) set into a *permanent invisible wall of iron*. Anyone flying down the corridor likely collides with the barrier and suffers 1d4 damage (+1 damage per 5 feet of movement over 15 feet per round), unless the person flying down the hallway sees the door (DC 25 Perception). In addition, anyone thusly striking the door must succeed on a Fortitude save (DC 10 + damage done) or be stunned for 1d4. A stunned character drops to the ground and contacts the poisoned surface. The only clue to the invisible barrier's presence is the small pile of debris at its base — dust blown down the corridor from outside and detritus from birds and other flyers who previously "encountered" the wall. If a PC who notices the debris receives a +2 bonus on their Perception check to see the door.

If that weren't trouble enough, the door is **trapped** and releases poison gas as per a *cloudkill* spell if it is opened by anyone other than Crane or someone wearing his amulet (which can be obtained from the berserk flesh golems; see above). In addition, brute force or any kind of magic used against the door triggers the trap. Failing a roll to pick the lock or disable the trap by more than 5 also triggers the trap.

Note: the amulets do not open the door; they simply prevent the trap from springing if the door is successfully unlocked. Crane endowed the golems with the amulets so that they could successfully convey his guests into the tower without setting off the *cloudkill* trap. At first, the *cloudkill* gas fills 30 feet of the corridor directly in front of the door. Then it billows forward at a rate of 10 feet per round, ultimately filling 90 feet of the corridor. The *cloud* lasts for 18 minutes before dissipating. The trap is permanent, resets instantly and can be triggered an unlimited number of times until it is disabled. Once the trap is disabled, the door may be opened safely. However, after the door is opened and closed, the trap automatically resets itself and must be disabled again; otherwise, opening the door again triggers the trap. PC's cannot permanently disable the trap, short of a *wish* cast by a wizard of higher level than Crane.

Trapped Iron Door and *Invisible Wall of Iron*: CR 8; 5 in. thick; Hardness 10; hp 180 (immune to spells and magic weapons or tools less than +5 enhancement); Perception DC 25; Break DC 38, Disable Device DC 30. Like the tower's exterior walls, the door and wall are immune to magic weapons and tools of less than +5 enhancement, are immune to spells, cannot be bypassed by *teleport*, etc. The door's trap releases poison gas, as per a *cloudkill* spell cast by an 18th level caster.

***CLOUDKILL* TRAP** **CR 7**
XP 3,200
Type magical; **Perception** DC 30; **Disable Device** 30

Type touch; **Reset** automatic
Effect spell effect (*cloudkill*, DC 17 Fort)

Once they bypass the door, the party can safely travel the remaining 30 feet of the corridor to the normal, locked door — the entrance to **Level 1** of the tower. This last stretch of corridor is not trapped with poison.

Locked Mundane Oak Door with Iron Bindings: 2 in. thick; Hardness 5; hp 20; Break DC 23, Open Lock DC 25.

Tower Level 1

The tower's basement is a large circular room about 40 feet in diameter. Set in the center of the room is a spiral, wooden staircase, which leads to a trapdoor in the ceiling. Barrels and boxes fill the room. A thick accumulation of dust has settled on the room's contents. This level contains various barrels, boxes and preserved foodstuffs stacked neatly along the walls of the room. A wooden staircase leads up to a locked trapdoor and **Level 2** of the tower. Nothing of value is present here.

Tower Level 2

This level appears to be a sitting room. Several pieces of beautifully crafted furniture tastefully appoint the room, which is further accented by rich tapestries. Again, a layer of dust covers everything. The masterwork-quality furniture can be removed by ambitious adventurers and sold in a city for 3d6 x 100 gp per piece. The magical fireplace, constructed of the same stone as the exterior walls, does not emit smoke when kindling is burned. Another wooden staircase leads up to a locked trapdoor and **Level 3** of the tower. Nothing else of real value is present here.

Tower Level 3 (CR 8)

This level of the tower is Crane's alchemical workshop. Opened and stoppered vials, jugs and bottles; pots, bowls, mortars, pestles and crucibles; many rusted tools, like pliers, scoops and tongs; braziers, censers, candles, oil lamps and bits of coal; a scale with weights; parchment, quills and inkpots; and glass piping, brass fittings and support apparatus litter four tables. Six locked cabinets stand against the walls, lined with shelves. Materials present in this laboratory would require several wagon trips to transport. There are, however, a number of rare, valuable items here, and the total setup would fetch well over 25,000 gp if sold to a wizard or alchemist. Another wooden staircase leads up to a **locked trapdoor** and **Level 4** of the tower.

A **secret, trapped compartment** behind one of the cabinets hides a **locked, trapped safe**. This safe contains some of Crane's monetary wealth as well as a few potions.

Trapped Secret Compartment: Perception DC 30; 2 in. thick; Hardness 5; hp 20; Break DC 20.

Alchemical Roulette

Randomly sampling alchemical materials can be very dangerous. If a PC does so, roll d% with the following results:

Roll d100	Result
01–12	Deadly poison (*Type* poison, ingested; *save* Fortitude DC 20; *onset* 10 minutes.; *frequency* 1/round for 6 rounds; *effect* 1d4 Con damage; *cure* 1 save).
13–25	Imbiber loses all body hair, though fingernails and toenails grow rapidly for 2 weeks.
26–35	Imbiber becomes delusional (believing that he is invisible, can fly, etc.) for 2d4 hours.
36–50	Mild poison (*Type* poison, ingested; *save* Fortitude DC 12; *onset* 10 minutes.; *frequency* 1/round for 4 rounds; *effect* 1 Str damage and 1 Con damage; *cure* 1 save).
51–80	No effect.
81–95	Tastes great! Imbiber is immune to *fear* effects for 2 hours.
96–99	Imbiber gains 1d3 temporary Str for 1 day.
00	Imbiber permanently gains an increase of 1 point in a random ability score. Roll 1d6 (1 = Strength, 2 = Intelligence, 3 = Wisdom, 4 = Dexterity, 5 = Constitution, 6 = Charisma)

ACID FLOOR TRAP **CR 6**
XP 2,400
Type mechanical; **Perception** DC 25; **Disable Device** DC 25

Trigger touch; **Reset** manual
Effect acid spill (5d6 acid damage plus 1d6 acid damage the following round, DC 20 Reflex negates); multiple targets (all targets in a 10-ft.-by-10-ft. area in front of the compartment)

PCs find the locked safe inside the secret compartment.

Locked, Trapped Safe: 4 in. thick; Hardness 10; hp 120; Break DC 45; Disable Device DC 30

***CLOUDKILL* TRAP** **CR 7**
XP 3,200
Type magical; **Perception** DC 30; **Disable Device** 30

Type touch; **Reset** automatic
Effect spell effect (*cloudkill*, DC 17 Fort)

Treasure: The safe contains 12,200 gp; six matched 100 gp gems (aquamarines); a *potion of protection from energy (cold)*, a *potion of nondetection*, and *elixir of hiding*, and *salve of slipperiness;* and a strange black talisman hanging from a pure adamantine chain. This talisman, a ruby-eyed, silver-tongued dragon twined around a ball, weighs four ounces and is exquisitely crafted of stone similar to that of the tower's exterior. It could be sold for as much as 1,000 gp. It detects faintly as magical, but does not reveal its true nature until the party reaches **Room N** of the dungeon.

This talisman — a *talisman of the sphere* — doubles the wearer's intelligence and level bonus when attempting to control a *sphere of annihilation.* In addition, this *talisman* is the key to freeing the *sphere* from the *forcecage* that contains it.

Tower Level 4 (CR 7)

This room appears to be Crane's bedroom, and it is lavishly furnished with tapestries, silk curtains and incense burners. The curtains around the canopied bed have been drawn back, revealing a beautiful woman of about 25 years, clothed in a fine red, silken robe, nestled amid the bedclothes. Pots of strange plants rest on tables around the room, filling the space with strange and exotic fragrances. Well-tended pots of **blue lotus flowers** clutter every table surface. Pollen from these flowers permeates the room, and any sudden or violent movement or disturbance stirs up a pollen cloud.

The beautiful woman is in reality a polymorphed **lilin devil**, named "Melissa" (her real name is Vaa'rankariziaalia). Melissa, once his consort, was summoned to this plane and bound to this room by Crane. She cannot leave the room, though she can summon friends, as noted below. These summoned friends are exempt from the prohibition against entering the tower by magical means. Crane *wanted* Melissa to summon help to defend his tower. However, she is bound never to summon them when Crane is present. She wears a *robe of blending*. Her beauty is flawless, and she is friendly if approached.

Hearing the approach of the PCs, Melissa disturbed the blue lotus flowers, filling the entire room with the narcotic pollen; all PCs entering the room are subject to its effects. Upon her discovery, Melissa engages the party in a dialogue, biding time until the pollen has taken effect. She rises from the bed and pretends to tend the potted plants as she speaks to the party, releasing more clouds of blue lotus pollen every round.

This room contains no stairs. A **secret trapdoor** in the ceiling, 8 feet above the floor and discoverable with a successful DC 20 Perception check, leads to **Level 5** of the tower.

Blue Lotus Poison

Blue lotus pollen has a narcotic effect on whoever inhales or ingests it, causing them to become drowsy and experience euphoric hallucinations.

Type poison, ingested/inhaled; *save* Fortitude DC 13
Onset 1 minute; *frequency* 1/minute for 4 minutes
Effect confusion (as the spell), –2 Str and Dex, –4 to Will saves versus enchantment and illusion spells and effects; *cure* 1 save

The pollen-induced hallucinations seem very real, appearing and disappearing at the GM's discretion. Whenever anyone under the influence has an adrenaline surge (becomes angry, enters combat, etc.), his hallucinations intensify, becoming more pronounced and horrific. Such a subject suffers an additional –2 hallucination modifier to all attack rolls. In addition, the subject imagines that several hallucinatory beasts attack him. Thusly afflicted PCs attack the hallucinatory dangers instead of actual dangers, unless the actual dangers attack them directly. Treat these additional images as though created by a *mirror image* spell. The hallucinatory effect of the pollen lasts 1d4 hours. Any temporary ability damage is regained when the narcotic effects wear off.

For additional details on blue lotus flowers, see the ***Creature Collection***, published by Sword and Sorcery Studios.

MELISSA (VAA'RANKARIZIAALIA) THE LILIN **CR 6**
XP 2,400
hp 73 (*Tome of Horrors Complete* 199 "Devil, Lilin")
LE Medium outsider (devil, evil, extraplanar, lawful)
Init +3; **Senses** darkvision 60 ft.; **Perception** +15

AC 20, touch 13, flat-footed 17 (+3 Dex, +7 natural)
hp 73 (7d10+35); regeneration 5 (good, silver)
Fort +7, **Ref** +10, **Will** +10
DR 10/silver; **Immune** fire, poison; **Resist** acid 10, cold 10; **SR** 17

Speed 30 ft., **fly** 50 ft. (average)
Melee *+1 longsword* +11/+6 (1d8+4/19–20) or 2 claws +10 (1d6+3)
Spell-Like Abilities (CL 9th)
At will—*charm monster* (DC 22), *greater teleport* (self plus 50 pounds of objects only), *protection from good, suggestion* (DC 21)
3/day—*animate dead*
1/day—*unholy aura* (DC 26), summon (level 3, 2d10 lemures, or 1d4 bearded devils or hellstokers, or 1 hellcat 50%)

Str 16, **Dex** 16, **Con** 20, **Int** 15, **Wis** 16, **Cha** 26
Base Atk +7; **CMB** +10; **CMD** 23
Feats Alertness, Iron Will, Lightning Reflexes, Persuasive
Gear In addition to her *robe of blending,* Melissa wears a *limited ring of mind shield,* which only masks evil alignments (thus lawful evil creatures appear detect as lawful neutral, and so on).

Tactics: As mentioned, Melissa disturbs the blue lotus flowers before the PCs enter the room. All PCs entering the level must save versus the effects of the pollen. Since veteran players should be immediately suspicious of the "trapped maiden" gag, GMs need to use a different tactic with Melissa. First, she detects as lawful neutral, which should throw players off the track, since most disguised demons and devils use lawful good disguises. Second, players are much less likely to kill something that is played well by a GM. Don't succumb to the "helpless, seductive woman lying on bed" routine. Though she is beautiful, she is clothed and not obviously vamping the party. Instead, try playing her as pissed off when the party enters. Think "Princess Leia," not "Mata Hari." She might voice her doubts about the party's power or competence: "Oh great. A group of adventurers finally gets past the poison corridor, but it must have been dumb luck. By the looks of you people, I will never be freed from this accursed tower." She may even aggressively grab one of the PCs, saying "I need you to free me from this place!"

Once discovered, Melissa uses her *charm monster* or *suggestion* abilities against the dumbest-looking, non-paladin fighter type in the party as she speaks, though she does not give him any commands yet. She tells the party that she is Crane's consort and that he extended her life with magic. She explains that she was a rival sorceress who lost a magical duel to Crane, and his prize was her servitude. Now that Crane is dead, she demands that the party free her from her captivity, her debt having been honorably satisfied. Of course, Melissa is just biding her time until the hallucinations begin. After one minute of real time, the fun starts. Melissa, familiar with the onset of the pollen-caused hallucinations — having seen Crane's reaction many times — knows which PCs have been affected.

Once the hallucinations begin, affected PCs begin seeing demon images. Melissa then *teleports* to another side of the room. She then uses her *charm monster* and *suggestion* abilities to telepathically instruct her victims to kill those who are not charmed. She then sits back and enjoys the ensuing slaughter.

Note: Melissa's poison immunity makes her immune to the pollen's effects. If attacked directly, Melissa simply *teleports* around the room at will. She uses her *unholy aura* if there are good-aligned PCs in the party. Melissa refrains from using her *summon* ability until the battle goes against her.

Treasure: Melissa wears a collar of finest gold and rubies, which functions as her soul gem and radiates evil, though it is masked by her *limited ring of mind shield*. The collar is worth 11,000 gp, but whoever possesses it will be visited by a barbazu in one month's time, at night, when he is asleep and helpless. Otherwise, the bedroom furnishings are worth over 3,000 gp if transported and sold.

Secret Locked Trapdoor in the Ceiling: Perception DC 20; 2 in. thick; Hardness 5; hp 20; Break DC 20; Disable Device DC 20.

Tower Level 5 (CR 8)

The walls of the tower's top level slope inward to meet at a pinnacle, creating a pyramid-shaped room. In the north wall, a **trapped secret door** opens into a 5-ft.-by-5-ft. room with a glowing crystal archway on the opposite, facing wall. This is a two-way portal that *teleports* anyone entering it to the dungeon of Crane. Those passing through this portal emerge through a similar portal in **Room A** of the dungeon (see below). A **vacuum trap** protects this secret door. If the trap is not disabled before the door is opened, the magic portal sucks all the air from the room, suffocating the PCs, and the trapdoor through which the PCs accessed this level closes itself airtight and locks with an *arcane lock* (cast at 18th level).

Trapped Secret Door: Perception DC 30; 2 in. thick; Hardness 5; hp 20; Break DC 20; Disable Device DC 20.

VACUUM TRAP **CR 8**
XP 4,800
Type mechanical; **Perception** DC 20;
Disable Device DC 20

Trigger touch; **Reset** none
Effect suffocation (see the "Environment, Suffocation" section of Chapter 13 of the *Pathfinder Roleplaying Game Core Rulebook*); suffocation; never miss, onset delay 2 rounds; multiple targets (all creatures in the room).

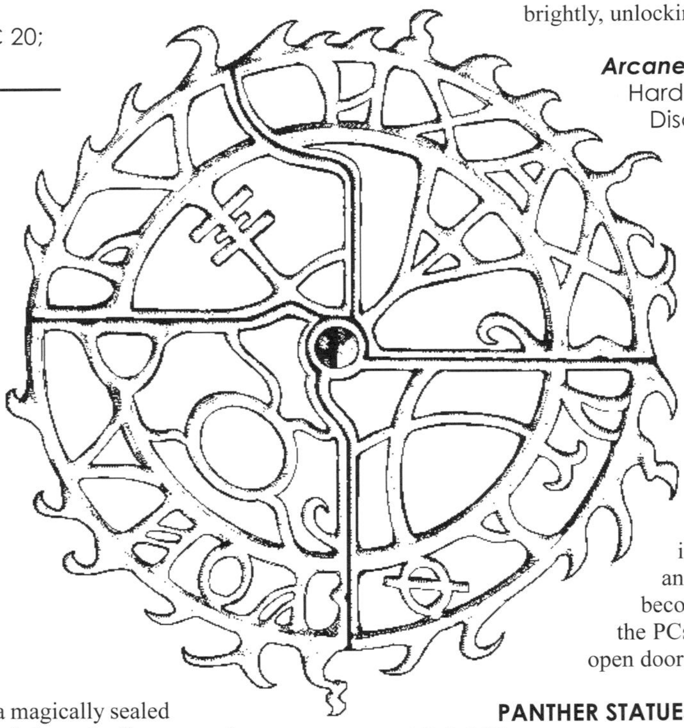

The Dungeon of Crane the Sorcerer

To protect his *sphere*, Crane hid it in a magically sealed chamber (**Room N**), to which he bound three devils as guards. Opening the seal to this chamber requires a fully assembled medallion, the four pieces of which Crane hid among the trapped and construct-populated corridors of his dungeon. No other way of opening the sealed chamber will succeed.

There are no wandering monsters in Crane's dungeon.

Entering the Central Chamber

Crane dispersed the medallion's four parts throughout the dungeon, thus securing the central chamber's integrity against intrusion — however unlikely the possibility. Fitting together tightly, the four pieces form a 10-inch-high flaming-sun-shaped medallion. Each magically sealed door to the central chamber bears an indentation into which a PC inserts the assembled medallion. Magic runes, read before the medallion's placement (using a *read magic* spell), activate the medallion, causing it to glow with a blue light. This glow lasts only 90 seconds, during which time the medallion must be placed in the door.

If a PC fails to set a *glowing* medallion in the door (i.e., the 90 seconds have elapsed or the runes were not read), that PC takes 6d6 points of damage. No save is allowed, and spell resistance does not apply. Three doors leading to the central chamber (**Room N**) are false doors; placing the medallion into these doors causes damage as described above, even if the PCs observed the proper procedure. Only the door in **Room L** opens into the central chamber. If the medallion is used correctly on that door, the glowing blue light engulfs the entire door, and it opens. The runes may be read a maximum of twice per day, after which they fade from existence for 12 hours.

The central chamber's walls and associated doors, like those of the tower's exterior, are immune to spells and to weapons and tools of less than +5 enhancement and may not be damaged. Literally, the only way to enter the central chamber is by placing the properly assembled medallion into the one, true door.

A. The Door Below

A magically sealed stone door, runes scratched across its surface, looms before the PCs. *Arcane locked* at an 18th level of ability, the door can only be forced opened with a *knock* or *dispel magic* spell. Alternatively, tracing the runes on the door with a finger causes the runes to glow brightly, unlocking the door.

***Arcane-locked* Stone Door:** 2 in. thick; Hardness 10; hp 80; Break DC 38, Disable Device DC40.

B. Guardians at the Gate (CR 6)

Beyond the locked door is a corridor leading into a trapezoidal room, its walls and floor constructed of red-veined white marble. Dominating the room are two awe-inspiring statues of large cats, sculpted from black stone. The southern and southwestern walls feature doors. If either unlocked door is opened, the **2 statues** come to life and attack until slain, at which time they become statues again. The statues pursue the PCs if they run, though the statues cannot open doors.

PANTHER STATUES (2) **CR 4**
XP 1,200
Giant panther (*Pathfinder Roleplaying Game Bestiary*, "Lion,")
N Huge animal
Init +6; **Senses** low-light vision, scent; **Perception** +9

AC 16, touch 10, flat-footed 14 (+2 Dex, +6 natural, –2 size)
hp 42 (5d8+20)
Fort +8; **Ref** +6; **Will** +2

Speed 40 ft.
Melee bite +8 (2d6+7 plus grab), 2 claws +8 (1d6+7)
Space 15 ft.; **Reach** 10 ft.

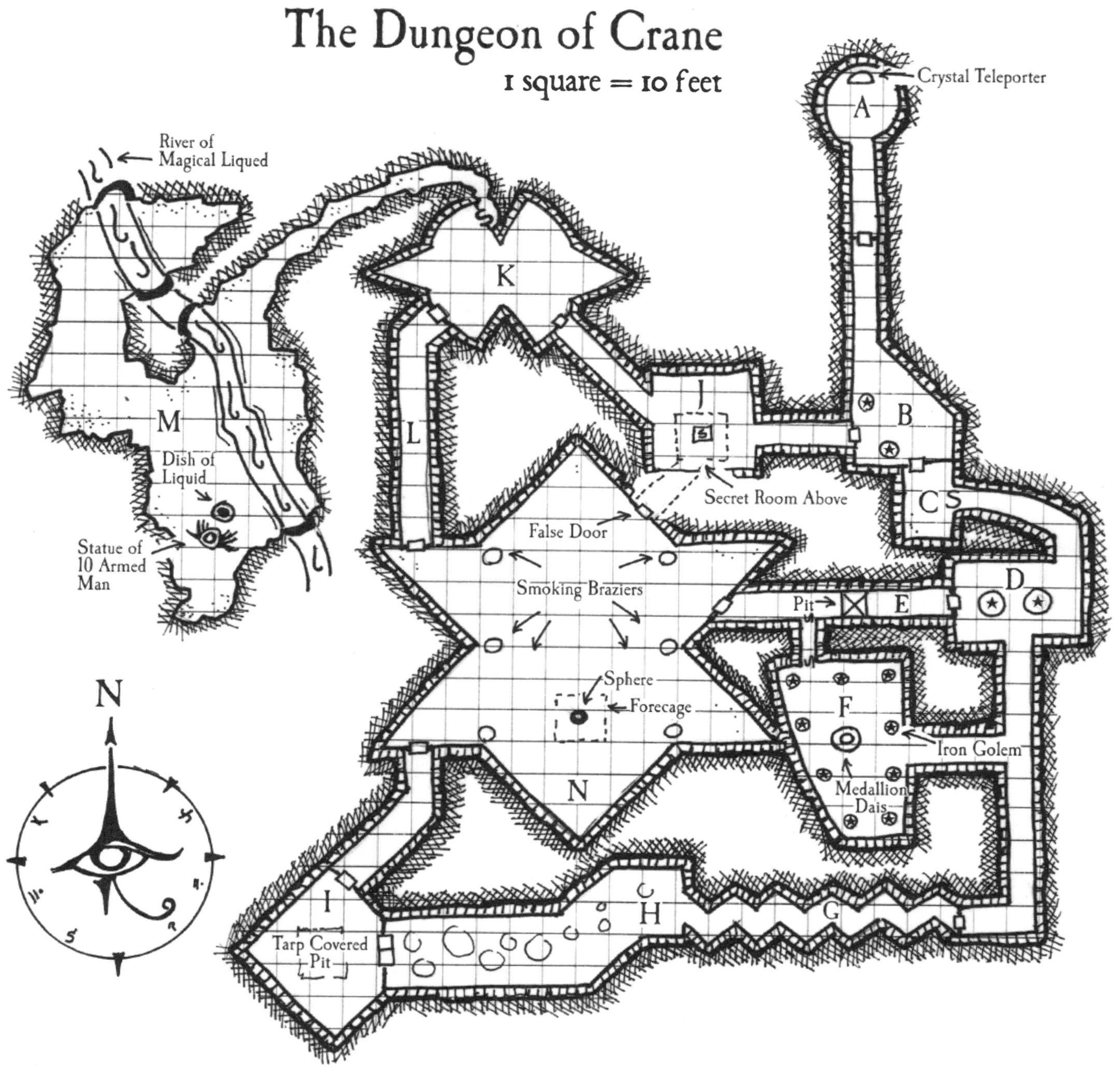

Special Attacks pounce, rakes (2 claws +8,1d6+7)

Str 25, **Dex** 15, **Con** 19, **Int** 2, **Wis** 12, **Cha** 6
Base Atk +3; **CMB** +12 (+16 grapple); **CMD** 24 (28 vs. trip)
Feats Improved Initiative, Run, Skill Focus (Perception)
Skills Acrobatics +10 (+14 jump, +14 to jump with a running start), Perception +9, Stealth +3 (+7 in undergrowth); **Racial Modifiers** +4 Acrobatics, +4 Stealth, +4 Stealth in undergrowth

C. The Sword Room (CR 9)

A brightly-glowing sword floats in midair in this room, which is carved entirely from black stone. This sword is an **animated object**. It immediately attacks anyone entering the room. A successful *dispel magic* allows the sword to be taken as treasure. "Killing" the sword destroys it. Magical cold makes it brittle (AC drops to 17; loses hardness ability). This *+2 wounding longsword* cannot leave the room while animated. A 10 ft. x 10 ft. pressure plate at the room's center activates a **poison gas trap**. A **secret door** on the east wall leads to **Room D**.

ANIMATED WOUNDING LONGSWORD **CR 5**
XP 1,600
Pathfinder Roleplaying Game Bestiary, "Animated Object"
N Small construct
Init +6; **Senses** blindsight; **Perception** +0

AC 23, touch 17, flat-footed 17 (+6 Dex, +6 natural, +1 size)
hp 26 (3d10+10)
Fort +1; **Ref** +7; **Will** +1
Defensive Abilities hardness 10; **Immune** construct traits; **Resist** fire 30

Speed fly 60 ft. (good)

Melee +2 *wounding longsword* +13 (1d8+2 plus 1 bleed)
Special Attacks wounding

Str 11, **Dex** 22, **Con** —, **Int** —, **Wis** 11, **Cha** 1
Base Atk +3; **CMB** +2; **CMD** 18 (can't be tripped)
Feats Weapon Finesse, Weapon Focus (longsword)

Wounding (Ex) A *wounding weapon* deals 1 point of bleed damage when it hits a creature. Multiple hits from a wounding weapon increase the bleed damage. Bleeding creatures take the bleed damage at the start of their turns. Bleeding can be stopped by a DC 15 Heal check or through the application of any spell that cures hit point damage. A critical hit does not multiply the bleed damage. Creatures immune to critical hits are immune to the bleed damage dealt by this weapon.

POISON GAS TRAP **CR 8**
XP 4,800
Type mechanical; **Perception** DC 20; **Disable Device** DC 20

Trigger location; **Reset** none
Effect cloud of poison gas (burnt othur fumes); never miss; onset delay (3 rounds); multiple targets (all creatures in the room).

Secret Door: Perception DC 20; 2 in. thick; Hardness 5; hp 20; Break DC 20; Disable Device DC 20.

D. The Statue Room

Two minotaur statues, 10 feet apart, occupy this room. A five-foot-diameter circle of red stones surrounds each statue. The south door features glowing runes. The west wall also contains a door. Both doors have intricate locks. The minotaurs are just what they appear to be: statues. The glowing runes read "Hall of Pools," if *read magic* is used on them. Both doors are locked.

Locked Wooden Doors: 2 in. thick; Hardness 5; hp 25; Break DC 28, Disable Device DC 25.

E. Gone Forever (CR 8)

In the center of the corridor, a **trap** plunges PCs into a pit linked to the astral plane. Magic has no effect after the 100-foot mark (allowing about 2 rounds for action). Anyone falling beyond that point risks being lost forever on the Astral Plane. Rescuing people thusly trapped requires plane travel abilities. A secret door leads past the pit to **Room F**. The door at the corridor's west end is one of the central chamber's false doors. See "**Entering the Central Chamber**," above.

PIT TRAP (BOTTOMLESS) **CR 8**
XP 4,800
Type mechanical; **Perception** DC 20; **Disable Device** DC 20

Trigger location; **Reset** none
Effect chute to a portal to the Astral Plane (DC 20 Ref avoids)

Secret Door: Perception DC 20; 2 in. thick; Hardness 5; hp 20; Break DC 20; Open Lock DC 20.

F. The Big, Mean Golem (CR 8)

Large iron statues, fully 10 feet tall and shaped as warriors, line this room on all sides, surrounding a raised dais in the center. Upon the dais rests a rune-encrusted golden triangle, intricately carved, its center accented with a jewel. The golden triangle is the **first piece of Crane's medallion**.

A single **flesh golem,** standing near the east entrance, guards against the piece's theft. The amulet piece is trapped with a ***lightning bolt* trap**. Touching either the amulet or the dais triggers the trap.

FLESH GOLEM **CR 7**
XP 3,200
hp 79 (*Pathfinder Roleplaying Game Bestiary* "Golem, Flesh")

Tactics: If damaged, the golem touches the dais and triggers the *lightning bolt* trap to heal itself. Should the party emerge through **Area E's** secret door, it can outrun the golem, who does not pursue the party through the secret passage to the north. Otherwise, if the amulet is disturbed, the golem positions itself to block the east exit and defends the room. When any person enters the room, the golem animates.

***LIGHTNING BOLT* TRAP** **CR 4**
XP 1,200
Type mechanical; **Perception** DC 28; **Disable Device** DC 28

Trigger touch; **Reset** none
Effect spell effect (*lightning bolt*, 5d6 electricity damage, DC 14 Ref half, CL 5th); multiple targets (all targets in a 120-ft. line)

Secret Door: Perception DC 20; 2 in. thick; Hardness 5; hp 20; Break DC 20; Open Lock DC 20.

G. Corridor of the Red Madness (CR 9)

When the PCs penetrate the paltry defenses of the simple wooden door to this corridor, they enter a zigzagging hallway with walls and ceiling composed of a red, spongy material. Small holes in the red matter emit curling wisps of reddish gas.

Locked Wooden Door: 2 in. thick; Hardness 5; hp 25; Break DC 28; Open lock DC 25.

The red-colored, spongy material that constitutes this corridor's walls and ceiling puffs out a small cloud of reddish gas with each touch or vibrational disturbance. The walls are so sensitive that even loud speech causes the material to pump out vision-obscuring quantities of this dreadful gas. Inhaling the gas, however, has a single, terrible consequence: insanity!

RED MADNESS TRAP **CR 9**
XP 6,400
Type mechanical; **Perception** DC 25; **Disable Device** DC 20

Trigger location; **Reset** repair
Effect poison gas (insanity mist); never miss; onset delay (1 round); multiple targets (all targets in a 10-ft.-by-40-ft. corridor); Touching the spongy material causes it to release gas in 10-foot-radius area. Anyone within the gas' area of effect must succeed on a DC 20 Fortitude save or suffer the effects of the gas: a horrible, mindless madness. Those struck insane grasp their head, fall to their knees and begin to scream. A victim's skin takes on a reddish sheen. Anyone stricken with madness must succeed on a second DC 20 Fortitude save or the insanity becomes permanent — curable only by a *heal, limited wish, wish* or *miracle* spell. Success, however, only means that the insanity lasts for 1d20 hours, though it too may be healed as described above.

H. Hall of Pools

This long hall is dotted every few yards with pools of bubbling, blue-green liquid. A huge set of double doors at the hall's far end seemingly bleeds this liquid; it drains into the various pools through a series of channels carved in the floor. Strange writing and a bas-relief carving of a scepter, covered in gold leaf with small ruby chips simulating dripping blood, ornament the door. A hollow sconce, next to the bas-relief scepter, appears large enough to receive an object of a size similar to the bas-relief scepter.

While the liquid's surface ripples only an inch or so below the level of the floor, the pools themselves measure over eight feet deep. This strange liquid actually constitutes some odd form of Earthpower, welling up from the depths. Any mortal touching so much as drop of this potent fluid becomes dizzy, finding it almost impossible to walk. Failing a DC 20 Fortitude save renders the subject unconscious for 1d6 days.

In the final pool is secreted a golden scepter, 8 feet below the surface. If the scepter is fished out, placing it into the sconce beside the bas-relief carving opens the door. The scepter then vanishes, returning to its resting place at the bottom of the pool.

The double doors at the hall's far end enjoy the same defensive immunities as the exterior walls of Crane's tower. Short of a *wish* or *miracle* spell, only by inserting the scepter into the sconce can the doors be opened, as previously described. The strange writing (in Celestial) decorating the door details this curse, explaining:

> *"None shall pass till the curse of the earth god is lifted."*

I. The Pit

Centered in the room, a 15-foot-square, covered pit rises about one foot above floor level. The cover — magically preserved leather — is pulled taut and is lashed down securely. At the bottom of the shallow, five-foot-deep pit, the PCs find a locked secret hatch; opening it reveals a 2-foot-long mahogany box with extremely detailed carvings along its entire surface. Within the small casket is hidden the **second piece of Crane's medallion**. The north wall's unlocked door leads to one of the central chamber's false doors; it does not open, even with the fully assembled amulet. See "**Entering the Central Chamber**," above.

Secret Hatch: Perception DC 20; 1 in. thick; Hardness 8; hp 20; Break DC 20; Disable Device DC 20.

J. "Seven Years Bad Luck"

When the PCs open the door adjoining **Room B** they hear the tinkling and jangling of glass, as though the room beyond were full of wind chimes. Multiple shiny objects reflect light back to the PCs, like a room full of twinkling stars. Dangling from the ceiling by long strands of thread, are thousands of shards of glass — as though a huge mirror had been broken and its remnants hung in this manner. From the ceiling 15 feet above, the shards dangle to every level of the room, to just about two feet above the floor.

Moving through the room requires a DC 15 Reflex save to avoid the shards. Small characters get a +2 on this save, since they can stoop beneath even the lowest-hanging shards. Characters who move at half speed get a +5 bonus on the save, and characters who move at double speed get a –5 penalty on the save. Characters who move at 1/4 speed don't need to make a save at all. A character moving at a run gets no save; he automatically fails. If a shard is broken or crudely mishandled, it explodes, giving off a thin wisp of smoke. This epicenter explosion initiates a chain reaction among the other shards, causing them all to shatter. The acrid smoke causes blindness and limits a person's ability to speak more than a whisper unless a DC 25 Fortitude save is made. Immunities and resistances to poison apply. This effect lasts 2d4 days.

There is an ***invisible* secret door** in the ceiling, shielded from view by the hanging shards (it's easier to locate if the hanging shards have been destroyed or if their support threads are carefully parted and secured). The door leads to a small chamber wherein a silver pedestal supports a red crystal staff. PCs can use the staff to form a crystal bridge in **Room M**. An image of a bridge spanning a river is inscribed on the staff.

***Invisible* Secret Door:** Perception DC 38 (DC 20 after glass is moved or destroyed); 1 in. thick; Hardness 5; hp 20; Break DC 20; Disable Device DC 20.

A corridor behind the pedestal heads south. This corridor leads to one of the central chamber's false doors; it does not open, even with the fully assembled amulet. See "**Entering the Central Chamber**," above.

K. The Final Guardians (CR 11)

Daggers, swords and shards of metal lie piled in the room's center. The PCs can feel a slight breeze. As the PCs enter, the breeze stiffens and a whirlwind suddenly forms, lifting the metal shards and weapons from the pile and sets them spinning through the air. Advancing through the room are three humanoid creatures draped in cruel, barbed chains.

Crane called forth these, his final guardians — **3 advanced kytons** — to protect the entrance to the strange Earthpower cavern (**Room M**) he discovered late in his life. These creatures will not leave the room. The locked southwestern door, made of iron, is trapped with a **poison needle**. A secret door leads to the north.

ADVANCED KYTONS (3) **CR 7**
XP 3,200
Pathfinder Roleplaying Game Bestiary, "Kyton"
LE Medium outsider (evil, extraplanar, lawful)
Init +9; **Senses** darkvision 60 ft.; **Perception** +16

AC 25, touch 15, flat-footed 20 (+4 armor, +5 Dex, +6 natural)
hp 76 (8d10+32); regeneration 2 (good weapons and spells, silver weapons)
Fort +10; **Ref** +11; **Will** +5
DR 5/good or silver; **Immune** cold; **SR** 17

Speed 30 ft.
Melee 4 chains +13 (2d4+4)
Special Attacks dancing chains, unnerving gaze

Str 19, **Dex** 21, **Con** 18, **Int** 15, **Wis** 16, **Cha** 16
Base Atk +8; **CMB** +12; **CMD** 27
Feats Alertness, Blind-Fight, Improved Initiative, Weapon Focus (chains)
Skills Acrobatics +16, Bluff +14, Climb +15, Craft (blacksmith) +13, Escape Artist +16, Intimidate +14, Perception +16, Sense Motive +5, Stealth +16
Languages Common, Infernal
SQ chain armor

Chain Armor (Ex) The chains that adorn a kyton grant it a +4 armor bonus, but are not treated as armor for the purpose of arcane spell failure, armor check penalties, maximum Dexterity, weight, or proficiency.
Dancing Chains (Su) A kyton can control up to four chains within 20 feet as a standard action, making the chains dance or move as it wishes. In addition, a kyton can increase these chains' length by up to 15 feet and cause them to sprout razor-edged barbs. These chains attack as effectively as the kyton itself. If a chain is in another creature's possession, the creature can attempt a DC 17 Will save to break the kyton's power over that chain. If the save is successful, the kyton cannot attempt to control that particular chain again for 24 hours or until the chain leaves the creature's possession. A kyton can climb chains

it controls at its normal speed without making Climb checks. The save DC is Charisma-based.
Unnerving Gaze (Su) Range 30 ft., Will DC 17 negates. A kyton can make its face resemble one of an opponent's departed loved ones or bitter enemies. Those who fail their saves become shaken for 1d3 rounds. This is a mind-affecting fear effect. The save DC is Charisma-based.

Locked Iron door: 2 in. thick; Hardness 10; hp 60; Break DC 48; Disable Device DC 25.

POISON NEEDLE TRAP **CR 2**
XP 600
Type mechanical; **Perception** DC 22; **Disable Device** DC 20

Trigger touch; **Reset** manual
Effect Atk +8 ranged (1 plus greenblood oil)
Secret Door: Perception DC 20; 2 in. thick; Hardness 5; hp 20; Break DC 20; Disable Device DC 20.

L. The Central Chamber's Entrance Hallway (CR 11)

Mirrors line the walls, floor to ceiling, along the corridor, but the view they offer is strangely distorted. A large rune-etched door marks the hallway's far end. At the corridor's 30-foot mark, a *mirror of life trapping* is affixed to the ceiling. A DC 19 Will save avoids the effects of the *mirror*. Shattering the mirror from the outside releases everything trapped inside. Crane imprisoned a **black pudding**, **2 wraiths** and a rival wizard named **Meldeth** in it before placing it here. No one knows how Crane ensnared the wraiths, as undead cannot normally be trapped by such an item.

A final inhabitant of the mirror, a poisoned and severely wounded wizard named **Toth A'karon**, dies from the poison in his veins as soon as he is released from stasis (no statistics provided). All creatures immediately attack the characters. Toth A'karon has the **third piece of Crane's medallion**. Barely alive, he uses his dying breath to relinquish the medallion piece to the PCs.

The command word for the mirror is *Seriwog*.

WRAITHS (2) **CR 5**
XP 1,600
hp 47 (*Pathfinder Roleplaying Game Bestiary* "Wraith")

BLACK PUDDING **CR 7**
XP 3,200
hp 105 (*Pathfinder Roleplaying Game Bestiary* "Black Pudding")

MELDETH, THE EVIL AND INSANE WIZARD OF THE VIOLET BROTHERHOOD **CR 8**
XP 4,800
Male human wizard 9
CE Medium humanoid (human)
Init +2; **Perception** +8

AC 12, touch 12, flat-footed 10 (+2 Dex)
hp 52 (9d6+18)
Fort +6; **Ref** +6; **Will** +5
DR 10/adamantine; **Resist** fire 10; **Immune** mind-effecting effects

---

Speed 30 ft.
Special Attacks metamagic mastery (1/day)
Universalist Spell-Like Abilities (CL 9th; ranged touch +6):
7/day—*hand of the apprentice*
Spells Prepared (CL 9th; ranged touch +6):
5th—*teleport*
4th—*lesser globe of invulnerability, phantasmal killer* (DC 18), *stoneskin* (already cast)
3rd—*displacement, fly, lightning bolt* (DC 17), *slow* (DC 17)
2nd—*acid arrow, invisibility, protection from arrows, see invisibility, web* (DC 16)
1st—*color spray* (DC 15), *grease, magic missile* (x2), *shield*
0 (at will)—*dancing lights, daze* (DC 14), *flare* (DC 14), *read magic*

Str 13, **Dex** 15, **Con** 15, **Int** 18, **Wis** 3, **Cha** 6
Base Atk +4; **CMB** +5; **CMD** 17
Feats Combat Casting, Iron Will, Maximize Spell, Scribe Scroll, Silent Spell, Skill Focus (Perception), Spell Mastery (*fly, lesser globe of invulnerability, lightning bolt, teleport*), Still Spell
Skills Craft (alchemy) +16, Fly +14, Knowledge (arcana) +16, Knowledge (dungeoneering) +16, Knowledge (planes) +16, Perception +8, Spellcraft +16, Stealth +11
Languages Abyssal, Aklo, Common, Infernal, Undercommon
SQ arcane bond (*ring of fire resistance [minor]*), insane
Combat Gear *wand of fireball* (CL 6th, 12 charges); **Other Gear** *cloak of resistance +1, ring of fire resistance (minor)*, jade unholy symbol of the frog-god Tsathogga (causes an *unhallow* effect in a 60-foot radius cast at 8th level, 12 charges), map to the Stoneheart Mountain dungeon with a cryptic reference to the Temple of the Frog (detailed in the dungeon module ***The Lost Lands: Stoneheart Valley*** from **Frog God Games**)
Spellbook: 0—all; 1st—*color spray, grease, magic missile, shield*; 2nd—*acid arrow, invisibility, mirror image, protection from arrows, see invisibility, spider climb, web*; 3rd—*displacement, fly, lightning bolt, slow, vampiric touch*; 4th—*confusion, lesser globe of invulnerability, phantasmal killer, stoneskin*; 5th—*summon monster V, teleport*.

Insane (Ex) Immune to all mind-affecting spells and effects due to insanity; attacks everyone in sight, including monsters, until slain.

Once the PCs assemble all the parts of Crane's medallion, they can open the door to **Room N**. See "**Entering the Central Chamber**," above.

M. The Earthpower Cavern

The secret door leads to a small cavern through which flows a stream of weird, shimmering blue-green liquid. Across the river towers a huge statue of a 20-armed man, a sword in each hand; inscribed in his chest is a rune symbolizing a long-forgotten lawful earth god of battle called Mocham. In front of the statue, is a 20-foot-diameter pool of red liquid.

Crane discovered this natural cavern while carving out his dungeon. This cavern, linked to a now-unknown earth god, was once sacred to clerics of that sect. The river that winds through this cavern is two feet deep and can be crossed easily (though at great cost). It radiates a strange antimagic effect; no magic functions within 20 feet of either bank. Spellcasters innately notice this antimagic aura. The red crystal staff, found in the secret chamber above **Room J**, forms a crystal bridge fording the river if waved over the liquid. The staff is the only magic item immune to the liquid's antimagic power. The liquid loses this antimagic ability when removed from the stream. Any characters crossing the river by any means other than the red crystal bridge are stricken as though a *mage's disjunction* had been cast on them and their possessions.

The giant statue — natural rock carved into the form of a 20-armed man — bears the weight of the ages upon his brow. Its expression inspires knee-bending humility, sadness and awe. At the monolith's feet is a two-foot-deep pool of opaque, dark-red-brown liquid that is very poisonous (*type* poison, contact; *save* Fortitude DC 22; *onset* 1 round; *frequency* 1/round for 6 rounds; *effect* 1d4 Con). Any characters moving to within 10 feet of any part of the monolith notices that the statue's eyes quickly pulse with blue light. If the warning is not heeded, the statue fires two *rays of lightning* at the transgressor's feet. Should the character persist, the statue fires directly at them (+11 ranged touch, 2d8 electrical damage) once every 3 rounds. Any good cleric may approach the statue without recrimination and is immune to the effects of the poison. The **fourth piece of Crane's medallion** lies hidden in the pool of the poisonous red liquid. Fishing the piece of the medallion out with a tool requires a successful attack against AC 20, with one attempt per round. While fishing, PCs count as flat-footed for rolls to be hit by the statue's *rays of lightning*.

N. The Central Chamber (CR 11)

When the medallion is properly inserted, the door ignites with searing blue light; its shape alters, forming a misty archway. The archway reeks with the stench of sulfur and brimstone. The room beyond is carved from living rock. Smoke and haze in the room obscures vision. At the far end is a strange glowing cube. Three men in black robes are present in the room. One is actually a **whip devil**. The others are **2 bearded devils**. When they see the PCs, one approaches cautiously. As he gets closer, he announces, "You are not my master!" He then transforms into his whip devil guise and attacks. The bearded devils join in the combat as well.

Crane bound these three devils to this room to guard his *sphere of annihilation*. Ordered to destroy all who enter the room but Crane, they neither negotiate nor bargain. If a priest casts *banishment, dismissal* or *gate* or if a wizard casts *banishment, freedom* or *gate*, the whip devils let the spell work (miss SR and saves on purpose), because it frees them from Crane's spell of *binding*.

Due to the magically burning brimstone, vision in this rather featureless room is limited to 50 feet; anything beyond that has concealment. Furthermore, living creatures can become quickly fatigued from breathing in the toxic, sulfurous fumes. Any character engaging in strenuous activity (such as combat) must succeed on a DC 15 Fortitude save at the start of their turn each round or be sickened nauseated for that round. Resistances and immunities to poison apply. Barefoot PCs take 1 point of fire damage per round from the hot floor. The distant glowing cube, a *(windowless-cell) forcecage*, contains Crane's *sphere of annihilation*. See **treasure**, below.

IGNUS the WHIP DEVIL **CR 10**
XP 9,600
hp 96 (see **Rescued from Oblivion** in "The Pit of Despair")

ALNUS and FEMUS,
the BEARDED DEVILS (2) **CR 5**
XP 1,600
hp 51 (*Pathfinder Roleplaying Game Bestiary* "Devil, Bearded")

Tactics: Very intelligent, the devils coordinate their attack. The whip devil attempts to *summon* more bearded devils to handle the brunt of combat, while the others attack lightly armored individuals first. They concentrate their efforts on one victim until that person is dead. If attacked by multiple opponents, the whip devil casts *fireball* on his own position. The bearded devils target wizards first, followed by clerics and thieves, and only thereafter fighters. The demons make no attempt to use the *sphere of annihilation*.

Treasure: Hovering in the center of the room, a *permanent windowless cell forcecage* contains Crane's *sphere of annihilation* — a two-foot-wide ball of absolute nothingness. To get the *sphere*, the *forcecage* must be brought down in one of two ways. First, destroy the *forcecage* with magic as per the spell description. Second, controlling the *sphere,* a PC can use it to destroy the *forcecage* from within (for which the dragon talisman, secreted in **Tower Level 3's** hidden safe, might be useful). Of course, this may happen accidentally if a character fails her attempt to control the *sphere* and it slides toward her, destroying the *forcecage* on contact. But then an uncontrolled *sphere of annihilation* would be loose…

The room contains no other treasure.

Ra's Evil Grin

By Clark Peterson and Bill Webb

Introduction

Designed for a party of at least 11th level, this module challenges adventurers seeking a powerful magic — the *Globe of Arden.* Any appropriate powerful item can be substituted as the final objective, as suits the GM's campaign. This dungeon culminates in a battle with named Dendorandra, a lesser marilith known as a dark daughter.

As a lead-in to this adventure, the GM may use a map from another treasure hoard showing the location of the *Globe* (detailed more fully in "The Legend of the Globe of Artden," below) or a priestly tome describing Arden, the long-dead avatar of Ra, and the wondrous powers of an unknown artifact called the *Globe of Arden.* Such a tome might mention that the *Globe* emits rays as intense as those of the sun, destroying all they touch. In any event, GMs should require consultation with sages or use of a *legend lore* spell to determine the location and history of the *Globe* and dungeon. A sage could also provide a map to the dungeon's location, referenced in the "The Legend of the *Globe of Arden*," below. Originally set on a small, remote island far across the sea, the dungeon can be relocated to meet the GM's requirements.

GMs will notice that the dungeon provides numerous puzzles, a few traps and only two monsters. Those monsters, though few in number, should ably challenge and threaten even the most combat-hardened party — particularly after the party encounters all the vicious creatures that inhabit the Island of the Globe.

The Legend of the *Globe of Arden*

Using *legend lore* or consulting sages uncovers the following information about the god, Arden, and the *Globe of Arden.* GMs should read this information to their players.

In days long past, the peoples of the eastern lands worshiped the sun god, Arden. Legend says that the gods of darkness destroyed Arden during divine combat. Arden's followers gathered their slain god's remains, storing them in his temples.

Legends tell that one such relic, the *Globe of Arden*, was originally the left eye of the god himself — ripped from its socket by Tsathogga, a vile frog-demon, during Arden's final, hopeless battle. However, the eye retained the powers of the sun, and the demonic servants of Tsathogga, attempting to steal it, were disintegrated by the power it contained. Priests of Arden eventually recovered the eye, which had solidified into a strange sphere seemingly made of cloudy, white glass, and renamed the divine artifact the *Globe of Arden.*

With Arden's destruction, his following waned. Yet the preserved relics — elements of his divine being — prevented Arden's foes from overcoming his temples. What the relics could not prevent, however, was the treachery of Asari. Then a high priest of Arden at the temple where the *Globe* was stored, Asari grew jealous and bitter over his loss of personal power, which followed the destruction of his deity. His spell powers failing and followers dwindling, he entertained the overtures of the frog-god Tsathogga, who promised to restore Asari's earthly power. As his final act of betrayal, Asari stole the *Globe of Arden* from the temple's inner sanctuary and fled before the priests detected his treachery. He delivered the *Globe* to the demon-priests who took the relic and hid it in a foreign and unpopulated land — a remote island, the legends say — in a complex designed to hide the *Globe* from Arden and his followers. Rumors suggest that the demon-priests of Tsathogga, a god of water and darkness, fashioned the complex' entrance to mock Arden, a god of air and light. Legends also caution that Asari, the fallen priest, received great rewards from the gods of evil: renewed earthly power and the gift of unlife. The followers of Arden, now greatly reduced in number and power, were unable to recover the *Globe*, and it fell out of all human reckoning.

After countless years' passage, the sands of the eastern deserts have long since consumed the "civilization" that once thrived there, while men and elves inhabit what were once the "unpopulated foreign lands" of Arden's time.

There exists an ancient map that allegedly depicts a possible location of the island on which the *Globe* was hidden. The coastline of those once "foreign lands" seems to correspond to an area of the currently civilized world, though no other maps refer to this island, nor have sailors spoken of it. The map also features these cryptic words, written in a long-forgotten language:

On an island within an island,
Beyond a door that is not a door —
Shielded by the grin of the hated sun —
Lies the Globe of Arden*, the eye of a dead god,*
Stolen long ago by the traitor Asari.

Perhaps this map holds a key to locating the ancient and powerful *Globe of Arden…*

In addition, characters succeeding on a DC 30 Knowledge (religion) check or consulting sages who specialize in ancient religions can obtain the information about Arden. Arden was once worshiped on this plane of existence as a lesser avatar of the sun god, Ra. He was commonly depicted as a hawk-headed, muscular man, wearing a short skirt of precious metals and jewels. He projects searing beams of sunlight from his eyes. His staff is tipped at one end with a bronze sphere, representing the sun and emblazoned with an ankh, and at the other end with a bronze hawk head. Arden also wields a bronze short sword. Evil deities, Tsathogga the frog-demon among their number, long ago destroyed Arden, but his worshipers gathered and treasured his remains as relics. Ages have passed, however, since Arden was worshiped on this plane.

Arriving at the Island of the Globe

The party may have acquired the ancient map from a previously looted treasure hoard or from the sage who related the *Globe's* legend. Obtaining the map might also constitute an adventure in its own right. Such an adventure is encouraged, though not detailed here. The map depicts an island located south of normal trade routes, off the coast of a sparsely populated area north of a southern jungle. In the **Lost Lands** campaign Setting of **Frog God Games**, this island lies at the edge of Great Oceanus, the main world-ocean of the planet, just north of where it becomes the Razor Sea in the vicinity of the Razor Coast. For more information on this area, see ***Razor Coast*** by **Frog God Games**.

Thick jungle and swampland cover the island. A large mountain, rising from the center of the island, is reflected in the waters of a lake to its south. Within that lake, a stone outcrop rises above the water's surface. On that inner island lies the entrance to the dungeon.

This module presumes that the PCs have gained the map and traveled

overland to a coastal city near the island. From the denizens of this city, skirting the northern border of a vast jungle, PCs can hire a boat to convey them to the island. GMs should spend multiple game sessions detailing this epic journey, foreshadowing trials yet to come.

If you wish to avoid the above trek, you may instead simply begin the module with the PCs having arrived at the island of the Globe, passed through the perils of the island and found the inner lake and the rock outcrop on which the dungeon entrance is located. If so, proceed to "**The Dungeon Entrance**," below.

The Dungeon Entrance (CR 10)

Once the PCs reach the lake's central island on the Island of the *Globe*, they immediately notice an unnatural depression ringed with 10-foot-tall, rune-covered stone pillars — the only evidence of a humanoid presence on the island. The pillars, heavily worn, have endured the passage of what must have been centuries. The runes are no longer legible. The pillars surround a deep hole, 30 feet in diameter and nearly 20 feet deep. Approaching the edge of the depression, more evidence of humanoid craftsmanship can be seen: the depression, lined with reflective tiles, has thousands of crystal beads set into its surface. PCs descending into the depression notice an inscription encircling a tiny ruby set in black stone. The inscription, shimmering in the sunlight, reads:

> *"Beware the noontime sun if you know not the puzzle behind RAS EVIL GRIN, which is tossed in the center of stone."*

Each PC perceives the inscription as written in their native language. Strangely, the inscription has not eroded over time.

The GM should write out the inscription and demonstrate how it fully encircles the small ruby; carefully capitalize all the letters of "RAS EVIL GRIN" to assist the PCs in solving the puzzle. If the party does not solve the puzzle by noon, determine whether anyone remains in the depression when the sun reaches its zenith.

At noon, the sun's intense rays strike the central ruby and trigger the **trap**: the ruby-refracted light bounces around the reflective, bead-encrusted depression, heating it to an incredible temperature. Any person in the depression when the trap is triggered takes 3d6 fire damage each round he remains in the depression. The intensified sunbeams lance around the depression for 5 rounds, after which the sun's angle changes and the heat rays subside. The only way to defeat this effect and enter the dungeon is to solve the puzzle of RAS EVIL GRIN. Tsathogga's priests created this trap to mock Arden, the sun god — harnessing the power of the sun to destroy those followers of Arden attempting to liberate the *Globe* hidden within the dungeon.

"RA'S EVIL GRIN" TRAP **CR 10**
XP 9,600
Type magical; **Perception** (not applicable); **Disable Device** (impossible, as only solving the puzzle deactivates the trap)

Trigger location; **Reset** none
Effect focused sunbeams (8d6 fire damage, DC 20 Ref half); 5 rounds; multiple targets (all targets within the depression)

Solving the Puzzle: "RAS EVIL GRIN" is an anagram for "A SILVER RING." Once the PCs figure this out, the rest of the solution should follow easily. The PCs need only "toss" a silver ring in the "center of stone" — that is, place a silver ring inside the letter "O" of the word "stone," since that letter is the center of the word "stone."

Helping the Players Along: If the players can't figure this puzzle out, encourage them to read the inscription closely. A successful DC 15 Perception check allows someone to notice a fine, silvery dust in the letter 'O' of the word 'stone.' Failing to grasp this obvious a clue, the PCs don't deserve the *Globe of Arden* (or whatever magical goodie awaited their discovery).

The Gems and Beads: An unknown type of magical protection prevents the amplified heat from damaging the gems and beads. Nor can the gems be pried out or removed in any way. PCs attempting such a theft must succeed on a DC 15 save for any prying tool used for this action. The item gets a +1 on its save if it is a masterwork item or a magic weapon; it gets a +2 for each "plus." If the save fails, the item breaks; if it succeeds, the item remains whole.

Opening the *Phase Door*: Having solved the puzzle, the players must still wait until noon. If the PCs have properly placed a silver ring in the "O" of "stone," when the sun reaches its zenith, a small crystal cylinder rises from the floor of the tiled depression. The noon sun's light strikes the ruby set in the depression's center, and a dazzling beam of energy immediately shoots from it, striking the crystal cylinder and refracting into a multicolored shower of light. This rainbow strikes the far wall of the depression and creates a shimmering doorway — a phase door that penetrates 10 feet of solid stone and opens into the catacombs below. When the sun passes its zenith, the *phase door* remains.

Unlike the *phase door* spell, an unlimited number of persons and creatures can pass through the door. In addition, the priests of Tsathogga enhanced the rocks that comprise the island; PCs cannot *teleport* or use other, similar means to enter or exit the dungeon (though teleporting within the dungeon is allowed). In addition, the priests enhanced the depression's walls to resist all spells except *disintegrate*. Thus, the only way into or out of the dungeon is the *phase door* or use of a *disintegrate* spell.

The *phase door* remains open for 24 hours, until the following noon. At that time, the cylinder drops into its housing, and the depression again heats like an oven, trapping any PCs still inside the dungeon complex. By recovering the *Globe of Arden,* the PCs could use its *disintegrate* power to blast a way out at the location of the *phase door*, since the stone there is only 10 feet thick. If the *Globe of Arden* is replaced with a different magic item, provide a *scroll of disintegrate* with the final treasure or create an alternative exit. The priests of Tsathogga intended that nothing ever leave this dungeon.

The Dungeon of the Globe

The *phase door* penetrates 10 feet of solid stone, extending from the depression to this location. From this point, the PCs can re-enter the *phase door* and return to the depression. The *phase door*, however, only remains open for 24 hours — from noon until noon. Remember: the only passages from the dungeon to the outside world are the *phase door* or a *disintegrate* spell. Teleporting is impossible.

When living matter passes through the *phase door*, an *alarm* spell triggers in **Rooms 3** and **9**, alerting Asari and Dendorandra, respectively, to the presence of intruders.

1. The Shifting Hallway (CR 11)

The corridor at this point contains large scrape marks on the floor, as if a huge stone block had been dragged over the hallway's paving stones. Anyone entering this corridor recognizes that a block within this corridor shifts. Further examination (a DC 10 Perception, Knowledge [dungeoneering], or Knowledge [engineering]) reveals which block: the easternmost 10 foot stone block in the south wall shifts, apparently sliding north and south. Since this is unusual stonework, remember to apply a dwarf's bonus form stonecunning.

The Stone Trigger: Careful search of the general area (Perception DC 16) reveals a stone trigger or button set in the north wall, about 4 feet up the wall, at "**A**" on the map. The button, a 1-cubic-foot stone block, can be pushed inward. Currently flush with the wall, pushing the button inward sets the blocks in motion. The button resets itself, flush to the wall, in one round. Pushing the button again causes the blocks to move in the opposite direction. If the blocks are moving when the button is pushed, the blocks stop for one round, then begin to move backward to their last position. There is no limit to the number of times the button may be pushed. However, there is a 1% chance (non-cumulative) each time the button is pushed that the button sticks and the mechanism malfunctions.

The pressure plate at area "**D**" also triggers the blocks, as described in **Room 2**, below.

The Shifting Blocks: Once the trigger at "**A**" is pushed, two blocks within the corridor shift. The first is block "**B**" — 60 feet of solid stone. It moves from its southern position (marked on the map as the solid block "**B**"), sliding 10 feet per round northward until it comes to rest against the far northern wall. The block's position when at rest at the north end is marked with dashed lines and the letter "**B**" on the map.

The second is block "**C**" — 30 feet of solid stone. Unlike block **B** which slides north and south, block **C** moves up and down. Initially in its down position, block **C** fills the corridor at the area marked "**C**." When the button is pushed, the block rises until flush with the ceiling. It takes 5 rounds for block **C** to either rise to the ceiling or return to the floor.

The blocks always move in tandem. They are always either "closed" (block **B** in its southern position and block **C** flush with the floor of the corridor) or "open" (block **B** in its northern position and block **C** flush against the ceiling). The two positions are named for their relation to **Room 2**. If the blocks are in the open configuration, the PCs can access **Room 2**; in the closed configuration, the blocks prevent access.

When initially encountered, the blocks are in the closed position, as described above. Pushing button "**A**" causes the blocks to shift to the open position — block **B** moves northward and block **C** rises to the ceiling. Because block **B** is still shifting by the time block **C** has stopped, the characters do not initially notice block **C**.

Finding Block C: If the characters venture down the hallway when the blocks are in the open position, the characters may spot block C (DC 20 Perception). In addition, PCs can make DC 10 Perception or Knowledge (engineering) checks to detect the location of block C, even though it is in its housing, flush with the ceiling. A further check using the same skill (DC 15) reveals that the block moves up and down. Dwarves receive a +2 bonus on this check thanks to their stonecunning ability.

Getting Caught Between the Blocks: If someone triggers the pressure plate at area "**D**" (see **Room 2**, below), the blocks return to the closed position. If the blocks are in the closed position when the plate is triggered, there is no effect. It is therefore possible that characters may be caught between the moving blocks if the plate is triggered when they are trying to escape the room.

After triggering the pressure plate (see below), the characters should make a DC 10 Perception check. Those who succeed hear the sound of grinding stone and realize that the stone blocks are moving; they can then make a DC 12 Reflex save to react this round. Any characters failing the Perception check or subsequent Reflex save cannot move during the first round that the blocks are in motion.

The blocks return to their original, closed position. Block **B** moves 10 feet per round until it returns to its original southern position. Block **C** descends 1/5th of the distance from the ceiling to the floor per round until it is flush with the floor of the corridor, which takes 5 rounds. Characters may be unable to exit the north/south corridor to the west, where the button is, because block **B** has moved back into place and closed off the passage; the characters may also be unable to pass descending block **C**, either into or out of **Room 2**.

Moving Past Block B: Presuming the blocks are in the open position when the pressure plate is triggered, the characters have 3 rounds to escape through the corridor to the west (presuming they are able to move the first round, which requires the Perception checks and Reflex saves detailed above). During the first and second rounds, because block **B** is not yet obstructing the exit to the western corridor, anyone may move freely through the passage. However, on round 3, the shifting stone block begins to block the passage; by the end of the round, the passage is fully blocked. Anyone attempting to move through the passage into the western corridor during this round must succeed on a DC 20 Reflex save. Those

The "Ra's Evil Grin" Dungeon

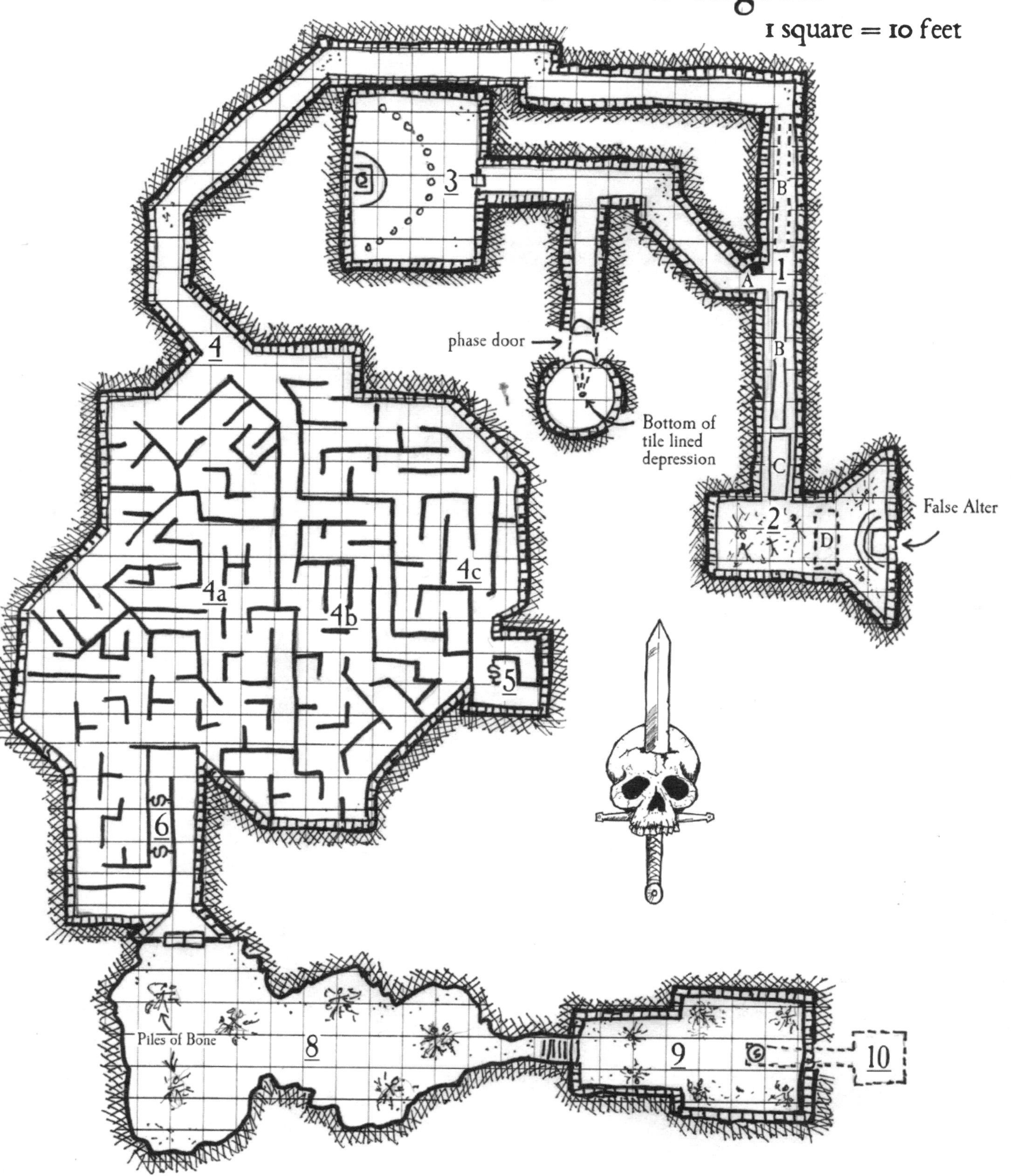

making the save tumble through the aperture just as the block closes off the corridor. Those failing the save are caught between the moving block and the opening and suffer massive damage; they must succeed on a DC 35 Fortitude save or be cut in half, killed instantly. Those who make the save still take 6d10 points of damage, managing to wiggle through the gap into the western corridor by sheer determination. Such PCs, their legs broken and useless, require assistance to move until fully healed.

Moving Past Block C: Presuming block **C** is in its raised, open position when the pressure plate is triggered, it takes 5 rounds for the block to descend fully to floor level. For the first two rounds, PCs can move under the descending block with no difficulty, requiring only a little crouching. On the third round of block **C**'s descent, PCs passing under must succeed on a DC 12 Reflex save. Success means they can move their full base movement under the block, and failure means they can only move half their base movement under the block. Running is impossible. On the fourth round, PCs must succeed on a DC 25 Reflex save. Success means they can move half their full base movement under the block, and failure means they are trapped under the block and cannot move. Small characters can add +2 to their saves, while Large characters suffer a –2. On the fifth round, the block settles flush against the floor. Any PCs trapped beneath must succeed on a DC 35 Fortitude save or be crushed and killed instantly. Those who make the save take 6d10 points of damage and continue to save and take damage every round they are trapped under the block.

"Caught in the Middle": A PC who can't quite make it out might get caught between block B moving south and block **C** descending. Obviously, block **B** comes to rest against block **C**, crushing any PCs caught in the middle. A PC in this situation normally has a few rounds of helpless immobility to contemplate his certain doom. Because block **B** only moves 10 feet per round, it takes six rounds for block **B**, after it prevents access to the western corridor, to come to rest against block **C**. Anyone caught between the blocks must succeed on a DC 35 Fortitude save or be crushed and killed instantly. Those who make the save take 6d10 points of damage and continue to save and take damage every round they are crushed between the blocks.

Stopping the Blocks: Physically preventing the blocks' movement is impossible. Pushing stone trigger "**A**" stops the blocks' movement and resets them to their last position. Thus, if the blocks were open and someone triggered pressure plate **D**, an alert character could reach the stone trigger at "**A**" and push it, sending the blocks — which were on their way to the closed position — back to the open position. Remember: after pushing stone trigger "**A**," the blocks remain still for one round before reversing direction.

Experience: Set the challenge rating of these blocks carefully. Pushing the button, watching the blocks move but never exploring anything shouldn't be worth anything above CR 2 for the characters. If the trap is triggered, jeopardizing the PCs' lives, GMs should consider treating the trap as CR 10 or more depending on the degree of peril.

2. The False Globe and the Block Trap (CR 11)

Dozens of skeletons are piled in this room. Several wear scraps of rusty armor; all have parts missing. Scratches and scrawling on the walls give evidence that some must have died here. Tooth marks mar some of the bones. These skeletons represent previous quests to recover the *Globe* as well as the servants of the priests of Tsathogga — entombed here once they finished constructing the labyrinth that houses the Globe, so that no one would ever learn its hiding place.

False Globe: At the far, eastern end of the room, an altar sits atop a dais, radiating evil. Symbols of the demon frog-god Tsathogga adorn the walls

A glowing globe sits upon the altar. Cautious PCs might feel as though this quest has proved too easy; their suspicion is warranted — this is a trap. The globe, enhanced with *magic aura,* radiates magic. It also radiates good. Anyone touching the false globe triggers the **trap**. Touching the globe to disarm the trap does not trigger it, unless the attempt fails by 5 or more.

FALSE GLOBE WITH *CHAIN LIGHTNING* TRAP **CR 11**
XP 12,800
Type magical; **Perception** DC 31; **Disable Device** DC 31

Trigger touch; **Reset** automatic
Effect spell effect (*chain lightning*, 13d6 electricity damage, DC 19 Ref half, CL 13th); multiple targets (up to 13)

Pressure Plate: Located in front of the altar at area "**D**" on the map is a pressure-plate trap. A weight of 100 or more pounds triggers the blocks at **Room 1** to return to their "closed" position. See **Room 1**, above, for details on how the stone blocks move.

3. The Evil Chapel (CR 12)

The door opens revealing an evil chapel with an altar carved in the form of a many-armed snake woman. Thirteen white stone pillars stand in a half circle in front of the blood- and skull-covered altar. A single priest chants arcane words as a silver glow envelops his body. Then all goes black.

The priest is **Asari** — the fallen high priest of Arden who long ago stole the *Globe of Arden* and delivered it to the priests of Tsathogga. Tsathogga rewarded Asari's treachery with eternal life as a powerful mummy, making him a consort to Dendorandra, the dark daughter. The chapel area detects as evil, and because of its utter evil, turning of the undead is impossible within its confines. In addition, all divine spellcasting has a 20% chance of failure, except that of chaotic evil priests.

ASARI THE MUMMY PRIEST **CR 12**
XP 19,200
Male mummy cleric of Tsathogga 8 (*Pathfinder Roleplaying Game Bestiary* "Mummy")
CE Medium undead
Init –1; **Senses** darkvision 60 ft.; **Perception** +24
Aura despair (DC 16)

AC 28, touch 9, flat-footed 28 (+9 armor, –1 Dex, +10 natural)
hp 128 (8d8+16 plus 8d8+16 plus 16)
Fort +10; **Ref** +3; **Will** +16
DR 5/—; **Immune** undead traits; **Resist** cold 10
Weaknesses vulnerability to fire

Speed 15 ft.
Melee slam +16 (1d8+4 plus mummy rot)
Special Attacks aura of destruction 8 rounds/day (+4), channel negative energy 5/day (DC 16, 4d6), destructive smite 7/day (+4)
Domain Spell-Like Abilities (CL 8th; ranged touch +11): 7/day—*icicle* (1d6+4 cold)
Spells Prepared (CL 8th; melee touch 15, ranged touch +11):
4th—*inflict critical wounds*[D] (DC 18), *poison* (DC 18), *spell immunity* (fireball, magic missile), *summon monster IV*
3rd—*bestow curse* (DC 17), *deeper darkness, meld into stone, protection from energy, rage*[D]
2nd—*desecrate, fog cloud*[D], *hold person* (DC 16), *shatter* (DC 16), *sound burst* (DC 16)
1st—*bane* (DC 15), *doom* (DC 15), *endure elements, entropic shield, obscuring mist*[D], *obscuring mist*
0 (at will)—*bleed* (DC 14), *guidance, resistance, virtue*
D Domain spell; **Domains** Destruction, Water

Str 17, **Dex** 8, **Con** —, **Int** 12, **Wis** 18, **Cha** 15
Base Atk +12; **CMB** +15; **CMD** 24
Feats Alertness, Armor Proficiency (Heavy), Combat Casting, Power Attack, Skill Focus (Perception), Spell Penetration, Toughness, Weapon Focus (slam)
Skills Diplomacy +9, Fly +0, Intimidate +13, Knowledge (planes) +12, Knowledge (religion) +12, Perception +24, Sense Motive +17, Spellcraft +12, Stealth +4
Languages Abyssal, Common
Combat Gear *eyes of doom;* **Other Gear** full plate, *robe of vermin* (worn by Asari, but has no effect on him), silver unholy symbol (Tsathogga), *helm of awareness* (magical helm that adds +4 awareness bonus to all Perception checks)

Despair (Su) All creatures within a 30-foot radius that see a mummy must make a DC 16 Will save or be paralyzed by fear for 1d4 rounds. Whether or not the save is successful, that creature cannot be affected again by the same mummy's despair ability for 24 hours. This is a paralysis and a mind-affecting fear affect. The save DC is Charisma-based.
Mummy Rot (Su) Curse and disease—slam; *save* Fort DC 16; *onset* 1 minute; *frequency* 1/day; *effect* 1d6 Con and 1d6 Cha; *cure* —. Mummy rot is both a curse and disease and can only be cured if the curse is first removed, at which point the disease can be magically removed. Even after the curse element of mummy rot is lifted, a creature suffering from it cannot recover naturally over time. Anyone casting a conjuration (healing) spell on the afflicted creature must succeed on a DC 20 caster level check, or the spell is wasted and the healing has no effect. Anyone who dies from mummy rot turns to dust and cannot be raised without a resurrection or greater magic. The save DC is Charisma-based.

Tactics: Asari begins combat by protecting himself from fire using his *protection from energy* spell, then casting *entropic shield, desecrate* and *spell immunity* as the party enters. The *alarm* spell, triggered by the PCs at the *phase door,* warned Asari of their arrival. After using his *summon monster IV* (3 dretches) spell, Asari advances to attack. Remember: Asari can use the *eyes of doom* each round as a free action. Asari uses *meld into stone* if seriously threatened and reappears a few feet away to resume his attack. He also enjoys using his *fog cloud* and *obscuring mist*.

The Altar: If Asari is killed, the face of the many-armed snake woman animates, and a female voice intones:

> "Little men, your powers are nothing to me. I would have destroyed all of you long before this, but I enjoy breaking such miserable creatures as you with my bare hands. Humans beg so wonderfully, shrieking and crying as I slowly pull them apart!" Looking at a spellcaster in the group, the female voice adds, "Perhaps I shall use you a replacement for my last companion — the one you so thoughtlessly destroyed."

The statue then re-solidifies amid distant laughter.

4. The Maze (CR 7)

It should be obvious to the PCs that they are about to enter a maze. Navigating this maze ultimately leads to **Area 8**. The maze does not present much difficulty and can be navigated by normal means. Note that, to pass through the doors at **Area 7**, the secret door at **Room 5** must eventually be discovered.

The maze is divided into three sections:

Section 4A leads eventually to the doors at **Area 7**. No monsters roam this section.

Section 4B leads nowhere; **2 ochre jellies** wander around this section. (There is a 1 in 1d6 chance per 5 rounds of encountering one of the jellies.)

Section 4C of the maze leads to the secret door at **Room 5**, below.

OCHRE JELLIES (2) **CR 5**
XP 1,600
hp 63 (*Pathfinder Roleplaying Game Bestiary* "Ochre Jelly")

5. Traps and Keys (CR 3)

A secret stone door, locked and trapped, bars entrance to this small room. Opening the secret door without disabling the **trap** triggers it.

Secret Spear Trapped Stone Door: Perception DC 20; 1 in. thick; Hardness 8; hp 20; Break DC 30; Disable Device DC 25.

SPEAR TRAP **CR 3**
XP 800
Type mechanical; **Perception** DC 20; **Disable Device** DC 20

Trigger location; **Reset** manual
Effect three Atk +12 ranged (1d8+4/x3, spear, 200 ft. maximum range)

Behind the secret door, on the far wall of this area, are four hooks, from each of which hangs a large key — one made of silver, one of bronze, one of lead and one of brass. PCs need them to open the iron doors at **Area 7**.

6. The Second False Globe (CR 11)

A secret stone door, locked and trapped, bars entrance to this small room, which holds a second false *Globe*. Opening the secret door without disabling the **trap** triggers it.

Secret Spear Trapped Stone Door: Perception DC 20; 1 in. thick; Hardness 8; hp 20; Break DC 30; Disable Device DC 25.

SPEAR TRAP **CR 3**
XP 800
Type mechanical; **Perception** DC 20; **Disable Device** DC 20

Trigger location; **Reset** manual
Effect three Atk +12 ranged (1d8+4/x3, spear, 200 ft. maximum range)

Opening the secret door reveals a small chamber. Its walls are barren and crudely worked, and the chamber's floor is unworked earth. Rudely placed in a stone basin set in the east wall, shrouded by a black cloth covered with evil runes, sits what appears to be an orb. The vile black cloth cannot mask the light emanating from the orb beneath.

The writing on the cloth, in Abyssal, appears to be some sort of curse of darkness. The cloth detects as evil and as magic. However, this is all a ruse (again), as the cloth is falsely enhanced to detect as evil and magic. Touching the cloth triggers the equivalent of a *poison* spell.

***POISON* CLOTH TRAP** **CR 5**
XP 1,600
Type magical; **Perception** DC 29; **Disable Device** DC 29

Trigger touch; **Reset** none
Effect spell effect (*poison*, DC 16 Fort negates, CL 7th)

The orb beneath glows with a bright holy light, as if radiating a *daylight* spell and good. This globe, like its predecessor, is enhanced with *magic aura*. Anyone touching the second false globe triggers the **trap**. Touching the globe to disarm the trap does not trigger the trap, unless the attempt fails by 5 or more.

FALSE GLOBE WITH *CHAIN LIGHTNING* TRAP **CR 9**
XP 6,400
Type magical; **Perception** DC 31; **Disable Device** DC 31

Trigger touch; **Reset** automatic
Effect spell effect (*chain lightning*, 10d6 electricity damage, DC 19 Ref half, CL 10th); multiple targets (up to 10); secondary effect (setting off this trap also sets off a *slay living* trap)

***SLAY LIVING* TRAP** **CR 7**
XP 3,200
Type magical; **Perception** DC 30; **Disable Device** DC 30

Trigger touch; **Reset** automatic
Effect spell effect (slay living, Atk +10 touch, 12d6+10 damage, DC 17 Fort save for 3d6+10 damage)

Northern Secret Door: At the north end of the chamber, a second secret door, this one expertly hidden and unlocked, opens into a passage that leads to the iron portals at **Area 7**, below.

Expertly Hidden Secret Door: 3 in. thick; Hardness 8; hp 45; Perception DC 35; Break DC 35.

7. Riddles at the Gate (CR 8)

A set of great iron portals bars the PCs way. The two doors, constructed of the finest material, are engraved with arcane writings. In the center of each door is an elaborate, rune-etched lock with several strange keyholes.

Each door is built from 4-inch-thick magical iron with 1-inch-wide internal channels that run both horizontally and vertically, through which adamantine bars have been inserted. These bars slide away when the locks are disengaged. The lock on the right-hand door causes the vertical bars to retract, and the lock on the left-hand door causes the horizontal bars to retract, thus unlocking the door. Attempting to pick the lock, instead of using the four keys from **Room 5**, triggers the **trap**. In addition, using the keys improperly subjects the PC(s) to electrical damage.

Trapped, Locked Adamantine-reinforced Iron Portals: 4 in. thick; Hardness 15; hp 130; spell immunity (except *wish* and *miracle*); Break DC 50; Disable Device DC 40.

Any failed attempt to pick the lock results in the character being stricken by a *slay living* spell; failing to use the keys in the proper manner or force the door subjects the PC to 2d6 electrical damage with no saving throw.

***SLAY LIVING* TRAP** **CR 7**
XP 3,200
Type magical; **Perception** DC 30; **Disable Device** DC 30

Trigger touch; **Reset** automatic
Effect spell effect (slay living, Atk +10 touch, 12d6+10 damage, DC 17 Fort save for 3d6+10 damage)

ELECTRIFIED KEYHOLE TRAP (x2) **CR 4**
XP 1,200
Type mechanical; **Perception** DC 25; **Disable Device** DC 25

Trigger touch; **Reset** automatic
Effect electric shock (2d6 electricity damage); never miss

Each of the two doors has four keyholes and a riddle that explains how to unlock it. Once both halves are opened, the doors can be swung wide into the cave at **Area 8**.

The Riddle on the Right-hand Door: Four colored metal plates in symbolic shapes comprise the lock in the door's center. The shaped plates, each with a keyhole at its center, are as follows: a brass table, a lead sword, a bronze coffin, and a silver diamond. Each lock appears designed to accept a normal-sized key. Surrounding the locks is the following inscription written in magical runes (requiring *read magic*):

> *"One man makes me, does not need me.*
> *One man buys me, does not use me.*
> *One man uses me, does not see me."*

Solution: The answer to the riddle is "coffin." When the bronze key is inserted into the coffin-shaped bronze lock, it slides back to reveal a second, coffin-shaped silver lock. If this is in turn opened with the silver key, it reveals a coffin-shaped lead lock, which when opened in turn reveals a coffin-shaped brass lock. Each lock must be opened with the key of similar metal. Using the keys in any other manner causes 2d6 electrical damage. Once all four locks are opened, the characters hear a loud, grinding sound, as the vertical interlocking adamantine bars within the doors slide away. PCs cannot yet open the doors until the left-hand door is unlocked.

The Riddle on the Left-hand Door: Four, square faceplates comprise the locks in the door's center — one each of silver, lead, bronze and brass. Surrounding the locks is the following inscription, written in magical runes (requiring *read magic*):

> *"I fall first the heaviest, and then heaviest from a man's purse."*

Solution: The answers are "lead" (because it is the heaviest of the four metals) and "silver" (because coins are made of it). Only by inserting and turning the lead key in the lead lock and the silver key in the silver lock does this half of the door unlock. Using the keys in any other manner causes 2d6 electrical damage. Once both locks are opened, the characters hear a loud, grinding sound as the horizontal interlocking adamantine bars within the doors slide away. PCs cannot yet open the doors until the right-hand door is unlocked.

Once both doors are unlocked — both sets of adamantine bars have withdrawn — they swing open freely, all traps disabled.

8. The Gloomy Cavern

This cave contains large piles of bones, loose rocks, rusty swords, armor and the rotten remains of packs and other soft goods. An eerie, howling wind blows through this place and an otherworldly light emanates from **Room 9**. There are no monsters here. The demon in **Room 9** can create animated servants from these bones.

Treasure: In one of the piles of bones, a *detect magic* spell reveals a *+2 heavy wooden shield* beneath a large pile of rusty metal.

9. The Guardian (CR 12)

A set of stairs, hewn from the red stone of the living rock of the cave itself, descends about 30 feet to a room of roughly worked stone. Strange crystals are set into its walls. A huge pile of silver and gold glitters and shines in the center of the room.

The monster in this room attacks once the PCs get close, revealing herself. Tsathogga commissioned **Dendorandra, the Dark Daughter** to guard the *Globe of Arden*. She knows that she will suffer eternal torment should she fail in her task.

DENDORANDRA, ADVANCED DARK DAUGHTER CR 13
XP 25,600
hp 112 (see **Rescued from Oblivion** in "The Pit of Despair")

Add advanced simple template (+2 on all roles and +4 to AC and CMD)
Melee *Xpatias* +17/+12/+7 (1d8+10/17-20), 3 Large +1 *longswords* +17 (2d6+8/17-20), 2 Large +1 *shortspears* +16 (1d8+8/x3), tail slap +8 (1d8+4 plus grab) or 6 slams +13 (1d6+7), tail slap +8 (1d8+4 plus grab)

Tactics: Dendorandra relishes combat. She fights with four longswords and two spears in her six arms — one is a *+3 longsword of speed*, named Xpatias (literally "frogsticker" in Abyssal; see **New Items** at the end of this adventure). The remaining swords and spears are all *+1*. Dendorandra uses *unholy blight* on the party. Dendorandra begins the melee with a *blade barrier*. She also attempts to *summon* 1d4 more dark daughters to occupy the fighters (she prefers her sisters as they serve her willingly, joining her in the frenzied bloodlust). She attacks lightly-armored individuals first and concentrates on one victim until that person is dead. If wounded to over half her hit points, she *teleports* into the large cavern to escape. If someone hits her with holy water, she flies into a rage and blindly attacks that person until one or both are slain.

Treasure: Other than the very magic sword, the pile of gold and silver consists of 4,000 gp and 20,000 sp. Under the pile of coins, a **secret hatch** opens into a passage — a 3-foot-diameter crawlspace of tiled stone — leading to **Room 10**. There is no magical way to detect the secret door.

Secret Hatch: Perception DC 25; 1 in. thick; Hardness 8; hp 30; Break DC 30; Disable Device DC 25.

10. The Treasure Room (CR 10)

A dim glow can be seen at the end of the tiny passage leading to this room. The PCs emerge into a 5-foot-square room containing a chest and a silver coffer. Both vessels look to be thousands of years old and are covered with ancient and arcane runic and hieroglyphic inscriptions. Fine locks of ancient construction on both items look untouched, as though undisturbed for centuries.

Treasure: Both vessels are locked and trapped. The chest, made of iron, is worth 1,000 gp intact. The coffer, made of mithral, is worth 4,000 gp intact. Their value drops to 1/5 the estimate if they are broken open.

The Chest: The chest contains the following 10 gems, sized from 1 carat to as large as a fist: a 10,000 gp uncut corundum sphere (the largest item); a 1,000 gp ruby; a 3,000 gp sapphire; a 6,000 gp emerald; a 2,000 gp garnet; a 8,000 gp opal; a 6,000 gp topaz; a 4,000 gp aquamarine; a large piece of jade worth 4,500 gp; and a 2,500 gp black opal.

Locked Iron Chest: 1 in. thick; Hardness 10; hp 40; Break DC 30; Disable Device DC 25.

POISON GAS TRAP **CR 8**
XP 4,800
Type mechanical; **Perception** DC 20; **Disable Device** DC 20

Trigger location; **Reset** none
Effect cloud of poison gas (burnt othur fumes); never miss; onset delay (3 rounds); multiple targets (all creatures in the room).

The Coffer: The coffer cannot be magically opened with an *open/close* or *knock* spell due to the unknown protective runes of a magic-retarding nature. Inside the coffer is an odd, unidentifiable and glowing gem, about 12 inches in diameter, made of a milky, glasslike substance. This is (finally) the *Globe of Arden* — a powerful artifact! See the **New Items** at the end of this adventure for more information on the *Globe of Arden.*

Locked Mithral Coffer: 1 in. thick; Hardness 15; hp 40; Break DC 40; Disable Device DC 35.

***LIGHTNING BOLT* TRAP** **CR 8**
XP 4,800
Type magical; **Perception** DC 28; **Disable Device** DC 28

Trigger touch; **Reset** none
Effect spell effect (*lightning bolt*, 10d6 electricity damage, DC 14 Ref half); multiple targets (all target in a 5 ft.-by-50 ft. line)

New Items

Globe of Arden (Artifact)

Aura strong evocation, divination, and transmutation; **CL** 20th
Slot none; **Weight** 5 lbs.

DESCRIPTION

The Globe has the following powers:

The Globe endows upon its owner one positive level while floating around his head (like an ioun stone). The Globe's owner gains a +1 bonus on all ability checks, attack rolls, combat maneuver checks, Combat Maneuver Defense, saving throws, and skill checks. In addition, the owner increases its current and total hit points by 5. The owner is also treated as one level higher for the purpose of level-dependent variables (such as spellcasting). Spellcasters do not gain spells or slots as a result of positive levels.

It continuously casts daylight. Its owner cannot cancel this effect, though the Globe can be put in a sealed container, which negates the daylight but also prevents use of any of the Globe's other powers.

It can cast shocking grasp (3/day) at its owner's level.

It can cast commune (1/month) with former allies of the god dead Arden. These connections include Arden's widow, the goddess Vionir, and Arn, the son of Arden and Vionir.

It can cast searing light (1/day) and sunbeam (1/ day) at its owner's level.

When the Globe's owner uses any of these powers, she loses all body hair permanently.

The Globe also has an incredible primary power (which can only be discerned by legend lore): it can cast a disintegrate beam (1/week). The user must invoke the name of Arden or Ra to use this power then make a ranged touch attack. Any target hit must succeed on a DC 31 Fortitude save. If the save fails, the object hit is utterly destroyed. If the save is successful, the target instead takes 10d10 points of damage and makes a massive damage check (see the Pathfinder Roleplaying Game). If the ranged touch attack misses its target, the attack still hits a randomly determined target. If used against nonliving matter, the beam disintegrates 20 cubic feet of it. Otherwise, the ray functions as per a disintegrate spell. Each time the primary power is used, the Globe's owner loses one point of Constitution permanently unless a successful DC 22 Constitution check is made. Evil creatures touching the Globe suffer 5d6 points of damage with no save.

DESTRUCTION

The Globe can only be destroyed if soaked in the blood of a sun deity and sealed within a chamber completely devoid of all light for 99 years.

Xpatias

Aura strong enchantment and transmutation; **CL** 15th
Slot none; **Price** 196,512 gp; **Weight** 4 lb.

DESCRIPTION

Xpatias is a +3 speed longsword: Int 15, Wis 13, Cha 18, Ego 22, AL CN, speaks, reads and telepathically communicates in Common, Infernal, and Celestial. Any chaotic creature may use Xpatias. Non-chaotic creatures touching Xpatias suffer 1d4 Con damage (Fortitude save DC 22 avoids) each time they touch the sword. It also has the following powers:

The wielder gains Blind-Fight as a bonus feat and has see invisibility constantly active.

The sword can detect amphibians within 60 feet and drives the wielder into a rage against those amphibians (as the spell except the effect doesn't end as long as there is a living amphibian in sight) if an ego test is failed (DC 22 Will save).

The wielder can cast shield on his person twice per day.

The sword's special purpose is to slay amphibians, including amphibian-like outsiders such as hezrous and greruor demons, and its special power is hold monster on all hits on amphibians and amphibian-like outsiders (DC 19 Will save as the spell).

CONSTRUCTION

Requirements Craft Magic Arms and Armor, *haste*, *hold monster*, *poison*, *rage*, *see invisibility*, *shield*; **Cost** 98,412 gp

The Pit of Despair

By Bill Webb and Clark Peterson

Introduction

Designed for a party of at least 13th level, this module details an adventure to recover the *Sword of Karith*, a *holy avenger longsword*. Not the straight-forward hack-and-slash treasure hunt your players will be expecting, this adventure is instead a trap laid by the forces of evil to corrupt and destroy their greatest enemy: paladins.

At the direction of Orcus, the demon-god of undead, a nalfeshnee demon named Caanara misappropriated the *Sword of Karith* and hid it in a desert temple, called the Temple of the Justicars. Adding to his villainy, Caanara also replaced the *Sword of Karith* with an *unholy reaver,* which Orcus heavily enhanced to mimic the *Sword of Karith*. Knowing paladins simply cannot resist a holy quest to recover a lost, magic sword, the forces of evil have created a win-win situation. Up-and-coming paladins attempting to find the temple and recover the sword will either be killed outright during their quest or be utterly corrupted when they inadvertently recover the *unholy reaver*, believing it to be the *Sword of Karith.* This adventure, then, has two possible outcomes: either the PCs all die or they recover an evil and corrupting *unholy reaver*. Cruel treatment of the characters, you say? Evil? Wicked? Dastardly? Exactly.

GMs thus must be at their most deceptive, skirting that thin line between gunning for your players and running a complex deception fairly. GMs must run this adventure with an understanding that it was crafted by extraordinarily intelligent deity-like demons whose goals are deception, corruption and slaughter. For instance, do not refer to this adventure as **The Pit of Despair**. Instead, call it **The Temple of the Justicars** or **The Quest for the *Sword of Karith***. Do nothing to tip off the do-gooding heroes to the presence of the trap.

The party's initial trip to the Temple of the Justicars most likely results in their defeating the demon guardians and recovering the false *holy avenger*, thus corrupting the party's paladin. This unlucky soul will then need to perform an act of *atonement* to cleanse himself of his unwilling sins and recover his paladinhood once he realized his corruption. Learning that the destruction of the false *holy avenger* is the only means of atonement, the PCs no doubt attempt a second trip to the temple, where they return with the *unholy reaver* in an attempt to destroy it along with the demon Caanara, and recover the true *Sword of Karith*.

GMs should feel free to replace Orcus, the demon-god of undead, and Thyr and Muir, the god of law and the goddess of virtue and paladins, respectively, with those gods most appropriate to their campaign.

The Legend of the *Holy Sword of Karith*

For the Players

Paladins are familiar with the legend of Karith — a heroic paladin of old who roamed the lands as a champion of good, wielding a wondrous sword of great power. Consulting a sage or casting a *legend lore* spell reveals the true history of Karith and his holy avenger.

Many years ago, a paladin of great renown, named Karith, roamed the world, righting wrongs, slaying dragons and protecting the innocent. The deeds of this great man border on the unbelievable. In fact, most common folk consider them great exaggerations, if not outright myth. In truth, Karith was less famous than he should have been, having done deeds far greater than even the most superstitious or pious would believe.

Karith wielded the mighty sword, *Entrancacor*, which in the ancient dwarven tongue means "slayer of demons." The finest dwarven smiths and enchanters forged this sword for the Holy Order of the Justicars — the paladins of the goddess Muir — over 1,000 years ago. Legend holds that no greater weapon was ever forged, before or since. Tales tell of demon armies recoiling from a lone man wielding this sword. The sword was passed from grandmaster to grandmaster within the holy order over many generations, and Karith was the last grandmaster of the Justicars.

As Karith neared the end of his life, the gods of good bade him wait patiently for his successor to appear. However, no paladin of the order then living was sufficiently worthy of bearing the sword and becoming grandmaster. Some held promise, yet none sufficiently distinguished himself from his peers. The high priests of the temple of Thyr and Muir — the god of law and the goddess of virtue and paladins, respectively — *communed* with their gods and were instructed to have faith. After several years passed with no worthy successor appearing, a female celestial of Muir visited the priests. In angelic splendor, the celestial instructed the high priests to relinquish the sword into her keeping. She revealed her plan to set the sword in a temple, hidden in a valley deep within a distant desert, where it would await discovery by a paladin worthy to retrieve it and bear it forth again. By its recovery, the celestial told the priests, they would know the new grandmaster of paladins. Legends call the resting place of the sword the "Temple of the Justicars." Though many brave paladins have attempted the sword's recovery, to this day, none has succeeded.

For the GM

The avatar mentioned above, who retrieved and hid the sword, was unrelated either to Thyr or Muir, and was instead Caanara, a nalfeshnee demon, sent by Orcus to steal the sword and place it beyond the reach of those serving Thyr and Muir. A master of deception, Orcus also gave his demon a false sword, called *Entranhumani* ("slayer of humans"), with which to dupe and despoil any paladins who successfully locate the hiding place of *Entrancacor*. Orcus bound his demon to the sword's resting place and commanded him to guard it. GMs should remember that nowhere in the legends are these demons mentioned; instead, convince any questing paladin that his god's avatar took the sword. The PCs should expect a "quest to find a sword belonging to the good guys" adventure, not an evil trap set by the worst enemies of law and good.

The methods by which the PCs discover the exact location of the Pit of Despair are up to the GM. The *holy avenger's* hiding place is a well-kept secret. Because demons do not want a powerful enemy running around slaughtering their kind with so powerful a weapon, even they go to great pains to keep the location a mystery — however fond they are of using the ruse to destroy up-and-coming paladins. And there are never any survivors of failed quests to question — their deaths mistakenly attributed to the paladin's excess pride or arrogant belief in his own worthiness to bear the sword. When in reality he was yet another victim of Orcus' and Caanara's treachery and deception.

Consultation with a sage is, perhaps, the best way to set the adventure

in motion. The sage could direct the PCs to a secluded sect of Muir's priests. Those priests, should they deem the party's paladin worthy, provide him with a copy of a map to the Valley of the Temple of the Justicars — the rumored hiding place of the *Sword of Karith*. They also inform the paladin that the legends reveal that "only someone who is prayerful and devout and who sees with the eyes of faith can find the entrance to the Temple."

Other methods of discovering the location of the Pit of Despair include a treasure map, a holy text found secreted away in a vast library, a message scratched into an abandoned shield or breastplate, a divinely bestowed vision, or consultation of the oracle at ***Rappan Athuk***.

Traveling to the Temple of the Justicars

After learning the location of the Temple of the Justicars, as described above, the PCs must travel to the edge of the desert and beyond to the Valley of the Temple. GMs should make this an arduous journey fraught with danger to provide the right "feel" for a holy quest. In the **Lost Lands** campaign setting by **Frog God Games**, the lost Temple of the Justicars lies in the mountains ringing the desert plateau known as the Sacred Table. The ruins of the holy city of Tircople still stand upon this plateau across the desert from the Crusader Coast.

To reach the general location of the Pit of Despair, the party must travel through a desert wilderness stretching beyond the last human settlement of the coast. The first third of the trip involves traveling into desert and should be dangerous, though not overly so. Once the PCs reach the edge of the plateau, they must then travel across its desert expanse, past the haunted ruins of Tircople until they reach the Valley of the Temple.

GMs wishing to avoid a prolonged wilderness trek can proceed directly to the section entitled, "**The Entrance to the Pit of Despair**," below. However, GMs are encouraged to run wilderness encounters as the PCs travel to the Valley of the Temple. This increases the "epic quest" feeling of the adventure, making the PCs more likely be duped when they recover the false *holy avenger* after their major battle in the Pit. Otherwise, the PCs might get suspicious if the quest is too easy.

The Entrance to the Pit of Despair

The PCs have traveled miles through the desert and have finally reached this forsaken place — the Valley of the Temple. Their map guides them into a cleft in the red-rock wall. They travel the narrow path in the shade of the looming walls for over an hour, and emerge from between the two large walls of rock into a small canyon, open to the sky.

The canyon ends in a worked wall of red stone, similar to that of the surrounding rock. The floor of the canyon is sand. Worked-stone entrances are set into the wall at various heights. The entrances all have the same general appearance: a 10-foot-high archway flanked by bas-relief statues of knights in mail. There is no detail that distinguishes one from the other. They do not detect as evil, good or magic.

To access the entrances — which do not have ledges in front of them

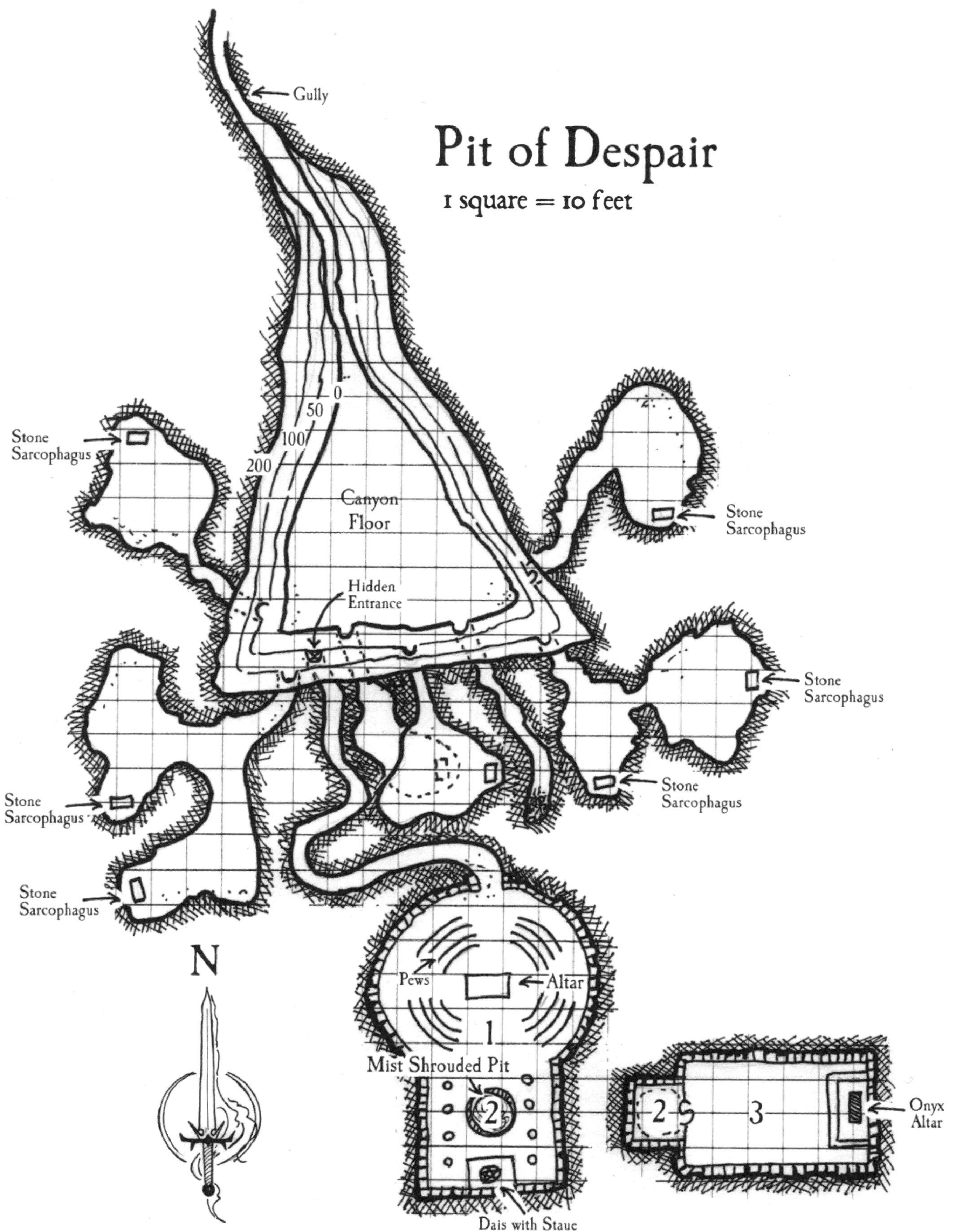
Gully
Pit of Despair
1 square = 10 feet
Stone Sarcophagus
0
50
100
200
Canyon Floor
Stone Sarcophagus
Hidden Entrance
Stone Sarcophagus
Stone Sarcophagus
Stone Sarcophagus
Stone Sarcophagus
N
Pews
Altar
1
Mist Shrouded Pit
2
2
3
Onyx Altar
Dais with Staue

— the PCs must find a way to climb the face of the canyon wall, which is nearly vertical. They can do this by climbing (Climb check at DC 25; DC 20 in the corners of the canyon) or using magic, such as *dimension door, fly, levitate* or *teleport*.

Climatic conditions in the Valley of the Temple run to extremes: unbearably hot during the day (exceeding 110° at noon) and freezing cold at night (dipping below 0° from 1 am to 3 am). This inhospitable region offers no source of water and no natural source of shade to shield the PCs from the sun. See the "Environment, Heat Dangers" and "Cold Dangers" of Chapter 13 of the *Pathfinder Roleplaying Game Core Rulebook*. In addition, the PCs may run short of food or water. If so, consult the "Environment, Starvation and Thirst" section of Chapter 13 of the *Pathfinder Roleplaying Game Core Rulebook*. Strong winds also plague the valley. Check once every hour on 1d20 with the following results: 1–10: no wind, 11–15: moderate wind, 16–17: strong wind, 18–19: severe wind, 20: windstorm. The winds in the canyon only last for 3d10 minutes. Any time strong or severe winds arise there is a 50% chance that a dust storm accompanies them. In addition, any windstorm is always accompanied by a dust storm, with a 75% chance of a greater dust storm. The winds themselves, of extreme temperature, do nothing to reduce the effects of heat or cold. See the "Environment, Weather" section of Chapter 13 of the *Pathfinder Roleplaying Game Core Rulebook* for the game effects associated with these winds and dust storms.

Wandering Monsters: Aside from the weather, one other danger threatens the PCs. There is a 1 on 1d10 chance per hour during the hours of darkness that **1d6 Huge scorpions** descend into the canyon to attack the PCs. There is an endless supply of these scorpions. They infest the surrounding hills.

HUGE SCORPIONS (1–6 OR MORE) **CR 6**
XP 2,400
Giant advanced giant scorpion (*Pathfinder Roleplaying Game Bestiary* "Scorpion, Giant")
N Huge vermin
Init –1; **Senses** darkvision 60 ft., tremorsense 60 ft.; **Perception** +4

AC 17, touch 7, flat-footed 17 (–1 Dex, +10 natural, –2 size)
hp 76 (5d8+40)
Fort +11; **Ref** +1; **Will** +2
Immune mind-affecting effects

Speed 50 ft.
Melee 2 claws +12 (1d8+8 plus grab), sting +12 (1d8+8)
Space 15 ft.; **Reach** 15 ft.
Special Attacks constrict (1d8+8), poison

Str 27, **Dex** 8, **Con** 20, **Int** —, **Wis** 10, **Cha** 2
Base Atk +6; **CMB** +16 (+20 grapple); **CMD** 25
Skills Climb +12, Perception +4, Stealth –5; **Racial Modifiers** +4 Climb, +4 Perception, +4 Stealth

---

Poison (Ex) Sting—injury; *save* Fort DC 21; *frequency* 1/round for 6 rounds; *effect* 1d2 Strength damage; *cure* 1 save. The save DC is Constitution-based and includes a +2 racial bonus.

False Entrances: All of the obvious entrances are false entrances, leading to caves and passages but not to the Temple of the Justicars. Each such cave has a 1–3 on 1d6 chance of being occupied by **1d4 Huge scorpions**, which immediately attack the PCs. Each cave also houses a sarcophagus of marble, carved to represent a knight in mail on the stone lid. Each such sarcophagus has a 1–4 on 1d6 chance of containing the remains of a knight in full plate mail with a sword (of random type) and shield. If remains are present, there is a 1 on 1d6 chance for each that the mail or the sword is enhanced. If enhanced, roll 1d6: 1–4: the item is *+1*, 5–6: the item is *+2*. These remains are, in fact, the corpses of paladins killed during their quest to recover the *Sword of Karith*. The demons have "entombed" the remains to look like the final resting place of revered heroes. The demons find this false reverence very entertaining.

The Real Entrance to the "Temple of the Justicars": The actual entrance to the Pit of Despair is hidden from mortal eyes. Only a paladin under the effects of a both a *prayer* (or who is performing some similarly extreme action, putting her in the proper religious frame of mind) and a *true seeing* spell even has a chance to see the entrance. Such a paladin must still make a DC 20 Perception check to see the entrance. Powerful magic prevents any other means of detecting the entrance, short of a *wish* or a *miracle*. Even *find the path* does not reveal the entrance. Once the real entrance is exposed, that paladin can thereafter see the entrance as plainly as the false ones. She can direct others to pass through the entrance.

The GM should make it very difficult — though not impossible — to locate the true entrance. Let the party search for several days and suffer the temperature extremes and begin to despair and contemplate abandoning the quest. After no fewer than 3 days' searching, the GM might take pity on the party and give it the following clue: between midnight and 2 am, a faint glow can be seen (Perception DC 25 without *true seeing*) from the portion of the cliff face where the true entrance is located. This clue doesn't let the PCs see the actual entrance; it just gives them a hint that there is something there they haven't discovered. They still need to cast *true seeing* and *prayer* on a paladin to see the real entrance. If the PCs still can't find the entrance, prod them to the proper solution by reminding them of the words of the priests that "only someone prayerful and devout and who sees with the eyes of faith can find the entrance to the Temple."

Once located, the entrance threshold may be crossed at will. There are no doors, locks or traps on the entrance. A winding, 10-foot-diameter, roughly worked tunnel leads 120 feet to **Area 1**.

Note: Because the Pit of Despair is a source of conflict between good and evil deities, any spells, such as *commune, divination* or *find the path,* cast in an attempt to learn the location of the entrance or the consequences of future actions will have no result. GMs might imply that Thyr and Muir want the PCs to find and recover the *sword* on their own merits, without guidance. Remind them: this is a test of faith and virtue, which can only be surmounted by noble, unguided, individual action. In reality, Orcus himself is watching the PCs and actively disrupting any contact with their good-aligned deities; he cannot, however, interfere with *miracle* spells.

The Pit of Despair

Three areas comprise the Pit of Despair. The first, a large underground amphitheater resembling a temple to Thyr and Muir, functions as the false "Temple of the Justicars." The second area, the pit itself, contains a false avatar of Muir (really an altered nalfeshnee) and the *unholy reaver*. The final area, an evil altar room, contains an unholy shrine to Orcus, with the *Sword of Karith* encased in blackest stone. The first two areas are enhanced with a strong magic that both masks alignment and projects a lawful-good alignment. This enchantment does not mask the alignment of the demons (though the *unholy reaver* masks Caanara's alignment). Additional shields prevent detection of the third area.

1. The "Temple of the Justicars"

The entrance room is a large temple, designed to resemble an amphitheater. Three tiered series of pews lead down to a flat central area that features an altar. A recessed area at the far side of the room is lined with columns, ending with a statue of Muir. The recess contains a large pit, 30 feet across, around which mists swirl, obscuring view within. The only inhabitants of the chamber — fifteen robed priests of Muir — chant and dance around the pit. The walls of the amphitheater and the pillars are worked with images of knights in full armor.

The First Visit (CR 14)

At first glance, the room resembles a temple of Muir — austere and dignified with clean, white marble columns, altars and statues. Holy runes and glyphs cover the walls. Careful inspection and a DC 15 Knowledge (religion) check reveals subtle defacement of the holy images, vaguely suggesting an evil presence. The room detects as good; however, the dancing priests clearly detect as evil — because they are, in fact, **5 vrocks** dancing their Dance of Ruin, attended by **10 dretches**. They attack immediately.

A PC succeeding on a DC 15 Intelligence check notices that five of the priests are a little too tall to be human, and ten are a little too short. Anyone succeeding on a DC 20 Knowledge (religion) check realizes that the priests' dance is not of any known ritual in the worship of Thyr or Muir. Anyone succeeding on a DC 20 Knowledge (planes) check recognizes the dance as the Dance of Ruin.

VROCKS (5) **CR 9**
XP 6,400
hp 112 (*Pathfinder Roleplaying Game Bestiary* "Demon, Vrock")

Tactics of the Vrocks: When the PCs first enter the amphitheater, the vrocks, disguised as robed priests of Muir, are gathered in a circle dancing around the pit and chanting. They started their dance when the party passed through the hidden entrance, completing it the first round the party is fully within the room — which becomes the first round of combat. If the characters have not yet grown suspicious of the dancing priests, the immediate discharge of crackling evil energy convinces them. Once the Dance of Ruin effect occurs, the vrocks on subsequent rounds cast *mirror image* (round 2) and attempt to *summon* another vrock (round 3), after which three vrocks *teleport* to their selected victims (spellcasters), use their stunning screech ability and attack. If the PCs engage them in combat, the vrocks switch to melee attacks and fight until slain, using stunning screech attacks. All vrocks use their special spores attack every third round as a free action against any targets in range. They *teleport* around the room to maintain their combat advantage. They focus their initial attacks on spellcasters and priests, dodging fighters and *teleporting* away from them. Once the spellcasters are eliminated, the vrocks concentrate on those heroic paladins. PCs killed in the Pit have their souls taken directly to the Abyss where Orcus himself feasts on them. They cannot be retrieved or *raised* without divine intervention, such as by a *miracle* spell, or by a *wish* or *limited wish*.

DRETCHES (10) **CR 2**
XP 600
hp 18 (*Pathfinder Roleplaying Game Bestiary* "Demon, Dretch")

Tactics of the Dretches: Dretches are pathetic, expendable pawns. The vrocks use the dretches to surround and occupy fighters while the vrocks concentrate on spellcasters. Immune to its effects, the dretches use their *stinking cloud* ability. They also use their *darkness* ability, which has no effect on the demons—they see right through it. They distract the fighters, so the vrocks can focus on killing the spellcasters.

The Arrival of the "Celestial": Caanara, the nalfeshnee demon, bides his time at the bottom of the pit (**Area 2** on the map; where Caanara's statistics are detailed). He monitors the battle between the PCs and the demons. If the characters kill three vrocks and it seems likely they will kill the remaining two, Caanara assumes the form of the female celestial of legend and ascends from the pit, bearing the *unholy reaver* (see below). If, however, the PCs are losing the battle, Caanara might interfere, emerging from the pit as "divine intervention." To maintain the charade, give the PCs a chance to defeat several demons, if possible.

Once Caanara ascends from the pit, the room brightens with a blinding, holy light. The demons freeze. Blasting away the mists covering the mouth of the pit, a beautiful, shimmering female figure wearing white robes rises from the pit, as if freed from ages of captivity. She levitates above the pit and holds in her hand a brilliant silver sword, encrusted with gems and inlaid gold and glowing with a holy light.

The vrocks recoil in terror, and the dretches slink away from her holy presence. Though she does not speak, each of the PCs hears a voice, so melodic and otherworldly it is almost painful.

> "May the goddess bless you for freeing me from my captivity," the celestial says. "Many ages ago I built this temple to house the Sword of the Justicars. When I returned to these halls to await the coming of the next grandmaster, hordes of demons and evil priests overcame me, imprisoning me in that pit. Your presence distracted them, allowing me to break free." She turns to the paladin in the party. "To you, great champion, I bestow this mighty weapon. Borne last by the great hero, Karith, and by all Justicar grandmasters before him, you are now chosen to succeed them. Hail to you, Grandmaster! May the lady of virtue bless you! Go forth and use this weapon to bring just retribution to creatures of evil and win glory for our lady's name."

Her great task completed, the celestial disappears in a blinding flash.

The vrocks, party to Caanara's deception, recoil from "her" in pretended fear. The vrocks work to convince the paladin and his party that they have, in fact, won the *Sword of Karith* and can return to the world, carrying with them an *unholy reaver*, thereby despoiling one of the world's more promising paladins. When Caanara "disappears," he really just *teleports* himself to **Area 3**, where he remains. Remember: Caanara has a 23 Intelligence and 22 Wisdom, as well as very high Bluff and Diplomacy skills. Play him as though he really were Muir's female celestial. The party should have no clue that this is a ruse — unless one of their number has *true seeing* (the *true seeing* on the paladin required to find the entrance should have long since worn off), in which case she sees Caanara as he truly is. If thusly discovered, Caanara and any remaining demons *teleport* to **Area 3**.

See the **New Items** at the end of the adventure for more information on the unholy reaver *Entranhumani*.

Once the paladin grasps the *unholy reaver* and Caanara *teleports*, the vrocks make no attempt to engage him, instead resuming their attacks against his companions. They flee from the paladin, acting as through afraid of him. If the paladin attacks them with the *unholy reaver,* it seems to cuts through the vrocks like butter. They pretend to die. They shriek and *teleport* to **Area 3** after they are struck twice by the sword. GMs should make fake rolls to convince PCs that this effect is some special power of the sword.

Conversion: At this point, the GM might choose to have the *unholy reaver* tempt the paladin, suggesting his conversion into an antipaladin (see the *Pathfinder Roleplaying Game Advanced Player's Guide*). The sword tells the PC that if he converts right now to chaotic evil, accepts Orcus as his god and joins with the demons in slaying his companions, he can become an antipaladin at two bonus levels of experience above his current paladin level. In addition, the sword promises the PC demon servants of great power, a suit of *demon armor* and a *+5 heavy steel shield*. If accepted, the sword delivers on these promises, *teleporting* the newly converted villain to a far-off cave where these items are hidden. The PC gains two hezrou servants, which are bound to serve the wielder of the *unholy reaver*. If the PC refuses to convert, the sword casts *forget* on him (no save), removing any memory of the solicitation from the wielder's mind. Of course, attempting this conversion tips off the paladin's player that the sword is not a *holy avenger* and something is amiss. Only attempt this conversion with a trusted roleplayer who will not reveal the sword's secret. GMs should roleplay this scenario away from the main group so that no one else is privy to the discussion. If other players ask questions, suggest that the sword was communicating privately with its new wielder, explaining its powers. Or you could decide to skip this conversion attempt and wait until the paladin leaves with the sword, as detailed below.

Return Visit

At some point in the future, when the PCs return to the Pit of Despair to destroy the *unholy reaver*, they find **3 vrocks** waiting for them, scattered about the room. The vrocks immediately attack the party — teaming up against one victim, *teleporting* next to him, grabbing him and carrying him to the bottom of the pit where all three rip him to pieces. Then they *teleport* out and do it again.

2. The Pit of Despair

With the demons finally destroyed, the mist shrouding the mouth of the pit dissipates. In the well below lies a massive treasure hoard. The pit, 40 feet deep and carved of stone, has no apparent exits.

The First Visit (CR 15)

Initially, the pit is shrouded with mists that serve no purpose save hiding Caanara from view. He lurks in the bottom of the pit, monitoring the battle above. If any PC is crazy enough to jump into the pit during combat, he encounters Caanara, who, if not expecting this action, will be in his original form. (If Caanara suspects a PC might enter the pit before defeating the demons, he changes into his celestial guise before his arrival and pleads with the PC to slay the demons so that "she" might be free and thus bestow the sword on the paladin.) If seen in his normal form, Caanara engages the PC in melee, using his meager skills. If the melee goes poorly, Caanara *teleports* to **Area 3**. Otherwise, Caanara acts as outlined above under "**The Arrival of the 'Celestial**."

CAANARA THE NALFESHNEE **CR 14**
XP 38, 400
hp 203 (Pathfinder Roleplaying Game Bestiary "Demon, Nalfeshnee")

Treasure: 6,200 gp, 36,000 sp, a gold cup set with emeralds worth 7,000 gp, inlaid masterwork harp of silver and elven hair worth 4,000 gp, *amulet of inescapable location* (cursed, identifies as an *amulet of proof against detection and location*), *bracers of defenselessness +5* (cursed, identifies as *+5 bracers of armor*) and a *periapt of foul rotting* (cursed, identifies as a *periapt of health*). Unless a *wish* is used, the cursed nature of the items cannot be detected while the PCs are within the Pit.

Secret Door: The secret door to **Area 3** is very difficult to locate, having been concealed with powerful magic. No magic short of a *wish* or *miracle* allows its detection. A *true seeing* spell does not even allow automatic detection; instead, reduce the Perception DC from 40 to 30. The secret door consists of an entire 40-foot section of the wall. When opened, the door swings upward 90 degrees, triggering a trap — a *symbol of death* inscribed on the reverse side of the door — and sealing the pit's mouth. If you wish, you could require a paladin be under the effects of *prayer* and *true seeing* spells to have a chance to detect the secret door, thus ensuring that the PCs leave the dungeon without finding the secret door on their first visit.

Secret Locked Stone Wall: Perception DC 40 (30 with *true seeing*); 12 in. thick; Hardness 15; hp 80; SR 28; Break DC 40; Disable Device DC 40. A *symbol of death* is inscribed on opposite face of door, revealed when door swings open.

***SYMBOL OF DEATH* TRAP** **CR 10**
XP 9,600
Type magical; **Perception** DC 33; **Disable Device** DC 33

Trigger spell trigger; **Reset** none
Effect spell effect (*symbol of death*, DC 22 Fort negates); multiple targets (up to 150 hp worth of creatures within 60 ft.)

False Ending

If the PCs do not find the secret door, the GM should smile, solicit feedback on how challenging the adventure was and congratulate the players on a job well done. Remark how incredible it was that the PCs defeated 5 vrocks (and possibly a blue dragon) to recover the *Sword of Karith*! Then take a break, quit for the night or start the next adventure. The *unholy reaver* will show its true colors later. Wait until the next playing session before beginning corruption of the paladin. See "**Atonement**," below.

Return Visit

Returning to destroy the *unholy reaver*, the PCs find the Pit of Despair empty. Any treasure left by the party during its previous visit has been moved to **Area 3**.

3. The Altar of Evil and Good

If the PCs find, open and survive the *symbol of death*-trapped secret door, they enter a large room. The secret wall, however, swings up and seals the pit's mouth with a foot-thick lid of stone. The large room houses an evil altar carved from onyx set upon a black dais. Strangely, the onyx, partially transparent, reveals the fabled *Sword of Karith*, pulsing with a holy white light, sealed within the altar.

At this point, the demons re-enter the picture, attacking the PCs en masse. Their sole purpose: preventing retrieval of the *holy avenger*. The forces of darkness include Caanara the nalfeshnee, as many vrocks as survived the initial encounter in **Area 1** above and 2 more vrocks if this is a return trip to the Pit of Despair. The party will also have to contend with the dretches that survived the initial encounter. Unlike before, all demons now concentrate their attacks on whoever wields the *unholy reaver.* They interpose themselves between the PC and the altar, preventing contact at all costs, even *teleporting* out of combat to do so.

During combat (but most likely after combat), the paladin can destroy the altar and *unholy reaver*, thus freeing the *holy avenger*, by striking the altar with the *unholy reaver*. The impact shatters both objects instantly! Destruction of the evil altar and *unholy reaver* nets each PC a 5,000 XP story award in addition to any combat experience.

Tactics of the Vrocks and Dretches: The vrocks act as described above in **Area 1**, except that they all *mirror image*, and then use stunning screech and melee attacks. All vrocks shoot spores every third round as a free action against any targets in range. The dretches surround fighters.

Tactics of Caanara the Nalfeshnee: When encountered in this room — whether by a resourceful party on its first visit to the Pit of Despair or by a party returning to the pit to undo his treachery — Caanara uses all his powers to slay all PCs. As soon as the secret wall is opened, he *summons* 1d4 hezrous (40% chance of success). The next round he casts *slow* at the party, followed by *call lightning* and his unholy nimbus until he is engaged. Once engaged, he *teleports* away and repeats the process until slain, possibly throwing in a *greater dispel magic* or using his unholy nimbus ability as appropriate. He only fights hand-to-hand as a last resort, and even then he uses *feeblemind* rather than his usual attacks. If reduced to less than 30 hit points, Caanara *teleports* to **Area 1** (above the pit, which is now sealed off by the open secret door). Defeating Caanara should be a feat that all of the surviving PCs brag about for years.

Treasure: The *holy avenger, Entrancacor* is inside the stone altar. See the **New Items** at the end of this adventure for more information. The sword can be moved from the altar block either by simultaneously casting a *wish* and a *miracle* spell on the altar or by striking the altar with the *unholy reaver, Entranhumani*, as described above. Doing so shatters the altar and *unholy reaver* and frees the *holy avenger* (the party can't have both!). No other way to remove the sword exists.

Atonement

If the PCs are successfully duped into believing they have recovered the *Sword of Karith*, there is a strong chance that the paladin will fall under the evil sword's sway. The PCs should have no encounters on their return trip. Returning to an area with a large (over 50) population of humans, the PCs might begin to note changes in the sword wielder. The sword waits until a good-sized group of low-level victims are available and, in the presence of few of the paladin's comrades, forces the character into a killing spree! Consider the common room of an inn or tavern, late in the evening after most PCs have retired and the paladin is telling the story of the sword's recovery to some locals, an appropriate venue. Or, more despicably, wait until the paladin visits the local church to pray. The character must succeed on a DC 27 Will save against the sword's ego or fly into a berserk, xenophobic rage (which he cannot willfully come out of), looking for humans to slay, including other PCs who stumble upon the enraged paladin. After the event, the paladin collapses and awakens a few minutes later. In the interim, the sword casts *forget* on the character. Should the PC paladin make the Will save, the *sword* immediately casts *forget* on him (no save) — erasing any memory of the failed attempt to control the PC.

GMs can find this highly entertaining. Imagine a paladin waking amid the gory remains of a dozen townsfolk — his sword bloodied and his paladin abilities no longer working. Any PC paladin succumbing to the will of the sword and committing the above-described atrocities loses his paladin status and cannot continue as a paladin without doing *atonement.* Any PC attempting to rid himself of the sword discovers that it continually *teleports* itself back to him.

The sword, of course, suggests an alternative. After the PC's paladinhood is lost, the sword tempts the paladin into becoming an antipaladin, as described under "**Conversion**," above. The only catch: he must slay all of his good- or lawful-aligned companions.

As GM, decide who might properly suggest *atonement* for such vile deeds. For example, require that the PC return to the priests of Muir from whom he obtained the map to the Temple of the Justicars. There, he can relate the story of the quest and its consequences. After much *prayer* and *communing*, the priests describe what must be done to restore paladinhood: the paladin must destroy the *unholy reaver!* There is only one way for this to be done: it must be smashed upon the altar on which it was forged. That altar, the PCs are informed, is hidden within the Temple of the Justicars, but no one knows exactly where. When this is done — the PCs are promised — not only will the *unholy reaver* be destroyed, but they will also free the true *Sword of Karith.* This act also restores the fallen paladin's status.

Most likely, amid feelings of doubt, hope and regret, the party gears up for a return trip to the Pit of Despair. Plan an appropriate number of wilderness encounters if it travels overland. Perhaps now the PCs might *teleport* to the canyon containing the temple's entrance. Once the PCs arrive at the Pit of Despair for the second time, GMs should refer to the above sections in **Areas 1** and **2** entitled "**Return Visit**" for details on how the Pit of Despair is different the second time around. Who knows? Maybe they will even succeed…

New Items

Entrancacor (Minor Artifact)

Aura strong abjuration; **CL** 20th
Slot none; **Weight** 4 lbs.

DESCRIPTION

Entrancacor is an intelligent *holy avenger*, a *+5 holy cold iron longsword* with the standard abilities of a *holy avenger* in addition to the following: Int 14, Wis 13, Cha 17, Ego 28, AL LG; telepathy; Primary Powers: *dispel*

The sword is only usable by lawful good outsiders, paladins, and clerics of Muir. The sword is insubstantial to all others, though it can cut through them if used against them in combat.

DESTRUCTION

Boil in the blood of three good dragons, killed within the hour, followed by taking the life of a good-aligned virgin with the sword.

Entranhumani (Minor Artifact)

Aura strong necromancy; **CL** 20th
Slot none; **Weight** 4 lbs.

DESCRIPTION

The sword *Entranhumani* is an intelligent *unholy reaver*, a *+5 unholy cold iron longsword*. It has the normal powers of a *holy avenger* in the hands of a paladin or antipaladin plus the following: Int 14, Wis 13, Cha 17, Ego 27, AL CE; no save,continuous G, DC 22 Will savely Short of a *miracle* or *wish*, the sword detects as a *holy avenger*.

The sword is only usable by paladins and antipaladins. The sword is insubstantial to all others; they cannot grasp it, though it cuts through them when used against them as a weapon. Note that this sword does no damage to demons unless wielded by an antipaladin!

DESTRUCTION

It must be shattered against the altar on which it was forged, as long as that altar contains a holy avenger (the players cannot have both!).

Rescued from Oblivion: The Original Demons and Devils

The revision of the rules for Our Favorite Game over 10 years ago brought us demons and devils that were much more powerful and dangerous than they were in the previous edition. In light of the new Pathfinder Roleplaying Game edition, **Frog God Games** is proud to present to you the **Lesser Demons and Devils**.

We went back to the first version of the d20 rules and salvaged those earlier versions of the demons and devils to bring them back to the game. Only those demons and devils that saw a drastic change in CR, HD, or abilities are re-introduced here as the "lesser" kin. We've updated them in such a way that they harken back to those earlier versions, but we've also scaled them to a degree that they "fit" within a hierarchy with their more powerful counterparts. Finally, we gave them new names to secure their own places in the existing hierarchy of demons and devils.

Demons

Boar Demon

A massive, boar-like head with fearsome tusks tops this demonic creature's bloated form. Two small bat-like wings sprout from its back, and its hands are tipped with sharp claws.

BOAR DEMON (LESSER NALFESHNEE) CR 10
XP 9,600
LE Huge outsider (chaotic, demon, evil, extraplanar)
Init +5; **Senses** darkvision 60 ft., *see invisibility*; **Perception** +28

AC 25, touch 9, flat-footed 24 (+1 Dex, +16 natural, –2 size)
hp 104 (11d10+44)
Fort +11; **Ref** +4; **Will** +15
DR 10/good; **Immune** electricity, poison; **Resist** acid 10, cold 10, fire 10; **SR** 21

Speed 30 ft., fly 40 ft. (poor)
Melee bite +15 (2d4+6/19–20), 2 claws +15 (1d4+6)
Space 10 ft.; **Reach** 10 ft.
Special Attacks unholy nimbus
Spell-like Abilities (CL 12th):
Constant—*see invisibility*
At will—*call lightning* (DC 16), *feeblemind* (DC 18), *greater dispel magic*, *slow* (DC 16), *greater teleport* (self plus 50 lbs. of objects only)
1/day—summon (level 5, 1 boar demon 20%, 1d4 vrocks 40%, or 1d4 nabasus 50%)

Str 23, **Dex** 13, **Con** 19, **Int** 22, **Wis** 22, **Cha** 16
Base Atk +11; **CMB** +18; **CMD** 29
Feats Cleave, Improved Bull Rush, Improved Critical (bite), Improved Initiative, Iron Will, Power Attack
Skills Bluff +17, Diplomacy +17, Fly +7, Intimidate +14, Knowledge (arcana) +20, Knowledge (planes) +20, Knowledge (any one other) +17, Perception +28, Sense Motive +20, Spellcraft +20, Stealth +7, Use Magic Device +17; **Racial Modifiers** +8 Perception
Languages Abyssal, Celestial, Draconic; telepathy 100 ft.

Environment any lawful evil aligned plane
Organization solitary or troupe (1 boar demon, 1 vrock, and 2–5 nabasus)
Treasure standard

Unholy Nimbus (Su) Three times per day as a free action a boar demon can create a nimbus of unholy light, causing nauseating beams of writhing color to play around its body. One round later, the light bursts in a 60-foot radius. Any non-demon creature caught within this area must succeed on a DC 18 Will save or be dazed for 1d10 rounds as visions of madness hound it. The save DC is Charisma-based.

Grossly obese and greedy for power, the boar demons are servile towards their masters, the nalfeshnees, but haughty and arrogant when dealing with other demons. Boar demons often indulge their desires to advance the cause of the Abyss, sometimes even against the wishes of their masters, hoping to gain the approval of some demon lord for its own personal gain. A boar demon is not above back-stabbing its master if such an act suits its purpose.

Dark Daughter

This demonic creature resembles a beautiful humanoid female with six slender arms, each bearing a longsword. Her lower torso tapers to a long, snake-like tail.

DARK DAUGHTER (LESSER MARILITH) CR 11
XP 12,800
CE Large outsider (chaotic, demon, evil, extraplanar)
Init +2; **Senses** darkvision 60 ft., *true seeing*; **Perception** +24

AC 26, touch 11, flat-footed 24 (+2 Dex, +15 natural, –1 size)
hp 94 (9d10+45)
Fort +11; **Ref** +8; **Will** +7
DR 10/good and cold iron; **Immune** electricity, poison; **Resist** acid 10, cold 10, and fire 10; **SR** 22

Speed 40 ft.
Melee longsword +14/+9 (2d6+5/17–20), 5 longswords +14 (2d6+5/17–20), tail slap +8 (1d8+2 plus grab) or 6 slams +13 (1d6+5), tail slap +8 (1d8+2 plus grab)
Space 10 ft.; **Reach** 10 ft.
Special Attacks constrict 1d8+2, multiweapon mastery
Spell-like Abilities (CL 13th):
Constant—*true seeing*
At will—*greater teleport* (self plus 50 lbs. of objects only), *project image* (DC 20), *telekinesis* (DC 18)
3/day—*blade barrier* (DC 19), *fly*, *unholy blight* (DC 17; replaced with *unholy aura* when the dark daughter advances to a full-fledged marilith)
1/day—summon (level 5, 1 hezrou 20%, or 1d4 dark daughters at 60%)

Str 21, **Dex** 15, **Con** 21, **Int** 18, **Wis** 18, **Cha** 17
Base Atk +9; **CMB** +15; **CMD** 27
Feats Combat Expertise, Combat Reflexes, Improved Critical (longsword), Power Attack, Weapon Focus (longsword)
Skills Acrobatics +14, Bluff +15, Diplomacy +15, Fly +16, Intimidate +15, Knowledge (engineering) +13, Perception +24, Sense Motive +16, Stealth +10, Use Magic Device +15; **Racial Modifiers** +8 Perception
Languages Abyssal, Celestial, Draconic; telepathy 100 ft.

Environment any chaotic evil aligned plane
Organization solitary or pair
Treasure standard

Multiweapon Mastery (Ex) A dark daughter never takes penalties to her attack roll when fighting with multiple weapons.

Dark daughters are the "younger sisters" of the marilith demons in the armies of the Outer Planes. They are mariliths that have yet to prove themselves worthy of servitude in the ranks of the demon lords. A dark daughter resembles her greater sisters, but her arms are more slender and she is not as hardy. Her lower rank and weaker powers make a dark daughter more subservient and more eager to follow orders in the hopes that her service will result in some later boon.

Balorog

This is a hulking brute of a demon, wreathed in flames and bearing huge smoky wings.

BALOROG (LESSER BALOR) **CR 13**
XP 25,600
CE Large outsider (chaotic, demon, evil, extraplanar)
Init +5; **Senses** darkvision 60 ft., *true seeing*; **Perception** +27
Aura flaming body

AC 26, touch 10, flat-footed 25 (+1 Dex, +16 natural, –1 size)
hp 123 (13d10+52)
Fort +12; **Ref** +5; **Will** +13
DR 15/cold iron and good; **Immune** electricity, fire, and poison; **Resist** acid 10, cold 10; **SR** 24

Speed 40 ft., fly 90 ft. (good)
Melee *vorpal longsword* +21/+16/+11 (1d8+8/19–20) or *vorpal longsword* +19/+14/+9 (1d8+8/19–20), whip +17 (1d4+3 plus entangle) or 2 slams +19 (1d6+7),
Space 10 ft.; **Reach** 10 ft. (15 ft. with whip)
Spell-Like Abilities (CL 20th):
Constant—*true seeing, unholy aura* (DC 22)
At will—*dominate monster* (DC 23), *greater dispel magic, greater teleport* (self plus 50 lbs. of objects only), *power word stun, telekinesis* (DC 19)
3/day—quickened *telekinesis* (DC 19)
1/day—*blasphemy* (DC 21), *fire storm* (DC 22), *implosion* (DC 23), summon (level 9, any 1 CR 12 or lower demon 100%)

Str 25, **Dex** 13, **Con** 19, **Int** 20, **Wis** 20, **Cha** 19
Base Atk +13; **CMB** +21 ; **CMD** 32
Feats Cleave, Combat Reflexes, Improved Initiative, Power Attack, Quicken Spell-Like Ability (*telekinesis*), Two-Weapon Fighting, Weapon Focus (longsword)
Skills Acrobatics +12, Bluff +18, Diplomacy +18, Fly +17, Intimidate +18, Knowledge (history) +16, Knowledge (nobility) +16, Knowledge (planes) +19, Knowledge (religion) +16, Perception +27, Sense Motive +19, Stealth +11 Use Magic Device +18 ; **Racial Modifiers** +8 Perception
Languages Abyssal, Celestial, Draconic; telepathy 100 ft.
SQ death throes, whip mastery

Environment any chaotic evil aligned plane
Organization solitary or troupe (1 balorog, 1 dark daughter, and 2–5 hezrous)
Treasure standard plus *+1 vorpal longsword*

Death Throes (Su) When killed, a balorog explodes in a blinding flash of fire that deals 50 points of damage (half fire, half unholy damage) to anything within 100 feet (Reflex DC 20 halves). The save DC is Constitution-based.
Entangle (Ex) If a balorog strikes a Medium or smaller foe with its whip, the balorog can immediately attempt a grapple check without provoking an attack of opportunity. If the balorog wins the check, it draws the foe into an adjacent square. The foe gains the grappled condition, but the balorog does not.
Flaming Body (Su) A balorog's body is covered in dancing flames. Anyone striking a balorog with a natural weapon or unarmed strike takes 1d6 points of fire damage. A creature that grapples a balorog or is grappled by one takes 4d6 points of fire damage each round the grapple persists.
Vorpal Sword (Su): Every balorog carries a *+1 vorpal greatsword*. The sword also has the spell-like ability to *detect good* as cast by a 12th-level sorcerer, except that its range is 30 feet.
Whip Mastery (Ex) A balorog treats a whip as a light weapon for the purposes of two-weapon fighting, and can inflict lethal damage on a foe regardless of the foe's armor.

Millennia ago, there were entire armies of balorogs in the Outer Planes. Recent wars between rival demon lords have severely decreased their numbers, however. These lesser kin of the mighty balor demons fight with a vorpal longsword in one hand and a mighty whip in the other.

Devils

Skull Devil

This devil is an emaciated, humanoid creature with a leering, skeletal face and a wide mouth filled with sharp teeth. A thin, scorpion-like tail arcs up over its head. Clutched in its bony hands is a wicked-looking barbed hook.

SKULL DEVIL (LESSER BONE DEVIL) **CR 6**
XP 2,400
LE Large outsider (devil, evil, extraplanar, lawful)
Init +4; **Senses** darkvision 60 ft., see in darkness; **Perception** +12
Aura fear aura (5 ft., DC 14, 1d6 rounds)

AC 17, touch 9, flat-footed 17 (+8 natural, –1 size)
hp 37 (5d10+10)
Fort +6; **Ref** +4; **Will** +3
DR 5/good; **Immune** fire, poison; **Resist** acid 10, cold 10; **SR** 17

Speed 40 ft.
Melee bite +9 (1d8+5), 2 claws +9 (1d4+5), sting +9 (3d4+5 plus poison) or hook +9 (1d3+5 plus entangle), sting +9 (3d4+5 plus poison)
Space 10 ft.; **Reach** 10 ft.
Special Attacks poison
Spell-like Abilities (CL 12th):
Constant—*fly*
At will—*dimensional anchor, greater teleport* (self plus 50 lbs. of objects only), *invisibility* (self only), *major image* (DC 15), *wall of ice*
3/day—quickened *invisibility* (self only)
1/day—summon (level 4, 1 skull devil, 35%)

Str 21, **Dex** 10, **Con** 15, **Int** 14, **Wis** 14, **Cha** 14
Base Atk +5; **CMB** +11 ; **CMD** 21
Feats Alertness, Improved Initiative, Quicken Spell-Like Ability (*invisibility*)
Skills Bluff +9, Diplomacy +9, Fly +9, Intimidate +10, Knowledge (planes) +9, Perception +12, Sense Motive +12, Spellcraft +9, Stealth +4
Languages Celestial, Common, Draconic, Infernal; telepathy 100 ft.

Environment any lawful evil aligned plane
Organization solitary, team (2–4), or squad (6–10)
Treasure standard plus skull devil hook

Hook (Ex): A skull devil can employ its hook to entangle

opponents of Large size or smaller. The hook has hardness 10, hp 10, Break DC 25.
Poison (Ex) Sting—injury; *save* Fort DC 14 ; *frequency* 1/round for 6 rounds; *effect* 1d3 Str damage; *cure* 2 consecutive saves. The save DC is Constitution-based.

If bone devils are the police and informers of the devil lords, then the skull devils are the rank-and-file snitches. A skull devil is a sycophantic, sniveling creature that exists only to please its masters. Skull devils are shorter than bone devils, standing only about 7 feet tall.

A skull devil fights with a large hook. A skull devil hook has an auto-locking, ratcheting joint midway along the shaft; one end of the hook has a spearhead, and the other has a curved barb like a fish hook. The favored tactic of a skull devil is to entangle an opponent in its hook and sting it repeatedly.

Spiked Devil

Spikes and spines of all sizes sprout from this demon's body, from the top of its pointed head to the tips of its clawed toes.

SPIKED DEVIL (LESSER HAMATULA) CR 6
XP 2,400
LE Medium outsider (devil, evil, extraplanar, lawful)
Init +0; **Senses** darkvision 60 ft., see in darkness; **Perception** +16

AC 20, touch 10, flat-footed 20 (+10 natural)
hp 58 (9d10+9)
Fort +7 ; **Ref** +6 ; **Will** +7 **Defensive Abilities** spiked defense; **DR** 5/good; **Immune** fire, poison; **Resist** acid 10, cold 10; **SR** 17

Speed 30 ft.
Melee 2 claws +12 (2d4+3 plus fear and grab)
Special Attacks fear, impale 3d4+4
Spell-like Abilities (CL 9th):
At will—*greater teleport* (self plus 50 lbs. of objects only), *hold person* (DC 15), *major image* (DC 15), *produce flame, pyrotechnics* (DC 16), *scorching ray* (2 rays only)
1/day—*order's wrath* (DC 16), summon (level 4, 1 spiked devil 35%), *unholy blight* (DC 16)

Str 17, **Dex** 11, **Con** 13, **Int** 12, **Wis** 14, **Cha** 14
Base Atk +9; **CMB** +12 (+16 to grapple); **CMD** 22
Feats Alertness, Cleave, Combat Reflexes, Iron Will, Power Attack
Skills Acrobatics +9, Diplomacy +8, Intimidate +14, Knowledge (planes) +10, Perception +16, Sense Motive +16, Spellcraft +12, Stealth +7, Survival +11
Languages Celestial, Common, Draconic, Infernal; telepathy 100 ft.

Environment any lawful evil aligned plane
Organization solitary, team (2–4), or squad (6–10)
Treasure standard

Fear (Su) A spiked devil's fear attack affects any creature it damages with its claws. A DC 16 Will save resists this effect, otherwise the victim becomes frightened for 1d4 rounds. This is a mind-affecting fear effect. The save DC is Charisma-based.
Grab (Ex) A spiked devil can use its grab attack against a foe of up to Medium size.
Impale (Ex) A spiked devil deals 3d4+4 points of piercing damage to a grabbed opponent with a successful grapple check.
Spiked Defense (Su) A creature that strikes a spiked demon with a melee weapon, an unarmed strike, or a natural weapon takes 1d8+3 points of piercing damage from the devil's spikes. Melee weapons with reach do not endanger a user in this way.

Assistants to the jailers of Hell, the spiked devils are cruel, sadistic creatures that take pleasure in torturing their prisoners. They are eager to please their immediate masters, the barbed devils, and constantly jockey for position in the hierarchy of their kind.

Whip Devil

This devil is lean but muscular, with great fiery wings and two curling horns on its head.

WHIP DEVIL (LESSER CORNUGON) CR 10
XP 9,600
LE large outsider (devil, evil, extraplanar, lawful)
Init +1; **Senses** darkvision 60 ft., see in darkness; **Perception** +16
Aura fear (5 ft., DC 17)

AC 25, touch 10, flat-footed 24 (+1 Dex, +15 natural, –1 size)
hp 93 (11d10+33); regeneration 5 (good weapons, good spells)
Fort +10; **Ref** +8; **Will** +7
DR 10/good and silver; **Immune** fire, poison; **Resist** acid 10, cold 10; **SR** 21

Speed 20 ft., fly 50 ft. (average)
Melee whip +16/+12/+6 (1d6+5 plus stun), bite +15 (1d4+5), tail +13 (1d3+2 plus wound) or 2 claws +15 (1d4+5), bite +15 (1d4+5), tail +13 (1d3+2 plus wound)
Space 10 ft.; **Reach** 10 ft.
Special Attacks infernal wound, stun
Spell-like Abilities (CL 12th):
At will—*dispel chaos* (DC 13), *dispel good* (DC 13), *magic circle against good, greater teleport* (self plus 50 lbs. of objects only), *persistent image* (DC 17)
3/day—*fireball* (DC 15), *lightning bolt* (DC 15)
1/day—summon (level 6, 3 bearded devils, 35%)

Str 21, **Dex** 12, **Con** 17, **Int** 14, **Wis** 14, **Cha** 15
Base Atk +11; **CMB** +17 ; **CMD** 28
Feats Improved Sunder, Iron Will, Multiattack, Power Attack, Vital Strike, Weapon Focus (whip)
Skills Bluff +16, Diplomacy +13, Intimidate +16, Knowledge (planes) +16, Perception +16, Sense Motive +16, Spellcraft +16, Stealth +10
Languages Celestial, Common, Draconic, Infernal; telepathy 100 ft.

Environment any lawful evil aligned plane
Organization solitary, team (2–4), or squad (6–10)
Treasure standard

Infernal Wound (Su) The damage a whip devil deals with its tail causes persistent wounds that deal 2 points of bleed damage. Bleeding caused in this way is difficult to staunch—a DC 18 Heal check stops the damage, and any attempt to heal a creature suffering from an infernal wound must succeed on a DC 18 caster level check or the spell does not function. Success indicates the healing works normally and stops all bleed effects.
Stun (Su) Whenever a whip devil hits with a whip attack, the opponent must succeed on a DC 20 Fortitude save or be stunned for 1d4 rounds. This ability is a function of the whip devil, not of the whip. The save DC is Strength-based.

Whip devils are infamous for their cruelty and sadistic tendencies. Like its more powerful masters, the horned devils, a whip devil is a strong creature that derives immense pleasure from causing pain—especially if it can use its whip to do so.

A whip devil fights primarily with its namesake weapon, a cruel barbed whip woven of some unknown infernal fibers. In melee, a whip devil never asks or gives any quarter, and fights until either it or its foe has been destroyed.

Winged Devil

This crimson-skinned devil is powerfully-built with bulging arms and legs and a mouth full of lethal fangs. Two massive wings drape from its back.

WINGED DEVIL (LESSER PIT FIEND) CR 13
XP 25,600
LE Large outsider (devil, evil, extraplanar, lawful)
Init +5; **Senses** darkvision 60 ft., see in darkness; **Perception** +17
Aura fear (20 ft., DC 19)

AC 30, touch 10, flat-footed 30 (+1 Dex, +20 natural, –1 size)
hp 136 (13d10+65); regeneration 5 (good weapons, good spells)
Fort +13; **Ref** +9; **Will** +11
DR 10/good and silver; **Immune** fire, poison; **Resist** acid 10, cold 10; **SR** 24

Speed 40 ft., fly 60 ft. (average)
Melee 2 claws +19 (1d6+7), 2 wings +17 (1d4+3), bite +19 (2d6+7 plus poison plus disease), tail slap +17 (2d4+3 plus grab)
Space 10 ft.; **Reach** 10 ft.
Special Attacks constrict 2d4+10
Spell-like Abilities (CL 13th):
At will—*blasphemy* (DC 20), *create undead, fireball* (DC 16), *greater dispel magic, greater teleport* (self plus 50 lbs. of objects only), *greater scrying* (DC 20), *invisibility, magic circle against good, hold monster* (DC 18; replaced with *mass hold monster* when the winged devil becomes a full-fledged pit fiend), *persistent image* (DC 18), *power word blind* (replaced with *power word stun* when the winged devil becomes a pit fiend), *scorching ray, unholy blight* (DC 17; replaced with *unholy aura* when the winged evil becomes a pit fiend), *wall of fire*
3/day—quickened *fireball* (DC 16)
1/day—summon (level 9, any 1 CR 12 or lower devil, 100%)

Str 25, **Dex** 13, **Con** 21, **Int** 20, **Wis** 20, **Cha** 17
Base Atk +13; **CMB** +21 (+25 to grapple ; **CMD** 32
Feats Cleave, Great Cleave, Improved Initiative, Iron Will, Multiattack, Power Attack, Quicken Spell-Like Ability (*fireball*)
Skills Appraisal +12, Bluff +19, Diplomacy +15, Disguise +12, Fly +11, Intimidate +19, Knowledge (arcana) +14, Knowledge (planes) +17, Knowledge (religion) +14, Perception +17, Sense Motive +17, Spellcraft +17, Stealth +9, Survival +14, Use Magic Device +15
Languages Celestial, Common, Draconic, Infernal; telepathy 100 ft.

Environment any lawful evil aligned plane
Organization solitary, team (2–4), or troupe (1–2 winged fiends, 2–5 whip devils, and 2–5 barbed devils)
Treasure standard

Disease (Su) *Devil Chills*: Bite—injury; *save* Fort DC 21 ; *onset* immediate; *frequency* 1/day; *effect* 1d4 Str damage; *cure* 3 consecutive saves. The save DC is Constitution-based.
Poison (Ex) Bite—injury; *save* Fort DC 21 ; *frequency* 1/round for 10 rounds; *effect* 1d6 Con damage; *cure* 3 consecutive saves. The save DC is Constitution-based.

Winged fiends are the sub-commanders of the armies of the Outer Planes. A winged fiend can often be found in the direct service of a pit fiend, either as a lieutenant, advisor, or common knee-breaker.

Winged fiends are every bit as resourceful and wily as their masters, and spare no expense in combat. If it is ordered to fight by a pit fiend, then fight it will, using every attack it its disposal to win the battle.

Giants & Dragons

The Dead from Above

By Michael Curtis

The Dead from Above is intended for use with four to six player characters of levels 10th to 13th. It likely takes two game sessions to complete. The adventure is set in (and above) a hilly region at the outskirts of civilization, presumably one near the base of a mountain chain. With a little work, the GM can place ***The Dead from Above*** wherever he or she desires in the campaign world. In the ***Lost Lands*** campaign setting, the adventure is set on the eastern border of Cerediun Province in southern Akados. It is situated in the foothills of the Scar-in-the-Sky Peaks in and around the village of Tagril near the headwaters of the River Sess. If you use the first option for introducing the PCs to the adventure, then it begins in the provincial capital of Trebes, some 100 miles northwest of Tagril.

Background

For centuries, the forbidding Scar-in-the-Sky Peaks were the demesne of the Stormbreaker Clan, a family of evil cloud giants. These giants long ago turned their backs on the path of righteousness and embraced the worship of the evil god Drahltuz, practicing dread arts and conducting foul rites in his honor. Despite their wicked ways, the Stormbreakers seldom troubled those dwelling outside the mountain region. They were content to remain in their high aeries and hold dominion over the lesser races that dwelled among the peaks.

In recent decades, however, the boundaries of mankind pushed closer to the mountains as civilization continued its march into the frontier. Many small villages arose in the foothills of the mountains, their growth spurred by discoveries of veins of precious ore and other resources. The Stormbreakers see this incursion into their ancient holdings as an infestation of lesser vermin that needs exterminating.

The cloud giants banded together with a tribe of hill giants led by mentally gifted necromancers and clerics to work an act of black magic and blasphemous ritual. First, they scoured the jagged mountains for the hidden burial grounds of their giant kin and great wyrms, prying the yellowed bones of dead titans from the earth and carting them back to their high peaks. The Stormbreakers called upon a long-forgotten ritual to tear the top from a mountain, transforming it into a floating island adrift on the winds. The collected bones were then used to build a mighty citadel on the broken peak, formed into a gleaming structure the giant necromancers dubbed "the Ossuary." This magical holdfast would serve as their engine of vengeance against the encroaching wave of mankind.

The Stormbreakers stocked the floating keep with the supplies their campaign required: rotting corpses of giants and dragons plundered from the secret cemeteries; reagents and concoctions of darkest magic; and as many of their blasphemous kin as the Ossuary would hold. They then departed the mountains, drifting down over the lands of mankind with hatred in their eyes.

The first villages had no inkling of the doom that awaited them. As the residents went about their business, the sun was suddenly blocked out by the floating Ossuary. The villagers watched in horror as giant zombies, the animated remains of the bodies unearthed in the graveyards, dropped down upon their settlement, destroying buildings and murdering the inhabitants. The Stormbreakers' chosen means of conveying their message that humanity was not welcome in the mountains was terrifyingly effective.

The giant necromancers are continuing their campaign of bombardment and destruction, intent on driving every last human out of the hills. Word of the attacks is spreading out of the hills and measures are being implemented to stop this terror before every town and village in the kingdom suffers from its predation. At this point, the adventurers become embroiled in the scheme to end the Stormbreakers' war on humankind.

Starting the Adventure

The GM can introduce ***The Dead from Above*** in one of two ways. The first is to have the party approached by local authorities to deal with the problem. This gives the characters a chance to prepare and plan their course of action. The second method is to thrust the adventure on them without warning, dropping the adventure — literally — onto the party! This section covers both possibilities.

Method 1: Hired Troubleshooters

This method works well if the characters are established adventurers in the region and have a reputation for thwarting evil. If they've done contract adventuring for local authority figures in the past, so much the better.

The party is approached by a representative of the lord-governor of Cerediun Province who informs them that a terrible evil is destroying the province's holdings in the eastern mountains. The Crown's provincial administrator is hiring brave adventurers to root out and destroy this evil before the death toll grows larger. In return, the lord-governor is offering a reward of 1,000 gp in gemstones (or other appropriate payment as the GM sees fit).

The agent knows the following information and freely presents it to the party:

A floating keep fashioned from bones and constructed in the shape of a rough humanoid skull appeared over outlying villages in the past week. Wherever it appears, it brings destruction and terror.

The occupants of the bony fortress have never been seen, but their attacks are terrifying and effective. Animated undead in the form of giant zombies and skeletal dragons are launched from the aerial holdfast onto the settlements below. These animated undead cause wholesale destruction, both by landing atop buildings and by tearing apart the villages' buildings and inhabitants.

Adding insult to injury, a flight of wyverns appears to be following the floating fortress like scavengers, feasting upon the dead and dying left in the wake of the attacks. It's not known whether they're allied with the fortress's inhabitants or are just taking tactical advantage of an opportunity.

The fortress has never been seen to touch down on the ground, making it impossible to lay siege to. Daring adventurers are needed to infiltrate the keep, identify who is responsible for the attacks, and end the threat before more lives are lost and more villages are destroyed.

If the party has its own means of flying (spells, magical items, etc.), the characters should be able to begin the adventure without difficulty, traveling to the western foothills and seeking out the Ossuary. Proceed to "The Wyvern Attack" below.

If the characters lack the means to take to the air, the lord-governor can assist them. The Crown's holdings in Cerediun includes a small stable of griffons, complete with trained handlers. The lord-governor loans the use of his flying mounts, along with their guides, to the party to aid their search and assault on the aerial fortress. He stresses that the mounts and their handlers should only help locate the holdfast and land the party on it, but shall not engage in battle other than in self-defense. Once the characters are in place, the griffons are to retreat to a safe distance until the party calls them back with a prearranged signal. The flying mounts are too valuable to risk in battle and, should the party fail, they'll be needed for subsequent attacks on the keep.

Method 2: The Call to Adventure Comes from Above (CR 10)

This option plunges the party directly into the events of the adventure without warning, forcing them to think fast and respond to an unexpected threat. It also provides a way to get a party without the means of magical flight up to the Ossuary to complete the adventure. Although this method is the author's preferred means of starting ***The Dead from Above***, some gaming groups respond poorly to being dragged into an adventure this way. You must determine how your players would react to this sudden immersion in events and whether it's right for your group.

The adventure begins while the party is engaged in mundane business in the small village of Tagril in the hilly region along the eastern border of Orediun Province. The adventurers might be resting overnight as part of a prolonged journey or they have arrived at the village for other reasons (seeking out the services of a local weapon smith, sage, wizard, etc.), or they might be following up rumors of a lost dungeon in the hills. It's ideal if you can seed rumors about recent attacks on nearby villages into whatever adventure the characters were on just before this one, but that isn't strictly necessary to begin the adventure. At some point during the day while the characters are inside a building, the Ossuary drifts over the village, having chosen it as the next target in its campaign of evil. Read the following:

> A tremendous crash echoes from outside, accompanied by an earthshaking tremor and the sound of screams. A moment later, the foul scent of decomposition and death washes over you. Villagers rush past the open doorway, obviously fleeing for their lives.
>
> As you emerge outside, you are confronted by a startling vista. A building lies in ruins, a tangle of shattered timbers and scattered thatching. Rising from the ruin is the walking, rotted corpse of a dead giant. The massive zombie has many broken bones, and cracked rafters protrude from its putrefying flesh. The creature must have plummeted from above!
>
> Looking skyward, you see other horrors overhead. The skeletal form of a dragon swoops about on tattered wings, its eyes burning like corpse candles. A network of glowing strands is interlaced throughout its bony form, twitching and vibrating as it soars above you. Floating directly above the village is what appears to be the top of a mountain, somehow sheared off its base and set adrift. A building fashioned from titanic bones rests atop the stony platform. As you watch, another immense figure steps from the edge of the drifting stone and plummets to earth, smashing a second building to flinders.

The village of Tagril is in chaos as residents flee in terror. The shock and awe of undead giants dropping atop them breaks their morale, and even the few armed militia panic and run. The heroes find themselves alone, facing three undead threats.

The first **stone giant zombie** strides toward the party to attack while the **red skeletal dragon** swoops down on them. The second **stone giant zombie** smashes into the ground, and it takes one round for the corpse to climb to its feet and another round to extract itself from the wreckage of the building.

STONE GIANT ZOMBIES (2) CR 6
XP 2,400
Pathfinder Roleplaying Game Bestiary, "Giant, Stone," "Zombie"
NE Large undead
Init +1; **Senses** darkvision 60 ft.; **Perception** +0

AC 24, touch 10, flat-footed 23 (+1 Dex, +14 natural, –1 size)
hp 77 (14d8+14)
Fort +4; **Ref** +5; **Will** +9
DR 5/slashing; **Immune** undead traits

Speed 40 ft.
Melee 2 slams +13 (1d8+9)
Space 10 ft.; **Reach** 10 ft.

Str 29, **Dex** 13, **Con** —, **Int** —, **Wis** 10, **Cha** 10
Base Atk +10; **CMB** +20; **CMD** 31
Feats Toughness[B]
SQ staggered

RED DRAGON SKELETON CR 7
XP 3,200
Pathfinder Roleplaying Game Bestiary, "Dragon, Red," "Skeleton"
NE Huge undead
Init +5; **Senses** darkvision 60 ft.; **Perception** +0

AC 12, touch 9, flat-footed 11 (+1 Dex, +3 natural, –2 size)
hp 67 (15d8)
Fort +5; **Ref** +6; **Will** +9
DR 5/bludgeoning; **Immune** cold, undead traits

Speed 40 ft., fly 60 ft. (clumsy)
Melee bite +18 (2d8+13), 2 claws +18 (2d6+9), tail slap +13 (2d6+13)
Space 15 ft.; **Reach** 10 ft.

Str 29, **Dex** 12, **Con** —, **Int** —, **Wis** 10, **Cha** 10
Base Atk +11; **CMB** +22; **CMD** 33 (37 vs. trip)
Feats Improved Initiative[B]

Flight (Su) Although it is a skeleton, this dragon can still fly thanks to a unique array of magical veins and cables (see **Aloft on Dead Wings**, below).

The stone giants have only one-half their normal hit points due to the damage suffered in their drop from the floating citadel. All three undead attack until destroyed. As the combat rages, the Ossuary slowly flies off, its objective complete. When the skeletal dragon is reduced to zero hit points, it collapses, its bony body emitting a pulsating, greenish glow for several minutes.

Reaching the Ossuary

Once the battle is over, villagers return to Tagril, praising the party for their valor. If the party is unaware of the recent attacks, the villagers inform them that this assault was just the latest in a series of similar abrupt bombardments of settlements in the area and that the local ruler is offering a 1,000 gp reward to whoever ends the attacks. The locals know all the details of the attacks as documented in Method 1 above. This should inspire the party to investigate the Ossuary and stop its menace. If not, the villagers plead with the characters to take the fight to the strange keep and avenge the deaths of the locals who died in the attack.

If the adventurers lack a means of flying in pursuit of the Ossuary, one possibility lies nearby. If characters investigate the still-glowing form of the battered but still relatively intact dragon, they discover the web of control veins laced throughout its body. If characters avoid the dragon or simply ignore it, some of the village children climb onto it and their curiosity impels them to start yanking cords, making the dragon's form respond to their plucking.

Aloft on Dead Wings

An examination of the skeletal dragon reveals a network of long, vein-like cables running throughout the interior of the dragon. This web of cables extends from the skull to the wings, legs, and tail, forming a skein of thick cords. The veins glow softly with a corpselike green color. Pulling on one of the veins causes the great skeletal beast to shudder as it responds to the tugging. One cord causes its wing to unfurl, another tucks in a skeletal leg, etc. A successful DC 10 Heal check identifies which veins connect to what portion of the dragon. A successful DC 10 Knowledge (arcana) check suggests that, if two heroes worked in concert, it'd be possible to make the skeletal dragon take flight once more — perhaps a useful way to pursue a certain drifting Ossuary!

With about an hour's worth of trial and error, two or more adventurers can get the dragon aloft, but it quickly becomes apparent that the magic holding the dragon together and empowering the vein network is slowly failing. A successful DC 15 Knowledge (arcana) check estimates the dragon has less than a day remaining in its useful life. If the party wishes to pursue the Ossuary, they need to go now.

So long as one or more characters succeeds in the Heal check and two heroes spend an hour practicing getting the dragon to fly, the skeletal craft takes to the air without problem, and can pursue the Ossuary.

The Wyvern Attack (CR 8)

Regardless of which method you use to introduce the adventure, the characters should ultimately close in on the Ossuary's location. If the heroes were hired by the local authority to seek out the fortress, a day or two of searching the skies above the hills (and surviving whatever random encounters you wish to add) locates the aerial keep flying through the sky in the distance. If the characters pursued the Ossuary after surviving the

Flying a Skeletal Dragon

The dragon can hold six Medium creatures, with up to three inside the dragon and another three riding atop it. Two Small creatures count as one Medium passenger. The two "pilots" (the characters tugging the skein to keep the dragon aloft) must be inside the dragon, nestled within its ribcage.

The dragon flies at a speed of 100 feet per round. It can move 20 feet per round on the ground, but it's ungainly. Making the dragon fly in a relatively straight line is easy with some practice, but if the pilots try to perform more intricate maneuvers (banking to attack the wyverns in the next encounter, for example), a DC 10 Dexterity check is required. The two adventurers piloting the dragon each make a roll. If both succeed, the dragon moves as they desire. If one or both fail the check, the dragon continues on its present course.

The pilots can also cause the skeletal dragon to bite an opponent. Doing so requires a standard action by one of the two pilots and an attack roll adding only the character's base attack bonus. The result of the check is used as the bite attack roll. The bite inflicts 2d8+13 points of damage on a successful hit. Note that the dragon cannot maneuver and attack in the same round, because both pilots are required to work in concert to move the dragon in anything other than a straight line.

Landing the dragon requires a DC 10 Dexterity check as if the pilots were maneuvering the skeleton. If one or both pilots fail the check, all aboard must succeed on a DC 12 Reflex save or take 2d6 points of bludgeoning damage as the dragon lands hard.

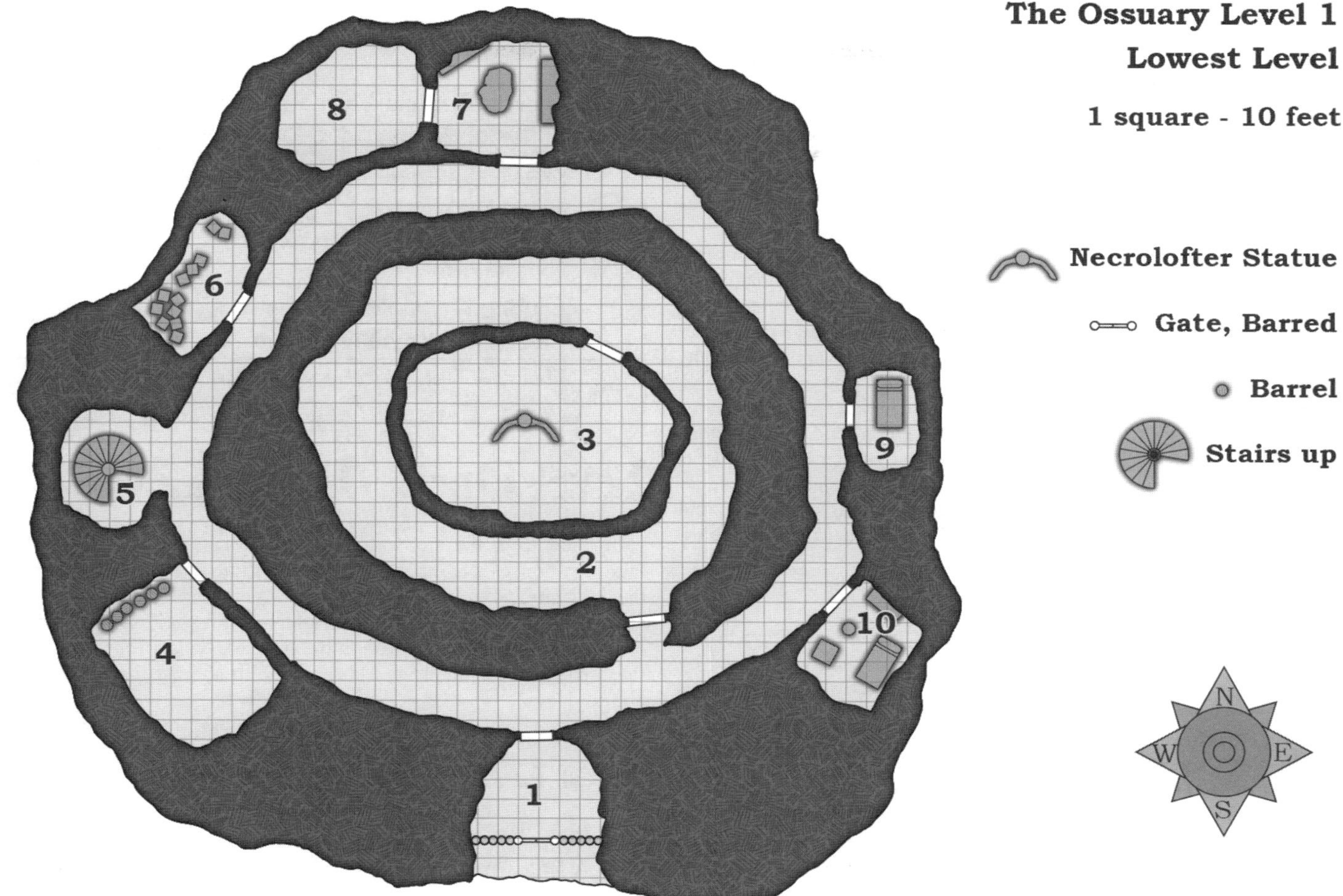

attack on the village, either via the skeletal dragon or through other flying measures, the party has little difficulty locating the fort, approaching it within an hour after beginning the pursuit.

As they approach the Ossuary but while it is still a few miles away, the party encounters a challenge that must be surmounted before they can begin their assault on the flying citadel. A **pair of wyverns** has taken to following the Ossuary as it travels, trailing it like sharks shadowing a ship seeking scraps. The small wyrms feed on the injured and dead the giants leave in their wake, and they soon spot the flying adventurers. They swoop down from out of the sun, requiring a DC 20 Perception check to notice them.

WYVERNS (2) CR 6
XP 2,400
hp 73 (*Pathfinder Roleplaying Game Bestiary* "Wyvern")

Note that casting spells while engaged in aerial combat can be taxing on spellcasters. If the spellcaster is mounted on a diving griffon or a skeletal dragon engaged in combat with one of the wyverns, the GM may rule that this counts as vigorous or even violent motion, requiring a Concentration check of the appropriate difficulty to cast spells. This is especially important if the spell being concentrated on is one holding the character or an ally aloft!

The Ossuary

The flying citadel known as the Ossuary is a squat structure fashioned from a humungous mass of bones. These bones range from small human femurs to the massive rib bones plundered from dragons, all assembled into a shape reminiscent of a humanoid skull. A parapet roughly resembling an extended jaw bone encloses a rocky courtyard set in front of the bony building.

The building rests atop a mass of rock that bears a truncated and upside-down teardrop shape. The stone foundation tapers to a point at its bottom and is flat at its top (it's the sheared-off top of a mountain, rotated upside-down), providing a firm and level base for the keep to rest upon. The Ossuary floats a constant 400 feet above the ground and moves at a speed of up to 80 feet per round.

The only obvious entrances to the Ossuary are via the great double doors visible in the courtyard and through the barred cavern mouth in the back of the fortress's rocky base. The Ossuary has no apparent windows, but some sections of bone are slightly translucent to allow sunlight to illuminate the interior.

The Ossuary's pilot, Morgosun, the cloud giant seated in the navigator's chair (see **Level Three, Area 3**), has a mental view of the area directly in front of the Ossuary and up to 90 degrees to the left and right. The fortress is effectively blind to creatures approaching from the rear, so a sneaky party can easily reach the cavern's mouth (**Level One, Area 1**) undetected. Heroes deciding on a direct frontal assault are automatically seen, and the Ossuary's inhabitants immediately prepare to repel the attackers.

Ossuary General Features

The entire fortress is fabricated from bones that are magically strengthened to the same durability as stone. Floors, walls, and ceilings of the fortress are constructed from hundreds of intertwined bones that form a solid, if somewhat uneven, surface. Ceilings average 25 feet in height and most corridors are 20 feet wide. The lower level of the Ossuary consists of room and hallways carved out of solid rock intermixed with natural caves and tunnels. The ceilings are slightly lower here, averaging 20 feet in height.

Doors: Doors inside the Ossuary, on the lower and upper levels, are fashioned from wood reinforced with metal and bone. Locks, when present, are integral parts of the door and not separate padlocks. Because of the large size of the locks, picking them is easier for Medium or smaller size creatures, requiring only a DC 15 Disable Device check. The doors are very sturdy, however, so a DC 25 Strength check is needed to bash them in. Even when unlocked, pushing open one of the great valves requires a DC 10 Strength check.

Illumination: During daylight hours, sunlight shines through semitransparent sections of the walls to provide bright illumination on the upper levels. Huge torches set in sconces resembling the skeletal hand and arm of a large humanoid are spaced throughout windowless inner chambers and lower levels of the fortress. Hill giant servants replace the brands as necessary.

Furnishings: All furnishings in the Ossuary are constructed for giants. The seat of a chair, for example, is 5 feet above the ground, and tabletops are located an average 9 feet in the air. Beds and similar accoutrements are also anywhere from 6 to 10 feet high. As such, man-sized and smaller creatures may not be able to see what lies atop certain furnishings and must make a successful DC 10 Climb check to clamber up onto tables, bunks, bookshelves, and similar objects.

Potions and Other Consumables: Any potion vials encountered inside the Ossuary or in the possession of one of the flying citadel's inhabitants are sized for giant consumption, making them three times larger than a standard vial. They effectively contain three doses each when used by Small or Medium creatures, and a single dose if drunk by a Large or larger creature.

Alarm: The Stormbreakers are intelligent foes who react to invaders using the best tactics available to them. If an alarm is sounded by the guards (in **Level Two, Area 2** or **Level Three, Area 1**) or by an Ossuary crewmember who encounters the party and flees for reinforcements, the Stormbreakers take the following steps:

The hill giants from **Level One, Area 4** are summoned to reinforce specific areas. If the alarm gong sounds in **Level Two, Area 2**, **4 giants** are sent to the hallway outside the kitchen and dining areas (**Level Two, Area 6** and **Level Two, Area 9**). They engage intruders encountered in the halls of Level Two or lie in wait to ambush invaders coming down the north-south hallway leading past the lounge and the kitchen (**Level Two, Area 4** and **Level Two, Area 6**).

Xurgal (**Level Two, Area 14**), Jezsyl (**Level Two, Area 16**), Oblugrim (**Level Three, Area 2**), and the remaining two hill giants from **Level One, Area 4** head directly to the last known location of the intruders.

The three young giants in the lounge (**Level Two, Area 4**) return to their quarters (**Level Two, Area 10**).

Tathhylia and her serpent (**Level Three, Area 2**) move to reinforce the guards in the Bridge (**Level Three, Area 3**).

Bregucar and Chandylbor continue their work, but they instruct the fire giant zombie in **Level One, Area 7** to patrol the main corridor on Level One.

The GM's judgment has final say over how the Stormbreakers react. The above directions should be used as a guideline. Stormbreaker casualties might mean some of the indicated NPCs aren't available to act as specified, leaving the GM to determine how the survivors act in the face of invasion.

Wandering Monsters

A check should be made every 30 minute to see whether characters encounter a random occupant of the Ossuary. There is a 10% chance for an encounter on Level One and a 20% chance for a random encounter occurring on Levels Two and Three every half-hour. If one occurs, the creature encountered depends on the adventurers' current location. A random encounter on Level One is always **1d4 hill giant guards** (see **Level Two, Area 2** for details). Encounters on Levels Two and Three are determined with a roll on the following table. A named NPC encountered and defeated during a random encounter is not met again at its keyed location or in subsequent random encounters. Defeating unnamed, randomly encountered monsters does not affect the number of giants aboard the Ossuary.

Ossuary Levels Two and Three Random Encounters

1d10	Encounter
1–5	**1d4 hill giant guards** (*Pathfinder Roleplaying Game Bestiary* "Giant, Hill")
6–7	**1 cloud giant** (*Pathfinder Roleplaying Game Bestiary* "Giant, Cloud")
8	**Xurgal** (see **Level Two, Area 14**)
9	**Jezsyl** (see **Level Two, Area 16**)
10	**Tathhylia** and **feathered snake** (see **Level Three, Area 2**)

Level One — Lower Level

Formed from the stony top of a mountain, the lower level of the Ossuary houses chambers for the creation of the zombie "bombs" the Stormbreakers use against humanity, the holdfast's weird engine, and living quarters. Prudent intruders begin their infiltration of the Ossuary by sneaking in through the barred cavern in the rocky base of the fortress rather than via a direct assault against the fortress's front doors.

Area 1. Bomb Bay

> A large cavern pierces the side of the rocky mass that serves as the base of the floating bone citadel. A massive row of bars with a closed double gate seals the cavern mouth from intruders. Beyond the great steel barricade, you can see burning torches that illuminate an apparently empty area.

The giants lead their animated dead to this area when approaching a new target, then open the gates and command the giant zombies to step out and plunge to the ground. When not preparing to bomb a target, the gates are closed and locked to keep aerial pests and intruders out.

The gate is locked by a tremendous padlock, but unfortunately for the giants, the size of the lock makes it easier to pick by man-sized or smaller creatures (a successful DC 15 Disable Device check springs the lock). Also, while the bars are spaced far enough apart to keep out human-sized or larger intruders, Small creatures can squeeze through with a successful DC 15 Escape Artist check.

The bomb bay cavern is empty when not in use. It contains six burning torches that light the large space and the faint smell of rotting flesh. A single door stands in the north wall.

Area 2. Sanguine Terror (CR 8)

> A heaving mass of partially coagulated flesh writhes in what appears to be a curved tunnel. The gelid heap struggles to rise, assuming a vaguely humanoid appearance. It slouches toward you.

The creature is the result of an experiment by Bregucar, who wanted to see if the coagulated blood of corpses could be chemically granted life and form, and thus used in the giants' campaign. The experiment was a success, giving birth to an abomination fashioned from blood: the **Sanguine Terror**, an advanced blood golem. It is currently contained in this circular room to serve as a security measure protecting the Necrolofter (**Area 3**), but the giant necromancers plan to put it to evil use in the near future. Bregucar has a modicum of control over the sanguine terror and it responds to his commands, allowing the giants to access **Area 3** when necessary.

The room surrounds the Necrolofter chamber. This area contains nothing but the sanguine terror and a few discarded bones of hill giant servants fed to the creature to keep it appeased.

SANGUINE TERROR **CR 8**
XP 4,800
Advanced blood golem (***The Tome of Horrors Complete***, 331)
N Huge aberration
Init +4; **Senses** darkvision 60 ft., tremorsense 60 ft.; **Perception** +19

AC 17, touch 8, flat-footed 17 (+9 natural, –2 size)
hp 75 (10d8+20 plus 10); fast healing 3
Fort +7; **Ref** +3; **Will** +7
DR 10/bludgeoning and magic; **Immune** mind-affecting effects; **Resist** fire 10
Weaknesses vulnerable to magic

Speed 30 ft., swim 30 ft.
Melee 2 slams +13 (2d6+7)
Space 15 ft.; **Reach** 5 ft.
Special Attacks blood consumption (DC 19)

Str 25, **Dex** 10, **Con** 14, **Int** 2, **Wis** 11, **Cha** 1
Base Atk +7; **CMB** +16; **CMD** 26 (can't be tripped)
Feats Great Fortitude, Improved Initiative, Skill Focus (Perception), Toughness, Weapon Focus (slam)
Skills Perception +19, Swim +15
SQ cell division

Blood Consumption (DC 19) (Su) Each time a blood golem hits a living opponent with a slam attack, it gains a number of temporary hit points equal to the damage dealt. These bonus hit points are added to the blood golem's total even if the addition takes it above its current maximum hit points allowed by its HD (not including any bonus hit points it may have from its Con score). For example, a 7-HD blood golem cannot gain more than 56 hit points.

If a blood golem successfully hits an opponent with both of its slam attacks in a single round, that opponent suffers catastrophic blood expulsion, taking 2d4 points of Constitution damage (DC 15 Fortitude save for half). A blood golem gains 5 hit points per point of Constitution damage it deals. The save DC is Constitution-based and includes a +2 racial bonus.

When a blood golem reaches its maximum hit points for its Hit Dice, it divides (see cell division, below).

Cell Division (Ex) When a blood golem absorbs enough blood to raise its hit points to the maximum for its HD, it splits into two identical blood golems, each with half the original's hit points. For example, a 7-HD blood golem that reaches 56 hit points splits into two 7-HD blood golems with 28 hit points each.

Vulnerability to Magic (Ex) A blood golem is *slowed* (as the spell) for 1d4 rounds by any cold-based attacks or effects. A *purify food and water* spell deals 1d6 points of damage per caster level (maximum 10d6) to a blood golem. A blood golem can attempt a Fortitude saving throw (DC 10 + caster's ability score modifier) to reduce the damage by half.

Area 3. The Necrolofter (CR 7–13)

The door to this room is locked. Bregucar (see **Area 7**) has the key.

> This rough-hewn cavern is dominated by a sizable piece of odd statuary. Fashioned from dark marble with striations of red throughout the stone, the statue depicts a figure that appears angelic at first glance. Large, feathered wings stretch from the robed figure's back. Its face is hidden by a shadowy cowl. The statue emerges from a large piece of rectangular stone, seemingly carved from the block. Haze hangs about the statue, making it difficult to pick out further details. What appear to be bones and clothing lie scattered about the area.

This statue is in truth a portion of a titan's gravestone plundered from an ancient cemetery. The headstone was magically altered to serve as a focus for necromantic power to be harnessed to levitate and drive the Ossuary. This mystical engine is known as the Necrolofter.

The Necrolofter draws its power from living souls fed to the hungry spirits surrounding the device. These indistinct souls are the haze encompassing the device. The Stormbreakers hurl a captured prisoner or poorly-performing servant in here once a week to keep the necromantic artifact energized. The inside of the door leading to this room bears numerous scratches and bloodstains as the "fuel" helplessly beat on it in an attempt to escape.

Tied to the Necrolofter are **4 wights**. They drain hit points from the victims forced into this room and channel the siphoned life into the device. The power of the Necrolofter keeps them contained within the confines of this room, ever-hungry and angry.

WIGHTS (4) **CR 3**
XP 800
hp 26 (*Pathfinder Roleplaying Game Bestiary* "Wight")

If the wights are destroyed, the Necrolofter cannot be refueled without removing the headstone and engaging in a new, prolonged ritual to repair the magical engine. Such a process takes at least two weeks to perform. Without the wights feeding the engine power, it slowly runs down. After seven days, the Ossuary drifts down from the sky, coming to rest wherever it is currently located. The descent is gradual (a safety measure inherent to the Necrolofter) so no damage is suffered by the Ossuary or its passengers.

Characters wishing to damage or destroy the device must first overcome the wights. Once the wights are gone, the Necrolofter can be attacked directly. While the wights exist, damage done to the Necrolofter is automatically repaired as the spirts shunt necrotic energy into the device. The engine has a hardness of 8 and 400 hit points. It automatically fails saving throws. If reduced to 200 or fewer hit points, safety protocols kick in and the Ossuary begins descending at a rate of 40 feet per round, reaching the ground after 10 rounds. If the Necrolofter is reduced to zero hit points before the Ossuary reaches the ground, the entire structure crashes to the ground catastrophically. All aboard suffer 10d6 points of bludgeoning as bones, rock, and rubble collapse atop them.

Any direct attack on the Necrolofter (not the wights) is detected by the pilot, Morgosun, in **Level Three, Area 3**. He feels the disturbance in the Ossuary's energy field and alerts his fellow giants. Immediately, a **cloud giant** and **3 hill giants** (assuming all the giants on the upper level haven't been slain) are dispatched to investigate, arriving 1d4+4 rounds later. Unsurprisingly, they are displeased with intruders attempting to crash the Ossuary, and they counterattack with brutal force.

CLOUD GIANT **CR 11**
XP 12,800
hp 168 (*Pathfinder Roleplaying Game Bestiary* "Giant, Cloud")

HILL GIANTS (3) **CR 7**
XP 3,200
hp 85 (*Pathfinder Roleplaying Game Bestiary* "Giant, Hill")

Area 4. Hill Giant Servants' Quarters (CR 10)

Any hero with Perception +1 or better automatically hears the sound of physical scuffling and deep, bass laughter coming from behind this door.

> Large beds and crude furnishing fill this room. Rugs of animal pelts line the floor and great hogshead barrels stand against one wall, a rack of tankards and drinking horns above it. The smell of body odor and stinky feet fills the air with a foul miasma.

The Stormbreakers subdued and conscripted a tribe of hill giants to serve as underlings and cannon fodder. The tribe bunks on the lower level of the Ossuary, where they can pursue their rough entertainments without disturbing their masters.

If the Ossuary isn't in a state of alarm, **3 hill giants** are present in this room, relaxing with dark ale drawn from the hogsheads and physical roughhousing.

HILL GIANTS (3) CR 7
XP 3,200
hp 85 (*Pathfinder Roleplaying Game Bestiary* "Giant, Hill")

The giants respond poorly to being interrupted during their rest and relaxation, but quickly decide beating the characters to death with their greatclubs provides ample entertainment. Two of the hill giants, a little deeper in their cups than their friends, grab barrels from the row of six lining the wall and hurl them (as rocks) at the party.

The room contains a dozen beds, six footlockers, and six open wardrobes. The wardrobes contain spare boots and crude shoes, dirty tunics, and fur vests. The footlockers hold a variety of dirty clothes and other items. Treat each footlocker as a giant's bag, rolling randomly to determine the unusual contents of the container.

The six barrels hold a dark, rich ale of vastly superior quality than what the hill giants are used to (thus they don't mind their servitude so much). Each barrel holds 54 gallons of ale. The brew is worth 4 sp per gallon (21 gp 6 sp per barrel). Thrown barrels break on impact and their contents are lost.

Area 5. Stairwell

> An open area beside the corridor forms a broad, rocky alcove here. The alcove holds a large spiral staircase carved from the native stone and winds upward clockwise through a hole in the ceiling. A single torch burns in a sconce at the base of the stairs.

The stairs measure 15 feet wide and rise 40 feet to connect with the upper level of the Ossuary at **Level Two, Area 8**.

If combat occurs on the staircase, creatures battling from the upper position have tactical advantage on attacks against lower opponents.

Area 6. Storage

> This chamber is roughly hewn from the surrounding rock and is densely packed with giant spools of rope and forged chain, crates and barrels, and other assorted containers. The smell of grease, oil, and other pungent scents mix to tinge the air with a potpourri of mundane, household odors.

This chamber is an unassuming storage area holding various everyday supplies used in the operation and maintenance of the Ossuary. Among the goods here are 2,000 feet of hemp rope, 500 feet of chain, 10 barrels of goose grease, assorted mops and brooms, bales of straw for bed ticking, 20 five-gallon kegs of lamp oil, sacks of lye, bags of sand, bolts of canvas, and other household goods. The contents of the room are flammable, but a blaze does not spread beyond this room.

Area 7. Animatorium (CR 13)

> Shelves bearing jars, retorts, beakers, and other oddly-shaped vessels of glass and ceramic line the walls of this room. A titanic stone slab occupies the center of the space, and the ghoulish corpse of an ice-blue giant sprawls on the tabletop. Crouched over him with long needles and thread are a pair of giants dressed in tattered black robes and high, pointed hoods. A second giant corpse, this one with rotting skin colored such a deep red that it's almost black, stands upright and unmoving in the corner.

The two robed giants are **Bregucar** and his apprentice, **Chandylbor**, hill giant necromancers and scholars of the funeral arts. It is their duty to produce the giant zombie "bombs." They are preparing another specimen now. This area operates under a permanent *desecrate* spell, thereby doubling the number of undead Bregucar can animate with a single casting of *animate dead* (up to 32 HD per casting).

The corpse on the slab is not yet animated, but the **fire giant zombie** in the corner is. The animated fire giant is a new prototype the necromancers designed to increase the destruction of their bombardment campaign. Before animation, the fire giant corpse was cut open and its body stuffed with containers of alchemist's fire. The intent is to create a zombie that explodes into flames upon impact, spreading fire as it shambles through a settlement. By using a fire giant corpse, the necromancers hope to prolong its "lifespan" and increase the destruction it causes.

BREGUCAR CR 11
XP 12,800
Male hill giant necromancer 8 (*Pathfinder Roleplaying Game Bestiary* "Giant, Hill")
CE Large humanoid (giant)
Init +3; **Senses** life sight (10 feet, 8 rounds/day), low-light vision; **Perception** +18

AC 21, touch 8, flat-footed 21 (+4 armor, –1 Dex, +9 natural, –1 size)
hp 145 (10d8+40 plus 8d6+32)
Fort +13; **Ref** +4; **Will** +11
Defensive Abilities rock catching

Speed 40 ft.
Melee dagger +15/+10/+5 (1d6+5/19-20) or mwk greatclub +17/+12/+7 (2d8+7) or 2 slams +10 (1d8+2)
Space 10 ft.; **Reach** 10 ft.
Special Attacks command undead 5/day (DC 12), rock throwing (120 ft.)
Necromancer Spell-Like Abilities (CL 8th; melee touch +15): 5/day—grave touch (4 rounds)
Spells Prepared (CL 8th; melee touch +15, ranged touch +9):
4th—*animate dead* (x2; already cast), *ice storm*
3rd—*protection from energy*, *ray of exhaustion* (DC 15) (x2), *sleet storm*
2nd—*acid arrow*, *command undead* (DC 14), *false life* (x2), *summon swarm*
1st—*cause fear* (DC 13), *chill touch* (DC 13), *feather fall*, *mage armor*, *protection from good*, *ray of enfeeblement* (DC 13)

0 (at will)—*light, ray of frost, read magic, touch of fatigue* (DC 12)
Opposition Schools Enchantment, Illusion

Str 20, **Dex** 8, **Con** 19, **Int** 14, **Wis** 10, **Cha** 7
Base Atk +11; **CMB** +17; **CMD** 26
Feats Arcane Armor Training, Cleave, Combat Casting, Command Undead, Craft Wondrous Item, Improved Initiative, Intimidating Prowess, Iron Will, Martial Weapon Proficiency (greatclub), Power Attack, Scribe Scroll, Weapon Focus (greatclub)
Skills Acrobatics –1 (+3 to jump), Climb +11, Heal +11, Intimidate +14, Knowledge (arcana) +20, Knowledge (religion) +13, Perception +18, Profession (Mortician) +11, Spellcraft +20
Languages Common, Draconic, Giant
SQ arcane bond (dagger), power over undead
Combat Gear *potion of cure serious wounds*; **Other Gear** *+1 studded leather*, dagger, masterwork greatclub, belt pouch, key ring, moonstone (worth 10 gp), silver ring (worth 25 gp), 76 gp

Bregucar carries a *potion of cure serious wounds*; a dagger that is his arcane focus; a key ring with keys to the gate in **Area 1**, the doors to **Area 3** and **Area 10**, and the trunk in **Area 10**; and a pouch containing 76 gp, a moonstone (10 gp value), and a silver ring (25 gp).

CHANDYLBOR **CR 9**
XP 6,400
Male hill giant necromancer 5 (*Pathfinder Roleplaying Game Bestiary* "Giant, Hill")
CE Large humanoid (giant)
Init –1; **Senses** low-light vision; **Perception** +13

AC 17, touch 8, flat-footed 17 (–1 Dex, +9 natural, –1 size)
hp 122 (10d8+40 plus 5d6+20)
Fort +12; **Ref** +3; **Will** +9
Defensive Abilities rock catching

Speed 40 ft.
Melee dagger +13/+8 (1d6+5/19-20) or greatclub +14/+9 (2d8+7) or 2 slams +13 (1d8+5)
Space 10 ft.; **Reach** 10 ft.
Special Attacks command undead 4/day (DC 10), rock throwing (120 ft.)
Necromancer Spell-Like Abilities (CL 5th; melee touch +13)
4/day—grave touch (2 rounds)
Spells Prepared (CL 5th; melee touch +13, ranged touch +7)
3rd—*ray of exhaustion* (DC 14), *slow* (DC 14)
2nd—*acid arrow, command undead* (DC 13), *ghoul touch* (DC 13)
1st—*cause fear* (DC 12), *chill touch* (DC 12), *magic missile, ray of enfeeblement* (DC 12), *shocking grasp*
0 (at will)—*acid splash, light, ray of frost, touch of fatigue* (DC 11)
Opposition Schools Enchantment, Illusion

Str 20, **Dex** 8, **Con** 19, **Int** 13, **Wis** 10, **Cha** 7
Base Atk +9; **CMB** +15; **CMD** 24
Feats Arcane Armor Training, Cleave, Combat Casting, Command Undead, Craft Wondrous Item, Intimidating Prowess, Iron Will, Martial Weapon Proficiency (greatclub), Power Attack, Scribe Scroll, Weapon Focus (greatclub)
Skills Acrobatics –1 (+3 to jump), Climb +11, Heal +8, Intimidate +16, Knowledge (arcana) +14, Knowledge (religion) +6, Perception +13, Spellcraft +14
Languages Common, Giant
SQ arcane bond (dagger), power over undead
Gear dagger, greatclub, belt pouch, keys, ancient gold coin (worth 100 gp), 67 gp, 18 sp

Chandylbor carries a dagger; keys to the trunk and spellbook in **Area 9**; and a pouch containing 18 sp, 67 gp, and a well-worn and ancient gold coin (1 gp face value, but worth up to 100 gp to collectors because of its antiquity).

The fire giant zombie has the special quality "Filled with Alchemist's Fire."

FIRE GIANT ZOMBIE **CR 7**
XP 3,200
Pathfinder Roleplaying Game Bestiary "Giant, Fire," "Zombie"
NE Large undead
Init –2; **Senses** darkvision 60 ft.; **Perception** +0

AC 18, touch 7, flat-footed 18 (–2 Dex, +11 natural, –1 size)
hp 93 (17d8+17)
Fort +5; **Ref** +3; **Will** +10
DR 5/slashing; **Immune** undead traits

Speed 40 ft.
Melee 2 slams +22 (1d8+11)
Space 10 ft.; **Reach** 10 ft.

Str 33, **Dex** 7, **Con** —, **Int** —, **Wis** 10, **Cha** 10
Base Atk +12; **CMB** +24; **CMD** 32
Feats Toughness[B]
SQ filled with alchemist's fire, staggered

Filled with Alchemist's Fire (Ex) An attack that causes slashing or piercing damage to the fire giant zombie triggers a burst of flame as one of the alchemist's fire containers inside the zombie spills its contents from the wound. If the damage came from a melee attack, the attacker must succeed on a DC 15 Reflex save or take 1d4 points of fire damage at the start of its turn, until it uses an action to extinguish the flames with a successful DC 15 Reflex save. If the damage came from a ranged attack, the alchemist's fire splashes onto one character adjacent to the fire giant zombie and on the same side of it as the ranged attacker; in this case, the saving throw to avoid the splash has a DC of 10 instead of 14.

The containers on the shelves hold various chemicals and reagents used to preserve dead flesh or retard its decay. They have no intrinsic value but can be treated as a spell components pouch for necromantic spells that don't require monetary components.

Area 8. Morgue (CR 4)

> The stink of rotting meat is overpowering in this large space. Piled in haphazard fashion are at least a dozen decaying corpses of giants. The dead creatures range in size, indicating that these corpses are of varying types and ages. Clouds of black flies fill the air, and swarms of maggots writhe on the exposed flesh.

The stench is so strong that each character who enters the chamber must succeed on a DC 12 Fortitude save or be sickened for as long as they remain in the room and for 10 minutes after leaving.

A total of 15 giant corpses are here: six hill giants, four stone giants, three fire giants, and two frost giants. All are in a state of great decay and dressed in rotting funeral garments or winding shrouds. One of the fire giants still bears a piece of funereal goods on its body, overlooked in the grave robbers' haste: a beaten gold bracelet bearing three fire opals (500 gp value). Finding this piece of jewelry requires a search of the bodies that stirs up the colony of **rot grubs** in the dead.

ROT GRUBS **CR 4**
XP 1,200
The Tome of Horrors Complete, 761
Type infestation; **Save** Fortitude DC 17
Onset immediate; **Frequency** 1/round
Effect 1d2 Con damage per grub

Area 9. Chandylbor's Quarters (CR 8)

A giant bed dominates this room, turning the otherwise spacious area into cramped living quarters. A writing table and chest clutter one corner of the room, and a high shelf littered with jars, boxes, and other containers hangs high overhead on the north wall.

These are the quarters of **Chandylbor**, the apprentice cloud giant necromancer. His room is not nearly as spacious as his master's but, like Bregucar, he spends much of his time in the animation area preparing new undead.

The shelf, hanging 15 feet above the floor, is affixed directly to the wall by bolts. Characters wishing to inspect its contents must climb the rough wall with a successful DC 15 Climb check or use magic to ascend.

The shelves contain:

- Six jars of ashes, bone fragments, teeth, and fingernail pairings;
- A glass beaker holding a clear liquid (concentrated acid equal to four vials of the substance);
- A box containing weathered and sweat-stained giant-sized tarot cards (no special properties, but worth 100 gp as a curiosity);
- An ogre skull turned into a candleholder. Inside the wax-sealed cranium is a *scroll of invisibility* that Chandylbor keeps as an escape plan should things ever fare poorly for him.

The writing table holds several jars of ink, a dozen large quills stored in a cup, and a box with a dozen sheets of foolscap.

The trunk is locked and trapped. Chandylbor's key safely unlocks it, but picking the trunk triggers the trap: A spray of acid strikes all targets in a 15-foot cone in front of the trunk. Those caught in the cone must succeed on a DC 20 Reflex save or suffer 3d6 points of acid damage.

ACID SPRAY TRAP **CR 8**
XP 4,800
Type mechanical; **Perception** DC 30; **Disable Device** DC 30

Trigger touch; **Reset** manual; **Bypass** key
Effect acid spray (3d6 acid damage, DC 20 Reflex save avoids); multiple targets (all targets in a 15-foot cone in front of the trunk)

The trunk holds a spare pair of low, soft boots, three sets of black robes with peaked cowls, a jar of hair pomade, a chased silver flask (50 gp value) holding three doses (or one giant-sized dose) of *potion of flying*, a leather sack with 378 sp and 297 gp, and a dagger in a brass sheath. Everything is giant-sized. It also holds Chandylbor's spellbook. A lock keeps the book sealed and requires either a successful DC 20 Disable Device check to pick or the key from Chandylbor's pouch (see **Area 7**). The spellbook contains the following spells:

0—all; 1st—*cause fear, shill touch, detect undead, grease, identify, mage armor, magic missile, ray of enfeeblement, shocking grasp*; 2nd—*acid arrow, command undead, darkness, false life, ghoul touch; 3rd—hold person, protection from energy, ray of exhaustion, slow*; 4th—*animate dead.*

Area 10. Bregucar's Quarters (CR 7)

The door to this room is locked. Bregucar (see **Area 7**) has the key.

A simple bedchamber carved from the surrounding rock, this room contains a large bed, a gigantic table, a solid wooden wardrobe, and a massive iron trunk. A carpet of ebon hue decorated with a pattern of white skulls covers the stone floor.

This room is Bregucar's chamber, but his duties give him little time to rest. The wardrobe contains half a dozen dark, tattered robes with high, pointed cowls and two pairs of giant-sized, high, soft boots. The table holds an assortment of writing implements, a score of giant sheets of paper measuring 10 feet square, a mighty tome, and a trio of long scroll tubes. The scroll tubes contain a blank scroll waiting to be inscribed, a scroll of *protection from undead*, and a scroll of *animate dead*. The tome is Bregucar's spellbook, and it is sealed with an *arcane lock* spell. The spellbook contains the following spells:0—all; 1st—*alarm, burning hands, cause fear, chill touch, expeditious retreat, feather fall, mage armor, magic missile, protection from good, ray of enfeeblement, shield*; 2nd—*acid arrow, arcane lock, command undead, darkness, false life, ghoul touch, summon swarm, web*; 3rd—*dispel magic, fly, haste, magic circle against good, protection from energy, ray of exhaustion, sleet storm*; 4th—*animate dead, black tentacles, fear, ice storm.*

The trunk's lid is inscribed with runes, but these are difficult to see unless a character climbs atop the large chest. The trunk is magical: A *detect magic* spell reveals an aura of conjuration and necromancy about the box. It is locked and requires Bregucar's key to open. However, if the lock is picked or even if the key is used and the opener does not press down on a certain rune on the trunk's lid (noticing the rune can be depressed requires an inspection of the writing and a successful DC 25 Perception check), a trap is sprung. Incorrectly opening the trunk causes a **ghost** to coalesce around the trunk and attack. The ghost prefers to possess a victim and cause it to walk off the ledge in **Area 1** (if the gate is unlocked). The ghost relinquishes control as the victim steps off the ledge, laughing hideously as the again-conscious subject plunges to its doom. The ghost then moves on to possess another victim.

GHOST **CR 7**
XP 3,200
hp 73; (*Pathfinder Roleplaying Game Bestiary*, "Ghost")
SA malevolence

The trunk contains the following treasures:

- A satin pouch (10 gp value) containing three garnets (50 gp value each), five sapphires (100 gp value each), and a blue diamond (500 gp value);
- A giant-sized ivory comb fashioned from a mammoth tusk (200 gp value);
- A leather sack containing 756 gp;
- A battered book. This text is a *golem manual (clay).*

The carpet is worn and dirty but still worth 50 gp if characters can find a way to clean it and cart it away.

Level Two — Main Level

This "ground level" of the Ossuary contains living quarters, food preparation and dining areas, storage, and an evil chapel, all of which cater to the Stormbreakers' day-to-day activities. Random encounters are more likely to occur on this level than on the lower one, and result in a

The Ossuary Level 2

1 square - 10 feet

more varied array of occupants moving about the fortress (see "Random Encounters," above).

Area 1. Courtyard (CR 9)

> A rocky courtyard lies exposed to the sky before the great bone building. The courtyard is encircled by a 40-foot-high rampart of fused bone on three sides and by the building itself on the fourth. A pair of skeletal dragons patrols the courtyard and scours the sky with glowing eyes. A set of double doors leads out of the courtyard and into the bony structure.

The doors are locked and of great size. Even unlocked, a DC 12 Strength check is required to push them open.

Defending the courtyard from intruders are **2 red dragon skeletons**. These skeletons have not yet received their magical flight apparatus, and cannot fly.

RED DRAGON SKELETONS (2) CR 7
XP 3,200
hp 97 (see **Method 2: The Call to Adventure Comes From Above**)

Area 2. Foyer (CR 10)

> Beyond the doors lies an entry hall fashioned from polished and interlaced bones of myriad sizes. Hanging from the east and west walls are unusual decorations. The west wall bears a massive plaque fashioned from bones and shaped into the semblance of a giant skull. A skeletal serpent is intertwined through the skull's eye sockets and nasal cavity. The east wall holds a gigantic shield decorated with the symbol of a fist grasping a turbulent storm cloud. Three exits leave this room: single doors in the east and west walls, and a pair of double doors in the south wall.

Stationed here are **3 hill giant guards** charged with defending the Ossuary and alerting its inhabitants in case of attack. If the heroes engage in battle with the skeletal dragons in the courtyard, these guards automatically hear the battle and sound an alarm by banging on the great shield hanging on the wall to put the inhabitants on alert (see Alarm under "General Ossuary Features" above). They then prepare to resist invaders.

If the party avoids battle with the courtyard dragons or approaches this area from within the Ossuary, the giants may be surprised. If taken unaware, one of their number attempts to sound the alarm on the first round of combat that the guards are able to react. Each of these giants also carries a skull bombard. These weapons are the skulls of large creatures (ogres are preferred) filled with clay containers of alchemist fire and weighted with lead. These hill giants use their skull bombards as ammo in their ranged attacks. On a successful hit, the skull bombard does damage as a rock. In addition, the skull bursts open when it hits a solid object and splashes alchemist's fire in a 5-foot radius area around the point of impact. Targets caught in the area of effect are set afire and take 1d4 points of fire damage at the start of each of their turns until they spend an action making a successful DC 15 Reflex save to put out the flames.

The giants have no coinage, but the squad leader wears a gold chain with a polished bone medallion (100 gp value) as a mark of his position.

The skull-headed plaque is the symbol of Drahltuz, the giants' god of fear and death, and patron of the Stormbreaker Clan. The fist-and-cloud plaque is the clan heraldry of the Stormbreakers. Neither item has any special property or value.

HILL GIANTS (3) **CR 7**
XP 3,200
hp 85 (*Pathfinder Roleplaying Game Bestiary* "Giant, Hill")

Area 3. Audience Hall (CR 12)

Beyond the doors is a vast hall. Four skeletal columns support a 40-foot-high cathedral ceiling. A raised dais stands against the far wall, a pair of bony thrones sized for giants resting atop it. Illumination comes from a half-dozen burning brands set in scones made from skeletal hands. The hall is otherwise empty.

The pillars are more than what they appear to be. Hidden in the skeletal patterns that decorate the columns are **4 bone golems**. The bone golems respond to Oblugrim's commands, serving to defend him and his consort when court is in session and to protect the hall from intruders when Stormbreakers are not present. The bone golems step from the columns to attack any unauthorized creature (e.g., the characters) entering this room.

BONE GOLEMS (4) **CR 8**
XP 4,800
hp 90 (*Pathfinder Roleplaying Game Bestiary 3* "Golem, Bone")

The bone thrones are used when Oblugrim and his consort, Tathhylia, hold court for the clan. Each contains a secret compartment in the left armrest. Locating the hidden cavity requires a successful DC 25 Perception check. Each compartment holds two glossy black vials, one with a white stopper and the other with a green stopper. The vials with white stoppers are *potions of cure serious wounds*, while those with green stoppers are *potions of detect thoughts*.

Area 4. Lounge (CR 10)

A plush rug of vibrant sky blue covers the bone floor of this brightly lit room. A large settee and three massive upholstered chairs are arranged around a low, dark-stained wooden table. Grand portraiture depicting picturesque landscapes and mountain vistas adorn the walls. Oversized candles mounted on mirror-backed holders hanging from the walls illuminate the room.

Unless an alarm sounds, the lounge is occupied by the **3 hill giant youths** named Tranimyz and Wylkun (male), and Sylzak (female). They enjoy the freedom and space of the lounge compared with their own cramped quarters. Sylzak has a longbow and 40 arrows.

TRANIMYZ, WYLKUN, and SYLZAK **CR 6**
XP 2,400
Male young hill giant (*Pathfinder Roleplaying Game* "Giant, Hill")
CE Medium humanoid (giant)
Init +1; **Senses** low-light vision; **Perception** +6

AC 18, touch 11, flat-footed 17 (+1 Dex, +7 natural)
hp 65 (10d8+20)
Fort +9; **Ref** +4; **Will** +3
Defensive Abilities rock catching

Speed 40 ft.
Melee greatclub +13/+8 (1d10+7) (Tranimyz and Wylkun only) or 2 slams +12 (1d6+5)
Ranged longbow +8/+3 (1d8/x3) (Sylzak only)
Special Attacks rock throwing (120 ft.)

Str 21, **Dex** 12, **Con** 15, **Int** 6, **Wis** 10, **Cha** 7
Base Atk +7; **CMB** +12; **CMD** 23
Feats Cleave, Intimidating Prowess, Martial Weapon Proficiency (greatclub for Tranimyz and Wylkun, longbow for Sylzak), Power Attack, Weapon Focus (greatclub)
Skills Acrobatics +1 (+5 to jump), Climb +11, Intimidate +10, Perception +6
Languages Giant
Gear greatclub or longbow and 20 arrows

Treasure: Tranimyz has a gold earring (100 gp value), 57 gp, and a rough opal (250 gp value).

Wylkun has a gold-and-silver torc (250 gp value), 78 gp in coins, and a charm bracelet with pieces of polished and shaped petrified wood hanging from it (150 gp value).

Sylzak has a silver circlet (200 gp value), matching gold and sapphire earrings (500 gp value), and 48 gp.

On the walls between the pictures are 12 candles and candleholders. Six pictures hang here, each done with accomplished skill. They are worth 250 gp each, but they measure 10 feet long, 5 feet high, and weigh 50 lbs. each.

Area 5. Decorative Archway

A decorative archway bisects the corridor at this location. Like the rest of the fortress, the archway is constructed of bones and assembled to depict a humanoid skull with a greatly exaggerated mouth. The skull's open mouth serves as the archway, requiring walkers to enter through the mouth to continue down the corridor. The long skeleton of a great serpent has been threaded through the skull archway's eye sockets to hang pendulously down over the corridor.

Four of these archways are on the upper level of the Ossuary. Two are simply decorative, while the other two are traps intended to slay or impede invaders lacking knowledge of the proper passcode.

Archway 5A (CR 6)

Failing to speak the word "*gulgrotha*" (the Giant word for boneyard) before entering the archway causes a pair of humungous skeletal arms to emerge from the surrounding walls of the corridor and attack the intruder.

Skeletal Arm Trap: Can be detected with a successful DC 20 Perception check, and disarmed with a successful DC 20 Disable Device check. If triggered, two Large skeletal arms emerge from the walls and attack each round. One arm grapples and the other arm pummels; the pummeling arm always targets a creature that is grappled by the other arm, if possible. Both arms are AC 8, and they have 50 hit points each. As skeletal arms, they have DR 5/bludgeoning. They automatically fail saving throws.

Pummeling Arm: +20 to hit (reach 20 ft.), 1d8+10 bludgeoning damage. A creature grappled by the grappling arm is hit automatically by this attack.

Grappling Arm: CMB +22 (reach 20 ft.).

Archway 5B (CR 6)

Failing to speak the word "*tromuldah*" (the Giant word for decay) before entering the archway causes the skeletal snake to animate and strike at intruders.

Skeletal Snake Trap: Can be detected with a successful DC 20 Perception check and disarmed with a successful DC 20 Disable Device check. If triggered, a **Huge anaconda skeleton** animates and attacks.

HUGE ANACONDA SKELETON **CR 6**
XP 2,400
Pathfinder Roleplaying Game Bestiary, "Snake, Constrictor," "Skeleton"
NE Huge undead
Init +7; **Senses** darkvision 60 ft.; **Perception** +4

AC 19, touch 11, flat-footed 16 (+3 Dex, +8 natural, –2 size)
hp 63 (14d8)
Fort +4; **Ref** +7; **Will** +9
DR 5/bludgeoning; **Immune** cold, undead traits

Speed 20 ft., climb 20 ft., swim 20 ft.
Melee bite +23 (1d8+15)
Space 15 ft.; **Reach** 15 ft.

Str 41, **Dex** 17, **Con** —, **Int** —, **Wis** 10, **Cha** 10
Base Atk +10; **CMB** +27; **CMD** 40 (can't be tripped)
Feats Improved Initiative[B]

Area 6. Kitchen (CR 9)

> The fixtures and furnishings of this sizable kitchen were designed for the use of large beings. Bubbling pots of stew rest atop the hot oven. A great tabletop is covered with diced vegetables and sliced meat awaiting their turn on the stove.

A **pair of hill giant servants** toils here preparing supper. They are present even if an alert is sounded, as they don't wish to anger their larger masters by delaying a meal. The stew is rich and tasty, and in sufficient quantity to feed up to eight giant appetites. The other prepared ingredients are normal and without interest or value.

HILL GIANTS (2) **CR 7**
XP 3,200
hp 85 (*Pathfinder Roleplaying Game Bestiary* "Giant, Hill")

Area 7. Pantry

> Foodstuffs, both fresh and preserved, fill this cramped room. Smoked sausages of unusual size hang from hooks in the ceiling. Jars of pickled fruits and vegetables line the shelves. Crates of potatoes, cabbages, and turnips sit beside sacks of flour and meal. Clusters of garlic, onions, and dried peppers add their own aromas to the melody of smells that perfumes the room.

Most of the ingredients for the meals prepared in **Area 6** come from here. Given the palettes of the diners, the array of viands is rather surprising and consists of quality goods. The pantry contains enough food to feed the equivalent of 50 men for one month.

Mixed in among the normal foodstuff is a small coffer containing 10 vials of spices, including cinnamon, cloves, cardamom, vanilla, and saffron. The coffer's contents are worth 200 gp to gourmands or spice traders. Finding the coffer requires a specific search of the shelves and a DC 15 Perception check because of its small size.

Area 8. Stairwell

The floor of this chamber is rough stone as opposed to the intertwined bone that makes up the walls and ceiling. An open spiral staircase descends through the floor, vanishing as it curves out of sight into the gloom.

The stairs terminate at **Level One, Area 5** on the lower level.

Area 9. Giant Dining Hall

Two titanic tables and many chairs occupy this room, providing seating for up to twelve giant humanoids. Each of the tables is covered with a woven tablecloth the size of a tapestry. The tables and chairs are carved with great skill from honey-colored wood. Six marble statues of exquisite fabrication, depicting nude male and female giants, are placed about the room in ascetically pleasing locales. A pair of humongous, open cabinets rest against the southeastern wall, and a door stands in the northeast corner of the room.

The statues are 15 feet tall and weigh 1,000 lbs. each, but they are worth 2,000 gp each for their artistic merit.

The cabinets hold a collection of giant-sized plates and eating ware, all of excellent fabrication. The eating ware is mostly pewter, but two silver spoons and three silver forks (50 gp value each) are mixed in among the utensils. Each utensil weighs 10 lbs.

The tablecloths are linen trimmed with silver and gold thread and weigh 100 lbs. apiece. Their manufacture makes them semi-valuable (25 gp each).

Area 10. Tranimyz, Wylkun, and Sylzak's Quarters

A trio of large beds occupies much of the floor space of this chamber. The massive divans are piled high with course woolen blankets of drab color. Two chests, one tremendous and the other merely huge, stand in opposite corners of the room. A table bearing a great silver decanter and washing bowls rests between two of the beds.

This room is the sleeping chamber of the three youngest members of the Stormbreaker clan. The relatively cramped confines of the room means the three are seldom encountered here. They can usually be found occupying the lounge or dining hall instead.

The chests hold clothing for the three. The largest trunk contains masculine garments for the brothers, Tranimyz and Wylkun, while the smaller chest holds feminine clothing for their cousin, Sylzak. In addition to clothing, the large chest has two random minor magic items and the small trunk has a single random item from the same table.

The decanter is worth 100 gp and the washing bowl has a 50 gp value.

Area 11. Xurgal's Quarters (CR 8 if Xurgal is present)

The walls of this room are lined with finely made weapons suited for giants. Bearded axes, long spears, greatswords, and a flanged mace hang in X-shaped patterns across the bone walls. A simple bed with an iron frame sits beside a closed wardrobe. The wardrobe bears a shield-shaped plaque across its doors. The floor is covered with woolly hides taken from the backs of unknown beasts.

This is the chamber of **Xurgal**, the Stormbreakers' master-at-arms, but he is seldom here. Xurgal instead spends most of his time in the company of Vyjelmot the Grim (see **Area 14**) discussing matters of death. He is here only if not encountered in the chapel and if there is no alert underway.

XURGAL **CR 8**
XP 4,800
hp 95 (see **Area 14**)

The weapons are all high-quality arms fashioned by cloud giant smiths of great skill. Two greatswords, three great axes, four long spears (treat as halberds), and a large mace are here. Each weapon is sized for Large creatures.

The shield-shaped plaque is a metal plate covered in dents and gouges. It hangs positioned over the wardrobe's handles so that it must be removed to open the door. The underside of the plaque is lined with needle-sharp barbs coated with deadly toxin (treat as wyvern poison). The barbs are easily noticed if the plaque back is examined before grabbing it. Once the barbs are noticed, they can be avoided easily. Anyone who grabs the plaque without caution is automatically jabbed by the barbs.

The wardrobe contains tunics, breeches, and boots. In addition, a spare suit of giant-sized chainmail hangs from a T-shaped post, and a gargantuan, fur-lined, silk dressing robe (300 gp value) is draped over an iron box. The box is locked but not trapped; it holds two giant-sized *potions of cure moderate wounds* (three doses each), a suede bag containing 10 amethysts (50 gp value) and 2 sapphires (100 gp value), and a decorative helmet inlaid with gold wire and pearls (500 gp value).

The floor is covered by three rugs made from wooly mammoth hide worth 250 gp each.

Area 12. Armory

The door to this room is locked. Xurgal and Oblugrim have keys.

Racks of weapons and stands bearing suits of armor fill this room. Several large, square crates are piled along the eastern wall. The air smells like leather, steel, and oil.

This room contains 20 halberds, 15 greatclubs, and 10 suits of chainmail sized for Large creatures. There are also 10 crates, each of which contains two skull bombards packed in straw and wool batting.

Area 13. Lavatory

An oversized privy is located beyond the door. Composed of a single-seat with a mahogany lid and a marble washing basin, this lavatory appears designed for functionality but with a touch of class. A gleaming silver spigot protrudes from the wall above the marble basin and a large cut-glass decanter rests beside the sink. Plush, sky blue towels hang from a rack on the wall.

This privy is positioned over an open shaft that exits the bottom of the Ossuary and allows waste to fall freely to the land below. The shaft is 3 feet in diameter and has a very nasty iron grate at the bottom to prevent animals (and intruders) from entering the ship via the latrine shaft. The spigot draws water from a rainwater-collecting cistern located at the top of the keep (not detailed).

Several of the items here have value. The silver spigot is worth 100 gp if extracted from the wall (which subsequently causes a torrent of water to pour into the basin). The decanter is worth 200 gp, and the four hand towels are worth 15 gp each. The mahogany toilet seat could fetch 50 gp as a curio.

Area 14. Chapel (CR 11, or 12 if Xurgal is present)

The bones that form the walls, ceiling, and floor of this room are a glossy ebony color, turning the boundaries of the chamber into a reflective, starless night. At the opposite end of the room is a circular depression filled with roiling mist. Rising from the mist, like an island in a stormy sea, is a column of white bones. These pale bones form a statue depicting a leering skull with a skeletal snake intertwined through its eye sockets and nasal cavity. A bowl of cloudy liquid rests beneath the statue's eyeless gaze.

This sanctum is dedicated to the worship of Drahltuz, the giants' god of fear and death, and the personal deity of the Stormbreaker clan. The statue rises 30 feet tall to scrape the ceiling and measures 15 feet in diameter.

The statue is surrounded by a circular moat that is 15 feet wide and 5 feet deep. Acrid, gray smoke from seven lit braziers placed along the moat's bottom fills the depression. A minor enchantment keeps the braziers burning and the smoke contained within the moat.

The idol produces an unholy aura that defends the worshippers of Drahltuz from specific magic. It provides the benefits of an *unhallow* spell, with *bane* as its secondary effect.

The dark bones have been treated magically and with natural dyes to produce their coloration and veneer, but they have no special powers or properties. The cloudy water in the bowl is magical and radiates divination and necromancy auras. Pouring 4 oz. of the liquid into the mouth of a creature that's been dead no more than one week allows the corpse to be questioned as if it was under the effect of a *speak with dead* spell. The font holds enough liquid to question five corpses.

The priest, **Vyjelmot the Grim**, is always present here. There is a 75% chance that **Xurgal**, the master-of-arms, is also here engaged in discussion with the cleric.

VYJELMOT THE GRIM **CR 11**
XP 12,800
Male hill giant cleric of Drahltuz 8 (*Pathfinder Roleplaying Game Bestiary* "Giant, Hill")
CE Large humanoid (giant)
Init –1; **Senses** low-light vision; **Perception** +9

AC 21, touch 8, flat-footed 21 (+4 armor, –1 Dex, +9 natural, –1 size)
hp 153 (10d8+40 plus 8d8+32)
Fort +17; **Ref** +4; **Will** +12
Defensive Abilities death's embrace, rock catching

Speed 40 ft. (30 ft. in armor)
Melee greatclub +18/+13/+8 (2d8+7) or 2 slams +12 (1d8+2)
Space 10 ft.; **Reach** 10 ft.
Special Attacks channel negative energy 1/day (DC 14, 4d6), rock throwing (120 ft.), scythe of evil (4 rounds, 1/day)
Domain Spell-Like Abilities (CL 8th; concentration +11)
6/day—bleeding touch (4 rounds), touch of evil (4 rounds)
Spells Prepared (CL 8th; concentration +11)
4th—*death ward, divine power, unholy blight* D (DC 17)
3rd—*animate dead, dispel magic, invisibility purge, magic circle against good*[D], *magic vestment*
2nd—*align weapon (evil only)*[D], *bear's endurance, hold person* (DC 15), *silence* (DC 15), *spiritual weapon*
1st—*cause fear* (DC 14), *cure light wounds, divine favor, protection from good*[D], *protection from good, shield of faith*
0 (at will)—*bleed* (DC 13), *guidance, read magic, resistance*
D Domain spell; **Domains** Death, Evil

Str 20, **Dex** 8, **Con** 19, **Int** 9, **Wis** 17, **Cha** 7
Base Atk +13; **CMB** +19; **CMD** 28
Feats Cleave, Combat Casting, Command Undead, Extra Channel, Improved Channel, Intimidating Prowess, Martial Weapon Proficiency (greatclub), Power Attack, Weapon Focus (greatclub)
Skills Climb +8, Intimidate +10, Knowledge (religion) +12, Perception +9, Sense Motive +12
Languages Giant
Gear hide armor, greatclub, *bracers of the spectres* (see the **New Magic Items Appendix**), ivory and pearl unholy symbol (worth 250 gp), keys to the door and the coffer in **Area 15**, polished bone prayer beads (worth 50 gp)

Vyjelmot uses his bracers to summon the spectres to assist in the defense of the chapel. He casts spells on subsequent rounds.

Xurgal, if present, hurls his bombards before closing into melee range with intruders.

XURGAL **CR 8**
XP 4,800
Male hill giant fighter 1 (*Pathfinder Roleplaying Game Bestiary* "Giant, Hill")
CE Large humanoid (giant)
Init –1; **Senses** low-light vision; **Perception** +6

AC 24, touch 8, flat-footed 24 (+4 armor, –1 Dex, +9 natural, +3 shield, –1 size)
hp 95 (10d8+40 plus 1d10+4 plus 1)
Fort +13; **Ref** +2; **Will** +3
Defensive Abilities rock catching

Speed 40 ft. (30 ft. in armor)
Melee *+1 warhammer* +15/+10 (2d6+8/x3) or 2 slams +14 (1d8+7) or light shield bash +15/+10 (1d4+7)
Space 10 ft.; **Reach** 10 ft.
Special Attacks rock throwing (120 ft.)

Str 25, **Dex** 8, **Con** 19, **Int** 6, **Wis** 10, **Cha** 7
Base Atk +8; **CMB** +16; **CMD** 25
Feats Cleave, Intimidating Prowess, Martial Weapon Proficiency (greatclub), Power Attack, Shield Focus, Weapon Focus (greatclub), Weapon Focus (shield, light)
Skills Climb +10, Intimidate +13, Perception +6
Languages Giant

Combat Gear *potion of cure moderate wounds*; **Other Gear** hide armor, *+1 light steel shield*, *+1 warhammer*, belt of tanned leather worked with polished bloodstones (worth 200 gp), gold bracers with chased platinum storm cloud engravings (worth 300 gp), keys to **Area 12** and to the box in **Area 11**

Area 15. Rectory

The door to this room is locked. Vyjelmot the Grim has the key.

> This secluded room is spartanly furnished and holds little ornamentation. A bed consisting of an iron plate resting atop four large, metal-plated skulls occupies much of the space. A ghastly-looking iron maiden, its features stained brown with old blood, rests in the corner. A lectern fashioned from yellowed bones holds crumbling pages of smeared and stained parchment.
> An open spiral staircase ascends to the ceiling, vanishing into a shaft leading upward.

The iron maiden has been converted to a wardrobe. It holds spare sets of vestments, sandals, and other personal objects. A locked coffer rests atop a high shelf inside the maiden's head. Fashioned from rusted iron, the coffer contains a mummified finger nearly as large as a human forearm. This is an unholy relic—the ring finger of one Drahltuz's first apostates. If handled by someone who is not a follower of the evil god, the person touching it becomes *cursed*. The curse manifests as rapid bodily decay similar to a supernatural leprosy. The victim suffers 3d6 points of necrotic damage and 1 point of Strength, Dexterity, and Constitution damage every 24 hours. If reduced to zero hit points or if an ability score drops to zero, the victim dies. A *greater restoration* or *remove curse* spell removes the curse.

Ten pages comprising a religious treatise penned centuries ago by a high priest of Drahltuz sit on the lectern. A DC 20 Knowledge (religion) check identifies the god and rites mentioned in the writings. Additionally, a DC 20 Knowledge (arcana) check discerns veiled passages relating to the construction of the Necrolofter (see **Level One, Area 3**). Although not detailed enough to be used to actually create a device, they do provide hints as to where to begin researching the process, at the GM's discretion. The final page of the treatise is actually a scroll of *speak with dead*.

The bed is horribly uncomfortable and has no special value or properties.

Area 16. Jezsyl's Quarters (CR 7)

> The delicate scent of jasmine incense wafts over you, flowing from the room beyond the door. Woven hangings depicting storm-wracked mountaintops and whirlwind-torn forests decorate the walls, and the floor is covered with a light cloth carpet. A small table holds smoking incense sticks and a dark idol. A simple sleeping pallet covered by a thin blanket rests in one corner.

If not encountered elsewhere, **Jezsyl**, a hill giant monk, is found here meditating before the small table shrine. She swiftly responds to intruders, leaping to her bare feet and using her monkish skills to incapacitate as many of the characters as possible while shouting for assistance. There is a 75% chance the occupants of the chapel come to her aid (if they are still able) and a 50% chance that a trio of hill giant guards respond to her cries in 1d4+2 rounds.

JEZSYL **CR 7**
XP 3,200
Female hill giant monk 1 (*Pathfinder Roleplaying Game Bestiary* "Giant, Hill")
LE Large humanoid (giant)
Init +0; **Senses** low-light vision; **Perception** +9

AC 22, touch 13, flat-footed 21 (+1 dodge, +3 monk bonus, +9 natural, –1 size)
hp 82 (10d8+30 plus 1d8+3)
Fort +12; **Ref** +5; **Will** +8
Defensive Abilities rock catching

Speed 40 ft.
Melee siangham +10/+5 (1d8+4) or siangham flurry of blows +2/+2 (1d8+4) or unarmed strike +10/+5 (1d8+4) or unarmed strike flurry of blows +2/+2 (1d8+4) or 2 slams +10 (1d8+4)
Space 10 ft.; **Reach** 10 ft.
Special Attacks flurry of blows, rock throwing (120 ft.), stunning fist (3/day, DC 18)

Str 19, **Dex** 10, **Con** 17, **Int** 9, **Wis** 16, **Cha** 7
Base Atk +7; **CMB** +12; **CMD** 26
Feats Cleave, Combat Reflexes, Dodge, Improved Unarmed Strike, Intimidating Prowess, Martial Weapon Proficiency (greatclub), Power Attack, Stunning Fist, Weapon Focus (greatclub)
Skills Acrobatics +5 (+9 to jump), Climb +10, Intimidate +9, Knowledge (history) +3, Knowledge (religion) +3, Perception +9
Languages Giant
Gear 2 sianghams, 144 gp

The idol is a representation of Drahltuz, the giants' god of fear and death. It is depicted as a squat, obese creature with a face resembling a serpent's skull. It is carved from rare black marble and weighs 100 lbs. (50 gp value). The incense is pleasant-smelling but has no special properties.

Beneath the sleeping pallet is a long, low wooden box containing a number of giantess-sized kimonos of simple manufacture and a spare pair of Large sianghams.

The four woven tapestries measure 15 feet long by 8 feet wide, and each weighs 150 lbs. They are skillfully made and worth 150 gp each.

Area 17. Stairs to Upper Level

> An open spiral staircase ascends to the ceiling, vanishing into a shaft leading upward.

These stairs lead 40 feet upward to **Level Three, Area 1**. The occupants of the Ossuary know to announce themselves before ascending. See the description of **Level Three, Area 1** for the consequences of failing to do so.

If combat occurs on the staircase, creatures battling from the upper position have tactical advantage on attack rolls against lower opponents.

Area 18. Treasury (CR 6)

The door to this room is locked, trapped, and alarmed. Bypassing the lock requires either the proper key (possessed by Oblugrim Stormbreaker in **Level Three, Area 2**) or a successful DC 30 Disable Device check. A DC 20 Perception check notices the trap: a spring lever that breaks a pair of small vials, one containing a clear liquid and the other containing a green liquid. The trap is triggered by any attempt to open the lock without the proper key, unless the trap is first disarmed with a successful DC 30 Disable Device check. If the trap is sprung and the vials are broken, their contents mix to create a flesh-devouring gas that fills a 20-foot-square space in front of the door. All creatures in the gas area can attempt a DC 20 Reflex save. Success indicates the character quickly jumps clear of the gas cloud. Those who fail the saving throw get a lungful of gas and take 3d8+3 points of acid damage at the start of each of their turns until they use an action to make a successful DC 20 Fortitude save against acid. A successful save stops further damage, as does any *cure* spell or other healing magic.

FLESH-DEVOURING GAS TRAP **CR 6**
XP 2,400
Type mechanical; **Perception** DC 20; **Disable Device** DC 30

Trigger touch; **Reset** none; **Bypass** key
Effect cloud of flesh-devouring gas (3d8+3 acid damage, DC 20 Reflex/Fortitude save negates); multiple targets (all targets within a 20 ft. cloud)

> Large iron chests stand along the walls of this room beside statuary, rolled cloth, and raw timber. Despite the contents, the room is largely empty, holding but a small portion of what it could contain.

The Stormbreakers planned to fill this treasury with loot plundered during their campaign, but so far their targets have been small agricultural villages possessing little that the giants desire. The contents of this chamber were won from early conflicts with the hill giants and other opponents in the mountains during the Ossuary's shakedown flight.

Six unlocked iron chests are here. Four are empty; the other two each hold 100 lbs. of unrefined gold ore (1,000 gp value).

The rolled cloth is actually two woven wool tapestries worth 100 gp each. Three carved stone statues depicting large and grotesque humanoid faces weigh 500 lbs. each. These idols are ancient and weathered, but they're worth 300 gp apiece to collectors, historians, or sages (they might hold clues to lost mysteries at the GM's choosing). The piled timber is all rare hardwood. The lumber weighs 1,000 lbs. and is worth 500 gp.

Level Three — Upper Level

This small level contains two important rooms: the quarters of the Stormbreaker leader and his consort, and the Ossuary's bridge. Adventurers seeking to end the cloud giant threat to the region likely find this level to be the site of the final battle.

Area 1. Guard Post (CR 9)

> At the top of the winding stairs is a simple space containing a table, three large chairs, and a hanging shield dangling from a cross brace on a wooden stand. A barrel stands near the staircase, and a large candle burns on the tabletop.

Always stationed here are **2 hill giant guards**, charged with defending this level. Standard protocol is for any occupant of the Ossuary to call out

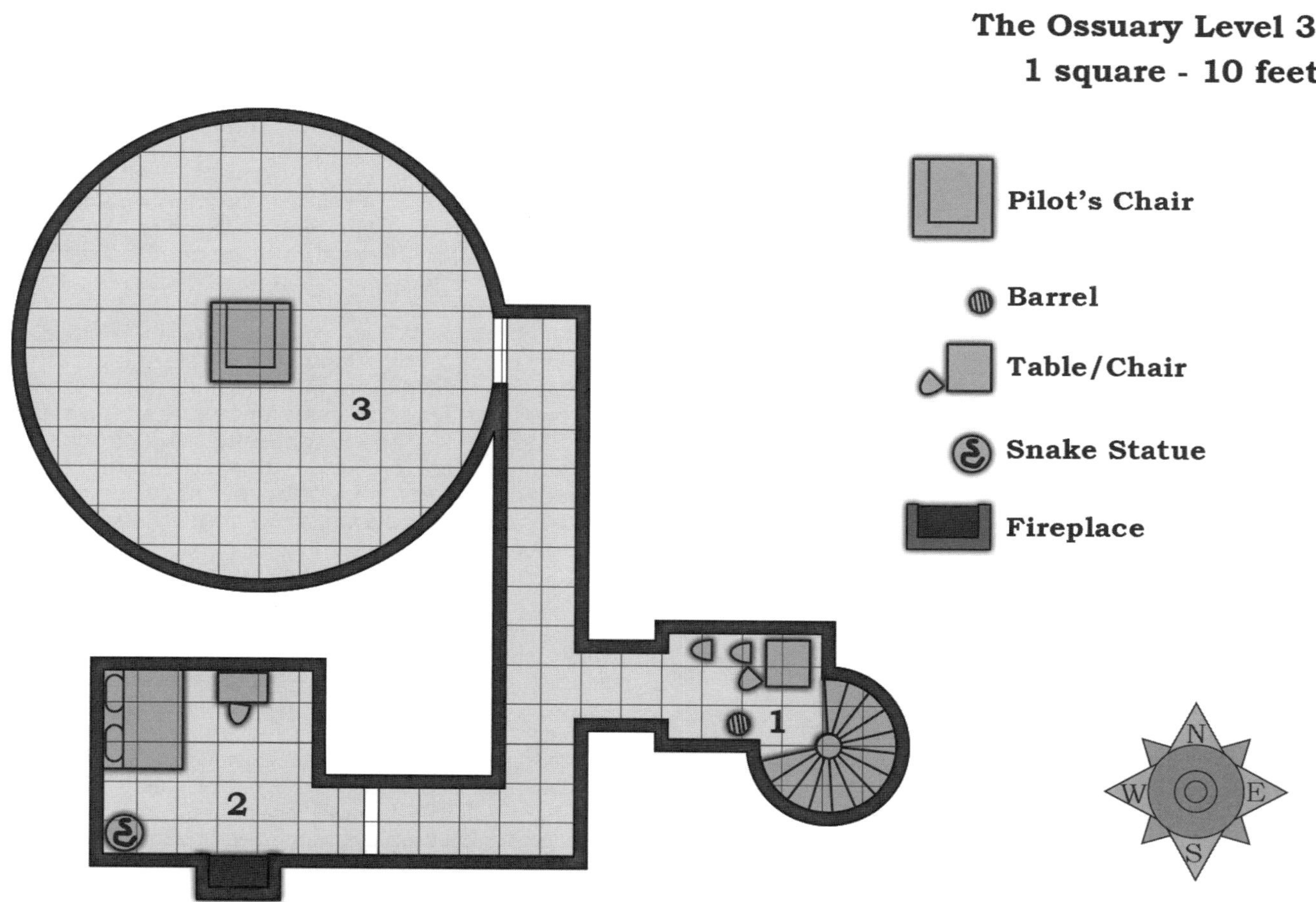

his or her name before climbing the staircase. If the guards detect creatures ascending that do not announce themselves, one of the guards pours the barrel of oil down the stairwell while the second stands by, preparing to hurl a skull bombard filled with alchemist's fire into the stairwell on the following round.

The barrel holds sufficient oil to coat the uppermost 30 feet of the stairwell, making the steps slippery and flammable. A creature wishing to climb the slick stairs must succeed on a DC 10 Acrobatics check to avoid slipping and falling down the stairs (suffering 2d6 points of bludgeoning damage in the fall). Any individual on the oil-coated stairs when they are set alight suffers 1d10 points of fire damage every time they begin their turn in the burning oil, for up to six rounds.

After setting the stairs alight, one of the guards pounds the shield alarm gong, alerting the giants in **Area 2** and the guards in **Area 3** that intruders are on their way. This giant carries a skull bombard (see **Level 2, Area 2**).

HILL GIANTS (2) **CR 7**
XP 3,200
hp 85 (*Pathfinder Roleplaying Game Bestiary* "Giant, Hill")

Area 2. Oblugrim's and Tathhylia's Quarters (CR 13)

This opulent chamber features a carved bedstead of rare wood situated on a plush carpet. Skillful portraiture and tapestries hang from the walls, and a large fireplace burns brightly in the bone wall. A table covered with jars and boxes stands before a large oval mirror on the north wall. A 15-foot-tall, serpentine-shaped post with a crossbar stands in the southwest corner of the room. The delicate scent of mountain flowers hangs in the air.

This chamber is home to the Stormbreaker patriarch, **Oblugrim**, and his consort **Tathhylia**, as well as their pet **advanced marble snake**. All three are found here if not encountered randomly elsewhere and no alarm is underway. Their pet usually rests on its post, entwined around the crossbar.

OBLUGRIM **CR 11**
XP 12,800
Male cloud giant (*Pathfinder Roleplaying Game Bestiary* "Giant, Cloud")
NE Huge humanoid (giant)
Init +1; **Senses** low-light vision, scent; **Perception** +17

AC 28, touch 9, flat-footed 27 (+4 armor, +1 Dex, +12 natural, +3 shield, –2 size)
hp 168 (16d8+96)
Fort +16; **Ref** +6; **Will** +10
Defensive Abilities rock catching

Speed 50 ft.
Melee *+1 frost morningstar* +23/+18/+13 (3d6+13 plus 1d6 cold) or 2 slams +17 (2d6+6)
Space 15 ft.; **Reach** 15 ft.
Special Attacks rock throwing (140 ft.)
Spell-Like Abilities (CL 16th; concentration +17);
At will—*levitate* (self plus 2,000 lbs.), *obscuring mist*
1/day—*fog cloud*

Str 35, **Dex** 13, **Con** 23, **Int** 12, **Wis** 16, **Cha** 12
Base Atk +12; **CMB** +26 (+28 bull rush, +28 overrun); **CMD** 37 (39 vs. bull rush, 39 vs. overrun)
Feats Awesome Blow, Cleave, Great Cleave, Improved Bull Rush, Improved Overrun, Intimidating Prowess, Iron Will, Power Attack
Skills Acrobatics –1 (+7 to jump), Climb +19, Craft (Enter Choice) +8, Diplomacy +9, Intimidate +26, Perception +17, Perform (string instruments) +8
Languages Common, Giant
SQ oversized weapon
Combat Gear 2 *potion of cure serious wounds*; **Other Gear** chain shirt, *+2 light steel shield*, *+1 frost morningstar*, keys to armory (**Level Two, Area 12**) and treasury (**Level Two, Area 18**)

TATHHYLIA **CR 11**
XP 12,800
hp 168 (*Pathfinder Roleplaying Game Bestiary* "Giant, Cloud")

ADVANCED MARBLE SNAKE **CR 4**
XP 1,200
The Tome of Horrors Complete, 419
N Large magical beast
Init +3; **Senses** darkvision 60 ft., low-light vision; **Perception** +13

AC 16, touch 12, flat-footed 13 (+3 Dex, +4 natural, –1 size)
hp 42 (4d10+20)
Fort +8; **Ref** +7; **Will** +3

Speed 20 ft., climb 20 ft.
Melee bite +9 (1d6+9)
Space 10 ft.; **Reach** 5 ft.
Special Attacks whistle (DC 14)

Str 22, **Dex** 17, **Con** 18, **Int** 2, **Wis** 14, **Cha** 15
Base Atk +4; **CMB** +11; **CMD** 24 (can't be tripped)
Feats Skill Focus (Perception), Toughness
Skills Acrobatics +15 (+11 to jump), Climb +22, Perception +13, Stealth +8

Whistle (Su) A marble snake can whistle, gaining the attention of any creature within 50 feet that hears it. All creatures (other than marble snakes) with the area must succeed on a DC 14 Will save or become entranced. This is a sonic mind-affecting charm effect. A creature that successfully saves cannot be affected again by the same marble snake's whistle for one day. The save DC is Charisma-based.

An entranced victim walks toward the marble snake, taking the most direct route available. If the path leads into a dangerous area, that creature gets a second saving throw. The effect continues for as long as the marble snake whistles and for 1 round thereafter. An entranced victim is effectively dazed (cannot attack, but can defend). If an entranced opponent is attacked, the effect is immediately broken. A bard's countersong ability allows the entranced creature to attempt a new Will save.

The paintings are oil portraits of the Stormbreaker Clan's former patriarchs. Each of the four paintings is worth 250 gp. They are sizable, however, measuring 10 feet long by 5 feet high and weighing 50 lbs. each. The tapestries are detailed landscapes of secluded mountain valleys surrounded by clouds and fog. Each of the three wall hangings is worth 150 gp.

The table contains personal grooming items and jars of makeup, perfume, and other hygiene products. One of the bottles is fashioned from cut jasper (50 gp value) and contains a delicate perfume that seems to change its scent depending on the person sniffing it. This perfume bears a slight enchantment and, when worn, increases the wearer's Charisma score by 1 for one hour. There is enough perfume for three uses.

Beneath the bed is a large iron chest. It has no lock and appears to be opened by simply pulling the knurled steel handle protruding from the lid's top. The chest is trapped, however. Unless the opener touches the handle with a *shocking grasp* spell before pulling the lid, a blast of electricity leaps from the chest, catching all creatures in a 30-foot radius around the box. Those in the blast take 8d6 points of electrical damage, or half as much with a successful DC 19 Reflex save (DC 17 for everyone but the one who touched the chest). Closely inspecting the handle and making a successful DC 25 Perception check reveals tiny runes etched along the handle's bottom, and anyone trained in Knowledge (arcana) can identify them as pertaining to electricity or lightning.

CHAIN LIGHTNING TRAP **CR 7**
XP 3,200
Type magical; **Perception** DC 31; **Disable** Device DC 31

Trigger touch; **Reset** none; **Bypass** *shocking grasp*
Effect spell effect (as *chain lightning*, 8d6 electricity damage, DC 19/17 Ref half); multiple targets (all targets within 30 ft. of the box)

The chest contains Oblugrim and Tathhylia's personal wealth. Inside are 1,046 cp, 768 sp, 477 gp, a large harp with electrum inlay (350 gp value), a robe of winter wolf fur (200 gp value), Tathhylia's spellbook (contains all her prepared spells), and an oversized crown of gold and sapphires (1,000 gp value).

Area 3. The Bridge (CR 12)

> This area is a massive, conical-shaped chamber with a cathedral ceiling. Dominating the chamber is a titanic, throne-like chair bearing a giant occupant. The seated individual wears only a white loin cloth, leaving the majority of his sky-blue skin exposed. Many rib-like bones and venous tubes protrude from the chair and are embedded in the flesh of the seated giant, effectively binding him to the seat. Five smaller giants dressed in mail armor and bearing large spears stand guard nearby.

The chair is the Ossuary's helm, and the figure attached to it is **Morgosun Stormbreaker**, the pilot of the Ossuary. Morgosun was not the most gifted or liked of the Stormbreaker clan, and when it was decided that someone needed to make the sacrifice to merge with the fortress to serve as its eternal captain, Morgosun was forcibly "volunteered" by Oblugrim. The only thing that has kept him from crashing the Ossuary and dooming his clan to death is Oblugrim's promise that once the humans are driven out of the mountains, Morgosun will be freed from his duty and restored to a normal life (this is a lie; Oblugrim considers the flying citadel far too valuable to give up). Nevertheless, as a precaution, Oblugrim stationed hill giant guards here to protect the pilot but also to slay him should he ever try to crash the Ossuary.

Gurgulash, the self-proclaimed sub-chief of the hill giants (under Xurgal), is here with **4 hill giants**. Gurgulash wears the *belt of bones* because he feels it gives him power and authority, even though it provides him no benefit.

GURGULASH **CR 8**
XP 4,800
Male advanced hill giant (*Pathfinder Roleplaying Game Bestiary*, "Giant, Hill,")
CE Large humanoid (giant)
Init +1; **Senses** low-light vision; **Perception** +8

AC 25, touch 10, flat-footed 24 (+4 armor, +1 Dex, +11 natural, –1 size)
hp 105 (10d8+60)
Fort +13; **Ref** +4; **Will** +5
Defensive Abilities rock catching

Speed 40 ft. (30 ft. in armor)
Melee greatclub +16/+11 (2d8+13) or 2 slams +10 (1d8+4)
Space 10 ft.; **Reach** 10 ft.
Special Attacks rock throwing (120 ft.)

Str 29, **Dex** 12, **Con** 23, **Int** 10, **Wis** 14, **Cha** 11
Base Atk +7; **CMB** +17; **CMD** 28
Feats Cleave, Intimidating Prowess, Martial Weapon Proficiency (greatclub), Power Attack, Weapon Focus (greatclub)
Skills Climb +12, Intimidate +19, Perception +8, Sense Motive +6, Survival +8
Languages Giant
Other Gear *belt of bones* (see the **New Magic Items Appendix**), hide armor, greatclub, gold bracelet (worth 250 gp), silver bracelet (worth 100 gp), silver snake-shaped ring (worth 100 gp), 54 pp, 178 gp, 200 sp

HILL GIANTS (4) **CR 7**
XP 3,200
hp 85 (*Pathfinder Roleplaying Game Bestiary* "Giant, Hill")

All of the hill giants carry one skull bombard apiece.

Morgosun Stormbreaker cannot physically attack the party; he is restrained by the Ossuary's helm. He can, however, defend himself with the necrotic energy field that powers the fortress under his command. He uses the standard cloud giant stat block, but his only means of attack is the Necrotic Blast.

Necrotic Blast (Su) Morgosun calls down a blast of withering energy that strikes a single target inside the bridge as a +6 ranged touch attack. The victim hit by the blast takes 4d8+4 points of damage, or half damage with a successful DC 20 Fortitude save.

If Morgosun is slain, the Ossuary immediately ceases moving. It hangs in place 400 feet above the ground until it runs out of power or the Necrolofter is destroyed (see **Level One, Area 3**). If the helm is attacked directly, it has AC 8 and 200 hit points. It fails all saving throws. Destroying the chair kills Morgosun instantly in a blast of necrotic energy, and the Ossuary comes to a dead stop.

This room contains only the helm, which is a huge seat fashioned from bone and rises 20 feet above the floor. A dozen bone spurs and vein-like tubes protrude from the chair, each ending in a sharp, hollow barb that can be inserted into skin and muscle. A living creature connected to the chair gains the ability to fly the Ossuary as well as to view its surroundings with limited clairvoyance. For more information on the role of the pilot, see the section "The Ossuary in the PCs' Hands."

Concluding the Adventure

The characters succeed in stopping the cloud giant's campaign of evil if they either kill the tremendous occupants of the Ossuary or incapacitate the flying citadel. The Lord-Governor of Cerediun Province accepts either circumstance as a victory and gratefully rewards the party the promised fee of 1,000 gp.

Should the adventure conclude with the Ossuary captured intact and operational, the lord-governor, seeing the military advantage of owning such a useful fort, offers to buy the flying citadel from the party. The exact amount he is willing to part with is left to the GM's discretion, but should not exceed 15,000 gp. Understandably, the party may wish to hold onto the keep for their own purposes. Refer to the section "The Ossuary in the PCs' Hands" in this case.

If the GM desires, the events of ***The Dead from Above*** can lead to additional adventures. The Stormbreaker Clan may not be the only cloud giant clan wishing to see humanity driven out of the mountains. Other giants might be planning their own vendetta against mankind, requiring the heroes to venture into the high peaks to stop these other campaigns before they begin.

If the characters successfully identify the important passages in the ancient texts found in **Level Two, Area 15**, they might be interested in learning more about creating fortresses like the Ossuary. This quest could spur numerous new adventures as the party tracks down lost lore or seeks out reclusive sages and wizards who possess the power and skill needed to tear mountains apart and make them fly.

And, of course, if any of the Stormbreakers survive the attack on the Ossuary, the characters should find themselves the target of giant vengeance, a revenge that begins with hurled boulders and powerful spells when they least expect it!

The Ossuary in the PCs' Hands

It is likely that if the characters defeat the Stormbreaker giants, they'll end the adventure in possession of the Ossuary. Not all GMs may want their players to own such a formidable base of operations, but luckily, being the sole entities standing inside the aerial holdfast does not automatically bestow command of the Ossuary on the party.

Firstly, the Ossuary requires a living creature in the role of the pilot. This is not so much an honor as a doom, because the pilot becomes permanently bonded with the magical helm in **Level Three, Area 3**. Not many beings are willing to give up their freedom and embrace such a ghastly existence to simply operate an artifact. NPCs will certainly refuse unless magically compelled. If *charm* spells are used to encourage an NPC to become the pilot, he seeks revenge once the enchantment wears off, likely crashing the Ossuary into the first convenient mountainside as suitable punishment for those who damned him!

If one of the characters volunteers to become the pilot, he (or others) need to first determine the proper way to connect a new pilot to the chair. This requires a successful DC 20 Knowledge (arcana) check and DC 20 Heal check. Divination spells can also help determine the proper process. Once the process is deduced, the would-be pilot suffers 8d6 points of piercing damage as the various bone spurs and tubes are inserted into his flesh. This damage can be halved if the person connecting the pilot to the chair makes a successful DC 15 Heal check. Lastly, the adventurer must succeed on a DC 20 Fortitude save to successfully integrate his mind and body with the Ossuary. If the save fails, the pilot dies, slain by necrotic energy feedback that tears his body apart. If the pilot survives the process, he gains full command of the Ossuary — including the ability to mentally see outside the Ossuary's confines and the power to summon the necrotic blast defense detailed in **Level Three, Area 3**.

Even with a living pilot on the bridge, the Ossuary requires constant refueling with souls, and this step should not sit well with characters who are not evil-aligned. As noted in **Level One, Area 3**, the Necrolofter requires the stolen life of living beings to operate. At least 8 HD of intelligent, living beings must be fed to the hungry spirits connected to the Necrolofter each week or the citadel loses power and settles to the ground until it is refueled. No other power source suffices.

While the characters might have moral issues with keeping the Ossuary running and under control, many NPCs suffer no such compulsions. If it becomes common knowledge that the party possesses the Ossuary, they can be certain that they'll find themselves targeted by all manner of bandit kings, evil wizards, foul priests, and other such ne'er-do-wells intent on claiming the Ossuary for themselves. The GM should make life very interesting for the characters for as long as they own the holdfast.

New Magic Items

Bracers of Spectres

Aura strong necromancy; **CL** 14th
Slot wrists; **Price** 60,000 gp **Weight** 1 lb.

DESCRIPTION

These ornamental brass bracers are covered with a patina of verdigris indicating their great age. Imagery depicting tombs, open graves, and plundered sarcophagi are inscribed on their surfaces. Leather straps hold them in place. Like many magical objects, the bracers of spectres resize to fit their wearer.

The *bracers of spectres* have a pair of undead spirits bound to them, forced to unerringly serve the bracers' owner when commanded. The owner can call upon either spectre to appear once per day, individually or together. When summoned, the spectre(s) appear to leap from the bracers, manifesting before the wearer. The spectre(s) follow any command spoken by the bracers' owner to the best of their ability for up to one hour. After that time, a spirit returns to the bracer until the following day.

A spectre that suffers damage while manifested is fully healed by resting in the bracers for 24 hours. If summoned before the period elapses, the spirit manifests in its damaged state and does not regain lost hit points until at least 24 hours have passed without it called forth. If a specter is destroyed while manifested, it is permanently lost and the owner cannot replace the destroyed spirit. Should both specters ever be destroyed while manifested, the bracers lose their enchantment and become ordinary objects.

CONSTRUCTION

Requirements Create Wondrous Item, *create greater undead*; **Cost** 30,000 gp

Belt of Bones

Aura moderate necromancy and transmutation; **CL** 7th
Slot belt; **Price** 10,000 gp **Weight** 1 lb.

DESCRIPTION

This object is a wide girdle fashioned from crudely-tanned leather of undetermined origin and decorated with aged, yellowing animal bones sewn to the leather backing. The belt rattles when worn, and the rattling increases in volume when the wearer calls upon the object's power.

The *belt of bones* provides the benefits listed below only if the wearer has the rage class ability; it is simply a decorative accessory in the possession of other classes.

Up to three times per day, the bones can instantly expand to cover the wearer's body and create a protective shell that functions exactly as the *shield* spell.

The wearer gains a +4 enhancement bonus to strength while the belt is worn.

If the belt is worn the entire day, once per day thereafter as a free action the wearer can grant herself 3 additional rounds of rage.

CONSTRUCTION

Requirements Create Wondrous Item, *rage*, *endurance*, *shield*, creator must have the bloodrage or rage class ability **Cost** 5,000 gp

Dread Dragon Temple

By James M. Ward

This adventure is inetended for 6th- to 8th-level characters with a bias toward spellcasters. In the **Lost Lands** campaign setting of **Frog God Games,** the adventure takes place on the island of West Talon at the Southern end of the Crescent Sea, just north of the Talanos Penisnula and its dread High Barrens. If you are adapting the adventure to your own campaign, it can be set on any temperate island that is large enough to support, not only a decent-sized fishing and farming population but a central desert and mountainous area as well.

Adventure Background

The small nation of Borss on the island of West Talon is renowned for the three mountains that rise from its central desert plateau, or more precisely for the massive stone temple shaped like a dragon that clings to the slopes of said mountains. Everyone the plies the waters of the Mouth of Akados knows about the Dragon Temple and its dire reputation of great treasures and even greater dangers.

Many a story has been told about the deadly temple, but the tale mothers tell their children the most is about a magical staff that is said to lie at the heart of the temple. The legends say the staff can transform its wielder into a great red dragon. The tales evolve, of course, as the children grow older, with larger and more terrible monsters guarding the staff; ever vaster treasures fill every corridor of the Dragon Temple with each retelling. Fearsome dragons of incredible size and magical power are said to prowl the temple halls ready to breathe fire on any being foolish enough to dare to enter their domain.

Other stories speak of wizards and heroes braving the challenges of the temple for a chance at the legendary *staff of the dragon*. All of these tales, however, share the same tragic ending for the impetuous bands of adventurers. One favored legend known to the peoples of the Crescent Sea speaks of the time King Col of the Ironskull Great Mountain Clan came down from his fastness in the Blackrock range with an army of mountain dwarf engineers and took a fleet of ships from Bret Harth to the island. After they landed, Old Col and his dwarves worked for more than a year to build a ramp from the mountains' base to the mouth of the temple. When they finished, the dwarven army climbed the ramp to invade, Old Col sure that the rumored treasures must overflow the storerooms of the temple. The legend says that before they could reach the temple mouth, a flight of red dragons flew down and incinerated the army, while another flight of dragons — these with scales of brass — destroyed the ramp so that no stone was left atop another. The legendary end of a legendary dwarven king.

Naysayers call this tale apocryphal at best and utterly preposterous at worst, but its proponents point out that King Col has inarguably been dead these hundreds of years and that there is plainly no ramp climbing to the temple's mouth and so claim it as proof of the tale's veracity, though no flight of dragons red, brass, or otherwise has ever been reported in the temple's vicinity before or since. Truth or no, this cautionary tale has ensured that no force of arms has challenged the temple since, and the nation of Borss' own small military has been able to ensure its own sovereignty from pirates and avaricious colonial powers at least partially on the reputation of the island's infamous — if perhaps exaggerated — guardians.

Of more recent and verifiable history, during the Year of Twelve Blue Moons, an ancient blue dragon flew down from the High Barrens to alight on the mountains of West Talon. With its lightning breath it is said that the dragon blasted out a lair in the sandstone cliffs of the mountains, creating a series of glass caverns for itself to live in. For a hundred years the blue dragon roared in the West Talon skies, eating its way through the giants and other monstrous denizens populating the central mountains and desert of the island.

The people of Borss long ignored the presence of the blue dragon; it tended to remain in the uninhabited central regions of the island and usually slept for decades after the few times it did raid a farm or ship in the nearby sea lanes. However, their complacency came to an abrupt end on the day the ancient beast flew down and destroyed the village of Sherss and all of its fishing vessels, devouring all of the inhabitants. The Draconic writing didn't have to appear on the wall for the citizens of the two largest cities, Borss and Kamis, and the other dozen-odd towns on the island to realize they needed help.

The sages and wizards of the realm researched the Dragon Temple to find out if the *staff of the dragon* from the children's stories existed and if its magic might allow heroes to challenge the dread blue dragon in its lair.

To their surprise, they discovered that the mythical staff of the dragon did indeed exist. The sages know nothing more of the relic but hope that brave adventurers can be found to enter the temple to retrieve the legendary staff — and then find a way to use it to end the island's new nightmare.

Challenges Outside the Temple (CR 6)

The mountains all around the temple are treacherous and near impossible to climb. The mountain rocks are ancient, crumbling sandstone, with reliable ledges and handholds few and far between, and constant winds coming from the sea and mixing with the desert thermals around the mountains make the weather tricky and unpredictable. What rain does fall on the highest peaks makes the rocks slippery, even as the moisture evaporates before it reaches the dry deserts encroaching on the mountains' rocky bases.

Most of the temple itself is high in the mountains and requires a lengthy climb to reach even the sides. In fact, the only part of the temple that is easy to get to is the tip of the tail. From any position along the mountainside near the temple, it is almost certain death to try a climb.

> The temple can be easily observed by anyone on the western side of the mountains. Even from a distance, it is clear the temple itself is shaped like a giant red dragon resting along the flank of the mountains. The structure forming the dragon's form is many miles long and wide, spanning possibly 15 miles from its snout to the tip of its tail. The four taloned limbs have giant claws of red granite several hundred yards long and high.

Climbing to any section of the temple is a deadly act for even the most experienced climbers. However, at the tip of the temple's tail, a slim path travels along the dragon's spine and takes a careful character right to the jaws and temple entrance 5 miles away. This path is purposely hard to see from anywhere around that section of the mountain. As the characters

Dread Dragon Temple

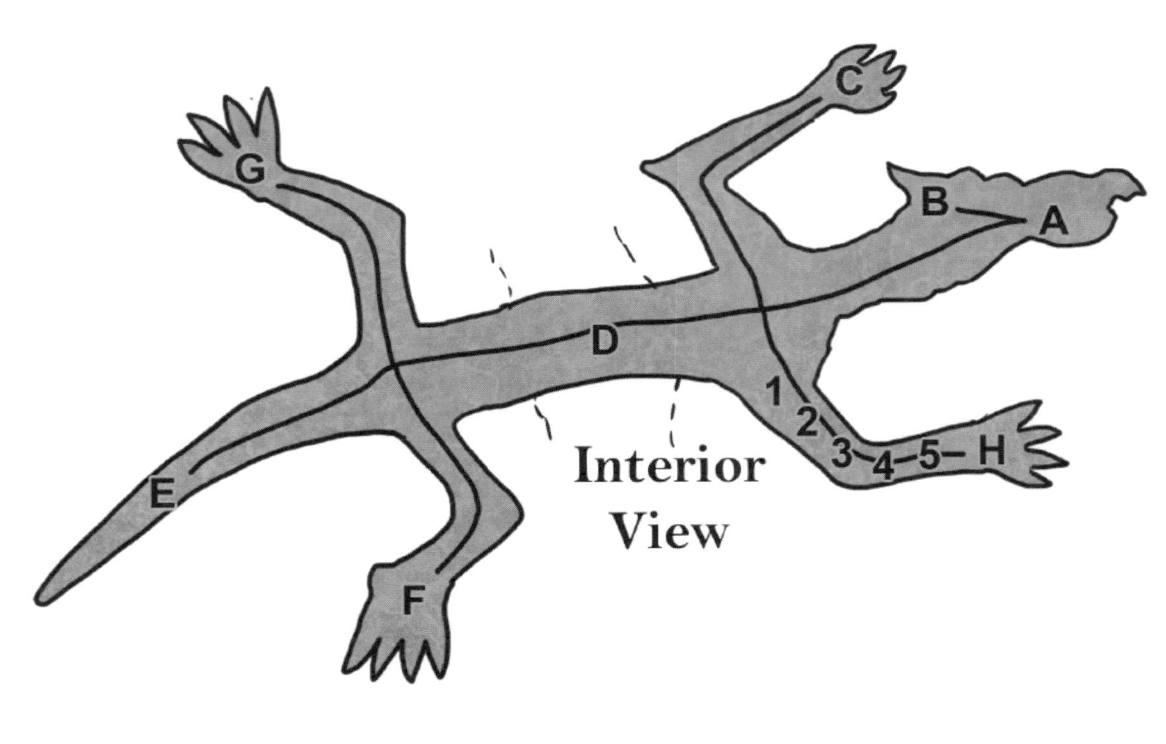

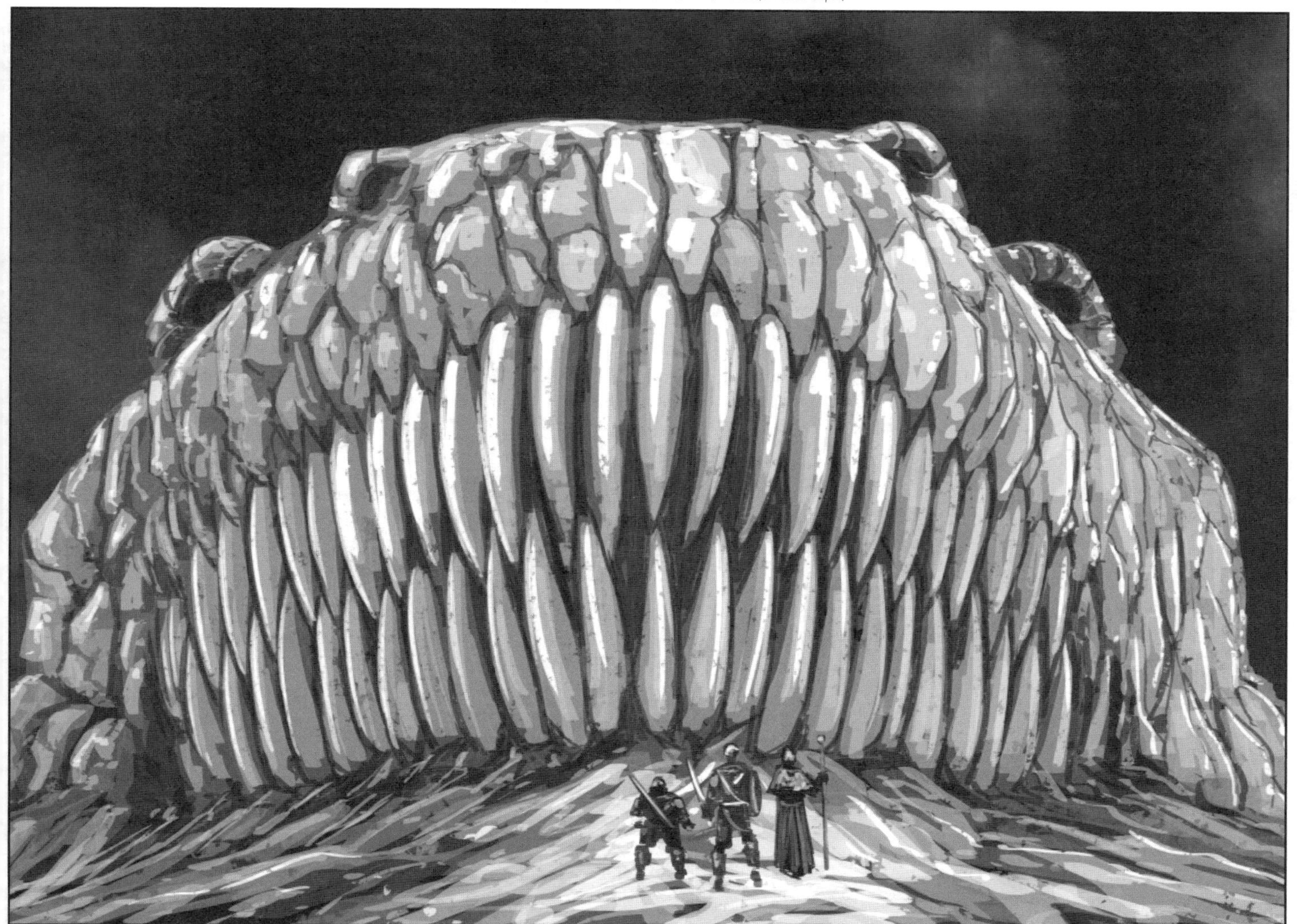

move along the path, grim portents give the wise traveler advance warning that this is a dangerous place. The blackest thunderclouds move over the mountains, and lightning strikes at random all over the path. Flurries of hailstones fall from the sky, creating a slippery carpet of ice on the trail. The roars of what sound like several different types of dragons echo down from the clouds above, and flashes of dragon fire and spouts of acid break through the clouds and fall near the characters.

The temple is carved directly into the rock of the mountain face. Efforts to break through its stone walls or use magic to dimensionally pass through them invariably fail as most of them are hundreds of feet thick at least and the winding interior does not provide obvious points of ingress to pinpoint. Important chambers are shielded with a layer of lead in the walls to prevent scrying, so it is virtually impossible to gain entry by means other than the main gates.

The tip of the tail offers the only safe spot where characters can climb up and onto a path that travels outside along the spine of the Dragon Temple.

The path provides a magical *bless*, as the spell, to all beings that walk the entire length to the head of the dragon. This blessing lasts as long as the characters are visiting the temple.

At the middle of the Dragon Path, a patrol of **6 lizardfolk** armed with halberds attacks the characters. The battle is to the death, and the fanatical lizardfolk pursue the characters until one group or the other is dead.

LIZARDFOLK (6) CR 1
XP 400
hp 11 (Pathfinder Roleplaying Game Bestiary "Lizardfolk")
Note Instead of morningstars, these lizardfolk are armed with halberds.
Melee halberd +2 (1d10+1/x3), bite +0 (1d4) or claw +2 (1d4+1), bite +2 (1d4+1)

Area A. Dragon Jaws Carnage (CR 6–9)

The huge stone head of the temple is carved in the image of an ancient red dragon. The head is over half-a-mile wide, over 1,000 feet high, and the long snout is a mile-and-a-half long. A flat plateau, canted at less of a grade than the slope, surrounds the head of the dragon. The rest of the carven stonework making up the dragon's body protrudes directly from the mountains' dangerous cliff faces.

Red sandstone covers the entire area around the head and claws, and dragon scales are carved into the stone surface.

Each of the dragon's carven fangs is hundreds of yards tall. Between the tightly fitted teeth can be seen a cave entrance that leads down the throat of the dragon. This is the obvious entrance to the Dragon Temple, but the edges of the great fangs are too close together to allow a person to squeeze between them.

Winds howl around this mountain face, and the smell of fresh blood blasts out of the throat entrance.

Spending the Night in the Temple

In this mysterious temple, the night is torn with the rage-filled roars of the ghosts of murdered dragons. It is lucky for the characters that these ghostly dragons have their own agendas. If talked to reasonably, the dragons reveal what they need from the party. They don't attack if the PCs agree to help the ghost dragon so it can flee the temple and go on to its afterlife. Although these ghostly dragons are intelligent, their powers are limited in the Material Plane; they function like haunts (Pathfinder Roleplaying Game GameMastery Guide, "Haunts"). Unlike other haunts, these dragons can be reasoned with.

If the party fights a dragon, they suffer the effects of dragon breath as the ghost furiously attacks. They can save to take no damage from the attack, but the attacks continue all night long unless the haunt is dispelled. Only one ghost dragon can interact with the party at a time. Helping a dragon allows its ghostly spirit to vanish and leave the temple.

DRAGON HAUNTS **CR 8**
XP 4,800
Haunt (40 ft. radius around the party) (*Pathfinder Roleplaying Game GameMastery Guide* "Haunt")
Notice Perception DC 10 to hear dragon roars
hp 36; **Trigger** location; **Reset** 1 day
Effect When this haunt is triggers, a random ghostly dragon appears (see below); each dragon can attack with a ghostly version of its breath weapon as if it were a young dragon of its type (see *Pathfinder Roleplaying Game Bestiary* "Chromatic Dragon")
Destruction A dragon haunt in this temple is only destroyed if it is helped to move on (see below)

Read the following if the characters decide to camp within the Dragon Temple:

> You set up camp in the safest area you can find. Early in the night, everyone wakes to the sound of multiple dragons roaring, each clearly coming from a different type of wyrm. Suddenly, a ghostly form appears near the camp. It's an ancient, ghostly dragon, and the creature doesn't look happy at your presence. "Why have you come here?" the ghost screams. You can almost feel its spectral breath.

All of the dragons are initially furious with the party. Each dragon claims it is going to kill the party for the terrible things done to it while it lived. In actuality, each dragon really wants to tell its story (except maybe for the blue dragon). If the party tries to talk to the ghost dragons at all, they can calm them down enough to finally hear their stories. Not all of these dragons died here, but all of their spirits were drawn here by the nature of the Dragon Temple.

Roll 1d10 to see which dragon appears to confront the characters each night. If the party has already helped a specific dragon, ignore that result if it is rolled again. Once all the dragons are helped, no new ones appear:

1. Gold Ghost Dragon's Story: Greedy dwarves killed the gold dragon. If a dwarf is in the party, the dragon ignores reason and attacks. The dragon didn't like that the dwarves also stole a unique dragon-slaying sword and took it to their hoard in the distant Blackrock Mountains. The dragon wants the characters to retrieve the sword from the dwarves. If they bring it to the temple and give it to any of the lizardfolk guards, the dragon helps them secure the *staff of the dragon* located in **Area E**.

Naturally, the dwarves don't want to give up the highly useful sword. However, if the dwarves receive enough gold in payment (at least 100,000 gp), they give the weapon to the characters.

2. Silver Ghost Dragon's Story: The silver dragon died at the hands of orcs. If a half-orc or orc is in the party, the dragon ignores reason and attacks. The dragon tells a story of a wave of orcs attacking its lair and slaying all of the dragon's guardian creatures. The orcs then made the lair their own. The silver dragon wants the party to go to that lair, which is located on the far side of the mountains 3 days' travel from the temple. The orcs must be removed from the lair. The silver dragon says the party can have any treasure they find except for a sacred 2-foot-long statue made of silver. The dragon statue belongs in the Dragon Temple. If the party does this, they receive help gaining the *staff of the dragon*. Ogres and orcs are in the lair, but the characters shouldn't have too many problems battling these monsters.

3. Bronze Ghost Dragon's Story: The bronze dragon died in a cave-in when making its lair. The dragon wants its skeletal head brought back to this temple. The cave-in area is 20 miles away in the same mountain range. The ghost dragon actually goes with the party and helps them find its dead body. If the group instantly goes on this quest, the ghost helps them find *plate armor of energy resistance (electricity)*.

4. Copper Ghost Dragon's Story: The copper dragon died when a band of stone giants attacked it. It helps the characters claim the *staff of the dragon* if the party frees the two fire elementals in the red corridor (**Area F**). If the group doesn't help the dragon, it appears when they try to retrieve the *staff of the dragon* on their own. It breathes its breath on them three times and then vanishes forevermore.

5. White Ghost Dragon's Story: The white dragon fell from the skies, its body pierced by the shafts from elven longbows. If elves are in the party, the temperature of the area drops to dangerous levels and the characters take 1d3 points of cold damage per round for as long as the ghost dragon keeps attacking. The dragon wants the party to free the white dragon trapped in the ice cave (**Area G**). The dragon tells the group that they have to pull the frozen dragon statue out of the cave to animate it. If the party agrees to do this task immediately, the ghost vanishes.

6. Black Ghost Dragon's Story: The black dragon died after lizardfolk attacked it in its home. The ghost doesn't care that lizardfolk now guard this Dragon Temple. If the party kills 12 lizard men, however, the ghost promises to give them *+1 dragon bane* weapons. This evil creature is lying, and the characters never see the ghost dragon again.

7. Green Ghost Dragon's Story: A goblin war band surprised the green dragon in its lair and managed to kill it. This green dragon's ghost hates goblins and wants revenge. If allowed to it leads the party to the forests on the western edge of the island. In the dragon's former lair is an ancient elven bow that is a *+1 dragon bane composite longbow (Str +2)*. A cluster of 11 emeralds worth 10,000 gold pieces each is also in the lair. The only hang-up is the 75 goblin warriors that remain in the lair.

8. Red Ghost Dragon's Story: The red dragon died in battle at the claws of a blue dragon centuries ago. The ghost dragon is elated if the characters tell him their reason for being in the temple. The ghost immediately retrieves the *staff of the dragon* and brings it to the party. However, if the party has taken anything from the temple, the ghost tells them they must return the items or it will never give them the staff. The ghost dragon also advises them not to fight the blue dragon in the sky. It tells them to change into red dragons (using the staff) and to go into its lair. It suggests spreading out and blasting the blue dragon with flame for as long as they can.

9. Blue Ghost Dragon's Story: The blue dragon ghost knows the party is trying to get the *staff of the dragon* to fight another blue dragon. It isn't happy and won't even consider helping the party. The

Spending the Night in the Temple (Continued)

ghost rages and tells them they should never have dared to enter this temple created for dragons. The dragon attacks relentlessly. The dragon turns into a mist and roars that such things happen when blue dragons are attacked.

10. Brass Ghost Dragon's Story: The brass dragon died at the hands of gnomes. If a gnome is with the party, the ghost attacks until the party flees the temple or it is driven off. The dragon tells the story of gnomes offering a huge treasure to the brass dragon for helping with three experiments. Two experiments went well and the brass dragon was very happy with the gold and silver it earned. In the last test, the gnomes were working with a massive steam cannon. The dragon was moving the device when it exploded and killed everything in the area. The ghost dragon wants the characters to go to the gnomes and demand the total treasure the dragon earned. The gnomes are a few weeks travel away in central Foere, and the dragon gives them a map if they say yes. If the characters retrieve the treasure, the dragon gives them the *staff of the dragon* and magically places 2 additional charges in it so it can create 7 red dragons. If the party refuses to help, the ghost dragon attacks three times with its dragon breath.

A number of ways exist to get into the stone mouth. If characters shout loudly and ask the mouth to open, the jaws open wide. Magically shrinking or turning to gas allows characters to slip between the stone fangs. "Showing" the great mouth a dragon of any type, living or carved or illustrated, causes the jaws to open.

Once past the fangs, characters are inside the mouth of the dragon. Among the stone fangs and the many stalactites and stalagmites are the nests of numerous rattlesnake swarms. These snakes strike at invaders as they defend their nests, which are often amid the high stone pillars. If characters try to avoid the snakes by moving along the inside of the jaws, more snakes strike from surprise. The party must pass through the area of 2d4+1 swarms to gain entry.

SNAKE SWARMS (2d4+1) **CR 2**
XP 600
hp 16 (*Pathfinder Roleplaying Game Bestiary 3* "Snake Swarm")

Inside the Temple

The Dragon Temple is 5 miles long in total. Each limb section that radiates off the main body is over 1-1/2 miles long. All corridors are semicircular in section (a flat floor beneath a smoothly arching, semicircular roof) and 70 yards wide. The walls and floor are carved to resemble dragon scales. The rough surface deadens sound, preventing noise from traveling far into the temple.

The apex of the ceiling is most likely hidden in darkness unless characters fly up to it (about 105 feet from the floor). Characters on the prowl for secret doors can check only one wall at a time because of the corridor's great width.

Lizardfolk

Dead bodies can be found in all parts of the inner temple. The lizardfolk that live here consider every slain explorer a sacrifice to Tiamat, so they never touch these bodies because doing so would defile the sacrifice. Along the same lines, the lizardfolk never talk to PCs. In the minds of the lizardfolk, all strangers inside the temple are unwelcome intruders who should be killed.

> Past the initial throat is a wide corridor of dressed sandstone carved to resemble dragon scales. The corridor is 70 yards wide, and the walls arch smoothly upward into darkness. The roof is beyond the limit of your light. The darkness here seems more intense than a simple absence of light.
>
> The stone floor and walls down the entire throat corridor are jet black. Dragon scales are carved into the stone, from the mouth down through the throat.

There is a slight downward slope to the corridor. The PCs can detect the slope only if they look for it specifically and make a successful DC 15 Perception check (a dwarf's stonecunning racial ability applies). Normal tests, such as a marble on the floor, don't work here because of the uneven, scaled texture carved into all surfaces.

A short distance down the throat, a passage branches off the main corridor to the northeast and ascends noticeably to Area B. The main corridor continues on to the southwest to the first (forelegs) crossroads.

Area B: Giant Rattler Ordeal (CR 5)

> Moving northeast off the main corridor, the side tunnel goes on for a mile into an open area where a small alcove contains a 10-foot-long carving of a black dragon. The dragon's back is flat, and on that platform is a mass of green, lightly glowing crystals.
>
> Four bodies wearing wizard robes are on the floor in front of the statue. The slimy robes hold the scent of dung, but the faint glow of magic still clings to the clothing. A sense of evil permeates the bodies.
>
> Suddenly, a deep rattling sound echoes through the area.

Stalactites and stalagmites fill this area located in the head of the Dragon Temple. Characters who search the bodies of the dead wizards before scouting the rest of the chamber are automatically surprised by a giant rattlesnake. The snake also attacks if characters check the chamber for danger before doing anything else, but then the usual procedures for determining surprise apply.

GIANT RATTLESNAKE **CR 5**
XP 1,600
hp 51 (*Pathfinder Roleplaying Game Bestiary 2* "Snake, Emperor Cobra")

The snake fights as long as characters stay in the area. Its nest is on a shelf above the entrance to the alcove. The reptile won't follow characters out of the area.

The dead wizards have all manner of equipment useful to experienced adventurers. Inside their expensive boots, each wears a *ring of protection +1* on his toe. A total of 57 gp and 22 gp can be found. Each spellcaster also was equipped with a short sword and four quality throwing daggers. Each has a scroll tube. Altogether, the tubes contain scrolls of *fireball*, *expeditious retreat*, *flaming sphere*, *blink*, *see invisibility*, *polymorph*, *dimension door*, and *stoneskin*.

On the back of the dragon statue are 88 glowing crystals. Each is a fairly worthless piece of crystal (1 gp each) in the shape of a 7-inch-long dragon scale. A slight bit of magic on the scales causes each one to dimly glow green. All dragons can sense these scales on a character and react violently to the desecration of their temple.

Area C. Torture of the Dragon Blades

Read the following when the characters reach the "shoulder" intersection that leads to the two forelimbs of the Dragon Temple.

> You've come to a four-way intersection in the broad corridor. Straight ahead, the black-walled corridor continues on. Other passages split off to the north and south.
> Dark green stone lines the northern corridor, and the air is stale and acrid.
> The southern corridor is lined with dark blue stone, and the air is extremely humid.

If the characters take the northern passage, they wind for several miles before arriving at **Area C**. The southern passage leads to **Area H**. Continuing down the "spine" of the dragon (the main corridor) takes characters to **Area D**.

The corridor to **Area C** grows more humid the farther characters travel. Eventually the atmosphere becomes so oppressive that the characters' clothes are drenched and everyone must make a DC 12 Fortitude save to avoid becoming fatigued. This fatigue can be removed by resting in a dry area (the main corridor suffices) and getting into drier clothing.

Read the following when the characters arrive at the end of the passageway:

> The corridor opens into an immense, dead-end chamber. The area is circular and at a guess it's in one of the taloned claws showing on the outside of the temple structure. The smell of dried blood permeates the area. Chunks of bodies and ripped equipment are all over the chamber. Severed heads and shoulders are spread over one part of the chamber, while hips and legs litter other areas. Splashes of dried blood cover the walls and floor.
> At the far end is the statue of a green dragon. It is 10 feet tall and twice that long. Its back is a flat platform. The only illumination in the area comes from a mass of orange crystals on the carving's back.

Slicing the Dragon (CR 8)

Grooves cover the walls, floor, and ceiling. If the characters look for a trap, they can quickly figure out the danger those wide grooves mean for them as they move through the chamber.

Stepping on any one of dozens of pressure plates scattered around the room triggers the trap. Spinning blades swing down from the ceiling and up from the floor. Rotating blades slice out from the walls at waist height (on a human). The blades affect the northeast quarter of the room on the first round, the southeast quarter on the second, the southwest quarter on the third, and the northwest quarter on the fourth. The blades then retract into the walls, floor, and ceiling. If someone steps on a pressure plate again, the trap activates all over.

WALL SCYTHE TRAP **CR 5**
XP 1,600
Type mechanical; **Perception** DC 20; **Disable Device** DC 20

Trigger location; **Reset** automatic reset
Effect Atk +20 melee (2d4+6/x4); multiple targets (all targets in the chamber)

A dragon-shaped pedestal sits at the end of the cave. On the pedestal are piles of orange crystal dragon scales. Each is 7 inches long, and closer inspection reveals they are nothing but cheap stones with a magical radiance that causes them to glow. However, taking even one orange scale from the pile trips another pressure plate that causes chlorine gas (as a dragon's breath attack) to fill the chamber. The characters have 2 rounds to leave the area before it's flooded by the gas. The gas floats in the area for 24 hours before it sinks through the floor.

CHLORINE GAS TRAP **CR 6**
XP 2,400
Type mechanical; **Perception** DC 25; **Disable Device** DC 25

Trigger touch; **Reset** none
Effect cloud of poison gas (6d6 acid damage, DC 20 Fort save half); onset delay (2 rounds); multiple targets (all targets in the chamber)

The dried husks of dead bodies show that killing has been going on for centuries in this chamber. Any surviving equipment is of excellent quality. A careful search of the bodies reveals 4 *potions of cure moderate wounds* in metal flasks. Scroll tubes are in several parts of the chamber, but they've been cut in half and most of the scrolls inside are destroyed. One intact tube contains still contains a scroll with 2 *polymorph* spells. Searching that same case reveals a hidden compartment in the cap that hides a masterfully cut red ruby worth 3,000 gold pieces.

Area D. Nightmare of the Dragon Throne

> Nothing changes for some distance as you walk down the corridor. Carved dragon scales continue to cover all of the black stone in the area.
> Finally, after you travel at least two miles, the area opens into a massive grotto too vast to decide just how big it could be without carefully pacing it off. In one area is a glowing throne carved into the shape of a blue dragon. The entire thing is made of some type of magnificent gemstone.
> The shape of the throne suggests a large human could sit upon it. A closer inspection of the area notes dried blood on the arms and seat. The stone of the carving is quite unusual and displays a gemlike quality as it magically glows. Veins of what appear to be gold and silver run through the carving.
> A mass of crushed bodies lies ten yards in front of the throne.

Sitting on the Dragon (CR 9)

A band of **6 lizardfolk** temple guards protect the throne. These guards immediately attack and follow the characters until one party or the other is dead.

LIZARDFOLK (6) **CR 1**
XP 400
hp 11 (*Pathfinder Roleplaying Game Bestiary* "Lizardfolk")
Note Instead of morningstars, these lizardfolk are armed with halberds.
Melee halberd +2 (1d10+1/x3), bite +0 (1d4) or claw +2 (1d4+1), bite +2 (1d4+1)

The massive dragon throne is made out of blue lapis lazuli. It takes heavy hammers to knock pieces from it. If the characters go wild and try to hack off pieces from the lower chair section, a glyph of warding (explosive runes) explodes, causing 5d8 points of lightning damage to everyone within 5 feet of the throne.

GLYPH OF WARDING TRAP **CR 5**
XP 1,600
Type magic; **Perception** DC 28; **Disable Device** DC 28

Trigger touch; **Reset** none
Effect spell effect (glyph of warding, 5d8 electricity damage, DC 14 Ref half); multiple targets (all targets within 5 ft. of the throne)

Each piece knocked off is worth 200 gold pieces, and about 90 head-sized pieces of lapis lazuli can be recovered. Under the outer covering of gemstone is a red granite mold of a chair with arcane symbols written all over the granite.

The throne is a deadly mechanical trap. If anyone sits on it, the arms and back collapse, doing 4d6 points of bludgeoning damage to the person in the seat. The trap then ejects the crushed victim onto the floor and resets.

CRUSHING THRONE TRAP **CR 6**
XP 2,400
Type mechanical; **Perception** DC 25; **Disable Device** DC 25

Trigger location; **Reset** automatic
Effect crushing stone (4d6 bludgeoning damage); never miss

A dozen crushed bodies lie 10 yards away from the front of the throne. Flesh-eating beetles rush out of the dead bodies if the corpses are moved. All their equipment is mostly crushed and destroyed, but characters can find some useful items if they take the time to search the bodies. These items are a *ring of protection +1*, a *ring of invisibility*, a *+1 silver dagger*, a *+1 dwarven waraxe*, 5 gems (500 gp each), 29 cp, 44 sp, 19 gp, and 11 pp.

As the throne trap resets, an ear-numbing roar issues from the throat of the dragon statue. This warning echoes up and down the miles of corridor.

Area E. Dragon Staff Bane (CR 11)

Read the following when the characters reach the "hip" intersection that leads to the two legs and the tail of the Dragon Temple.

> You stand at another four-way crossroads. The northern corridor shows white scales carved into the stones. The corridor to the south has red stones carved with dragon scales. The blue stones of the western corridor are at least three feet thick on the walls, floor, and ceiling.

If the characters proceed along the main corridor (toward **Area E**) they hear a quickly moving group coming up behind them and making a bit of noise once they are about a half-mile from the *staff of the dragon*. The strangers hail the group and ask for a parley. These four experienced adventurers carry

high-quality equipment. A great deal of that equipment glows from spells cast by the group before they shouted to the player characters.

The strange party consists of a **wizard**, a **cleric of the draconic deity Moash-Sirrush**, and **2 fighters**.

CLERIC **CR 7**
XP 3,200
Male human cleric of Moash-Sirrush 8
NE Medium humanoid (human)
Init +6; **Perception** +11
Aura destructive aura (30 ft., +4, 8 rounds/day)

AC 19, touch 12, flat-footed 17 (+7 armor, +2 Dex)
hp 64 (8d8+8 plus 16)
Fort +7; **Ref** +4; **Will** +9

Speed 30 ft. (20 ft. in armor)
Melee *+1 morningstar* +8/+3 (1d8+2)
Special Attacks channel negative energy 3/day (DC 16, 6d6), destructive smite (+4, 6/day)
Domain Spell-Like Abilities (CL 8th):
At will—*master's illusion* (8 rounds/day)
6/day—*copycat* (8 rounds)
Spells Prepared (CL 8th; melee touch +7)
4th—*giant vermin, inflict critical wounds* (DC 17), *poison*^{D} (DC 17)
3rd—*contagion* (DC 16), *cure serious wounds, magic circle against good, prayer, rage*^{D}
2nd—*barkskin*^{D}, *cure moderate wounds, hold person* (DC 15), *resist energy, summon monster II*
1st—*cause fear* (DC 14), *comprehend languages, cure light wounds, detect good, inflict light wounds* (DC 14), *true strike*^{D}
0 (at will)—*bleed* (DC 13), *detect magic, read magic, resistance*
D Domain spell; **Domains** Destruction, Trickery

Str 13, **Dex** 14, **Con** 12, **Int** 8, **Wis** 17, **Cha** 10
Base Atk +6; **CMB** +7; **CMD** 19
Feats Combat Casting, Command Undead, Improved Channel, Improved Initiative, Toughness
Skills Acrobatics –1 (–5 to jump), Knowledge (religion) +6, Perception +11, Spellcraft +6
Languages Common, Elven
Combat Gear 2 *potions of cure light wounds*; **Other Gear** *+1 breastplate, +1 morningstar, phylactery of negative channeling*, gold holy symbol of Moash-Sirrush (75 gp)

AXE FIGHTER **CR 6**
XP 2,400
Male human fighter 7
CG Medium humanoid (human)
Init +5; **Perception** +8

AC 21, touch 11, **flat-footed** 20 (+7 armor, +1 Dex, +3 shield)
hp 71 (7d10+14 plus 14)
Fort +8; **Ref** +4; **Will** +4 (+2 vs. fear)

Speed 30 ft.
Melee *+1 battleaxe* +13/+8 (1d8+6/x3)
Ranged composite longbow +8/+3 (1d8/x3)
Special Attacks weapon training (axes +1)

Str 18, **Dex** 12, **Con** 14, **Int** 13, **Wis** 8, **Cha** 10
Base Atk +7; **CMB** +11 (+13 trip); **CMD** 22 (24 vs. trip)
Feats Alertness, Combat Expertise, Improved Initiative, Improved Trip, Iron Will, Persuasive, Power Attack, Toughness, Vital Strike
Skills Climb +9, Diplomacy +5, Handle Animal +4, Intimidate +9, Perception +8, Ride +2, Sense Motive +8
Languages Common, Halfling
SQ armor training 2
Combat Gear 2 *potions of cure moderate wounds*; **Other Gear** *+1 chainmail, +1 heavy steel shield, +1 battleaxe*, 20 arrows, composite longbow, *cloak of resistance +1*, 35 gp

SWORD FIGHTER **CR 5**
XP 1,600
Male human fighter 6
CG Medium humanoid (human)
Init +2; **Perception** +7

AC 22, touch 13, **flat-footed** 19 (+7 armor, +2 Dex, +1 dodge, +1 natural, +1 shield)
hp 39 (6d10+6)
Fort +7; **Ref** +5; **Will** +2 (+2 vs. fear)

Speed 30 ft. (20 ft. in armor)
Melee *+1 bastard sword* +12/+7 (1d10+7/19–20)
Ranged light crossbow +8 (1d8/19–20)
Special Attacks weapon training (heavy blades +1)

Str 17, **Dex** 14, **Con** 12, **Int** 10, **Wis** 8, **Cha** 13
Base Atk +6; **CMB** +9; **CMD** 22
Feats Alertness, Dodge, Exotic Weapon Proficiency (bastard sword), Mobility, Power Attack, Weapon Finesse, Weapon Focus (bastard sword), Weapon Specialization (bastard sword)
Skills Acrobatics +3 (-1 to jump), Climb +7, Intimidate +7, Perception +7, Ride +3, Sense Motive +7
Languages Common
SQ armor training 1
Combat Gear 6 *potions of cure light wounds*; **Other Gear** masterwork field plate, masterwork light steel shield, *+1 bastard sword*, 10 crossbow bolts, dagger, light crossbow, *amulet of natural armor +1, cloak of resistance +1*, 142 gp

WIZARD **CR 8**
XP 4,800
Male human evoker 9
N Medium humanoid (human)
Init +5; **Perception** +9

AC 14, touch 12, flat-footed 13 (+1 armor, +1 deflection, +1 Dex, +1 natural)
hp 71 (9d6+18 plus 18)
Fort +6; **Ref** +5; **Will** +7

Speed 30 ft.
Melee *+1 dagger* +4 (1d4/19–20)
Special Attacks intense spells (+4 damage)
Arcane School Spell-Like Abilities (CL 9th; concentration +12)
At will—*elemental wall* (9 rounds/day)
6/day—*force missile* (1d4+4)
Spells Prepared (CL 9th)
5th—*cone of cold* (DC 20), *elemental body II*
4th—*dimension door, fire shield, wall of fire*
3rd—*fireball* (DC 18), *fly, lightning bolt* (DC 18), *lightning bolt* (DC 18), *greater thunderstomp**
2nd—*false life, flaming sphere* (x2) (DC 17), *glitterdust* (DC 15), *rope trick*
1st—*burning hands* (x2) (DC 16), *grease, magic missile* (x2), *shield*
0 (at will)—*detect magic, light, mage hand, read magic*
Opposition Schools Enchantment, Necromancy
*See the *Pathfinder Roleplaying Game Advanced Class Guide*

Str 8, **Dex** 13, **Con** 14, **Int** 17, **Wis** 10, **Cha** 12
Base Atk +4; **CMB** +3; **CMD** 15
Feats Brew Potion, Combat Casting, Greater Spell Focus (evocation), Improved Initiative, Nimble Moves, Scribe Scroll, Spell Focus (evocation), Toughness
Skills Appraise +11, Craft (alchemy) +7, Fly +11, Intimidate

+2, Knowledge (arcana) +15, Knowledge (religion) +10, Perception +9, Spellcraft +15, Use Magic Device +10
Languages Common, Draconic, Elven, Gnome
SQ arcane bond (ring of protection +1)
Combat Gear *potion of bear's endurance, potion of cure moderate wounds, potion of darkvision, potion of invisibility, arcane scroll (CL 9: alter self, cone of cold, expeditious retreat)* ; **Other Gear** *+1 dagger, amulet of natural armor +1, bracers of armor +1, cloak of resistance +1, ring of protection +1, spellbook* (contains all prepared spells plus 1d4 random spells of each level up to 5th), spell component pouch, 610 gp

The strangers try hard to persuade the player characters that nothing of value is down the corridor and that they should leave before the moon is full in the sky. Legends tell of ghost dragons moving out of the temple and into the sky during the time of the full moon. If the characters don't buy this story and leave, the strangers attack. They fight until one of their number dies. The rest then retreat into the darkness.

As the characters get closer to the staff of the dragon (within 100 yards of **Area E**), they soon hear the sound of heavy boots marching toward them from the darkness. The battle cry of a dragon echoes down the corridor from the direction they are moving toward. The corridor feels heavy as the air pressure increases.

The dragon's roar and the increase in air pressure are designed to fill the characters with fear. Both are magical effects (similar to ghost sound and magic mouth) that are meant to scare but not harm the characters.

The blue stone corridor finally ends in a 50-yard-diameter chamber. A glowing dais sits in the middle of the chamber at the top of seven steps. Each step is a foot tall and three feet deep. A glowing staff with a golden dragon head at its top is atop the dais.

Each of the seven steps is a different color stone: red, green, white, blue, black, purple, and orange. A number of long-dead bodies lie on the steps. The equipment you see would seem to note practitioners of many different professions, from warriors in full-plate armor to a cleric in brown robes with a staff in her dead hand. You can't tell how they died from the condition of their bodies. The dead aren't burnt from spells or ripped apart by monsters.

The dried husks of meat-eating beetles cover the first step of the dais.

The Dragon's Goal (CR 10)

The real prize in the chamber is the staff of the dragon.

Each of the seven steps of the dais does 2d6 points of sonic damage anytime someone touches a step. If the characters instead step on the many dead bodies on the steps instead of the magical stone of the dais, they can safely reach the staff and take it without taking physical damage. The first step is littered with flesh-eating beetles that surged up the riser to get to the corpses and died from the magical damage.

MAGICAL STEPS TRAP (7) **CR 4**
XP 1,200
Type magical device; **Perception** DC 25; **Disable Device** DC 25

Trigger location; **Reset** automatic
Effect magical energy burst (2d6 sonic damage); never miss*
***Note** Although this trap never misses, it is easy to avoid by simply stepping on the corpses instead of the steps. Thus, its CR is 2 lower than it should be.

The staff is casually sticking in a holder in the center of the dais. The staff could be lassoed from the floor and pulled out of its stand with ease. Flying characters could also reach the staff without touching the dais. Even levitation might do the trick if characters are clever about maneuvering (using ropes or gusts of wind).

The Staff of the Dragon (Minor Artifact)

Aura strong transmutation; CL 20th
Slot none; **Weight** 15 lbs.

DESCRIPTION

The *staff of the dragon* is an ornate staff carved from a single rib bone of an adult red dragon. It is covered in gold filigree and encrusted in rubies, diamonds, and topaz.The staff currently has 5 charges and imparts knowledge on its use to whoever picks it up. Each charge changes one Small or Medium creature into a young adult red dragon as per the spell *form of the dragon III*. The character can remain in this form for as long as they want to use that shape.

DESTRUCTION

The *staff of the dragon* is destroyed when all charges are expended from it. Once the charges are expended, it becomes a non-magical staff worth 20,000 gp due to the precious metals and stones that decorate it.

The dead bodies appear to have died rushing up the steps to gain the staff. If characters examine or search the bodies, **rot grubs** pour out of the faces and arms.

ROT GRUB **CR 4**
XP 1,200
(*The Tome of Horrors Complete*, 761, "Rot Grub")
Type infestation; **Save** Fortitude DC 17
Onset immediate; **Frequency** 1/round
Effect 1d2 Con damage per grub

Characters can find many treasures around the bodies: a *+1 short sword*, a *+1 thundering quarterstaff*, a *+2 light steel shield*, a *minor cloak of displacement*, *potion of protection from energy (fire)*, *scroll of protection from energy (electricity)*, and a *+1 dragon bane bastard sword*. Most of the bodies also have backpacks filled with highly useful equipment such as candles, flint & steel, canteens, sleeping bags, extra clothes, needle and thread, sharpening tools, and extra weapons such as throwing daggers, throwing axes, and warhammers.

Area F. Bloodbath at Talon Rock

Read the following the characters head south from the hip crossroads toward **Area F**:

The red stones of the corridor hint at something fiery at its end. The corridor runs for a mile, and in all that time, the temperature grows hotter as you move down the passage.

Eventually, you see steam in the distance. The heat is such that metal armor is very uncomfortable to wear. A steamy fog obscures the way ahead.

Steamy Fog of Lizardfolk (CR 6)

Hidden in the steam, and quite enjoying the heat, is a squad of **6 lizardfolk** with halberds. The characters travel a hundred yards in the dense fog before the lizardfolk attack from surprise.

The creatures never leave the fog and don't follow the characters.

LIZARDFOLK (6) **CR 1**
XP 400
hp 11 (*Pathfinder Roleplaying Game Bestiary* "Lizardfolk")
Note Instead of morningstars, these lizardfolk are armed with halberds.
Melee halberd +2 (1d10+1/x3), bite +0 (1d4) or claw +2 (1d4+1), bite +2 (1d4+1)

If the player characters run from the battle, they have a 50% chance of running headlong into the lava pool at the end of the corridor. Check to see if the characters left any markers to guide them back the way they came. If they didn't, roll a die for each member of the group. Make sure to tell them if some of the party members run in a different direction from other party members because they are shouting and trying to help each other as the melee progresses. The lizardfolk follow characters back the way they came until the fog ends. The creatures do not follow the characters into the lava pool. With a 70-yard-wide corridor, it's very possible the characters could even retreat to a side wall and not go down the length of the corridor at all.

> Moving carefully from the ambush site, you travel several hundred yards in the steamy fog. Finally, the steam clears to reveal a dead-end chamber. The chamber is at least a hundred yards in diameter. A pool of lava covers the entire area of the round chamber.
>
> At the center of that pool is a twenty foot long and tall carving of a red dragon done in red crystal and floating on a pedestal. The back of the dragon is flat and holds a pile of the purest white crystals. The heat of the area is nearly unbearable.
>
> Forty yards of lava surrounds the dragon carving.

Dragon Fire (CR 8)

Those wearing plate mail or chainmail are likely to be in a great deal of pain when they reach the lava chamber. this room counts as extreme heat (see *Pathfinder Roleplaying Game Core Rulebook*, "Heat Dangers). Touching the lava or trying to walk in the lava causes instant death. On the back of the dragon are 33 white crystals. Each crystal protects the holder once against one white dragon breath attack.

Before the characters can get to the pedestal, however, **2 Large fire elementals** rise from the lava to talk with the characters. The elementals tell a story of forced labor to keep the lava hot in this pool. They want to get out of the lava and back to their home. If the characters take out the ruby eyes of the dragon statue and throw the gems into the fire, the elementals can leave for home. The elementals offer 4 potions of energy resistance (fire) if the characters help them.

LARGE FIRE ELEMENTALS (2) **CR 5**
XP 1,600
hp 60 (*Pathfinder Roleplaying Game Bestiary* "Elemental, Fire")

Each eye in the statue has hardness 8 and 40 hp. All the while, characters within 5 feet of the statue take 1d6 points of fire damage per round.

The elementals never allow characters to attack them. If the group tries to do battle with the elementals, the creatures sink into the lava and the entire chamber becomes even hotter, inflicting 1d6 points of heat damage per round for nine hours. The elementals aren't very bright. They make the same offer to the players every 10 hours, even if the characters tried to fight them previously.

Area G. Carnage at the Dead-End

Read the following if the characters head north toward **Area G** from the hip crossroads.

> The white stones of the corridor would seem to represent the influence of a white dragon. The temperature in the corridor does indeed steadily drop to freezing and below. All too soon, those of you in plate armor are very uncomfortable in the extreme cold. Your feet and hands grow numb as you travel.
>
> After walking for a mile, the corridor opens into a large cavern at least a hundred yards in diameter. A statue of a white dragon at least thirty yards tall and long is against the west wall. On its back is a flat platform that contains a mass of gems of many colors.

Cold Heart of the Dragon

This chamber counts as severe cold (see Pathfinder Roleplaying Game Core Rulebook, "Cold Dangers"). The extreme cold also slows the characters as the spell unless they succeed on a DC 15 Fortitude save. This effect persists while the characters are in the chamber and for 10 minutes after leaving the room. The mass of gems on the platform are all useless glass.

The real treasure in the chamber is the white dragon statue. It's a living ancient white dragon of good alignment paralyzed to stay in the chamber. The characters have no way of knowing the true nature of the dragon, but they can figure out that it is a living creature if they rap on it or test it in other ways. If the dragon is taken out of the chamber, it returns to life and is very grateful. It grants each character in the party one boon.

The icy floor makes moving the dragon out of the chamber easy as it slides on the ice. The instant the creature is out of the chamber, it animates and talks with the party, telling them its long life story. The white dragon, unlike most of its kin, is actually good and likes humanity. For centuries it helped the tribes living up north in the cold regions near the dragon's former lair. However, when the white dragon helped the tribesmen kill an old black dragon, a curse fell upon it and brought it here to this temple.

The dragon is so grateful at being released that it gives each party member a ring made of magical ice. The dragon explains that if the character speaks a request into the ring, it will answer the call and, if it can, fulfill the request. If the dragon succeeds, the ice ring vanishes. If the dragon fails to honor the request, it explains that its powers are not up to the task and grants another boon before it vanishes.

GOOD ANCIENT WHITE DRAGON **CR 15**
XP 51,200
AL CG
hp 283 (Pathfinder Roleplaying Game Bestiary, "Chromatic Dragon, White")

Area H. Living with the Dragon

The characters face several encounters before they reach Area H. Read the following once they enter the southern tunnel in the dragon's four-way shoulder crossroads that leads to **Area H**:

A wet sheen covers the dark blue stones. Even the floor, with its carved dragon scales, is slippery. There is little doubt that running is dangerous and might result in slipping. Just ten steps into the corridor, wet clothes already drag you down. Those in plate mail have it the worst as their padding becomes more like a sponge full of water.

Area H1. Lizard Man Nests (CR 10)

The tunnel opens into a vast chamber several hundred yards long at least. Sconces on the walls hold blazing torches that help display the hall's size. It's clear the corridor continues southeast through the room. Strange objects like ten-foot-diameter nests fill the chamber in three different rows. Smeell is stAt least a hundred or more of these nests are in this area. The smell of the marsh and swamp is strong here.

More than 100 yards into the area, the nests are filled with sleeping lizardfolk. It is difficult to tell how many contain sleepers, but the party sees at least 10 full nests.

These lizardfolk stay asleep if characters don't cause a commotion in the area. Any fighting wakes the **20 lizardfolk** who throw their javelins at the characters. Each nest contains 4 large javelins. The lizardfolk have no problem throwing ranged weapons into melee as other lizardfolk fight hand-to-hand. Each of these reptilian warriors also has a large bandoleer with a silver belt, more shield than buckle, at its center. The silver ornament is an image of the Dragon Temple in the mountains. Each is worth 100 silver.

After the lizards throw their javelins, they swarm the characters and use their talons and jaws in hand-to-talon fighting. These lizardfolk won't retreat. They are serious temple guards filled with the importance of their jobs. If the characters run, the guards follow them until the characters are either out of the temple or killed in battle.

LIZARDFOLK (20) **CR 1**
XP 400
hp 11 (*Pathfinder Roleplaying Game Bestiary* "Lizardfolk")
Note Instead of morningstars, these lizardfolk are armed with halberds.
Melee halberd +2 (1d10+1/x3), bite +0 (1d4) or claw +2 (1d4+1), bite +2 (1d4+1)

Area H2. Lizardfolk Pool (CR 9)

You move several hundred yards down the corridor and again the area to the south opens up to reveal a very large pond. The water is several hundred yards in diameter and very murky. The place once again smells like a swamp. In the shadows are lumps of things, but it's impossible with the present light to make out what is down there.

Brightly glowing forms swim in the pond, making it easy to estimate how long and wide the water is.

Suddenly, the excited splashing of many fish churn up the water. Fish leap into the air, and some even land on the stone floor. Several of the larger fish glow brightly and light the area.

Waiting under the water are **15 lizardfolk**. The lizardfolk organizing under the water scares the fish and causes them to jump. When the characters are 50 feet away, the lizardfolk rise out of the water and hurl their javelins. Each has 3 javelins. The lizard people do not follow the characters, but they roar out a warning that echoes up and down the corridor. The lizardfolk stay half-submerged in the water and continue throwing javelins. If the characters continue the fight after taking three volleys of missiles, the lizardfolk come out of the water and fight hand-to-talon to the death. Once the fighting begins, these lizardfolk follow the characters until the characters are dead or the lizardfolk perish.

LIZARDFOLK (15) CR 1
XP 400
hp 11 (*Pathfinder Roleplaying Game Bestiary* "Lizardfolk")
Note Instead of morningstars, these lizardfolk are armed with halberds.
Melee halberd +2 (1d10+1/x3), bite +0 (1d4) or claw +2 (1d4+1), bite +2 (1d4+1)

Numerous benches at the other end of the pond hold 15 high-quality halberds and 15 magical cloaks that make the wearer nearly invisible when he stands in shadows of any kind (as half-value *cloaks of elvenkind*, but the Stealth bonus only applies in dim or dark lighting).

Area H3. Lizardfolk Eating Area (CR 5)

> You travel quite a ways before another large area opens to the south. Magical glowing rods light the area. Two hundred yards to the back of the chamber are ten large crocodiles gutted and hung on meat hooks. Nearby are several square stones covered in dried blood. On the stones are large butcher knives. Thirty large rectangular stones also covered in dried blood are in this open area. The eating tables have 10 to 20 feet of space around each one. It's clear the lizardfolk use this section for eating their meals of crocodile meat. No cook fires are in the chamber, so the lizardfolk must eat their food raw.

Crocodiles are raised by the lizardfolk for food in caverns deeper in the mountains. Off to the far side of this room are **4 lizardfolk** who are just finishing lunch when the characters arrive. They wear cloaks that hide them in the shadows along the wall. As the party leaves the area, these four lizardfolk throw javelins at the backs of the party. They get off two surprise attacks before the party can respond. The lizardfolk follow the group and keep attacking if the party doesn't stay and do battle. The fight continues until one party or the other is dead.

LIZARDFOLK (4) CR 1
XP 400
hp 11 (*Pathfinder Roleplaying Game Bestiary* "Lizardfolk")
Note Instead of morningstars, these lizardfolk are armed with halberds.
Melee halberd +2 (1d10+1/x3), bite +0 (1d4) or claw +2 (1d4+1), bite +2 (1d4+1)

Area H4. Lizardfolk Leader Chambers (CR 8)

> You find two large leather doors along the east wall. The leather is cured, boiled, and quite stiff on each door. Each door has a center latch.

Read the following if the characters open the left door:

> Opening the door on the left reveals a large chamber where a huge lizard man is chopping a large block with a halberd. The chamber contains a nest, a dragon statue, and ceremonial equipment in front of the statue. The powerfully built lizard man charges to attack!

The **lizardfolk leader** has *+1 chainmail* and a *+1 halberd*. He chases the party if they run and continues attacking as long as even one character remains alive. The lizardfolk leader even follows the party out of the temple if needed. He can also track and use magical skill. If the characters escape the temple using magic, the leader and **6 lizardfolk** find each party member and attack within a few weeks.

On and around the green dragon statue at the back of the chamber are holy relics made of gold and encrusted in jewels. Dragon images cover each relic. These items include a large bowl, a large chalice, a small sphere of silver with several embedded gems, an empty jeweled gold box, and a small gold hammer with a bell. Each item is worth 5,000 gold pieces.

LIZARDFOLK LEADER CR 4
XP 1,200
Male Lizardfolk fighter 3 (*Pathfinder Roleplaying Game Bestiary*, "Lizardfolk")
NE Medium humanoid (reptilian)
Init +5; **Perception** +1

AC 23, touch 11, flat-footed 22 (+7 armor, +1 Dex, +5 natural)
hp 38 (2d8+4 plus 3d10+6 plus 3)
Fort +8; **Ref** +2; **Will** +1; +1 vs. fear

Speed 30 ft., swim 15 ft.
Melee *+1 halberd* +9 (1d10+5/x3), or bite +5 (1d4+1), 2 claws +5 (1d4+1)
Ranged javelin +5 (1d6+3)

Str 16, **Dex** 12, **Con** 15, **Int** 10, **Wis** 10, **Cha** 12
Base Atk +4; **CMB** +7; **CMD** 18
Feats Cleave, Improved Initiative, Multiattack, Power Attack, Weapon Focus (halberd)
Skills Acrobatics +2, Climb +5, Handle Animal +5, Intimidate +7, Perception +1, Sense Motive +2, Survival +4, Swim +8;
Racial Modifiers +4 Acrobatics
Languages Draconic
SQ armor training 1, hold breath
Gear *+1 chainmail*, *+1 halberd*, 3 javelins

LIZARDFOLK (6) CR 1
XP 400
hp 11 (*Pathfinder Roleplaying Game Bestiary* "Lizardfolk")
Note Instead of morningstars, these lizardfolk are armed with halberds.
Melee halberd +2 (1d10+1/x3), bite +0 (1d4) or claw +2 (1d4+1), bite +2 (1d4+1)

> Opening the door reveals a large chamber. Skulls from many intelligent races are mounted on the walls. The chamber has a nest at its center, a dragon statue at the back, and a large chest by the statue. Nothing else is in the room.

The room belongs to the chieftain of all of the lizardfolk. The creature is out and about currently and won't engage the characters. In his chamber are the normal things for lizardfolk except for the large leather-bound chest.

The leather-bound chest is trapped. Opening it fills the chamber with deadly chlorine gas. At the back of the chest, currently hidden because the chest is pushed against the wall, is a secret drawer at the bottom. Inside the drawer are a *ring of invisibility*, a *helm of telepathy*, a *mattock of the titan*, and a 3-foot-tall platinum holy symbol of a celestial dragon with large emeralds for eyes (10,000 gp).

CHLORINE GAS TRAP **CR 4**
XP 1,200
Type mechanical; **Perception** DC 25; **Disable Device** DC 25

Trigger touch; **Reset** none
Effect cloud of chlorine gas (3d6 acid damage, DC 20 Fort half); multiple targets (all targets in a 10 ft. cube centered on the chest)

Area H5. Lizard Man Hall of Honor

Another chamber opens to the south. The hall is 75 feet wide, 300 feet long, and filled with mounted heads and stuffed bodies of dangerous foes the lizardfolk have fought in and around the Dragon Temple. More than 100 heads or skulls are on the walls, with a number of intelligent races represented. Against the back wall is a 15-foot-tall stone statue of a lizard man with a brass club in his hand.

The mounted and stuffed beings are not dangerous. If the characters do anything with the heads and bodies, however, the **stone golem** steps off its pedestal and attacks. The animated statue follows the characters for 1 mile from the hall. If the characters come back, the golem immediately steps off of its pedestal and attacks again. Very little of value is in the hall, but the drow figures wear boots that cancel sound the wearer makes as he moves across the floor. The drow figures also have +2 longswords, but the weapons lose their magical powers after they are used in two battles.

STONE GOLEM **CR 11**
XP 12,800
hp 107 (*Pathfinder Roleplaying Game Bestiary* "Golem, Stone")

Area H6. Dragon Inner Temple

You've traveled more than a mile to the end of this corridor to an area easily two hundred yards in diameter. At the center of the chamber is a massive dragon statue with ten heads, each in a different color: gold, silver, brass, bronze, copper, white, black, green, red, and blue.

The statue is 50 feet tall and its body is 100 feel long.

The area is damp and the temperature is warmer as well, especially around the giant dragon statue.

There is something holy about the place. It's a feeling that isn't just evil, neutral, or good. Then you notice the hundreds of eggs along the walls in all shapes, colors, and sizes. There is no doubt that every type of dragon appears here in this mass of eggs.

If the characters break or fool with the eggs, the entire statue moves nearer the eggs. The black dragon head then bends down and splashes all of the characters near the eggs for 6d6 points of acid damage. If that doesn't stop the characters from handling the eggs, the black dragon head spits acid again as the blue dragon head animates and spits out a lightning bolt. Both attacks inflict 6d6 points of damage of the appropriate type (acid, electricity, etc.). The characters take half damage with a successful DC 15 Reflex save. Only divine attacks and spells have any affect on the huge dragon statue, and melee attacks with magical weapons do nothing to chip or mar its surface. The statue has 100 hit points per head and 500 hit points in the body. It won't follow characters that retreat from the area. Any damage done to the statue heals after 24 hours.

Each dragon head can animate, and their attacks never miss no matter what the characters might do to protect themselves. Each strike does 6d6 points of damage.

The dragon statue won't give characters any second chance at the eggs. If they retreat and then return, the dragon statue instantly attacks.

If the characters are wise and do not touch the eggs or the statue, they hear a loud command of "wait" before they leave the chamber. The gold dragon head lowers and opens its maw. On the dragon head's tongue are fist-sized gems, one for each of the characters. All of the gems are worth 25,000 gold pieces apiece. Randomly pick a few from the following list: star-aquamarine, star-chrysoberyl, star-red garnet, star-moonstone, star-ruby, star-dark blue-sapphire star-pink spinel, and star-sunstone. The characters can receive these stones only once in their lifetime.

Facing the Blue Dragon

If the characters recover the staff of the dragon, they have the relic needed to finally stop the blue dragon from terrorizing the island. The character who carries the staff knows that the relic can change 5 characters into young adult red dragons to fight the creature. How the characters fight the dragon is up to them, although the ghost red dragon may have suggested possible strategies if they met him.

You step forward and spread out for the upcoming transformation. The staff waves and the five volunteers transform into powerful young adult red dragons, leaping into the sky.

The *staff of the dragon* can transform up to 5 characters (7 if the characters helped the brass dragon ghost) into young adult red dragons so they can fly out to challenge the blue dragon. The ancient blue dragon is a tough fight, but multiple red dragons might survive the battle. The transformation allows the characters to adjust easily to their new dragon bodies. Whatever protective magic items they carried still lend their protections to the characters. Items such as wands and magical weapons, however, meld into the body of the transformed dragon and cannot be used. The character regains any lost hit points and is totally healed in his new dragon form. The characters also now attack and make saving throws as young adult red dragons. The characters have no spell abilities but can now speak Draconic. The characters remain in their dragon form as long as they wish, and can transform back any time.

The Final Dragon Battle

Read the following when the red dragon characters confront the blue dragon. Adjust the text accordingly if they attack the wyrm before it leaves its cave.

The ancient blue dragon flies into the air and roars out a challenge. The creature is massive for its kind and darkens the sky with titanic wings.

ANCIENT BLUE DRAGON **CR 18**
XP 153,600
hp 324 (*Pathfinder Roleplaying Game Bestiary* "Chromatic Dragon, Blue")

YOUNG ADULT RED DRAGON (The transformed PC) CR 13
XP 25,600
Pathfinder Roleplaying Game Bestiary, "Chromatic Dragon, Red"
AL varies Huge dragon (fire)
Init +4; **Senses** dragon senses, smoke vision; **Perception** +20
Aura frightful presence (150 ft., DC 19)

AC 26, touch 8, flat-footed 26 (+18 natural, –2 size)
hp 172 (15d12+75)
Fort +14; **Ref** +9; **Will** +13
DR 5/magic; **Immune** fire, paralysis, sleep; **SR** 24
Weaknesses vulnerability to cold

Speed 40 ft., fly 200 ft. (poor)
Melee bite +22 (2d8+13), 2 claws +22 (2d6+9), tail slap +20 (2d6+13), 2 wings +20 (1d8+4)
Space 15 ft.; Reach 10 ft.
Special Attacks breath weapon (50 ft. cone, 10d10 fire, every d4 rds, DC 22 half)
Spell-Like Abilities (CL 15th):
At will—*detect magic, pyrotechnics* (DC 14)
Spells Known (CL 5th):
2nd (5/day)—*invisibility, resist energy*
1st (7/day)—*grease, magic missile, shield, true strike*
0 (at will)—*arcane mark, light, mage hand, message, prestidigitation, read magic*

Str 29, **Dex** 10, **Con** 21, **Int** 14, **Wis** 15, **Cha** 14
Base Atk +15; **CMB** +26; **CMD** 36 (40 vs. trip)
Feats Cleave, Improved Initiative, Improved Iron Will, Improved Vital Strike, Iron Will, Multiattack, Power Attack, Vital Strike
Skills Acrobatics +0 (+4 to jump), Appraise +20, Bluff +20, Fly +10, Intimidate +20, Perception +20, Sense Motive +20, Spellcraft +20, Stealth +10.

The Blue Dragon's Cave

The blue dragon has an unusual hobby. The creature likes to use its lightning to melt precious metals and add them to spheres of the various metals. Characters find a 1-foot-diameter sphere of gold worth 21,000gp. A 1ft diameter sphere of silver is worth more than 2600gp, while a 2ft-diameter sphere of copper is worth 900gp. Finally, a small sphere of platinum is worth 4000gp. The dragon also has a magical wooden cupboard that looks like it can hold just 10 potion bottles, but is actually capable of holding up to 100 potions. The cabinet currently holds 12 random potions.

Concluding the Adventure

The *staff of the dragon* cannot be recharged (except by the brass dragon ghost as previously mentioned). The gold and gems on the staff make it worth 20,000 gp, however. But even though it is worthless as a magical item, more roleplaying opportunities exist with the exhausted staff. It seems that all dragon types take great exception to any non-dragon owning the staff. Every dragon encountered insists that the staff be returned to the dais in the Dragon Temple. The temple is an ancient spiritual center for dragons of all kinds sacred to both Tiamat and Behemoth, the Celestial Dragon.

Emeralds of Highfang

By Ed Greenwood

Wise rogues join the government, where their larceny has the cover of "legality" and the cash comes in heaps and piles from deceitful receipts and pocketed procurements rather than in small, bloodstained purses from breaking windows, scaling walls, and risking traps and long-fanged guard dogs.

Wise rogues do *not*, by choice, go up against towering giants armed with clubs larger than the tallest rogue in the guild. Nor do they try to nick treasure from dragons without a group of powerful fellow adventurers behind them who can hurl mighty spells, hack and hew toe to toe with an angry wyrm, heal the injured, and (when things go as they usually do), resurrect the dead.

There are wise rogues, and then there are player characters. ***Emeralds of Highfang*** awaits them with open arms, offering special challenges and rewards to rogue characters — but as always, the prospects are much better for a party of adventurers from a variety of classes, with wide skills and experience, and high level. Some might find that a broad base of experience is not only helpful, but essential for survival.

Emeralds of Highfang is a Pathfinder Roleplaying Game adventure. It is designed for a party of characters of levels 15–17.

Foreword

Emeralds of Highfang leads characters into the caldera of an extinct volcano that has become the lair of an ancient red dragon. The dragon, however, isn't alone; it is allied with a clan of fire giants, who in turn have hill giants and ettins in their service. The volcano, therefore, is every bit as dangerous a place after its death as it was while it was actively spewing lava.

The potential reward for defeating an ancient red dragon and a clan of giants is immense, but so is the risk. This adventure should prove particularly rewarding for rogue player characters, both because the grandest treasure in the dragon's hoard is especially valuable to a rogue, but also because there's more opportunity — and more need — here for stealth, scouting and sneakiness than in most adventures. All too often, rogues who'd like to be out front performing reconnaissance are forced to walk in the middle of the marching order while paladins and barbarians lead the way. In ***Emeralds of Highfang***, brash warriors who barge into chambers relying on their armor and their hit points won't survive long. After one or two encounters, they'll be glad to let the rogues lead from the shadows.

Adventure Hooks

A party of adventurers can be introduced to this adventure in several ways. The events take place in a remote area of the Forlorn Mountains. The most natural manner to begin the adventure (i.e., the least suspicious) is for characters to innocently draw close to Highfang Peak, a long-dormant volcanic caldera that from below looks like a rounded mountain soaring to a high, narrow spike on one side (somewhat like a splinter jutting upward from one side of an immense, sawn-off tree stump). If viewed from the lip or from the air, Highfang is revealed to have a deep, verdant green crater at its heart where wild cattle roam and cascading streams are plentiful.

Characters can be pulled into the area with the usual rumors of unplundered tombs or wealthy bandits, or they can be pushed in by severe weather. In winter, you can rely on a howling blizzard with bad visibility, slick footing under deep, wet snow, and the threat of severe frostbite or hypothermia if they spend the night exposed to the elements. In summer, a blinding, pelting rainstorm with lightning crashing all around, wind tearing trees from the ground, and hailstones the size of cockatrice eggs can do the trick. In either case, a pack of dire wolves or other hungry, desperate creatures shadowing the characters is a nice bit of added motivation for the travelers to seek a safe refuge.

In short, the characters must find shelter or face dire peril — and they find **Area 1**: **The Cavern of the Club**.

Alternatively, characters who begin the adventure in an urban setting or a rural town find, in some dark alley, shed or vacant warehouse, one shattered end of a gigantic club — as thick as a tree trunk, battered into

Glowflow

These mindless, harmless fungi range in size from the span of a human hand to about as large as the top of a dining table; whatever their area, most are about as thick as a human adult's wrist. They can join and divide at random or in response to attacks. They are ambulatory, creeping very slowly toward sources of warmth and movement. When no such sources are present, they flow slowly over stone, readily sticking to walls and ceilings, to reach the highest points in an area or the apex of a cavern ceiling.

If characters sleep in a glowflow-infested cavern without a sentinel, or if they try to remove the fungus (it can be scraped from the stone easily with a stick or a shield), they might awaken with the fungus on them. The fungus likes to cover the faces of living creatures because of the warm breath, but it won't suffocate the sleeper.

Glowflow tastes rather like beef fat, and it does no harm at all if ingested. It does cause the skin of the ingester to glow softly with the same steady, faint, brownish-white luminosity of the glowflow for 1d6+2 days. Glowflow avoids areas of rushing or open water but can be found just about everywhere else underground, throughout all subterranean areas in Highfang Peak and the surrounding mountain range.

Knowledge (nature)

DC	Result
DC 10	Glowflow are harmless fungi found throughout subterranean areas.
DC 15	Glowflow can join together or divide at random or in response to attacks. They are also ambulatory.
DC 20	Glowflows taste like beef and are edible, but will cause the ingester's skin to glow a faint, brownish-white.
DC 25	Glowflows move towards warm and will sometimes seek to cover sleeping individual's mouths, but will not cause suffocation.

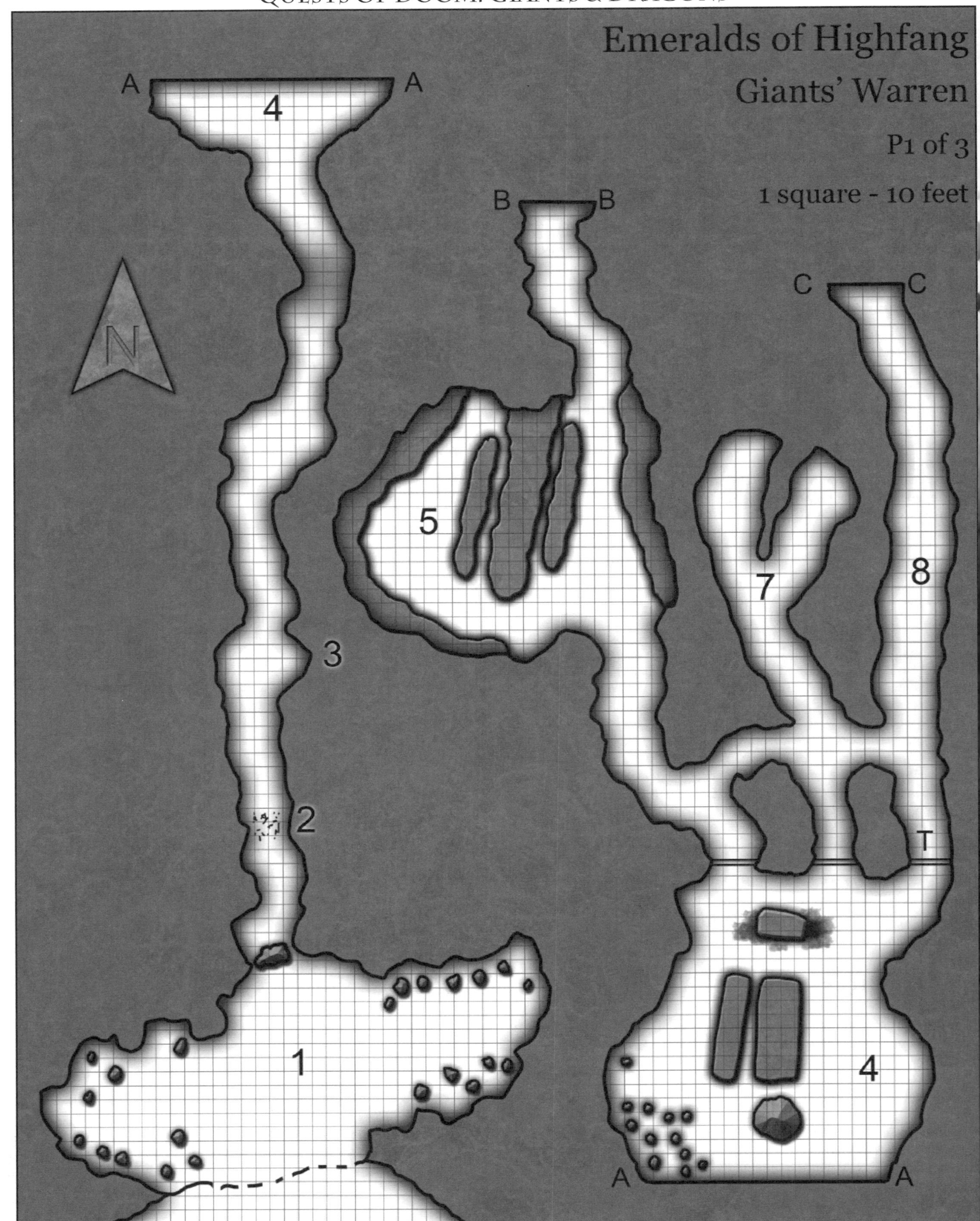
Emeralds of Highfang
Giants' Warren
P1 of 3
1 square - 10 feet
A
A
4
B
B
C
C
N
5
7
8
3
2
T
1
4
A
A

roundness, hardened by fire and studded with iron spikes. It is lying abandoned, apparently discarded and forgotten, and pulsing with a faint, eerie, purple-white magical glow.

If the club is touched, moved, or even approached too closely, it triggers a *teleport* effect that relocates all of the characters and the club fragment to **Area 1** of the giants' warren.

Giants' Warren

Area 1. The Cavern of the Club (CR 4)

Characters espy (DC 20 Perception check) a dark opening in the mountainside, a tall, narrow crack in Highfang Peak. It leads into a huge, irregularly-shaped cavern that's lit faintly by patches of phosphorescent fungus on the walls and ceiling — furry, amorphous, jellylike masses that emit a steady, pale, brownish-white glow.

Strewn around the cavern lie the crushed and rotting bodies of 6 dead orcs who were felled by the blows of a huge, blunt weapon — perhaps a giant's club (DC 10 Heal check to confirm blunt impact damage to the orcs). Amid them are the two halves of the broken giant's club that slew them, dropped by the disgusted giant when it broke. (If the characters were brought here magically by a glowing, broken club, it is one of the halves. It flashes brightly upon arrival, then goes dark, its magic exhausted.)

The dead orcs have a few weapons and some treasure.

Orc 1 gear: Lice-ridden, rotting hide armor, leather belt with crude, rusty dagger in sheath, and pouch containing 6 cp and an orc tooth (his) wrapped in a scrap of bloody cloth. He has a greataxe with broken shaft.

Orc 2 gear: Hide armor in good condition, leather belt with a masterwork dagger in sheath (salvaged from a past human victim), and a pouch containing 1 gp and 4 cp. He has a greataxe in good condition.

Orc 3 gear: Hide armor in good condition, leather belt with *+1 dagger* in sheath (salvaged from a past human victim), and a pouch containing 3 pp and 1 gp. He has an intact javelin.

Orc 4 gear: No armor but has a black metal shield, brittle and pounded flat by a club (the orc's arm, still strapped to the shield, is shattered) and starting to rust, a good leather belt with empty sheath (the dagger is missing and nowhere to be found in the cavern), and pouch containing seven 2-foot-long leather thongs, an ornate leather garment button, and 2 gp. He has a greataxe in good condition.

Orc 5 gear: Lice-ridden, rotting hide armor that was poorly made to begin with (many gaps spanned by knotted, crisscrossing leather thongs), a rotting leather belt with crude but not rusty dagger in sheath, and a pouch containing 2 gp and a fist-sized bundle of soft leather tied up with thongs (inside is a deep red, faceted gemstone about the size of a man's thumbnail, that looks valuable: It's a rose-cut ruby worth 3,000 gp). He has a javelin in good condition.

Orc 6 gear: Hide armor in good condition, leather belt with a good dagger in sheath (salvaged from a past human victim), and a pouch containing 6 sp and 1 cp. He has a greatsword in good condition.

At the back of the cavern is a huge cleft, about 50 feet tall and 20 feet wide. It is blocked by a boulder that is wedged into the cleft and is a little more than 20 feet tall. The boulder was placed here by the giants to keep out wolves and casual intruders. The boulder can be climbed over easily (DC 10 Climb check), or it can be dislodged by characters make a successful DC 15 Strength check due to its precarious position. If the boulder tumbles into the cavern, it makes enough noise that every creature in the next two encounter areas is alerted to the presence of intruders. It also has the potential to crush anyone foolishly standing in front of it when it breaks free. Everyone in its path must make a successful DC 20 Reflex save to avoid 20d6 points of bludgeoning damage.

The first character that climbs to the top of the boulder comes face to face with a **wolf-spider**. It pounces and attacks without hesitation.

WOLF-SPIDER **CR 4**
XP 1,200
The Tome of Horrors Complete 652
NE Large magical beast
Init +7; **Senses** darkvision 60 ft., low-light vision, scent; **Perception** +11

AC 15, touch 12, flat–footed 12 (+3 Dex, +3 natural, –1 size)
hp 45 (6d10+12)
Fort +7; **Ref** +8; **Will** +2

Speed 40 ft., climb 20 ft.
Melee bite +8 (1d8+3 plus poison plus trip)
Space 10 ft.; **Reach** 5 ft.
Special Attacks web (+9 ranged, DC 15, 6 hp)

Str 15, **Dex** 17, **Con** 14, **Int** 8, **Wis** 10, **Cha** 2
Base Atk +6; **CMB** +9; **CMD** 22 (34 vs. trip)
Feats Alertness, Improved Initiative, Weapon Finesse
Skills Acrobatics +3, Climb +10, Perception +11, Sense Motive +2, Stealth +8 (+16 in its webs), Survival +2 (+6 tracking by scent); **Racial Modifiers** +4 Perception, +4 Stealth, +4 Survival when tracking by scent
Languages Common, Goblin

Poison (Ex) Bite—Injury; *save* Fort DC 15; *frequency* 1/round for 6 rounds; *effect* 1d4 Str; *cure* 2 consecutive saves. The save DC is Constitution-based.

Beyond the boulder, the cleft becomes a passage with a rocky, uneven floor covered by fallen and wedged boulders. Moving along this floor is more akin to climbing than to walking; the entire stretch is considered difficult terrain.

The route is roomy enough for giants to traverse, though its difficult terrain for them, too. The rough-walled, irregular passage bends to the right, then curves left again, for 70 feet.

Area 2. Bats and the Drift (CR 5)

At this point, the rough, rocky floor becomes strewn with scattered human and demihuman bones, the remains of unfortunate earlier intruders.

There are **2 mobat bats** that roost here on the passage's ceiling, above a ledge high up on the right side (relative to creatures moving inward along the passage, deeper into the mountain). They swoop to attack anything smaller than a giant that enters the passage.

The bats are jet black with blazing red eyes, large fangs, long tails and wide black leathery wings 15 feet across that make them resemble manta rays, though they are simply a rare subspecies of bat. They shriek as they attack, their wide and many-fanged maws gaping wide. These cries are so high-pitched that they are like needles in the ears of those nearby, but are almost inaudible more than 70 feet away.

MOBAT BATS (2) **CR 3**
XP 800
hp 34 (*Pathfinder Roleplaying Game Bestiary* 2 "Bat, Mobat")

Development: The bats are hungry, so they attack intruders to slay and feed, but they flee to high ledges or out into **Area 1** to roost high up when down to 3 or fewer hit points or when one of the bats is killed. Surviving bats might attack again if characters pass through this area later on their way out.

The Drift

When characters enter the area of bones, they disturb an ancient magical effect called "the Drift," a gentle *reverse gravity*-like field that causes bones to "fall" slowly but steadily upward to the roof of the passage, remain there for four or five minutes, and then gently descend again.

Characters who struggle against the effect can remain grounded with a successful DC 15 Reflex save. Characters who relax and let the effect take hold of them can ride it as if they're affected by a *levitate* spell. Going aloft makes them easier targets for the mobats, which get tactical advantage when attacking "drifting" targets. By using ropes with grapnel hooks, 10-foot poles, or just by pulling themselves along the walls and ceiling with their hands, characters can reach various high ledges (varying from 7 feet wide to just over 2 feet) that run along the passage walls. From these ledges, they can fight giants in the passage and in the Fang Cavern beyond at giant-head-level.

The Drift was established by magic long ago. Now it exists only in a 40-foot-long stretch of the passage, as shown on the map. The boundaries are "soft." PCs who leave the Drift while aloft don't plummet to the ground, but float gently down.

Area 3. Passage Sentinels (CR 9)

Some 80 feet beyond the Drift, the passage widens briefly, creating an alcove in both walls. A large, round brass gong hangs from the center of the ceiling on a massive chain that vanishes up between ceiling-boulders to an unknown anchor point. Under it sit **2 male hill giants**. They are mean, nasty, smelly individuals clad in uncured and reeking hides of various mountain beasts. They are armed with great clubs like the broken one in **Area 1**.

HILL GIANTS (2) **CR 7**
XP 3,200
hp 85 (*Pathfinder Roleplaying Game Bestiary* "Giant, Hill")

The hill giants have orders to kill any intruders. For every intelligent creature or large and dangerous monster (not the mobats nor anything smaller) whose body they display to the fire giants who dwell deeper inside Highfang Peak, those giants reward this pair of brutes by letting them move "closer to Highfang," which the hill giants have been led to believe is a paradise where they can gorge themselves on all they can eat in the company of friendly female hill giants. They are under orders never to both sleep at the same time.

They have been at this wide spot in the passage for almost a year, and it reeks of their dung. (They trudge huge buckets of the stuff out of the caverns to dump as seldom as possible; three huge buckets occupy one alcove, with massive slabs of stone laid across them to form a bench or table.) The fire giants bring them food (usually roasted bull carcasses), and they drink water from the natural spring that trickles down the wall behind the dung buckets and seeps away through the floor.

The giants are dimwitted but enthusiastic in a fight — so much so that they might comically injure each other or bump and stumble over each other (considered them at a –2 while attacking), trying to move into positions from where they can better smear enemies over the rock walls, floor and ceiling with their huge clubs. They are also under orders to strike the gong hanging from the ceiling with their clubs whenever they see an intruder. This alerts the stone giants to (very unhurriedly) come and check the situation.

To keep the hill giants from bashing the gong into smithereens out of anger or boredom, the dragon long ago reached an agreement with some wizards to enchant it so the gong now **trapped**. It emits a weak *lightning bolt* in a line straight toward whoever strikes the gong. The hill giants know this and hate it, so they strike the gong only if they decide they're losing this fight and could use some help. They're smart enough to stand where the *lightning bolt* hits a few enemies in addition to the giant who triggers it.

LIGHTNING BOLT TRAP **CR 4**
XP 2,400
Type mechanical; **Perception** DC 20; **Disable Device** DC 28

Trigger touch; **Reset** automatic
Effect spell effect (*lightning bolt*, 4d6 damage, DC 15 Reflex save for half damage)

Area 4. Fang Cavern (CR 16)

From the widening occupied by the hill giants, the passage runs another hundred feet to a similar widening that's untenanted, then descends gently for 80 feet to another widening of the passage, before rising a further 90 feet beyond it to open out into this large cave.

This rough-walled natural cavern has a ceiling 90 feet up that's dominated by many stalactites (none more than 12 feet long). Most have been crudely pierced so small oil-lamps can be hung from them. More than 40 such lamps are burning in the chamber, giving off smoke that has coated the stalactites with soot, making the room oppressively hot, and seeming to carpet the ceiling in flames. The cave's many stalagmites have all been smoothly cut off to form seats or the supports for stone tabletops. The tables formed this way resemble large, flat-topped stone mushrooms.

One huge central stalagmite has been left alone. It sweeps up from the floor in a thick, sharp, tapering curve that echoes the shape of the lower fang of a gigantic feline.

Here sit **6 fire giant guards**. At any time, two are sleeping, two are cooking and cleaning, and two are on guard duty (which usually means they're sitting with weapons ready and playing stoneguard, a simple dice game; three rolls against three rolls, highest total wins, difference between totals is how many spaces the winner can advance the Dead Giant marker along a straight track of 20 spaces; whenever the marker reaches one end of the track, the giant sitting at that end loses the game).

FIRE GIANTS (6) **CR 10**
XP 9,600
hp 142 (*Pathfinder Roleplaying Game Bestiary* "Giant, Fire")
Gear see below

The two on-duty guards sit on cut-down stalagmites, with a stone table (also formed by a stalagmite) between them. The stoneguard board is carved into the top of the table. They're playing for gold coins. An open sack containing 448 gp sits on the floor beside the table. The two stoneguard players might not notice someone pilfering coins at first (passive penalty Perception –4), but a second trip to the sack by anyone the giant is considered on alert.

Behind the fang is a stone table (a socketed slab placed atop three lopped-off stalagmites), a bench (massive rectangular stone block laid beside the table), and in a slight depression in the cavern floor, a cooking hearth full of smoldering charcoal surrounded by a ring of ready firewood (short but, to humans, quite large and heavy logs). Above the hearth is a blackened metal frame of heavy roughcast iron on which rest three spits, each transfixing the carcass of a whole bull now partly roasted, sizzling and dripping fat into the fire. Each spit has six metal wedges that can be placed on the frame at either end to hold the spit and its meat in a particular position. To humans, these metal wedges are each about the size of a large chair, and are *very* heavy (requiring a DC 20 Strength). Near the hearth is a reeking bucket (about the size of a human bathtub) of eel oil, which the giants use as a fire starter and a baste. Above the hearth, the cavern rises in a natural chimney, a shaft that rises for fully 240 feet beyond the 90-foot height of the cavern to emerge high atop one of the rising arms of Highfang Peak. The chimney is never less than 20 feet wide, and its walls are caked with soot and slippery grease, making it nearly impossible to climb. A successful DC 30 Climb check is needed at the beginning, middle and end of the climb to ascend the chimney.

Three arch-topped, lockless, giant-sized doors of fitted, sculpted stone are set into the back wall of this cavern, spaced well apart. The doors swing into this cavern when opened.

The door on the left leads to a huge hot cavern where the fire giants live, the one in the center to a privy, and the one on the right opens into a long passage that penetrates deeper into Highfang Peak. The tunnels behind these three doors are all linked by a cross-passage.

The fire giants all have crimson beards and eyebrows and jet-black hair. They wear well-oiled black armor over hide jerkins and breeches, and have armored boots and black metal open-face helms.

They are:

Horlond (awake, on duty, winning at stoneguard, jovial): Paunchy and the possessor of a wide smile, large and merry eyes, and crooked teeth; over his armor, he wears a baldric with three metal knives (to humans, greatswords) ranged down it in sheaths with pommel straps (loops of thick leather sewn to the baldric, that the pommels of the knives are confined within, to help keep them falling free of the sheaths), pouch sewn to baldric under chin that contains scrap muslin sacks of 17 gp, 33 sp, and 12 cp. Horlond's principal weapon is his greatsword, scabbarded at his hip.

Marl (awake, on duty, losing at stoneguard, testy): Broad-shouldered and burly (even for a giant), with an ugly slab of a face and a flattened nose (looking rather like the stone faces of real-world Easter Island); garbed and equipped identically to Horlond, greatsword and all, except that Marl's pouch holds sacks containing 6 gp, 14 sp and 27 cp (he loses at stoneguard a lot).

Haelath (awake, cooking, slow and methodical): Handsome for a fire giant, with weathered features and a perpetually stern expression; garbed and equipped identically to Horlond, but his helm, sword, armor, baldric and jerkin lie in a neat pile on the bench by the table. Haelath's pouch contains sacks of 22 gp, 4 sp and 11 cp. Consider his AC 16 if he is unable to don his armor before combat.

Gararl (awake, cutting up vegetables and fetching spices from a row of jars along two neat ledges carved into the wall): Ugly and with snarled, curly, light-hued hair and a nose that was badly broken in the past; garbed and equipped identically to Haelath, his helm, sword, armor, baldric and jerkin lie in a neat pile on the bench by the table beside Haelath's. Gararl's pouch contains sacks of 8 gp, 29 sp and 15 cp. Consider his AC 16 if he is unable to don his armor before combat.

Kalikh (asleep on the floor to one side of the cavern, wrapped in a dusty blanket of many sewn-together overlapped hides, initially hidden from characters [DC 20 Perception check] by stalagmites unless characters are up on a wall ledge): Hook-nosed, scar-faced (cut by at least two swords), and ugly to start with, Kalikh has a sour, sarcastic disposition to match his looks; garbed and equipped identically to Haelath (except that his boots are off, and standing beside his gently snoring head); his helm, sword, armor, baldric and jerkin, wrapped in a second blanket, serve him as his pillow. Consider his AC 16 if he is unable to don his armor before combat.

Loruth (asleep on the floor to one side of the cavern, wrapped in a blanket, initially hidden from characters [DC 20 Perception check] by stalagmites unless characters are up on a wall ledge): Youngest of the giants and with a handsome baby face and soft-hued brown hair and eyes; garbed and equipped identically to Kalikh; boots off and helm, sword, armor, baldric and jerkin, wrapped in a second blanket, serving as his pillow. Consider his AC 16 if he is unable to don his armor before combat.

(If the characters never learn the names and traits of these giants, you can use them to flesh out any other fire giants encountered later in their explorations. Feel free to adjust the giants' hit points up or down for variety.)

The giants are likely to catch sight of anyone walking along the wall ledges, which are near their typical eye level. It is also a habit for them to frequently glance down the passage to **Area 3** (toward the hill giant sentinels). The slope of that passage, however, could enable a Medium or Small creature crawling on the floor to reach the lip without being seen (considered concealment). From there, any intruder notes the stony forest of lopped-off stalagmites that begins, on the intruder's left, right where the passage enters the large cavern. Quiet, stealthy characters who crawl up the passage and immediately slip into the field of stalagmites have a good chance to avoid being noticed by the stone giants.

All six fire giants, like most of their kind, are expert rock hurlers. Just because this cavern has been cleared of loose rocks doesn't mean they don't have things they can throw: on the floor behind the bench are stacks of stone platters (two piles of eight each) and plates (five stacks of twelve each). These platters and plates are thrown just like stones but cause less damage (1d6+15 plus 1d6 fire).

Area 5. Hot Cavern (CR 18 or varies)

From the door, a 20-foot-wide irregular passage (a natural cleft, long ago chiseled wider) runs 60 feet into the solid rock of Highfang Peak before it is joined by a side passage to the right. Beyond that junction, the tunnel continues for 80 feet until it opens out into this huge cavern where the majority of the fire giants of Highfang dwell.

Mindful of the possible wrath of the dragon, the giants, who are all of the Narlohrind tribe, brought no children or pregnant tribal members to Highfang. There are elders and wives, not just male fire giants in the prime of life. Counting the six guards in the Fang Cavern (**Area 4**), 38 fire giants reside in all of Highfang. When not working the quarry or forges, on guard duty, or cooking or dining, they dwell here.

At any given time, the typical job roster for the fire giants has 4 giants cooking, 6 working the quarry, 6 on guard duty, 2 at the forge, and 6 in the mill, leaving **8 fire giants** and **6 fire giant children** in this room. If weakened characters try to hide or take refuge here, you might decide that 12 of these 14 have gone to dine.

Aside from mothers and children dwelling in deep magma-warmed caves far from Highfang, these Narlohrind are the last remnants of a once numerous and powerful fire giant tribe that was almost wiped out in a terrible war with frost giants. Facing extermination and desperate, they agreed to serve the red dragon Haeraglondrar in return for the wyrm's protection. Thus far, they haven't regretted doing so.

FIRE GIANTS (8) **CR 10**
XP 9,600
hp 142 (*Pathfinder Roleplaying Game Bestiary* "Giant, Fire")

FIRE GIANT CHIDREN (6) **CR 9**
XP 6,400
Male and female young fire giant (*Pathfinder Roleplaying Game Bestiary* "Giant, Fire")
LE Medium humanoid (fire, giant)
Init +0; **Senses** low-light vision; **Perception** +14

AC 24, **touch** 10, **flat-footed** –1 (+8 armor, +0 Dex, +6 natural)
hp 112 (15d8+45)
Fort +12; **Ref** +5; **Will** +9;
Defensive Abilities rock catching; **Immune** fire;
Weaknesses vulnerability to cold

Speed 40 ft. (30 ft. in armor)
Melee greatsword +18/+13/+8 (2d6+11) or 2 slams +17 (1d6+6)
Ranged rock +12 (1d6+15 plus 1d6 fire)
Space 5 ft. **Reach** 5 ft.
Special Attacks heated rock, rock throwing (120 ft.)

Str 23, **Dex** 11, **Con** 17, **Int** 10, **Wis** 14, **Cha** 10;
Base Atk 11; **CMB** 19; **CMD** 30
Feats Cleave, Great Cleave, Improved Overrun, Improved Sunder, Iron Will, Martial Weapon Proficiency (greatsword), Power Attack, Weapon Focus (greatsword)
Skills Climb +12, Craft (any one) +8, Intimidate +11, Perception +14
Languages Common, Giant
Gear half-plate, greatsword

Heated Rock (Su) Fire giants transfer the heat of their bodies to rocks as part of an attack action when they throw rocks. A heated rock deals 1d6 points of additional fire damage on a hit.

The ranking tribal elder is **Klarrouth**, who stands a head taller than the other fire giants, he wears two greatswords, one made of adamantine in a scabbard on a baldric down his back and one in a scabbard at his hip. He wears the intricately detailed half-plate armor and helm. Klarrouth is a veteran tactician who is far less hot-tempered and more prudent and far-sighted than most fire giants, and he has little time for flattery, courtesy or deference.

KLARROUTH **CR 16**
XP 76,800
Fire giant fighter 6 (*Pathfinder Roleplaying Game Bestiary* "Giant, Fire")
LE Large humanoid (fire, giant)
Init +5; **Senses** low-light vision; **Perception** +20

AC 27, touch 9, flat-footed 27 (+10 armor, +8 natural, –1 size)
hp 208 (15d8+60 plus 6d10+24 plus 19)
Fort +18; **Ref** +8; **Will** +12
Defensive Abilities rock catching; **Immune** fire
Weaknesses vulnerability to cold

Speed 30 ft.
Melee +2 *flaming burst greatsword* +32/+27/+22/+17 (3d6+23/17-20 plus 1d6 fire) or 2 slams +28 (1d8+12)
Space 10 ft.; **Reach** 10 ft.
Special Attacks rock throwing (120 ft.), weapon training (heavy blades +1)

Str 34, **Dex** 13, **Con** 19, **Int** 13, **Wis** 16, **Cha** 14
Base Atk +17; **CMB** +30 (+32 overrun, +32 sunder); **CMD** 41 (43 vs. overrun, 43 vs. sunder)
Feats Blind-fight, Cleave[B], Critical Focus, Great Cleave[B], Improved Critical (greatsword), Improved Initiative, Improved Overrun, Improved Sunder, Iron Will, Persuasive, Power Attack[B], Toughness[B], Weapon Focus (greatsword), Weapon Specialization (greatsword)
Skills Bluff +5, Climb +18, Craft (Weapons) +20, Diplomacy +16, Intimidate +20, Knowledge (dungeoneering) +10, Perception +20
Languages Common, Draconic, Giant
SQ heated rock
Other Gear +2 *half-plate*, +2 *flaming burst greatsword*, *boots of speed*, *ring of feather falling*, gold crown (350 gp value)

This cavern was named for its warmth, which fire giants find comfortably hot (and most other races consider uncomfortably so). The warmth comes from magma flows beneath the floor and behind the western wall of the cavern.

The northern, western and southern walls of the room have been dug out to form stone bed-shelves for the giants. Rows of small cubbyholes at floor level are used for storage. In these, the giants keep changes of clothing and footwear, dice and cards for idle time, walking sticks, vials of oil and sharpening stones for the maintenance of their weapons, tools, armor, sewing kits and the rest of their belongings.

This cavern was once two smaller side-by-side caves, but the wall between them was carved down to form two immobile benches with backs, with a stone table (a continuous pedestal that supports a tabletop, all carved out of solid, unbroken stone) between them. These occupy the center of the cavern.

A dozen braziers of welded metal fashioned by the fire giants stand around the room. They each have a 5-foot-square metal base supporting a 15-foot-tall straight metal column about as thick around as an average adult human's thigh, topped by a stone bowl with a 1-foot-high lip that holds sarduik [subterranean fish oil, DC 15 Knowledge (nature) to identify] about 8 inches deep, in which floats a flaming wick. These braziers give off more smoke than heat and more heat than light, but their massed effect in this cavern is bright and hot.

The air stinks of sarduik, a smell like overheated copper, underlaid by fire giant sweat, which smells like overheated, impure iron. It is hot enough to make humans sweat after a few seconds of exposure. After two minutes or so, a typical human is slick with sweat, which causes tactical disadvantage of –4 to Climb skill checks.

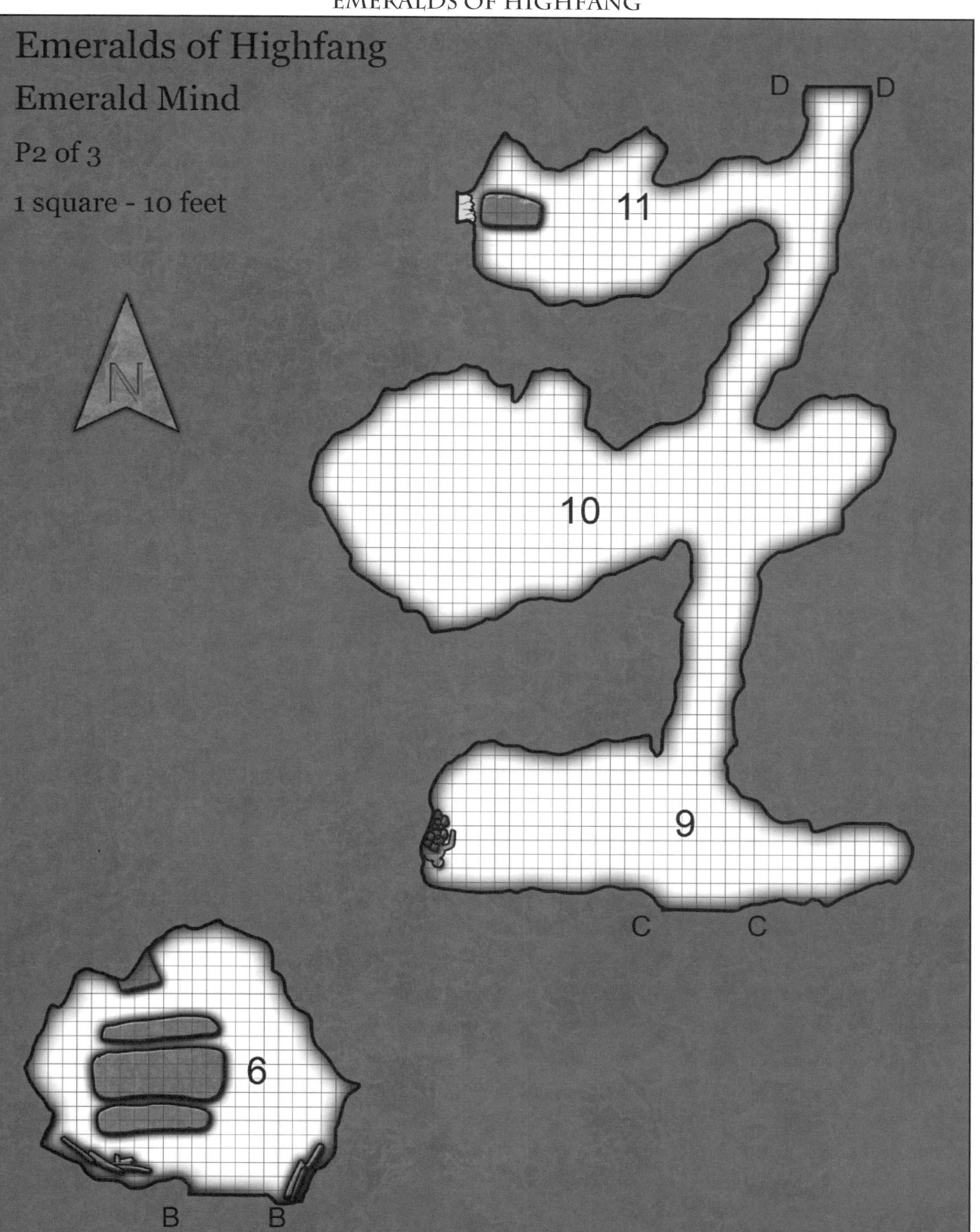
Emeralds of Highfang
Emerald Mind
P2 of 3
1 square - 10 feet
N
D
D
11
10
9
C
C
6
B
B

Area 6. Fire Giant Kitchen

From **Area 5**, a 20-foot-wide passage bends and twists 120 feet back into the rocky heart of the mountain, then opens out into this combined kitchen and larder.

The back of this cave is a huge roasting hearth containing three parallel, horizontal metal spits, each held up on its own pair of metal stands. The 30-foot-long spits rest in a "Y" at the top of a 15-foot-tall vertical column welded to a 10-foot-square base. Each spit has a pointed end and a "T" end with crossbar handles. In a pinch, the spits can be used as improvised spears by the giants, doing 2d6 points of piercing damage.

Above the hearth is a natural chimney extending up through Highfang Peak to the sky above. It rises 210 feet beyond the 60-foot height of the cavern, to emerge between two pinnacles of one of the rising arms of Highfang Peak. The chimney is 30 feet in diameter and the walls are caked with soot and slippery grease, making it nearly impossible to climb. A successful DC 30 Climb check is needed at the beginning, middle and end of the climb to ascend the chimney.

On the right side of the cavern is a larder consisting of 20 huge sacks of flour (each sack is three times the size of an average adult human and weighs close to a ton) and 18 barrels of sarduik (whole fish, orange and eyeless, naturally blind, and exuding their own oil; each barrel weighs well over a ton, and they have been sealed on the outside by being dipped in mortar that coats them with crumbling concrete that they constantly shed as deposits of grit).

Thirty-five iron hooks are hammered into the rocky ceiling, where hang the smoked carcasses of everything from wolves to captured humans to horses to cattle. If any characters are captured, they are likely to be hung up by their ankles from these hooks, alive, until Klarrouth gets around to questioning them. When characters first see this cavern, only five hooks are empty.

At the end of the larder, the cavern sidewall vanishes behind a ceiling-high stack of split firewood that covers much of the cavern walls.

The left-hand wall of the cavern is home to a stone shelf or counter where many large, soot-covered skillets sit, alongside blackened iron cooking racks for placing over the spits, above the hearth. The shelf ends before the hearth begins, and in the space between stand a sarduik oil press and two empty sarduik barrels used as trash cans. Characters might not immediately recognize the press for what it is [DC 15 Knowledge (engineering)]. The device resembles an enormous metal hinge with drain holes in the bottom plate. It's welded to four legs that straddle a square catch-bucket with a pour spout. Oil is squeezed from fish into the bucket then poured into the braziers. On close inspection, characters see the orange fish scales and clotted blood coating the press.

In the center of the room is a stone dining table with stone benches on both sides. Unlike those in the Hot Cavern (**Area 5**), these were not carved in place from the solid bedrock. They were instead carved elsewhere and brought into this room.

Area 7. Giants' Privy

The reek from this open latrine isn't bad because it drains into a magma flow far beneath that chars everything that goes down it. The privy consists of two adjacent caverns at the end of the passage, one for females and one for males. Flushing is done by buckets of water, a dozen of which line either side of the wall dividing the two caverns. The privy likely is empty when characters investigate it.

Area 8. Inner Passage (CR 12)

This natural crevice is chiseled out to form a tunnel 40 feet wide and 70 feet high. The irregular walls are studded with small storage niches at waist to shoulder height for a giant. The giants keep things such as unlit oil lamps on them. None of the niches joins with the ledges or "go anywhere," so although a stealthy human could hide here, the niches are of little use for traversing the length of the passage by avoiding the floor. The passage descends slightly as it travels some 400 feet from the Fang Cavern (**Area 4**) to the Emerald Mine (**Area 9**).

This passage is **trapped** starting 10 feet beyond the door from the Fang Cavern. Weight of 40 pounds or more on the floor causes a block to fall from the ceiling. The giants simply hold the block in place with their hands over their heads as they pass; once they step off the trigger plate, the block again locks in place.

FALLING BLOCK TRAP **CR 12**
XP 19,200
Type mechanical/magical; **Perception** DC 20; **Disable Device** DC 25

Trigger touch; **Reset** repair
Effect falling block (8d6 bludgeoning damage, DC 25 Reflex save for half damage); multiple targets (all targets in a 20-foot-square area)

The trap can be spotted with a successful DC 20 Perception check, or automatically if someone sees a giant walking through the passage. The floor plate and the ceiling block are rather obvious, as such things go, but they fill the full width of the passage and extend for 20 feet, making them difficult to avoid. When the trap is triggered, four 1-ton stone blocks drop from the ceiling on chains; the chains halt the blocks 6 inches above the floor. The rattling chains give plenty of warning that a trap has been triggered, and the long drop of the stone accounts for the relatively easy avoidance saving throw. If, however, characters are burdened in a way that prevents them from quickly exiting the 20-foot-long danger space — if they're carrying heavy sacks of dragon loot or the body of a fallen comrade, for example — they have tactical disadvantage on this save.

Area 9. Emerald Mine (CR 13)

The passage intersects here with a dark gray vein rich in emeralds, which the giants have been digging out for the dragon for a year or so — until they encountered a problem they haven't yet summoned up the courage to tell the dragon about. Klarrouth is pondering starting a side tunnel from the upper reaches of this cavern to dig around the problem, but he fears the dragon suspects the giants of stealing emeralds if they dig for any length of time without yielding more gems. If the vein is as narrow as it looks to be, a side tunnel will traverse a long stretch of gem-free bedrock. So no giants will be found at work here.

The inner passage (**Area 8**) crosses a huge, giant-dug cavern before vanishing into a tunnel mouth on the other side. The crossing is 120 feet long, with a ceiling 120 feet up, and the passage running on from the cavern is 45 feet wide by 70 feet tall. To the right of someone entering the mine cavern from the inner passage, the mine has a level floor that extends only 100 feet, narrowing toward its end.

To the left of such a traveler, the mine cavern descends steeply and is almost 100 feet wide. It ends 80 feet below the floor level of the passage. Torches and lanterns won't illuminate the far end of the cavern from the passage, and even most creatures with darkvision can't see that far.

At the lower (left) end, the diggings broke through into an ancient cavern that suffered a ceiling collapse long ago, entombing an **iron golem** on its back under tons of boulders and stone rubble. The giants uncovered its head, chest and one arm, and in doing so — as it perceives — "attacked" it with their prybars, picks and hammers. Its ancient instructions, given to it by a long dead and forgotten mage, were to defend the cavern against intruders, and it still considers that its mission. It belched poison gas onto the giants trying to dig it loose and fought them with its free arm.

The giants retreated, leaving the golem lying there, trapped on its back beneath the rubble as it had been for ages. Since then, it is ever-so-slowly digging itself free by clawing with its one arm. Its head, chest, left shoulder and left side down to its waist are now bare; its right shoulder and side, sword arm, and its lower body are still pinned.

PCs entering the mine won't at first see the golem (DC 30 Perception check), which is lying still in the dark with its face turned toward the

passage (facing the approaching characters). Its upper arm lies flat and motionless on the rubble, but bent 90 degrees at the elbow so the forearm points straight up, its hand balled into a fist. The iron golem looks like a full-body suit of black plate armor, with a full-face helm pierced only by two thin, dark "eye" slits above four vertical "breathing" slits.

The moment anyone gets within 15 feet of it, the golem exhales a cloud of poison gas. If any character gets closer, it lashes out with its arm in a sideways punch.

IRON GOLEM **CR 13**
XP 25,600
hp 129 (*Pathfinder Roleplaying Game Bestiary* "Golem, Iron")

Treasure: No one who gets within 50 feet of the golem fails to notice that a dozen raw, uncut emeralds as large as a dwarf's fist are heaped on its chest. They were gathered there by the golem as it lay in the darkness (its orders tell it not to damage emeralds). Uncut, each is worth about 200 gp; once expertly cut and polished, each would be worth 4d4x100 gp.

Area 10. Quarry (CR 15)

The passage from the Emerald Mine crosses one end of a vast cavern where the fire giants are quarrying out large, rectangular blocks of stone for the Mill (**Area 12**). The ceiling of this cavern is studded with the broken-off roots of stalactites, and the floor is entirely smooth where block after block has been removed. The fire giants are neat, methodical stonecutters.

At work in the quarry, as far away from the passage crossing as it's possible to get, are **6 fire giants** without helms, armor or swords, but armed with mattocks, hammers, picks and huge prybars that they swing like greatswords.

FIRE GIANTS (6) **CR 10**
XP 3,200
hp 142 (*Pathfinder Roleplaying Game Bestiary* "Giant, Fire")

If the giants notice intruders, they rush to attack. One giant tries to thunder past the characters and on down the passage toward **Area 11** to warn the dragon. After past incidents, the dragon has issued firm "no exceptions" orders to the giants that it is to be informed of the presence of any sentient intruders or large and dangerous creatures of any kind. PCs pursuing the giant see that it races past **Areas 11** and **12** to **Area 13**, where it first stammers, hems and haws for several moments before finally blurting out a warning about "humans in our halls." The dragon is asleep, so the giant's first attempt at a message awakens it, but it doesn't hear the message properly. A fast-moving PC who uses the side opening to get into the speaking tube can completely block the giant's second attempt, so all the dragon hears is muffled rumblings. It assumes it's hearing the mumblings of a drunken giant rather than a warning and goes back to sleep, now in a sour mood.

If characters don't stop the giant before it reaches **Area 13** or block its message, they'll likely reap the consequences in **Area 11**.

Unbeknownst even to the giants, a **mimic** has crept into this cavern from the wilds of Highfang. It is posing as part of the rough stone around the edges of the cavern, near the passage crossing, where the giants haven't yet gone in their cutting. It stalks characters if it gets the chance, drawing closer (as a stone) when it thinks it isn't being watched.

MIMIC **CR 4**
XP 1,200
hp 52 (*Pathfinder Roleplaying Game Bestiary* "Mimic")

If the PCs defeat or drive off the giants and then decide to sleep or rest here, the mimic becomes immobile and waits until the maximum number of characters is asleep, or when it can catch someone alone, before it attacks. If characters suddenly move to depart, it immediately attacks the rearmost character.

Area 11. Forge (CR 15)

A side-passage branches off the inner passage to the left. This tunnel is 45 feet wide by 70 feet high, and it runs 80 feet (descending slightly) before opening into a natural cavern 100 feet across and 140 feet long. The air in this chamber stinks of hot metal, and is hot enough to make humans sweat after only a few seconds of exposure. After two minutes or so, a typical human is slick with sweat, which causes tactical disadvantage of –4 to Climb skill checks

The heat in this cavern comes from a hole in its western wall, farthest from the passage, which opens into a magma flow. Magma slides slowly and endlessly past this cavern, from right to left as seen by someone standing facing the hole.

This "hot hole" serves the fire giants as a forge fire. They work here with tongs, hammers and long iron bars that end in flat paddles, moving continually between the hole and a gigantic, scarred, flat-topped slab of noqual ("starmetal," a fallen meteor) that serves them as an anvil. The fire giants forge, repair and temper their weapons and mining tools (picks, hammers, mattocks and prybars) here.

When PCs first peer into this room, a **fire giant** apprentice and his master, **Toroth** (the fire giants' most talented smith) are working the forge. Toroth loves to fight bare handed and as soon as he spots the PCs he smiles, drops his smithy hammer, cracks his knuckles and starts swinging.

FIRE GIANT **CR 10**
XP 9,600
hp 142 (*Pathfinder Roleplaying Game Bestiary* "Giant, Fire")

TOROTH THE BLACKSMITH **CR 14**
XP 38,400
Fire giant brawler 4 (*Pathfinder Roleplaying Game Bestiary* "Giant, Fire"; *Pathfinder Roleplaying Game Advanced Class Guide* "Brawler")
LE Large humanoid (fire, giant)
Init +2; **Senses** low-light vision; **Perception** +13

AC 26, touch 12, flat-footed 23 (+6 armor, +2 Dex, +1 dodge, +8 natural, -1 size)
hp 245 (15d8+105 plus 4d10+28 plus 23)
Fort +20; **Ref** +11; **Will** +9
Defensive Abilities rock catching; **Immune** fire
Weaknesses vulnerability to cold

Speed 40 ft.
Melee unarmed strike +28/+23/+18 (2d6+15)
Space 10 ft.; **Reach** 10 ft.
Special Attacks brawler's flurry, knockout 1/day (DC 25), maneuver training (bull rush +1), martial flexibility 5/day, rock throwing (120 ft.)

Str 36, **Dex** 14, **Con** 24, **Int** 13, **Wis** 12, **Cha** 13
Base Atk +15; **CMB** +29 (+30 bull rush, +31 overrun, +31 sunder); **CMD** 42 (43 vs. bull rush, 44 vs. overrun, 44 vs. sunder)
Feats Cleave, Great Cleave, Improved Overrun, Improved Sunder, Improved Unarmed Strike, Iron Will, Power Attack^B, Toughness^B, Weapon Focus (greatsword), Weapon Focus (unarmed strike), Weapon Specialization (unarmed strike)
Skills Acrobatics +2 (+6 to jump), Appraise +7, Climb +24, Craft (armor) +20, Craft (Weapons) +16, Intimidate +12, Knowledge (dungeoneering) +10, Perception +13
Languages Common, Giant, Ignan
SQ brawler's cunning, heated rock, martial training
Other Gear +2 *mithral shirt*

This cavern has a small but almost straight natural chimney to the surface, a 170-foot vertical shaft that begins as a 10-foot-diameter hole in the center of the ceiling in the side passage that links the forge cavern with the inner passage (**Area 8**).

If PCs were spotted in the quarry (**Area 10**) and a giant fled from there and alerted the dragon, then while characters are scouting or exploring this chamber, the dragon leaves its bed and is sitting on a lesser pinnacle of Highfang right beside this chimney, listening intently. If it hears talking or whispering that isn't coming from a giant (the dragon can easily tell the difference, and the chimney acts like a megaphone for sounds from below), it breathes fire down the chimney. The chute confines and focuses the flames so they reach past the bottom of the shaft and flood out into a 30-foot stretch of the side-passage centered on the shaft. All creatures in this area take 20d10 points of fire damage, or half that with a successful DC 25 Reflex save.

Area 12. Mill (CR 16)

The Inner Passage branches to the left in another side passage 60 feet wide, 70 feet high and 100 feet long, with a smooth, downward-sloping ramp for a floor that is worn slippery-smooth by the endlessly repeated passage of something that created two parallel grooves or "slides" (which are sized more like troughs). The cavern descends and widens out into a long chamber. A deep, ceaseless, rumbling, groaning sound comes up from below, overlaid fairly often by high-pitched screeches.

A PC who sets foot in either groove in the floor must make a DC 20 Reflex save. Failure indicates the character slips, falls and slides helplessly down the groove for the full length of the passage, alerting the giants in the mill space below.

A strong, steady breeze blows from the passage down into this cavern. The rumbling and screeches would be much louder throughout other areas inside Highfang if it didn't.

This cavern has been denuded of stalactites and stalagmites. It houses the main coin-earning industry the fire giants are running for the dragon. Characters who look down into this cavern from the side passage see an underground spring gushing high out of the cavern wall on their right, at the end of the cavern. It plunges into the buckets of an undershot mill wheel made of welded iron, mounted sideways to the observer on a massive stone axle. The turning wheel is the source of the rumbling sound as it turns endlessly under the goad of the constant fall of water.

A metal axle protrudes from the wheel to jut into the room, where it powers a spinning, tapered-point cutting drill. Working in the chamber are **6 fire giants** who are manipulating one of the blocks from the quarry by brute strength as the cutter slowly grinds away at it. Five giants are holding and turning the stone, while the sixth is using a huge stone paddle to deflect some of the falling water onto the stone at the spot where the cutter is at work, to cool the stone and wash away what would otherwise be blinding clouds of rock dust.

FIRE GIANTS (6) **CR 10**
XP 9,600
hp 142 (*Pathfinder Roleplaying Game Bestiary* "Giant, Fire")

The giants are slowly transforming the rectangular blocks they quarried in **Area 10** into smooth, cylindrical stone columns. These are sold for cash to merchants, who market them as roof supports for massive palaces and public buildings.

Finished columns are loaded onto high-sided sledges and dragged up the slope out of this cavern and on to **Area 15** by teams of captive ettins. No ettins are in the mill cavern when characters first see it. Ettin teams are brought here only when a sledge is filled with four columns securely lashed into wooden cradles. At the moment, one sledge sits off to the side of the milling area with just one finished column loaded. A glance at the sledge confirms that this is what wore the grooves into the floor.

Any character who examines the water wheel closely notices (DC 28 Perception check) that the side of the turning wheel nearest the wall has something welded to it: metal fan blades that turn with the wheel, between it and the stone wall. These blades drag air down into this cavern from the passage above to push air through a tunnel behind the turning water wheel, in the cavern's end wall. This gently ascending tunnel is oval in

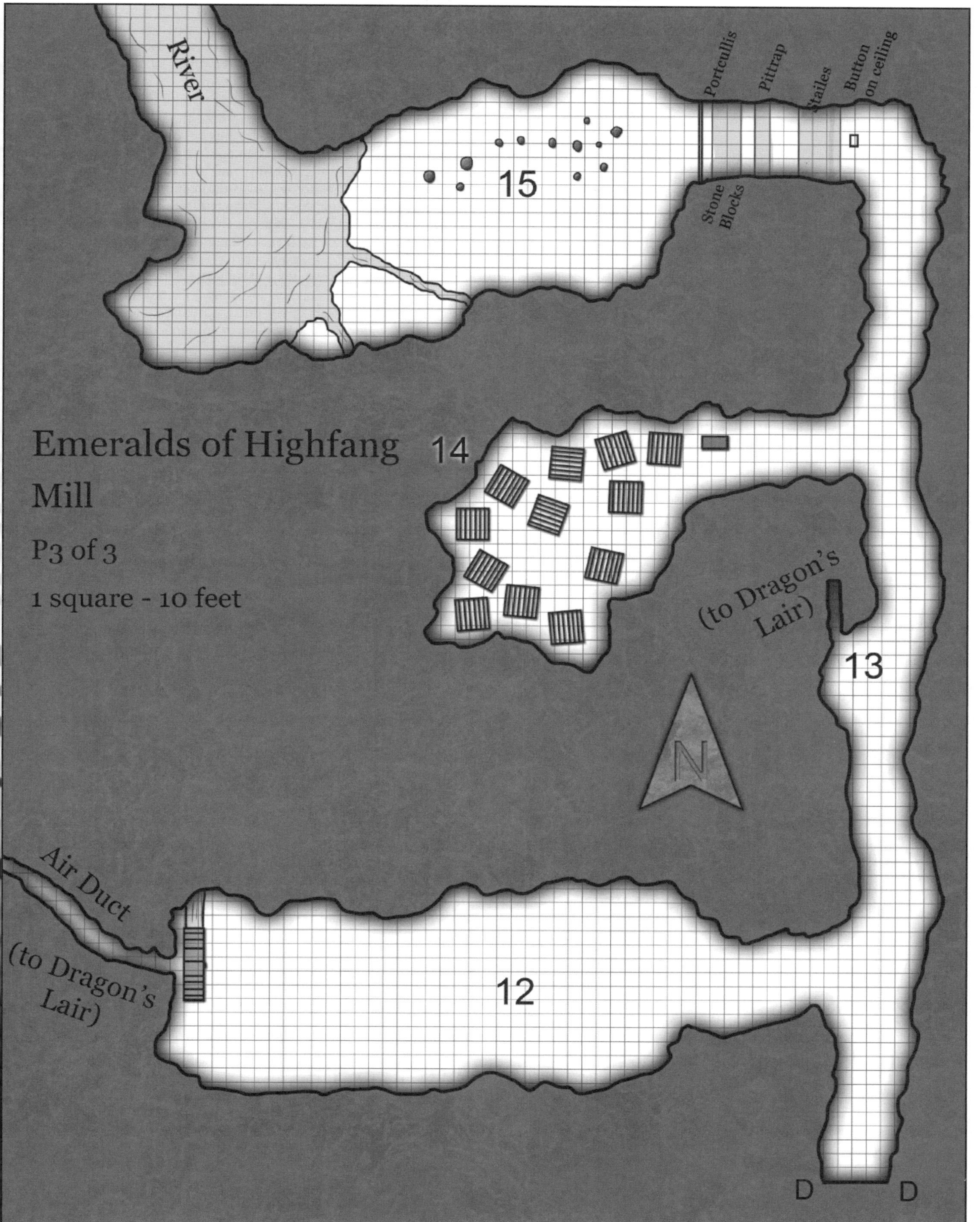
River
Portcullis
Pittrap
Stailes
Button on ceiling
Stone Blocks
15
14
13
12
Emeralds of Highfang
Mill
P3 of 3
1 square - 10 feet
(to Dragon's Lair)
N
Air Duct
(to Dragon's Lair)
D
D

cross-section, about 15 feet across and 30 high, and carries fresh air up into the dragon's lair (**Area 19**). This air channel is the stealthiest way into the lair.

Area 13. Speaking Tube

The passage widens here into a natural, rough-walled alcove, roughly 50 feet long and 20 feet wider than the rest of the passage, with the same 70-foot ceiling as the adjoining passage. Long ago, emerald delvers of much smaller stature than the giants (probably dwarves) bored a long shaft high up in one wall that ascends steadily into the Dragonslumber Cavern (**Area 19**) of the dragon's lair.

It is currently used as a speaking tube. The pipe amplifies what the giants shout, speak or whisper into it, so the dragon can hear them clearly in its lair. If a giant flees from the quarry to here, he uses the speaking tube to warn the dragon. The speaking tube's creators also cut a second hole into the wall below and to the left of the larger one the giants use. This secondary hole connects to the main sound passage after a climb of about 15 feet. A human can fit through either one.

The speaking shaft is not just a narrow crawlspace. It is 5 feet tall and 3 feet wide. An adult human can squeeze through it easily, but can also block it with their body, clothing and gear sufficiently to muffle any sounds coming through [DC 20 Knowledge (engineering) check or DC 15 Wisdom check]. Blocking the tube this way won't stop all sounds, but it utterly garbles any speech through the tube that is more complex than single, short, simple words (such as "Help!") shouted by a giant.

Area 14. Ettin Pens (CR 16)

This large, irregular, natural cavern contains a spare, empty sledge (a duplicate of the one in **Area 12**) and a dozen massive cages made from welded iron bars. Slave teams of captive ettins are imprisoned here, three to a cage, permanently wearing welded iron harnesses (**36 captive ettins** total). The room reeks of ettin dung, which is heaped knee deep (to a human) throughout the cages. Mixed in are the bones of the cattle carcasses thrown to the ettins by their fire giant captors.

The giants select ettins when needed and drag them out, one by one, clip their harnesses together by means of the rings that are part of each harness, beat any uncooperative ettins into near-senseless submission, then drag the assembled teams to **Area 12**, hitch them to a loaded sledge, and force them to drag the tons of stone up the steep slope to **Area 15**. If one of the giants makes it to this room, he could potentially release the ettins against the PCs. The ettins have no intention of turning on the brutal giants and if told to, will attack the PCs relentlessly.

CAPTIVE ETTINS (36) **CR 6**
XP 2,400
hp 65 (*Pathfinder Roleplaying Game Bestiary* "Ettin")

Area 15. Raft Sally Port (CR 17)

The Inner Passage turns left and descends, to end in this large cavern studded with the stumps of broken-off stalactites and stalagmites. From where the passage turns to where it enters the wider cavern is a descent of 20 feet. The walls, floors and ceiling are made of smooth stone blocks with large seams between them. The floor is paved with 10-foot-long paving stones, and the ceiling and walls are covered with 4-foot-square blocks.

Several small springs weep down the walls of this cavern and join together in a pool where a dozen rafts wait. Each raft is fitted with a trio of wooden cradles into which a single stone column can be lashed. The giants push loaded rafts out into the pool and let the current flowing from the pool carry the columns downriver to human merchants in the Domain of Hawkmoon who work for the dragon.

Spare cradles, rope for lashing (as thick around as small barrels, to a human; a very short length of rope could serve as flotation for one person), a cleaver (treat as greatsword) for lopping off lengths of rope, and the chopping block that the cleaver rests in, all wait here for the giants' use.

The descending stretch of the Inner Passage into this cavern is fitted with traps and guarded by a portcullis (hardness 10, hp 60, Break DC 30), to keep intruders out and enslaved ettins in.

The **first trap** (from the viewpoint of someone entering the chamber, moving east to west) is located just where the Inner Passage completes its turn and starts to descend. An obvious button for deactivating the trap can be seen in the ceiling (DC 20 Perception). A fire giant can easily reach it, but anyone else must climb the wall and somehow cross 30 feet of ceiling to reach it. If someone moves through this area without pressing the button, a row of iron stakes springs out from the walls and the ceiling 10 feet farther on. The stakes imperil a 30-foot-long stretch of passage and the trigger is in the final 10 feet, so many characters might be in the area when the trap goes off if they are sticking close together. The spikes spring out from the seams in the walls and ceiling to their full length. The ceiling spikes drop 65 feet, so someone less than 5 feet tall in the danger area is safe from them. The wall spikes thrust out far enough so that they leave only a 1-foot-wide safe lane between their points. Pushing the button sets off audible whirring and ticking sounds (cogs spinning behind the stone). The sound continues for five minutes, during which time the trap is safe, then it resets with a loud click.

IMPALING SPIKES TRAP **CR 15**
XP 51,200
Type mechanical; **Perception** DC 20; **Disable Device** DC 35

Trigger location; **Reset** automatic
Effect Atk +15 melee (16d6 piercing and slashing damage); multiple targets (all targets in a 30-ft.-long passage)

The **second trap** is a 60-foot-deep pit that fills the corridor from side to side, covered with a hinged lid that blends seamlessly with the real floor. Pushing a specific spot on the wall locks the lid closed for five minutes. The spot is discolored by grease and soot from the fire giants' hands, so it can be noticed with a successful DC 20 Perception check. When a body strikes the floor of the pit, a puff of poison gas is released from the floor.

PIT FALL, POISONED **CR 14**
XP 38,400
Type mechanical; **Perception** DC 20; **Disable Device** DC 30

Trigger location; **Reset** manual
Effect 60-ft.-deep pit (6d6 falling damage; DC 20 Reflex avoids); impact releases poison gas (Nightmare Vapor*); multiple targets (all targets in a 10-ft.-square area)
*see *Pathfinder Roleplaying Game Ultimate Equipment*

The third trap is similar to the trap in **Area 8**. It consists of a pressure plate and ceiling sections concealing spike-studded stone blocks on chains. The stones plummet down, imperiling a 20-foot stretch of passage across its entire width. This trap is better hidden; it can be spotted with a successful DC 30 Perception check. The rattling chains give plenty of warning that a trap has been triggered, and the long drop of the stone accounts for the relatively easy avoidance saving throw. If, however, characters are burdened in a way that prevents them from quickly exiting the 20-foot-long danger space — if they're carrying heavy sacks of dragon loot or the body of a fallen comrade, or if they're trying to move up the slope rather than down — they have tactical disadvantage of a –4 on this save.

FALLING BLOCK TRAP **CR 12**
XP 19,200
Type mechanical/magical; **Perception** DC 30; **Disable Device** DC 25

Trigger touch; **Reset** repair
Effect falling block (8d6 bludgeoning damage, DC 25 Reflex save for half damage); multiple targets (all targets in a 20-foot-square area)

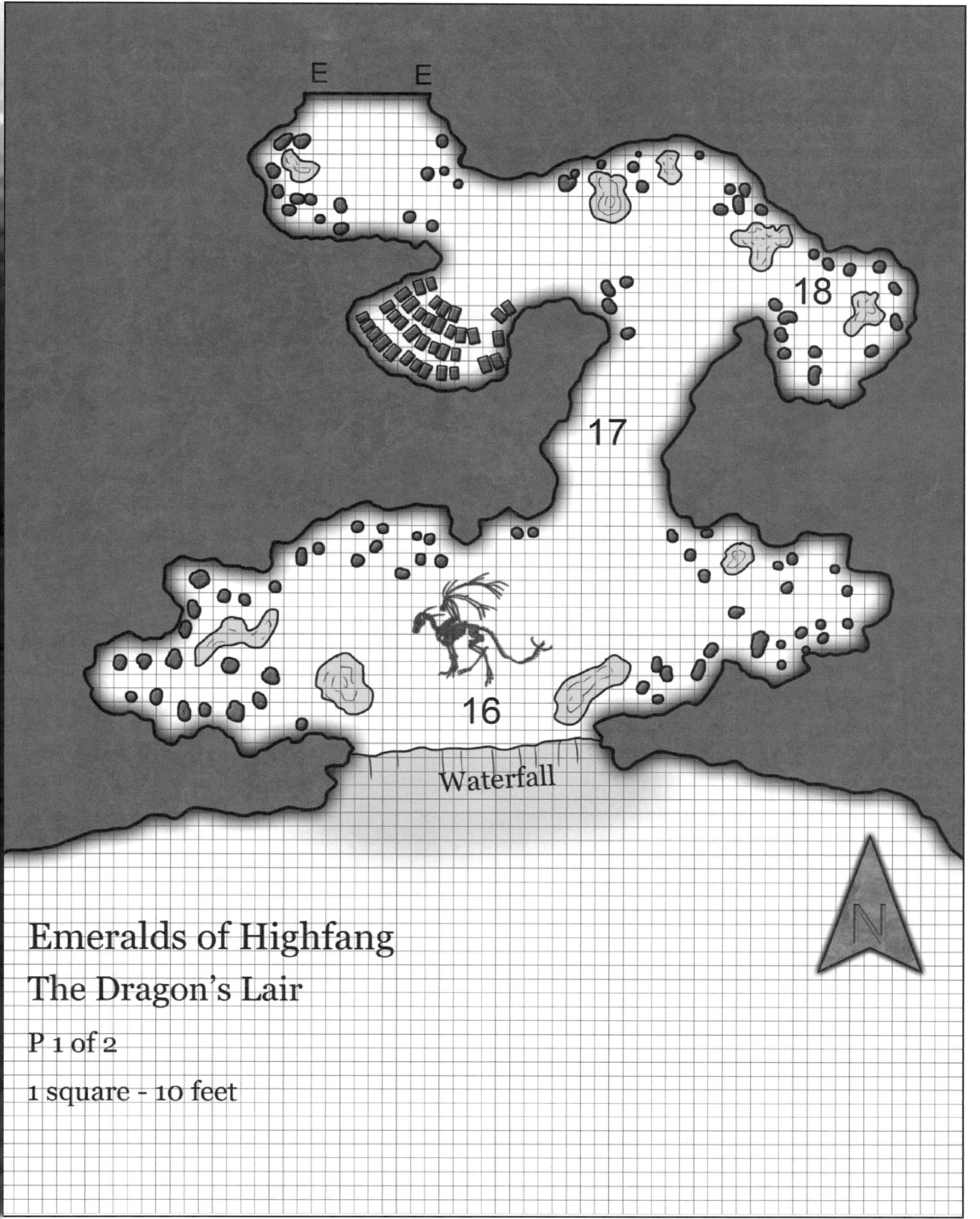
E
E
18
17
16
Waterfall
N
Emeralds of Highfang
The Dragon's Lair
P 1 of 2
1 square - 10 feet

Finally, a portcullis (hardness 10, hp 60, Break DC 30) can close off the passage at the bottom of the slope where it opens into the cavern. It is made of massive welded iron bars in a lattice with 1-foot-square openings. Heavy gouge marks can be seen readily on the floor where the portcullis slams when it drops, and the portcullis itself is not camouflaged against the ceiling. On both side walls, just east of where the portcullis drops, are two identical, unmarked buttons, one above the other (two on the north wall and two on the south wall). The upper button on both walls causes the portcullis to winch itself back up into the ceiling (noisily, by clockwork). The lower button on the south wall causes the portcullis to crash down immediately, whereas the lower button on the north-hand wall causes the portcullis to stay up for 15 minutes before dropping (a ticking sound is heard if characters are quiet). It can still be dropped instantly by pushing the button on the south wall. Jamming a normal weapon or tool into the wall below the portcullis won't accomplish anything other than destroying the tool if the portcullis drops; it is far too heavy to be held up by anything smaller than giant-sized implements, and large ones at that.

The Dragon's Lair

The red dragon Haeraglondrar (which is an "it" to the giants, not a he or she) is an adult red dragon, a "she" masquerading as a "he" in all dealings with non-dragons. Although Haeraglondrar is every bit as arrogant and vain as others of her kind, her worldview is that accepting her superiority as a given means that she shouldn't waste her time preening and doing nothing, nor in assailing lesser creatures (including other red dragons) to take what they have amassed, when she could be fulfilling her innate superiority by creating wealth for her hoard and at the same time steadily increasing her influence and dominance among non-dragons by trading with them.

So she treats with the most sly, enterprising and energetic human merchants to sell emeralds (in tiny amounts, to discerning buyers, firmly controlling supply and therefore maintaining high prices) and stone building columns. She pounces on, slays and plunders the wealth of merchants who try to swindle or deceive her, of course.

Haeraglondrar won't hesitate to use violence when it seems the best tactic, but prefers to know what talents and expertise she's destroying, rather than slaying first and discovering what she's lost and wasted afterward.

She has a healthy respect for adventurers, and she happily avoids direct battle with them when she can use the properties of her lair and the strengths of her underlings to reduce or even shatter such potentially dangerous foes.

At the center of Highfang Peak is the caldera or bowl-shaped heart of the slumbering volcano, where the giants keep a herd of cattle as food for themselves and for the dragon.

Area 16. Dead Dragon Cave (CR 13)

This large natural cavern is a forest of stalactites and stalagmites, many of which have joined into stone columns that stretch unbroken from the irregular stone floor to the jagged stone ceiling.

The mouth of the cave is the lowest end of the cavern. Water that percolates through the stone and drips down the many stone "teeth" here drains out through the cave opening into the central caldera of Highfang Peak in a trickle that keeps the rock face perpetually wet and slick. The entrance is a huge, irregular opening large enough for Haeraglondrar to fly through with wings fully spread. Such openness means the front cavern is difficult to defend, so it's never a preferred spot for Haeraglondrar to rest or bide her time, particularly in cold or wet weather.

Intruders wanting to enter the dragon's lair from the caldera, or vice versa, need to climb about 80 feet of rock face. Despite the trickling water, it's an easy DC 15 Climb check, thanks to plenty of ledges, handholds and crevices — unless, of course, an angry dragon on the wing catches an intruder in mid-ascent.

The most striking feature in this area fills the smooth floor at the center of the cavern: the charred skeleton of a white dragon. Haeraglondrar defeated and slew this wrym long ago to claim this lair. She left the carcass here as a trophy and to lull intruders into wondering whether the dragon that lived here has already perished. The skeleton is burned and strategically crushed to make it almost impossible to confirm what type of dragon it was; a successful DC 25 Knowledge (arcana) check is needed to identify the bones as having been a white dragon rather than some other kind.

The skeleton lies twisted amid a deep drift of black ash. Visible in the depths (DC 25 Perception check) of these ashes is a ruby-red glow. Upon closer examination it can be seen to be a faceted, clear gemstone as large as a human's head, and the glow is coming from within it! This gemstone is an illusion, and it is part of a *glyph of warding* **trap** triggered by touching, poking, lassoing or otherwise moving the gem through mundane or magical means.

GLYPH OF WARDING (BLAST) CR 13
XP 25,600
Type magic; **Perception** DC 31; **Disable Device** DC 31

Trigger proximity; **Reset** none
Effect spell effect (*glyph of warding, greater*, 10d8 fire damage, DC 20 Reflex save for half damage); multiple targets (all targets in a 20-ft.-radius burst)

A family of **4 mobats** roosts on high ledges near the cavern ceiling. They swoop to attack anything smaller than a giant that examines the dragon skeleton or that passes through the central area of the cavern floor. The bats are jet black with blazing red eyes, large fangs, long tails and wide black leathery wings that make them resemble manta rays, though they are simply a rare subspecies of bat. They shriek as they attack, their wide and many-fanged maws gaping wide. These cries are so high-pitched that they are like needles in the ears of those nearby, but are almost inaudible more than 70 feet away.

MOBAT BATS (4) CR 3
XP 800
hp 34 (*Pathfinder Roleplaying Game Bestiary 2* "Bat, Mobat")

The bats attack characters to slay and feed, but flee to high ledges or out into the caldera if injured to 6 hit points or less. The death or one bat retreating won't affect the others.

Warm, fouled water with a strong mineral aftertaste collects in several small, shallow pools scattered across the cavern. Intruders who drink this water vomit it in minutes as it is tainted (DC 15 Survival check to identify). The "air duct" tunnel from **Area 12** opens up in a corner of this cave, bringing a strong rush of air and the rumbling, screeching din of the mill with it.

The highest end of this cavern becomes a natural passage leading farther into Highfang. This "Wyrmcrawl" passage is roughly oval, being about 80 feet wide and about 100 feet high. Although it's a natural tunnel, it shows obvious claw gouges where the dragon enlarged it and smashed out stalagmites and stalactites over the years.

Area 17. Wyrmcrawl

Whenever Haeraglondrar thinks intruders may be in Highfang (thanks to a warning from the giants or from hearing the sounds of fighting or of intruders whispering through the air vent or speaking tube), the red dragon goes on the defensive at the north end of this tunnel. When intruders enter the passage, it retreats backward along the passage, watching the intruders and taking lair actions to trigger magma eruptions or tremors or spheres of poisonous volcanic gas in **Area 17**. It can't cause the same effect in successive rounds. Its preferred defensive routine is to use tremors and gas clouds to immobilize or slow intruders, hit them with magma eruptions, then repeat the process, wearing them down as they advance.

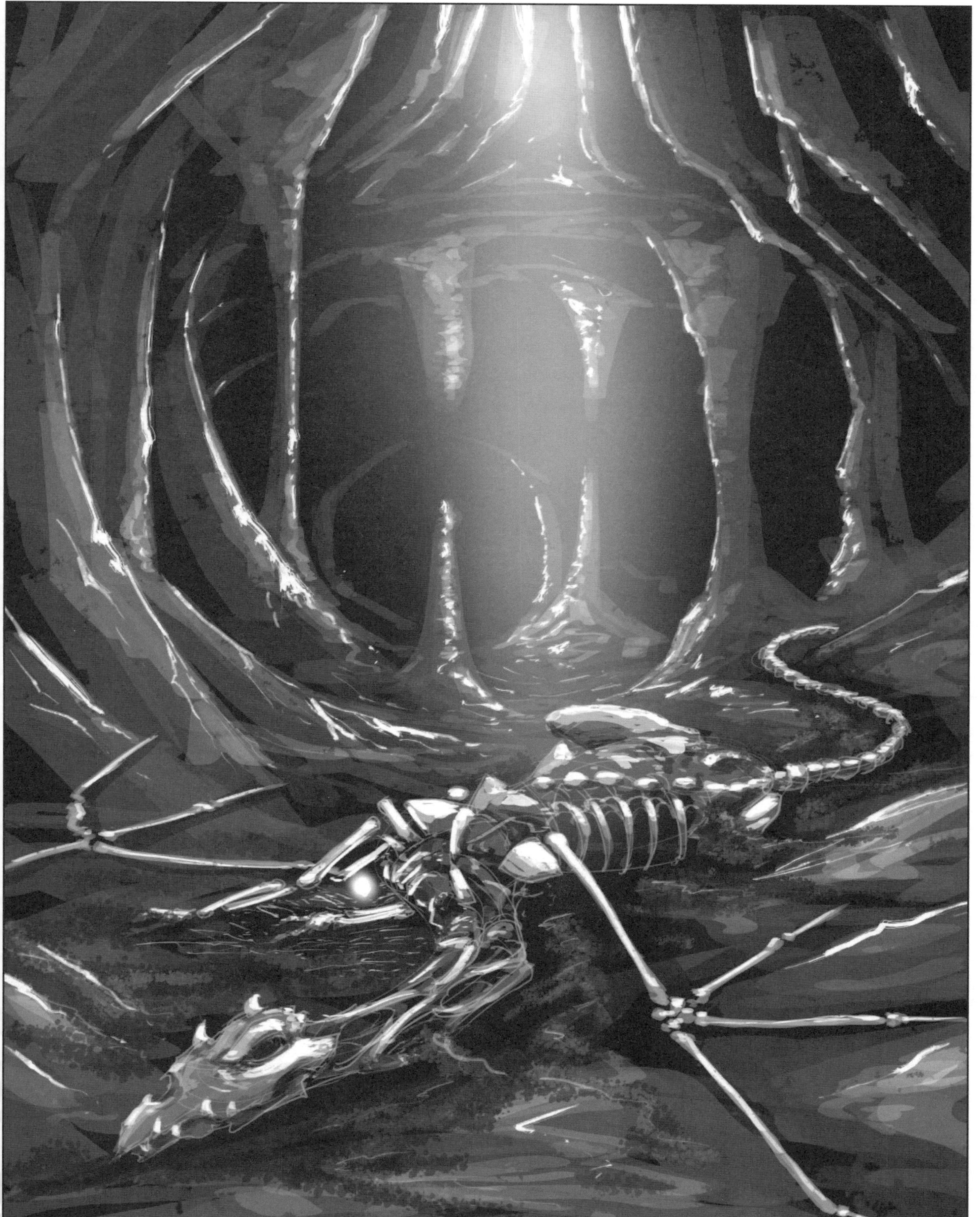

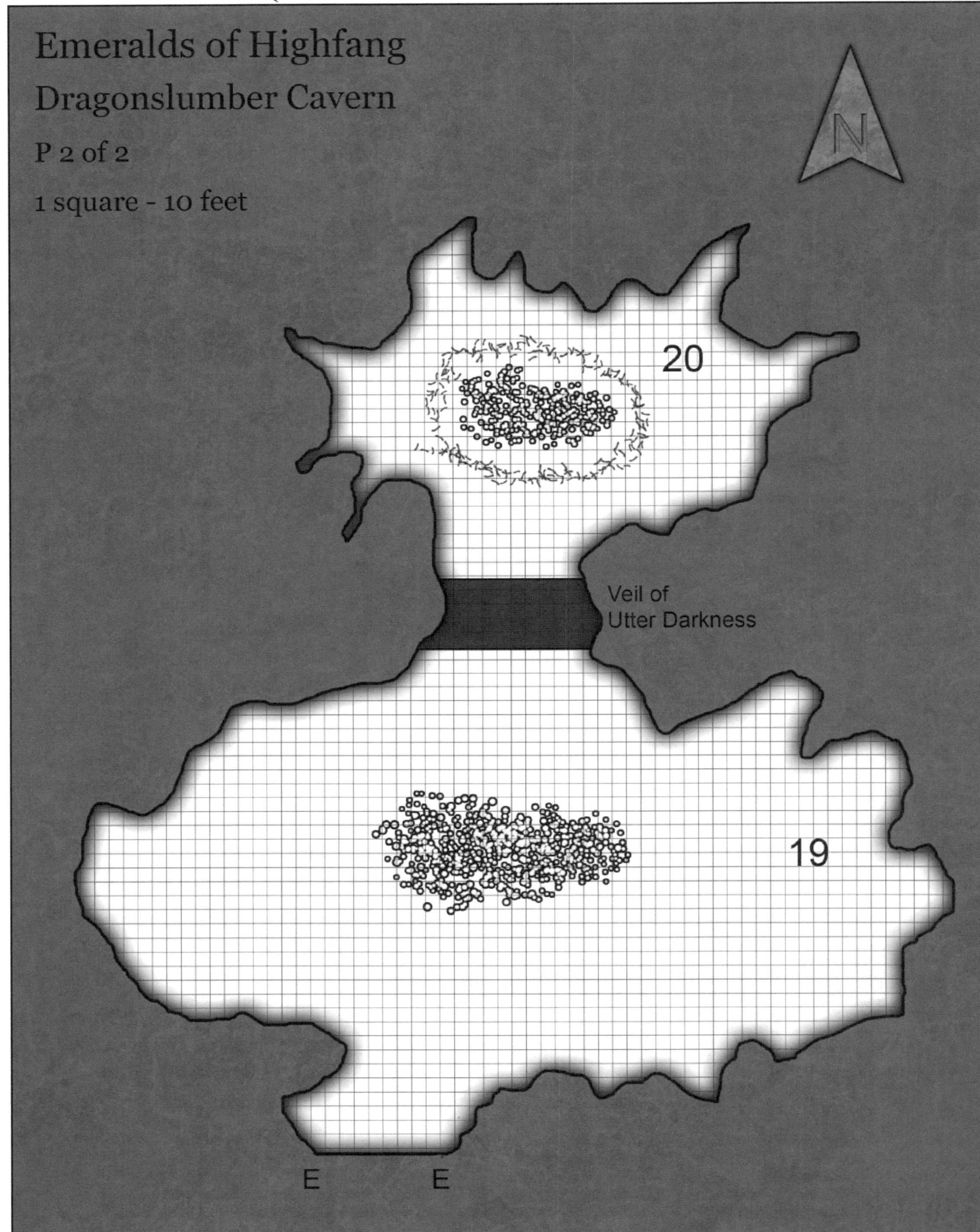
Emeralds of Highfang
Dragonslumber Cavern
P 2 of 2
1 square - 10 feet
N
20
Veil of
Utter Darkness
19
E
E

Area 18. The Spending Hoard (CR 17)

This cavern, minus the dragon skeleton and the resident bats, is similar in appearance and properties to the Dead Dragon Cave (**Area 16**), right down to the shallow pools of water. Haeraglondrar retreats slowly through this cavern, using the plentiful stone columns and stalagmites for cover, and continues wearing intruders down with lair actions. Advancing characters can't help but notice a large alcove that opens to the left, where 30 sealed chests are clustered. These are large, hooped, brassbound, locked chests in the classic "pirate" style, all with end-handles and large enough that it would take two strong people to carry them.

These are one big trap. The chests are all locked and bolted (from the inside) to the floor. The locks are intricate and sturdy; one can be opened with a set of lock picks and a successful DC 30 Disable Device check or with a successful DC 25 Str check (allow tactical advantage if characters use a prybar). Only one attempt can be made per chest, but there are **30 trapped chests** to work on. A character who inspects just one chest needs a successful DC 30 Perception check to notice the trap, but if characters inspect several chests beforehand, it drops to DC 15.

Raising the lid of just one chest releases the lids on all of them, allowing the starving stirges inside (**8 stirges** per chest, or **240 stirges** in all!) to fly out. Slamming a lid back down has no effect on any other lids. There is no treasure here. Aside from the stirges, the chests are empty.

STIRGES (240) **CR 1/2**
XP 200
hp 5 (*Pathfinder Roleplaying Game Bestiary* "Stirge")

At the far end of the cavern from the Wyrmcrawl, this cavern opens directly into another vast cave: the Dragonslumber Cavern. The natural archway between the two caverns has a floor of crushed and strewn stone rubble, and a ceiling of jagged stalactites.

It, too, is a **trap**, which Haeraglondrar can trigger at will to cause the stalactites to plunge to the floor. She triggers this trap when the characters she judges most formidable are passing through the archway. If the dragon thinks the intruding characters are powerful and largely unscathed, she uses her fiery breath on them at the same time. The trap can be noticed with a successful DC 25 Perception check under normal circumstances; if the check is made in the midst of a battle against the dragon, characters have –4 to Perception tactical disadvantage on it.

STALACTITE TRAP **CR 15**
XP 51,200
Type mechanical; **Perception** DC 25; **Disable Device** DC 20

Trigger location; **Reset** manual
Effect Atk +15 melee (16d6); multiple targets (all targets in a 10-ft. square)

Area 19. Dragonslumber Cavern (CR 19)

This large, irregular natural cavern is cleared of stalagmites and stalactites. Even their broken-off stumps have been worn down and smoothed over the years. The **ancient red dragon Haeraglondrar** customarily slumbers here on a heap of gold and silver coins (39,667 gp in all).

HAERAGLONDRAR, ANCIENT RED DRAGON **CR 19**
XP 204,800
hp 362 (*Pathfinder Roleplaying Game Bestiary* "Chromatic Dragon, Red")

The cavern floor has been graved with claw marks to divide it into more-or-less regular 10-foot squares. Some of these lines bisect the roots of shorn stalagmites. By counting lines, any intruder can see at a glance that this cavern is *big* — large enough for the dragon to move with ease, slap with its tail, spread its wings, and so on. Another huge, dark opening at the rear of the cavern suggests that there's another cave beyond this one.

The dragon naps lightly, awakening in an instant if voices come up the speaking tube from **Area 13** that opens in one corner of this cavern.

Atop her heap of coins, one of the dragon's hindclaws dangles down an open "well" amid the coins, where it rests on a final trap control. By means of it, Haeraglondrar can open any 10-foot square on the surrounding floor in a 20-foot-wide oval ring all around the heap of coins, plus a 30-foot-wide swath of floor leading from that ring to the mouth of the passage from **Area 18**. Every one of these 10-foot sections covers a pit trap.

PIT TRAPS **CR 12**
XP 19,200
Type mechanical; **Perception** DC 25; **Disable Device** DC 20

Trigger location; **Reset** manual
Effect 50-ft.-deep pit (5d6 falling damage); pit spikes (Atk +15 melee, 1d4 spikes per target for 1d6+5 damage each plus poison [Shadow Essence*]); DC 25 Reflex avoids; multiple targets (all targets in a 10-ft.-square area)
*see *Pathfinder Roleplaying Game Ultimate Equipment*

Development: Haeraglondrar loves her treasure but not to the point that she will die for it. If she judges the characters too formidable after she's worn them down on the way here, tried to catch them in these pit traps, and breathed fire on them a few times, she'll shift her effort to flying away. The intruders need time to pack up all this treasure, after all, and she might be able to get it back soon by arranging a second battle more to her liking. Perched on a promontory on Highfang, she can swoop down on the characters at her leisure while they are climbing down the cliff at the entrance or rafting away on the river. Anyone who plunders her hoard must die, but she is patient. She is vain and greedy, but not stupid or suicidal.

Area 20. Hoard Cavern (CR 12)

This small, innermost cavern is veiled by a curtain of *darkness*: a magical field of chill air that drinks all light, permitting no radiance to pass through and no light to function within it. The curtain also confines **2 mobats** inside its area of effect. They are ravenous, and swoop at and viciously attack any creature other than the dragon that enters the 50-foot-thick *curtain*.

MOBAT BATS (2) **CR 3**
XP 800
hp 34 (*Pathfinder Roleplaying Game Bestiary 2* "Bat, Mobat")

The veil also magically foils all *teleport*, *dimension door* and similar translocation magic through it and into or out of **Area 20**.

Treasure: Beyond the veil lies the dragon's real hoard: a huge heap of coins and gems, 450 rubies (each worth 2,000 gp); 144,000 gp; 210,000 sp; and 1,600 cp that the dragon didn't bother to throw away while sorting out more valuable coins.

Around the entire heap is an ominous fence: a continuous ring of human bones, all jumbled together and including scraps of rusty armor, weapons and adventuring gear (but no magic items).

Two items float above the heap: a ragged, dirty, moth-eaten *purple cloak* floats upright, obviously empty, and a smooth, ovoid stone nearly as large as a person's palm that gives off a soft, beige glow. The gem appears to be lighting the entire cavern with dim light: an illumination radius of more than 250 feet!

Neither of these floating items responds to the presence of intruders.

The stone is simply an ordinary, polished stone on which has been cast a modified *continual flame* spell. With the proper housing, it could be useful as a lantern or a signaling device. Its light can't be dimmed or quenched by magical means (outside a *wish* spell), but it can be shrouded by metal, wood or heavy cloth. It illuminates a radius of 300 feet with dim light, and it can be seen as a soft, beige speck in the darkness for many miles.

The cloak looks like cloth, but anyone who touches it immediately understands that it is actually a suit of armor. It is +2 *glamered leather armor of the shadows*, highly useful to rogues or anyone else with stealthy intentions as it gives the added benefit of *shadow* ability granting a +5 competence bonus to Stealth checks.

This precious hoard is not unguarded: The ring of bones animates if disturbed or crossed over, rising in a whirling cloud of bones that quickly resolves into skeletons wearing the scraps of armor and wielding the rusty weapons intermingled with the bones. These skeletons are *not undead*, so they can't be turned or destroyed by clerics. Rather, they are animated objects. Treat them in every way as **18 animated armors**, except for how you describe them to players.

ANIMATED ARMORS (18) CR 3
XP 800
N Medium construct (*Pathfinder Roleplaying Game Bestiary* "Animated Object")
Init +0; **Senses** darkvision 60 ft., low-light vision; **Perception** –5

AC 14, touch 10, flat-footed 14 (+4 natural)
hp 36 (3d10+20)
Fort +1; **Ref** +1; **Will** -4
Defensive Abilities hardness 5; **Immune** construct traits

Speed 30 ft.
Melee 2 slams +5 (1d6+3)

Str 14, **Dex** 10, **Con** —, **Int** —, **Wis** 1, **Cha** 1
Base Atk +3; **CMB** +5; **CMD** 15
SQ 2 construction points (additional attack, grab)

A Last Gasp

If characters begin shifting or digging into the heap of coins and gems, something large suddenly stirs from beneath the pile, rising ominously and shedding coins and gems in all directions: another dragon!

Or rather, the skeleton of a dragon. It rears up, opens its jaws, spreads its wings, reaches with its claws for the characters — and then collapses into its component bones, puffing dust from every joint as it tumbles into ruin. This was a half-finished project of Haeraglondrar's, another animated object intended to someday be a last-ditch guardian of the hoard, not an undead dragon, but she never got around to perfecting it.

Lycanthropes & Elementals

Bad Moon Rising

By Steve Winter

This adventure is for characters of levels 6 to 8. The default setting is the Barony of Loup-Montagne, but any remote, heavily wooded principality with highly superstitious residents will do.

Barony of Loup-Montagne

The Barony of Loup-Montagne is a remote region of densely forested hills cut by steep-banked streams, rocky outcrops, and darkly shadowed dales. In the **Lost Lands** campaign setting of **Frog God Games**, the barony lies in the western portion of the Duchy of Mains, a semi-independent vassal of the Crown of Foere. Any similar area in your campaign world can fill in, with or without the French-sounding names used here.

Roulune

The center of Loup-Montagne is the town of Roulune. It is home to about 500 residents in roughly 80 households. Roulune is hardly a metropolis, but it is the biggest town for miles around, thanks largely to the remoteness of the region. Only a few roads of any consequence pass through the town. The main route is a trade road through the tangled, wooded hills that dominate this region. Baron Chaput exacts a toll on traders who use the road, in exchange for keeping it safe from bandits and monsters. The toll is not excessive, and most traders pay it willingly because the road is considered safe, by and large. Incidents of robbery and violence along the highway are rare within the barony.

What's Going On

As is normal in a gothic horror tale, the true situation in Roulune is different from what it seems. Figuring out the real story and the real connections between people is key to the player characters' success in this adventure. For the GM's convenience, this section lays out the straight facts.

NPCs in Loup-Montagne

Grandfather Nicodeme

This evil old man is the ultimate source of all the trouble.

What's Told: Baron Nicodeme ruled the barony for more than 40 years, and they were good years. The baron had a reputation for being strong-willed and pitiless, but not unnecessarily cruel. He was harsh toward those who broke his laws, but his laws were clear and generally considered fair. A year ago, while hunting, wolves attacked Nicodeme. The baron's lieutenant (Paschal Moreau) fought his way through the wolves. According to Moreau's account, the baron ordered him to ride out on the only surviving horse and bring help. By the time help arrived, Nicodeme and two other men-at-arms were already dead. With his legs torn apart so he couldn't walk, the baron had put his back to a tree and fought heroically to the end. Only two bodies were recovered. A blood trail indicated that one of the men-at-arms was dragged away by the wolves. His body was never found.

What's True: The baron and his three companions were attacked while hunting. The attackers were wolves led by a werewolf. The hunters fought off the attack, but both men-at-arms were killed and the baron was badly wounded by the werewolf. Knowing what would happen to him, the baron and Moreau switched the baron's clothing and belongings for those of one of the dead men mangled beyond recognition. As Paschal rode away with news of the baron's "death," the bleeding baron dragged himself into the woods. With his wounds healing rapidly, his blood trail soon petered out. He headed for the ruins of St. Ulrich Abbey, where Moreau was to meet him later. Nicodeme has been living in the vicinity of the abbey ever since, growing more evil and bloodthirsty with each passing month. Moreau visits him occasionally when he thinks he can do so without being discovered. Although he is an afflicted werewolf, some strange confluence of fates has enabled him to pass on the curse of lycanthropy as if he were a natural werewolf.

Nicodeme raised Ghislain after Renard's death, but he never liked his grandson. He thinks Ghislain's rule will bring ruin to the barony and stain the family name. He has decided to murder Ghislain since that will clear the way for Jules Brisbois to claim the mantle.

Renard Chaput

As the only son of Baron Nicodeme, Renard should have succeeded his father to be the baron now — if he'd lived long enough

What's Told: Renard was handsome, dashing, and lively. He would have made a good baron, if he'd outlived his father, but he died 12 years ago in a tragic incident. Renard, his wife, Seraphine, and their son, Ghislain, were riding in the forest when wolves attacked them. Only seven-year-old Ghislain survived; he was found unconscious beneath the bloody bodies of his parents.

What's True: The common story is true, but it's only part of the story. Renard was a philanderer with one illegitimate son (Jules Brisbois) whose existence was publicly acknowledged, and probably others he didn't acknowledge. The existence of a bastard son is a problem because of the legend concerning the Barony of Loup-Montagne (see "The Legend" below). Renard was popular among the young men of the barony because he enjoyed popping into taverns, buying drinks for everyone, and turning the evening into a raucous party. But he was strongly resented by the many married men he cuckolded.

Wolves really killed Renard and Seraphine, but if characters dig into this story, they hear persistent rumors that the wolf attack was a cover-up, and that Renard was assassinated by a conspiracy of jealous husbands fed up with his behavior; it was simply bad luck for Seraphine that she was riding along at the wrong time.

Ghislain Chaput

Ghislain is the current Baron Chaput.

What's Told: Ghislain is liked well enough by the citizenry, but he's very young (19 years old) and has been baron for only a year. It's common knowledge that the former baron (Ghislain's grandfather) didn't like Ghislain and was trying to arrange for Jules Brisboi to become his heir, but Nicodeme died before such an arrangement could be formalized. Hence, tradition had to be followed and Ghislain was anointed the new baron.

Most citizens of Loup-Montagne like Ghislain well enough, but they also know the legend — that tragedy will follow if the barony doesn't pass to the eldest surviving son. A heated debate erupts anytime this topic comes up in a tavern or public place. One side argues that Ghislain is the legitimate heir, so everything is fine. The other side argues that Jules Brisboi is Renard's eldest son, legitimate or not, so trouble will follow if he doesn't carry the title. This camp is already blaming the recent surge in wolf attacks on flouting the legend.

Ghislain's right leg was severely mangled in the attack that killed his parents. No magical healers were on hand, and Nicodeme refused to allow doctors to amputate it, but the boy surprised everyone by surviving the wound. He needs a crutch to walk, and walking or riding a horse are extremely painful. He is carried in a chair most of the time, walking or riding only when he goes out in public.

What's True: Ghislain is a decent young man who takes his position seriously. He trusts his half-brother Jules and places no credence in the legend. Even if he did, Ghislain's attitude is that he is Renard's eldest legitimate son, so whatever power the legend has (which he believes is none), it should be satisfied. Ghislain is greatly troubled by the wolf attacks, but he believes they are the work of hungry wolves and nothing more.

Ghislain vehemently denies the rumor that angry husbands murdered his father if asked about the incident. He was only seven, but he clearly remembers being attacked by wolves, and he angrily strips off his stocking to show his withered, mangled right leg. Anyone with training in Nature can confirm that they are the bites of large canines. Anyone with training in Medicine is amazed that a child survived such a wound without magical healing.

Jules Brisbois

Baron Ghislain's half-brother is an important officer in the barony. His position is informal, but he acts as an advisor and confidante to Ghislain and as a lieutenant to Moreau.

What's Told: Brisbois is something of an enigma in Roulune. He is boisterous and lusty like his father, and he's well-liked by the young men of the town for the same reasons Renard was liked. If characters press for more information than that, they are mostly met with stony silence; the people of Roulune are obviously reluctant to talk about Brisbois in too much detail, other than to say things like, "Well, you know how men like him can be." Residents are more willing to talk about Brisbois' role in the legend than about any dark aspect of his personality. About a third of the town would prefer Brisbois as baron over Ghislain. If the wolf attacks grow worse, that percentage is bound to grow.

What's True: The "secret" that townsfolk are reluctant to discuss is that Brisbois has a vicious temper, and when it gets out of control, he becomes dangerous. He has come close to killing people with his bare hands while in a fury, including a few of his friends. Because of his position in the barony, people who get hurt in his rampages are paid off in gold and the incidents aren't spoken of. The innkeeper at the Wolf's Pelt Tavern is one of the few locals willing to open up to characters about this, but only if he can't be overhead by other locals.

Brisbois's temper is a red herring, meant to mislead characters into suspecting that he is the werewolf. If characters raise that possibility around any townsfolk, even in jest, at least a few are bound to nod their heads in dark agreement.

Brisbois's real offense against the barony is that he's fallen in league with a group of poachers and occasional highwaymen. In exchange for a cut of the profit, he provides them with information about where the baron's foresters plan to patrol for poachers each week and when particularly rich or vulnerable merchants are traveling through the barony. These bandits can be encountered at Travers Castle, and if handled properly, they might implicate Brisbois in their crimes.

Paschal Moreau

Moreau was the former Baron's right-hand man. Ghislain considers him a trusted family deputy and employs Moreau as head of the militia and as an advisor.

What's Told: Moreau is "the last of the old breed," a gentleman warrior who can be relied on to always do the right thing. A few people whisper accusations of cowardice over him leaving Baron Nicodeme when the wolves attacked, but most accept Moreau's account of what happened at face value. A man like him never would have left the baron willingly under those circumstances unless the baron ordered it directly, and leaving the baron to ride for help must have been the hardest thing Moreau ever did.

What's True: Moreau is every bit the rock of determination and strength that people believe him to be, but his account of what happened to the baron is false. He is the only person in Loup-Montagne (who is not also a werewolf) to know that Nicodeme, in werewolf form, is behind the recent killings. Moreau is genuinely conflicted about the secret he's hiding, but his unswerving loyalty to Nicodeme blinds him to the great evil the old baron is committing.

Absalon Dufort

Dufort serves as the barony's treasurer. He also manages the baron's household and runs the manor as superintendent and castellan. He is in his 60s, with wild hair, a wispy beard, and a slight but noticeable twist to the left caused by an injury to his spine when he was a young soldier. Everyone simply calls him Dufort. He is the only person besides Moreau to have a key to the treasury, where Moreau stores all the town's silver collected through taxes.

The treasurer has an incredible head for numbers, but his thinking about most other topics is muddled and confusing at best. Dufort has noticed the preponderance of silver in the treasury and has been meaning to ask Moreau about it for months, but he's a busy man with many things on his mind, and Moreau is never around when Dufort is thinking about it.

The Legend

A legend has circulated through the Barony of Loup-Montagne for hundreds of years concerning the order of inheritance for the title of baron. The legend holds that if the title is passed to someone who is not the eldest heir, the spirits of the forest will lash out against the people of the barony. Citizens of Roulune can cite any number of historical incidents to "prove" this claim. All of them happened before any living person in Roulune was born, and most are highly dubious if not completely spurious.

The few citizens who aren't overwhelmingly superstitious see this legend as nothing more than a story meant to ensure that every baron sets up a clean transfer of power upon his death — an outcome greatly desired in a world where any doubt about the line of accession can lead to bloody murders between brothers, sisters, aunts, uncles, and grandchildren.

In this regard, Renard Chaput's philandering created a problem. Jules Brisboi is older than Ghislain, and Renard acknowledged Jules as his son. The custom of the barony is that a legitimate son has primacy over an illegitimate one, but this is only a custom, not an explicit law, and illegitimate offspring have ruled on other occasions.

Because the exact form of retribution the forest spirits will seek isn't specified, any unfortunate incident that happens in or near the woods can be blamed on the legend. Likewise, people who oppose or dislike a particular baron can point to any unusual death or injury and claim it as proof that a different person should hold the title. If fate doesn't cooperate by providing mysterious mishaps, it's easy enough for clever schemers to arrange a few and blame them on the legend.

Current events have stirred up plenty of talk about the legend and motivated Jules Brisbois' circle of friends to mumble about replacing Ghislain with Jules. A minority of citizens supports this idea, but most believe that Ghislain is the proper heir. Only a small group blames Brisbois for causing the trouble, and they do so quietly and mostly in private out of fear for his temper.

Silver

Paschal Moreau knows that silver is one of the few things that can harm Nicodeme. To protect the werewolf, Moreau makes it his mission to keep silver out of the hands of the people of Loup-Montagne. This is done mostly through taxation. People who pay their taxes in silver rather than copper are given a small discount. Silver items such as jewelry and plate are accepted in lieu of coins at greater than their face value. Moreau

doesn't care about a few silver coins or lockets; he is concerned about larger items such as silver plates, pitchers, picture frames, mugs, and other articles that contain enough silver to turn into knives, spearheads, or swords.

Roulune is a poor town, and Moreau personally collects taxes door-to-door (with a militia backup). The process involves a fair amount of haggling under any circumstance, so the slow disappearance of silver has gone unnoticed by most people. The jeweler (a dwarf named Beaumont) is curious why less silver jewelry is crossing his table for repair than in years past, and innkeepers and shopkeepers who are paid in silver stare at the coins for a few moments before making offhand comments such as "Don't see many of these anymore" or "You *are* new around here." If a character questions the scarcity of silver in a public place, it sets off the usual round of arguing and superstitious theorizing common in Roulune.

The silver is stored under lock and key in the treasury at Chaput Manor. Only Moreau (as chief tax collector) and Dufort (as treasurer) have keys to that chamber.

Roulune

Roulune is a medium-size town filled with typical homes and shops for bakers, cobblers, bowyers, candlemakers, potters, ropemakers, blacksmiths, tailors, and all the other businesses a medieval town requires. Four locations stand out among the rest, being of special interest to traveling adventurers.

ROULUNE
N small town
Corruption +2; **Crime** –6; **Economy** –4; **Law** +1; **Lore** +2; **Society** –5
Qualities rumormongering citizens, superstitious
Danger +20
Disadvantage hunted*

Government overlord
Population 500
Notable NPCs
Ghislain Chaput, Baron (male human aristocrat 6)
Jules Brisbois, Advisor (male human aristocrat 2/bard 2)
Paschal Moreau, Captain of the Guard (male human fighter 7)
Absalon Dufort, Accountant (male human expert 7)

Base Value 800 gp; **Purchase Limit** 5,000 gp; **Spellcasting** 2nd
Minor Items 3d4; **Medium Items** 1d6; **Major Items** —

*If the werewolf threat to Roulune is ended, it loses the hunted disadvantage. Its Economy, Law, and Society modifiers each go up by +4, its danger decreases to 0, and its base value increase to 1,000 gp.

Wolf's Pelt Tavern

The Wolf's Pelt is the only tavern in Roulune with rooms for rent to travelers. It's also the biggest and most welcoming to outsiders, and it's where the locals come when they want to hear news from the outside world.

The proprietor is a friendly young man named Hugues who does everything he can to make strangers feel welcome. His wife Lilou is almost twice his age and is seldom seen by customers. She is painfully shy, so she spends most of her time in the kitchen. If someone tries to talk to her, she becomes flustered and calls for Hugues.

Fewer travelers come through Roulune these days thanks to news of the wolf attacks, so the inn has plenty of room available if characters choose to stay here.

The Church of the Forest

This temple can serve whatever good-aligned deity is most appropriate in your campaign, or several at once. In the **Lost Lands**, the temple is dedicated to Cerunnos, the Green Father. The cleric of the temple is Frere Emilé. He can cast *cure moderate wounds* twice per day, but he expects strangers to make a donation to the church's coffers in return (at least half the cost of a *potion of cure moderate wounds* in your campaign). He keeps two scrolls of *lesser restoration* and one of *greater restoration* in a secret compartment beneath the altar in case of emergency. Again, he expects the church to be compensated if they must be used to benefit outsiders.

"Nicodeme's" body was brought to Frere Emilé after the attack. Everyone accepted it as the baron's based on the clothes and Moreau's testimony. But Emilé knew Nicodeme well, and in preparing the corpse for burial, he saw the body of a much younger man. That weighs on his mind, and he talks to the characters about it if they establish a level of trust with him.

Gervaise the Astrologer

Gervaise the Astrologer is the most-educated person in Roulune. The more she learns, the more she abandons the town's traditional superstitions. It's getting to the point where she even has doubts about astrology.

This dwarf is neither a spellcaster nor an alchemist. She doesn't sell magic items, potions, or magical services. What she has is an amazing store of knowledge on almost any subject the characters have questions about. You can use Gervaise as a reliable source of information, a skill bank, a rumor source, and as the characters' general sounding board in Roulune.

Gervaise can give accurate directions to any location in the barony, along with basic background information about it. Most importantly, she can direct the characters accurately to Travers Castle, St. Ulrich's Abbey, and the Witches' Den. Directions to the Witches' Den come with a warning that the site still has magical power. For further details, see "The Witches' Den" below.

Gervaise puts no stock in the legend about the eldest heir. She doesn't know what's behind the recent attacks, but based on the bodies she's seen and the reports she's heard, she's pretty sure a werewolf is involved. She hasn't shared that opinion with other townsfolk because, given how superstitious they are, talk of a werewolf would be sure to set off ridiculous behavior if not outright panic.

In light of that, Gervaise advises the characters to arm themselves with wolfsbane before venturing into the deep forest. The only spot she can be certain wolfsbane grows is Duval's Meadow. The best time to harvest it is under the light of a full moon (which is, of course, tonight and the following two nights). She offers characters two pieces of advice regarding wolfsbane. First, Gervaise cautions them that they should wear gloves when handling it and avoid inhaling the flowers' scent; too much exposure causes fatigue (characters who ignore this precaution must make a successful DC 10 Con saving throw at the end of an hour's exposure or gain one level of exhaustion). Second, wolfsbane is also prized by hags, so characters should be on the lookout for those vile creatures when they visit Duval's Meadow.

Wolfsbane: Wolfsbane smeared onto a piercing or slashing weapon gives the weapon a +1 damage bonus against lycanthropes. Even a weapon that lycanthropes have DR against cause 1 point of damage if coated with wolfsbane. Also, a lycanthrope must succeed on a DC 10 Wills ave before attacking someone who prominently displays a bunch of wolfsbane (wearing it as a garland, tucked into a belt, waving it in the hand, etc.). Once the werewolf makes a successful save, it can ignore the wolfsbane for the rest of that encounter.

Yannick's Candle Shop

Yannick is a very rare breed: a mix of halfling and elf. He looks like most other halflings at a glance, but anyone who spends more than a few moments conversing with him notices the delicate features, slender grace, and musical speech of a half-elf.

Yannick's shop is famous for its "infused candles." These are mildly magical items that produce minor magical effects when lit, similar to a cantrip. A few types that adventurers might find useful are listed below; feel free to expand this list with any other types you like, at comparable prices.

Candle Drifting Light
Length 30 mins
Price 10 gp

The person holding the candle can cause its light to drift away at a speed of 5 feet/turn, to a distance up to 60 feet from the candle. The drifting flame casts dim light in a 10-foot radius.

Candle Friends
Length 30 mins
Price 20 gp

Everyone within 15 feet of the lit candle has generally positive feelings toward the person who lit it; that person gets tactical advantage on Charisma-based skill checks that target humanoids in the candle's radius. These candles are very popular among storytellers and romantic young men.

Candle Light the Path
Length 30 mins
Price 5 gp

If the person holding the lit candle thinks about a place he or she has been to, and the flame flickers toward the direction of that place. These are popular among folk who must travel at night and are anxious about losing their way back home. Hugues keeps a box of them at the Wolf's Pelt tavern for revelers who overindulge.

Candle Mending
Length 30 secs
Price 15 gp

If the wax from this rapid-burning candle is dripped onto a broken object, the object repairs itself exactly as it would if a mending spell had been cast on it. One candle can repair one object.

Candle Message
Length 1 min
Price 30 gp

A message is whispered to the candle while it is lit, then the candle is extinguished. The next time the candle is lit, it repeats the message verbatim. The total burning time of the candle is one minute, so a message that's more than 30 seconds long is truncated on delivery. The candle works only once, regardless of how short the message is.

Candle Restfulness
Length 1 hr
Price 30 gp

If a character lights this candle and spends an hour basking in its light, he or she recovers from one level of exhaustion. Only the character who lit the candle gets the benefit, and the benefit can be gained only once in a 24-hour period.

Candle Witching Hour
Length 8 hrs
Price 10 gp

The flame of this candle turns blue for one minute precisely at sunset, midnight, and dawn. It is popular among witches, astrologers, and diviners. Yannick usually keeps these under the counter because they upset some of the most superstitious residents of Roulune.

Candle Wolfsbane
Length 1 hr
Price 40 gp

This candle fills a 30-foot radius with the scent of wolfsbane. The components harmful to people have been refined out; only those that irritate lycanthropes remain. All lycanthropes must withdraw from the candle's radius unless they make a successful DC 10 Fortitude save. This is an experimental item not yet available for sale. Yannick offers it only if characters mention werewolves, wolfsbane, or that they plan to go hunting wolves.

Superstition in Roulune

The people of Roulune are tremendously superstitious. They interpret every little occurrence as an omen of good or bad tidings based on centuries-old traditions that no outsider has much hope of understanding. Every conversation with villagers should be peppered liberally with superstitious declarations such as those below. If two or more villagers are involved, it's common for arguments to break out about the meaning and interpretation of omens.

- "The last fort-moon was blood red, and I saw the shadow of a rabbit on it clear as a bell. Bad times are coming for sure."
- "My Gran' tripped on the lintel three times last week. Now I'm afraid to keep a fire burning in the hearth for fear that the house will burn down."
- "I heard a raven call while I was milking the cow this morning. Had to dump the whole pail of milk. Can't have it poisoning the baby."
- "All the flowers on the ivy were facing north this morning. I'm keeping my doors and windows locked until after the harvest."
- "The worst time to be confronted by wolves is at midnight. You can tell when that is because the flame from a candle turns blue at the witching hour." (This bit of myth is true for the candles from Yannick's shop, and it may be useful to characters during the adventure.)
- "A hare chased a cat across my path last week. There's a witch prowling these woods, that's now a proven fact."
- "I heard hedgehogs whining at dusk. They were telling our secrets to witches. You can't trust anybody these days."
- "When I was hunting, I saw a wolf staring at me from the brush, and it was missing its left ear. There's always something like that wrong with a werewolf, you know. Always."
- "I stopped my brother-in-law from cutting down a thorn tree last week. He would've angered the faerie folk even more and brought bad luck on us all."
- "If you're concerned about ghosts or werewolves, bring a rooster with you, and be ready with a needle to make him crow. Ghosts and werewolves hate the crowing of roosters; it drives them away." (This belief derives from the fact that ghosts and werewolves tend to cease their activity at dawn, which is coincidentally when roosters start crowing. A rooster crowing in the middle of the night has no supernatural effect.)
- "Johann ate three eggs for breakfast last week, and his horse died, just like I warned him it would. Eating an odd number of eggs is just inviting death into your home."

Locations in the Barony of Loup-Montagne

The locations below play important roles in the adventure, and characters are likely to visit most of them in the course of resolving events in Loup-Montagne. Everyone knows where the baron's manor is, of course, at the edge of town. Likewise, everyone knows that Travers Road on the south of town leads to the ruin of Travers Castle, but no one goes there anymore. Residents of Roulune give conflicting accounts about the location of St. Ulrich Abbey — those who hunt or travel are more likely to get it right than those who farm or run shops in town. The Witches' Den is little more than a legend, and any group of three or more people won't be able to agree on whether it even exists.

Moreau and Gervaise know all three hidden locations, but only Gervaise gives correct directions to all three. Moreau's directions to the abbey and the Witches' Den lead characters to a random point along the river since he doesn't want them to find those spots. Dufort claims to know all three locations if asked, but characters realize that his muddled directions are impossible to follow even as he's giving them.

Baron's Manor

The baronial manor is a grand home, but that's "grand" on a medieval scale. It is not a palace or a mansion. It's a large, well-appointed, half-timber construction. Important rooms (entrance hall, great hall) and family sleeping rooms have wood paneling for warmth and appearance; other rooms have plaster walls and exposed timber beams. The stable and the barracks are similar, but much plainer. The whole compound is enclosed inside an 8-foot-high stone wall.

Unless they reach some arrangement with the Baron to inspect his home, characters have no good reason to wander unescorted through the manor. If they do so, or if a guest disappears for an unusual length of time, it rouses suspicion. Guests in an aristocrat's home are expected to behave appropriately.

Area 1. Main Entrance

The main entrance hall is a grand chamber designed to impress visitors. It's two stories tall, paneled in oak, and paved with flagstones. Portraits of former barons and their families line the walls, along with close to a hundred weapons: mainly polearms, but with a score of swords, maces, and morningstars mixed in. The most arresting of the portraits is one that shows a man in his thirties with piercing silver eyes and a halo of unruly, gray-streaked hair: Baron Nicodeme in his prime.

Area 2. Great Hall

Most of the entertaining and business of the barony is conducted in this chamber. Tables are put up when needed using smooth planks laid across trestles, and taken down and stored along the walls with their benches when not needed. The hall is empty most of the time. A low platform (one step up) lines one wall for the table of the baron and honored guests.

Area 3. Kitchen and Storage

During the day, two cooks and a half-dozen teenage helpers work in this chamber. At night, the helpers sleep here.

Area 4. Treasury

Most of the baron's wealth is stored here: coins, jewelry, and plate are the most common, with silver predominating because of Moreau's policy of collecting taxes in silver whenever possible. Only Moreau and Dufort have keys to the massive lock that seals the heavy door. The lock can be picked with a set of thieves' tools and a successful DC 20 Disable Device check. If the check fails, a *magic mouth* appears above the lock and shouts "Thieves at the treasury! Thieves at the treasury! Thieves at the treasury!" for 30 seconds, which is sure to bring Moreau, Brisbois, the baron, and an armed escort to investigate.

If someone succeeds in breaking into the treasury chamber, it contains a total value of 20,000 gp: 1,800 gp (36 lbs.), 80,000 sp (1,600 lbs.), and 10,200 gp worth of silver plate, silver candlesticks, silver picture frames, silverware, jewelry, and other items with a total weight of 1,000 lbs. (average of 1 lb. per 10 gp value, but with considerable variance; jewelry has much higher value at low weight, while silver hair brushes and mirrors are heavy for their value).

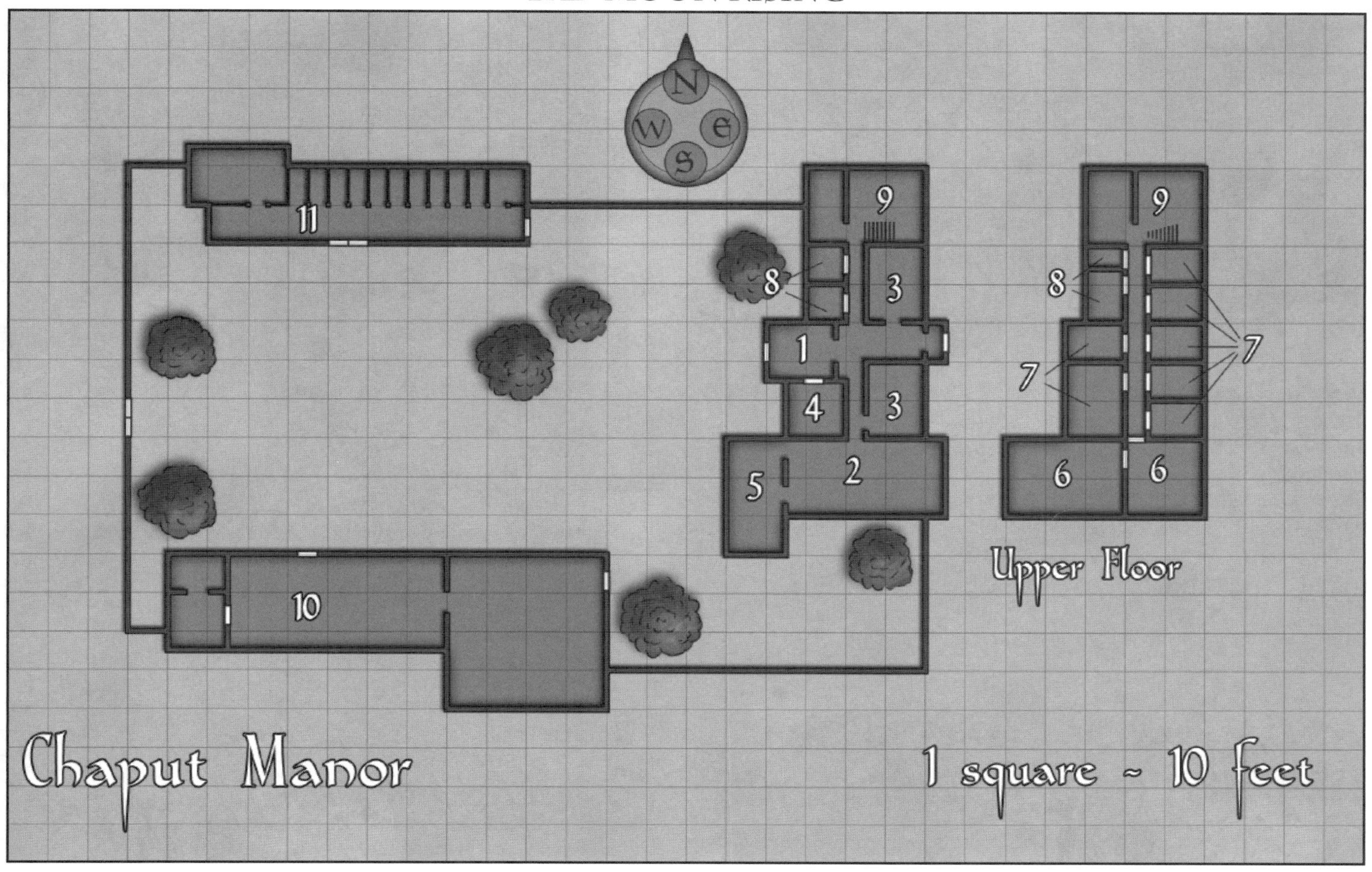

Area 5. Trophy Room

This resembles a room in a hunting lodge, with dozens of trophy heads of wild boar, elk, bears, and many wolves (including a few dire wolves and worgs) mounted on the walls. Rugs of bear and wolf pelts are scattered on the floor.

Area 6. Baron's Chambers

A comfortable sleeping chamber adjoins a writing chamber (the baron's office).

Area 7. Family and Guest Chambers

Baron Ghislain has no wife or children, so most of these chambers are empty. Only Jules Brisbois has a permanent room here, and he uses it only about half the time. If characters are invited to stay at the manor, they'll be assigned rooms in this area.

Area 8. Servant's Quarters

Dufort and the household staff (one butler, two maids, and two cooks) reside in these rooms.

Area 9. Day Rooms

These airy rooms are available for whatever purpose the family needs at the time. They've served as children's playrooms, sewing rooms, schoolrooms, workrooms, and many other functions. Since Ghislain is unmarried and has no family as yet, they're used chiefly as workrooms by the servants on the ground floor and as sitting rooms on the upper floor.

Area 10. Barracks (CR 11, if taken all at once)

Paschal Moreau and the **20 men and women** who make up the full-time core of the Loup-Montagne militia live in this structure. It is divided into several dormitory-like sleeping and living chambers, an armory, and a private room for Moreau.

Most areas of the barracks are neat and tidy, but one stands out for its almost animal-like squalor: beds are unmade and covered with reeking animal skins instead of blankets, and belongings and leftover food are strewn around the floor. Three men and one woman of the militia share this chamber. They are **4 werewolves** infected by Nicodeme and under his control. Moreau is aware of their state and tolerates it because of his loyalty to Nicodeme, but other members of the militia resent what they see as a handful of Moreau's favorites being given special privileges (they don't know the four are werewolves). They'll share their complaints with PCs if asked in private. They feel the situation is becoming intolerable, and they're beginning to question Moreau's leadership because of it. If characters search this room (not just examine it from the doorway) after Enzo's murder, they find a pair of bloodstained, embroidered gloves of the type Enzo was transporting.

PASCHAL MOREAU **CR 6**
XP 2,400
Human fighter 7
LN(E) Medium humanoid (human)
Init +5; **Perception** +7

AC 19, touch 12, flat-footed 17 (+7 armor, +1 Dex, +1 dodge)
hp 64 (7d10+14 plus 7)
Fort +7; **Ref** +3; **Will** +2; +2 vs. fear
Defensive Abilities bravery +2

Speed 30 ft.
Melee *+1 greatsword* +14/+9 (2d6+10/19–20)
Special Attacks weapon training (heavy blades +1)

Str 18, **Dex** 13, **Con** 14, **Int** 12, **Wis** 10, **Cha** 8

Base Atk +7; **CMB** +11; **CMD** 23
Feats Cleave, Combat Reflexes, Dodge, Great Cleave, Improved Initiative, Power Attack, Vital Strike, Weapon Focus (greatsword), Weapon Specialization (greatsword)
Skills Diplomacy +6, Handle Animal +9, Intimidate +9, Perception +7
Languages Common
SQ armor training 2
Gear *+1 chainmail, +1 greatsword*

GUARDS (16) CR 1
XP 400
hp 16 (*Pathfinder Roleplaying Game GameMastery Guide* "Caravan Guard")

WEREWOLF GUARDS (4) CR 2
XP 600
hp 19 (*Pathfinder Roleplaying Game Bestiary* "Lycanthrope, Werewolf")
Note These guards are afflicted werewolves, and have **DR** 5/ silver in their hybrid and animal forms.

Area 11. Stables

Twelve horses are stabled here, along with all their riding tack and a primitive coach that is seldom used. Four stablehands sleep in a cozy corner of the hay loft.

Area A. Travers Castle (CR 10 if taken all at once)

Many generations ago, the original barons of Loup-Montagne ruled the barony from Travers Castle. The castle was sited to control an important river crossing, and the barons grew rich on the tolls they charged to use the bridge. When the bridge was washed out in a flood, wagon traffic diverted to a ferry crossing upstream. By then, the baronial families had relocated to the more comfortable manor in Roulune anyway, and the decision was made not to rebuild the bridge.

The castle has been abandoned for almost a hundred years. No one has much reason to make the trek there, so the castle and the road to it are overgrown by the forest. The walls of the castle still stand, but the thatched roofs of the buildings have collapsed and the gates sag on their hinges.

The pile is not entirely forgotten, however; a group of poachers and sometime highwaymen use it as an occasional hideout. The gang consists of **bandit captain Thibault Voclain, 12 bandits, 3 scouts**, and **2 mastiffs**. They are present when characters come to investigate. They post guards, but because they aren't expecting visitors, their sentries aren't especially alert.

THIBAULT VOCLAIN, BANDIT CAPTAIN CR 6
XP 2,400
hp 53 (*Pathfinder Roleplaying Game GameMastery Guide* "Highwayman")

BANDITS (12) CR 1/2
XP 200
hp 11 (*Pathfinder Roleplaying Game GameMastery Guide* "Bandit")

SCOUTS (3) CR 3
XP 800
hp 30 (*Pathfinder Roleplaying Game GameMastery Guide* "Trapper")

MASTIFFS (2) CR 1
XP 400
hp 13 (*Pathfinder Roleplaying Game Bestiary* "Dog, Riding")

Area A1. Overgrown Clearing (CR 1)

Long ago, this was a cleared space around the castle. Now it's heavily overgrown with brush and trees, although it's obviously not old-growth forest like the rest of the surroundings. The poachers take few pains to conceal their presence, so their tracks toward the castle are plain to see. Someone can discern their numbers to be between 12 and 18 with a successful DC 15 Survival check.

There are always **2 bandits** on watch, both of them standing above the main gate and looking north. Characters sneaking through cover toward the castle go unseen if their Dex (Stealth) checks are better than the guards' passive Perception scores of 10.

BANDITS (2) CR 1/2
XP 200
hp 11 (*Pathfinder Roleplaying Game GameMastery Guide* "Bandit")

Area A2. Main Gate

The gate sags on its hinges and doesn't close all the way anymore. People at the gate can't be seen by the guards above because of the overhanging wall. A character trying to slip silently through the slightly ajar gate must make a successful DC 10 Stealth check. A failed check indicates that the character brushes against the gate and causes it to squeak. The first time this happens, the guards assume it is the wind and don't bother to investigate. The second time it happens, they become suspicious; from their perch atop the wall, one starts scanning the courtyard carefully and the other scans the area before the wall. If it happens a third time, they raise a cry of alarm.

Area A3. Courtyard (CR 6–7)

This area is mostly bare ground. Depending on the weather, it might be hard-packed dirt or churned mud. A disintegrating wagon with a broken wheel is tipped against one wall. Two tables and four benches have been thrown together by placing planks across barrels and stumps. A fire pit sits between the tables. During daytime, **2d4 bandits** and **1 scout** are in the courtyard, butchering a deer that they poached a few days before and are preparing for the evening meal, with the **2 mastiffs** lying nearby, waiting for scraps. At night, the courtyard is empty except for the deer carcass hanging from a post.

BANDITS (2d4) CR 1/2
XP 200
hp 11 (*Pathfinder Roleplaying Game GameMastery Guide* "Bandit")

SCOUT CR 3
XP 800
hp 30 (*Pathfinder Roleplaying Game GameMastery Guide* "Trapper")

MASTIFFS (2) CR 1
XP 400
hp 13 (*Pathfinder Roleplaying Game Bestiary* "Dog, Riding")

Area A4. Great Hall

The great hall lost its roof decades ago, so it's now just four walls and a skeletal staircase to a mezzanine that rings the hall 10 feet above the floor. Weeds grow profusely between the old flagstones, and a great fire pit dominates the center of the floor. A few poachers sometimes sleep here under the stars in fine weather, but most prefer to sleep in the chapel.

The stairs up to the mezzanine are rotted from exposure. Anyone climbing them must make a successful DC 8 Acrobatics check to reach the top safely. On a failed check, the staircase collapses, dropping the character 10 feet to the ground. Everyone in the castle hears the collapse.

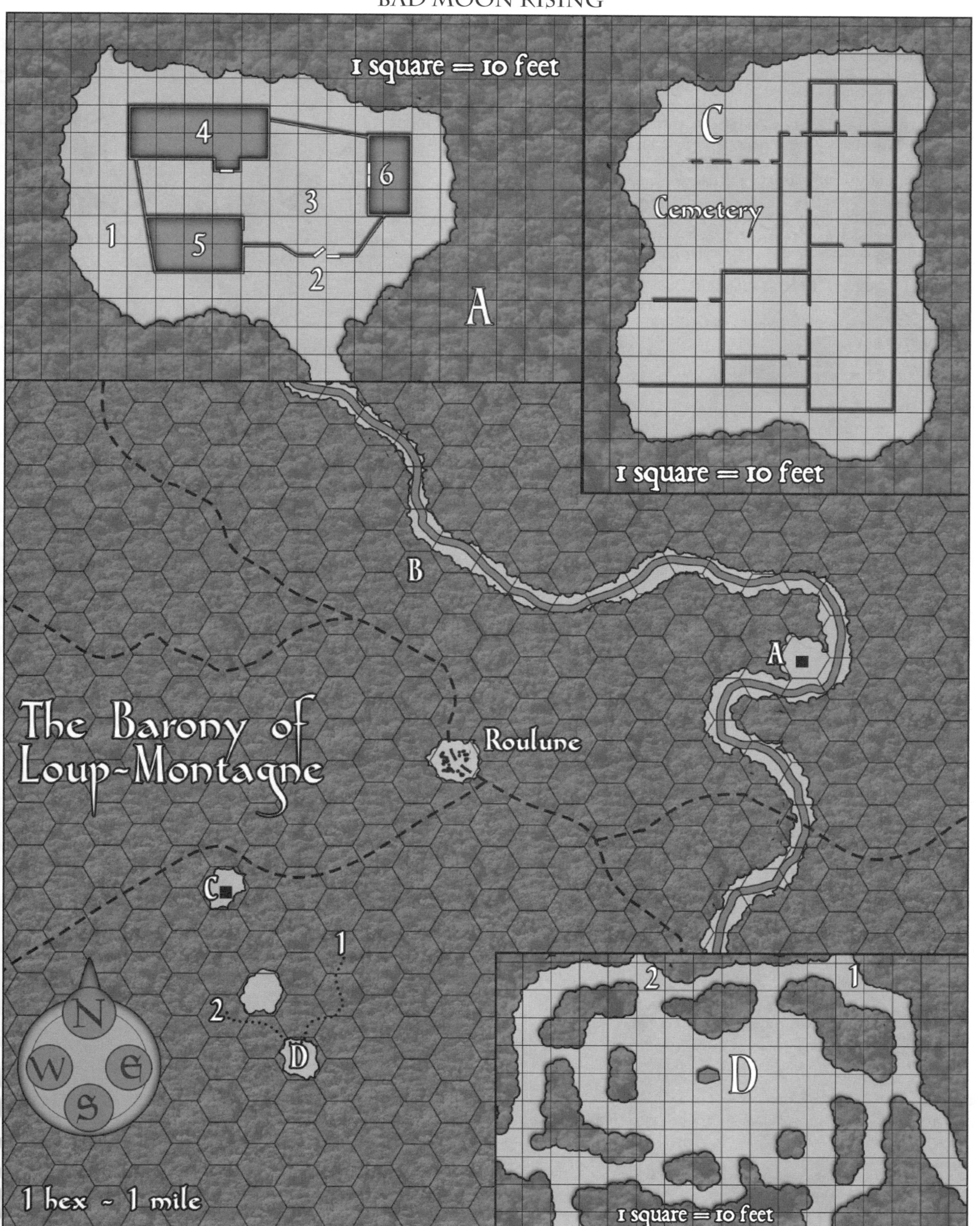

1 square = 10 feet
4
6
3
1
5
2
A
C
Cemetery
1 square = 10 feet
B
A
The Barony of Loup-Montagne
Roulune
C
1
2
D
N
W
E
S
2
1
D
1 hex - 1 mile
1 square = 10 feet

Area A5. Chapel (CR 8–10)

This is the poachers' chief residence when they stay in the castle. They repaired the roof by covering it with canvas looted from merchants' wagons. It leaks in heavy rain, but most of the time it stays warm and comfortable enough for their purposes.

During the daytime, **2d4 bandits** and **Thibault Voclain** are here, resting and planning their next robbery or poaching expedition. At night, the entire gang, including the mastiffs, is here asleep, except for **2 bandits** on the wall and **1 scout** who got up to relieve himself from atop the east wall. If fighting breaks out, he tries to ambush someone from behind if it might make a difference in the outcome; otherwise, he slips away into the forest. If this adventure is taking place during summer in your campaign, **1d4 bandits** could be sleeping in the great hall instead.

THIBAULT VOCLAIN, BANDIT CAPTAIN CR 6
XP 2,400
hp 53 (*Pathfinder Roleplaying Game GameMastery Guide* "Highwayman")

BANDITS (2d4) CR 1/2
XP 200
hp 11 (*Pathfinder Roleplaying Game GameMastery Guide* "Bandit")

SCOUT CR 3
XP 800
hp 30 (*Pathfinder Roleplaying Game GameMastery Guide* "Trapper")

MASTIFFS (2) CR 1
XP 400
hp 13 (*Pathfinder Roleplaying Game Bestiary* "Dog, Riding")

Area A6. Stables

The bandits' **4 riding horses**, **4 draft horses**, and **2 mules** are stabled here. They pay no attention to anyone who enters.

Area B. Duval's Meadow (CR 6)

This is a small clearing in the forest, unremarkable in all ways except for the wolfsbane plants that flourish here. Their blooms stay open during the day, but they are at their fullest under the light of a full moon. See the entry "Gervaise the Astrologer" above for information on wolfsbane's effect against lycanthropes.

If characters come here during a night of the full moon, they encounter a **green hag** named **Savine** on the same mission as them (harvesting wolfsbane). Disguised as a human druid via her *alter self* ability, she does her best to persuade the characters that she also intends to find and slay the werewolf. She offers to join the characters on their quest. If the characters fall for this ploy, Savine does indeed join them and help in their fight against the werewolves. But the moment it appears that the werewolves are beaten, she turns against the characters. Savine is accompanied by a **swarm of poisonous snakes** that should be treated as invisible until they attack.

SAVINE THE GREEN HAG CR 5
XP 1,600
hp 58 (*Pathfinder Roleplaying Game Bestiary* "Green Hag")

SNAKE SWARM CR 2
XP 600
hp 16 (*Pathfinder Roleplaying Game Bestiary 3* "Snake Swarm")

Area C. St. Ulrich Abbey

Nicodeme and his small coterie of werewolves use the abandoned abbey as a gathering place. They don't spend all their time there, but it's the one place they return to regularly between hunts.

> A century ago, the area around the abbey might have been a larger clearing, but the encroaching forest has swallowed it and crept nearly to the ancient building's walls. An overgrown cemetery with headstones tilting at all angles stands outside the crumbling, roofless, fieldstone walls. The structure must have been impressive in its day, but now the leaning, moss- and vine-covered walls form a small maze in the forest.

All areas of the abbey are essentially the same: open, roofless spaces surrounded by crumbling walls with large, arched doorways. The doors are long since rotted away. Only the old chapel has a flagstone floor; all other areas have packed dirt floors spotted with patches of waist-high grass, weeds, and thin bushes. Only a few saplings have taken root inside the structure.

The remains of several of the werewolves' victims are strewn around. They consist mainly of gnawed bones, torn and bloodstained clothing, and a few meager possessions such as copper coins, rusted knives, tacky jewelry, and tarnished belt buckles. Little is left to identify the victims, but if everything is gathered up and brought back to Roulune, Frere Emilé at the Church of the Forest does his best to figure out who the werewolves killed and devoured. If characters search for bodies, each area contains the remains of 1d6–3 victims. If characters search this area after Enzo's murder, they find a pair of bloodstained, embroidered gloves of the type Enzo was transporting.

If characters come here at night, the abbey is abandoned (the werewolves are out hunting). During the day, characters encounter two or three ragged-looking humans. They are filthy, their clothing is tattered (if they wear anything at all), and their hair is matted with twigs and mud, creating an appearance of desperate poverty, and that's the story they tell; they are peasants who were kicked off their land, and are now trying to eke out a subsistence living in the forest by scrounging for roots and nuts. If asked about the bones, they claim that wolves sometimes bring their prey here. When that happens, these humans flee into the forest for a day or more before returning. A character who examines them closely and makes a successful DC 10 Heal check recognizes that despite their apparent destitution, beneath the filth and rags, these people appear very healthy, muscular, and well fed.

Scratched on one of the interior walls of the abbey is a crude representation of a six-sided stele in a forest clearing with wolf-like creatures prancing around it beneath a full moon. The rendering is almost life-size, judging from the figures. If the scene is described to Gervaise, Frere Emilé, or Moreau, they recognize it as the Witches' Den. Any other resident of the barony has a 50% chance to guess that it's the Witches' Den based on stories they've heard. Otherwise, there's an even chance that they'll guess something else or admit that they don't know.

Area D. The Witches' Den

The Witches' Den is the site of an ancient, pagan altar where renegade witches and evil warlocks performed sacrifices. The warlocks and witches who used the altar were killed or driven out of Loup-Montagne long ago, but the altar hangs onto its evil power. Nicodeme uses it for much the same purpose — when he wants to bring someone new into his troop of werewolves, the recruit is brought here to be ritualistically "killed" and reborn as a werewolf.

Physically, the Witches' Den is just a clearing in the woods about 80 feet in diameter and with a stone stele or column at its center. The stele is 12 feet tall and 3 feet across at the base, but it tapers to 2 feet across at the top. It has six roughly-cut sides. The druids and witches carved mystic runes into the stone, but those are completely hidden now by a few centuries' growth of moss and lichen. Not even Nicodeme is aware of the runes or their power, or of what's concealed inside the stele.

The clearing sits in a natural bowl surrounded by some of the most tangled forest the characters have ever plowed through. The clearing can be considered open ground, but the paths around it are treated as difficult terrain. The surrounding forest is nearly impassable; creatures of Huge and Medium size can move just 5 feet per move action off a path, Small creatures can move 10 feet per move action, and Tiny creatures are unimpeded.

Finding the Witches' Den

It would take months of searching to find the Witches' Den without directions. Aside from the werewolves, only Gervaise and Moreau know its location. Moreau, if asked, is likely to give false directions that lead to a random point along the river, then apologize later, saying he must have been mistaken about where it is. He gives accurate directions only if he's been able to arrange for Nicodeme to ambush the characters when they arrive.

Gervaise gives accurate directions to the player characters if asked, along with a brief history of the place and a warning that although it was abandoned long ago, it still has magical power. If characters ask her to explain what that means, Gervaise asks for 24 hours to conduct some research. Characters trained in Knowledge (arcana) or Knowledge (history) can help Gervaise plow through her books and scrolls; each helper can make one DC 15 check, and each successful check cuts five hours off the research time. At the end of that time, Gervaise can tell the characters about the runes on the stele, what they do, and how to activate them. She suspects there may be more to the story, but that's all she could uncover from the available resources. She doesn't know about the *fearsome mask of Lo-Athard* inside the stele or how to release it.

The paths into the Witches' Den begin at forest landmarks that are largely forgotten (since no one comes here anymore) but are not difficult to find if the searcher knows what to look for. Gervaise tells characters how to find "the great oak on the bluff," meaning characters enter the clearing along Path 1 if they get directions from her. If Moreau gives accurate directions, they are from "the boulder that resembles a skull," meaning Path 2, from which they'll more easily be spotted. The paths can be found easily from either of those landmarks.

The Runes On the Stele

Although they're completely overgrown by moss and lichens, the runes carved into the stele have lost none of their power. Because of the runes, anyone touching the stone column can cast the spells *banishment*, *bestow curse*, *enthrall*, and *hypnotic pattern* as if he or she were using a scroll. Each spell can be cast once per week. If a casting attempt fails, the spell is still available in the stone and the casting can be attempted again, but the character who failed to cast the spell must make a successful DC 15 Fortitude save to avoid being stunned for one round by backlash from the stele.

As soon as one of the spells is cast, the stele begins vibrating softly but audibly in a toneless drone that sounds almost like many distant voices chanting in an unknown tongue. If two spells are cast in a 24-hour period, the droning grows louder and the words become more distinct (but remain unintelligible). If three or four spells are cast in a 24-hour period, the runes carved into the stone glow with an orange light that can be seen through the covering of moss. The droning and the glow become gradually weaker as the hours go by until both disappear after 24 hours.

The Fearsome Mask of Lo-Athard

Aura moderate transmutation; **CL** 8th
Slot head; **Price** 5,500 gp; **Weight** 1 lb.

DESCRIPTION

The *fearsome mask of Lo-Athard* is a mask of beaten silver and bronze sculpted to resemble an ugly, scowling human face. When a character dons the mask, it becomes almost invisible, but the wearer's face gains a more threatening aspect than it had before.

The wearer of the *fearsome mask* gains a +2 enhancement bonus to Charisma for as long as the mask is work. Additionally, 3 times per day the wearer can cause himself to be more attractive or frightful, acting as *charm person* and *cause fear*, respectively.

CONSTRUCTION

Requirements Craft Wondrous Item, *eagle's splendor*, *cause fear*, *charm person*; **Cost** 2,790 gp

The Treasure in the Stele

If the patterns of the glowing runes are traced with a finger across the stele while it is glowing and vibrating, the stone splits in half, then shatters into dozens of pieces that tumble to the ground. Hovering in the air where the stele stood is the *fearsome mask of Lo-Athard*, a long-dead cultist who worshipped in this grove centuries ago and whose followers erected the stele.

Key Events

Three incidents set off the events of *Bad Moon Rising*. Once the three lead-in events are over, characters have complete freedom to investigate the strange occurrences around Roulune however they choose. If characters turn down Ghislain's request for help, they could be approached afterward by Gervaise, by a committee of citizens or merchants concerned about the wolf attacks, by Frere Emilé from the Church of the Forest, or even by Jules Brisbois if they look like the sort of scoundrels who'd be good additions to his band of highwaymen. (Marauding wolves in the forest motivate merchants to rout their wagons around Loup-Montagne, and that's bad for the highway robbery business, too.)

Wolf Attack (CR 8+)

The characters get their first taste of wolves while on the road to Roulune. Trigger this event when they are on the road through the forest.

> Arching branches of ancient trees form a continuous roof over the narrow roadway you're on, locking it in eternal twilight. The surrounding forest is a tangle of closely spaced tree trunks with low branches, boulders, fallen trees, thorny brush, and twisting vines. The road twists like a serpent; you haven't seen a straight stretch longer than 50 yards since you entered this forest. The mood isn't improved by the cold, thin drizzle that's been misting down through the trees all day. Picking your way along the muddy, rutted surface is an exhausting way to travel.
>
> Thoughts like those are interrupted by shouts of "Help! Help!" from beyond the next bend in the road, followed by animal snarls — quite a few snarling animals, from the sound of it.

About 100 yards ahead is a merchant's wagon with a broken wheel. Characters can't see it from their current location because of the dense trees and the winding of the road. They need to advance another 80 yards to bring the wagon into view. When they do, read the next description to players.

A wagon with a broken wheel blocks the road. Two terrified draft horses rear and buck in the traces while an old man and a young boy try to keep their balance atop the barrels and crates stacked in the wagon box. They are using spears to fend off a pack of wolves that's circling the wagon, but the wolves seem more interested in the horses than in the passengers.

The wolf pack contains **1 dire wolf** and **1d2+1 wolves** per player character, depending on how tough you judge the characters to be. Surviving wolves flee into the woods when the dire wolf is slain or when half the entire pack is down.

DIRE WOLF **CR 3**
XP 800
hp 26 (*Pathfinder Roleplaying Game Bestiary* "Wolf, Dire")

WOLVES (1d2+1 per PC) **CR 1**
XP 400
hp 13 (*Pathfinder Roleplaying Game Bestiary* "Wolf")

The merchant is Enzo Martel, and the boy is his grandson, Eric. They are on their way to towns farther east with a load of nails, mirrors, embroidered gloves, and fine saddles to sell. They plan to spend the evening in the next town up the road, which is Roulune. Right now, they could use some help replacing their broken wheel with one of the spares. Enzo explains that the horses shied violently when the wolves appeared, twisting the wheel in a rut on the road and snapping it.

There's nothing nefarious about these two. They are grateful for whatever help the characters give them. As payment, they offer a ride on their wagon into Roulune, which is still several miles ahead. A ride would be a big improvement over walking in the mud.

Tax Collectors (CR 8)

Characters arrive in Roulune about 30 minutes before sunset. Read the description to players when they arrive.

Roulune looks much like other towns you've visited in this part of the world. The single road you've been traveling on branches out into a small network of roads that wind through a maze of homes and shops. On the outskirts, the houses stand apart and have fenced gardens and animal pens. Farther into town, the buildings lean against one another and overhang the street. But the streets are wide and the forest stops at the town's edge, so at least you can see the sky again.

"Ahead is where we're bound," says Enzo, pointing to a pleasant-looking inn with an enormous, shaggy wolf's pelt draped like a sign above the doorway. "I'll stand you each an ale if you join us later."

He drops his voice before adding, "There's a piece of misfortune." With a slight nod of his gray head, he indicates a knot of men-at-arms farther up the street. "I was hoping we might miss the tax collectors, but today has not been a lucky day — other than meeting you, of course."

The tax collectors are **Paschal Moreau** and **4 men-at-arms** of the town militia (guards) on a routine patrol of Roulune. Moreau is fulfilling his role as a combination of tax-man and town sheriff: collecting tolls from merchants on their way through and taking the measure of strangers to decide whether they're peaceable travelers or troublemakers.

Before the characters can hop down and get their gear off Enzo's wagon, Moreau and his soldiers march up. They aren't threatening, but they are professionals with plenty of practice at this drill.

Moreau looks over Enzo's wagon and tells him that the toll on the load is 500 cp, with a 20 percent discount on any portion he pays in silver. Characters should know that this is a reasonable toll for use of private roads; Enzo isn't happy to pay it, but he doesn't complain that it's unfair. If characters try to make an issue out of this with Moreau, Enzo makes it clear that he'd prefer they not make trouble for him. If, however, they bring up the wolf attack on the road as a reason why the toll should be reduced or waived, Moreau drops the toll to 200 cp as recompense for Enzo's trouble, provided the merchant spends some of the savings getting the broken wheel repaired at the local wainwright's shop.

After that business is taken care of, Enzo bids the characters farewell while he tends to his horses and wagon, with a promise to meet them later in the inn. Moreau invites the characters inside the Wolf's Pelt for food and conversation.

None of this should seem suspicious, nefarious, or threatening. Moreau comes off as a reasonable man going about his job in a professional way. He admires freelance adventurers. It's his job to know why they came to his town, but he isn't looking for trouble; there won't be a confrontation unless the characters start it.

Moreau answers most questions frankly, unless they're impertinent. Characters can learn quite a bit about the barony, the baron, and the current problem with wolves simply by conversing with Moreau. As long as they aren't rude or antagonistic, Moreau invites them to come to the baron's manor for dinner; the baron is always interested in meeting educated travelers with stories to tell. If characters' behavior toward Moreau is not the sort that leads someone to invite strangers to dinner, then they receive an invitation to dinner directly from the baron the following day, brought by a young page from the manor.

PASCHAL MOREAU **CR 6**
XP 2,400
hp 64 (see **Area 10: Barracks**)

GUARDS (4) **CR 1**
XP 400
hp 16 (*Pathfinder Roleplaying Game GameMastery Guide* "Caravan Guard")

Dinner with the Baron

Baron Ghislain hopes to find adventurers from outside his domain whom he can trust. His household militia has proven itself incapable of stopping the wolf attacks that plague the barony, so it's time to bring in outside experts.

The dinner scene can be as extended or as abbreviated as you like, depending on whether your players enjoy roleplaying this type of social interaction. It will be a small gathering, not a large party: just Ghislain, the characters, Jules Brisbois, and a few servers wandering in and out of the Great Hall. Moreau is not present since the baron can't discuss the wolf problem without talking about Moreau's failure to solve it, and he sees no reason to embarrass his lieutenant that way.

Read the following when characters arrive at the baronial manor.

> The baron's manor is not palatial, but it's clearly the home of someone powerful and important. The two-story structure sits inside a walled enclosure — not a castle, but a well-tended, fortified estate. You're greeted by a servant and shown immediately to the great hall, which is mostly empty. Tables are disassembled and stacked along the walls. Only the head table is prepared, standing across the front of the room on a low platform. The servant asks you to seat yourselves. As he's filling your goblets with wine, two men of noble bearing — one barely more than a lad and walking with crutches — enter the hall and join you at the table.

The younger man welcomes the characters to his home, introduces himself as Baron Ghislain and the other man as "his brother, Jules Brisbois," and joins them at the table without ceremony. During dinner, he reveals all of the following information, however you care to impart it. Jules allows the baron to do most of the talking, but he answers direct questions and adds clarifications to the baron's statements as you see fit.

- "My father died when I was young, so I was raised by my grandfather, Baron Nicodeme. He was blessed with a long life, but when he died in a hunting mishap about a year ago, I inherited the barony."
- "Jules is older than I — very astute of you to notice — but my father's wife was not his mother. That leaves me as the most direct line of accession in the Chaput family, hence I hold the title. Jules is my brother and my right hand. I trust him completely."
- "Yes, there is a legend about tragedy befalling the barony if the oldest heir doesn't inherit the title. Like any legend, it's mostly nonsense — a parable meant to keep the baron honest and ensure a smooth transfer of power. I'm told that a few people have pointed to recent trouble as evidence that Jules should have inherited before me, but our most learned scriveners agree that the legend must refer to the oldest *legitimate* heir. Otherwise, the laws of accession would be meaningless."
- "For the last several months, the barony has been plagued by wolf attacks. There have always been wolves in the forest, and there have always been wolf attacks, but the current situation is worse than ever. These wolves don't just take sheep and cattle; they attack people, too. They seem almost to prefer people over other prey. They've even broken into remote farms and slaughtered entire families. Some people are killed outright, others simply disappear. We can only assume that they, too, are victims of this pack."
- "My huntsmen conclude this is the work of a single pack that has become uncharacteristically aggressive."
- "My huntsmen and soldiers have conducted massive hunts and set numerous traps, to no avail. The attacks continue unabated. My citizens are becoming greatly upset, and tales leaving the barony are beginning to disrupt trade, on which we rely."
- "I've concluded that for this job, I need people with … special skills. Adventurers such as yourself. I don't imagine these creatures are any more supernatural than this table, but they've proven exceptionally wily. They don't follow the predictable patterns wolves follow, and they don't fall for the tricks wolves fall for. That's why I believe hunters with experience battling unnatural foes might succeed where normal field craft has failed."
- "If you're up for such a challenge, I offer you 10 pounds of gold apiece (500 gp each). You can discuss it among yourselves, or sleep on it if you like and give me an answer in the morning."
- The characters are offered comfortable lodging in the baron's manor for the night. If they accept his offer, they can stay in the manor during their entire sojourn in Loup-Montagne.

The Situation Worsens

After their meeting with the baron, characters are free to investigate the wolf attacks however they choose. Brisbois and Moreau are available to answer questions and to provide some material aid, such as guides to the forest and a militia escort if characters want more muscle backing them up. But the deeper characters dig, the more suspicious they should become of those two.

During their time in Loup-Montagne, any of the following events can occur, spurring on the characters' investigation.

Murdered Merchant: As Enzo Martel and his grandson are leaving the barony, they are attacked on the road east of Roulune. Eric straggles back to town with an arrow in his arm. He claims that their wagon was set upon by bandits. His grandfather argued with the bandits, but the robbery was interrupted by the howling of wolves nearby. That frightened some of the bandits terribly, and the boy took advantage of their distraction to run away. One of the bandits loosed an arrow that caught him in the arm, but he kept running, hoping to bring help from town.

If characters head east along the road, they find the ambush spot about four miles from town. Enzo is dead, along with both horses and one bandit;

all apparently killed by wolves. The bandit is one of Thibault Voclain's band from Travers Castle, but no one is able to identify him. The killers were Nicodeme and a few of his werewolves. If characters subsequently search St. Ulrich Abbey or the barracks room used by members of the pack, they find a bloody pair of embroidered gloves that they recognize as similar to those Enzo was hauling. Gloves should be found in one location or the other, but not both.

Leader of the Pack: One of the Baron's woodsmen brings the corpse of an immense wolf to town and displays it in the square. He claims that it must be the pack leader, and many townsfolk agree with him. It truly is a monstrous wolf, with a body six feet long. If someone thinks to cut it open and examine its stomach contents, it is found to have eaten only rabbits and deer meat in the last 24 hours. That doesn't prove it's not the killer, of course, just that it hasn't killed anyone in the last day or two.

Home Besieged: A teenaged boy comes to the baron's manor asking for help. He is the son of a hunter who lives in the forest four miles west of Roulune. Their home was besieged by wolves, or wolflike creatures, for two nights and a day. When his father tried to slip out to the stream to fetch more water, the creatures attacked him and dragged him away into the forest.

The cabin is four miles due west of town. The wolves' trail away from the farm is easy to follow because they were dragging the bleeding body of the hunter. They dragged him about two miles west, then stopped and ate him. The grisly remains are easily found.

By examining the area around the cabin and around the hunter's body, a character who also makes a successful DC 12 Survival check can determine that three creatures were involved, and they were larger than typical wolves. They split up when they finished with the body: one went south, one went southeast, and one went northeast. This behavior is highly uncharacteristic of wolves. Unfortunately, their trails become impossible to follow after a quarter mile.

Omens: If characters haven't uncovered rumors and become curious about St. Ulrich Abbey or the Witches' Den on their own after a few days, they are called to one of the dayrooms in the baron's manor. There they find Ghislain, Moreau, and Brisbois awaiting them, along with Gervaise the Astrologer and Frere Emilé. Gervaise and Emilé approached the baron with startling news: Omens in the sky and elsewhere make it clear that a werewolf is plaguing the barony, and the best place to catch it would be at the Witches' Den during a full moon (which should occur this night or the next). Gervaise provides all the pertinent astrological details, but this is pure smokescreen. Gervaise and Frere Emilé pieced the clues together on their own and decided that this story was the best way to frame their findings to the baron.

The Baron is less superstitious than his subjects, but he understands the power of such beliefs in the barony. He also respects Gervaise and Frere Emilé as the town's two most-educated citizens; he concludes that they're trying to tell him something important without revealing everything, and he wisely plays along.

The problem in the room is Paschal Moreau. The details of any plan that's discussed in his presence finds its way to Nicodeme (probably through a message passed to one of the werewolves in the militia). Even if he's excluded from planning, he alerts his master to be on his guard, because hunters are closing in.

Like the baron, characters should have the opportunity to sense that Gervaise and Frere Emilé aren't telling the whole truth in this meeting. One of the NPCs might surreptitiously pass a note to a character, or you could slyly convey something through your roleplaying. Alternatively, a character might make a DC 12 Knowledge (arcana) check to realize that Gervaise's astrological reasoning is subtle nonsense, or a DC 12 Sense Motive check to realize that the pair's statements are highly guarded.

Bad Moon Rising

Ultimately, through their own investigation or someone's advice, characters should wind up at the Witches' Den. What happens there depends on when they come and whether Nicodeme is expecting them:

If characters are unexpected and arrive during the day (CR 5–6): They find **1 or 2 werewolves** plus **2d3 wolves** sleeping around the column. Nicodeme is not among them.

WEREWOLVES (1d2) **CR 2**
XP 600
hp 19 (*Pathfinder Roleplaying Game Bestiary* "Lycanthrope, Werewolf")
Note These are afflicted werewolves, and have **DR** 5/silver in their hybrid and animal forms.

WOLVES (2d3) **CR 1**
XP 400
hp 13 (*Pathfinder Roleplaying Game Bestiary*, "Wolf")

If characters are expected and arrive during the day: The area is abandoned.

If characters are unexpected and arrive at night (CR 9–10): They find **Nicodeme**, **2 or 3 werewolves**, and **2d3 wolves** prancing and howling around the stele in the clearing.

NICODEME (HYBRID FORM) **CR 7**
XP 3,200
Male human natural werewolf aristocrat 3/fighter 4 (*Pathfinder Roleplaying Game Bestiary*, "Lycanthrope, Werewolf")
NE Medium humanoid (human, shapechanger)
Init +2; **Senses** low-light vision, scent; **Perception** +11

AC 24, touch 13, flat-footed 22 (+5 armor, +1 deflection, +2 Dex, +4 natural, +2 shield)
hp 60 (3d8+9 plus 4d10+12 plus 4)
Fort +8; **Ref** +4; **Will** +8; +1 vs. fear
Defensive Abilities bravery +1; **DR** 10/silver

Speed 35 ft.
Melee *+1 scimitar* +11/+6 (1d6+5/18–20) or dagger +10/+5 (1d4+4/19–20) or bite +5 (1d6+2 plus curse of lycanthropy)
Special Attacks curse of lycanthropy

Str 19, **Dex** 15, **Con** 17, **Int** 13, **Wis** 14, **Cha** 7
Base Atk +6; **CMB** +10; **CMD** 23
Feats Blind-fight, Combat Expertise, Fleet, Intimidating Prowess, Iron Will, Persuasive, Power Attack, Skill Focus (Perception)
Skills Bluff +4, Diplomacy +6 (+10 to change attitude vs. animals related to lycanthropic form), Handle Animal +2, Intimidate +12, Knowledge (history) +5, Knowledge (local) +7, Knowledge (nobility) +5, Perception +11, Ride +6, Sense Motive +8, Stealth +9, Survival +8; **Racial Modifiers** +4 to survival when tracking by scent
Languages Common, Halfling
SQ armor training 1, change forms, lycanthropic empathy
Gear *+1 chain shirt, +1 light steel shield, +1 scimitar,* dagger, *ring of protection +1*, courtier's outfit, 430 gp

WEREWOLVES (1d2+1) **CR 2**
XP 600
hp 19 (*Pathfinder Roleplaying Game Bestiary* "Lycanthrope, Werewolf")
Note These are afflicted werewolves, and have **DR** 5/silver in their hybrid and animal forms.

WOLVES (2d3) **CR 1**
XP 400
hp 13 (*Pathfinder Roleplaying Game Bestiary* "Wolf")

If characters are expected and arrive at night (CR 10): They find **1 werewolf** and **1d3 wolves** prancing and howling around the stele. **Nicodeme**, another **werewolf**, **1d3 wolves**, and **Paschal Moreau** are hidden in the forest, waiting in ambush for characters to arrive.

NICODEME **CR 7**
XP 3,200
hp 60 (as above)

PASCHAL MOREAU **CR 6**
XP 2,400
hp 64 (see **Area 10: Barracks**)

WEREWOLVES (2) **CR 2**
XP 600
hp 19 (*Pathfinder Roleplaying Game Bestiary* "Lycanthrope, Werewolf")
Note These are afflicted werewolves, and have **DR** 5/silver in their hybrid and animal forms.

WOLVES (2d3) **CR 1**
XP 400
hp 13 (*Pathfinder Roleplaying Game Bestiary* "Wolf")

Resolution

If Nicodeme is killed, the barony's wolf problem ceases, even if other werewolves are still on the loose. Without Nicodeme to hold them together, surviving werewolves fall to bickering and fighting among themselves, and the pack disintegrates. If the pack is wiped out but Nicodeme survives, the problem appears to go away for a few months, but eventually it resurfaces — probably long after the player characters move on. In either case, having one or more of the vengeful werewolves cross the characters' path months later makes a memorable encounter.

As long as the problem seems resolved, the baron gladly pays the promised gold. If Moreau's role in events is uncovered, it leaves a vacancy at the head of the barony's militia that Ghislain offers to one of the characters.

Death in Dyrgalas

By Skip Williams

Dyrgalas Raiders

In ancient times, the area now known as the Dyrgalas Fens was home to a sect group of Hyperborean nature worshippers who adopted the practices of the Ancient Ones before them and wrested a living from the depths of the Harwood Forest, built open-air temples, and generally did well. Over the centuries, a series of natural disasters (some say a series of foolish magical experiments) led to a rising water table and turned their home in the forest into a vast swamp.

As the waters rose, most of the people left. Today, a few stalwart humans remain in the fens, living off the land through hunting, fishing, trapping, and even some agriculture. In addition to these honest folk, the Dyrgalas has some less savory residents, including black and green dragons, trolls, hags, escaped criminals, and a host of lycanthropes. Most of these creatures prey on travelers foolish or unlucky enough to enter the fen and sometimes raid inside and outside the fens.

This adventure deals with one group of raiders that makes its lair in the Dyrgalas. A weretiger called Gavriil has formed a group of assorted lycanthropes into a group of cunning brigands. The lycanthropes favorite caper involves infiltrating a merchant caravan, posing as travelers, merchants, or swords for hire, then leading an attack from within. Gavriil and his servants also take on kidnappings, murder for hire, and any other unsavory tasks that might come their way.

In the ***Lost Lands*** campaign setting, the Dyrgalas Fens lie in the central Harwood south of the Wolf Hills. There is little civilization in the region, the closest true authority being the Duchy of Mains from its duchal seat in distant Arbo. However, there is some trade in the region between the loggers and trappers of the surrounding forest and more civilized lands, so the duke does take an interest in the area, insofar as it lines his coffers.

Adventure Hooks

An adventuring party might have any number of reasons for tangling with Gavriil and his minions:

- The party is traveling with a merchant caravan when Gavriil's lycanthropes attack. A group of lycanthropes posing as merchants attack the caravan from within one night. After dealing with the infiltrators, the group can track them back to the fens.
- A merchant or aristocrat of Arbo hires the group to recover a stolen

robe of blending. The medusa Theronia actually stole the robe, but Gavriil's brigands have captured her in turn.

• The group is hired to recover someone Gavriil's group has kidnapped. The PCs might be charged with delivering a ransom and recovering the victim, or simply to rescue the person. There's a very good chance that the lycanthropes try to seize the ransom without releasing the captive

• The Duke of Mains has decided that Gavriil's activities have become intolerable. He doesn't wish to expend the resources to send his own soldiers into the wild depths of the Harwood and instead hires the party to smoke him out.

• A sage, antiquarian, or spellcaster wishes to acquire a detailed map of the ruins where Gavriil makes his lair. This person might seek the knowledge for its own sake or might need the information for some ritual or experiment.

Ruined Pavilion

The ancients built the pavilion as a place where the faithful could rest and find serenity. It was once a stately edifice of butter-colored limestone filled with tranquil pools and ringed with soaring spires. Much of the complex was open to the sky, but a series of partial roofs provided shade (and modest shelter from the weather) for meditating visitors. In times of peril, clerics used the pavilion as a site for summoning elementals, which they sent forth to meet any approaching threat.

Today, the low mound where the pavilion stands has become an island in the Dyrgalas, and the once-proud building has degenerated into a crumbled ruin, half flooded, and shrouded in moss, creepers, vines, and even a few trees. A handful of the ruin's trees are truly immense.

The weretiger Gavriil finds the tumbledown pavilion a convivial place to live and work. He's made the place his personal stronghold and he's gathered a formidable collection of fierce animals, rogue elementals, and fellow lycanthropes to help him defend it.

Conditions and Features

Although aboveground, the pavilion's walls, decaying roofs, leafy trees, and flowing water make the place as dark and damp as any a dungeon. Whenever a condition or feature requires a save or check, pavilion residents have advantage on that save or check (thanks to long familiarity with the place and its quirks), even when the text specifies a disadvantage for a visitor.

Doors: The pavilion's original wooden doors rotted away long ago. Gavriil, however, has replaced them with new doors made from rough planks. The unfinished wood warps and swells in the humid atmosphere, and PCs must succeed a DC 15 Strength check to shove open a door. These doors are hung so that they tend to swing shut on their own. A door opened and not deliberately closed remains ajar for 1d4+1 rounds before slamming shut.

Foliage: Though vines and creepers cover almost every inch of the pavilion that is not flooded, in some places, the growth is taller and thicker. Creatures or objects in these areas have concealment and partial cover against most attacks. The cover value drops to half against attacks coming from above. Movement costs are doubled in foliage due to difficult terrain.

Floors: When new, the pavilion's floors were smooth marble. Today, the marble floor slabs remain mostly undamaged, but the land subsiding under the stonework on the ground floor has played havoc with them. They now tilt crazily in random directions, and creepers sprout from every crack. Making a double movement requires a successful DC 15 Acrobatics check. Visitors have disadvantage on this save. If the save fails, the character can still move, but only at normal speed. Floors in the upper stories remain flat.

Light and Sight: There's plenty of shade inside the pavilion thanks to the walls, trees, and partial roofs. Even on a bright day, the interior is dimly lit and lightly obscured unless otherwise noted in an area description (or if someone provides artificial light). When twilight falls outside, the pavilion's interior is completely dark.

Pools and Flooded Areas: Springs deep under the pavilion flow sluggishly, keeping the water from becoming completely stagnant, though a thick layer of leaves, twigs, and other floating debris blankets most wet areas. Geothermal activity in the area keeps the water at about 82 degrees Fahrenheit year-round (fairly warm to the touch for most warm-blooded creatures). Characters can easily wade in water that is less than waist deep (no loss of speed). Movement costs are doubled for wading in water more than waist deep, and characters must swim in water that's at least as deep as they are tall. Characters wading or swimming are disadvantaged on stealth checks unless they have swimming speeds.

Rubble: Heaps of loose rubble fill many areas within the pavilion. Movement in these areas cost doubled in rubble and is considered difficult terrain. If PCs wish to run or charge they must succeed in a DC 15 Acrobatics check, failing the save, the character moves roughly five feet, then falls prone, suffering 1d6 points of damage.

Walls: The pavilion's stonework is heavily weathered. Here and there, a patch of the original, cheerful yellow remains, but on the whole the walls are darkened to a muddy brown streaked with black and gray. The weathering created plenty of handholds, but the covering moss and vines make climbing tricky. Scaling the walls requires a successful DC 10 Climb check. Those pesky vines and moss make the walls uncannily resistant to grappling hooks; they tend to either slide off the moss or get caught in the vines, where they tear loose at the slightest pull.

Approaching the Pavilion

A road, of sorts, winds through the fens, crossing many islands, causeways, and decaying bridges. Some of the locals can direct the party to the ruin. They don't visit the place thanks to the elementals that still prowl the grounds, but they know where it lies. A reconnaissance from the air reveals the pavilion's towers rising from amid the trees from several miles away.

Area 1. Main Entrance and Façade

The following text assumes the party approaches the area from outside the pavilion. Adjust accordingly if the group first sees this area upon leaving the ruin.

> A weedy trail of crushed stone leads to a massive pile of mud-colored stone as large as any provincial temple. The facade looks to be at least 30 feet high and composed of crumbling, vine-covered blocks. Round towers, each at least twice as tall as the main structure, mark the facade's ends. Onion domes, well punctured with irregular holes and gaping cracks, cap the towers. Two banks of narrow, glassless windows are visible in each tower. The lower bank is perhaps 25 feet aboveground, with the second back an equal distance above that.
>
> Off to the left stands a massive tree whose wide canopy presses hard against the nearest tower, a span of 20 feet or more.
>
> A low portico of gleaming marble slabs fronts the place. It has its own freestanding roof that looks as tattered as the onion domes above it.
>
> The portico's stonework might once have lain as flat and smooth as a dining table. Now they look more like a deck of cards haphazardly spread in a single layer and left to sink randomly into the soggy ground. No two slabs seem to meet on the flat. Tangles of creepers grow in the spaces left between the slabs, and snake their way over the stonework. Just a few paces from where the pavement begins lies a pool of water cloaked in a thick mantle of floating debris.
>
> The ruin's stone facade rises behind the pool. Four archways pierce the facade, and an open space seems to lie beyond.

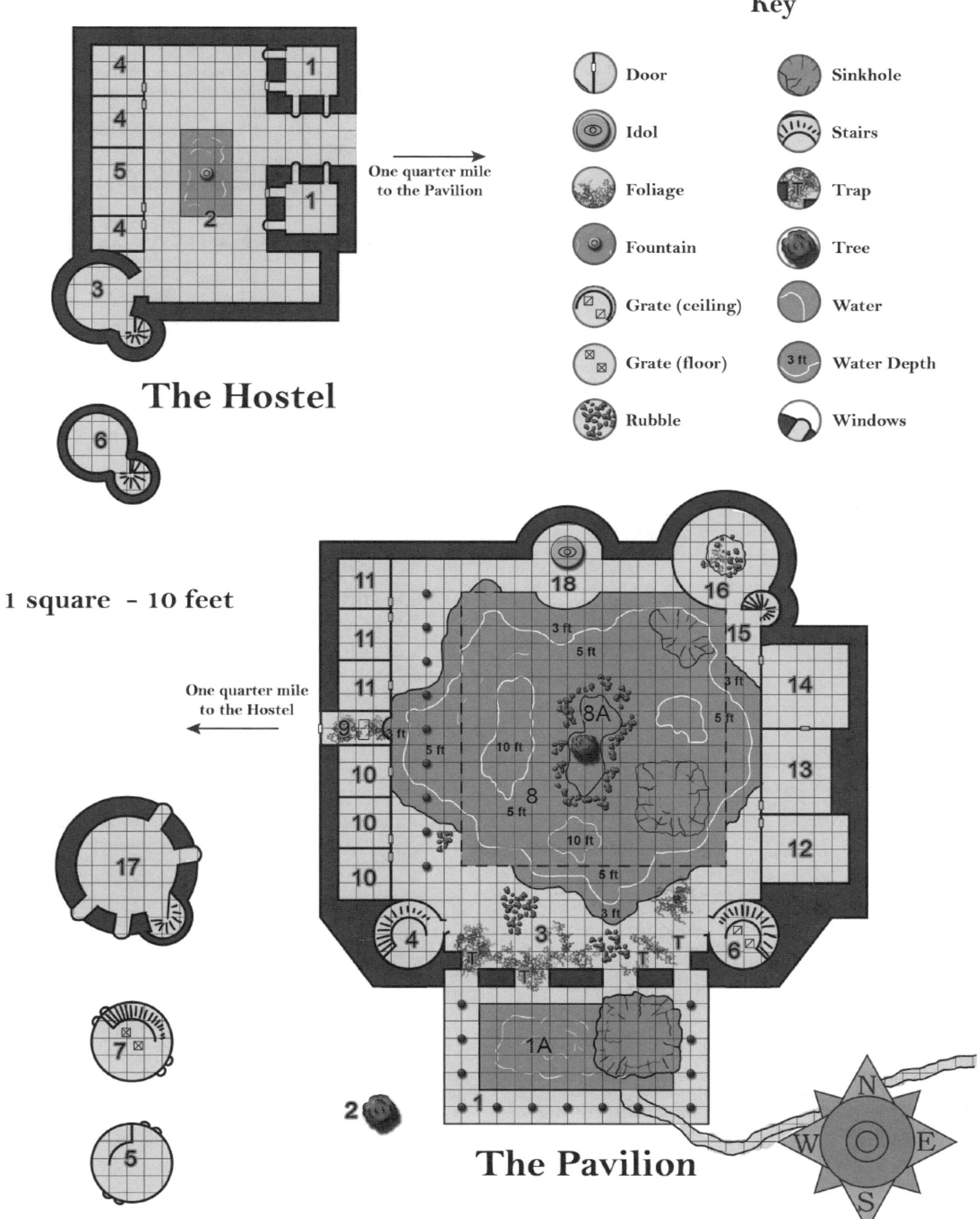

Key
Door
Idol
Foliage
Fountain
Grate (ceiling)
Grate (floor)
Rubble
Sinkhole
Stairs
Trap
Tree
Water
Water Depth
Windows
The Hostel
One quarter mile to the Pavilion
One quarter mile to the Hostel
1 square - 10 feet
The Pavilion
N
E
S
W

Area 1A. The Pool (CR 7)

Very little open water remains visible in the pool. A layer of twigs, leaves, lily pads, and a few waterlogged branches mostly obscures the surface. The whole pool smells of soggy leaves, with a hint of rotting meat. A weak current sets the lighter debris astir, and a thin, winding rivulet exits through a crack near the pool's near right-hand corner and meanders away toward the surrounding fens.

The pool is about 5 feet deep, with a bottom covered with waterlogged twigs, leaves, and branches (the weak current here isn't quite strong enough to carry away everything that falls in). At the pool's east end lies a sinkhole 40 feet deep. At the sinkhole's bottom lies a 10-foot passage that connects to the south sinkhole in **Area 8**.

Floating mostly submerged among the twigs and leaves covering the pool are **3 saltwater crocodiles**. Gavriil took them from a distant nest and brought them here as part of a group of more than two dozen hatchlings. He released the youngsters into the pool and left them to fend for themselves. These three are the only survivors. They've vicious and always hungry. From time to time, Gavriil comes here to talk with them (via spell) and feed them just enough to keep them healthy. The pavilion's other denizens know enough to toss the crocodiles a few morsels and hurry away if they need to pass.

SALTWATER CROCODILE (3) CR 5
XP 1,600
Pathfinder Roleplaying Game Pathfinder #58"Crocodile, Saltwater"
N Huge animal
Init +4; **Senses** low-light vision; Perception +9

AC 18, touch 8, flat-footed 18 (+10 natural, –2 size)
hp 57 (6d8+30)
Fort +10; **Ref** +5; **Will** +3

Speed 20 ft., swim 30 ft.
Melee bite +8 (2d6+6 plus grab), tail slap +3 (1d8+3)
Space 15 ft.; **Reach** 15 ft.
Special Attacks death roll, lunging bite

Str 23, **Dex** 10, **Con** 20, **Int** 1, **Wis** 13, **Cha** 2
Base Atk +4; **CMB** +12 (+16 grapple); **CMD** 22
Feats Improved Initiative, Skill Focus (Perception, Stealth)
Skills Perception +9, Stealth +2 (+10 in water), Swim +14;
Racial Modifiers +8 Stealth in water
SQ hold breath

Death Roll (Ex) When grappling a foe of its size or smaller, a saltwater crocodile can perform a death roll upon making a successful grapple check. As it clings to its foe, it tucks in its legs and rolls rapidly, twisting and wrenching its victim. The crocodile deals its bite damage and knocks the creature prone. If successful, the crocodile maintains its grapple.
Hold Breath (Ex) A saltwater crocodile can hold its breath for a number of rounds equal to 4 times its Constitution score before it risks drowning.
Lunging Bite (Ex) Once per minute, a saltwater crocodile can extend the reach of its bite attack by 5 feet without taking the normal penalties to AC associated with the Lunge feat. This extended reach applies only to the crocodile's bite attack and lasts until the start of the creature's next turn.

Whether they're fed or not, the crocodiles lunge out of the pool and attack anyone who remains within their reach for more than a few seconds (except for Gavriil). They have advantage on Stealth checks to remain unnoticed and attack with surprise if their foes don't see them coming. When attacking, they try to grab the nearest creature and haul their prey to the bottom sinkhole for a death roll.

If badly wounded (less than half hit points), or if attacked from a distance, they retreat down the sinkhole and through the passage to **Area 8** and from there to **Area 8A**.

Development: The wererats in **Area 5** and the medusa in **Area 7** quickly notice combat here, especially if the crocodiles are splashing in the pool or if their foes use any flashy spells. They make no attempt to intervene (the roof over the pool tends to make ranged combat against anyone fighting the crocodiles difficult), though the wererats might attempt to sneak out a window and into **Area 2** to get a better look. See the appropriate area descriptions for other actions these creatures might take.

Area 2. Sentinel Tree (CR 8)

The tree standing here looks like a true giant. It has a trunk wider than a hogshead and a crown that tops out at least a bowshot overhead. Many of its branches push hard against the ruined tower several yards away.

The tree is nothing special, just very large. It takes a DC 15 Climb check to climb the trunk. A character could easily toss a grapple into the tree's lower branches and find a firm anchor point.

The lower branches reach all the way to a window in **Area 5**, and anyone who can climb up there can just walk along a thick limb and step right into the chamber beyond. Gavriil and his allies know about the connection, and have arranged an unpleasant surprise for anyone who tries to enter the pavilion by this route. They've stripped, sharpened and bent several branches to act as a battery of maces **trap**.

BRANCHES TRAP CR 8
XP 4,800
Type mechanical; **Perception** DC 25; **Disable Device** DC 25

Trigger location; **Reset** manual
Effect branches snap down (all targets on connecting branch within 10-ft. area of the window, 6d6 damage, DC 20 Reflex save for half damage)

Area 3. Entry Hall (CR 8)

This area resembles **Areas 1** and **1A**. It sports a freestanding roof, but has no pool. The text below assumes the party enters through one of the arches leading to **Area 1**.

Beyond the arch lies another expanse of pale, broken pavement. A decaying roof rests on a double row of slender pillars. Piles of rubble, and thickets of young trees, vines, and brambles are everywhere. Just north of the covered area lies a somewhat turbulent pool covered in a thin mist.

The rubble and foliage in here has accumulated more or less naturally, though Gavriil and his crew have made a few additions. At each area marked with a "T" they have bent saplings that resemble the **trap** in **Area 2**, except that a creature struck also must make a successful DC 20 Reflex save or be knocked 15 feet to the north and into the pool at **Area 8**.

BRANCHES TRAPS CR 8
XP 4,800
Type mechanical; **Perception** DC 25; **Disable Device** DC 25

Trigger location; **Reset** manual

Effect branches snap down (all targets within 10-ft. area, 6d6 damage, DC 20 Reflex save for half damage)

Development: The wererat guard in **Area 4** keeps an intermittent watch over this area (Gavriil has ordered the wererats to watch constantly, but their attention wavers if the weretiger isn't on hand to keep them focused). Still, the guard notices intruders in here unless they're being stealthy. If anyone triggers one the traps in here, the wererats in **Area 4** and **Area 5** notice automatically, as does the medusa in **Area 7**. Any other loud or flashy activity in here, such as ranged combat, spellcasting, or an extended conversation among several characters also alerts the neighbors.

Area 4. West Tower Ground Floor (CR 8)

The staircase here rises 25 feet to **Area 5**. The text below assumes characters are viewing the chamber from **Area 3**.

> A narrow arch pierces a curved section of wall here. A circular chamber lies beyond. A staircase spirals around the wall and vanishes into darkness overhead. An untidy mass of twigs, grass, fur, and who knows what else fills the chamber's whole floor and rises taller than a peasant cottage.
>
> Above the arch, perhaps 25 feet above the floor, is a pair of barred windows, with a second pair about another 25 feet above that.

The "untidy mass" is the resident wererats' nest. The whole construction is about 15 feet wide and nine feet high. Calling this place home are **8 wererats**, but only three are present at any given time. Two of the current occupants rest while the third keeps a lazy eye on **Area 3**.

The windows above the chamber entrance lead into **Area 5**.

WERERATS (8) **CR 2**
XP 600
hp 20 (*Pathfinder Roleplaying Game Bestiary* "Lycanthrope, Wererat")

When a wererat notices intruders in **Area 3**, he quickly rouses his companions and resumes his watch on **Area 3**. Unless the intruders trigger one of the traps in **Area 3**, one of the wererats quietly slips up the stairs to warn his companions in **Area 5**. The two remaining wererats hunker down in the nest, where they have concealment and advantage on stealth checks. The pair waits until foes enter the chamber, then pop out of the nest and make sneak attacks. If intruders spot them and attack from outside the chamber (with spells or ranged attacks), the wererats fire their crossbows once each, then retreat up the stairs to **Area 5**.

If a party manages to catch all three wererats here unawares, the trio fights as well as they are able. They'll maneuver to use their sneak attacks as best they can and try to hold out until help arrives from **Area 5**.

Development: If the party defeats the wererats, they can tear apart the nest and recover a *+1 corrosive rapier** (Gavriil allows the wererats to accumulate a few trinkets).

*See *pathfinder Roleplaying Game Ultimate Equipment.*

Any fighting here alerts the wererats in **Area 5** after two rounds (or sooner if a wererat escapes up the stairs). Once alerted, the wererats in **Area 5** join the fight here (see the **Area 5** description for details).

If a fight starts in **Area 5**, the wererats here notice the ruckus after 2–3 rounds. Once alerted, all three wererats scramble upstairs to join the battle.

If the party captures and questions a wererat, the prisoner is reluctant to answer any questions, and claims to be a mere slave. If the PCs make an Intimidation check or make the prisoner friendly with a Diplomacy check, or by magical coercion they reveal the following in response to the appropriate questions:

- A weretiger called Gavriil lords it over this place.
- Gavriil lives in the northeast tower with two companions, Inessa and Zhanna (they're weretigers, too).
- Gavriil can do some magic and spends a great deal of his time talking to animals and other beings. He even talks to the water in the central pool (Area 8). **Note:** Gavriil talks to the water elemental in **Area 8**, but the wererats don't really understand what the weretiger is doing. The wererats know that Gavriil uses magic, but they're not sure what kind.
- Gavriil keeps his mistress/personal assassin in the west tower (**Area 7**). If someone offends Gavriil, the poor fool visits the tower and is never seen again. Her name is Theronia, and she's probably some kind of demon.

Note: Theronia is a medusa Gavriil has conscripted. Theronia usually keeps herself masked, both to conceal her true nature and to keep from petrifying too many of Gavriil's servants. See **Area 7** for more details.

- Gavriil has collected all manner of creatures to serve as raiders. The weretiger is making a fortune robbing caravans, kidnapping merchants, and all manner of other foul deeds. Of course, everyone here would be happy to be mere hunters, woodsmen, and even farmers. **Note:** The wererats and other lycanthropes fear Gavriil, but serve him more or less willingly.

Area 5. West Tower Upper Floor (CR 7)

The staircase here descends 25 feet to **Area 4**. This area once was only one of two upper floors in the tower. Today, most of the tower interior has collapsed, leaving this chamber open all the way to the tower's decaying onion dome.

> Mounds of rubble choke most of this wide, circular, dusty space, though the center seems clear. A crumbling staircase corkscrews around the outer wall. The steps leading down seem fairly intact, but the set leading up quickly dwindle away to mere shards. At about floor level, two sets of windows look southwest and northeast. The northeast pair is barred, but the southwest pair merely gape open. Two pairs of windows, identical to the pairs at floor level, are about 25 feet farther up the walls. Above that soars a great, but ragged dome.
>
> The chamber's clear space contains a rough table with a few crudely woven wicker chairs, a few casks and barrels, and a brazier filled with dying coals.

The bars in the northeast windows are hinged and swing outward like doors. The wererats here keep the bars padlocked shut. A key to the locks hangs from a hook under the table.

There are always **5 wererats** on duty here. Gavriil has tasked them with keeping watch over **Area 8**. The wererats, however, treat this chamber as their place to indulge in human vices such as gambling and drinking. Usually, a single wererat hides in the rubble next to a window and keeps watch over **Area 8** (this guard occasionally waves at one the weretigers watching from **Area 17**). The other four sit at the table, playing knucklebones and sipping liquor from their supply of casks. They're careful not to become inebriated — they'd never survive Gavriil's wrath if caught drunk — but hardly keep a vigilant watch.

WERERATS (5) **CR 2**
XP 600
hp 20 (*Pathfinder Roleplaying Game Bestiary* "Lycanthrope, Wererat")

If forewarned, the wererats hide, with one or two ducking under the table, and the rest taking to the rubble. If a fight develops, the wererats try to attack their foes from as many different directions as they can manage. They use melee or ranged weapons as necessary.

If they detect a threat outside their chamber, 2 wererats move to the windows and fire their crossbows. The barred windows overlooking **Area 8** provide them half cover. The unbarred windows facing outside also provide half cover. The remaining wererats rush down the stairs to **Area 4** and out to meet the threat. If the threat is in **Area 4**, 2 wererats use the stairs and the others open the windows and use ropes to rappel down to **Area 3**.

Development: The wererats notice any traps triggered or combat in **Areas 3**, **8**, or **9** the round after the action happens. They notice a fight in **Area 4** after two rounds (or sooner if a wererat from there comes to warn them). If a fight starts here, the wererats in **Area 4** notice the ruckus after 2–3 rounds and scramble up the stairs to join the battle. The wererats eventually notice fighting in **Area 1A**; however, they do little to intervene beyond going to **Area 2** so they can get a better look at any intruders. If any of these wererats is captured and questioned, they react as noted in the description for **Area 4**.

Area 6. East Tower Ground Floor (CR 7)

The staircase here rises 25 feet to **Area 7**. The text below assumes characters are viewing the chamber from **Area 3**.

> A narrow arch pierces a curved section of wall here. A circular chamber lies beyond. A staircase spirals around the wall and vanishes overhead. A substantial mound of mossy rocks and dirt fills most of the chamber. Masses of brambles, vines, and saplings grow from the dirt. Here and there among the stones and leaves, a metallic gleam or crystalline sparkle is visible.
>
> Above the arch, perhaps 25 feet above the floor, is a pair of barred windows, with a second pair about another 25 feet above that.

The foliage growing here gets light from the open archway and also from two gratings in the ceiling 25 feet overhead.

The pile of stone and dirt is home to a **Huge earth elemental** Gavriil recruited to serve as a combination jailer and guardian for the medusa in **Area 7**.

HUGE EARTH ELEMENTAL **CR 7**
XP 3,200
hp 95 (*Pathfinder Roleplaying Game Bestiary* "Elemental, Earth")

The gleams and sparkles visible here come from several bits of iron pyrite (essentially worthless), plus a scattering of coins (22 gp, 38 cp) and 8 bits of polished quartz (5 gp each). Gavriil scattered these odds and end here to please the elemental and to tempt and delay intruders.

The elemental spends its time blended into the mound. It can detect anyone setting foot inside the chamber or on the stairs or trying to climb the walls. It rears up and slams away at any trespassers, gaining surprise. Thanks to its ability to glide through earth, it ignores the effects of the debris in here. It fights to the death.

Development: The elemental won't notice anyone flying through the chamber, unless the intruder touches something. Neighboring creatures don't pay much attention to what goes on in here, except for the medusa in **Area 7**. The medusa notices a battle in here immediately. Once alerted, she quietly observes the action for one round by peering through the gratings or down the staircase. After that, she lets loose a few spells.

The elemental ignores everything going on outside its chamber, except for **Area 7**. The elemental notices in 1–2 rounds when the medusa is involved in a fight or even if her usual pattern of movements change. It charges upstairs and attacks as quickly as it can.

Area 7. East Tower Upper Floor (CR 9)

The staircase here descends 25 feet to **Area 4**. This area is similar to **Area 5**. It's open all the way to the ruined dome 60 feet overhead. It also has windows overlooking the pavilion's exterior and interior as noted in the **Area 5** description. The medusa Theronia calls the chamber home (at least for the moment), and her living arrangements are considerably different from what the wererats in the neighboring tower have.

> Colorful rugs cover most of the floor in a wide, circular space here. Metal grates lie in the stone floor at two places where there are no rugs. A crumbling staircase corkscrews around the outer wall. The steps leading down seem fairly intact, but the set leading up quickly dwindle away to mere shards. At about floor level, two sets of windows look northwest and southeast. The northwest windows have bars. The southeast pair has no bars, but light curtains cover them. Two pairs of windows, identical to the pairs at floor level, are about 25 feet farther up the walls. Above that soars a great, but ragged dome.
>
> The chamber's furnishings include a canopied bed, a desk of brightly polished wood, several shelves of books, a pair of divans, a loom draped with many skeins of yarn, and a massive bronze brazier flanked by two big amphorae. The crumbling steps leading up hold an assortment of art objects, including several vases, delicate lamps, and realistic sculptures of birds and small animals.

The windows here are just like the windows in **Area 5**, right down to the hinged bars. **Theronia** keeps the key to the windows in her desk.

THERONIA **CR 9**
XP 6,400
Female medusa wizard 5 (*Pathfinder Roleplaying Game Bestiary* "Medusa")
LE Medium monstrous humanoid
Init +8; **Senses** all-around vision, darkvision 60 ft.; **Perception** +16

AC 19, touch 14, flat-footed 15 (+2 armor, +3 Dex, +1 dodge, +3 natural)
hp 126 (8d10+40 plus 5d6+25)
Fort +8; **Ref** +11; **Will** +11

Speed 30 ft.
Melee *+1 dagger* +15/+10 (1d4/19-20) or bite +9 (1d4–1)
Special Attacks hand of the apprentice (7/day), petrifying gaze, poison
Spells Prepared (CL 5th; concentration +9):
3rd—*fireball* (DC 17), *lightning bolt* (DC 17)
2nd—*invisibility*, *levitate*, *see invisibility*
1st—*lock gaze**, *mage armor*, *magic missile*, *shield*
0 (at will)—*detect magic*, *light*, *message*, *read magic*

Str 8, **Dex** 18, **Con** 20, **Int** 18, **Wis** 13, **Cha** 19
Base Atk +10; **CMB** +9; **CMD** 24
Feats Blind-fight, Brew Potion, Combat Casting, Dodge[B], Improved Initiative, Point-blank Shot, Precise Shot, Scribe Scroll, Weapon Finesse
Skills Acrobatics +13 (+6 to jump), Appraise +15, Bluff +12, Craft (alchemy) +10, Disguise +13, Intimidate +15, Knowledge (arcana) +15, Knowledge (planes) +10, Knowledge (religion) +8, Perception +16, Sense Motive +10, Spellcraft +15, Stealth +15, Survival +10; **Racial Modifiers** +4

Perception
Languages Abyssal, Common, Draconic, Elven, Ignan
SQ arcane bond (*+1 dagger*)
Gear mask, spellbook, *+1 dagger*, *bracers of armor* +2, 98 gp

Poison (Ex) Poison—Injury; save Fort DC 19; freq 1/rd for 6 rds; effect 1d3 Str; cure 2 cons saves.
*see *Pathfinder Roleplaying Game Ultimate Combat*

The gratings in the floor pull out easily, allowing movement (for a Medium or smaller creature) or attacks into **Area 6**. The gratings are made of soft steel and actually somewhat flimsy. If someone weighing more than 50 pounds steps on one, roll 1d6.

On a roll of 1, the grating gives way, dumping the character 25 feet into **Area 6**. A character can attempt a DC 25 Reflex save to grab the opening and avoid the fall. If the grating does not give way, it groans and bends. Repeat the die roll each round a character remains atop the grate, increasing the chance it gives way each round (to a maximum of 1–5).

Theronia spends all her time in here. She studies her books (including her spellbooks), works at her loom, and keeps watch over **Areas 3** and **8**. When awake, she usually goes masked. She sleeps during the darkest part of each night, leaving her pet **basilisk** to stand watch. She takes off her mask when she goes to bed.

BASILISK **CR 5**
XP 1,600
hp 52 (*Pathfinder Roleplaying Game Bestiary* "Basilisk")

When possible, Theronia attacks from a distance with *lightning bolt* spells as she deems most appropriate. She uses her basilisk as a distant guard to watch the stairs or windows.

If foes close to melee range, she doffs her mask, unleashing her gaze attack. If necessary, she fights with her dagger and snakes.

If reduced to 10 hit points or less, Theronia surrenders, covering her face and begging her attackers to have mercy on a poor slave (see the Development section for more information).

Therona mostly ignores disturbance outside her chamber, except in **Areas 3** or **8**, where she uses her spells to attack anyone fighting the elementals in those areas.

Development: The wererats in **Areas 4** and **5** notice when Theronia begins slinging spells, but they don't intervene. The weretigers in **Area 17** also notice any disturbances here, but they use the time to prepare their defenses.

Likewise, Theronia notices any fighting in **Areas 4** or **5** (or if someone triggers a trap in **Area 3**), but does nothing to intervene except to ready her own defense. Theronia also notices any fighting in **Area 8** and begins her ranged spell assault against any intruders there as soon as she can. She uses the barred windows in her chamber for three-quarters cover. Likewise, she notices if someone triggers the trap in **Area 9** and attacks intruders with her spells as they emerge from the passage there.

If the party captures Theronia or induces her to surrender, the medusa claims to be a mere slave. She has much the same information that the wererats in the West Tower do, plus additional tidbits as noted in the list that follows. She's careful about revealing what she knows, and tries to bargain with the group. Theronia is mostly interested in escaping the confrontation alive, but she'd also like to get the magical robe Gavriil took from her (read on). Theronia might reveal the following to her captors in response to the right questions (if the party catches any of her omissions, Theronia claims to have simply forgotten to mention the missing details):

- Theronia came to serve here after being captured when a horde of lycanthropes attacked the caravan in which she was traveling. The other captives were either ransomed or sold, but the lycanthrope leader decided to keep her here. **Note:** This is only partially true. In fact, the lycanthropes infiltrated the caravan and cut a deal with the medusa to attack the caravan from within. Theronia was to receive a cut of the spoils. Later, Gavriil double-crossed the medusa by insisting that her property was part of the spoils. Theronia is now working to get her things back, in particular a *robe of blending*. Theronia was returning to her lair after a quest to recover the *robe of blending* when Gavriil attacked her caravan.

• The weretiger Gavriil is the mastermind behind all the activity around here. He seems to be some kind of cleric and favors spells involving the elements. He's friendly with all the elementals lurking around here and talks to animals. **Note:** Theronia has it right: Gavriil is a druid who can speak with elementals.

• Gavriil lives in the large tower at the ruin's northeast corner. He has a pair of weretiger bodyguards. A spiral staircase leads up to the weretigers' chamber just to the south of their tower. Gavriil likes to watch the pool (**Area 8**), however, so it would be hard to sneak up on him. **Note:** This is mostly true. Theronia knows about the guardian tigers in **Area 14**, but does not mention them to the party.

• Gavriil uses the idol at the north side of the pool (**Area 8**) to store his ill-gotten gains. **Note:** This is true as far as Theronia knows. She neglects to mention the fire elemental that erupts from the idol.

Treasure: If the party loots the chamber, they find Theronia's spellbooks on the bookshelves. The collection of art objects on the ruined staircase includes six rare vases worth 150 gp each and one gold lamp set with amber and rubies (750 gp). The small sculptures are real birds and little animals that Theronia petrified (she's fond of doing that). The petrified creatures might have some value as curiosities, at the GM's option. Eight of the rugs in here are valuable; they each weigh 18 pounds, and each is worth 150 gp.

Area 8. Central Pool (CR 7)

Originally, the pool served as a place where the faithful could wade or simply lounge at the edges. Short roofs projected over the pavements surrounding the pool, with the pool itself open to the sky. The pool's edges have mostly collapsed; transforming the original rectangular pool into an irregular shape (the dotted line on the map shows the original outline and roof line). During the day, this area is well lit.

A pool that looks about as long and wide as a village square lies here, its waters lapping against the weathered stonework surrounding it. In several places, the remains of a fairly narrow pavement that must have once formed a veranda of sorts round the pool remain, but the pool's waters reach all the way to the walls, and a few doors, that once fronted on the missing veranda. The remains of short roofs with gentle slopes surround the pool on all four sides, and here and there the stumps of broken support pillars stick up like rotten teeth.

Many piles of rubble form tiny islands all over the pool, and one very large pile of debris near the center sprouts a massive tree that rises past the old roofline.

The original pool was about 3 feet deep. Today, the pool's bottom has broken up and subsided, leaving an uneven bottom of hard and jagged stones. However, a vast accumulation of debris and silt about a foot thick covers it all. The combination gives the pool a varying depth, as shown by the contour lines on the map.

In addition, two sinkholes are in the southeast and northeast corners. The southeast sinkhole is about 40 feet deep, with a 10-foot passage at the bottom that leads to the sinkhole in **Area 1A**. The northeast sinkhole is about 20 feet deep.

Currently living in the pool are **2 Large water elementals**. They spend most of their time resting at the bottom of the northern sinkhole, rising occasionally to speak with Gavriil.

LARGE WATER ELEMENTALS (2) CR 5
XP 1,600
hp 68 (*Pathfinder Roleplaying Game Bestiary* "Elemental, Water")

Though out of sight and underwater, the elementals notice if any activity occurs near the pool (such as fighting in one of the adjacent areas) or when anyone does anything in or with the water in the pool (such as swimming, wading, or tossing anything in). They prefer to attack foes touching the water. If no such target is available, an elemental tries to knock someone into the water. Anyone standing on rubble and adjacent to water is vulnerable. The elemental moves within reach of the rubble and uses a slam attack to jostle the rubble. The elemental attempts to bull rush the target creature, pushing them and having them fall into the adjacent water. If more than one space exists where the target could fall into the water, the elemental decides where the target falls. After a fall, the target is prone in the water and must swim or wade during its next turn. An elemental uses its slam attack against single opponents and its vortex attack when it faces multiple foes in the pool.

The elementals fight to the death.

Development: A *ring of ferocious action** is hidden in the silt at the bottom of the north sinkhole (mostly items Gavriil tosses in the water for safekeeping).

*see *Pathfinder Roleplaying Game Ultimate Equipment*

All the pavilion residents in **Areas 5**, **7**, and **17** notice any fight with the elementals, and most make ranged attacks against any foes that they can see, as the terrain and the combatants relative positions allow.

Area 8A. Tree Island (CR 8)

A tree has taken root in a big pile of debris here and grown to massive size.

A substantial mound of rock and organic debris rises from the water.

A massive tree with a trunk at least as wide as a human is tall grows from the mound. It has a crown wider than a village street and nearly as tall as the domed towers that ring it. A layer of moss makes the trunk look shaggy and green. Some of the tree's lower branches are thicker than a man's leg and a few of these droop low, hanging just a few feet above rock or water.

The mound is the remains of a tower, now collapsed and utterly destroyed. As shown on the map, the mound has a fringe of rubble that forms its shoreline. Near the center, the mound is dirt covered in creepers and ferns.

Making their home in the tree are **2 girallons**. Gavriil struck an uneasy truce with the pair. He tosses them some food now and then, and generally leaves them alone.

GIRALLONS (2) CR 6
XP 2,400
hp 73 (*Pathfinder Roleplaying Game Bestiary* "Girallon")

The girallons wait in the tree's lower branches and stay hidden (they have full concealment in the foliage). They emerge only if someone comes within reach or touches their island or tree. The immediately attack such trespassers, hanging down from the tree and flailing away with their claws.

The girallons notice most of what goes on near the pool, but do not break their cover or intervene at all.

Development: Wounded crocodiles from **Area 1A** retreat here (to the mound's north side) if they escape a fight in their pool. The girallons don't like that, but do nothing.

If the crocodiles are here when characters approach the mound, they attack again. The girallons watch the fight, waiting for a chance to catch someone unawares when they reach the mound.

Treasure: A few trinkets lie beneath the water just off the mound (discarded gear from the girallons' victims), including a *+1 frost dagger*.

Area 9. Side Entrance (CR 7)

Priests and pilgrims once used this doorway to enter the pavilion from their quarters. The priests' quarters have sunk into the fens, but the ruins of the pilgrims' hostel still stand. The remains of a path running from here to **Area 1** at the hostel are very faintly visible. It takes a successful DC 15 Perception to locate the path. If the PCs search for the path, they have advantage on the check.

The text below assumes the party is viewing the area after opening the door from the west.

> A passage, some 10 feet wide, with walls of cracked rock, extends east from the door. The corridor has an arched stone ceiling. Enough blocks are missing to show patches of sky.
>
> Some 20 feet in from the door is a thicket of saplings and vines that seems to grow from the very stones of floor.

The foliage is natural; it grows from dirt-filled cracks in the floor.

Gavriil had his servants add a deadly **rock fall trap** in the corridor. Anyone passing through the foliage triggers the trap. The narrow rectangle on the map shows the trigger. The trap has two effects. First, the rock falls into the 10 foot area that border the trigger. Second, the character triggering the traps triggers a **net trap**. A netted character winds up wrapped in the net and suspended from the ceiling.

ROCK FALL TRAP **CR 5**
XP 1,600
Type mechanical; **Perception** DC 20; **Disable Device** DC 20

Trigger location; **Reset** manual
Effect Atk +15 (10 ft. stone; 6d6 damage); multiple targets (all targets in a 10-ft. square)

NET TRAP **CR 5**
XP 1,600
Type mechanical; **Perception** DC 25; **Disable Device** DC 20

Trigger location; **Reset** manual
Effect Atk +15 (5 ft. net, DC 25 Reflex save to avoid being snared)

Development: Triggering the trap alerts the residents in **Areas 4**, **7**, and **17**. These creatures watch the passage's east end. If nobody emerges after a round or two, the pair of weretigers from **Area 17** go to see if anyone has been caught in the net. If intruders emerge from the passage, the residents attack, as noted in their area descriptions.

Area 10. Larders

Through some trick of nature (or perhaps an extraplanar connection), these chambers remain at about 40 degrees Fahrenheit around the clock. The pavilion's original staff opened the room's doors from time to time to provide a cool draft for anyone using the central pool's west side (**Area 8**). Gavriil merely uses the chambers as larders.

> A wave of shivery cold laced with the stench of blood and sudden death rolls over you as the door opens. A mass of skinned and dressed carcasses hang from the ceiling in the chamber beyond.

The carcasses are from animals Gavriil's servants killed in the fens. The smell comes from the carcasses, which are not very well cleaned, though mostly unspoiled.

Area 11. Storage

These areas once were very cold, though now their temperature stays near 60 degrees. Gavriil uses them to store beverages and dry goods.

> A cool, somewhat dry, puff of air washes over you as the door opens. The draft carries a faintly pleasant scent. The chamber beyond does not seem to contain anything except a mass of crates and barrels.

Treasure: The crates and barrels contain supplies for Gavriil and his servants. There are salt, spices, and beverages plus some preserved food (smoked meat and dry fruit and vegetables) and some butter, lard, and flour. A few crates contain valuable trade goods, including about 100 square yards of very fine cotton cloth (worth 500 gp) and 200 square yards of silk (worth 2,000 gp).

Area 12. Hall

This chamber once was one of several small chapels provided for the faithful. An altar and idol once stood at the east end, but Gavriil removed them. Today, the residents use the place as a dining hall (when they have a taste for cooked food) and meeting hall. It usually stands empty.

> The odor of stale smoke fills the air. A table of rough planks, lined with wicker chairs, fills much of the space in this narrow chamber. Fairly solid looking chests lie against the north and south walls. At the back of the chamber is an uneven dais covered in ash and bits of half-burned wood. Stacks of firewood lie near the circle of ash.

The dais is where the altar and idol once stood. The residents use it as a crude fireplace now. The firewood is nothing special and is somewhat green.

Treasure: The chests were taken from a caravan. They're not locked. Inside are several sets of pewter and silver plates. The whole lot weighs 55 pounds and is worth 500 gp. There also are a few bottles and casks of wine and liquor, all drinkable, but of no particular value.

Area 13. Kitchen (CR 4)

Like the hall (**Area 12**), this chamber was once a chapel. Now the residents use it as a kitchen.

> A smoky fire atop a raised, open hearth at the eastern end of this small chamber fills the air with haze. A few covered pots and clay vessels lie in the smoldering coals. Closer at hand, a very sturdy looking table looks rather like an overturned cart or wagon. An assortment of bloodstained wooden slabs, crusty knives, and scraps of food sit on the table. A few slabs of meat (cooked and raw) and several bunches of herbs hang from the smoke-stained ceiling. There's one other exit, a door to the north.

Three servants always stay in here, cleaning game or preparing food. Two of the servants are human women, kidnapped from one of the villages in the fens. The third servant is a male **wereboar**. He's nominally the head cook, but he's really here to keep an eye on the women.

The cooks are busy and tend not to notice any fighting elsewhere unless it occurs right on their doorstep — in **Area 14** or right outside the door connecting this room to **Area 8**.

WEREBOAR **CR 4**
XP 1,200
hp 46 (*Pathfinder Roleplaying Game Bestiary 2* "Lycanthrope, Wereboar")

The wereboar hustles the women out if he notices any disturbances in the pavilion. He herds them through **Area 14** and into **Area 16** unless the trouble seems to be in **Area 14**, in which case he ushers them through **Area 3** and outside. If caught unawares, the wereboar pretends to be just another kidnapped servant. Add the following text if the cooks are still here when the party enters.

Three bedraggled-looking humans stand between the fire and the table, two women and a man. They're all dressed in soiled smocks, and their faces and arms are smeared with grease. When the door opens, the trio freezes in place and stare at you with wild eyes.

The kitchen holds nothing of interest or value, except, perhaps, the trio of cooks.

The humans don't fight, and merely shriek and cower if attacked. The wereboar follows suit, initially. He tries to bluff the party into leaving him behind along with his two charges. If that doesn't work, he looks for a chance to throw open the door to **Area 14**. Thereafter, he changes form and attacks the closest foe.

Development: Once the party deals with the wereboar, they can question the women (they won't talk in the wereboar's presence). They have the same information as the wererats in **Area 4**. The women are terrified of the tigers in **Area 14**.

Area 14. Guardpost (CR 7)

Like **Areas 12** and **13**, this chamber was once a chapel.

This chamber reeks with an overpowering, musky smell. Soiled rushes cover the floor. There's a deeper mound of rushes at the chamber's east end, or perhaps that area is raised a bit. There's not much time to study the architecture, however, as a veritable pride of striped, shaggy felines each about a big as a pony regard you with hungry eyes.

Gavriil keeps a group of **3 tigers** here to guard **Areas 15** and **16**.

TIGERS (3) **CR 4**
XP 1,200
hp 45 (*Pathfinder Roleplaying Game Bestiary* "Tiger")

The tigers attack anyone entering here except lycanthropes or visitors accompanied by lycanthropes. The tigers don't thinking much during combat. One or two tigers attack the nearest foe while the others try to circle around to the flanks.

Development: The tigers don't pay attention to what's going on elsewhere in the pavilion. Any disturbance here alerts the wereboar in **Area 13** and the weretigers in **Area 17**.

Area 15. Spiral Stairs

These stairs rise 25 feet to **Area 16**, then a few more feet before they crumble away to a broken shaft, with the top open the elements.

Area 16. Northeast Tower Ground Floor (CR 7)

This chamber once served as a bath. Today, Gavriil uses it as a prison.

Faint light filters down into this circular chamber through gratings in ceiling. A round pit, mostly filled with leaves, twigs, and masonry debris, takes up most of the floor. A cage of blackened iron bars hangs from the ceiling over the pit.

The pit once served as the bath. It's about four feet deep and filled nearly to the top with leaves and other detritus. The pool is home to **2 vipers** that Gavriil keeps here with regular offerings of live prey.

VIPERS (2) **CR 5**
XP 1,600
hp 51 (*Pathfinder Roleplaying Game Bestiary 2* "Snake, Emperor Cobra")

Gavriil added the iron cage to hold valuable prisoners (he keeps the key). The combination of locked cage and venomous snakes discourages escape attempts.

The vipers have full concealment in the pit. They wait quietly unless someone disturbs their nest or the cage.

Development: The vipers pay no attention to what's going on outside their chamber. Any fighting in here alerts the weretigers in **Area 17**. The wereboar in **Area 13** might come here if flushed out. The wereboar knows about the vipers and gives them the widest possible berth when sheltering here.

Area 17. Northeast Tower Upper Floor (CR 10)

This chamber looks much like **Areas 5** and **7**. It has windows in the same configuration as **Area 5** (though the weretigers keep the lower set of bars unlocked) and a floor with gratings similar to **Area 7**. Gavriil uses the place as a living space for himself and his weretiger bodyguards and as a guardpost.

A quartet of metal grates lie in this circular chamber's stone floor. At about floor level, two sets of windows look southeast and northwest. The southeast windows have bars, while the northwest pair are open and bare. Two pairs of windows, identical to the pairs at floor level, are about 25 feet farther up the walls. Above that soars a great, but ragged dome.

The chamber's furnishings include a very large canopied bed, a jumble of cushions, and at least a half dozen low planters overflowing with flowering vines, and a few brightly colored rugs.

Gavriil, his **tiger** animal companion and his 2 female weretiger bodyguards, **Inessa** and **Zhanna**, spend nearly all their time here. Usually, one keeps an eye on **Area 8** (through the barred windows) and the other watches the archway to the staircase outside (**Area 15**).

When possible, Gavriil and his guards attack from a distance. Gavriil uses spells such as *produce flame, chill metal,* or *call lightning bolt* spells as he deems most appropriate. The bodyguards stand at the windows firing their bows.

If foes manage to close to melee range, Gavriil uses *entangle* and *summon swarm* to slow up foes. Inessa and Zhanna do their best to protect Gavriil from melee attacks. Gavriil supports them with *magic fang* and even a few *cure wounds* spells. If forced to fight, Gavriil uses his natural weaponry.

Inessa and Zhanna fight to death, at least as long as Gavriil is still alive and kicking. Gavriil fights as long as both bodyguards are still on their feet. If forced to fight alone, Gavriil fights for a round or two, then dives out of window and into the pool in **Area 8** (the barred windows in here are kept unlocked). Once in the water, Gavriil stays submerged and tries to escape through the south sinkhole and out the pool at **Area 1A**.

INESSA AND ZHANNA (HUMAN FORM) CR 6
XP 2,400
Female human natural weretiger fighter 6 (*Pathfinder Roleplaying Game Bestiary 2* "Lycanthrope, Weretiger")
LE Medium humanoid (human, shapechanger)
Init +5; **Senses** low-light vision, scent; **Perception** +6

AC 15, touch 12, flat-footed 13 (+2 armor, +1 Dex, +1 dodge, +1 natural)
hp 55 (6d10+12 plus 6)
Fort +7; **Ref** +3; **Will** +4 (+6 vs. fear)
Defensive Ability bravery +2

Speed 30 ft.
Ranged mwk composite longbow +8/+3 (1d8+3/×3)
Special Attacks curse of lycanthropy, weapon training (natural +1)

Str 17, **Dex** 13, **Con** 15, **Int** 10, **Wis** 10, **Cha** 10
Base Atk +6; **CMB** +9; **CMD** 21
Feats Blind-fight, Dodge, Improved Initiative, Iron Will, Point-blank Shot, Power Attack, Weapon Focus (claw), Weapon Specialization (claw)
Skills Acrobatics +5, Perception +6, Sense Motive +2, Stealth +7
Languages Common
SQ armor training 1, change forms, lycanthropic empathy
Gear mwk composite longbow (+3 Str), *amulet of natural armor +1*, *bracers of armor +2*

INESSA AND ZHANNA (HYBRID FORM) CR 6
XP 2,400
Female human natural weretiger fighter 6 (*Pathfinder Roleplaying Game Bestiary 2* "Lycanthrope, Weretiger")
LE Large humanoid (human, shapechanger)
Init +6; **Senses** low-light vision, scent; **Perception** +8

AC 20, touch 12, flat-footed 17 (+2 armor, +2 Dex, +1 dodge, +6 natural, –1 size)
hp 67 (6d10+24 plus 6)
Fort +9; **Ref** +4; **Will** +6 (+2 vs. fear)
Defensive Ability bravery +2; **DR** 10/silver

Speed 30 ft.
Melee bite +13 (2d6+8), 2 claws +14 (1d8+10 plus grab)
Ranged mwk composite longbow +8/+3 (1d8+3/×3)
Space 10 ft.; **Reach** 10 ft.
Special Attacks curse of lycanthropy, pounce, rake (2 claws +9, 1d8+6 plus grab), weapon training (natural +1)

Str 17/25, **Dex** 13/15, **Con** 15/19, **Int** 10, **Wis** 10/14, **Cha** 10
Base Atk +6; **CMB** +14 (+18 grapple); **CMD** 27
Feats Blind-fight[B], Dodge[B], Improved Initiative[B], Iron Will[B], Point-blank Shot, Power Attack, Weapon Focus (claw), Weapon Specialization (claw)
Skills Acrobatics +10, Perception +8, Sense Motive +4, Stealth +8; (+12 in undergrowth) **Racial Modifiers** +4 Acrobatics, +4 Stealth
Languages Common
SQ armor training 1, change forms, lycanthropic empathy
Gear masterwork composite longbow (+3 Str), *amulet of natural armor +1*, *bracers of armor +2*

INESSA AND ZHANNA (ANIMAL FORM) CR 6
XP 2,400
Female human natural weretiger fighter 6 (*Pathfinder Roleplaying Game Bestiary 2* "Lycanthrope, Weretiger")
LE Large humanoid (human, shapechanger)
Init +6; **Senses** low-light vision, scent; **Perception** +8

AC 20, touch 12, flat-footed 17 (+2 armor, +2 Dex, +1 dodge, +6 natural, –1 size)
hp 67 (6d10+24 plus 6)
Fort +9; **Ref** +4; **Will** +6 (+8 vs. fear)
Defensive Ability bravery +2; **DR** 10/silver

Speed 40 ft.
Melee bite +13 (2d6+8), 2 claws +14 (1d8+10 plus grab)
Space 10 ft.; **Reach** 10 ft.
Special Attacks curse of lycanthropy, pounce, rake (2 claws +14, 1d8+10 plus grab), weapon training (natural +1)

Str 25, **Dex** 15, **Con** 19, **Int** 10, **Wis** 14, **Cha** 10
Base Atk +6; **CMB** +14 (+18 grapple); **CMD** 27
Feats Blind-fight, Dodge, Improved Initiative, Iron Will, Point-blank Shot, Power Attack, Weapon Focus (claw), Weapon Specialization (claw)
Skills Acrobatics +10 (+14 to jump), Perception +8, Sense Motive +4, Stealth +8 (+12 in undergrowth); **Racial Modifiers** +4 Acrobatics, +4 Stealth in undergrowth
Languages Common
SQ armor training 1, change forms, lycanthropic empathy
Gear *amulet of natural armor +1*, *bracers of armor +2*

GAVRIIL (HUMAN FORM) CR 9
XP 6,400
Male human natural weretiger druid 9 (*Pathfinder Roleplaying Game Bestiary 2* "Lycanthrope, Weretiger")
NE Medium humanoid (human, shapechanger)
Init +2; **Senses** low-light vision, scent; **Perception** +10

AC 16, touch 14, flat-footed 13 (+1 deflection, +2 Dex, +1 dodge, +2 natural)
hp 62 (9d8+9 plus 9)
Fort +9; **Ref** +7; **Will** +12; +4 vs. fey and plant-targeted effects
Immune poison

Speed 30 ft.
Special Attacks curse of lycanthropy, wild shape 3/day
Spells Prepared (CL 9th; concentration +11):
4th—*earth glide***, *flame strike* (DC 16)
3rd—*call lightning* (DC 15), *cure moderate wounds*, *jolt* (DC 15)
2nd—*chill metal* (DC 14), *elemental speech**, *flaming sphere* (DC 14), *heat metal* (DC 14), *soften earth and stone*
1st—*cure light wounds*, *longstrider*, *obscuring mist*, *produce flame*, *speak with animals*
0 (at will)—*detect magic*, *know direction*, *mending*, *read magic*

Str 10, **Dex** 14, **Con** 13, **Int** 15, **Wis** 14, **Cha** 10
Base Atk +6; **CMB** +6; **CMD** 20
Feats Blind-fight, Combat Casting, Dodge, Iron Will, Natural Spell
Skills Acrobatics +6, Handle Animal +10, Knowledge (nature) +15, Knowledge (planes) +10, Knowledge (religion) +10, Linguistics +3, Perception +10, Sense Motive +8, Spellcraft +10, Stealth +10, Survival +10
Languages Aquan, Common, Druidic, Ignan, Terran
SQ change forms, lycanthropic empathy, nature bond (tiger—Zalissa), nature sense, trackless step,

wild empathy +9, woodland stride
Gear *amulet of natural armor +2*, *cloak of resistance +2*, *ring of protection +1*, spell component pouch, 85 gp
*see *Pathfinder Roleplaying Game Advanced Player's Guide*
**see *Pathfinder Roleplaying Game Advanced Race Guide*

GAVRIIL (HYBRID FORM) CR 9
XP 6,400
Male human natural weretiger druid 9 (*Pathfinder Roleplaying Game Bestiary 2* "Lycanthrope, Weretiger")
NE Large humanoid (human, shapechanger)
Init +2; **Senses** low-light vision, scent; **Perception** +10

AC 20, touch 13, flat-footed 17 (+1 deflection, +2 Dex, +1 dodge, +7 natural, –1 size)
hp 89 (9d8+36 plus 9)
Fort +12; **Ref** +7; **Will** +12; +4 vs. fey and plant-targeted effects
DR 10/silver; **Immune** poison

Speed 30 ft.
Melee bite +12 (2d6+7), 2 claws +12 (1d8+7 plus grab)
Space 10 ft.; **Reach** 10 ft.
Special Attacks curse of lycanthropy, pounce, rake (2 claws +12, 1d8+7 plus grab), wild shape 3/day
Spells Prepared (CL 9th; concentration +11):
4th—*earth glide***, *flame strike* (DC 16)
3rd—*call lightning* (DC 15), *cure moderate wounds*, *jolt* (DC 15)
2nd—*chill metal* (DC 14), *elemental speech**, *flaming sphere* (DC 14), *heat metal* (DC 14), *soften earth and stone*
1st—*cure light wounds*, *longstrider*, *obscuring mist*, *produce flame*, *speak with animals*
0 (at will)—*detect magic*, *know direction*, *mending*, *read magic*

Str 10/25, **Dex** 14/15, **Con** 13/19, **Int** 15, **Wis** 14, **Cha** 10
Base Atk +6; **CMB** +14 (+18 grapple); **CMD** 28
Feats Blind-fight[B], Combat Casting, Dodge, Iron Will, Natural Spell, Rending Claws**
Skills Acrobatics +10, Handle Animal +10, Knowledge (nature) +15, Knowledge (planes) +10, Knowledge (religion) +10, Linguistics +3, Perception +10, Sense Motive +8, Spellcraft +10, Stealth +10 (+14 in undergrowth), Survival +10; **Racial Modifiers** +4 Acrobatics, +4 Stealth in undergrowth
Languages Aquan, Common, Druidic, Ignan, Terran
SQ change forms, lycanthropic empathy, nature bond (tiger—Zalissa), nature sense, trackless step, wild empathy +9, woodland stride
Gear *amulet of natural armor +2*, *cloak of resistance +2*, *ring of protection +1*, spell component pouch, 85 gp
*see *Pathfinder Roleplaying Game Advanced Player's Guide*
**see *Pathfinder Roleplaying Game Advanced Race Guide*

GAVRIIL (ANIMAL FORM) CR 9
XP 6,400
Male human natural weretiger druid 9 (*Pathfinder Roleplaying Game Bestiary 2* "Lycanthrope, Weretiger")
NE Large humanoid (human, shapechanger)
Init +2; **Senses** low-light vision, scent; **Perception** +10

AC 20, touch 13, flat-footed 17 (+1 deflection, +2 Dex, +1 dodge, +7 natural, –1 size)
hp 89 (9d8+36 plus 9)
Fort +12; **Ref** +7; **Will** +12; +4 vs. fey and plant-targeted effects
DR 10/silver; **Immune** poison

Speed 40 ft.
Melee bite +12 (2d6+7), 2 claws +12 (1d8+7 plus grab)
Space 10 ft.; **Reach** 10 ft.
Special Attacks curse of lycanthropy, pounce, rake (2 claws +12, 1d8+7 plus grab), wild shape 3/day
Spells Prepared (CL 9th; concentration +11):
4th—*earth glide***, *flame strike* (DC 16)
3rd—*call lightning* (DC 15), *cure moderate wounds*, *jolt* (DC 15)
2nd—*chill metal* (DC 14), *elemental speech**, *flaming sphere* (DC 14), *heat metal* (DC 14), *soften earth and stone*
1st—*cure light wounds*, *longstrider*, *obscuring mist*, *produce flame*, *speak with animals*
0 (at will)—*detect magic*, *know direction*, *mending*, *read magic*

Str 25, **Dex** 15, **Con** 19, **Int** 15, **Wis** 14, **Cha** 10
Base Atk +6; **CMB** +14 (+18 grapple); **CMD** 28
Feats Blind-fight, Combat Casting, Dodge, Iron Will, Natural Spell, Rending Claws**
Skills Acrobatics +10 (+14 to jump), Handle Animal +10, Knowledge (nature) +15, Knowledge (planes) +10, Knowledge (religion) +10, Linguistics +3, Perception +10, Sense Motive +8, Spellcraft +10, Stealth +10 (+14 in undergrowth), Survival +10; **Racial Modifiers** +4 Acrobatics, +4 Stealth in undergrowth
Languages Aquan, Common, Druidic, Ignan, Terran
SQ change forms, lycanthropic empathy, nature bond (tiger—Zalissa), nature sense, trackless step, wild empathy +9, woodland stride
Gear *amulet of natural armor +2*, *cloak of resistance +2*, *ring of protection +1*, spell component pouch, 85 gp
*see *Pathfinder Roleplaying Game Advanced Player's Guide*
**see *Pathfinder Roleplaying Game Advanced Race Guide*

ZALISSA CR —
XP —
Female tiger animal companion (*Pathfinder Roleplaying Game Bestiary* "Tiger")
N Large animal
Init +8; **Senses** low-light vision, scent; **Perception** +8

AC 23, touch 14, flat-footed 18 (+4 Dex, +1 dodge, +9 natural, –1 size)
hp 68 (8d8+32)
Fort +10; **Ref** +10; **Will** +4 (+8 vs. enchantment)
Defensive Abilities evasion

Speed 40 ft.
Melee bite +12 (1d8+7 plus grab), 2 claws +12 (1d6+7 plus grab)
Space 10 ft.; **Reach** 5 ft.
Special Attacks pounce, rake (2 claws +12, 1d6+7 plus grab)

Str 25, **Dex** 18, **Con** 18, **Int** 2, **Wis** 15, **Cha** 10
Base Atk +6; **CMB** +14 (+18 grapple); **CMD** 29 (33 vs. trip)
Feats Dodge, Improved Initiative, Multiattack, Power Attack, Toughness
Skills Acrobatics +10 (+14 to jump), Perception +8, Stealth +5
SQ tricks (attack, come, defend, down, fetch, fighting, guard, heel, seek, stay, track)

Development: If captured, Inessa and Zhanna say nothing if they think Gavriil is still alive. If convinced Gavriil is dead, the pair answer questions. They know the area fairly well, though they don't know where Gavriil hides all his loot.

If Gavriil fails to escape, he'll try to bargain for his life by revealing where he concealed all his treasures. He insists that he cannot call off any of his guards. He offers to help the party with some of the combat, but only as a cover for another escape attempt.

If the party asks Gavriil about the idol in **Area 18** (as they might if they've questioned Theronia in **Area 7**), he says he's hidden the coins and gems in a hollow space below the idol. In fact, Gavriil drops a gem in there from time to time to keep the gate that the idol marks open (see **Area 18**). If he thinks he can get away with it, Gavriil offers to "open" the idol for the group. In reality, he plans to summon a fire elemental to attack the party.

Treasure: Gavriil and his guards keep little in here except personal gear. The *robe of blending* Gavriil took from Theronia the medusa (see **Area 7**) is spread out atop the bed canopy. One of the cushions holds 18 red garnets worth 10 gp each (Gavriil uses these in the idol at **Area 18**).

Besides his gear, Gavriil carries keys to all the locks in the pavilion and the hostel.

Area 18. Idol (CR 7)

The hollow, bronze shell of some forgotten ancient deity stands here. The people who built the pavilion used it as a focus for summoning elementals.

> Water laps against a low stone apron, still mostly intact, here. A semicircular dais rises above the rippling water. A wide bronze shell, green with verdigris, is atop the dais. The shell's outside resembles some kind of birdlike (or perhaps amphibious) creature. Apparently, the shell was once a hollow bronze statue.

When the pavilion was new, the idol served as a summoning device for elementals of all kinds. Today, with the idol broken, the idol can summon only a single fire elemental once a month. To stay active, the idol must receive a live coal each day and a red gem worth at least 10 gp each month. If these offerings stop for even a day, the idol becomes inactive for at least a year. If the elemental the idol summons is killed, the idol likewise falls inactive for at least a year. Once inactive, the idol must receive offerings each day (and month) to become active again. If red gems worth at least 50 gp are placed in the idol, a **Huge fire elemental** erupts from its hollow interior.

HUGE FIRE ELEMENTAL **CR 7**
XP 3,200
hp 85 (*Pathfinder Roleplaying Game Bestiary* "Elemental, Fire")

Gavriil keeps the idol active. A look inside reveals a pile of gray ash and half-burned coals.

Gavriil has gotten to know the elemental from the idol and the creature attacks anyone else it meets, even if the character used the idol to summon it. In battle, the elemental tries to set as many foes afire as it can. The elemental fights to the death, or until all its foes retreat into the water. In the latter case, the elemental waits one round, then returns to its home plane if no one exits the water to carry on the fight.

Pilgrims' Hostel

The ancients built the hostel as a companion to the pavilion. Pilgrims who came from afar to visit the place were housed here.

The hostel lies about a quarter mile west of the pavilion. The faint remains of a path that once connected the two can still be seen. The path connects **Area 9** in the pavilion with **Area 1** in the hostel.

Gavriil uses the hostel as a prison for captives and as a hiding place for some of his loot.

Conditions and Features

The hostel has architecture similar to the pavilion and is as decayed and overgrown as the pavilion. Conditions inside are identical to those within the pavilion.

Approaching the Hostel

The party can reach the hostel by hacking through the undergrowth on the island, or by using the path leading from the pavilion. If they don't use the path, the island's guardian earth elemental attacks them, as noted in the **Approaching the Pavilion** section. In either case, the trees on the island tend to screen the group from view if they're traveling overland. The guard in **Area 6**, however, might see them as they enter. The guard makes a Perception check opposed by each character's Stealth check as the group enters the hostel. See **Area 6** for more details.

If the party tries the climb the hostel's walls or approach from the air, the air elemental in **Area 6** notices them and attacks unless the group is *invisible*. The guard in **Area 6** also sees visible aerial visitors.

Area 1: Entrance

> A weedy trail of crushed stone leads to a tumbledown pile of mud-colored stone as large as an aristocrat's villa. The place has a walled compound with three towers. Two of those are square and flank a narrow gateway that looks to be the only entrance. It's hard to tell how tall these entrance towers once were. All but the ground floors have fallen away now. The third tower is round, and it rises from the compound's southwest corner. It seems to be two floors high, with a tattered roof over the upper floor.

Area 1A. Entrance Towers (CR 9)

Priests and guards once used these chambers to keep an eye on the place. Gavriil's servants use them for much the same thing. Visitors can get a look inside by opening the doors or peering through the windows.

> The space in here is a square chamber with windows facing the complex's gateway and courtyard. Inside, there's a crude wooden table with a couple of wicker chairs and a few crates and barrels. There seems to be a spiral stair leading upward, but it's blocked with rubble. Opposite the stair lies a big mass of leaves, twigs, and old rags.

The staircases are indeed blocked. They once led to an upper floor, now gone.

Living in each tower are two guards or **4 elite wererats** in total. The pair in one tower rests while the other pair keeps watch. It's possible to duck past the guards using a Stealth check; however, the guard in **Area 6** also might see the intruder.

ELITE WERERATS (HUMAN FORM) CR 5
XP 1,600
Male human afflicted dire wererat slayer 5 (*Pathfinder Roleplaying Game Bestiary* "Lycanthrope, Wererat"; *Pathfinder Roleplaying Game Advanced Class Guide* "Slayer")
CE Medium humanoid (human, shapechanger)
Init +3; **Senses** low-light vision, scent; **Perception** +8

AC 17, touch 14, flat-footed 13 (+3 armor, +3 Dex, +1 dodge)
hp 52 (5d10+10 plus 10)
Fort +6; **Ref** +7; **Will** +3

Speed 30 ft.
Melee mwk rapier +9 (1d6/18-20)
Special Attacks sneak attack +1d6, studied target +2 (2nd, move action)

Str 10, **Dex** 16, **Con** 15, **Int** 14, **Wis** 10, **Cha** 10
Base Atk +5; **CMB** +5; **CMD** 19
Feats Combat Reflexes, Dodge, Iron Will, Toughness, Weapon Finesse
Skills Acrobatics +11, Climb +8, Disable Device +8, Intimidate +8, Perception +8, Sense Motive +8, Sleight of Hand +8, Stealth +11, Survival +8
Languages Common, Goblin, Orc
SQ change forms, lycanthropic empathy, slayer talents (fast stealth, finesse rogue), track +2
Gear masterwork studded leather, masterwork rapier

ELITE WERERATS (HYBRID FORM) CR 5
XP 1,600
Male human afflicted dire wererat slayer 5 (*Pathfinder Roleplaying Game Bestiary* "Lycanthrope, Wererat"; *Pathfinder Roleplaying Game Advanced Class Guide* "Slayer")
CE Medium humanoid (human, shapechanger)
Init +3; **Senses** low-light vision, scent; **Perception** +10

AC 19, touch 14, flat-footed 15 (+3 armor, +3 Dex, +1 dodge, +2 natural)
hp 57 (5d10+15 plus 10)
Fort +7; **Ref** +7; **Will** +5
DR 5/silver

Speed 30 ft.
Melee mwk rapier +9 (1d6+1/18-20) or bite +3 (1d4 plus disease)
Special Attacks sneak attack +1d6, studied target +2 (2nd, move action)

Str 12, **Dex** 17, **Con** 17, **Int** 14, **Wis** 15, **Cha** 10
Base Atk +5; **CMB** +6; **CMD** 20
Feats Combat Reflexes, Dodge, Iron Will, Toughness, Weapon Finesse
Skills Acrobatics +11, Climb +9, Disable Device +8, Intimidate +8, Perception +10, Sense Motive +10, Sleight of Hand +8, Stealth +11, Survival +10
Languages Common, Goblin, Orc
SQ change forms, lycanthropic empathy, slayer talents (fast stealth, finesse rogue), track +2
Gear masterwork studded leather, masterwork rapier

ELITE WERERATS (ANIMAL FORM) CR 5
XP 1,600
Male human afflicted dire wererat slayer 5 (*Pathfinder Roleplaying Game Bestiary* "Lycanthrope, Wererat"; *Pathfinder Roleplaying Game Advanced Class Guide* "Slayer")
CE Small humanoid (human, shapechanger)
Init +3; **Senses** low-light vision, scent; **Perception** +10

AC 20, touch 15, flat-footed 16 (+3 armor, +3 Dex, +1 dodge, +2 natural, +1 size)
hp 57 (5d10+15 plus 10)

Fort +7; **Ref** +7; **Will** +5
DR 5/silver

Speed 40 ft., climb 20 ft., swim 20 ft.
Melee bite +4 (1d3 plus disease)
Special Attacks sneak attack +1d6, studied target +2 (2nd, move action)

Str 12, **Dex** 17, **Con** 17, **Int** 14, **Wis** 15, **Cha** 10
Base Atk +5; **CMB** +5; **CMD** 19
Feats Combat Reflexes, Dodge, Iron Will, Toughness, Weapon Finesse
Skills Acrobatics +11 (+15 to jump), Climb +19, Disable Device +8, Intimidate +8, Perception +10, Sense Motive +10, Sleight of Hand +8, Stealth +15, Survival +10, Swim +11
Languages Common, Goblin, Orc
SQ change forms, lycanthropic empathy, slayer talents (fast stealth, finesse rogue), track +2

The piles of leaves and rags are wererat nests. When resting, the wererats hide themselves in their nests. When "on duty" the wererats sit at the tables, glancing out the windows and occasionally rising to take longer looks out the windows.

The two active wererats attack the moment they see intruders. They spread out as much as they can, trying to use their sneak attacks. The pair of resting rats joins the fray one round later.

Development: The guard in **Area 6** notices any fighting here after two rounds, and might see intruders even before a fight (see the Approaching the Hostel section). If alerted, the guard does not intervene, but sees to his own defenses.

If captured and questioned, the wererats can reveal much the same information as the wererats in the pavilion, plus the following:

- They know the hostel's layout and denizens, but not about Gavriil's caches of treasure (**Area 4**). They'll reveal the location of the prison (**Area 5**) and the kennels (**Area 4**), but insist they hold only mangy dogs.
- They know about the air elemental in **Area 6**, but not about the water elemental in **Area 2**.
- They tell the party that **Areas 3** and **6** house human mercenaries. They know these people are werewolves, but conceal that information if they can.

Area 2. Courtyard (CR 9)

> Beyond the gates is a smallish courtyard paved with muck-covered stones. Here and there, cattails and other water-loving plants grow in the pavement's gaps. At the courtyard's center stands a burbling fountain with a basin covered in lily pads.

The fountain is home to a **greater water elemental**. The elemental is concealed in the basin and attacks anyone except a hostel resident or someone in a resident's company. When the elemental attacks, the fountain spews water all over the courtyard (that's why the yard is soggy and covered in muck). While the fountain sprays, everyone in the courtyard is considered touching water for purposes of combat with the elemental. The spray also gives anyone light concealment at a distance of 10 to 20 feet and heavy concealment at a distance of 25 feet or more. The elemental fights to the death, and the fountain stops spewing one round after the elemental is killed or stops fighting.

GREATER WATER ELEMENTAL **CR 9**
XP 6,400
hp 123 (*Pathfinder Roleplaying Game Bestiary* "Elemental, Water")

Development: Everyone in the hostel notices when the fountain sprays. They avoid the blinding spray, but prepare for ranged combat against the invaders if they defeat the elemental.

Area 3. Tower Ground Floor (CR 6)

This area was once a bath similar to **Area 16** in the pavilion. Gavriil's servants turned it into a barracks of sorts. Gavriil fitted the current door with an arrow slit. The text below assumes the party is peering through the slit or opened the door.

> Faint light filters down into this circular chamber through gratings in the ceiling. A round pit in the floor's center looks mostly filled with rock. A dying fire smolders atop the rocks. Four crude bunks are arranged around the pit. Each bunk has a crude chest with a flat top at its foot. An open arch to the left reveals a spiral stair going up.

The stairs rise 25 feet to **Area 6**.

Living here are **4 werewolves**, but one is on guard duty in **Area 6** at any given time. Two of the three werewolves snooze in their bunks or pass the time gambling, using a chest as a table.

WEREWOLVES (4) **CR 2**
XP 600
hp 21 (*Pathfinder Roleplaying Game Bestiary* "Lycanthrope, Wererwolf")

If forewarned, one werewolf runs up the stairs to **Area 6** to make ranged attacks at any intruders. The remaining two try to hold the door. They keep their door closed, and one uses the arrow slit. If foes manage to breach the door, they switch to melee attacks. After the werewolves fight for a round or two, the dire wolves from **Area 4** break out of their kennels and join the fray. In battle, bloodlust quickly overcomes the werewolves and they fight to the death. If intruders break into **Area 4** and attack the dire wolves there, the werewolves join the fight after a round.

Development: The guard in **Area 6** notices a fight here immediately, and makes ranged attacks against any foes he can see.

If captured and questioned, the werewolves have the same information as the wererats in **Area 1**. If asked about the pavilion, they reveal much the same information as Theronia the medusa (see **Area 7** in the pavilion), though they try to bargain for their lives and freedom before revealing it.

Area 4. Kennels (CR 6)

These areas once served as dormitories for visiting pilgrims. Gavriil's servants converted them into kennels (none too clean) for **3 dire wolves**.

> Tiers of wooden bunks, sans mattresses, line the walls in this dank, stinky chamber. An uneven layer of twigs and soiled rushes covers the floor.

One dire wolf lies in each kennel, snoozing until a disturbance elsewhere in the hostel awakens it.

DIRE WOLVES (3) **CR 3**
XP 800
hp 37 (*Pathfinder Roleplaying Game Bestiary* "Wolf, Dire")

A dire wolf confronted in its kennel attacks the closest foe using its trip attack. As the battle continues, the wolf tries to trip as many foes as it can, attacking foes still on their feet when possible. Any fighting in a kennel or in **Areas 3** or **6** brings out all the dire wolves (they can easily burst the doors). When fighting in the open, the wolves try to surround a foe so they can fight as much as possible from the rear or flanks.

Development: The dire wolves and the werewolves is **Areas 3** and **6** support each other as noted in the **Area 3** description.

Treasure: Gavriil buried 2,600 gp under the floor of kennel 1, *belt of mighty constitution +2* and a *+1 greatsword* under kennel 2.

Area 5. Storage

This area once served as a meeting and dining hall for visiting pilgrims. Now it serves as a storage room similar to **Area 11** in the pavilion. It's not as cold as the pavilion's storage area, but it has a similar collection of trade goods.

If the party came to the area to rescue captives, any commoners who are not likely to bring any ransom payments are imprisoned here. Gavriil keeps them manacled and chained to rings set into the floor. He carries the keys with him.

Area 6. Tower Upper Floor (CR 9)

The staircase here descends 25 feet to **Area 3**.

The people who built the hostel used this area as a space for quiet reflection and meditating. Gavriil's servants use it as a guard post.

> This area is mostly open to the air. A circle of arches supports a badly damaged roof. There's a stone seat under each arch.

A **werewolf** stands guard here all the time. He keeps watch on **Area 1** and the courtyard. A **greater air elemental** also hovers here, near the peak of the roof.

The werewolf uses his bow against any foes he sees approaching. The werewolves there rally and attack when the guard does, along with the dire wolves from **Area 4**. The elemental has orders to attack anyone approaching the hostel from the air or trying to scale the walls. The elemental stays out of any fight unless someone takes to the air or climbs the walls, or if it is attacked itself. It generally uses its slam attacks, but uses its whirlwind power if it can do so without affecting any allies.

Once in combat, the elemental fights to the death, as does the werewolf.

WEREWOLF **CR 2**
XP 600
hp 21 (*Pathfinder Roleplaying Game Bestiary* "Lycanthrope, Wererwolf")

GREATER AIR ELEMENTAL **CR 9**
XP 6,400
hp 123 (*Pathfinder Roleplaying Game Bestiary* "Elemental, Air")

Development: If the party manages to capture the werewolf, he has the same information as his comrades in **Area 3**.

The Darkening of Namjan Forest

By Michael Curtis

The Darkening of Namjan Forest is an adventure intended for use by six to eight 6th- 8th-level PCs. The PCs encounter a lot of shadows in this adventure, so they should be well-equipped with magic weapons and *restoration* spells; nearly everything in this adventure drains Strength or inflicts negative levels. This is an exceptionally dangerous adventure! In the course of the adventure, the party explores the Namjan Forest, a woodland threatened by the creeping advance of the Plane of Shadow made manifest through the presence of a rare shadow elemental. This creature, a pure embodiment of the gloomy substance that underlies the Plane of Shadow, has escaped a long imprisonment within an ancient artifact known as the *darkling lanthorn*. The party must investigate the phenomenon affecting Namjan Forest, trace the Darkening back to its source, and destroy the agent seeking to infect the Material Plane with the touch of shadow.

The adventure is assumed to occur in a temperate forest region bordered by hills on the edge of a small duchy. The GM can alter the adventure to better fit his campaign world if necessary. In the ***Lost Lands*** campaign setting, the Namjan Forest is a region of the great Haunted Wood on the Frontier of the Grand Duchy of Reme. It lies in the gap between the Ashen Hills and the Gryphon Hills, some 150 miles north of the village of Dreikeng.

Background

The Namjan Forest is a modest-size woodlands growing in the fork between two chains of hills forested along the verge of civilization. The Namjan is an old wood, but not a pristine one. The residents of the realm

have long felled its trees, hunted its wildlife, and made charcoal within its borders. They've even gone so far as to live within it, and a small village stands upon the shores of the Fehlween River, the large waterway that flows through the Namjan. In short, the Namjan Forest was a place that seemed to harbor few mysteries. This impression, however, was horribly wrong.

Eons ago, when the hills were higher and the Fehlween wilder, the land now filled by the woodland was held by a sorcerer-warlord named Dyraxl Uhl-Kal-Totten. Uhl-Kal-Totten built his fortress upon an easily defensible rise of land near the center of the hill-bordered lands. From this keep, the sorcerer-warlord ruled over the small farms and villages that lay under his gaze and conducted arcane experiments to increase his magical prowess. Uhl-Kal-Totten, like many a man who carved his way to despotism, desired to expand his holdings, dreaming of an empire that spanned from distant shore to far-flung shore. And, like many a would-be tyrant, Uhl-Kal-Totten's dreams never came to fruition.

The circumstances that led to Uhl-Kal-Totten's fall are long forgotten. The few scraps of lore surviving from that distant time record that the sorcerer-warlord's enemies laid siege to his fortress, tearing down its walls with magic and hurled boulders. Uhl-Kal-Totten fought to the last, ultimately calling down powerful sorceries onto his own head to decimate himself, his keep, and the multitude of invaders who thirsted for his blood. When the smoke cleared and the dust settled, all that remained of the warlord and his fortress were scorched bones and broken stones. His enemies returned to their homelands and the dreams and accomplishments of Uhl-Kal-Totten were forgotten.

As the centuries rolled along, the lands that had been tamed under Uhl-Kal-Totten's rules grew wild once more. Seedlings became mighty trees, the high hills wore down like old teeth, and the Fehlween grew slow and tired. Where once was tilled fields and a towering keep, now only old trees and shallow gullies remained. But this placid landscape hid a dark secret.

Not all of Uhl-Kal-Totten's dreams died in the conflagration. When his fortress fell, the rubble buried his deepest cellars and undercrofts under a mountain of blasted debris. Deep underground slumbered magic long forgotten by history, relics the sorcerer-warlord planned on tapping to achieve his dreams of empire. Among those forgotten objects was the *darkling lanthorn*, a lamp that threw not light, but gloom, and contained an obscure and titanic elemental drawn from the Plane of Shadow.

The *darkling lanthorn* may have laid in quietude for millennia more had it not been for a tree. A mighty oak sprang up in the ruins above the forgotten foundations, its bole growing from the now nearly vanished stones that once formed Uhl-Kal-Totten's keep. As the tree grew, its roots dug deep, burrowing through the ground to seek out nutrients and support the tremendous trunk and branches that towered over the land. One of these probing roots wound its way through a gap in the masonry walls of Uhl-Kal-Totten's cellar and — perhaps by chance or perhaps guided by supernatural powers not fully understood — curled about the handle of the *darkling lanthorn*.

With the long deferred touch of a living creature, the *darkling lanthorn's* slumbering occupant awoke. The devastation that destroyed the fortress above had long since caused the protective barriers and wards placed around the *lanthorn* to weaken and the shadow elemental within the lamp easily shook off the feeble defenses that remained. With nothing left to contain it, the *darkling lanthorn's* power climbed out of its moldering erstwhile prison and snaked its way into the oak above.

The once-mighty tree is now ground zero for an infectious gloom spreading throughout the Namjan Forest, a plague known as the Darkening. Tendrils of darkness and wisps of misty gloom flow outward from the tree, staining everything they brush against with the touch of Shadow. The Fehlween's waters have turned ebony and the animals that once frolicked within the woods have… changed. Hunters and loggers have disappeared in the now-dark forest and those who survived speak of a relentless and every-hungry gloom intent on plunging the entire wood — and perhaps even the lands beyond it — into shadow.

The power within the *darkling lanthorn* is just beginning to grow and, unless someone can root out the source of this tangible darkness, the fate of those living outside the Namjan soon hangs in the balance. It is up to a band of intrepid adventurers to find the heart of darkness before it is too late.

Starting the Adventure

First alerted to the threat by the survivors of the Darkening of Stillwater (see **Namjan Forest, Area 4**), the Duke of the Northmarches sent a company of soldiers into the Forest to investigate the matter. When these well-armed veterans, led by the ranger, Egrihl, failed to return, seemingly swallowed up by the ill-omened woodland, his grace declared a standing reward of 2,500 gp and the promise of a noble claim on the Namjan to whoever discerns the origin of the gloomy menace and puts an end to it before it spreads across the duchy. With an offer of that magnitude, it is hoped the PCs devote themselves to finding and stopping the insidious taint afflicting Namjan Forest.

If the PCs are renowned adventurers, an agent of the duke seeks them out and explains his grace's offer. The agent can provide the information below and, if the PCs succeed in a DC 15 Diplomacy check, arranges an audience with the duke to further elaborate on the offer.

Gathering Information

A wise party seeks out further information about Namjan Forest and the mysterious events occurring within it before beginning its investigation. The PCs can obtain information by either questioning occupants of the nearby settlements of Dreikeng or Nerimar or through the duke or his agents. The following information is gleaned:

The shadowy infestation was first noticed about a week ago when the Fehlween turned dark. The river's discoloration was originally thought to be sedimentation flushed down from the hills, but the water soon had strange effects on the animals and people who drank from it.

In addition to the darkened waters of the Fehlween, the forest itself has grown dim. Shadows cling to branches like vines and pool in thickets, exuding an aura of menace. The sound of animal noise has diminished and even the air has grown heavy and still as if tainted by an invisible weight.

According to the refugees fleeing the forest, this encroaching darkness spreads like a sickness, infecting those exposed to its touch over several days. The creeping shadow drains away vitality from living creatures. Those touched by the gloom either vanish utterly, fading away as if ghosts, or are transformed by the darkness. Transformed creatures grow a dusky ash in color and manifest unnatural powers. Their minds become evil and they revel in violence.

Several areas of interest are in Namjan Forest, including two permanent settlements called Stillwater and Thistlehill; a low, stone-covered hill known as the Tumbles; a natural cave called the Gullet; and the ruins of an old watchtower of amazing age.

Stillwater is a human hamlet located on the western shore of the Fehlween River deep in the forest. According to refugees, it has been overwhelmed by the Darkening and the fate of its inhabitants is unknown.

Thistlehill is a small gnomish community situated near the western edge of the forest. The gnomes mine a rich quartz vein and trade the shining stones at Stillwater. No one knows if Thistlehill has been touched by the darkening or if the gnome miners are even aware of the threat.

The Gullet is a small cave located near the middle of the forest and is said to be home to various monsters. Legends conflict, and trolls, orcs, demons, and even a dragon have all been said to live within it.

The riverside hamlet of Stillwater is perhaps the best place for the party to begin its investigation of the Namjan. The village can be reached by either paddling up the Fehlween River or, if the party lacks water transport, by following a horse trail that runs along the east side of the river.

Random Encounters

The PCs are subject to random encounters while traveling through the Namjan and on the Fehlween River. There is a 20% chance of an encounter occurring at select intervals depending on whether the party is in the woods or on the river. The GM should check for random encounters twice a day while venturing through the forest, once in the late morning and once in the evening. If the party is traveling on the water, a random encounter check is made every hour while on the river. Use the following tables to determine the random encounter if one occurs.

Namjan Forest Random Encounters

1d8	Encounter
1	**Encroaching shadow** (see below)
2	**1d3 shadow elk** (see **Namjan Forest, Area 9**)
3	**1d3 grimseems** (see **Appendix: New Monsters**)
4	**Shadow owlbear** (see **Namjan Forest, Area 10**)
5	**Shadow wolf** (see below)
6	**Advanced shadow** (see **Area 1**)
7–8	**1d4 shadows**

Fehlween River Random Encounters

1d6	Encounter
1	**Encroaching shadow** (see below)
2	**Advanced shadow** (see **Appendix: New Monsters**)
3	**1d3 shadow alligator gar** (see **Namjan Forest, Area 3**)
4	**1d3 grimseems** (see **Area 1**)
5–6	**1d4 shadows**

Random Encounter Notes

Shadow Creatures: Animals and monsters that succumb to the Darkening gain frightening new powers. The GM should refer to the *Pathfinder Roleplaying Game Bestiary 4* for details on converting a typical creature a shadow creature and the changes made to their stat block.

Encroaching Shadow: A long, thin finger of shadow creeps out to wrap itself around a random PC. Treat the tendril as having a Stealth check result of 15. The targeted PC must succeed on a DC 13 Reflex save to avoid being touched by the shadow tendril. If the tendril is noticed by the PC or an ally who sees the tendril's approach and warns him, he makes the saving throw as normal. If unseen, the character has a –2 penalty on the save. On a failed saving throw, the finger latches onto the PC, siphoning his energy. The touched PC gains one temporary negative level.

The tendril continues to drain the PC on subsequent rounds, requiring the character to make a DC 12 Fortitude save or gain another temporary negative level. The affected PC or his allies can cut the tendril with silver or magical weapons (treat as AC 10 and 5 hit point) or can break free by making a DC 15 Strength check. Once broken or cut, the tendril dissipates into sooty mist.

The Darkening

Shadow's taint is slowing expanding across the forest, spreading from its epicenter of the Darkling Oak (see **The Namjan Forest, Area 12**). The forest map shows what portion of the woodland is already under Shadow's sway and what has yet to succumb to the creeping gloom. PCs can rest in a hex untouched by Shadow, allowing them to recoup and perhaps shake off Shadow's touch (see "The Danger of Shadow Inflection" below).

Once the adventure begins, the GM rolls 1d4+1 at the start of each day. The result is the number of hexes on the forest map that Shadow spreads to. The GM then determines which hexes are affected and marks them to chart Shadow's progress. The GM can choose the afflicted hexes randomly, using whatever means he desires, or pick areas that are most dramatically appropriate and heighten tension among the PCs (the party awakens to discover Shadow surrounded them during the night, forcing them to venture through affected land to escape, for example).

If Shadow ever claims the entire Namjan Forest, its grip become absolute. Even the destruction of the *darkling lanthorn* and its elemental defender is insufficient to break Shadow's hold on the land and further troubles are bound to affect the region (see **Concluding the Adventure** for further details and ideas).

The Danger of Shadow Infection

The influence of the *darkling lanthorn* pervades Namjan Forest, insinuating itself into every living creature within its borders. The PCs are subject to this infection as they explore the tainted woodlands and, should they fail to root out the source of the corruption quickly, may succumb to its effects.

Each day (or portion thereof) a PC is within the boundaries of the forest, he must succeed on a DC 10 Fortitude save or become drained of vitality. This drain manifests as a temporary negative level. Negative levels gained through exposure to the Darkening cannot be relieved by resting while inside any portion of the Namjan Forest under Shadow's hold. A PC suffering from temporary negative levels due to the Darkening can be cured only by resting in an unaffected area of forest or outside its boundaries. A *restoration* or *greater restoration* spell removes the temporary negative levels normally.

PCs directly exposed to the spreading gloom also lose vitality. A PC drinking from the tainted waters of the Fehlween River or eating the flesh of a shadow-infected creature must succeed on a DC 15 Fortitude save or gain a temporary negative level.

A creature reduced to 0 levels from exposure to the Darkening does not die as normal, but is instead completely overcome by the shadow taint. An overcome creature either fades away to the Plane of Shadow (75% chance) or becomes a shadow creature (25% chance). In either event, the character becomes an NPC no longer under the player's control.

Namjan Forest

Namjan Forest is predominately first- and second-growth trees of maple, oak, spruce, and pine. The forest floor is covered by a thick layer of rich, dark loam that supports small plants and shrubs, as well as growths of mushrooms, mosses, and similar low flora. Deadfalls are common away from the trails that snake through the woods. Close to these paths, fallen limbs and dead trees have been cleared for firewood and charcoal-making.

General Features

Atmosphere: The Forest is much quieter than normal. Little animal noise is heard inside the forest, and the few sounds that are present echo from areas not yet overcome by the Darkening. The air is still and unmoving, and travelers experience a sense of being watched from the ever-present shadows.

Trails: Two types of paths wander through the forest: main trails and secondary footpaths. The trail links the settlements of Thistlehill and Stillwater with the outside world, while the smaller footpaths leave the main trail to reach smaller sites of interest inside the woodlands. The main trail is wide enough to accommodate two horses and riders traveling side-by-side, while the footpaths are narrower, forcing riders into a single file. The main trail is largely clear of forest debris, and the occasional sign points in the direction of Thistlehill and Stillwater. Footpaths lack signage and tend to be partially overgrown by brush.

Illumination: Due to the effects of the Darkening, portions of Namjan Forest are permanently cloaked in dense shadows. These shades are ominous and seem to almost possess a physical heft. Draperies of gloom dangle like hanging moss from tree limbs and darkness collects in drifts like fallen snow beneath the canopy. This cloak of shadows means that even in daylight the forest is considered to have dim lighting. Additionally, as a result of the overall gloom, targets farther than 60 ft. away from the party are considered to have concealment.

The Fehlween River: The river averages between 60 and 100 ft. in width and is 30 ft. deep at its center. The waters of the Fehlween are

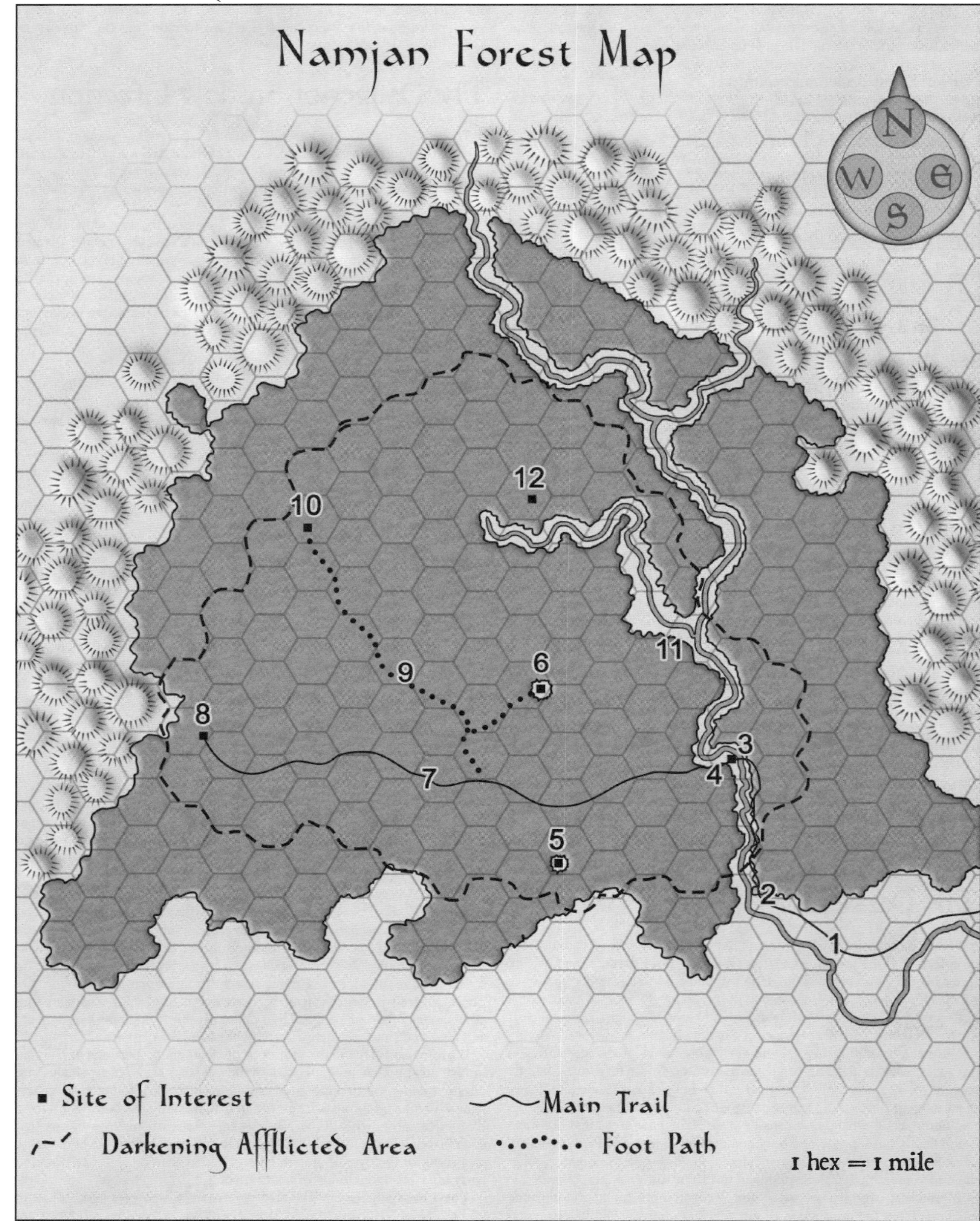
Namjan Forest Map
N
W
E
S
12
10
11
9
6
8
3
7
4
5
2
1
Site of Interest
Main Trail
Darkening Affllicted Area
Foot Path
1 hex = 1 mile

pitch black due to the Darkening as shadow creeps down its length. An individual putting his hand in the water discovers the fluid has an inexplicable heft as if filled with sediment, but there is no gritty feel to the river. In fact, the waters feel almost silky, but it is a silkiness that has no place on this earth. Physical contact with the water is not hazardous, but see **The Danger of Shadow Infection** for the consequences of drinking from the river.

Namjan Forest

Area 1. Shadow Attack

> The sound of screams rings from the riverbank. A small boat packed with bags, tools, and similar goods rests on the shore among reeds and mud. A body lies sprawled besides the boat, looking curiously drained and ashen. A human male dressed in homespun clothing stands over the body swinging a wood axe wildly. Looming over the panicked man is a patch of deep darkness that possesses a vaguely humanoid shape.

The woodsman and his now-dead companion are refugees fleeing the Darkening by traveling down the Fehlween River when they encountered an **advanced shadow**. They took to the shore to escape the creature, but it killed one of them and is set on slaying the other.

The advanced shadow concentrates its attacks on the woodsman, killing him in 2 rounds unless destroyed or driven off. It attacks the party if they intervene.

ADVANCED SHADOW **CR 4**
XP 1,200
Pathfinder Roleplaying Game Bestiary, "Shadow"
CE Medium undead (incorporeal)
Init +4; **Senses** darkvision 60 ft.; **Perception** +12

AC 19, touch 19, flat-footed 14 (+4 deflection, +4 Dex, +1 dodge)
hp 25 (3d8+12)
Fort +5; **Ref** +5; **Will** +6; +2 bonus vs. channeled energy
Defensive Abilities channel resistance +2, incorporeal; **Immune** undead traits

---

Speed fly 40 ft. (good)
Melee incorporeal touch +6 (1d6 Str damage)
Special Attacks create spawn

Str —, **Dex** 18, **Con** —, **Int** 10, **Wis** 16, **Cha** 19
Base Atk +2; **CMB** +6; **CMD** 21
Feats Dodge, Skill Focus (Perception)
Skills Fly +14, Intimidate +10, Perception +12, Stealth +10 (+14 in dim light, –4 in bright light); **Racial Modifiers** +4 Stealth in dim light, –4 in bright light
SQ create spawn, strength damage

If the woodsman survives the fight, he thanks the party and provides any information listed under "Gathering Information" above, as well as directions to the various places of interest (see Namjan Forest map). He has no desire to join the party and only wishes to escape. He insists on burying his dead companion, unaware that the man rises as a shadow in 1d4 hours. Unless *gentle repose* is cast upon the corpse, it crawls from its grave as a newborn shadow and the woodsman later becomes its first victim. If the woodsman dies from the advanced shadow's attack and *gentle repose* is not cast on the bodies, the two newly spawned shadows track down the party and attack after dark during the PCs' first night inside the forest (treat as an automatic nighttime random encounter).

The boat is packed with clothes, tools, and other household goods the two owned. The only objects of value or interest are a pair of lanterns (full), a shovel, a wood axe, two daggers, a shortbow and 20 arrows, a small barrel half filled with whiskey, a pipe and full tobacco pouch, and a leather sack containing 56 cp, 24 sp, and 6 gp.

Area 2. Forest Trail

> A dirt path wide enough to accommodate two riders traveling side by side leads into the forest. The branches above form a tunnel of leaves that hang motionless in the still air. The hairs on your neck stand up as you view the forest, for it feels as if something inexplicable is missing from the woods.

This main trail enters Namjan Forest at this point and winds its way through the woods until it ends at Thistlehill (**Area 8**). Traveling on the trail is considered normal terrain. PCs walking or riding through the forest proper move as if traversing difficult terrain.

Area 3. River Bridge (CR 4)

> A 100-foot-long wooden bridge crosses the inky waters 20 feet above the river. Fashioned from rough timbers lashed and nailed together, the bridge is wide enough to allow wagons to cross. A pair of thin-looking railings run along the edges of the span, providing some protection against falling into the river below.

This bridge once allowed traffic to and from Stillwater to cross the river, but the corruption of shadow has undermined its purpose. The touch of shadow has weakened the bridge's pilings, and the span is now a hazard to travelers. Besides its failing condition, **2 Large shadow alligator gars**, tainted by shadow, swim around the bridge's supports and are drawn to individuals in the water. The savage fish immediately attack any creature that falls into the river.

The bridge has a cumulative 10% chance per person of collapsing. Thus, the first person to travel across it has a 10% chance of causing a collapse, while the fourth risks a 40% chance. A party of six faces a 60% chance of collapsing the bridge if they all cross it together. A large transport such as a horse or cart automatically causes the bridge supports to fail.

If a collapse occurs, the person or creature causing the collapse and anyone within 10 ft. must succeed on a DC 10 Reflex save or fall into the Fehlween River and take 1d6 points of damage from the fall.

GIANT SHADOW ALLIGATOR GARS (2) **CR 3**
XP 800
Male shadow giant gar (*Pathfinder Roleplaying Game Bestiary 2* "Gar,";*Pathfinder Roleplaying Game Bestiary 4*, "Shadow Creature")
N Large outsider (aquatic, augmented animal, native)
Init +5; **Senses** darkvision 60 ft., low-light vision; **Perception** +6

AC 14, touch 10, flat-footed 13 (+1 Dex, +4 natural, –1 size)
hp 17 (2d8+8)
Fort +7; **Ref** +4; **Will** +1
Defensive Abilities shadow blend; **Resist** cold 5, electricity 5; **SR** 9

Speed swim 60 ft.
Melee bite +4 (1d8+6 plus grab)
Space 10 ft.; **Reach** 10 ft.

Str 18, **Dex** 12, **Con** 19, **Int** 1, **Wis** 13, **Cha** 2

Base Atk +1; **CMB** +6 (+10 grapple); **CMD** 17 (can't be tripped)
Feats Improved Initiative
Skills Perception +6, Swim +12

Shadow Blend (Su) In any illumination other than bright light, a shadow creature blends into the shadows, giving it concealment (20% miss chance). A shadow creature can suspend or resume this ability as a free action.

Area 4. Stillwater (CR 7)

A cluster of small cottages stands along the western shore of the dark river. These rude huts appear dim and indistinct, their edges blurred by shadows. The structures almost seem as if they are fashioned from gossamer scraps of gloom rather than wood and plaster. The air surrounding the hamlet is also dim and heavy with darkness as if a cloud of soot and ash clings to the village with an unrelenting grip. You detect no signs of life.

Stillwater succumbed to the Darkening swiftly as its residents and its existence depended on the Fehlween River. The hamlet is entirely corrupted by shadow and is no longer part of the Material Plane.

Most of the two-score residents of Stillwater died from shadow's infection, but a half-dozen emerged from the blight as servant of the Darkening. Lurking along the gloomy edges of town are **4 shadows** that ambush anyone who enters the village.

SHADOWS (4) **CR 3**
XP 800
hp 19 (*Pathfinder Roleplaying Game Bestiary* "Shadow")

The cottages of Stillwater are insubstantial, being nothing more than dark reflections of the Shadow Plane. Solid objects pass through them and even magical weapons and spells have no more effect than slicing a shadow with a knife. PCs peering inside the buildings observe that the Darkening overcame Stillwater suddenly. Half-eaten, shadowy meals sit atop gossamer tables and chores appear to have stopped mid-task. A successful DC 12 Perception check discerns that the occupants of buildings on the southeast end of the village had some warning before being overcome by the march of shadow, suggesting the encroachment came from the north or west.

Area 5. The Charcoal-Maker's Shack

The smell of burnt wood hangs heavy in the gloomy air. Before you is a small clearing containing a single hut made of cut timbers and sod. A ring of charred wood, dead coals, and ash surrounds the clearing, encompassing the entire area within its blackened embrace.

Until recently, the hut was home to one of the charcoal-makers who dwelt in the forest. As the Darkening spread through the woods, the charcoal-maker and his family found themselves surrounded by the encroaching shadows. Seeking to save themselves, they heaped wood in a ring around their home and set it alight to drive back the darkness. This worked well until nightfall when the burning barrier threw more shadows than it drove away, and the charcoal-maker, his wife, and their son watched in horror as the Darkening reached for them. Determined not to fall to it embrace, the man killed his wife and child, then took his own life, denying the shadows more victims.

The ashes surrounding the hut are cool to the touch, having burned out a few days ago. Inside the burned area, tendrils of shadow lurk in depressions in the ground and crouch by the timber and cut-sod hut. Despite their presence, the hut can be entered without danger.

Inside the small, two-room hut are the three bodies of the charcoal-maker and his family. Clouds of blowflies fill the air in the dark hovel, and the smell is ghastly. From their wounds, it is apparent that the wife and son died from slit throats and the husband perished from a single stab to the heart. The knife's hilt juts from his chest, his stiff hand still on the handle.

Little can be learned from this place, but PCs who don't mind pilfering the dead find a gold wedding band (50 gp value) on the wife's finger and a carved wooden box containing 67 cp and 14 sp if they search the hut.

Area 6. Ancient Watchtower Site (CR 4)

> In a dark clearing stands the broken remains of an old watchtower. The structure is missing its upper floors and is gutted by fire and time, leaving only the shell of a once-formidable redoubt. The ruin seems to stand like a tombstone to some forgotten age.

A crumbling relic from the days when Dyraxl Uhl-Kal-Totten ruled the land, the watchtower survived the collapse of his rule and served as a safe refuge for travelers for centuries before falling utterly into decay. The ruin later provided shelter for woodsmen and sometime bandits, but is now home to some of shadow's spawn.

Lurking inside the watchtower's shell are **2 grimseems** (see **Appendix: New Monsters**). They hide during the daytime, but attack if the ruin is entered while the sun is high. After nightfall, the two elementals emerge to hunt and attack the PCs if the party camps nearby.

GRIMSEEMS (2) **CR 2**
XP 600
hp 32 (see **Appendix: New Monsters**)

The watchtower's interior is 50 ft. square and filled with mounds of fallen masonry, underbrush, and vines. A small fire pit containing cold ashes and charred wood is dug at the center of the ruin.

Overlooked by travelers, a forgotten treasure still resides inside the shell. A bandit gang once buried their loot here, but internal squabbling and eventual murder ensured the trove was forgotten, its location lost with the death of the bandits. A successful DC 20 Perception check discerns a few odd scratches on a large slab of fallen stone. Lifting the stone — which requires a DC 15 Strength check — uncovers a shallow hole containing a large bundle wrapped in oilskin. Inside the parcel is a wrapped stack of 10 beaver pelts (2 gp value each), an ermine-trimmed coat (25 gp value), a pair of silver candelabras (15 gp value each), a longsword scabbard wrapped with gold wire wrapped and adorned with semi-precious stones (200 gp value), a sack containing 27 sp and 15 gp, and a glass vial filled with a *potion of cure light wounds*.

Area 7. The Soldiers' Fate (CR 6)

> The faint glimmer of steel is visible on the narrow trail that winds through the gloom. A closer look reveals it to be several chainmail shirts, metal shields, spears, and swords strewn about the path. Mixed in among the discarded arms and armaments are tunics, breeches, and boots. It is as if the wearers decided they no longer wished to be encumbered by raiment and weapons and hastily shed them.

The duke's men succumbed on this spot to the Darkening and either perished or were consumed. Those absorbed by shadow's grasp left their gear behind. Their equipment and clothing, however, is not all that remains of them. While some of those devoured by shadow sought out the *darkling lanthorn* (see **The Cellars, Area 10**), a few remained and have gorged themselves on the living energy of creatures in the woods, growing fat and fearsome in their feasting.

Along the sides of the path are **2 advanced shadows**. They first devoured some of their fellow soldiers, but now subsist on the occasional animal that survives in the forest. They haunt this stretch of path until destroyed.

ADVANCED SHADOWS (2) **CR 4**
XP 1,200
hp 25 (See **Area 1**)

The discarded weapons and equipment along the path consist of chainmail shirts, spears, longwords, and shields for a dozen men. There are also four light crossbows and four bolt cases with 10 bolts remaining in each. Besides the arms and armor, PCs find a dozen sets of travelers' clothes and 12 small sacks holding water skins and three days of rations. Among the mundane supplies are pouches containing a total of 46 cp, 77 sp, 15 gp, two silver rings (10 gp value each), a gold hoop earring (5 gp value), and a small garnet (50 gp value).

Area 8. Thistlehill

> The ground rises slightly here to form a 10-foot-high hillock in the midst of a gloomy clearing. In the side of the hill is a wide, low door bracketed by thick timber posts and lintel. A well-worn path leads up to the shut door.

This is the main entrance to the gnome burrow of Thistlehill, the other settlement inside Namjan Forest. Like their neighbors in Stillwater, Thistlehill fell to the spread of the Darkening, and most of its residents were carried off or corrupted by the touch of shadow. A bastion of hope remains in Thistlehill, however. The gnomes mined a small vein of gemstones that absorb and release light. This makes the gems potent weapons against shadow. More information on the gnome burrow is presented in the Thistlehill chapter.

Area 9. Hunter and Hunted (CR 6)

> The sound of howling and the thump of hooves on the soft forest floor ring out around you. Bursting from out of the trees comes a pack of wolves, their eyes bright with panic. A moment later, another beast rushes from among the boles, branches tearing free from trees in its passing. Pursuing the pack is a large elk, its fur a dusky ash color. Strands of writhing shadows dangle from its horns.

The elk succumbed to the Darkening, turning it fearsome and hungry for vitality. When the wolf pack encountered the afflicted animal, they found themselves going from predator to prey. Now they flee the elk and their flight brings them into the party's path.

Emerging from the woods are **4 wolves** and a **shadow elk**. The wolves are panicked and may attack the party if PCs fail to get out of their path. The elk, seeing more vitality in the party than the wolves, ceases its pursuit to siphon life from the PCs.

WOLVES (4) **CR 1**
XP 400
hp 13 (*Pathfinder Roleplaying Game Bestiary* "Wolf")

SHADOW ELK **CR 2**
XP 600
Pathfinder Roleplaying Game Bestiary 3 "Herd Animal, Elk"; *Pathfinder Roleplaying Game Bestiary 4* "Shadow Creature"
N Medium outsider (augmented animal, native)
Init +3; **Senses** darkvision 60 ft., low-light vision; **Perception** +7

AC 13, touch 13, flat-footed 10 (+3 Dex)
hp 15 (2d8+6)
Fort +6; **Ref** +8; **Will** +2
Defensive Abilities shadow blend; **Resist** cold 5, electricity 5; **SR** 8

Speed 50 ft.
Melee gore +3 (1d6+2), 2 hooves –2 (1d3+1)

Str 14, **Dex** 17, **Con** 16, **Int** 2, **Wis** 15, **Cha** 7
Base Atk +1; **CMB** +3; **CMD** 16 (20 vs. trip)
Feats Lightning Reflexes, Run[B]
Skills Acrobatics +3 (+7 to jump with a running start, +11 to jump), Perception +7

Shadow Blend (Su) In any illumination other than bright light, a shadow creature blends into the shadows, giving it concealment (20% miss chance). A shadow creature can suspend or resume this ability as a free action

It is possible for the wolves to be magically-induced to aid the party via spells such as *animal friendship* or *dominate beast*, but the canines have advantage on their saving throw due to their frenzied state. If charmed successfully, the wolves calm and act according the parameters of the spell.

Area 10. The Gullet (CR 5)

> Large rocks protrude from the forest floor in this vicinity, leaning upon one another like staggering drunkards. Two especially large outcroppings form an upside-down V with a dark cave mouth visible in the gap between them. The air here smells foul and rank.

A careful inspection of the area accompanied by a DC 15 Perception check reveals several large footprints winding among the rocks. A DC 9 Knowledge (nature) or Survival check identifies the tracks as bear tracks, but a DC 14 check instead recognizes them as owlbear tracks.

The cave measures roughly 30 ft. square and is home to a **shadow owlbear**. It remains inside its cave during daylight hours, emerging to hunt only after dark.

SHADOW OWLBEAR **CR 5**
XP 1,600
Pathfinder Roleplaying Game Bestiary "Owlbear"; *Pathfinder Roleplaying Game Bestiary 4* "Shadow Creature"
N Large outsider (augmented magical beast, native)
Init +5; **Senses** darkvision 60 ft., low-light vision, scent; **Perception** +12

AC 15, touch 10, flat-footed 14 (+1 Dex, +5 natural, –1 size)
hp 47 (5d10+20)
Fort +10; **Ref** +5; **Will** +2
Defensive Abilities shadow blend; **DR** 5/magic; **Resist** cold 10, electricity 10; **SR** 11

Speed 30 ft.
Melee bite +8 (1d6+4), 2 claws +8 (1d6+4 plus grab)
Space 10 ft.; **Reach** 5 ft.

Str 19, **Dex** 12, **Con** 18, **Int** 2, **Wis** 12, **Cha** 10
Base Atk +5; **CMB** +10 (+14 grapple); **CMD** 21 (25 vs. trip)
Feats Great Fortitude, Improved Initiative, Skill Focus (Perception)
Skills Perception +12

Shadow Blend (Su) In any illumination other than bright light, a shadow creature blends into the shadows, giving it concealment (20% miss chance). A shadow creature can suspend or resume this ability as a free action.

If PCs enter the cave during the day, the owlbear is asleep 50% of the time. It automatically awakens if attacked, but suffers disadvantage on its initiative check due to its sudden rousing. It mauls any PC in melee range. If the party is out of range, it uses its shadow-ripping ability for 2 rounds before closing the distance and fighting with beak and claws.

The cave contains bones and owlbear scat. Mixed in among the detritus are a rusty chain shirt, a *+1 dagger*, a set of ivory gaming dice (15 gp value), and a gold belt buckle with amethyst stone (200 gp value) attached to a rotting leather belt.

A crude and extremely old map is scratched on the cave wall. This map dates back to the time of Dyraxl Uhl-Kal-Totten and depicts the region as it was then. The Fehlween River is easily identifiable and, with that as a guide, the PCs can deduce the approximate locations of the Watchtower (**Area 6**) and the Darkling Oak (**Area 12**). Each site is depicted as a crude tower and keep, and may hint at further locations in need of exploration to find the source of the Darkening.

Area 11. Shadows Merge

> A small tributary flows into the Fehlween River from the west, its waters just as inky dark as the shadow-rich liquid of the main river. Stands of soot-colored reeds cling in clusters to the riverbanks, their tufted stalks unmoving in the still air.

A DC 15 Perception check notices a punt pulled up to the northern bank of the tributary and mostly hidden among the reeds. PCs inspecting the long, narrow boat find the bottom of the punt stained with copious amounts of blood. Resting in the midst of the gore is a human leg severed at the shin and a blood-stained fishing knife. Writing is carved into the seat of the punt, scratched into the wood by a shaky hand. The writing is in Common and reads:

"The dark crept in and touched my leg. Cut it off, but too late. I'm going, going dark and light. Came down the thinny way, out of the Tumbles. Can't st…"

The scratched message ends abruptly.

The message was written by the unfortunate former owner of the severed leg who became infected by the Darkening as it crept down this narrow tributary ("the thinny way") from the tree. The infected boatman severed the appendage but shadow overtook him and his body faded away. He had just enough time to scrawl his warning before his physical body dissipated.

If the party continues past the meeting of the waters, they soon see that the waters of the Fehlween clear, losing their dark taint. It is obvious that the source of the river's Darkening is the tributary, which perhaps spurs them deeper into the forest toward the source of the shadows.

Area 12. The Darkling Oak

The ground rises slightly here, forming a low island among the gloomy forest floor. This small hillock appears formed by a mass of ancient, fallen stones. Tumbled together and half-buried under centuries of forest loam, the moss-covered stones are weathered by storms and time. Sprouting among the broken masonry is a titanic oak rising 50 ft. into the air. Its trunk is dusky ash in color, its leaves glossy obsidian. Hanging from the branches are thick coils of shadow that drip slowly down toward the ground like black honey.

This tree is in direct contact with the *darkling lanthorn* and the conduit to shadow. It is responsible for awakening the relic's power and starting the Darkening. As such, the oak is entirely infected with shadow's touch and only partially exists on this plane. Any attack or destructive spell targeting the oak temporarily damages it, but the tree heals its massive trunk and limbs moments later as the injury patches over with shadow stuff.

The dripping coils of shadow are dangerous, and the tree instinctively lashes out with the viscous substance at any creature approaching within 20 ft. The tree has a +2 modifier to initiative checks and it makes up to four attacks each round, striking with a +6 incorporeal touch attack and draining 1d4 points of Strength damage with a successful hit. There is nothing the PCs can do to destroy this tree or its shadow coils. Once they sever its connection with the *darkling lanthorn*, it becomes a normal tree again and can be destroyed by any method that would destroy a tree.

The earth-covered mound of broken rubble is all that remains of Dyraxl Uhl-Kal-Totten's stronghold. This rise of land measures 100 ft. in diameter and 20 ft. tall at its highest point. The Shadow Oak sprouts from the western end of the hillock. Slightly south of the tree at a distance of 20 ft., a narrow, dark tunnel mouth is visible between two massive pieces of masonry. It appears to lead to a cave or similar descent within the mound. This tunnel connects to **The Cellars, Area 1.**

Thistlehill Gnome Burrow

This small burrow was home to two dozen gnomish miners and woodworkers. They did a brisk trade with their human neighbors of Stillwater, selling their wares to dealers there in return for the necessities and luxuries the gnomes desired. When the Darkening spread through the Namjan, the gnomes barred their doors and hoped to withstand the infection. They failed and were afflicted by shadow's touch. Only one gnome remains untouched, surviving thanks to the strange properties of the sunbreath quartz the gnomes mined.

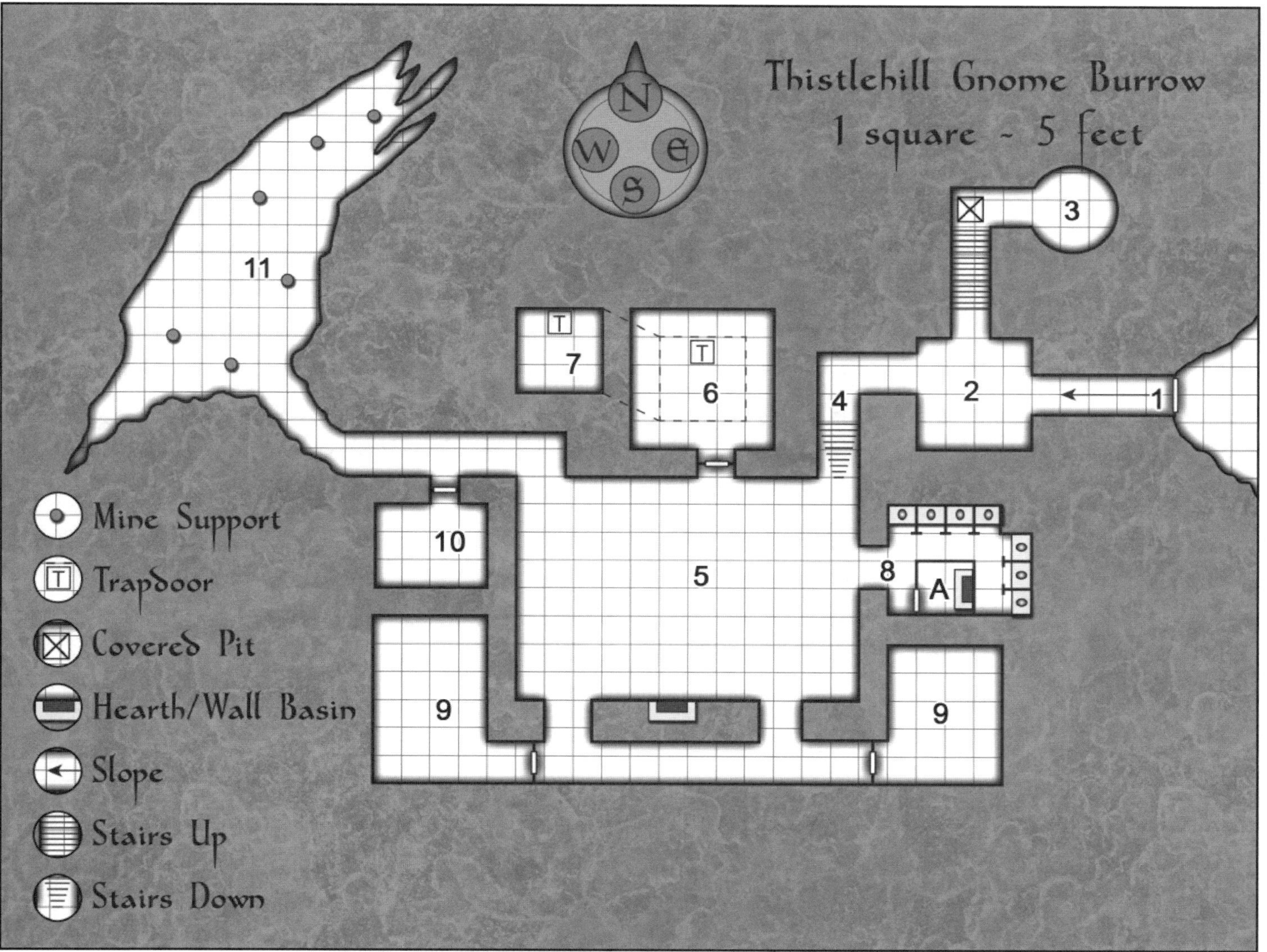

General Features

Thistlehill is excavated out of the rocky soil beneath the forest, but it's no series of earthen caves and tunnels. The floors, walls, and ceilings of Thistlehill are lined by stout timber planks, planed smooth and pegged firmly into place. The air is dry and cool, and holds only a trace of rich earthy scents.

Interior Dimensions: Thistlehill is a gnomish home and sized accordingly. Ceilings stand 6 ft. high and corridors are 8 ft. wide at the most. Human-sized creatures can move and act without penalty inside Thistlehill, but find the place cramped and uncomfortable after long.

Illumination: In better days the interior of Thistlehill was lit by thick beeswax candles set in wall holders or hanging chandeliers. These are still present, but the taint of shadow makes the interior a place of full darkness and prevents candles from being lit. If lit, the flame struggles feebly for a moment then fails. Other sources of illumination function normally inside Thistlehill, unlike in the cellar (see below).

Area 1. Front Door

The door measures 6 ft. high and 8 ft. wide and is made from stout oak bound with iron. A small closed peephole pierces the left-hand door, looking out at gnome-eye level. The door is barred from within, but the bar holding it closed is small (better to be managed by the gnomes). Bashing the door open is achieved with a DC 20 Strength check or the use of a *knock* spell.

No one is guarding the door, but multiple unsuccessful attempts to force open the portal alerts the gloom gnomes at **Area 2** to prepare to attack intruders.

Area 2. Guard Post (CR 6)

> A cramped square room stands at the end of a sloping, plank-lined hallway. The space holds a small table and three chairs, a little sealed barrel, and a pair of doors leading out. One door stands in the north wall, the other in the west wall.

Former guards are still stationed here, but the **3 gloom gnomes** (see **Appendix: New Monsters**) continue their vigil out of hunger not duty. If the party bursts open the front door and immediately proceeds here, the guards are present and preparing to attack. If the PCs dallied before entering or needed multiple attempts to breach the front door, the shadow gnomes are merged with the gloom and attack from ambush, likely surprising the party.

GLOOM GNOMES (3) **CR 3**
XP 800
hp 32 (see **Appendix: New Monsters**)

The barrel contains 5 gallons of watered brandy. The doors exiting this room are closed, but not locked.

Area 3. Observation Post

> A small round room stands at the top of a narrow flight of stairs. Small observation windows are cut in the walls of the room at the eye level of a short observer, granting a 360-degree view of the forest outside. An unlit brazier filled with coal sits in the center of the room.

This place once allowed the gnomes a hidden vantage point to observe travelers approaching Thistlehill's front door. It is no longer manned, but may still present a threat to the PCs.

The coal in the brazier is thoroughly infected by shadow stuff. If set alight, the coal bursts into brilliant deep blue flames that immediately suck the warmth from this room. All within 15 ft. of the brazier must succeed on a DC 12 Reflex save or suffer 1d8+2 points of cold damage (half damage on a successful saving throw). The coals continue to burn, inflicting additional damage each round the PCs remain within its area of effect. Once lit, the brazier cannot be extinguished by mundane means until it exhausts itself one hour later.

Area 4. Pit Trap

A 20-ft.-deep covered pit bars passage here. A DC 20 Perception check notices the concealed trap. Failing to detect the pit forces the first rank of the party to succeed on a DC 15 Reflex save or plunge into the trap. A hidden switch, detectable with a DC 20 Perception check, is located behind a knothole in the corridor's plank walls. Throwing the switch seals the pit cover, allowing it to be crossed without danger.

Area 5. Common Room (CR 8)

> This large room holds carved wooden chairs, tables, and cupboards, each fashioned with exquisite skill. A plush woven carpet of forest green and autumn gold covers the plank floor. A wide, cold hearth stands in the south wall, and a curious low-walled box rests beside it.

The central gathering place for the gnomes, this common room was the hub of life within Thistlehill. It is now home to the worst of the shadow-afflicted residents.

Dwelling here are **4 gloom gnomes** and their pet, a **shadow dire badger**.

GLOOM GNOMES (4) **CR 3**
XP 800
hp 32 (see **Appendix: New Monsters**)

SHADOW DIRE BADGER **CR 3**
XP 800
Pathfinder Roleplaying Game Bestiary 2 "Badger, Dire";
Pathfinder Roleplaying Game Bestiary 4 "Shadow Creature"
N Medium outsider (augmented animal, native)
Init +6; **Senses** darkvision 60 ft., low-light vision, scent;
Perception +10

AC 14, touch 12, flat-footed 12 (+2 Dex, +2 natural)
hp 22 (3d8+9)
Fort +6; **Ref** +5; **Will** +2
Defensive Abilities shadow blend; **Resist** cold 5, electricity 5;
SR 9

Speed 30 ft., burrow 10 ft.
Melee bite +4 (1d4+2), 2 claws +4 (1d3+2)
Special Attacks blood rage

Str 14, **Dex** 15, **Con** 17, **Int** 2, **Wis** 12, **Cha** 9
Base Atk +2; **CMB** +4; **CMD** 16 (20 vs. trip)
Feats Improved Initiative, Skill Focus (Perception)
Skills Escape Artist +6, Perception +10; **Racial Modifiers** +4
Escape Artist

Shadow Blend (Su) In any illumination other than bright

light, a shadow creature blends into the shadows, giving it concealment (20% miss chance). A shadow creature can suspend or resume this ability as a free action.

The room contains normal furniture for the warren's inhabitants. The curious, low-walled box is filled with straw and wood chips, and served as the badger's bed before the coming of shadow.

Area 6. Kitchen

The smell of many old and fine meals seeped into the wooden walls of this well-kept kitchen. Clay ovens stand against the north wall, facing low tables covered with bowls, plates, and kitchen implements. A closed trapdoor lies in the floor next to the preparation tables.

This ordinary kitchen is free from danger. The table holds several bowls, wooden spoons, a butcher's knife, cleaver, a pair of paring knives, and a pewter salt cellar. The ovens are cold and empty, but the faint smell of freshly baked bread is detectable when the doors are opened.

The trapdoor is unlocked and opens to reveal a short ladder leading down to the pantry (**Area 7**).

Area 7. Pantry

Sacks, barrels, and boxes fill this cramped root cellar. The smell of flour, smoked meat, and earth is rich here.

This room holds enough food to feed two dozen small appetites for two weeks. The pantry holds sausages, wheels of cheese, flour, corn meal, pickled vegetables, dried fruit, and salted fish. Four dusty bottles rest atop a high shelf, requiring a DC 12 Perception check to see them under the dust and cobwebs. Each bottle holds an old gnomish fortified wine spiced with restorative herbs and flowers. Drinking the lavender wine of a full bottle acts as a *potion of lesser restoration.*

Area 8. Lavatory

This rooms serves the burrow's basic sanitary needs. Seven stalls with single-hole latrines line the walls and an enclosed bathing area (**A**) is used for washing. A natural spring flows into a clay basin in the bathing area, providing water for basic needs. Nothing of interest or value is in this area.

Area 9. Dormitories

Numerous small bunks, tables, chairs, and wardrobes fill this room, providing sleeping quarters for the warren's occupants.

Each of these rooms holds 12 bunks and wardrobes, along with small tables and chairs for sitting and eating. The wardrobes are filled with small-sized clothing and the personal effects of Thistlehill's miners, as well as a handful of common tools. The two dormitories are largely identical and their differences in contents are listed below.

Area 9A.

A band of **6 gloom gnomes** (CR 8) slinks about in the darkness, waiting to ambush the curious.

GLOOM GNOMES (6) **CR 3**
XP 800
hp 32 (see **Appendix: New Monsters**)

Among the mundane contents of this room are a small pouch of six moonstones (10 gp value each), a pair of small boots with silver heels (10 gp value), 75 cp, 49 sp, and 55 gp in mixed coins, and a small barrel of good brandy (10 gp value).

Area 9B.

This dormitory is free of dangerous inhabitants. A minor treasure consisting of a silver drinking decanter (25 gp), four copper cups (10 gp value total), a pouch containing 12 freshwater pearls (10 gp value each), and 96 cp, 66 sp, and 63 gp in mixed coins can be found.

Area 10. Storage

This room is crammed with crates, barrels, spools of rope, boxes, and tools. The smell of grease and wax fills the air. Cobwebs dangle in the dark corners of the room.

Sunbreath Quartz

Sunbreath quartz appears identical to clear quartz except when exposed to light over several hours. After such time, sunbreath quartz glows naturally, producing illumination equal to a candle for 12 hours. The emitted light is always a pale yellow glow similar to sunlight regardless of the origin of the absorbed illumination. This property makes it valuable to tailors who adorn clothing with sunbreath quartz, as well as jewelers, who use the glowing stones in their creations. A single sunbreath quartz crystal is worth 25 gp.

Sunbreath quartz can be "charged" with magical light to create an effective weapon against certain creatures. By casting a *light* cantrip on a single sunbreath quartz crystal, the stone absorbs and retains the spell, becoming a miniature "light bomb" that can be employed against creatures affected by bright light. The magical light is retained by the crystal for up to one hour and, due to the strange properties of the stone, continues to maintain its light even if another *light* cantrip is cast by the same spellcaster (this effect supersedes the spell's description). A spellcaster can cast the *light* cantrip on multiple sunbreath quartz stones and each retains its illumination until an hour passes or the stone is used offensively.

A charged sunbreath quartz can be thrown as an improvised weapon up to 20 ft. If it strikes a target or hard surface, the stone shatters, releasing the *light*. The explosion of illumination has one of two effects: If the creature possesses eyesight and is not a shadow-based creature, it must make a Constitution saving throw vs. the spellcaster's spell DC or be blinded for one round. Shadow creatures, including shadows, advanced shadows, shadow creatures, grimseems, shadow elementals, and gloom gnomes, struck by the blast suffer 1d6+spellcaster's spell ability modifier damage. Regardless of effect, the explosion shatters the crystal and it cannot be used again.

A sunbreath quartz crystal can also be used to focus a *light* cantrip and transform it into a ray attack capable of damaging shadow-based creatures. The spellcaster casts the *light* cantrip while holding a sunbreath crystal in his hand, aimed at his target. On a successful ranged touch attack, the creature suffers 1d8 points of radiant damage. This attack "burns out" the crystal and it cannot be used as a focus or charged again.

The chamber contains mundane supplies necessary for the day-to-day operations of the warren and adjacent mine. There are spare lanterns, 500 ft. of rope, picks, shovels, buckets, barrels of grease, crates of candles, lumber and timbers for building mine supports, wheelbarrows, and similar items. No danger or treasure is present.

Area 11. Gemstone Mine (CR 6)

> The plank-lined corridor gives way to an excavated area hewn from the surrounding earth and stone. Timber braces support the earth-and-stone ceiling, creating a low, wide cavern underneath the ground. Buckets, tools, and wheelbarrows lean against the walls of the room. Flickering shadows with malicious smiles crowd around the edge of a glowing circle of light at the cavern's northeastern end. Huddled within the light is a pale, thin gnome that watches the shadows in terror. Several pools of melted wax surround the gnome.

The gnomes of Thistlehill mine a rare form of crystal known as sunbreath quartz from a vein that runs beneath the forest. Although not as valuable as many precious stones, sunbreath quartz is highly desired by jewelers and tailors for its unique property. Most of the stone has been extracted and only a small bit of the original vein remains.

This area contains **3 shadows** and **Mevlyn Butteroak**, the sole remaining resident of Thistlehill unaffected by the Darkening. When the Darkening spread through the community, a handful of gnomes fled to the mine where they discovered the absorbed light of the sunbreath quartz could stymie the encroaching shadows. Over the past few days, most of the gnomes made a desperate attempt to gather supplies or escape the burrow, but succumbed to the Plane of Shadow's minions. Only Mevlyn remains, and he has run out of candles to keep the sunbreath crystal illuminated. Unless rescued, the crystals' glow soon expires and the shadows claim Mevlyn. The shadows turn to attack the PCs, hungry for long-delayed sustenance.

SHADOWS (3) CR 3
XP 800
hp 19 (*Pathfinder Roleplaying Game Bestiary* "Shadow")

MEVLYN BUTTEROAK CR 1/2
XP 200
Male gnome fighter 1
CG Small humanoid (gnome)
Init +1; **Senses** low-light vision; **Perception** +3

AC 15, touch 13, flat-footed 13 (+2 armor, +1 Dex, +1 dodge, +1 size)
hp 13 (1d10+3)
Fort +5; **Ref** +1; **Will** +1; +2 vs. illusions
Defensive Abilities defensive training

Speed 20 ft.
Melee short sword +3 (1d4+1/19–20)
Ranged sling +3 (1d3+1)
Special Attacks hatred

Str 13, **Dex** 13, **Con** 16, **Int** 10, **Wis** 12, **Cha** 10

Base Atk +1; **CMB** +1; **CMD** 13
Feats Dodge, Mobility
Skills Acrobatics +1 (-3 to jump), Craft (weapons) +2, Handle Animal +4, Perception +3, Ride +5, Survival +5; **Racial Modifiers** +2 Craft (weapons), +2 Perception
Languages Common, Gnome, Sylvan
SQ gnome magic
Other Gear leather armor, short sword, sling, 20 sling bullets, trail rations (3 days)

Mevlyn is overjoyed if the shadows are vanquished. He has been trapped in the mine for several days and is severely dehydrated and malnourished. Mevlyn, saddened by the loss of his friends and home, wants nothing more than a meal and to get as far away from Shadow's reach as possible. He explains how he remained untouched by the shadows for so long, telling the party of sunbreath quartz's power (see **Sidebox**) and suggests they take as many of the stones as possible if they are brave enough to fight the Darkening's power. Unfortunately, only 20 quartz crystals large enough to be used offensively remain in the vein.

Mevlyn tells the party that the Darkening flowed over Thistlehill from the northeast, corrupting everything in its path. If they seek the source of Shadow's power, he suggests they head deeper into the forest in that direction.

Mevlyn is traumatized by his experience and has no desire to join the party in their quest. However, if the PCs play upon his love of his home and friends, convincing him to avenge their loss, a successful DC 12 Diplomacy check causes him to swallow his fear and dedicate himself to stopping the Darkening. He gathers his possessions from **Area 9A** (assuming the gloom gnomes have been dispatched), which include leather armor, a short sword, a sling with 20 stones, traveler's clothes, and food and water for three days, and joins the party.

The Cellar of Dyraxl Uhl-Kal-Totten

Buried beneath the ancient rubble and thick forest loam are the surviving catacombs of the sorcerer-warlord, Dyraxl Uhl-Kal-Totten. It was in these chambers that he conducted his eldritch research and stored his prized magical artifacts — including the *darkling lanthorn* which is the source of the Darkening of Namjan Forest. It is here that the PCs must venture to end the shadow infection, but the task is not easy as formidable foes are arrayed against them.

General Features

The cellar is hewn from the bedrock that underlies the forest, carved from the stone eons ago by magical incantations and physical labor. Much of the cellar is in ruins or buried under tons of rubble, victim to the original destruction called down by Uhl-Kal-Totten and the march of time.

Illumination: The cellar is dark — even more so than can be attributed to the lack of illumination. The encroachment of the Plane of Shadow has veiled the entire undercroft in an unnatural gloom. Light sources that normally create bright light struggle against this darkness, casting only dim light in their area of effect. Areas that are normally considered dim light (the edges of a lantern's illumination range, for example) are treated as darkness in the cellars. These shadows even affect *darkvision*. All *darkvision* ranges are reduced by one-third, rounded down, while in the cellar (e.g. a dwarf's *darkvision* only has a 40 ft. range in the cellar).

Wandering Monsters

Several shadowy occupants of the cellar prowl its corridors, constantly seeking to assuage their hunger and increase the shadow's hold, and the PCs may encounter these wanderers during their exploration. There is a 20% chance of encountering a wandering monster or other random encounter every 30 minutes while inside the cellar. If a wandering monster encounter is indicated, the GM should roll on the table below to determine the type and number of creatures encountered.

Cellar Random Encounter Table

1d6	Encounter
1	**1d4 shadow spiders** (see **Area 1**)
2	**1d6 shadows**
3	**1d4 grimseems** (see **Area 5**)
4	**Miasmic death** (see **Appendix: New Monsters**)
5–6	**Advanced shadow** (see **Area 1: Shadow Attack**)

The Cellar of Dyraxl Uhl-Kal-Totten

The entrance to the cellar is a steep, angled tunnel filled with fallen blocks of masonry and old forest earth. It connects to the surface in the lee of the Darkling Oak that unwittingly serves as guardian to the cellar. Once the Darkling Oak is evaded, the PCs can venture down the shaft's 50-ft. length to arrive in **Area 1.**

Area 1. Spider Wine (CR 4)

> The steep shaft terminates in a dark chamber, its contents largely obscured by the almost-physical gloom that fills the space with shadows. A collapsed wooden rack and smashed barrels are vaguely discernable in the dark and the stone floor is littered with shards of broken, dusty glass.

Once a wine cellar, this chamber is now home to a **2 shadow giant spiders**. Ever hungry, they scuttle close to the party, seeking to ambush them from the dark.

SHADOW GIANT SPIDERS (2) **CR 2**
XP 600
Pathfinder Roleplaying Game Bestiary "Spider, Giant"; *Pathfinder Roleplaying Game Bestiary 4* "Shadow Creature"
N Medium outsider (augmented vermin, native)
Init +3; **Senses** darkvision 60 ft., low-light vision, tremorsense 60 ft.; **Perception** +4

AC 14, touch 13, flat-footed 11 (+3 Dex, +1 natural)
hp 16 (3d8+3)
Fort +4; **Ref** +4; **Will** +1
Defensive Abilities shadow blend; **Immune** mind-affecting effects; **Resist** cold 5, electricity 5; **SR** 8

Speed 30 ft., climb 30 ft.
Melee bite +2 (1d6 plus poison)
Special Attacks poison, web (+5 ranged, DC 12, 3 hp)

Str 11, **Dex** 17, **Con** 12, **Int** —, **Wis** 10, **Cha** 2
Base Atk +2; **CMB** +2; **CMD** 15
Skills Climb +16, Perception +4 (+8 in webs), Stealth +7 (+11 in webs); **Racial Modifiers** +8 Climb, +4 Perception, +4 Stealth, +4 Stealth in webs, +4 perception in webs

---

Poison (Ex) Bite—injury; *save* Fort DC 14; *frequency* 1/round

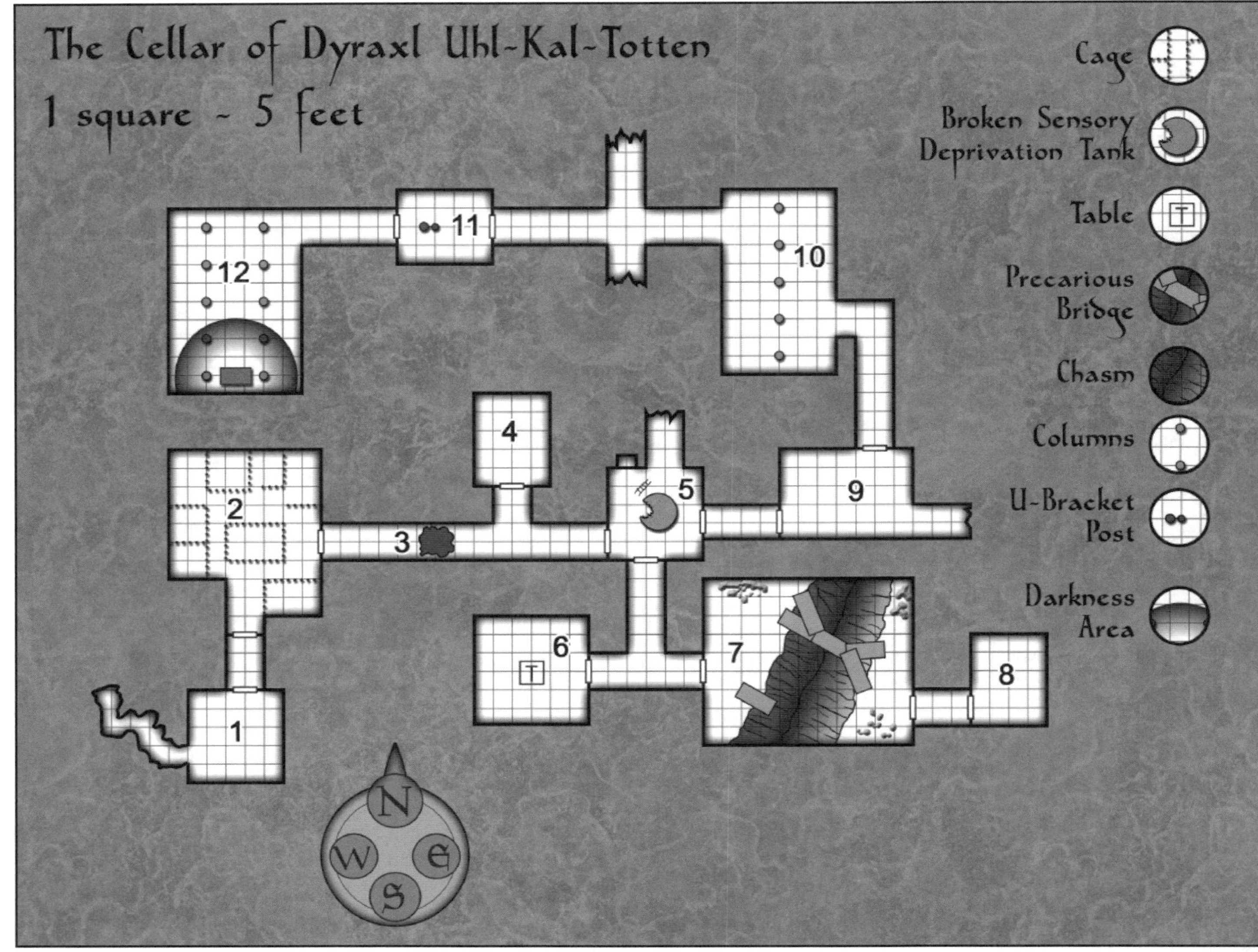

for 4 rounds; *effect* 1d2 Strength damage; *cure* 1 save.
Shadow Blend (Su) In any illumination other than bright light, a shadow creature blends into the shadows, giving it concealment (20% miss chance). A shadow creature can suspend or resume this ability as a free action.

The contents of this room are in ruins. Barrels and bottles that once held fine vintages from long ago are now broken and empty. The tall wooden racks are either dust or riddled with dry-rot and collapse into punky wood with a touch. A careful search of the chamber accompanied with a DC 15 Perception check uncovers an intact bottle fashioned from cut crystal. The bottle alone is worth 50 gp. The vessel contains a *potion of lesser restoration*.

Area 2. Ruined Menagerie

> Rusty bars form several caged-off areas of varying sizes in this chamber. Yellowed, moldering bones lie in haphazard fashion within the cages. Open doors on rusty hinges moan slightly, pushed by faint subterranean draughts.

Dyraxl Uhl-Kal-Totten kept his most fearsome and fascinating pets in this chamber, intent on experimenting and crossbreeding them. The mystical creatures died during the siege and their bones remained undisturbed here ever since.

There are eight cages, all composed of rusting bars with doors that are ajar. Skeletal remains of great age, some nearly fossilized by mineralization, are scattered across the floor inside the cages. A DC 20 Knowledge (arcana) check identifies the remains as belonging to a bulette, a catoblepas, a gorgon, an owlbear, a peryton, and a unicorn.

The unicorn's horn is still intact and worth up to 2,000 gp.

Area 3. Snatching Darkness

This location conceals a pool of semi-intelligent darkness that is a conduit between the material realm and the Plane of Shadow. It clings to the ceiling, nearly undetectable (requiring a DC 25 Perception check to notice) until the party passes beneath it. It then strikes, lashing down with its two 20-ft.-long shadow tentacles to grab random passers-by. The pool cannot move from its position.

The pool attacks twice as an action, making grapple attacks against two targets. The pool has a CMB of +6 and a CMD of 16. Once it successfully grapples an opponent, it drags the victim upward to the ceiling, pulling him inside its body. The pool's form exists in the Material Plane and the Plane of Shadow. Victims pulled into its form seem to disappear as if dropped into a dark hole in between the planes. The pool's mass is large enough to hold two Medium victims at a time.

Any creature enveloped by the pool's body takes a cumulative –1 penalty to Strength-based attack rolls, Strength checks, and Strength saving throws for each round it is immersed in the pool. If the creature's penalty and normal Strength modifier ever equal –5, the creature perishes, its life force absorbed by the shadows. An 8-hour rest ends the penalty.

Grappled creatures can attempt to break free as normal. Allies can assist a grappled creature, granting them advantage to their opposed check to break the grapple or attempt to sever the tentacles. Each tentacle is AC 10 and has 10 hit points. A missed attack on a tentacle has a 50% chance of potentially hitting the grappled PC. On a d100 roll of 50 or less, the attacker makes another attack roll with all the normal modifiers against the grappled PC's AC, doing damage to his ally if the attack hits.

It must be noted that PCs dragged into the pool are 15 ft. above the corridor's floor, and the distance likely hampers their allies' attempts to aid them.

The pool cannot be killed by weapons or most spells, but if subject to a *daylight* spell, the searing light banishes the pool back to the Plane of Shadow.

Area 4. Alchemy Lab (CR 3)

Broken glassware covered by a thick blanket of dust is strewn about this small chamber. The floor is stained by the spills of a hundred strange chemicals and reagents. The air seems to roil and swirl, casting a rainbow of dull hues as if soap bubbles were caught in a draft.

The countless spilled chemicals combined with the arcane destruction called down by Uhl-Kal-Totten and now infused with shadow has created a unique life form in this room — a **miasmic death**. The gaseous creature drains nutrients and the breath of those it envelops, seeking to reproduce itself and spread beyond the confines of this small chamber.

MIASMIC DEATH **CR 3**
XP 800
hp 31 (see **Appendix: New Monsters**)

The contents of this room are largely beyond salvage. The various alchemical instruments and materials are rusted and rotted or smashed to flinders. However, mixed among the debris are three iron beakers sealed with ill-smelling wax. The beakers each contain a potion, but the elixirs have undergone "magical spoilage" down the millennia. Now, each potion produces a harmless but interesting side-effect when consumed. The side effect lasts for as long as the potion is functioning. They are:

- A *potion of flying;* side effect: turns the drinker's skin a vibrant green color;
- A *potion of gaseous form;* side effect: the gaseous form throws tiny, harmless blue lightning bolts that cause the drinker to be at a disadvantage on stealth-related checks;
- A *potion of heroism;* side effect: the sound of cattle lowing accompanies the drinker wherever he goes.

Area 5. Former Sensory Deprivation Chamber (CR 6)

A large spherical vessel resembling a round amphora occupies this room. The 10-ft.-diameter container has a large hole in its side, allowing a glimpse into its empty interior. The flagstone floor is stained by some ancient spillage and covered by dust. The remains of a corroded iron ladder lie beside the grand vessel.

Lurking inside the round vessel are **3 grimseems** that are hidden by the gloom and the remaining sides of the container. They flutter out on shadowy, bat-like wings and attack.

GRIMSEEMS (3) **CR 2**
XP 600
hp 32 (see **Appendix: New Monsters**)

The spherical vessel was a sensory deprivation tank. Uhl-Kal-Totten drifted inside the tank, floating in warm water and shrouded in darkness, allowing his mind to visit unseen dimensions and contemplate the mysteries of magic. The stain on the floor comes from the heavily salted water that once occupied the tank.

A search of the north wall accompanied by a successful DC 10 Perception check discovers a concealed compartment. This tall, narrow cubby once contained dressing robes and towels, as well as certain substances Uhl-Kal-Totten imbibed before entering the tank. On a small shelf is a crystal box (10 gp value) containing a gummy black resin. This substance is extract of the night hyacinth flower, a mystical drug that affects spellcasters. A single dose of resin is in the box.

Any spellcaster consuming the resin must make a DC 15 Fortitude save. If the save fails, the character suffers 3d8 points of damage but no further effect. On a successful save, the caster falls unconscious for 1d4 hours, during which time nothing can awaken him. The caster has fearsome dreams while unconscious, his mind glimpsing strange vistas at the far ends of the multiverse. When he awakens, he does so with the understanding of how to bolster his magic with his own body.

The spellcaster can effectively increase the level of an expended spell slot by permanently reducing his Constitution by 1 point. For example, a 3rd-level wizard could cast a spell using one of his 2nd-level spell slots and, by permanently decreasing his Constitution score by one, cause the spell to take effect as if cast with a 3rd-level spell slot. Lost Constitution cannot be restored by any magic less than a *wish* spell. Expended Constitution can be regained when using the Ability Score Improvement feature during leveling.

Expended Constitution to increase a spell slot's power does not allow the caster to use magic beyond his level ability. A caster cannot expend more than 1 point of Constitution per round to increase a spell slot level.

Area 6. Golem Forge

A massive table fashioned from a single stone slab occupies much of this room's floor space. Scraps of punky, dry-rotted wood and rusty nails indicate tables or other furnishings that once lined the western wall, but they long ago succumbed to age. A large stone box, its exterior inscribed with strange sigils, rests atop the slab table.

Golems and constructs were once fashioned in this chamber and Uhl-Kal-Totten was preparing to create a new model when his stronghold fell. All that remains is a single component sealed inside a magically-warded box.

A PC who can speak Terran or who succeeds in a DC 15 Knowledge (arcana) check identifies the writing as pertaining to the Plane of Earth. The box is sealed shut and bears no obvious lock or closure. It weighs 300 lbs. The chest resists attempts to break it open, its rocky surface "healing" damage and shrugging off most magical spells. Its contents can be access only via three ways: 1) A *disintegrate* spell destroys the box, revealing its contents; 2) a *stone shape* spell allows an opening to be molded in the box's side; and 3) an earth elemental can reach inside using its *earth glide* power and extract the box's contents.

The box contains an oversized humanoid left hand made from solid stone. Originally intended for a stone golem, the hand is magical and usable by one daring enough to pay the price. If the hand is affixed to the freshly severed (within 12 hours) stump of a left arm and a *regenerate* spell is cast on the hand, it potentially fuses with the flesh, allowing the creature to use it as his own, natural appendage. When the *regenerate* spell is cast, the subject must make a DC 10 Fortitude save. If the save is successful, the limb attaches itself without any side effects. If the saving throw fails, however, the fist rejects its owner's natural flesh and replaces it with solid rock, petrifying the subject. If restored to normal, the hand separates from the now un-petrified owner and can never be used by the subject.

The fist, when successfully fused to flesh, grants the owner a +2 Strength bonus in his left arm. He can also smash his hand upon the ground to create a *tremor* twice per day. The *tremor* is trip attack against all creatures within 20 ft. using the wielder's CMB and with enhanced Strength score. The rocky fist has hardness 10 and 20 hp.

Area 7. Slippery Stones (CR 6)

> A jagged hole tears the stone floor of this chamber in two. Collapsed ceiling stones are piled in tumbled fashion, forming a crude bridge across the gap. Mounds of dark forest earth have partially buried the chamber, having poured into the room from the holes in the roof. Debris or broken furnishings are dimly visible on the far side of the room, as is a closed door.

The destruction long ago severely damaged this room, opening an 80-ft.-deep, 30-ft.-wide rift in the floor while dumping tons of earth and rock into the room from the compromised ceiling. By sheer chance, several of the ceiling slabs fell to form a delicately balanced bridge across the gap. They remain there, but are precariously positioned.

Flittering about in the darkness are **3 shadows**, greedy for the PCs' lives. They wait until the party begins to cross the haphazard bridge before attacking.

SHADOWS (3) CR 3
XP 800
hp 19 (*Pathfinder Roleplaying Game Bestiary* "Shadow")

Combatants battling on the stone slab bridge risk a very real chance of collapsing the precarious span. The GM rolls 1d6 each round combat occurs on the bridge; if the result is less than or equal to the number of rounds the fighting has lasted, the slabs fall, pitching all on the makeshift bridge into the chasm. PCs falling into the pit suffer 8d6 points of bludgeoning damage. Falling individuals that make a DC 15 Reflex save grab a protrusion and save themselves from the fall, but are left dangling over the pit. The assistance of an ally or a DC 10 Strength check on a subsequent round allows them to climb back onto solid ground. PCs struck while dangling over the chasm must make a Strength check with a DC equal to 5 + damage suffered or fall into the chasm.

The broken debris on the eastern side of the room are all that remains of display and trophy cases that once housed prizes Uhl-Kal-Totten wrested from his enemies. An inspection of the ruined wood, glass, and rusty iron uncovers shattered bits of bone, corroded bits of armor, and scraps of cloth that crumble to dust with a touch. One object survived the destruction, however: a human tibia inscribed with odd glyphs and wrapped with decaying reptile hide. This is a *staff of radiance* (see **Appendix: New Magical Items**). A successful DC 13 Perception check discovers the intact wand among the debris.

Area 8. Map Room

> Collapsed shelves and crumbling chests of drawers slouch in this small room, covered with eons of dust and smelling of great age and mildew. A faint, old stink of rotting flesh is barely discernable among the other pungent subterranean smells.

Uhl-Kal-Totten stored his library of maps, charts, and other such documents in this room, but age destroyed them all. The smell of rot comes from the decayed animal hides that once bore ancient maps of a long-vanished land. Most surviving materials in the room fall to pieces if handled. The exception is a bone scroll case sealed with a mithral cap (200 gp value).

The case contains a rolled piece of thin metal bearing a number of seemingly randomly spaced rectangular holes (similar to an old time computer punch card). The sheet measures 1 ft. square and is of an unidentifiable metal. This object serves as a key to open the vault door in **Area 11** and to bypass the trap protecting it.

Area 9. Funeral Trophies

> This chamber appears to have been furnished by tomb raiders and grave robbers. More than a dozen sarcophagi in various styles and condition are placed about the room. Some stand upright, while others lie flat on the cracked flagstones. The caskets all bear the covers, obscuring what, if anything, they may contain. One sarcophagus glows an eerie green color, like foxfire in a dismal mire.

Uhl-Kal-Totten plundered many tombs and cemeteries to acquire lost lore and the ghastly material components he needed for his spells and experiments. He took to collecting the sarcophagi of his lootings as macabre trophies, speculating he might be able to use their funereal power in his experiments. One of the stone caskets was an obvious source of magical power and Uhl-Kal-Totten claimed it to further experiment on, but his research was foiled by the collapse of his demesne.

The glowing sarcophagus possesses an unusual and possibly beneficial magical power, but only to the PC who is brave enough to climb in. If the lid is removed, odd hieroglyphics are found to line the interior of the casket. A DC 20 Knowledge (history) check reveals them to be ancient writing concerned with rebirth, but their exact meaning is vague. If a living creature climbs inside the sarcophagus and closes the lid, the green glow increases in brilliance, becoming nearly blinding to those outside the coffin. The person within the sarcophagus undergoes a vivid hallucination of a hundred faces of strangers racing past his eyes, many of whom are dressed in outlandishly ancient (or perhaps future?) fashions. The enclosed PC must then make a DC 15 Fortitude save. If he succeeds, nothing happens and the light subsides. Should he fail, however, a strange contingency magic affects him.

Should the PC die an untimely death, he immediately returns to life as if the subject of a *reincarnate* spell, restored to existence in the form of one of the countless individuals who once interacted with the magical sarcophagus.

While the coffin's contingency magic is in effect (i.e. before the PC's untimely demise), the character radiates necromancy and transmutation magic if subjected to a *detect magic* spell. There is no other indication of what the sarcophagus's effect is. A *remove cure* followed by a *dispel magic* negates the contingency magic and the PC is not reincarnated in a new form if he dies prematurely.

The remaining 14 sarcophagi in the room are old, but otherwise unremarkable.

Area 10. Egrihl's Lair (CR 8)

> Shallow niches in the walls of this dark chamber still bear rotted picture frames indicating this was once a galley where art was displayed. Thin decorative columns divide the room in two, and the floor is covered in the dusty, decayed remains of a once-grand carpet.

Lurking in the darkness is a victim of the Darkening known as **Egrihl**, formerly a scout for the duke's soldiers who succumbed to shadow. Unlike his fellows, however, Egrihl became a shadow lord. The fallen ranger and his companion dog **Marko** were lured by the shadows and now reside close to the source of the Darkening's power. They defend the approach to the Vault of Shadows (**Area 12**), attacking from ambush from the shadows.

EGRIHL THE SHADOW LORD **CR 8**
XP 4,800
Male human shadow lord ranger 6 (*Pathfinder Roleplaying Game Bestiary 4* "Shadow Creature")
NE Medium outsider (augmented humanoid, human, native)
Init +5; **Senses** darkvision 60 ft., low-light vision, see in darkness; **Perception** +11

AC 21, touch 15, flat-footed 16 (+5 armor, +4 Dex, +1 dodge, +1 shield)
hp 55 (6d10+12 plus 6)
Fort +7; **Ref** +10; **Will** +4
Defensive Abilities incorporeal step, shadow blend; **DR** 10/magic; **Resist** cold 15, electricity 15; **SR** 14

Speed 30 ft. (20 ft. in armor)
Melee *+1 battleaxe* +6/+1 (1d8+2/×3) or handaxe +5 (1d6/×3) or touch attack +7 touch (1d6+1)
Special Attacks cloying gloom burst 3/day (30 ft. cone, DC 15), combat style (two-weapon combat), favored enemies (animals +2, magical beasts +4)
Spell-Like Abilities (CL 6th; ranged touch +11):
At will— *ray of sickening* (DC 12)
3/day—*shadow conjuration, shadow step*
1/day—*shadow walk* (DC 16)
Ranger Spells Prepared (CL 3rd):
1st—*delay poison, entangle* (DC 13)

Str 12, **Dex** 21, **Con** 14, **Int** 10, **Wis** 14, **Cha** 12
Base Atk +6; **CMB** +7; **CMD** 23
Feats Dodge, Endurance, Mobility, Spring Attack, Toughness, Two-weapon Defense, Two-weapon Fighting
Skills Acrobatics +3 (–1 to jump), Climb +8, Handle Animal +10, Heal +11, Intimidate +10, Knowledge (nature) +9, Perception +11, Stealth +20, Survival +11; **Racial Modifiers** +8 Stealth
Languages Common
SQ favored terrain (forest +2), hunter's bond (dog named Marko), planar thinning 1/day, track +3, wild empathy +7
Gear *+1 hide armor*, *+1 battleaxe*, handaxe, *hunter's mask*

Cloying Gloom Burst (Su) Three times per day, the shadow lord can unleash a 30-foot cone of cloying gloom. On a failed Fortitude saving throw, creatures in the cone are affected by a slow spell (caster level equal to the shadow lord's Hit Dice) and are blinded for the duration of the slow effect.
Incorporeal Step (Su) When a shadow lord moves, it gains the incorporeal subtype and quality, including a deflection bonus to AC equal to its Charisma bonus. It loses the incorporeal subtype and special ability when it stops moving.
Planar Thinning (Su) Once per day as a full-round action, a shadow lord can thin the barriers between the Material Plane and Shadow Plane, making it considerably easier for creatures to cross between the two. This functions like the planar travel aspect of the gate spell (CL 6th). This planar thinning is immediately dispelled if in an area of normal or bright light.
Shadow Blend (Su) In any illumination other than bright light, a shadow lord blends into the shadows, giving it concealment (20% miss chance). A shadow lord can suspend or resume this ability as a free action.

MARKO **CR —**
Male dog (Pathfinder Roleplaying Game Bestiary "Dog")
N Small animal
Init +4; **Senses** low-light vision, scent; **Perception** +8

AC 19, touch 15, flat-footed 15 (+4 Dex, +4 natural, +1 size)
hp 19 (+6)
Fort +5; **Ref** +7; **Will** +2
Defensive Abilities evasion

Speed 40 ft.
Melee bite +6 (1d4+3)

Str 14, **Dex** 18, **Con** 15, **Int** 2, **Wis** 12, **Cha** 6
Base Atk +2; **CMB** +3; **CMD** 17 (21 vs. trip)
Feats Skill Focus (Perception), Weapon Focus (bite)
Skills Acrobatics +4 (+12 to jump), Perception +8, Survival +3; **Racial Modifiers** +4 to survival when tracking by scent
SQ tricks (come, defend, fetch, fighting, guard, track)

Egrihl uses the *hunter's mask* ability to cast *bear's endurance* on himself at the start of combat to gain temporary hit points. He then wades into the thickest concentration of foes and uses his horde breaker ability to strike as many targets as possible. Marko attacks foes Egrihl isn't engaging.

If Marko is slain and Egrihl is still alive, he flees to **Area 12**, using his *shadow step* or *shadow walk* ability to do so. He waits with the shadow elemental to defend the *darkling lanthorn* and the conduit to Shadow.

Area 11. Vault Door (CR 6)

This chamber is largely bare, holding only a strange contraption near the western end of the room. A stone post rises 4 ft. from the floor and ends in a U-shaped bracket. A small round protrusion extends from the post on its east side, giving it a lopsided appearance. Set in the western wall is an intimidating-looking stone door. Numerous small tiles cover its face.

This room protects the Vault of Shadows (**Area 12**) with its well-secured door and a secret trap.

The door is solid stone and measures 8 ft. square. More than 60 1-inch-by-2-inch steel tiles cover its exterior, all of which are rusty but still solid. The door is locked and can only safely be opened by pushing the correct combination of tiles. A pressed tile slides into the door's face, creating a 1-inch-deep divot. Depressing the proper 15 tiles disarms the trap (see below) and unlocks the door.

The stone post is situated 6 ft. away from the door and is the key to determining the proper combination of tiles to be pushed. Each end of the U-shaped bracket has a small slot running down its length as if it is intended to hold something. If the metal sheet from **Area 8** is unrolled and slid into the grooves, the PCs discover it fits perfectly. The round protrusion extending from the eastern side of the post is a stone ring sized large enough to hold a torch or fat candle. Placing a lit torch or candle into the ring causes light to pass through the punched holes in the metal sheet, throwing small rectangles of light on the door's face. Each rectangle shines directly on one of the 15 tiles that unlocks the door and deactivates the trap. There is no set order in which the tiles must be pressed; simply depressing all 15 safely opens the vault.

A party failing to find the key sheet in **Area 8** can attempt to deduce what tiles unlock the door with a successful DC 25 Perception check. If successful, the party notices certain tiles show slightly more signs of wear. A *knock* spell also unlocks the door, but does not disarm the trap defending the vault.

If the trap is triggered, a cloud of once-lethal acid gas floods the chamber from miniscule vents in the ceiling (a DC 25 Perception check notices the vents if a PC specifically inspects the ceiling and has sufficient light to do so). Luckily for the PCs, the toxicity of the gas has diminished over the eons. Each PC suffers 2d8 points of acid damage, or half that with a successful DC 15 Fortitude save. The gas persists for three rounds and PCs who failed their initial save must attempt to save again on subsequent rounds or suffer damage. Once a PC successfully saves, he is no longer affected by the gas.

ACID GAS TRAP **CR 6**
XP 2,400
Type mechanical; **Perception** DC 25; **Disable Device** DC 25

Trigger location; **Reset** none; **Bypass** proper key
Effect cloud of acid gas (2d8 damage per round for 3 rounds, DC 15 Fort half); multiple targets (all within the vault)

Area 12. The Vault of Shadows (CR 7, or 9 if Egrihl is present)

The high, vaulted ceiling of this chamber suggests a large size, but the depths of the room are swathed in stygian blackness. A few thick pillars march away from the door only to vanish into the gloom. Somewhere in the darkness comes a hideous rustling sound as if the very fabric of reality was undulating in unnatural rhythm.

Uhl-Kal-Totten kept his most prized treasures in this secure vault, where they remained undisturbed for millennia. But when a single, stray root brushed across the *darkling lanthorn*, that contact with vitality was enough to rouse it from its long slumber. The shadow elemental within escaped its prison and now oversees the conduit between the Plane of Shadow and the material world.

The far end of the room is covered in the magical *darkness* created by the *darkling lanthorn*, and neither the artifact nor the shadow elemental who lurks within it is visible. The *darkness* can be circumvented as normal (a *daylight* spell, for example), which temporarily banishes the gloom and makes the *lanthorn* visible (see sidebox).

The **shadow elemental** dwells in the vault, restrained in this room by an innate connection to the *lanthorn* and its need to protect the conduit to the Plane of Shadow. It waits until one or more PCs approach the magical *darkness* and then rushes from the gloom to attack.

If Egrihl fled here after confronting the party in **Area 10**, he, too, waits within the darkness, ready to strike.

HUGE SHADOW ELEMENTAL **CR 7**
XP 3,200
hp 105 (see **Appendix: New Monsters**)

EGRIHL THE SHADOW LORD **CR 8**
XP 4,800
hp 55 (see **Area 10**)

If the *darkness* is dispelled, the party glimpses an incredibly old lantern forged from black iron and lit with blue-black flame. This is the *darkling lanthorn*. It rests atop a stone table, a large root coiling around its handle and vanishing into a crack in the stone wall. The air around the *lanthorn* ripples with shadows, creating the audible rustling noise. The occasional glimpse of a dark, gloomy world is visible in the cut crystal windows of the *lanthorn*. The *lanthorn* can be targeted by attacks and spells if visible and, if destroyed, seals the conduit and puts an end to the Darkening (see sidebox for more information).

Destroying the *darkling lanthorn* before the Darkening fully envelops the forest (see **Concluding the Adventure** below) causes the conduit to break apart, creating a brief but powerful suction of ethereal wind as the breach tears apart. All creatures within 40 ft. of the *lanthorn* when it is destroyed must make two DC 12 Strength checks. If the individual fails both checks, the failing conduit sucks him into it as it collapses, sending the unlucky creature tumbling into the Plane of Shadow. The fall does not injure the individuals, but does leave them stranded on another plane with no easy way to return. They must survive the shadowy threats long enough to discover another means to return home.

With the *darkling lanthorn* vanquished, the pervasive gloom filling the cellar vanishes and the party discerns several large stone chests lined against the wall in the southwest corner of the room. These chests are locked (DC 25 Disable Device check to pick) but not trapped. They contain:

- Chest #1: 1,506 cp and 997 ep.
- Chest #2: 57 gp and 160 pp.
- Chest #3: a small coffer holding 4 emeralds (100 gp value each), 8 sapphires (150 gp value each), 4 white opals (200 gp value each), and 2 pink diamonds (300 gp value each).
- Chest #4: A gold trinket box (500 gp value), an electrum statuette of an ancient tribal chieftain (200 gp value), a breastplate adorned with moonstones (400 gp value), a gem-encrusted sundial (700 gp value), and a gold and ruby ring (1,200 gp value).
- Chest #5: A *staff of striking* and a *ring of wizardry*.

Concluding the Adventure

The destruction of the *darkling lanthorn* likely closes the conduit (see below) between the Material Plane and the Plane of Shadow, halting the Darkening and preventing Namjan Forest from become a beachhead of darkness. Destroying the *lanthorn* closes the conduit, the gate, and banishes the shadow elemental back to the Plane of Shadow if it is still alive and outside the confines of the *lanthorn*. With the *lanthorn* gone, the effects of the Darkening slowly subside, vanishing like shadows at noon. Creatures infected by the touch of the Plane of Shadow do not revert to normal, however, and remain affected until their deaths. Whether it's possible for them to pass on these traits to their offspring remains to be seen (and may play a role in further adventures). The party that ends the Darkening are rewarded as promised by the duke, earning the 2,500 gp bounty and are named "Wardens of Namjan Forest," a minor noble title that also allows them the right to build a stronghold within the woodlands and act as local overseers of this frontier domain.

It is possible, however, that the spread of shadow grows too large to be easily broken with the *lanthorn's* destruction. If the party tarries too long and the daily growth of the Darkening infiltrates every forest hex on the overland map, the Plane of Shadow succeeds in establishing a claim on the Material Plane. In this event, destroying the *darkling lanthorn* is insufficient to seal the conduit. Like an avalanche racing downhill, the Plane of Shadow gains too much momentum and the artifact is no longer necessary to keep the conduit open.

In this case, the Darkening continues to spread across the land, moving beyond the boundaries of the forest and infecting whatever it touches. The encroaching shadows grow daily, and the forces of light and hope are pushed back before the advance. Powerful magic, perhaps in spell form or residing in ancient relics, is necessary to seal the conduit and halt the invasion. However, with the conduit now stable, shadow denizens begin pouring through the gate and its now not just shadow creatures the defenders of light must face. Eventually, an entire shadow army marches out of Namjan Forest to lay siege to the world. Only an equally powerful force of Good and Light has a hope of stopping them. The PCs likely see conflict on the front lines whether they want to or not, as their previous fight against the touch of shadow makes it likely they'll be approached to help end its invasion.

The Darkling Lanthorn (Minor Artifact)

Aura strong conjuration; **CL** 18th
Slot none; **Weight** 5 lbs.

DESCRIPTION

This magical artifact resembles a black iron lantern with cut crystal panes. When visible, the *lanthorn* burns with a black-blue light. The *lanthorn* naturally produces a permanent *darkness* effect in a 15-ft. radius around it, but this blackness can be temporarily negated with a *daylight* or similar spell. If countered, the *darkness* fades for as long as the negating spell is in effect, returning once the spell ends.

The *darkling lanthorn* has three magical properties. First, a rare shadow elemental is linked to the artifact, residing within its housing. The elemental can emerge from the *lanthorn* to protect it and to defend the conduit (see below) the artifact produces. The elemental can return to the *darkling lanthorn* when injured, healing all damage after spending 24 hours within the artifact.

Secondly, the *darkling lanthorn* acts as a *gate* as per the 9th-level spell. The *gate* leads solely to the Plane of Shadow and is permanent as long as the *darkling lanthorn* exists. Any creature speaking the phrase, "Lethel marr d'clatik" (a phrase in Aklo meaning, "Behold the Dark," which is inscribed on the base of the lanthorn), is transported to the Plane of Shadow as per the *gate* spell. The *gate* works in both directions.

Lastly, the *darkling lanthorn* has the power to form a conduit between the Material Plane and the Plane of Shadow. This conduit allows the basic essence of shadow to slowly invade the Material Plane with its pervasive darkness. This "Darkening" begins slowly, assimilating a 2-mile area per day at first, but quickly begins to advance at an almost geometric rate. The effects of this darkening are detailed above.

If reduced to 25 hit points or less, the *darkling lanthorn* attempts to summon 1d4 advanced shadows to help protect it. There is a 33% chance this summoning is successful. Other than this power and the shadow elemental guardian, the *darkling lanthorn* cannot defend itself.

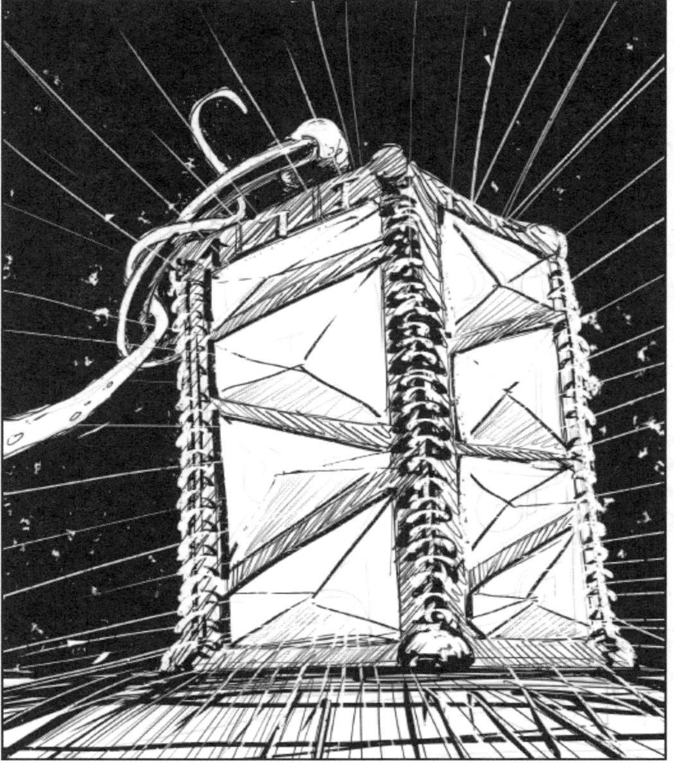

DESTRUCTION

The *darkling lanthorn* is subject to physical and magical attacks. The *darkling lanthorn* has a hardness of 10 and 100 hit points. It is immune to cold and electricity, and can only be damaged by magic weapons.

New Magical Items

Hunter's Mask

Aura moderate transmutation; **CL** 6th
Slot head; **Price** 20,000 gp **Weight** 1 lb.

DESCRIPTION

This object is a wooden mask carved from darkest mahogany and bearing inlaid ebony to form winding sigils across its face.

The hunter's mask provides the benefits listed below only if the wearer has the favored enemy class ability; it is simply a decorative accessory in the possession of other classes.

If the wearer does not already possess darkvision, the ranger gains that ability with a 60-ft. range.

The wearer gains a +4 bonus to Survival checks when tracking, regardless of quarry. This benefit stacks with the ranger's usual advantage when tracking favored enemies. Once per day, the wearer can cast *aspect of the wolf* and *bear's endurance* on himself.

CONSTRUCTION

Requirements Create Wondrous Item, *aspect of the wolf, bear's endurance, darkvision,* **Cost** 10,000 gp

Staff of Radiance

Aura strong evocation; **CL** 14th
Slot none; **Price** 40,000 gp **Weight** 5 lb.

DESCRIPTION

This staff is crafted from an ancient human tibia wrapped with crumbling reptile hide. Prehistoric glyphs are carved down the length of the bone

- *light*: 1 charge
- *burning gaze*: 1 charge
- *daylight*: 3 charges

If the staff's last charge is expended, roll 1d20. On a result of a 1, the staff crumbles into dust, destroyed.

CONSTRUCTION

Requirements Craft Staff, *burning gaze, daylight, light*; **Cost** 20,000 gp

New Monsters

Gloom Gnome

A short humanoid with dusky ash skin and glittering black eyes slinks out of the.

GLOOM GNOME **CR 3**
XP 800
NE Small outsider (elemental, native)
Init +2; **Senses** darkvision 120 ft.; **Perception** +8

AC 13, touch 13, flat-footed 11 (+2 Dex, +1 size)
hp 32 (5d10+5)
Fort +2; **Ref** +6; **Will** +4
Immune elemental traits
Weakness light sensitivity

Speed 20 ft.
Melee shadow blade +8 (1d4+2)
Ranged necrotic ray +8 (Fort DC 13)
Special Attacks sneak attack (+2d6)

Str 14, **Dex** 15, **Con** 13, **Int** 12, **Wis** 11, **Cha** 9
Base Atk +5; **CMB** +6; **CMD** 18
Feats Dodge, Mobility, Spring Attack
Skills Acrobatics +10, Bluff +7, Climb +10, Knowledge (planes) +9, Perception +8, Sense Motive +8, Stealth +14 (+18 in areas of dim light or darkness); **Racial Modifiers** +4 Stealth in areas of dim light or darkness
Languages Aklo, Common, Gnome

Environment any undeground
Organization solitary or small group (1d6+1)
Treasure NPC Gear (heavy pick, light crossbow with 10 bolts, other treasure)

Necrotic Ray (Su) The gloom gnome throws a beam of dark, scintillating energy as a ranged touch attack. The ray drains the victim of its vitality; a living creature struck by a gloom gnome's necrotic ray must succeed on a DC Fortitude save or be fatigued. A fatigued creature struck again by a necrotic ray, even if from another gloom gnome, becomes exhausted. On a third successful attack, the creature goes unconscious.

Grimseem

This creature is an inky black blot resembling a headless bat with a pair of long tentacles trailing behind.

GRIMSEEM **CR 2**
XP 600
CE Small outsider (chaotic, elemental, evil, extraplanar)
Init +3; **Senses** darkvision 120 ft.; **Perception** +7

AC 14, touch 14, flat-footed 11 (+3 Dex, +1 size)
hp 32 (5d10+5)
Fort +2; **Ref** +7; **Will** +3
Immune elemental traits
Weakness light sensitivity

Speed 10 ft., fly 40 ft. (average)
Melee bite +6 (1d4), 2 slams +7 (1d6)

Str 10, **Dex** 16, **Con** 12, **Int** 5, **Wis** 8, **Cha** 8
Base Atk +5; **CMB** +4; **CMD** 17
Feats Flyby Attack, Hover, Weapon Focus (slam)
Skills Fly +13, Perception +7, Stealth +15 (+19 in areas of dim light or darkness); **Racial Modifiers** +4 Stealth in areas of dim light or darkness
SQ shadow form

Shadow form (Ex) While in dim light, a grimseem can move through any opening regardless of width without squeezing.

Miasmic Death

A cloud of dim oblong bubbles throws a pale rainbow light as it drifts along.

MIASMIC DEATH **CR 3**
XP 800
N Medium ooze
Init +2; **Senses** blindsight 60 ft.; **Perception** –5

AC 12, touch 12, flat-footed 10 (+2 Dex)
hp 31 (7d8)
Fort +2; **Ref** +4; **Will** +3
Defensive Ability amorphous; **DR** 5/magic; **Immune** ooze traits

---

Speed 20 ft. fly (average)
Melee swarm (2d6)
Special Attacks distraction (DC 13)

Str 2, **Dex** 14, **Con** 10, **Int** —, **Wis** 12, **Cha** 10
Base Atk +3; **CMB** -1; **CMD** 11 (can't be tripped)
SQ misty form

Environment any
Organization solitary
Treasure none

Misty Form (Ex) A miasmic death's body is composed of a semisolid mist similar in consistency to thick foam. The miasmic death does not have a Strength score, and it cannot manipulate or wear solid objects. This form grants it the amorphous defensive ability, and allows it to move through areas as small as 1 inch in diameter with no reduction to its speed. A miasmic death cannot enter water or other fluids, and is treated as a creature two size categories smaller than its actual size (Tiny for most miasmic deaths) for the purposes of how wind affects it.
Swarm (Ex) A miasmic death can occupy the space of another creature, and is treated like a swarm for the purposes of its melee attack and distraction ability. A miasmic death doesn't make standard melee attacks. Instead, it deals automatic damage to any creature whose space it occupies at the end of its move, with no attack roll needed. A miasmic death's attack is not subject to a miss chance for concealment or cover.

Elemental, Shadow

Looming out of the darkness is a vaguely humanoid shape, entirely black, with pale purple pits for eyes and arms that end in glowing purple claws.

Languages Common

Environment the Plane of Shadow

Organization solitary
Treasure standard

Strength Damage (Su) A shadow elemental deals Strength damage with a successful slam attack. A creature reduced to Strength 0 dies and becomes a shadow in 1d4+2 rounds. Shadows are not under the control of the shadow elemental that created them.
Shadow Blend (Su) During any conditions other than full daylight a shadow elemental can disappear into the shadows, giving it total concealment. Artificial illumination, even a *light* or *continual flame* spell, does not negate this ability but a *daylight* spell does.

SMALL SHADOW ELEMENTAL **CR 1**
XP 400
N Small outsider (elemental, extraplanar)
Init +0; **Senses** darkvision 120 ft.; **Perception** +7

AC 17, touch 11, flat-footed 17 (+6 natural, +1 size)
hp 13 (2d10+2)
Fort +1; **Ref** +3; **Will** +3
Defensive Abilities shadow blend; **Immune** elemental traits

Speed 20 ft.
Melee slam +5 (1d3+3 plus 1d3 Str)
Special Attacks 1d3 Strength damage
Spell-like Abilities (CL 6th):
At will—*shadow walk*
3/day—*shadow evocation* (DC 15)

Str 14, **Dex** 10, **Con** 13, **Int** 4, **Wis** 11, **Cha** 11
Base Atk +2; **CMB** +3; **CMD** 13
Feats Alertness
Skills Perception +7, Sense Motive +7, Stealth +9

MEDIUM SHADOW ELEMENTAL **CR 3**
XP 800
N Medium outsider (elemental, extraplanar)
Init +1; **Senses** darkvision 120 ft.; **Perception** +9

AC 19, touch 11, flat-footed 18 (+1 Dex, +8 natural)
hp 34 (4d10+12)
Fort +4; **Ref** +5; **Will** +4
Defensive Abilities shadow blend; **Immune** elemental traits

Speed 20 ft.
Melee slam +7 (1d4+4 plus 1d4 Str)
Special Attacks 1d4 Strength damage
Spell-like Abilities (CL 8th):
At will—*shadow walk*
3/day—*shadow evocation* (DC 15)

Str 16, **Dex** 12, **Con** 17, **Int** 4, **Wis** 11, **Cha** 11
Base Atk +4; **CMB** +7; **CMD** 17
Feats Alertness, Power Attack
Skills Perception +9, Sense Motive +9, Stealth +8

LARGE SHADOW ELEMENTAL **CR 5**
XP 1,600
N Large outsider (elemental, extraplanar)
Init +2; **Senses** darkvision 120 ft.; **Perception** +13

AC 20, touch 11, flat-footed 18 (+2 Dex, +9 natural, –1 size)
hp 76 (8d10+32)
Fort +6; **Ref** +8; **Will** +6
Defensive Abilities shadow blend; **DR** 5/magic; **Immune** elemental traits

Speed 20 ft.
Melee 2 slams +13 (1d6+5 plus 1d6 Str)
Space 10 ft.; **Reach** 10 ft.
Special Attacks 1d6 Strength damage
Spell-like Abilities (CL 12th):
At will—*shadow walk*
3/day—*shadow evocation* (DC 15)

Str 20, **Dex** 14, **Con** 19, **Int** 6, **Wis** 11, **Cha** 11
Base Atk +8; **CMB** +14; **CMD** 25
Feats Alertness, Cleave, Power Attack, Weapon Focus (slam)
Skills Knowledge (planes) +9, Perception +13, Sense Motive +13, Stealth +9

HUGE SHADOW ELEMENTAL **CR 7**
XP 3,200
N Huge outsider (elemental, extraplanar)
Init +8; **Senses** darkvision 120 ft.; **Perception** +17

AC 21, touch 12, flat-footed 17 (+4 Dex, +9 natural, –2 size)
hp 105 (10d10+50)
Fort +8; **Ref** +11; **Will** +7
Defensive Abilities shadow blend; **DR** 5/magic; **Immune** elemental traits

Speed 30 ft.
Melee 2 slams +16 (1d8+7 plus 1d8 Str)
Space 15 ft.; **Reach** 15 ft.
Special Attacks 1d8 Strength damage
Spell-like Abilities (CL 14th):
At will—*shadow walk*
3/day—*shadow evocation* (DC 15)

Str 24, **Dex** 18, **Con** 21, **Int** 6, **Wis** 11, **Cha** 11
Base Atk +10; **CMB** +19; **CMD** 33
Feats Alertness, Cleave, Improved Initiative, Power Attack, Weapon Focus (slam)
Skills Knowledge (planes) +11, Perception +17, Sense Motive +17, Stealth +9

GREATER SHADOW ELEMENTAL **CR 9**
XP 6,400
N Huge outsider (elemental, extraplanar)
Init +9; **Senses** darkvision 120 ft.; **Perception** +20

AC 22, touch 13, flat-footed 17 (+5 Dex, +9 natural, –2 size)
hp 121 (13d10+50)
Fort +9; **Ref** +13; **Will** +8
Defensive Abilities shadow blend; **DR** 10/magic; **Immune** elemental traits

Speed 30 ft.
Melee 2 slams +20 (1d8+8 plus 1d8 Str)
Space 15 ft.; **Reach** 15 ft.
Special Attacks 1d8 Strength damage
Spell-like Abilities (CL 17th):
At will—*shadow walk*
3/day—*shadow evocation* (DC 15)

Str 26, **Dex** 20, **Con** 21, **Int** 8, **Wis** 11, **Cha** 11
Base Atk +13; **CMB** +23 (+25 sunder); **CMD** 38 (40 vs. sunder)
Feats Alertness, Cleave, Great Cleave, Improved Initiative, Improved Sunder, Power Attack, Weapon Focus (slam)
Skills Intimidate +16, Knowledge (planes) +15, Perception +20, Sense Motive +20, Stealth +13

ELDER SHADOW ELEMENTAL **CR 11**
XP 12,800
N Huge outsider (elemental, extraplanar)
Init +10; **Senses** darkvision 120 ft.; **Perception** +23

AC 23, touch 14, flat-footed 17 (+6 Dex, +9 natural, –2 size)
hp 168 (16d10+80)

Fort +10; **Ref** +16; **Will** +10
Defensive Abilities shadow blend; **DR** 10/magic; **Immune** elemental traits

---

Speed 30 ft.
Melee 2 slams +24 (1d8+9 plus 1d8 Str)
Space 15 ft.; **Reach** 15 ft.
Special Attacks 1d8 Strength damage
Spell-like Abilities (CL 20):
At will—*shadow walk*
3/day—*shadow evocation* (DC 15)

Str 28, **Dex** 22, **Con** 21, **Int** 10, **Wis** 11, **Cha** 11
Base Atk +16; **CMB** +27 (+29 bull rush and sunder); **CMD** 43 (45 vs. bull rush and sunder)
Feats Alertness, Cleave, Great Cleave, Improved Bull Rush, Improved Initiative, Improved Sunder, Power Attack, Weapon Focus (slam)
Skills Intimidate +19, Knowledge (arcana) +19 Knowledge (planes) +19, Perception +23, Sense Motive +23, Stealth +17

Shadow elementals inhabit the Shadow Plane, being as fundamentally connected to that plane as an earth elemental is bound to the Plane of Earth. Comprised of the essence of their plane, shadow elementals are shadowstuff made manifest — much like a shadow transformed into rock.

Shadow elementals play many roles on their home plane, constantly plotting and scheming to advance through the ranks of their elaborate hierarchy. The largest shadow elementals are usually the leaders of powerful armies of shadows, though they have been known to enter into pacts with mortal wizards, serving as powerful enforcers in exchange for certain wondrous items.

Shadow elementals have solid bodies, as the shadowstuff has coalesced into tangible form and been inhabited by the elemental spirit. Their great strength, coupled with their special abilities, makes them lethal opponents.

Men & Monstrosities

Deep in the Vale

By James M. Ward

Deep in the Vale is a Pathfinder Roleplaying Game adventure. It is designed for a party of characters of 1st level.

Game Master's Notes

In this adventure, your player characters should start at 1st level with zero experience points. As they run through each encounter, give them the experience points they earn instead of waiting until the entire adventure is over. As the GM, you want your characters to gain a level or two and the hit points those levels add to the character sheet.

The characters have lived their whole lives in the Vale. The pleasant valley is a peaceful place with few things bothering the inhabitants. Thirty years ago, orc and goblin wars occurred that the oldsters of the village still talk about. However, life is easy for the people of the Vale — but that is about to change. This adventure is not about acquiring gold and vast treasure. It instead presents many fighting situations with enough choices so that the players know they are roleplaying and that their decisions move the action along.

The player characters are exposed to encounters coming into the Vale looking to do the inhabitants harm. Some roleplaying is involved where the players have to figure out how to best defend themselves from danger. Don't assume each of these encounters happens day after day in the Vale. Let a few days or even weeks pass between encounters.

Give the characters time to think of ideas to prepare for the greater dangers coming into their peaceful valley. The players should roleplay the various jobs they have in the Vale. The blacksmith is going to make shields and warhammers. The hunters are going to look for deer in the woods to the north. Life must continue to flow in the Vale, no matter what problems affect the villagers.

At the end of all of these encounters, the ealdorman in the burh of Warsley, a fortified city 20 miles to the south, having heard of the exploits of the players characters, could easily order them to come to his hall and deal with a problem in another part of his shire.

In the ***Lost Lands*** campaign setting, the Vale is nestled among the lower slopes of the Cumbrian Mountains just north of the burh of Warsley. It lies on the western edge of the Helcynngae Peninsula, though it has largely been isolated from most of the turmoil of the Helcynn over the last few centuries. The residents of the Vale are hard-working Heldring folk, fair of face and long of limb with flaxen or red hair. The men favor beards while the women tend to wear their hair in long braids, with both genders wearing arm-rings and ornamental brooches to display their affluence. The rest of the world may see the Heldring as peerless warriors and pitiless sea raiders, but to the folk of the Vale they are just neighbors and friends who leave the wars and raiding to others of the Helcynn.

Introduction

In any beginner game, the GM needs to help his players learn how to roleplay and react to his descriptions. Many battles are in this adventure, but to get to them, the GM should encourage the characters to reach the proper conclusions. Encouragement is done through the use of NPC villagers of the Vale. A new GM must know inside and out the "combat rules" and the "experience rules" for this adventure to work properly.

The PCs are all from the Vale. This is a simple place where the equipment needed to live is sparse. No suits of armor or warhorses are available to buy in the local area. If the characters want that material, they must go many miles away to the city. The equipment that can be purchased is found in the farms and homes of simple people. The tinker and his wagon supply things such as daggers, pots, and pans, and some useful chemicals and leather goods. The people of the village are capable of making backpacks, fur cloaks, lanterns and the like. These goods appear at the market in the village square. The blacksmith player character is able to make shields, but swords and more complex weapons are beyond him. The leatherworker can make boiled-leather chest plates, but more complex armor is beyond him.

The player characters could expect to have things made by farmers and blacksmiths. Assume in this adventure that each of the player characters has a job in the village. The strongest of the player characters is the blacksmith. Parcel out jobs for the rest of the group. Suggestions include: farmer, orchard grower, herdsman, dairyman, innkeeper, leatherworker, and woodcarver. Have the characters in their late teens. All of the characters work successfully at their own jobs.

The central figure, the blacksmith, is the fighter type and has a war club his father carved from a piece of oak that lightning struck. The others in the group have quarterstaffs. If there is a magic-user, he has several throwing daggers. Their parents gave them their backpacks, which include things such as mirrors, flint and steel, waterskins, pots, metal plates and cups, blankets, heavy cloaks, changes of clothes, bandages, and skins of wine. A cleric worships Thor and keeps up the shrine at the entrance to the Vale.

As the GM, your task is to describe people, places and things so well that they come alive in the minds of your players. You want to make the encounters interesting. If your players enjoy themselves, they keep coming back and all of you can enjoy the fun of this experience. One of the most important things you can do as a GM is to maintain a sense of excitement.

You live and work in the Vale. Each of you has your own home and has been on your own for several years, making a good living and growing to adulthood. The Vale has been good to you, and you like the land and the people who live in this area. You have a group of friends that you like to tip a few ales with at the local inn. As teenagers, you all have dreamed about being brave heroes just like in the legends the oldsters talk about at the inn.

It's Thor's Day, and you and your friends are up before the dawn. Thor's Day happens in the middle of every week. You all stand with weapons in hand at the shrine of Thor, at the top of the hill. You wait for the dawn sun to peek over the hill to the east. To the west is your valley and homes.

As the blacksmith, you are the strongest member of your group. As the son of a blacksmith, you have been shaping metal for most of the seventeen years of your life. You smile at the rest of the group. They are farmers, dairymen, and orchard growers. Every week, you all get together for this run. The rest of your friends want to beat you in this race, but none has been able to do so in the last five years.

Dawn's light comes over the hill. "Go," you shout. Heading north, you all enjoy the feel of your muscles working. The first part of the run is five miles to the ridges on the west side of the valley. You jog around the valley three times, as fast as you can for the exercise running provides for the group. As you run these ridges, you look down at the cabins. The largest of the homes holds Amber. She is eighteen, and constantly on your mind.

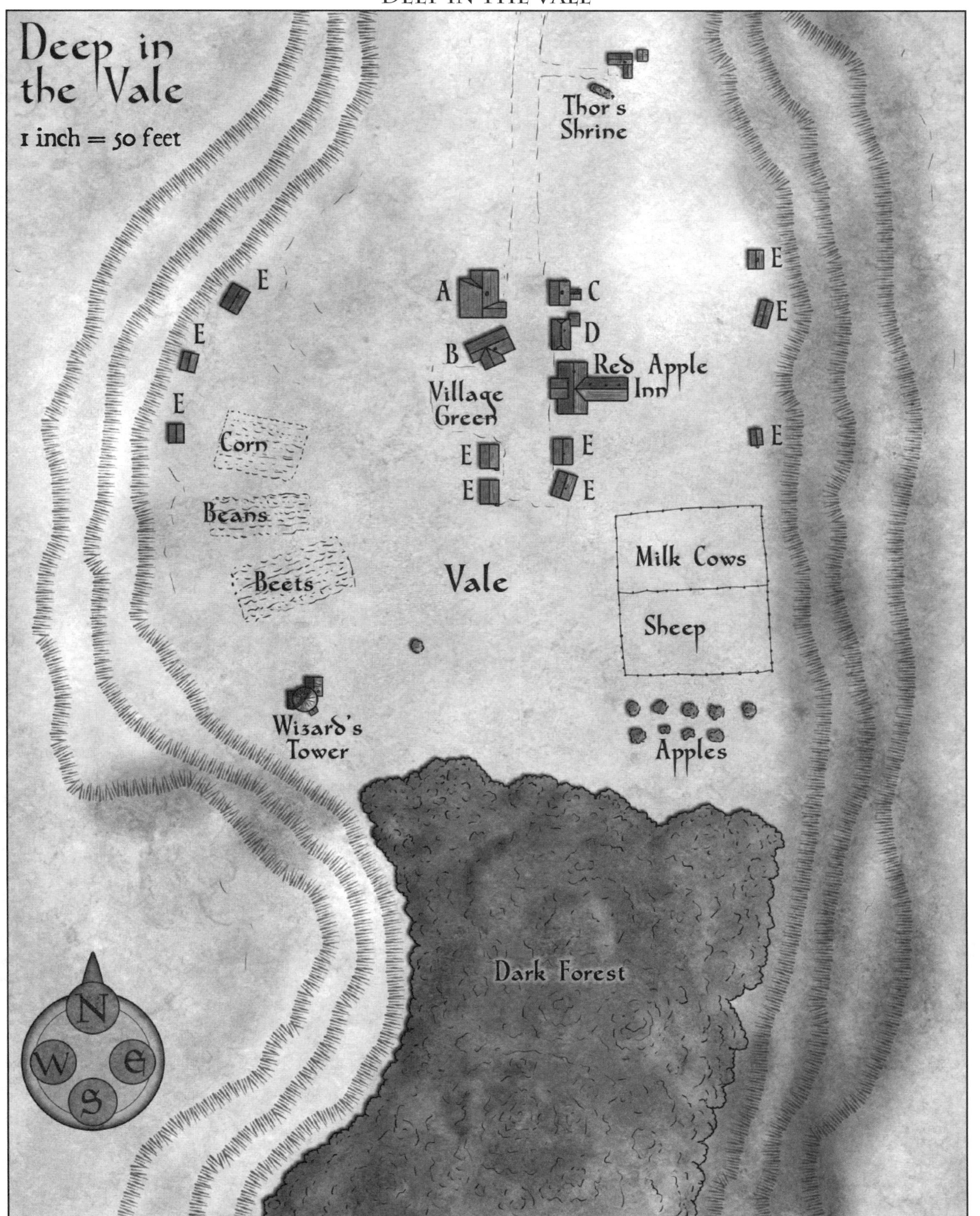
Deep in the Vale
1 inch = 50 feet
Thor's Shrine
A
B
C
D
E
E
E
E
E
E
E
E
E
E
E
Red Apple Inn
Village Green
Corn
Beans
Beets
Vale
Milk Cows
Sheep
Wizard's Tower
Apples
Dark Forest
N
W
E
S

In minutes, you and your friends run past the fields of parsnips, cabbages, and beans along the western side of the valley. Donal rushes past, and you laugh. Your friends know he has rushed ahead way too early.

As the group runs near the black tower in the southwest end of the valley, everyone gives that mass of magical stone a wide margin. A wizard lives in that tower. As children, you dared each other to slap the tower door and run away. That stopped when Devon turned to stone for 24 hours.

The south end of the valley is filled with the dark forest. Even the hunters avoid that place. The group runs east past the huge apple orchard. The red apples are thick and large on the many trees. Stomachs grumble at the thought of apple pies baking and placed on cabin windowsills for cooling.

The reason for your weapons on this run becomes clear as the howls of the wolves and bleats of the sheep hit your ears. The sheep and cow pens are large and right together on the east side of the Vale. Running up, you see the four large wolves feasting on four different sheep. The beasts aren't paying any attention to your group.

A Run Around the Valley (CR 5)

The group is running for exercise. They come across a pack of wolves feasting on sheep in a large grazing pen. The wolves are hungry and just started eating the sheep. They aren't paying attention to the PCs. These wolves won't run from battle and fight over the bodies of the sheep they are eating. The characters get in the first strike at each wolf and then the battle begins in earnest.

WOLVES (4) **CR 1**
XP 400
hp 13 (*Pathfinder Roleplaying Game Bestiary* "Wolf")

Treasure: These are unique wolf pelts and make fine cloaks for the player characters. In two weeks, the leatherworker can make cloaks that have a +1 armor bonus.

The Vale

The Vale is a very prosperous place. Everyone works and enjoys life in the peaceful valley. For more than a hundred years the wizard (see "Talk to the Wizard" below) of the Vale, has secretly protected the land around his tower. He's getting old and isn't as capable as he was when he was only a hundred years old. The old wizard still has plenty of power, but he relies on magic items he creates. If a spellcaster is in the group, (as the wizard is currently friendly, if he could be made helpful by a PC wizard DC 15 Diplomacy check) the old wizard finds a way to reward the younger mage with a valuable magic item to (GM's discretion) protect the people of the Vale.

The player characters all know exactly what is useful in any given cabin and have no problem asking to borrow these items. As the GM, feel free to suggest they take this equipment to fight the Vale's battles.

Amber's Cabin (CR 2)

Amber is 18 years old and the true beauty of the Vale. She works as a barmaid at one of the local taverns. She has always liked the blacksmith of the Vale. Everyone figured she would marry him when she turned 18. Her log cabin is the largest of the cabins of the Vale. This vinter's cabin has six large rooms and a loft above half of it. She and her father live there. Her father grows grapes on the hillsides east of the Vale. His red and white wines age in barrels in the root cellar of the cabin.

AMBER **CR 1/2**
XP 200
hp 7 (*Pathfinder Roleplaying Game GameMastery Guide* "Barmaid")

Amber also works with the sheep and spins wool to make very warm clothing and blankets. She is skilled with a sling and iron bullets the blacksmith makes for her. Amber is a useful NPC. She flirts with all the members of the group, and is perfect for giving suggestions that move the adventure along. She is also the focus of a quest during the adventure.

Her father, **Durus**, was in the Warsley Fyrd (the militia army) 20 years ago. He has a halberd and a steel half-plate he wears when gearing up for battle. He is an old man, however, and wouldn't be much use in a real combat situation.

DURUS **CR 1**
XP 400
hp 18 (*Pathfinder Roleplaying Game GameMastery Guide* "Guard")

Farmer's Cabin (CR 1/2)

The **farmer** grows parsnips, cabbages, and beans in three large fields. He can be a player character or another NPC run by the GM. His home is a large four-room log cabin. Out back is a pair of large horses that pull plows over the fields. His root cellar is the largest in the Vale and is stores the produce he doesn't sell in Warsley. He has a wagon for taking his crop to town. Two short swords hang above the mantel in his cabin. The farmer's two grandfathers used these weapons in the Mountain War with the goblin tribes 30 years ago. The weapons are a tad rusty, but could be made battle-ready with a little care.

FARMER **CR 1/2**
XP 200
hp 10 (*Pathfinder Roleplaying Game GameMastery Guide* "Farmer")

Herdsman's Cabin (CR 1/2)

While Amber turns wool into yarn, the **herdsman** tends the sheep and moves them about the hillsides to crop the grass. He can be a PC or an NPC. His cabin has two large rooms. An adjoining shed is used to store the wool after shearing. Four adult sheep dogs obey the character's commands and are extremely useful in battles in the Vale. Currently, 100 sheep are in a very large pen east of the cabin. Every morning, the sheep are taken to a different section of the gentle sloping hills and allowed to crop the grasses in those areas.

HERDSMAN **CR 1/2**
XP 200
hp 10 (*Pathfinder Roleplaying Game GameMastery Guide* "Farmer")

Dairy Cattleman's Cabin (CR 3)

The **dairyman**'s cabin is large with two rooms. An adjoining milk barn is where the cows are milked and their milk stored for sale or processing. Other workers help the dairyman milk the cows. He then gets more help making butter and cheese. A total of 20 dairy cows are in a very large pen. A group of **5 teenagers** take the cows out each day to let them feed to the north of the Vale. All of these boys carry slings and river stones for sling bullets. They constantly test each other's skills. In a battle in the Vale, they go to a ridge line and hurl sling stones down at an enemy.

DAIRYMAN **CR 1/2**
XP 200
hp 10 (*Pathfinder Roleplaying Game GameMastery Guide* "Farmer")

TEENAGERS (5) **CR 1/3**
XP 135
hp 6 (*Pathfinder Roleplaying Game GameMastery Guide* "Village Idiot")

Worker's Family Cabin (CR 1)

Each of these cabins has two large rooms and a large loft above the rooms. These **workers** do whatever jobs are needed in the Vale. Each has two or three children of varying ages. In times of danger, the kids go into the root cellars while the mother and father stay above to protect the entrance. The workers wield quarterstaffs and are unusually adept with the weapons as they practice weekly on Thor's Day on the common green.

These workers all have large beekeeping areas. The Vale's honey is famous for its reported healing properties. Besides its value as food, the honey cooks into mead that is sold for extra income. When the farmer goes into town on his wagon, he always takes several bottles, jars, and even small casks of honey and mead for sale.

WORKERS (2) **CR 1/2**
XP 200
hp 10 (*Pathfinder Roleplaying Game GameMastery Guide* "Farmer")

Red Apple Inn (CR 3)

The Red Apple Inn is a large two-story building. The upper story has six bedrooms and a bath chamber. The lower floor has a common chamber and bar, a kitchen with a pantry, and a bedchamber for the **innkeeper** and his **wife**. The inn is famous for apple ale and meat pies. The innkeeper's five children and his wife help run the inn. A small stable is at the side of the inn and a good-sized paddock sits behind it. At any given time, four sound horses are for sale. Everyone in the Vale eats here at lunchtime, when they get together to talk about the events of the week. It's a little known fact that the innkeeper and his wife are expert marksmen with a heavy crossbow, and that they've taught their sons and daughters this skill. The entire family is capable of sitting on the roof of the inn and firing down on advancing enemies.

INNKEEPER AND WIFE **CR 1**
XP 400
hp 13 (*Pathfinder Roleplaying Game GameMastery Guide* "Shopkeep")

Village Green

The village green is the Vale's social center. Every week, the adults practice quarterstaffs here while the children train with slings. At the end of the week, if the weather is pleasant, music is played on the green. Sometimes, when danger is in the area, everyone comes to the village green to band together and protect the Vale.

Thor's Shrine

The shrine has been at the entrance to the Vale for as long as anyone can remember. Maintaining the shrine has customarily been the job of the Vale's blacksmith. Once a day, the stones are wiped down with raw wool and mistletoe is spread out evenly on the marble arch. If the hammer bell isn't ringing because of the wind, the caretaker chimes the bell a few times a day.

The blacksmith shop with its anvil and furnace are in a large one-room cabin behind the shrine. This person can be a PC, and the party's main fighter. If this character doesn't have a 17 or 18 for strength, tell the player *that working with metal all his life gives him great strength to equal 17.* The blacksmith is gifted by the Heldring gods with the ability to make warhammers quickly. He also can make stout shields with his skill bonus Craft (blacksmith) +4.

The Shrine's Warning

Clerics put the shrine to Thor at the top of the rise hundreds of years ago. The shrine is a white marble arch with mistletoe growing all over the sides and top. A small bell in the shape of a hammer hangs down from the top of the arch. A good-sized white marble bench is below the arch so people can rest their tired bodies and enjoy the view down into the Vale. The creators of the shrine hoped the gods would look favorably on the valley and give the people their blessing.

As the blacksmith, you have come to the top of the rise to look for the tinker and his cart. He's been expected for several days. During the past week, you started making shields and wondered if the tinker could sell them for you. As you neared the shrine, you sent up a prayer to Thor, the deity of combat and strength, and the shrine started to glow. On the bench appeared a warhammer. You couldn't help but wonder at this message, as you have never seen the shrine glow before. When the hammer is picked up, the glow vanishes.

The glow has no explanation. Thor knows the Vale is under attack by several different forces and gives the blacksmith player character a high quality, warhammer to defend the valley.

Development: As the GM, you need to create a sense of danger that wasn't present before in the Vale. As the characters work at their various jobs, they sense that they are being watched. The hackles on the backs of the characters' necks rise for no reason.

The villagers gossip about crops stolen in the night. They discuss how farm animals are being killed and parts of them carried away into the Dark Forest. They also worry that fall has come a bit early, and all the crops are ready for picking.

Dark clouds come out of the south, blotting out the sun and making things very dark in the Vale. Thunder and lightning fill the sky day and night as a goblin shaman causes the clouds so the sun doesn't cause a glare for the goblins and orcs who might attack during the day. If the party has a cleric, that player knows the dark clouds [DC 10 Knowledge (religion)] are an evil sending.

Introduce the charming daughter of the winemaker of the Vale. Amber is interested in the blacksmith. She flirts with other player characters to make the blacksmith jealous. If she hears the blacksmith describe the unusual hammer and the glowing shrine, she insists on being taken there. When she urges the blacksmith to sit with her on the bench, she glows with Thor's favor. This scares the wits out of her and she rushes home. This foreshadows her abduction in a later encounter.

Treasure: The weapon acts a *masterwork warhammer* that glows when it is within 30 feet of any monster humanoid or undead. From now on, the blacksmith can make these weapons although they won't have *Thor's favor*.

Zombies Smashing in the Door (CR 5)

In the middle of the night, a pounding sounds on the door of the blacksmith's cabin. As the GM, make sure you know exactly what the player character is holding and wearing. Do not allow him to gear up. If he over-prepares, make the first encounter an NPC who needs help birthing a cow. The player should feel silly that he had a weapon in hand.

Days later, the real encounter occurs as the pounding at the door turns out to be **2 zombies** coming in to attack. The zombies should be easy to kill. They strike last in the combat round. They move slowly and don't defend themselves at all.

ZOMBIES (2) **CR 1/2**
XP 200
hp 12 (*Pathfinder Roleplaying Game Bestiary* "Zombie, Human")

After the battle, find out exactly what the blacksmith character wants to do because more zombies are attacking other houses this night. The blacksmith hears shrieks in the night. His first thoughts imagine Amber in trouble. He also might want to alert his friends in their houses.

Attacking the other cabins are **6 zombies**. Each is an easy battle, especially if other PCs join the action. Thor's hammer glows in the darkness as the wielder comes within 30 yards of the monsters, but it displays no other magical properties.

The goblin shaman sent the zombies to attack the Vale. Creating the zombies was a lot of effort for the shaman, and he rests afterward for several weeks.

ZOMBIES (6) **CR 1/2**
XP 200
hp 12 (*Pathfinder Roleplaying Game Bestiary* "Zombie, Human")

The Tinker's Demise

On another Thor's Day, the player characters are waiting at the top of the rise. The talk is about the zombies that invaded two nights ago. There was no trail to show where the zombies came from. As the sun rises in the dawn sky, in the distance down the Shire Road everyone can see the Tinker's unmoving wagon. The group runs to the wagon to note the horses killed by arrows that appear to be of orc make. The tinker's head is on a pole by the wagon. The pole is covered in blood and has strange stones and raven claws attached to it. No one knows what it means. The goods in the wagon are thrown all around the area.

The orc arrows are all alike, with large shafts more than three feet long and painted in the colors of Hooked-Fang orc tribe. Each uses raven feathers and has an obsidian arrowhead. The orcs like the damage the razor-sharp volcanic stone does to the target. Orc raiders haven't been seen in the area in years. The people of the Vale need to be warned.

Many fun roleplaying situations can be had with this discovery. The GM should use the people of the Vale to present options for the player characters to consider as the population of the Vale meets at the inn.

Development: Do the player characters pack up everything and take the wagon and the body down into the Vale? Or do they plunder the wagon since the tinker isn't going to do anything with the materials?

The Vale populace needs to be warned about the orcs. This roleplaying situation has the player characters get all of the people of the Vale together at the inn.

Should the wizard of the tower hear news of this danger? Could Amber like the blacksmith more for revealing this new encounter? What are the people of the Vale supposed to do? Is there a need to set up a night watch? Should someone go to The burh of Warsley to raise the fyrd and bring help? What is the significance of that strange pole the orcs left behind?

The player characters are not good trackers. They couldn't find the trail the orcs left after they attacked the tinker. But should the PCs sweep the area looking for signs of the orcs?

Treasure: Many useful items are in the wagon and include, but are not limited to, throwing daggers, axes, lanterns, oil for the lanterns, holy symbols of many types, trail rations, and kitchen items such as cups, plates, and cutlery. Enough items are available to supply all the player characters with useful equipment.

Danger at the Heart of the Forest (CR 7)

All the villagers talk about the problems presented by the tinker attack. Everyone thinks scouting the camp of the orcs and reporting back to the Vale is necessary. With heavy hearts, the entire town knew that going into the Dark Forest was a dangerous part of this task. This was the place where monsters collected.

As the village folk talk about the tinker's death, the innkeeper serves up free drinks of apple cider. Suddenly, the door opens and a stranger walks in. The elf fighter is wearing the furs of a wolf.

Smaragdus the elf is here to stimulate the action in the adventure and help the player characters survive. As the GM, you need to think how to roleplay this character. Think of a movie character you like that is aggressive and interesting and make Smaragdus like that character. You could make him a Robin Hood character or a sarcastic comic book character you like. Accents can be amusing, with the elf saying things like, "Well, I don't know now," over and over again. The elf's agenda is to find a very special wolf he has been seeking for years. When he describes the beast, the elf gets a far-away look on his face. The description makes it sound very dangerous as he describes a huge wolf with white fur on all its legs. Sounding very sad, Smaragdus explains that the wolf killed his younger brother. When the party goes into the forest, they find an unusual number of wolves. Smaragdus doesn't let the group search the woods after sunset.

The elf should also suggest setting traps along the edge of the Dark Forest. This defensive planning takes place with the help of the townspeople. What type of traps would best stop the orcs? The player characters should think of traps and then lead the way in getting those traps made.

SMARAGDUS **CR 2**
XP 600
Male elf ranger 3
NG Medium humanoid (elf)
Init +3; **Senses** low-light vision; **Perception** +9

AC 16, touch 13, flat-footed 13 (+3 armor, +3 Dex)
hp 27 (3d10+3 plus 3)
Fort +5; **Ref** +7; **Will** +3; +2 vs. enchantments
Immune sleep

Speed 30 ft.
Melee mwk longsword +5 (1d8+1/19–20)
Ranged mwk composite longbow +8 (1d8+1/×3)
Special Attacks combat style (archery), favored enemy (monstrous humanoids +2)

Str 12, **Dex** 17, **Con** 12, **Int** 12, **Wis** 13, **Cha** 8
Base Atk +3; **CMB** +4; **CMD** 17
Feats Endurance, Point-blank Shot[B], Precise Shot[B], Weapon Focus (longbow)

Skills Acrobatics +5, Climb +5, Handle Animal +4, Heal +5, Knowledge (dungeoneering) +5, Knowledge (geography) +5, Knowledge (nature) +7, Perception +9, Sense Motive +2, Stealth +9, Survival +7; **Racial Modifiers** +2 Perception
Languages Common, Elven, Orc
SQ elven magic, favored terrain (forest +2), track +1, wild empathy +2
Gear mwk studded leather, dagger, mwk composite longbow (+1 Str), mwk longsword, *cloak of resistance +1*, 88 gp

> Even if the elf is leading, chills go down your spines as you enter the Dark Forest. This is the place of scary legends for you. All your life, your family and friends have filled you with stories of the dangers of the forest. Right away, the elf pushes the group off the animal trail you were following. In seconds, four orcs come into view. Each is armored and ready for war, not 30 feet from the edge of the forest. The elf signals the group with a question: Attack them or leave them alone?

If the PCs attack and slay the **4 orcs**, read the following textbox. If they decide to let the orcs be, however, modify the text to omit any mention of the orcs.

ORCS (4) **CR 1/3**
XP 135
hp 6 (*Pathfinder Roleplaying Game Bestiary* "Orc")

> The fight with the orcs is resolved, so the group travels several miles into the Dark Forest using the animal trails. The elf gathers the group together. "There is goblin sign all over this area. I fear there is a large tribe of them somewhere near. We can search them out or go wide of this area. What do you all wish to do?"

If the group wants to travel to the goblin camp, the elf leads them along the ridges of the Dark Forest. In the late afternoon, the group finds the tribe of goblins at a massive cave opening on the side of the hill. There is no way to tell how many goblins are in that cave. At any one time, the group notes at least **20 goblins** in total maintaining a huge fire as others chop up the forest to fuel the blaze. And **3 goblin shamans** hold the totems that are exact copies of the one found near the tinker's wagon. Just this little evidence makes it clear that the goblins and orcs are working together.

GOBLINS (20) **CR 1/3**
XP 135
hp 6 (*Pathfinder Roleplaying Game Bestiary* "Goblin")

GOBLIN SHAMANS (3) **CR 1/2**
XP 200
Male or female goblin shaman 1 (*Pathfinder Roleplaying Game Bestiary* "Goblin"; *Pathfinder Roleplaying Game Advanced Class Guide* "Shaman")
CE Small humanoid (goblinoid)
Init +1; **Senses** darkvision 60 ft.; **Perception** +2

AC 14, touch 12, flat-footed 13 (+2 armor, +1 Dex, +1 size)
hp 11 (1d8+2 plus 1)
Fort +2; **Ref** +1; **Will** +4

Speed 30 ft.
Melee sickle +1 (1d4)
Spells Prepared (CL 1st; concentration +3):
1st—*burning hands* (DC 13), *sleep* (DC 13); *enlarge person*[S] (DC 13)
0 (at will)—*bleed* (DC 12), *know direction*, *read magic*
S spirit magic spell; **Spirit** Battle **Wandering Spirit**

Str 10, **Dex** 12, **Con** 14, **Int** 10, **Wis** 15, **Cha** 11
Base Atk +0; **CMB** –1; **CMD** 10
Feats Combat Casting
Skills Acrobatics +2, Knowledge (nature) +4, Knowledge (religion) +4, Ride +5, Spellcraft +4, Stealth +9; **Racial Modifiers** +4 Ride, +4 Stealth
Languages Goblin
SQ battle spirit, spirit animal
Gear leather armor, sickle

While the party watches the camp, the shaman are working on some sort of altar, speaking their prayers directly to the stone. The large rectangular block glows with a hellish light. Several types of wild animals are dead on the stone. Once they bleed out, the bodies are thrown in the large fire. The goblins are preparing several sacrifices.

The elf takes the party back to the village. In the discussion that follows at the inn, the elf is sure the goblins pose a growing danger to the Vale. The elf is sure the creatures are going to make some type of important sacrifice. He says that after such a sacrifice, the goblins transform into more dangerous creatures.

If the Characters Don't Want to Head Toward the Goblins (CR 7)

If the party doesn't want to follow the goblins, the elf leads them in another direction and, hours later, discovers an orc tower that is under construction. Watching the tower for an hour reveals at least **20 orcs** working on the structure. The tower's half-built walls are already formidable. A large **ogre** shows itself as the leader. Also **3 goblin shamans** are casting spells on the finished walls.

GOBLIN SHAMANS (3) **CR 1/2**
XP 200
hp 11 (see **Danger at the Heart of the Forest**)

ORCS (20) **CR 1/3**
XP 135
hp 6 (*Pathfinder Roleplaying Game Bestiary* "Orc")

OGRE **CR 3**
XP 800
hp 30 (*Pathfinder Roleplaying Game Bestiary* "Ogre")

The tower is located by a large pool of water and a 100-foot-tall waterfall. The orcs are quarrying stones from the hillside by the waterfall and have already dug a deep cliff into the hillside. At least a hundred finished square blocks sit by the tower. With the right effort, those stones might be pushed into the tower to ruin the half-built structure.

Back at the Vale, the elf talks with the townspeople about the problems with the growing bands of goblins and orcs. The villagers look to the player characters as leaders. Talk continues long into the night about how best to defend the Vale if any bands of monsters attack. This is a great roleplaying opportunity. The NPC villagers ask a number of difficult questions of the player characters, such as:

1. How many goblins can the village fight and expect to beat?
2. What can a goblin shaman do when it casts spells?
3. When will an orc band or a goblin band attack?
4. Should the village send someone to the ealdorman to ask for help?
5. What type of attacks do the goblins and orcs use in battle?

If the player characters can't answer the questions, that isn't a problem. They should do their best and tell the group when they don't know the answer.

Spider in the Apples (CR 4)

In the morning, the villagers are up and milling about nervously as they stare at a quarter section of the apple orchard that is covered in unusually thick webs. The webs are so dense that looking past them reveals only a deeper web wall of white. A three-foot-wide section of webs extends from the orchard to the sheep pens. A quick count of the sheep reveals five adult sheep missing.

The villagers are terrified and hysterical. They don't know what to do about the webs in the orchard but hope the PCs can figure something out.

The elf suggests the easiest effort is burn the webs and kill whatever comes out to escape the fire. The orchard owner hates that idea as too much of the ripe fruit is covered in the webs.

The elf is not happy, but comes up with another idea. If the villagers use sticks to poke at all sides of the webbing, a group of determined adventures can go into the middle of the webs with a chance of surprising the spiders. The elf knows such creatures use the vibration of the webs to track victims. If the webs are moving all over the area, the spiders won't know which way to turn in their attacks. Villagers with quarterstaffs stand by youngsters who hold sticks to jiggle the webs. If the spiders appear at an edge, the quarterstaffs should keep the spider away until attackers with better weapons can arrive.

In the webbing are **3 giant spiders**. The dead bodies of blood-drained sheep reveal the dangerous spiders in the webs. The yelling villagers and poking sticks distracts the arachnids, making it easy to surprise the spiders, which are on the ground in half-dug holes. Hundreds of web strands lead into the holes.

GIANT SPIDERS (3) CR 1
XP 400
hp 16 (*Pathfinder Roleplaying Game Bestiary* "Spider, Giant")

Talk to the Wizard

After the spider attack, the villagers think the wizard of the tower should help defend the Vale. The oldest villagers remember the wizard helping the last time the orcs appeared and attacked from the Dark Forest.

Naturally, they want the PCs to ask the wizard for help. There is some danger in this act; the last time the wizard made his presence known, he turned a child into a stone statue for 24 hours.

The elf wants nothing to do with wizard ways and refuses to go with the PCs to the ancient spellcaster's tower. He vows to wait at the inn for the group.

This wizard and his tower are useful for the GM. The wizard pays a good price for anything magical that the group acquires. This same wizard is also able to use spells the player characters can't cast. For a fee (see "Goods and Services" in Chapter 6 of the Pathfinder Roleplaying Game , the wizard can neutralize poison with a potion, can turn a statue back into a character with a *stone to flesh* scroll, or he can sell the characters useful potions for twice the normal cost.

Arcanius has noted the wolves and giant spiders coming into the valley.

If the characters think of the tinker, they can tell the wizard what happened. The death of the tinker surprises the wizard, and he becomes very concerned about the villagers of the Vale. He feels he is too old to go with the group into the Dark Forest. But Arcanius wants to do his part defending the valley. He offers the group some special potions and says they are free for the taking. They include *2 potions of cure light wounds*, a *potion of invisibility*, a *potion of bull's strength*, and a *potion of neutralize poison*.

ARCANIUS **CR 5**
XP 1,600
hp 33 (*Pathfinder Roleplaying Game GameMastery Guide* "Battle Mage")

On a final note, the wizard says, "If you get your enemies to follow you to the Vale, I can shoot *fireballs* at them." If a spellcaster is in the group, the wizard gives that character a *wand of sleep*. The wand has 10 charges left and is very powerful against goblins and almost as good against orcs. With that, the wizard closes the door.

Player characters can't go into or use the wizard's tower. Attempts to sneak into the tower are met with many magical traps and enchanted guardians that include golems to animated statues.

Wizard Arcanius

The wizard is 300 years old but looks older. Standing a little over 6 feet tall, he is almost doubled over from stooping due to old age. He uses a staff with an eagle's head at the top to help him move about. When the wizard gets angry, the eyes of the eagle glow brightly. The wizard dresses in black silk robes and wears two ruby rings on his fingers. He has a faintly glowing medallion of a scarab beetle on his chest. A green glass dagger is worn at his hip.

He could be a useful NPC for the GM. Whenever the PCs face a large problem, they can expect something useful from the wizard — assuming they can pay for the help.

After the encounter, the wizard expects his pick of the treasure and any magic items found. In this way, the GM can keep his game balanced.

When the player characters report back to the inn, the wizard's attitude amuses the elf. He suggests that if the wizard intends to fight only if monsters come near his tower, then the villagers should erect a large wooden fence to force the monsters in that direction. Everyone thinks this is a great idea. The tinker's wagon contained a couple of axes and saws to help cut down the trees if the characters decide to put this plan into action.

Wolves in the Night (CR 7)

In the middle of the night, when the moons are at their highest, the wolves strike. The night fills with howls. In a few heartbeats, the dairy cows and sheep cry out in pain and fear as wolves race around the village.

A large number of wolves attack the village. Smaragdus leads most of the villagers to fight the wolves attacking the cows and sheep. During the course of the battle, the elf notes burn marks on the backs of the wolves. The elf surmises the wolves were driven into the village with torches from the direction of the Dark Forest.

During the battle, **8 wolves** generally ignore the people in favor of quickly killing animals and dragging them off into the darkness. A **dire wolf** is amongst the attackers and seems to be the alpha of the pack. The wolf attack is just a diversion so the lovely Amber can be kidnapped. After the attack, PCs find a totem of a goblin shaman at the door of her home, and her father killed by attackers. Amber is missing, but no one knows where she is or why she was taken.

Have the dire wolf that the elf hunts appear out of the darkness and do some damage. The beast then vanishes in the direction of the homes — specifically Amber's home. The elf ignores the many wolves in the area in favor of looking for the dire wolf. The people of the village beg the player characters to help drive off the wolves attacking the animal pens.

DIRE WOLF **CR 3**
XP 800
hp 37 (*Pathfinder Roleplaying Game Bestiary* "Wolf, Dire")

WOLVES (8) **CR 1**
XP 400
hp 13 (*Pathfinder Roleplaying Game Bestiary* "Wolf")

Amber is Kidnapped

Using torches, the wolves are driven out of the Vale. The wounded cows and sheep are tended to. The dead animals are skinned and the smoking huts are filled with fresh meat to cure.

Suddenly, an anguished cry splits the night. The door of Amber's home has been smashed in. The kitchen and living room looks like a battle took place there. Even worse, neighbors who entered the house found her father dead inside. A goblin totem like the one left at the tinker's wagon stands outside the cabin's front door. Amber is nowhere to be found, and her body was not among the few villagers slain.

Everyone in the Vale has searched the land in and around the village, but no sign of the pleasant Amber can be found.

The kidnapping is a big deal. During the wolf attack, the goblins invaded the village and took Amber away. They hid their trail well as they fled, using wolves as mounts. A few of the goblins died in traps at the edge of the forest, which is how the people of the Vale know goblins likely kidnapped Amber.

During her kidnapping, Amber thought fast and dropped one of her large amber necklace stones at the forest's edge (a successful DC 15 Perception check finds these). She then dropped nine more stones along an animal trail that the goblins followed during their escape. The elf leads the PCs into the forest along the trail. When he nears the goblin lair on a hill in the Dark Forest, they come across a strange scene.

Goblins of the Dark Forest (CR 5)

The elf moves quietly through the pitch darkness. By staying close, everyone is able to keep up. Coming to the goblin's hillside cave, many strange sights can be seen. Above the cave is a high mound of boulders that looks ready to tip and cover the cave entrance. You can't tell, but the elf says it's possible goblins are guarding the boulders. A constant flow of male and female goblins go in and out of the cave. Those going out carry food to a banquet area near the cave entrance.

Twenty yards away from the cave, on the flat part of the forest, is a huge fire maintained by young goblins. These creatures don't have armor and weapons like the adults guarding the cave entrance. The forest is cut away here, and a large stack of wood is used for the fire. Patches of trees cover the rest of the area. Stumps rise out of the ground near the cave entrance, but everywhere else, old trees fill the area.

Amber struggles on a black stone altar. A sickening glow surrounds the altar as four goblin shamans chant spells around her. A strangely shaped, gaseous head slowly takes form above the stone.

Amber obviously needs to be saved, but how? The elf warns that charging into the mass of goblins would be certain death. The group moves back into the woods to talk about what they saw.

GOBLINS (8) **CR 1/3**
XP 135
hp 6 (*Pathfinder Roleplaying Game Bestiary* "Goblin")

GOBLIN SHAMANS (4) **CR 1/2**
XP 200
hp 11 (see **Danger at the Heart of the Forest**)

The group needs a plan to quickly save Amber since they don't know when the magic of the goblin shaman will finish. If the players don't come up with any ideas, the elf can suggest some options. They include the following:

Rush In and Throw Burning Logs Everywhere (CR 5)

The group talks about fires all around the cave and what such blazes might do to the goblins and the shaman. The idea involves the elf taking a burning bush around the perimeter of the cave entrance. Once fires start and the goblins move away from the flames, the player characters go to the large fire and throw the burning logs at the cave entrance and the surrounding countryside. The elf uses his bow on the four shamans. One of the PCs unties Amber and pulls her away from certain death.

The goblins are indeed very disturbed by the flames. The light is also too bright for them, putting them at a disadvantage. Most of the goblins hide in the cave or try to put out the fires. The player characters are barely noticed at all. The elf kills at least **2 shamans** and **10 goblins** before the player characters go to the altar to free Amber. The PCs face a battle, with a chance the remaining shamans kill the player character.

GOBLINS (10) **CR 1/3**
XP 135
hp 6 (*Pathfinder Roleplaying Game Bestiary* "Goblin")

GOBLIN SHAMANS (2) **CR 1/2**
XP 200
hp 11 (see **Danger at the Heart of the Forest**)

If the group frees Amber, they race for the Vale and purposely move toward the wizard's tower. Some of the goblins chasing the PCs are caught in the deadly traps at the edge of the Dark Forest. *Fireballs* from the tower finish off the remaining goblins.

Moving back to the goblin base days later reveals it destroyed and dead goblins. The rest of the tribe has left the area. If the player characters think of it, they could destroy the goblin altar to avoid trouble later.

Sneak to the Boulders and Push Stones Down into the Cave (CR 9)

At the top of the boulders are **2 goblin guards**. They have to be dealt with before the rocks can be toppled into the cave. The falling rocks are a great diversion as all of the goblins outside the cave immediately begin moving rocks. Sneaking into the camp is easy for any character who wants to cut Amber free. Once Amber is freed, the entire party runs to the Vale. The elf rings the gong at the village green to warn the villagers of a large pack of goblins coming out of the darkness. This attack happens long before dawn.

GOBLINS (2) **CR 1/3**
XP 135
hp 6 (*Pathfinder Roleplaying Game Bestiary* "Goblin")

The player characters should lead the defensive efforts, moving Vale defenders around the area to protect the village. The idea of sending goblins close to the wizard's tower is brought up, and the wizard is warned what could happen. He claims he is more than ready to stop large bands of goblins, which is good as **40 goblins** and the **2 goblin shamans** come out of the Dark Forest to attack. Many fall prey to traps set at the edge of the forest. If the characters think ahead, they might position villagers or obstacles to move the goblins past the wizard's tower. Several *sleep* spells and *fireballs* finish off the goblins.

GOBLINS (40) **CR 1/3**
XP 135
hp 6 (*Pathfinder Roleplaying Game Bestiary* "Goblin")

GOBLIN SHAMANS (2) **CR 1/2**
XP 200
hp 11 (see **Danger at the Heart of the Forest**)

Days later, scouting the goblin cave reveals that all the creatures have left. The stone altar is destroyed, cracked wide open by rolling boulders.

Create a Diversion and Lead Goblins to the Wizard's Tower (CR 1/2)

The group thinks a diversion could cause the goblins to chase the characters back to the Vale. The wizard has also claimed he can kill large groups of goblins. The group agrees the elf should go to warn the wizard. He will leave burning torches along the path to the tower for PCs to follow as they lure the goblins away.

Almost all the goblins follow the characters, but **1 goblin shaman** remains behind to watch Amber. Once the goblins leave their camp, the remaining player characters can attack the shaman and try to free Amber.

GOBLIN SHAMAN **CR 1/2**
XP 200
hp 11 (see **Danger at the Heart of the Forest**)

The diversion works, causing many of the goblins to die in the traps set at the edge of the Dark Forest. The monsters come close enough to the wizard's tower for him to use *sleep* and *fireball* spells to wipe them out.

Rush in and Surprise Attack the Goblin Shaman (CR 9)

This approach won't work as **60 adult goblins** come out of the cave to attack the characters with javelins and short swords. The **4 goblin shamans** use their spells against the characters. As the fight progresses and characters are injured, give them an opportunity to escape and vanish into the forest. If they stay and fight, however, they'll likely be overwhelmed and killed. The GM should help the players roll up new characters from the Vale. Amber is lost and never seen again. Such is the price of failure. If you are feeling generous, let the new characters try some other way to save Amber.

GOBLINS (60) **CR 1/3**
XP 135
hp 6 (*Pathfinder Roleplaying Game Bestiary* "Goblin")

GOBLIN SHAMANS (4) **CR 1/2**
XP 200
hp 11 (see **Danger at the Heart of the Forest**)

Orcs of the Dark Forest (CR 2)

> A week passes uneventfully. Then one morning, two cattle herders find two dead orcs in a pit trap at the edge of the forest. The orcs' bodies are pierced by stakes at the bottom of the pit. Both orcs wear a treasure in weapons and armor, and include a shortbow with two quivers of arrows, a long orc blade made of bronze, and a bronze breast plate and a helm. They each had 11 silver coins. Gossipers in the village say these were scouts for a bigger attack group.

The villagers decide to post guards near the forest each night, and they also discuss building more traps along the edge of the Dark Forest to snare any other orcs.

Nine days after the orcs' bodies were discovered, the night guards again summon the characters. An orc tripped another trap at the edge of the forest. The guards summon aid after finding **3 orcs** noisily trying to free their trapped brother.

The entire village swarms to defend the Vale, with men and women rushing to their assigned spots. The elf readies fire arrows to use against the orcs.

The people of the Vale attack the surprised orcs under the light of the full moon, which means the darkness doesn't count against the characters' combat abilities. After two orcs die, the other two try to run away. Ask your players if they want their characters to follow the orcs into the much darker forest.

Once again, the orcs are ready for battle. They are well armored in bronze chain and shield and carry several different types of bronze weapons. These weren't hunters; they were ready for battle.

ORCS (4) **CR 1/3**
XP 135
hp 6 (*Pathfinder Roleplaying Game Bestiary* "Orc")

Unexpected Aid (CR 3)

One morning, an unexpected visitor rides a wagon into the Vale. The ealdorman has heard of the ongoing troubles in the Vale and sends the experienced warrior **Sergeant Rolaesc** to assist the villagers. He brings a wagon loaded with weapons and armor, including 15 pole-axes and 20 steel breast plates. This equipment is a gift from the ealdorman to the villagers to use in their defense of the Vale. The sergeant's orders are to stay and train the people in use of the weapons and armor.

The old warrior explains that the ealdorman is very sorry that he can't raise the fyrd and send it to aid the Vale. The ealdorman acknowledges the danger to the Vale, but trouble brewing with giants in the east end of the shire requires the fyrd to defend the lands there.

SGT. ROLAESC **CR 3**
XP 800
hp 34 (*Pathfinder Roleplaying Game GameMastery Guide* "Guard Officer")

The GM could encourage the player characters to use the equipment provided. Now, the talented elf and the old warrior can help the characters and the villagers survive. When roleplaying the crusty old warrior, the GM should think of an old fellow he knows and use that person's mannerisms and accent. The warrior is not a patient man and expects the people of the valley to work hard to get ready for more orc attacks.

The People of the Vale Must Make a Decision

The people of the Vale have gathered at the inn to discuss what to do about the orcs. Everyone is certain bands of orcs are coming to attack the Vale. The defenses are as strong as the villagers can make them at the edge of the Dark Forest. Rolaesc wants the people to make a decision: Should the villagers attack the orcs at their base in the forest or wait for the largest band of orcs to attack the Vale?

By this point in the adventure, numerous deadly traps cover a line 50 yards out from the edge of the Dark Forest. A stout fence also flows from one end of the Vale to the other on the southern end of the valley, but stops before it reaches the wizard's tower. Everyone knows the wizard can take care of monsters coming near his tower.

Ten yards into the southern edge of the Dark Forest is a line of dried leaves and twigs. During an attack, fire arrows can be used to set these piles burning. The fire behind their ranks prevents the orcs from retreating and also blinds them. The orcs' night vision is ruined, while the villagers can clearly see the monsters as the band of orcs charges out of the forest.

Another line of defense is a hedgerow of thorny plants. The villagers searched the countryside for the thorny vines and planted them along the fence line. Again, an open space with no plants exists by the wizard's tower.

The villagers have practiced rapidly banding together when guards ring a gong on the Village Green. All defenders with sling skills go to the ridge on the eastern end of the Dark Forest. Bowmen and spear carriers take up positions in the middle of the fence line to keep monsters from climbing the fence. The player characters can roam the entire line and back up difficult battles. Everyone in the Vale thinks the next batch of orc attackers will appear as a large group. The biggest debate is whether to attack the orcs' tower or wait until the invaders come in force and have the people defend the Vale with the hope that the wizard can destroy the orc group.

Attack the Tower (CR 4)

It has been decided that you and the elf should look over the orcs' base. At dawn of the next day, your band moves out. As you travel through the Dark Forest, the elf points out where the orcs have been scouting the Vale.

By noon, you arrive at another forest's edge and can view what the orcs are doing. A partially built tower stands near a pond of water fed by a waterfall. The water rushes over a cliff wall of granite. The orcs are mining stone from the cliff and cutting it into blocks of stone for the tower. A large pile of stones sits beside the partially built tower. Pulleys and cranes on the cliff face and the tower allow the orcs to maneuver the stone blocks from the pile to the rising tower. The ogre leader seen earlier directs the orcs efforts.

The elf has two ideas and presents them to the group. You could cut down a tree, but leave the limbs on the trunk so it is easier to carry. Most of the orcs are in the tower during the day as orcs don't like sunshine. A tree battering ram might topple the pile of stones into the half-built tower, leaving the surviving orcs susceptible to attack as they rush out of the ruined tower. Or, the party could wait until dark when most of the orcs are unarmed and cutting stone in the quarry then attack the workers with surprise before attacking the orcs remaining in the tower.

You all talk among yourselves, picking one of the ideas.

In either choice, the Vale must win to eliminate the danger. When the **ogre leader** and **10 orcs** are killed, the rest retreat in fear. They are never seen again at this base or in the Vale.

ORCS (10) **CR 1/3**
XP 135
hp 6 (*Pathfinder Roleplaying Game Bestiary* "Orc")

OGRE **CR 3**
XP 800
hp 30 (*Pathfinder Roleplaying Game Bestiary* "Ogre")
Gear *+1 shield*

Wait for the Orcs to Attack the Vale

The people of the Vale talk most of the day about what is best for the Vale. The consensus is that the Vale's defenses are such that they should let the orcs attack. The pit traps and fence line are designed to drive the orcs toward the wizard's tower. Before the people make a final decision, however, you are encouraged to go to the wizard and get a promise of support from the spellcaster. The looks of fear on the villagers' faces show that no one wants to face the wizard. The party must trek to the wizard's tower to talk with him.

Talk with the Wizard

The old wizard comes to his tower door looking extremely angry. After you present the needs of defending the Vale, he begins shouting at your group.

"I see no reason to help this Vale. Foolish orcs can't get into my tower. Why should I help the people of the valley?"

You are all surprised by the wizard's brief speech. If you can't talk him into helping, the Vale is doomed.

The situation with the old wizard is supposed to occur as a fun roleplaying experience. The players must use their best roleplaying skills to think of reasons why the wizard should help. It won't take much convincing to get the wizard to agree to lend help with his powerful spells. The group can even get him to tell them how far from the tower he can throw his *sleep* and *fireball* spells. The party should leave the wizard feeling that they have done a good job. Now, all they have to do is wait for the orcs to invade. That attack comes the next night.

Attack in the Night (CR 6)

The growls in the night testify to the orcs moving in. The clang of the warning gong puts everyone on alert. The elf laid alarm traps deeper into the forest that the orcs tripped in their passing. This allows the people of the Vale to move to their defensive positions long before the orcs near the edge of the forest.

The elf fires flaming arrows into the dry leaves and sticks. In a few heartbeats, an **ogre** and a mass of well-armored **15 orcs** are backlit by the firelight. The burning brush startles the orcs, causing them to rush blindly forward into the deadly traps at the edge of the forest. Pits, springing vine traps, and other hidden surprises take out some of the monsters.

A hail of iron sling bullets and arrows drive the band of orcs to the west. The battle is on.

ORCS (15) **CR 1/3**
XP 135
hp 6 (*Pathfinder Roleplaying Game Bestiary* "Orc")

OGRE **CR 3**
XP 800
hp 30 (*Pathfinder Roleplaying Game Bestiary* "Ogre")
Gear *+1 shield*

This is supposed to be a learning experience for the player characters. They should face one or two orcs at a time. When the ogre leader shows up to fight, the entire party, the elf and Rolaesc should take the fight to the monsters. When the ogre dies, it knocks the fight out of the remaining orcs. Further decimating their ranks are exploding *fireballs* and a stone golem sent by the wizard to mow through the orcs. Thirty minutes into the battle for the Vale, only one or two orcs are left to flee into the Dark Forest.

A cheer goes up from the people of the Vale. The player characters are regarded as heroes and treated to a heroes' welcome at the inn. The old wizard comes out of his tower and rewards each player character with gold and useful potions and scrolls. Later in the week, the ealdorman summons the player characters with a problem in another part of the shire that he could use their help solving.

Irtep's Dish

By Casey W. Christofferson
additional material by Scott Greene

Irtep's Dish is an adventure for characters of 6–8 level. This adventure requires the skills of a rogue or some other expert at traps, a cleric or character that can heal allies and offer beneficial bonuses to the team, a wizard or other master of the arcane arts, and a fighter to take care of "the heavy lifting."

Background

Irtep is an eccentric wizard, recently as well known for his issues with wine, women, and gambling as for his skill at wizardry, which is substantial. His marker at the Fortune's Fool gambling house in Bard's Gate has been rescinded by Fat Julie, and he has even been banned from the tables at Blazing Bones. The bookies are now hot on Irtep's heels. His tower appears to be guarded by unmanned arcane defenses. There is speculation (and wagering) that Irtep is no longer in the city at all but has pulled a disappearing act to a different city, country, or even dimension.

Despite his personal and moral failings, Irtep is an important wizard whose closely guarded research is sought after by high-ranking officials in the Dominion Arcane. It was widely believed (within narrow wizardly circles) that Irtep was on the verge of a huge breakthrough before his collapse into the dens of ill repute. Dominion and independent magic-users are desperate to learn the spells Irtep was allegedly working on, and many are willing to pay any price to discover his secrets.

Even now, assassins, bounty hunters, thieves, wizards, and creditors of every stripe are hot on Irtep's trail, though none has managed to infiltrate his tower and recover their money or his secrets.

At the start of the adventure and at various points during it, player characters are contacted by any number of sources seeking to hire them to discover Irtep's whereabouts. Their investigation eventually leads to Irtep's tower, which they explore in search of the missing wizard or some clue to his whereabouts.

In the course of their exploration, the characters are transported to the Minzoa — a tiny world discovered by Irtep and hidden within "Irtep's Dish," where they must battle the elements, strange microscopic creatures, and other assassins and bounty hunters who are also striving to locate Irtep. Through their explorations, characters discover what truly happened to Irtep, for good or ill.

Part 1: The Missing Wizard

A variety of methods can be used to involve characters in the quest to locate Irtep and his hidden magic. The most straightforward are rumors, or direct contact from Irtep's friends, colleagues, or debt collectors. Use whatever method is most likely to hook your players' interest to get the adventure started.

Rumors

Rumors are most useful for motivated parties of experienced players who enjoy pursuing leads on their own. When handing out initial rumors, have each character make a Diplomacy check to gather information and consult the table below. Consider making these die rolls yourself, behind your screen. That way, players won't know whether they got an especially high or low roll, and they'll need to use some judgment when deciding what to believe.

Another option is to have all characters make a d20 roll without telling them what the roll is for. Instead, use their rolls as a secret check, adding their Diplomacy skill bonus and relaying the information to the players afterward.

Either of these methods helps avoid the "I rolled a 20, so we know my rumor is true" effect.

Result	Rumor
10 or less	There's nothing going on in town. If it were any more boring in Bard's Gate right now, the place would be abandoned. (FALSE.)
11	An old friend of Irtep the Wizard hired killers to assassinate him over an old grievance (Osgood Flumph, Faisal Dhaken, or Michalena Goddeau are named as the hiring NPC). (FALSE. But assassins are actually claiming to have been hired by these people.)
12	"When the wind blows, we're all going to die. I don't know what it means but I heard some wizard rambling about it." (NEUTRAL. This rumor is most effective when it's uttered by a blind hobo who reappears at odd times to repeat the message.)
13	Tuvio at the Blazing Bones hired someone to kill Irtep over bad debts. (FALSE. Tuvio is owed money, but he's leaning toward giving the thieves' guild a finder's fee to recover his money.)
14	The Dominion Arcane is actively hiring mercenaries. Inquire at the Wizard's Familiar for more information. (FALSE. Asking about this attracts the Dominion's attention, which is not necessarily a good thing. The Dominion typically summons its aid. The rumor is likely perpetrated by the Society of Arms to annoy the Dominion.)
15	Gamblers who show a little skill can get themselves a no-interest line of credit in most of the gaming houses in the city. (NEUTRAL. Credit is usually available, but there is always interest on it.)
16	Fat Julie is offering a reward for Irtep the Wizard's head over excessive gambling debts. (FALSE. Julie is looking for Irtep, but his own gang is doing the legwork. He offers no reward to outsiders.)
17	Irtep racked up massive gambling debts. Even his favorite good luck charm, Michalena Goddeau, refuses to speak to him. (TRUE.)

Result	Rumor
18	Several gangs have already tried to break into Irtep's tower. Nobody has seen them since. (TRUE)
19	"Irtep is a minzoologist, whatever that means. I heard him brag about it once." (TRUE. A successful DC 15 Knowledge (arcana or nature) check reveals that a minzoologist studies tiny life forms.)
20	Irtep was romantically involved with Michalena Goddeau, but she hasn't been seen since his disappearance. The lowdown is that when he ran out of money, she ran off with a charming sell-sword. She used to frequent the Fortune's Fool. She spent a lot of time at his tower while they were together, so she might know some of its secrets. (TRUE.)
21	Irtep used to drink with Osgood Flumph at the Wizard's Familiar and the Blazing Bones till they had some sort of falling out. Some say it was over a woman, others that it was over Irtep's arcane studies. Either way, Osgood has spent plenty of time inside Irtep's tower. Since their friendship fell apart, Osgood's been holed up at the Wizard's Familiar. (TRUE.)
22	Sources within the Dominion and among several of the temples who have been asked to investigate Irtep's disappearance are reasonably sure that he has not fled the city. Attempts to locate him magically keep pointing toward his tower, though there's no sign that anyone is there. (TRUE.)
23	Irtep made enemies of a wizard named Faisal Dhaken by beating him at a game of cards, stealing his woman, and co-opting his research. (NEUTRAL. Irtep might have beaten Faisal at cards at some point, but the other two items are incorrect. Faisal has a strong dislike for Irtep, however, arising from years of jealousy over Irtep's successes.)
24	All this drinking and gambling is a recent thing for Irtep. He used to be a stable, sober guy. Maybe his research put a curse on him or something. (TRUE. Irtep was cursed by Osgood Flumph, who hoped that Irtep's downfall would gain him access to Irtep's secret laboratory.)

Irtep's Associates

It is always possible that no matter how deeply the GM attempts to set the hook of adventure in his players, they refuse to take the bait. In this event, introduce the player characters to associates of Irtep as a way of moving the plot along and engaging the characters in the story. Hearing rumors at the onset of the adventure about a bounty on Irtep can lead characters directly to associates of Irtep and a glorious quest for treasure. Players are typically skittish about unverified rumors, however. This can be especially true if they've played other **Necromancer Games** adventures! In this case, a more direct approach is sometimes needed to kick the adventure into high gear. If characters don't follow up on any rumors, have hunters in search of Irtep or associates of Irtep looking for a hand in solving the wizard's disappearance approach the characters.

Michalena Goddeau

Goddeau is a girl who frequently works the Blazing Bones. Irtep considered her his lucky charm until his luck (and money) ran dry and she moved her affections to a mercenary flush with cash from a campaign in the Stoneheart Mountains. Michalena visited Irtep's tower on occasion, and it is suspected that she might know the password. Unfortunately, Michalena went missing within hours of Irtep's disappearance.

She might approach the characters through an intermediary. Her desire is to get the assassins and thieves off her back. Without much money of her own, she figures the only way of doing that is to get an item from Irtep's laboratory to pay off the hunters so that they leave her alone. She is agitated beyond belief, angry with Irtep, and annoyed that his problems are interfering with her life and livelihood.

Michalena is currently hiding out with her boyfriend at the Pride of Waymarch. This knowledge can be gained after questioning her associates at the Blazing Bones or Fortune's Fool and making a successful DC 12 Diplomacy or Intimidation check and/or some believable roleplaying.

If contacted, or if Michalena seeks out the characters, she asks that they bring her a magic bowl from Irtep's laboratory. She tells them they can keep and sell anything else they find; she only wants the bowl. If characters agree, she gives them the password that gets them in the front door.

If characters take Michalena up on her offer but don't deliver the bowl to her, she puts out a "harlots all-points bulletin" on the characters. Bounty hunters and assassins within 200 miles make the characters' lives miserable until the characters are dead or Michalena receives 5,000 gp worth of compensation for her trouble. As they say in the business, "that's a lotta chedda." Fortunately for the player characters, most of the bounty hunters who respond to such a call are wannabes, has-beens, and other low-rent hoods.

Osgood Flumph

Osgood is a doughty, overweight wizard known to have shared similar lusts for wine, ladies, and rich food when Irtep was on his long winning streak, mostly as a hanger-on or toady. Since Irtep's fall from grace in the gambling community and his subsequent disappearance, Osgood has lost his main source of free food and drinks.

He is currently hiding out at the Wizard's Familiar, where he worries that assassins, kidnappers, or powerful members of the Dominion Arcane may seek him out and work him over for knowledge of Irtep's research and whereabouts.

Osgood could use magic to contact the characters and ask them to meet him at the Wizard's Familiar. Once there, he makes a case, begging the characters to help him avoid the assassins by retrieving the *sextant of Minzoa* from Irtep's secret laboratory. Osgood helped Irtep craft the sextant and figures that he could trade it to the Dominion Arcane for their protection, or at least for a promise that they won't harm him. Osgood is unsure of the actual password to enter Irtep's tower, but he is familiar with the trap on the first floor.

If the characters take Osgood's deal, he expects to receive the *sextant*, and he insists on using a scroll inscribed with a special *geas* spell on it to make sure the characters remain on the up-and-up with him. He offers the characters the following magic items to help them in their task: a *potion of fly*, a *scroll of lightning bolt*, 1,000 gp apiece, a 500 gp diamond, a *wand of magic missiles* (10 charges), a *potion of invisibility*, and a *+1 weapon* of the group's choice. He also suggests that they help themselves to any of the antiquities Irtep collected, which he keeps crated on the sixth floor of his tower (this is a lie; no treasures are there, only a charmed troll).

Not What He Seems

Osgood is not whom he presents himself to be. In fact, Osgood is the one who placed the curse on Irtep by blending a curse into the *sextant* specifically set to *geas* poor Irtep into destructive behavior. Faisal suspects Irtep was cursed and he further suspects that Osgood is behind it, but he has no proof with which to trap the treacherous Osgood. If Irtep is brought to Faisal, the foreign wizard can break the curse.

Osgood is particularly suspicious of Faisal Dhaken (an old associate of his and of Irtep), and he warns the characters against meeting with the wizard. He complains that Faisal is one of the reasons Osgood is hiding in the Wizard's Familiar, since the inn offers protection against magical assault.

Folk who know Osgood from the bars and gaming halls might suggest that he is hiding at the Wizard's Familiar with a successful DC 13 Diplomacy or Intimidation check. As Osgood is aware he is being sought by bounty hunters, assassins, and guards, he might reach out to the characters on his own, desperate for protection.

Osgood's statistics are located in the **Appendix**.

Faisal Dhaken

Faisal is a foreign wizard with exotic features and a forked beard. He wears a brilliant black turban with a precious ruby affixed in its center and carries a twisted staff inlaid with silver magical symbols. Faisal has a reputation for dark deeds. Whether this reputation is warranted remains to be seen. He is caustic, haughty, and quick to anger. Faisal was an associate of Irtep in gambling and magical research. He assisted Irtep in enchanting the *pipes of Minzoa* but was horrified by the demonstration of their use. He begged his friend to destroy the pipes. Irtep refused, and the two parted ways.

Some weeks passed before Faisal found Irtep gambling at the Fortune's Fool. He joined the table to play a hand, hoping time and their mutual love of gambling would allow him to broach the subject of the pipes once more. Irtep again refused to destroy them, and the two had a loud and vocal argument that everyone assumed was over gambling. Because of Faisal's dark reputation, many observers assume Faisal hired assassins to slay his former friend over the incident. Faisal has quietly offered a substantial reward for finding Irtep, but he wants his friend brought back to safety, not murdered. Faisal may approach the characters and offer them 1,000 gp each, a *potion of invisibility*, a *potion of haste*, a *potion of bull's strength*, and a *potion of spider climb*, as well as a *scroll of lightning bolt* and a *scroll of slow*. He asks that the characters find Irtep and bring him back alive and unmolested.

Faisal is not hiding. He can be found at his apartment in Turlin's Well.

Faisal's statistics are in the **Appendix**.

Gynnen Valzoe

Gynnen is a skilled musician and member of the Bard's College. Gynnen, probably more than any other associate or panderer of Irtep's favor besides Faisal, is honestly worried about Irtep and his well-being. Gynnen and Irtep became drinking buddies during Irtep's winning streak, when Gynnen performed regularly at the Fortune's Fool. Irtep insisted on taking lessons in pipe playing from Gynnen. Eventually, Irtep persuaded Gynnen to craft a set of pipes for Irtep from mithral, silver, ivory, and rare hardwood. Gynnen understood that Irtep meant to make the pipes magical, but he knows nothing about the specific nature of the enhancement. The bard is afraid that the pipes were enhanced with a malevolent purpose. He would like to see them turned over to the authorities or destroyed.

Mostly, though, Gynnen just misses his drinking buddy and wants to make sure that Irtep is alive and safe. If the characters can bring Irtep to him alive, he intends to smuggle the wizard out of the city to start over again in another city with a new identity.

Gynnen Valzoe's statistics are in the **Appendix**.

Location Scouting and First Contacts

Somehow, characters must be set on the path of locating Irtep. Rumors and NPCs set the stage for locations the characters should visit in the course of the adventure, as well as suggesting locations the player characters might visit on their journey to Irtep's tower. Listed here are brief descriptions of the likely locations that the characters might visit in their search for Irtep and his associates. Each location also includes a potential first contact with an NPC that can get the characters access to Irtep's tower.

The Blazing Bones

This establishment is a generic, rectangular gaming hall. No special map or floor plan is needed.

If the characters head off to the Blazing Bones, they arrive at a darkened establishment. The harlots and streetwalkers normally found near its busy front door are absent. A sign on the door reads "Gone fishing, come back tomorrow. The Mgt." Attempting to peer through the place's filthy windows reveals that the inside is indeed dark and empty.

The door is locked with a stout lock, and careful inspection (or picking the lock with a DC 20 Disable Device check) reveal that it's also barred from the inside. If the characters persist at trying to get through the door, a half-orc opens the door from inside and tells them to beat it. If asked about Irtep or Michalena, the half-orc grins and says. "Don't worry, the boss is out lookin' for 'em!" He then slams the door in their faces, bars it again, and goes back to whatever he was doing before.

Fortune's Fool

Fortune's Fool is a massive casino and entertainment parlor in the Thieves Quarter of Bard's Gate. It features a renowned indoor theater and outdoor unarmed fighting arena. Further details on the exact floor plan of the Fortune's Fool can be found in ***Bard's Gate*** from **Necromancer Games**, but we provide enough information here for you to use the location.

Gathering Information

If characters wander through Fortune's Fool, talking to patrons and eavesdropping on conversations, you can use the rumors table from above to determine what additional tidbits they gather. Their efforts should lead eventually to a suggestion (friendly or otherwise) that Ayelyln the Barkeep is the best source of information in the place.

Assuming that the characters ask the barkeep about Irtep, Faisal, Michalena, or other characters they've encountered during their investigation, they are directed to a backroom guarded by a pair of menacing half-orcs (Choli Bonesnapper and Colic) dressed in fine doublets and brandishing greataxes. If the characters don't seem interested in checking out the backroom, a squad of four or more half-orcs surrounds them and insistently escorts them to the backroom.

Public Brawling

Starting a bloody battle in Bard's Gate's largest casino is a very rash idea. Fortune's Fool is a popular place, and its customers don't want to see it wrecked. Such shenanigans attract the guard, sheriffs, and wandering adventurers of comparable level to the player characters, who harry and assault player characters foolish enough to start trouble here. Characters won't be killed, but they'll be pummeled into unconsciousness and handed over to Fat Julie to deal with.

Fat Julie

If the player characters meet with Fat Julie, he greets them in a backroom and offers to pay them to track down Irtep and relieve the wizard of at least 15,000 gp worth of property — that's what the halfling bookmaker is owed by the deadbeat spellcaster. Fat Julie is polite to characters (unless they started trouble in his place), but he's absolutely clear that Irtep owes him a debt and no one welches on Fat Julie. That's just good business.

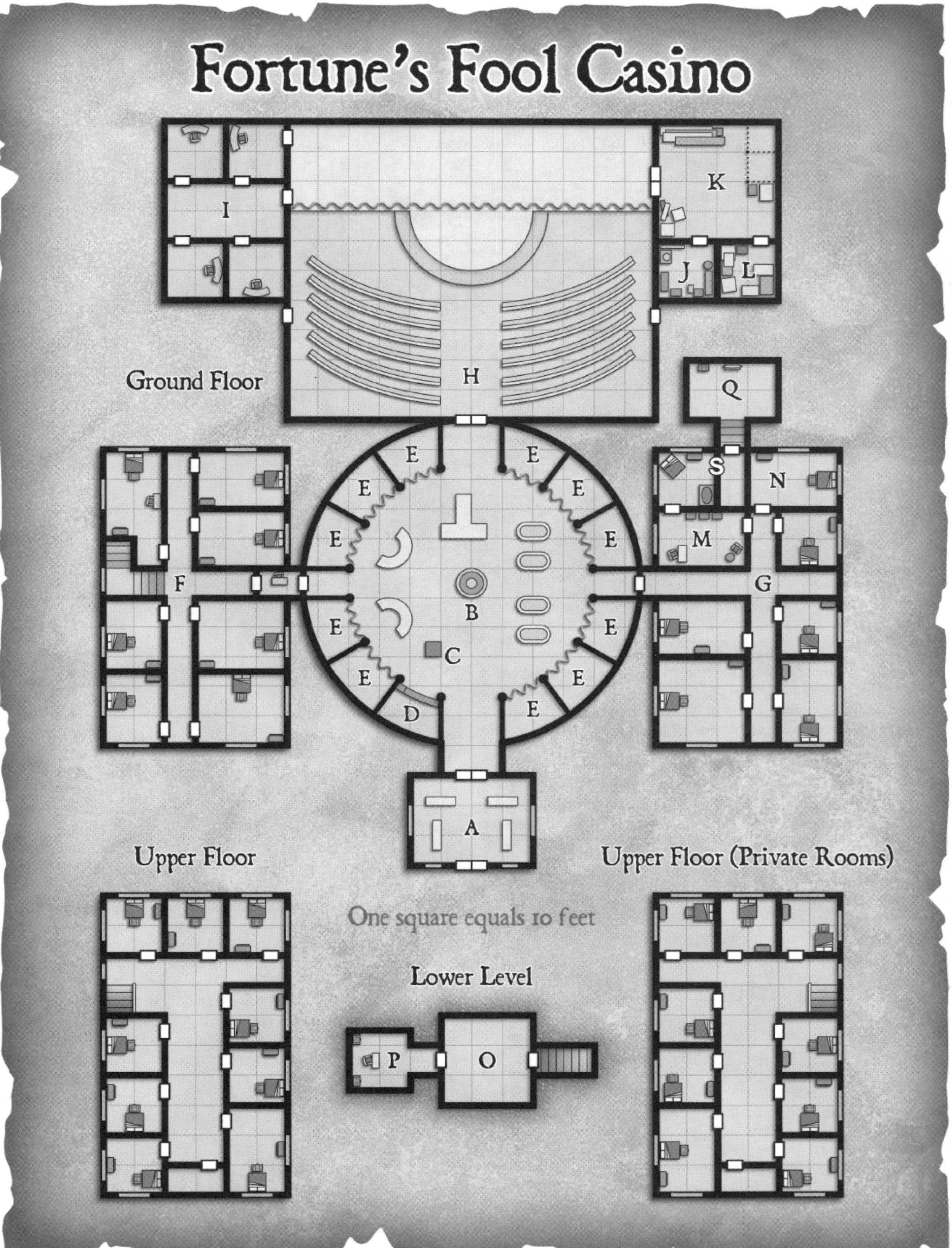
Fortune's Fool Casino
Ground Floor
Upper Floor
Upper Floor (Private Rooms)
One square equals 10 feet
Lower Level
A
B
C
D
E
F
G
H
I
J
K
L
M
N
O
P
Q
S

Characters can take Julie's deal or leave it. Taking the deal may give the characters an added ally or contact in the city whom the GM can use when setting up further adventures. Refusing Julie's offer won't necessarily earn the characters an enemy. Either way, Fat Julie sends his agents to tail the characters through the city to see which other contacts they end up making.

If characters take the deal, they are directed to track down Irtep's one-time girlfriend at the Pride of Waymarch, or his old buddy Osgood Flumph at the Wizard's Familiar. Julie's agents haven't been able to make much progress at either establishment because of the Pride's low tolerance of any being with "half" in their name, and the Wizard's Familiar's low tolerance of non-magicians.

If the characters end up meeting more than one additional contact without accepting Fat Julie's deal, a second meeting with Julie's gang of half-orcs happens just after the characters leave Irtep's Tower. See the "Conclusions" section of this adventure for more details.

Leaving the Fortune's Fool

Upon leaving the Fortune's Fool, the characters are approached by a dark figure in a turban. He asks the characters to quickly follow him into a nearby alley across from the Fool where he introduces himself as Faisal and tells the characters that they are in great danger. If they follow him into the alleyway, he directs their attention to the front door of the Fortune's Fool just as a pair of half-orcs leave the place. A successful DC 10 Intelligence check allows the characters to recognize them as some of Julie's thugs that they encountered in the casino.

As the characters watch, the half-orcs sniff at the air and turn almost immediately toward the alley where Faisal and the characters are hiding. Faisal quietly casts a spell, and the air around the characters fills with the smell of roses and manure. Immediately the orcs lose the characters' scent.

Faisal's Offer

Faisal admits that he was an ally of Irtep, and that Irtep is being sought by Julie and also by members of the Dominion Arcane and Red Blades Assassins. He begs the characters to find a way into Irtep's Tower and to recover the *pipes of Minzoa* before they fall into someone else's hands and cause even more trouble. He offers to pay the characters 1,000 gp apiece, plus a few select magic items from Irtep's collection (but nothing outrageous).

If questioned about the rumor that he is the one who wants Irtep killed, he explains that he is Irtep's friend and that their falling out was his reaction to the evils that the pipes could have been used to commit.

If characters take Faisal up on his offer, he suggests that they visit the Pride of Waymarch to track down Michalena Goddeau. Faisal is certain that Irtep gave her a special password that reveals the door of his tower.

Faisal is unaware of the ground floor trap in Irtep's Tower, as the trap was devised by Osgood and Irtep. Osgood does not have the password to enter the tower, because this was given only to Irtep's concubines.

If Fat Julie learns that the characters accepted Faisal's offer after turning his down, he won't be interested in pursuing any further deals with them.

If the characters say no to Faisal, he is annoyed and refuses to offer them any help. He suggests that if they are unwilling to help, they should steer far clear of him and forget they knew the name of Irtep or Faisal Dhaken. See the section "Conclusions" for further details on Faisal's actions.

At The Wizard's Familiar

A map is provided of the ground floor for the Wizard's Familiar.

Rumors may have set the characters on the course of the Wizard's Familiar in search of Osgood Flumph. It is also possible that the characters

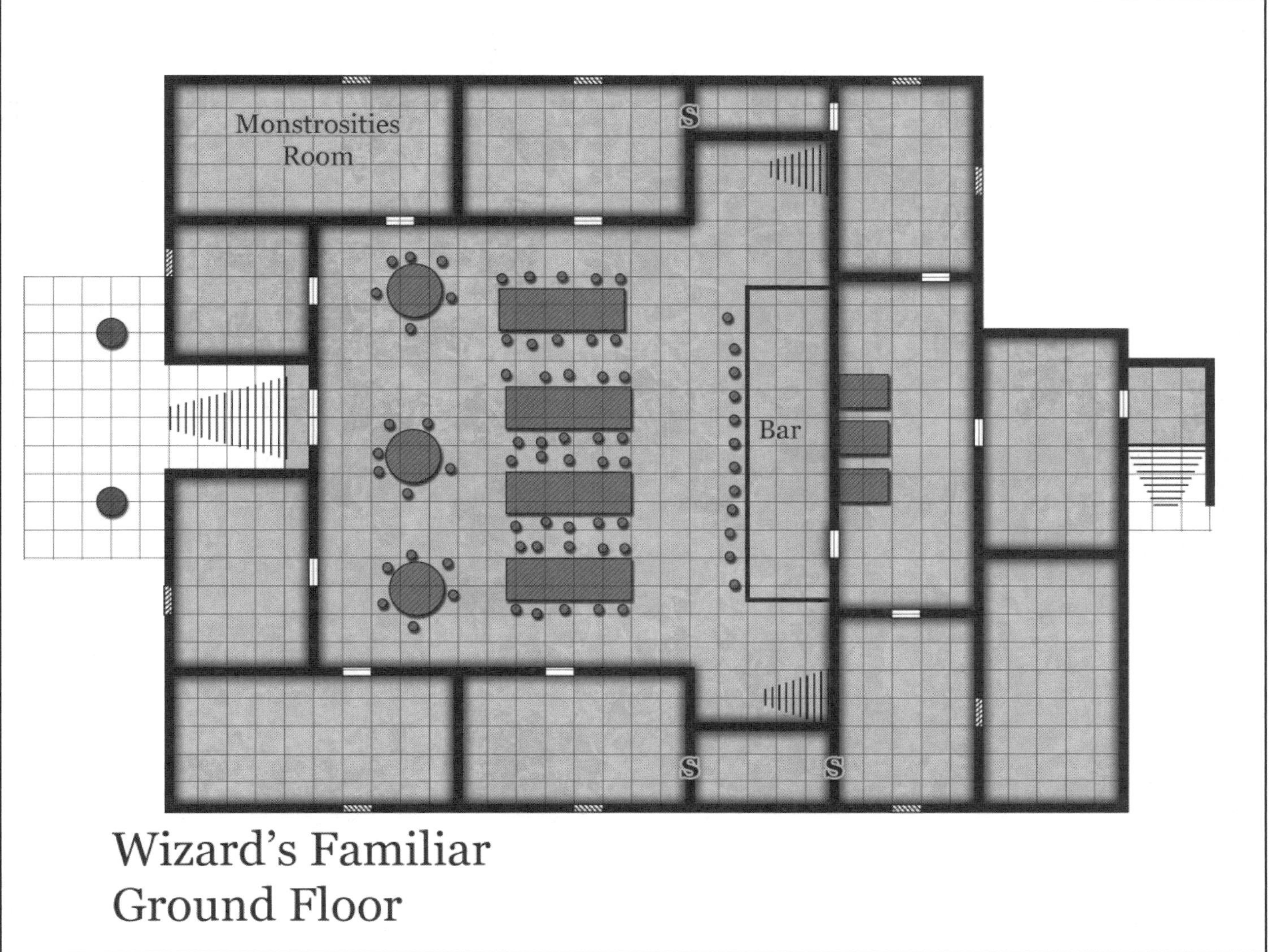

have already encountered Faisal Dhaken, Fat Julie, or Michalena Goddeau, and one of them might have put the characters on the trail of Osgood.

The Wizard's Familiar is a grand inn and landmark in the Turlin's Well District of Bard's Gate. The Familiar, as it is called, is an exclusive establishment, open to arcanists or by invitation only. The inn is covered in illusions to make it appear as nothing more or less than high-class apartments common in the area.

Its front stair is guarded with spells that steer riff-raff away from the club. Luckily for the characters, the Wizard's Familiar is well known to most locals who are in the know. The typical laborer in the street won't know its location, but anyone who is more highly placed in society or who dabbles in the magical arts can direct them to the correct building, even if most people have never seen the inside of the place.

The stairs to the doorway are hidden by an illusion that appears to be a permanent wall; a successful DC 14 Perception check is needed to spot the door. Beyond the illusory wall is a small courtyard leading to a set of stairs that end at a pair of massive, oaken double doors decorated with carvings of crows, cats, dogs, bats, fish, birds, small dragons, and other creatures that throughout the ages have served wizards as familiars.

The entrance is flanked by a pair of statues of grim-faced wizards whose features are hidden by the brims of their broad hats. The statues trigger a magical *fear* trap on any being who is not an arcane spellcaster. Those who step onto the stairs must succeed on a DC 16 Will save or become frightened of the entire building for 24 hours. Those who succeed are allowed entry to the Grand Parlor of the Wizard's Familiar, though they are not allowed access to any chamber beyond save by permission of the proprietor, Folsum Judduk.

FEAR TRAP **CR 6**
XP 2,400
Type magical; **Perception** DC 29; **Disable Device** DC 29

Trigger location; **Reset** automatic; **Bypass** be an arcane spellcaster
Effect spell effect (*fear*, DC 16 Will save negates)

Gathering Information

The Grand Parlor of the Wizards Familiar is a combination taproom, meeting lounge, and general common chamber one would find in any upscale inn. Here, however, the patrons are all wizards who are sitting and chatting, puffing their pipes, stroking their beards, scratching behind their familiars' ears, or generally ruminating on the mysteries of the universe. If the characters engage them in conversation, you can pull additional rumors off the rumors table (above). Questions involving Irtep, Faisal, or Osgood attract the attention of a quartet of young but stern wizards in black silk and velvet attire with the design of the Wizard's Familiar embroidered on their tunics. The wizards are armed with wands and are quite humorless.

If characters approach the bar, they are met by Folsum Judduk, who introduces himself as the innkeeper of the Wizard's Familiar. He is aware of Irtep, and has thrown the wizard out for bringing trouble to his establishment. He hopes that he will not also have to throw the characters out for similar reasons. If the characters are sincere and respectful in their investigation and questioning, Folsum directs them to the Monstrosities room just off the main parlor, indicating they may find answers to their questions there. If characters get pushy or try intimidating the bartender or his patrons — well, they're trying to start something in a room filled with high-level magic-users. That ploy won't end well for the characters.

Monstrosities Room, Osgood's Offer

The private room is adorned with parts and pieces of various creatures such as manticores, perytons, and the stuffed heads of a chimera. It has a view of the street through crystal glass windows and fine velvet curtains. The walls are lined with bookcases on various supernatural beasts.

Sitting in one corner smoking a pipe is a portly wizard who introduces himself as Osgood Flumph. He apologizes for all the previous questioning and the subterfuge required to meet him at the Wizard's Familiar, but indicates that his life may be in danger because of his association with Irtep. Osgood claims to be a good friend of the wizard, though they recently had a falling out over Irtep's drinking and womanizing.

Osgood suspects that Faisal Dhaken had something to do with Irtep's disappearance, but the only evidence he offers is Faisal's reputation for being devious and a member of an "evil" sect of the Dominion Arcane. He thinks Faisal is trying to steal Irtep's secrets for himself, and that he needs Osgood to get him past a particularly nasty arcane trap located on the ground floor of Irtep's tower. Osgood claims he would go to Irtep's tower, overcome the trap, and gather the *sextant* himself, but he does not know the password to enter the tower. Each time he entered the tower in the past, he was accompanied by Irtep.

Osgood offers to pay the characters with a *potion of fly*, a *scroll of lightning bolt*, 1,000 gp apiece, a 500 gp diamond, a *wand of magic missiles*, a *potion of invisibility*, and a *+1 weapon* of the characters' choice if they recover an item called the *sextant of Minzoa* that he helped Irtep to create. He does not go into detail about the item, other than that it looks like a sailor's sextant, it is located somewhere in Irtep's laboratory, and that unless he can get it into the hands of his allies in the Dominion Arcane, he may be trapped in the Wizard's Familiar, a de facto prisoner of a wizard's power play for the rest of his days.

If the characters take his offer, Osgood suggests that Michalena Goddeau, a lady companion of Irtep, has the password that would gain access to Irtep's tower. She was frequently seen entering the tower during her and Irtep's time together.

If the characters refuse Osgood's offer, he tells them that they are making a grave mistake and that he will not be able to protect them from rumors that they are on the trail of Irtep's treasures. He may allude that the Red Blades would not be as congenial as he, and that Faisal certainly would do "terrible things" should he find the *sextant* or Irtep's research notes. From that point on, Osgood is hostile to the characters and interferes with their attempts at gaining access to Irtep's Tower. See "Conclusions" for further details on Osgood's actions.

Leaving the Wizard's Familiar

Regardless of the outcomes or their experiences in the Wizard's Familiar, the characters are eventually approached by a handsome bard who begs their time to play a song for them. The bard is quite persistent to the point of annoyance. If the characters pay him off, he draws forth a set of pipes and begins performing a song for them.

Upon completion, he smiles and introduces himself as Gynnen Valzoe and indicates that he is aware that the characters are looking into Irtep's disappearance. He has heard good things about the characters and wants to offer them some advice. Gynnen suggests that none of the former friends of Irtep are as they seem. He distrusts Osgood Flumph and Faisal Dhaken equally. He claims he was Irtep's best friend, and that he fashioned a set of fine pipes for the wizard just before Irtep fell head over heels in love with Michalena Goddeau. He begs the characters to do whatever they can to find his friend and to bring him secretly to the docks, where Gynnen intends to spirit the wizard safely out of town, perhaps to Reme or somewhere in the Grand Duchy where he can start over.

Recently, because of his suspicions, Gynnen followed Faisal and saw him entering and leaving known hangouts of "dark" members of the Dominion Arcane. Around the same time he came across Osgood as he was leaving the residence of a wizard named Manisool — a man of evil reputation — with a clutch of papers and scrolls in his hands. When he approached, Osgood grew agitated and took great pains to prevent Gynnen from seeing what was on any of the items, but the bard is certain that some of them were magical scrolls.

Gynnen is convinced that one or both of those characters have cursed his friend, and he has spent a goodly amount of the coin Irtep paid him for crafting the pipes to purchase a powerful scroll of his own to break what he assumes is a curse on his friend. This is a specialized scroll of *greater restoration*, bought with Irtep's money and associated to him through personal possession so that it can automatically break the *geas* on Irtep even if the caster is not normally able to cast that spell.

Gynnen can offer little in the way of payment, though he points out that aside from Irtep's notebook and his life, the wizard is unlikely to take any of his possessions with him when he assumes his new identity. Anything in his tower might as well go to the characters who saved his life as to the scavengers who will inevitably follow.

Gynnen knows that only Michalena Goddeau has the current password. He is also aware of a particularly nasty arcane trap allegedly built into the first floor of the tower, which Osgood Flumph had some knowledge of. Gynnen suggests that the characters avoid any of Irtep's other associates and "work it out on their own" as the safest policy. The fewer people who know about their mission, the better.

The Pride of Waymarch

The Pride of Waymarch is a simple, square tavern. No map is provided.

If rumors or NPC interactions lead the characters to the Pride of Waymarch, they find themselves at a tavern in the Market District of Bard's Gate catering to military, ex-military, and mercenaries of all stripes. The shield of Waymarch hangs above the lintel and a sign indicates "Private Club — Spellcasters and other undesirables unwelcome."

A pair of mercenaries wearing old campaign badges of the armies in which they served sit flanking the doorway with tall tankards of ale. They ask anyone who even resembles an arcane spellcaster to move along. Other newcomers are given the choice of dueling either of the two fighters for a chance at a membership.

Characters who agree are escorted to a courtyard set along the side of the inn where a series of racks of blunted practice weapons sit. Characters can choose their weapon and proceed to battle. Use the statistics for CR 3 guard officer in the *Pathfinder Roleplaying Game GameMastery Guide* for their opponent (or any other humanoid NPC in the CR 2–4 range, if you prefer). If the character wins the fight, or lasts at least three rounds against the opponent, the character is vouched for and can join the club for 2 gp. Once inside the Pride of Waymarch, the characters find themselves in the company of hard-bitten fighting men. Some are retired, while others are young sell-swords looking for work. Most are drinking, sharing stories, and lying about their exploits to a coterie of attractive trollops.

If the characters start asking questions, use the rumors table (above) to see what the "word on the street" is. Should their line of questioning directly relate to Irtep, Faisal Dhaken, or Osgood Flumph, they are directed to the bar owner, Sergeant Vassale. The sergeant suggests that characters who are seeking wizards should go look in the types of pest-holes where wizards hang out; otherwise, they should shut their traps and enjoy their whiskey and ale. If characters ask for directions, Vassale tells them how to find the Wizard's Familiar, the Tower of Irtep, and the apartment of Faisal Dhaken. If trouble develops, Sergeant Vassale is a standard human guard officer as referred to above.

If characters inquire about Michalena Goddeau, a burly young fighter stands up and demands to know who is asking and why. The fighter is Gustas, Michalena's new sugar daddy. He just returned from an expedition to the Stoneheart Mountain Dungeon with a nice sack of gold. Gustas gets mouthy with the character(s) asking questions about his girl. While Gustas keeps the characters occupied, his girl is slipping out the back exit from the taproom. Characters who make successful DC 10 Perception checks notice a young brunette woman sidling toward the rear exit.

Gustas is hot-blooded and may want to go to blows over people making any disrespectful comments about his girl. This, of course, leads Sergeant Vassale to suggest they "take it outside" to the courtyard to settle their issue. Use the stats for a raider in the *Pathfinder Roleplaying Game GameMastery Guide* for Gustas.

If a character ends up dueling Gustas and appears poised to win the fight, Michalena returns immediately and tries to stop the beating. She agrees to talk to the characters if they don't hurt Gustas anymore. Gustas is humiliated, but he stops fighting for Michalena. He insists on being present for any questioning and continues to hold a chip on his shoulder against the characters. (See the section "Conclusions," below.)

Pursuing Michalena

Michalena is easy to track with a DC 10 Survival check. She simply found a hiding spot in the alleyway and is waiting for the characters to leave the Pride so that she can return to her boyfriend. If cornered, she threatens to scream for the constables. She can be calmed down with a DC 10 Diplomacy or Intimidation check or a bribe of at least 50 gp.

Michalena is a gold-digger who was only interested in Irtep's money. When she met the younger Gustas and his sack of gold, her heart and her avarice followed. She wants nothing more to do with Irtep or his crazy ways, and she's willing to sell the password to his tower for 1,000 gp and a crystal dish that Irtep owns. She figures that he spent more time with "the dish" than he spent with her, so it would be ironic justice if she get the dish and he had nothing but his debts, the bounty hunters, and a broken heart. She finds Osgood "creepy" and feels that Faisal is definitely a villain. Her opinion of Gynnen is that he is "dreamy" but broke, and therefore not worth wasting her time on.

If the characters make a deal with her, she gives them the password ("*Irtep is a love machine,*" she says with a sigh) and reminds them that if she doesn't get the dish, Gustas's mercenary friends will come looking for them. It should be noted that taking Michalena's deal means crossing Fat Julie, which becomes important in the "Conclusions" section of the adventure.

The password can also be gotten from Michalena through a successful DC 15 Diplomacy or Intimidation check, a 5,000 gp bribe, or through use of a spell such as *charm person*.

Should any character be heartless enough to get into a duel with Michalena, she uses the stats of a barmaid from the *Pathfinder Roleplaying Game GameMastery Guide*, but fights with a dagger instead of a serving tray or frying pan.

Leaving the Pride of Waymarch

Upon leaving the Pride of Waymarch, the characters are stopped by a trio of half-orc ruffians led by a thin, shifty human male with dark hair and a wicked, fine-handled rapier in his belt. The man asks if he can buy the characters a drink from a local wine cart while they walk and talk. If the characters refuse, his half-orcs crowd around and try to look intimidating, but the man waves them back.

He introduces himself as Tuvio, proprietor of the Blazing Bones. He knows that the characters have managed to get an audience with Michalena and would like to know what they learned about Irtep and whether or not Michalena gave up the password.

Tuvio explains that Irtep owes him a cool 5,000 gp, and that if the characters are looking for Irtep, they are in fact looking for his money. Since the characters are hunting for Irtep anyway, there's no reason why they can't cooperate for mutual benefit. Tuvio isn't even angry at Irtep — he likes the wizard and understands that gamblers have up times and down. The 5,000 gp isn't even everything Irtep owes him; it's what Tuvio is willing to settle for.

Tuvio's kind feelings toward Irtep (which are at least partly genuine) don't extend to Michalena, Osgood, or Fiasal. He considers the first two to be worthless sponges and the last to be a dangerous meddler in dark arts.

Like everyone else, Tuvio wants the characters to get inside Irtep's tower, find out what became of the wizard, help him if they can, and retrieve Tuvio's debt. For payment, Tuvio extends the characters 1,000 gp each in credit at the Blazing Bones and offers to introduce them to some of the best and most important folk of local society. He sweetens the deal by offering to fence anything they retrieve from Irtep's tower at top value, so long as he gets his 5,000 gp cut from the deal.

If the characters refuse Tuvio, he informs them that they are making a mistake and that he has friends that shouldn't be crossed. See "Conclusions" for possible attention from Tuvio and his associates at the end of this adventure.

Part 2: On to Irtep's Tower

Eventually the characters should have enough material and information to make a go at entering Irtep's Tower.

The use of the password is important in entering the tower but is by no means the only means of entry. A few enterprising thieves and members of the Red Blades have already found alternate entrances. What isn't widely known (because the Red Blades and the thieves' guild aren't talking) is that none of these experts has managed to leave the tower once they got in.

Tower Features

Doors: All doors are locked with *arcane lock* spells unless otherwise. Picking such a lock requires a set of thief's tools and a successful DC 25 Disable Device check (that includes the 10-point penalty for *arcane lock*), and breaking down such a door requires a DC 25 Strength check, unless noted otherwise.

Windows: Windows line the sides of the tower on the 2nd, 3rd, 4th, 5th, and 6th stories. The outdoor windows are locked with *arcane locks* and require the same rolls as doors to open, unless noted otherwise.

Electricity Trap: The windows are trapped. Anyone touching a window and everyone else within 15 feet takes 3d6 points of electricity damage, or half that much with a successful DC 14 Reflex savs. This trap can be discovered with a DC 28 Perception check and bypassed with a DC 28 Disable Device check, but failing the check sets off the trap.

ELECTRICITY TRAP **CR 4**
XP 1,200
Type magical; **Perception** DC 28; **Disable Device** DC 28

Trigger touch; **Reset** automatic
Effect spell effect (*lightning bolt*, 4d6 electricity damage, DC 14 Reflex save half); multiple targets (all within a 120 ft. line)

Light: The tower is brightly lit by sconces of magical flame placed at 10- to 20-foot intervals unless otherwise noted.

Outside the Tower (CR 10)

The tower sits in a decent area of the Old Temple District not far from the Kings Bridge.

It is an octagonal tower for the most part, with six stories, standing roughly 80 feet high. The roof tapers to a point. The tower is surrounded by a decorative moat with a bridge that leads to the doors of the ground floor.

Irtep's Tower

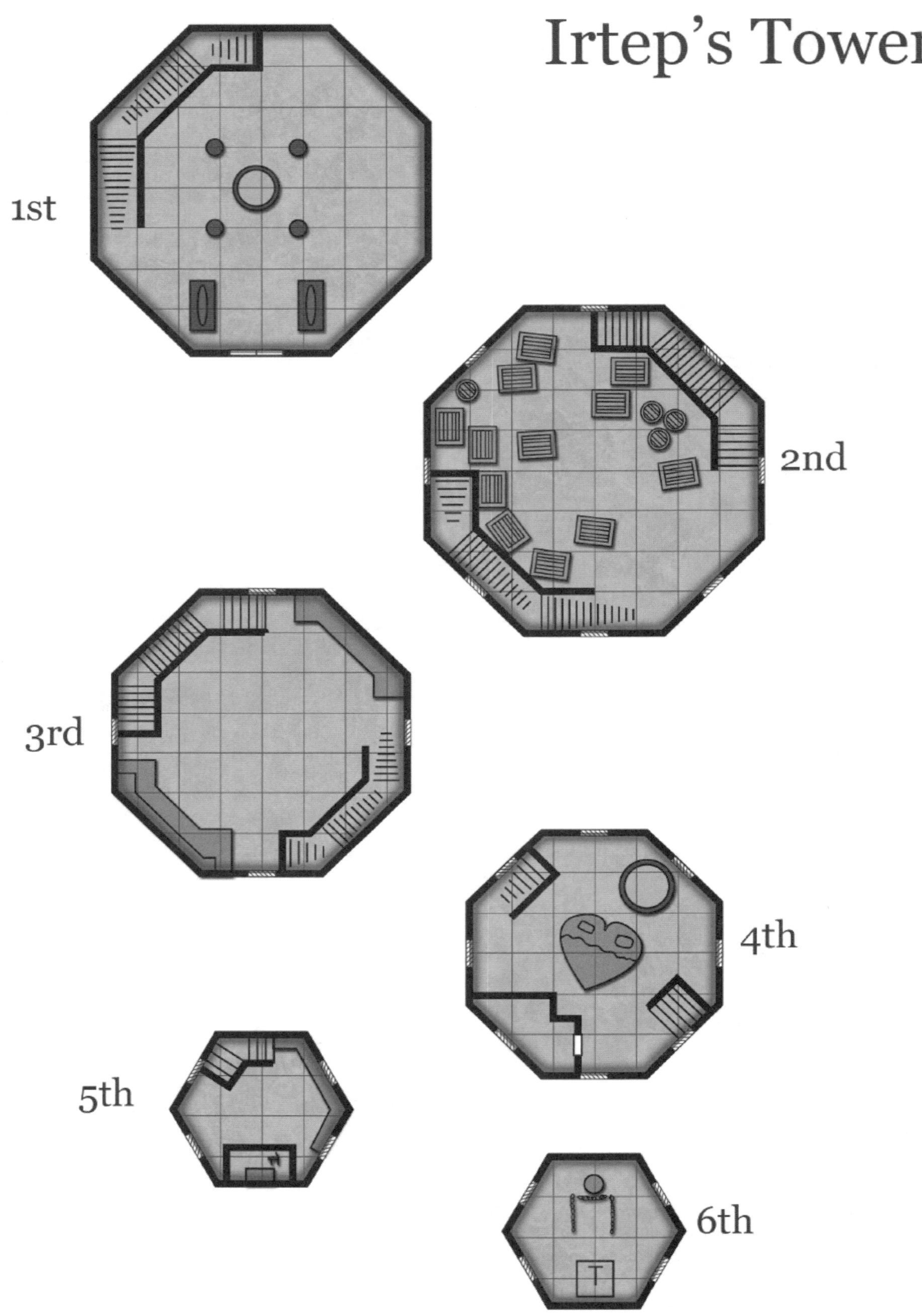

A group of **4 Lyreguards** with **4 guard dogs** under the command of a no-nonsense veteran named **Officer Gralme** patrol the moat. The guardsmen steer folk away from the tower and are serious about pursuing any would-be thieves. The tower is currently considered something of a public hazard, and the guardsmen are here to safeguard the citizenry.

Because this is a unique situation, this guard detachment is accompanied by a specialist named **Finly**, a 6th-level wizard who often works with the Lyreguards on jobs that are likely to meet magical foes or to need magical backup. Finly obviously is not a soldier — he isn't wearing armor or carrying military weapons — but nothing immediately identifies him as a mage. He finds that going incognito often gives him an essential edge when dealing with troublemaking spellcasters. Characters who've lived in this town for several months might know who Finly is by reputation if not by sight. Newcomers assume he's just a citizen chatting with the guardsmen.

If characters approach the tower without first attempting to scout it stealthily, they are stopped by Officer Gralme and his special squad. Officer Gralme asks what the characters' business is near the Tower of Irtep. If he doesn't care for their answer, he orders them to leave the area immediately, and he'll send a few soldiers to escort them away. Obviously, if the soldiers don't come back in a few minutes, Gralme knows that evil is afoot, and he's not a fool. Where adventurers are concerned, he always calls for backup first and then plans his attack.

OFFICER GRALME CR 6
XP 2,400
hp 57 (*Pathfinder Roleplaying Game GameMastery Guide* "Watch Captain")

LYREGUARDS (4) CR 1
XP 400
hp 19 (*Pathfinder Roleplaying Game GameMastery Guide* "City Guard")

FINLY CR 5
XP 1,600
hp 33 (*Pathfinder Roleplaying Game GameMastery Guide* "Battle Mage")

MASTIFFS (4) CR 1
XP 400
hp 13 (*Pathfinder Roleplaying Game Bestiary* "Dog, Riding Dog")

Getting Into the Tower

Some form of subterfuge or magic is needed to get across the bridge to Irtep's Tower without being noticed by Gralme, Finly, and the soldiers and dogs. Possibilities include but are not limited to a *charm* effect, invisibility, stealth, or an especially clever distraction (tossing a rock into the bushes won't do it). If the PCs gain entry to the tower without fighting Gralme and his men, award them full xp for the encounter.

Talking their way past Gralme: A Bluff or Diplomacy check opposed by Gralme's Sense Motive check.

Stealth: A DC 20 Stealth check coupled with a thorough description of how the characters are going to dodge the patrols to make it to the tower undetected.

Charm: A *charm person* spell might be used to persuade Gralme to let the characters pass, though casting a spell is likely to start a fight with the Lyreguard patrol if it's noticed. This could land the characters in jail if it doesn't pan out.

Disguise: Characters could use a disguise to dress as a relieving patrol, or to pass off one of their members as a town officer who has official clearance to access Irtep's property. This requires a successful Disguise check opposed by Officer Gralme's Perception check.

Organized Distraction: Characters could come up with a plan to stage a distraction that pulls the guard patrol away from the doorway long enough for characters to slip inside. This could involve hiring a troupe of performers or beggars, an illusion of a rampaging monster, a fire that threatens a nearby building, or some other pressing event. Use your best judgment to determine whether Gralme falls for the trick, remembering that he's a seasoned officer of the law who used to be an adventurer himself.

Windows: Someone is bound to have *boots of flying*, a *ring of invisibility*, a *scroll of passwall*, and the willingness to leave all of his or her friends on the sidelines and go it alone inside the tower. Such characters create a welcome addition to the official **Frog God Games'** rolls of the dead. Characters can feasibly fly up to a window, overcome the trap, open the lock, and get inside without being noticed by the guards. Surviving to fly back out the window again is another question entirely.

The Bridge: The bridge is a simple stone arch that crosses the decorative moat. It's not meant for defense. There are no railings or sidings to hide behind.

The Moat: The moat surrounding the tower is filled with koi fish and lily pads. The water is 10 feet deep and 10 feet wide around the entire circumference of the tower. A grate at the bottom of the pond on the north side of the tower could be forced opened with a successful DC 15 Strength check. Characters could then swim through 50 feet of culvert with a DC 10 Swim check and find themselves below the drain in the fountain in the center of the first floor of Irtep's Tower.

Drain: The drain is clogged with pieces of at least three bodies and some items of thiefly gear. The equipment includes a broken rapier, a *+1 short sword*, a *+1 light crossbow*, 10 quarrels, two sets of thieves' tools, and three waterlogged black leather masks of the type commonly worn by members of the Shadow Masks. The bodies have been bitten and clawed savagely and also are singed.

A secret button slides the fountain to the side, affording access to the first floor, and activating the first-floor trap. The button requires a successful DC 15 Perception check to notice.

Area 1. Front Door (CR 5)

The front door to Irtep's estate is carved in an image that looks like a willow tree surrounded by leaves. On close examination or with a successful DC 15 Perception check, the tree appears to be eating the leaves, and the leaves appear to be eating smaller leaves.

The door is reinforced with steel and locked with an *arcane lock* and a very complicated mechanical lock that requires a successful DC 25 Disable Device check to pick. Picking the lock requires several minutes, and unless the lock picker is invisible, covered by an illusion, or some other distraction is keeping the guardsmen from doing their jobs, the lock picker is easily spotted. A DC 20 Strength check can force the door in, but this ruins any chance for getting in unnoticed. A *knock* spell suppresses the *arcane lock* normally (lowering the DC for picking the lock by 10), but the sound from the spell is certain to attract the guards' attention.

The best and easiest way in is by using the password ("*Irtep is a love machine*"), known only to Irtep and Michalena.

Additionally, the door is protected by a mechanical trap. It can be spotted with a successful DC 17 Perception check. If the lock is picked or the door is forced or *knocked* without first disarming the trap with a successful DC 17 Disable Device check, a large, yellow, 500-pound iron ball attached to a gigantic chain drops from the top story of the tower onto anyone in the doorway. Each creature near the door takes 8d6 points of bludgeoning damage, or no damage with a successful DC 15 Reflex save to jump to safety. The ball also smashes the bridge and gets the attention of everyone within 300 feet. Afterward, an automatic winch drags the gore-smeared ball back up the side of the tower. Characters notice a cruel, smiling face painted on the ball.

SMASHING BALL TRAP CR 5
XP 1,600
Type mechanical; **Perception** DC 17; **Disable Device** DC 17

Trigger location; **Reset** automatic; **Bypass** proper key

Effect crushing ball (8d6 bludgeoning damage, DC 15 Reflex save negates); multiple targets (all within a 10 ft. square by the door)

Area 2. Irtep's Tower: Ground Floor (CR 6)

This large chamber is octagonal and 40 feet in diameter. The doors are flanked by a pair of stone statues of coppery koi fish. A circular inscription is inlaid in silver in the polished marble floor. The circle of the inscription connects four pillars that surround a fountain. Each pillar is a different color and has a sconce affixed to it with a different colored candle. As the last character enters the dimly lit chamber, a voice calls down from high above:

"If intruders to my home are thee, be dissuaded from my property.
If thou art friend then know the score — match the hue of yon stair-top door.
Pillar to candle, candle to wick, hurry now and make it quick,
For if water touches flame, your days are ended, down the drain."

When the voice ends, the fountain begins bubbling, and a gurgling, flushing sound can be heard as water spills over the fountain's edge onto the floor.

The door at the top of the stairs is brown. To open it, characters must match its shade of brown by swapping candles around the pillars. Placing a candle on a pillar of a different color changes the color of the pillar or the candle. Creating two orange pillars and one green pillar solves the puzzle.

If characters took the deal from Osgood Flumph, he told them the correct matching of colored candles to colored pillars to produce brown, and they should be able to deactivate the trap easily. If they have not, their options are trial and error, magic, or death!

Water is filling the room quickly. When it reaches the top of the sconces on the pillars, none of the candles can be lit, and the characters are likely to drown.

When characters trigger the trap, the arrangement of candles and pillars is as follows:

Pillar	Pillar Color	Candle Color
1	Red	Red
2	Blue	Blue
3	Yellow	Yellow
4	Black	White

Moving candles to different pillars has the effect of blending those colors, as listed below.

Candle	on Pillar	Changes
Red	Blue	Pillar turns Purple
Red	Yellow	Pillar turns Orange
Blue	Red	Pillar turns Purple
Blue	Yellow	Pillar turns Green
Yellow	Blue	Pillar turns Green
Yellow	Red	Pillar turns Orange
White	Any	Candle matches Pillar
Any	Black	Candle turns White

No matter what color a pillar is at the moment, it always reacts to the presence of a new candle as if the pillar was its original color. For example, assume that a red candle was placed on the blue pillar, turning the pillar purple. Characters then experimentally replace the red candle with a yellow candle. The yellow candle turns the pillar green, the same way it would have if it had been placed there while the pillar was blue.

To produce brown and unlock the door, characters must make two pillars orange and one pillar green.

This puzzle will be much more enjoyable for everyone if you draw the four pillars on a sheet of paper or on your battle mat and label the colors or indicate them with colored markers. Use colored beads or dice to represent the candles, swapping them for different ones when their colors change. Without this visual aid, everyone (including the GM) is likely to become hopelessly confused.

The "correct" method is listed below:

- Remove the candle from the blue pillar and hold it.
- Move the yellow candle to the blue pillar, turning that pillar green.
- Replace the white candle on the black pillar with the blue candle, turning the blue candle into a second white candle.
- Move the newly-made white candle to the yellow pillar, turning that candle yellow.
- Replace the red candle on the red pillar with the newly made yellow candle, turning that pillar orange.
- Replace the yellow candle on the yellow pillar with the red candle, turning that pillar orange. At that point, there are two orange pillars, one green pillar, and one black pillar, and someone should be holding a yellow candle.
- Place the remaining yellow candle on the black pillar.

Placing the last candle on the black pillar causes the new colors in the chamber to mix in the air and create a dark brown color that matches the door at the top of the stair, at which point the door opens. When the door opens, the fountain slides to the side and the water quickly drains through a grate in the floor.

Moving the candles around should take a party of four no more than two rounds to accomplish. Obviously, players who remember what they learned about color in third grade will have an easier time of it than others. If players insist on applying skills to get a clue (or are floundering hopelessly and need all the help they can get), then with a successful DC 15 Intelligence check, a character recalls learning that brown paint is made up of two parts orange pigment and one part green pigment. Alternately a character with an applicable Craft or Profession skill (such as Profession [painter]) can use that skill to solve the puzzle.

The Flow of Water and Other Dangers

Water is being sucked out of the moat and into the ground floor quickly. Exactly how quickly is up to you. The decision should be based on how well your players deal with these types of puzzles. Rather than trying to adjudicate the situation with game rounds, we recommend real time. Even a slow, deliberative group should be able to find a solution in five minutes. Two minutes should be enough for most groups, and those that thrive on such puzzles might be done in less than one minute. If you're unsure how much time to give, you can play it by ear, describing the water rising faster or slower as you get a better grip on how quickly your players will find the solution. The key is to keep the situation exciting and to give the characters a near-death thrill without needlessly killing everyone because you misjudged their color-mixing capability.

For descriptive purposes, by the time the water is 1 foot deep, the floor is difficult terrain for Small or smaller creatures. When the water is 2 feet deep, it is difficult terrain for everyone.

When the water's depth reaches 4 feet, the **2 copper koi statues** animate. They dive into the water, crackling with electricity, and attack the characters from under the water.

When the water is 6 feet deep, everyone must begin swimming. Swimming with a lit candle and keeping the wick dry requires a successful DC 15 Swim check.

If the characters have not managed to fix the candles by the 8th round, there is no way that they can keep the candles lit as the water puts out the flame. In 18 rounds the water reaches the ceiling. Unless characters can breathe underwater, drowning and suffocating rules apply. Water stays at the top of the ceiling for five rounds at which point the fountain slides to the side and the water drains back into the moat outside the tower.

COPPER KOI STATUES (2) **CR 3**
XP 800
N Medium construct
Init +2; **Senses** darkvision 60 ft., low-light vision; **Perception** –1
Aura electricity (5 ft., 2d6 electricity damage, DC 13 half)

AC 16, touch 12, flat-footed 14 (+2 Dex, +4 natural)
hp 53 (6d10+20)
Fort +0; **Ref** +2; **Will** –1 **DR** 5/adamantine; **Immune** cold, construct traits, electricity

---

Speed 30 ft. swim
Melee bite +7 (1d6+1 plus 1d6 electricity)
Special Attacks electricity (1d6)

Str 13, **Dex** 15, **Con** —, **Int** —, **Wis** 8, **Cha** 2
Base Atk +6 ; **CMB** +7; **CMD** 19 (can't be tripped)
Skills Swim +9

Upstairs Door

The upstairs door is built like the entrance. It is a steel-reinforced door that prevents any of Irtep's things in his storage area from getting wet. The door can be opened only by arranging candles in the proper sequence as described above, but powerful magic such as *passwall* can bypass the doorway.

Second Story: Storage

This dark, octagonal chamber is similar in size and shape to the floor below. It is filled from floor to 15-foot-ceiling with crates and boxes that must barely fit through the doorways or windows. A staircase opposite the first-floor landing leads to a door and the floor above.

Several leather-bound and wooden trunks and cases are here, as detailed below.

Crate A (CR 5): The largest crate in the chamber is about 8 feet long, 5 feet tall, and 5 feet wide. The lid is partially stove in and a pair of legs is sticking out of the broken section, with dried blood on the floor.

Within the case is a **mummy**, partially unwrapped from a ceramic urn, and the mummy's victim, an unfortunate member of the Red Blades assassins' guild who made the mistake of looking for a little loot. He broke the seal of protection keeping the mummy in suspended animation. If characters investigate the crate or the corpse sticking out of it, a mummy bursts free and attacks.

MUMMY **CR 5**
XP 1,600
hp 60 (*Pathfinder Roleplaying Game Bestiary* "Mummy")

Hidden within the desiccated wrappings of the mummy are various baubles and amulets that were precious to the mummy in life. Among them are 10 golden amulets of various Khemitian gods worth 25 gp each, a gold bracelet with inset agates worth 200 gp, and a turquoise inlaid pectoral of an ibis that is an *amulet of nautral armor +2*.

The corpse belongs to Ralek Marn, a Red Blades assassin, which is obvious from the tattoo that can found on the fellow's ankle. His neck is broken and his face is purple from the stranglehold the mummy placed upon him. He has a *scroll of dispel magic*, a *scroll of knock*, a *potion of neutralize poison* (crafted by a druid), 2 vials of arsenic, a poisoned *+1 saber*, a *potion of invisibility*, and a *potion of levitate* in his pack.

Crate B: This crate is marked "Inner Water Sample."

Within the crate is a ceramic cask, its lid sealed with thick tar. If the cask is opened, every character within a 10-foot radius must succeed on a DC 15 Fortitude save as foul liquid and gas splatter from the jar. Those that fail their save are sickened for 1d2 days. A *lesser restoration* or

similar magic ends the effect.

Crate C: This crate is filled with a large amount of earth. It is labeled "Minzoa Experiment 2, Graveyard Dirt — Contagious." The crate is roughly 5 feet by 5 feet. Disturbing or digging in the dirt rouses a **sporozoan** buried in a cyst in the dirt. The cyst breaks open if the dirt is disturbed, and 1d4 tentacles lash out, seeking a target. Roll randomly to determine which nearby party members are attacked. Stats for the giant sporozoan are in the **Appendix**.

Characters recognize immediately that this creature is unlike anything they have encountered before. It has the aspects and characteristics of an ooze, but also the characteristics of other creatures with limbs or, at the very least, tentacles.

Crate D: This crate is filled with several crystal bottles of water listed from various locations throughout the Lost Lands. One names Blood Creek, others the Stoneheart River, and even the Ice River in the distant Northlands. The water is of no special value, but the names of far-off, exotic places might stir the characters' curiosity.

Crate E: This crate is filled with pieces of mechanical equipment, including powders for grinding and polishing glass, plus various glass lenses about the size of a silver coin and metal tubes of varying lengths. The bits and sundries have a total value of 400 gp and a street value of 250 gp if fenced through the proper channels.

Third Story: Irtep's Laboratory

This laboratory holds the bulk of Irtep's scientific and arcane equipment. The walls are lined with test tubes, beakers, vials, potion bottles (empty), jars of unguents, reagents, other components, and many books on arcane theory.

A DC 10 Perception check notes a breeze blowing in from the open southern window, carrying the smell of charred flesh. Lockpicks are scattered on the floor in a cone-shaped pattern expanding into the room from the windowsill. A careful search of the area or a DC 19 Perception check locates the invisible corpse of a halfling woman hanging across the sill, head and shoulders inside the room and legs dangling outside. A ring on the halfling's left hand is the source of her *invisibility*. The body is Traedie Jane, who was an up-and-coming halfling burglar until she was electrocuted on her way through Irtep's window. Traedie inherited the ring and her career from her mother Gwennie Jane, who passed away a year ago. Tradie's other gear includes a pair of *+1 daggers* and a hand crossbow with 20 bolts.

The cupboards and shelves contain enough ingredients to make any potion based on a wizard spell, up to two times. Another cupboard contains 100 pages of vellum and 10 pots of ink, enough to scribe a full spellbook or write 100 scrolls containing spells of level 4 or below.

Three devices that look like sextants are lined up on one of the shelves. Several glass dishes sit beneath the sextants. The dishes are filled with a variety of filthy liquids that look and smell like sewer water, or water with something unpleasant growing in it. Peering into the sextant devices reveals nothing unless a light source is placed beneath them, as the objects are in fact microscopes. A DC 15 Intelligence check reveals the purpose of the "sextants" and that a light source is helpful. None of the items tests as magical, but the microscopes are worth 300 gp each. Peering into them with a light beneath reveals a world invisible to the naked eye, including protozoan creatures swimming around in the filthy water. Characters who saw the sporozoan on the second floor recognize its similarity to these creatures.

Fourth Floor: Irtep's Love Den

This room is plush and contains all of the creature comforts one could imagine: a polished silver mirror ceiling, a tub sunk into the floor filled with warm bubbling water, a private bathroom, and a huge, heart-shaped bed on a slowly revolving turntable in the center of the room. The walls are adorned with naughty paintings of cherubs, nymphs, elven maidens, and the like cavorting with centaurs, minotaurs, and middle-aged wizards. The paintings are incredibly tacky; all five together might fetch 100 gp from a collector with no taste and/or a ribald sense of humor.

Irtep's Commode

The restroom off the bedchamber is a complex affair of carved, polished marble. A foot pedal on the floor pumps water for the bidet, and a second pump flushes into the moat outside the tower.

A side table next to the commode holds a notebook titled *"My Experiences in the Minzoa,"* by Irtep. The notebook details the construction of the *sextant of Minzoa* and its use to enter a vaguely defined "inner world" Irtep calls the Minzoa. Irtep's first explorations led to the death of some hired hands, and Irtep barely escaped the Minzoa with his life. The wizard next commissioned his friend Gynnen to fashion a set of pipes with which to charm the Minzoan creatures and later, to summon them to our world. The summoning terrified his friend Faisal, whom Irtep describes as weak-willed and lacking in understanding of the potential power that the Minzoa could unleash.

Most other entries in the notebook are love poems dedicated to various harlots, including lengthy opining for the love and attention of Michalena Goddeau. Other entries detail his collapse into drunkenness and gambling, with lists of his many debts and the threats made against him by Fat Julie and Tuvio. Irtep has spent his entire fortune on Michalena Goddeau, the *sextant of Minzoa*, and the *pipes of Minzoa*. Like any gambling addict, Irtep's writing is filled with excuses on how just "one big win" will set him up for life, if only someone will advance him the necessary cash.

Fifth Floor: Irtep's Library

Irtep's library stands on the penultimate story of the tower. Books line the walls from floor to ceiling. Found here are many spellbooks, each containing 2d6 cantrips, 1st-, or 2nd-level spells. Other books contain 1d8 spells of 3rd and 4th level. A single book contains the remainder of Irtep's spell collection: 1d4 5th-level spells.

Each spellbook is trapped with a curse that blinds and deafens the reader unless the reader is Irtep, or if the reader is studying the books with Irtep's permission as an apprentice or other student. A DC 15 Will save negates the curse, and a *remove curse* spell cast on the target ends the curse.

Other books lining the walls of the chamber cover all manner of life, including a detailed, illustrated treatise written by Irtep himself on a hidden realm called the "Minzoa." Locating this book requires a successful DC 18 Perception check, or 30 minutes spent browsing the shelves. Illustrations in the book show nightmarish creatures that resemble oozes with tentacles and hooks, and dripping with slime. Most of the creatures are shown in water or some other liquid. The illustrations portray a broad, shallow sea with bits of land rising from the water. The sky appears very bright and the horizon is very flat. Few land masses larger than low hills can be seen anywhere. The plant life is bizarre and alien, seemingly composed of vines or growths resembling seaweed snaking out of the water.

The Study (CR 5)

A locked chamber within the library faces the south wall. A wizard's mark written above the door reads, *"It ain't the size of the boat ..."*

The door is trapped to deal 8d6 points of electricity damage to anyone who touches the doorknob. A successful DC 16 Con saving throw reduces the damage by half. The trap can be discovered with a DC 28 Perception check, and disarmed with a DC 28 Disable Device check.

ELECTRIFIED DOOR TRAP **CR 5**
XP 1,600
Type magical; **Perception** DC 28; **Disable Device** DC 28

Trigger touch; **Reset** automatic; **Bypass** proper key
Effect spell effect (as *lightning bolt* but single-target, 8d6 electricity damage, DC 14 Reflex save half)

Beyond the door is a small chamber containing a desk on which sits a "sextant" like those in the lab, but with several notable differences. This sextant is made from silver, platinum, and gold, and is inlaid with arcane inscriptions. A magical disk of light glows from the sextant's base. Sitting in front of the disk is a fine crystal dish filled with fetid water. A chair is knocked onto its side behind the desk.

The dish is etched with the family crest of Irtep and is emblazoned with a tree whose roots dig deep into the earth and whose leaves blow freely in the wind. The dish has special sentimental meaning to Irtep: It was his mother's favorite candy dish.

If any character looks through the sextant at the bowl of water, he and anyone within 10 feet of him are instantly teleported into the fungus forest of Irtep's Dish (see "Part 3. Irtep's Dish and the Minzoa") unless a successful DC 20 Will save is made.

The Sextant of Minzoa

Aura moderate conjuration (teleportation) and transmutation; **CL** 10th
Slot none; **Price** 51,500 gp; **Weight** 3 lbs.

DESCRIPTION

When aimed at a dish of water, this sextant allows for the microscopic viewing of life forms smaller than the eye can see. Through arcane forces, the sextant can also serve as a conduit from the normal world into the tiny world viewed through the microscope. In effect, it allows travel into the Minzoa, the microscopic world of protozoan life forms.

Once per day the *sextant of Minzoa* can transport all creatures and objects in a 30 ft. cone emanating from the eyepiece into the Minzoa. To activate this function, the *sextant's* user must simply rotate a special magical reducing lens into the lens array and look into the eyepiece. The viewer and everything within the area of effect behind him are immediately miniaturized and transported to a random location in the Minzoa as if by use of the *teleport* spell.

By examining a small object and rotating the magical passkey lens into the array, the object is transformed into a *passkey*. The holder of the *passkey* can use it to return all creatures and objects within a 30 ft. radius back into the normal sized world. If both the reducing lens and the passkey lens are in place, the *sextant of Minzoa* does not function. One *passkey* can be created per day in this manner.

Use of the *sextant of Minzoa* offers a number of other startling possibilities. It could be used to shrink creatures to such a tiny degree that they could hide in a flask of water or carefully packed box of soil, allowing a thief or assassin (for example) to be smuggled into almost any location, then released with a word by the carrier of the sextant or the bearer of the *passkey of Minzoa*. The sextant can also be set as a trap of sorts to capture unwitting creatures and teleport them into the Minzoa by leaving the reducing lens in place and its eye-cap uncovered.

CONSTRUCTION

Requirements Craft Wondrous Item, *clairvoyance, enlarge person, planar adaptation, reduce person, shrink item, teleport*; **Cost** 25,750 gp

Sixth Floor: Top Floor (CR 6)

The top floor of the tower is accessed by a trapdoor at the top of the stairs from Level 5. Little is here except the chain and winch system attached to the giant yellow iron ball trap. A trapdoor in the ceiling leads to the roof of the tower.

The iron ball trap is maintained by **Beagle, a charmed troll** kept by Irtep who dines on rats and thieves. As far as Beagle is concerned, anyone who enters this chamber (other than Irtep) is a thief, which equates to dinner.

BEAGLE THE TROLL CR 5
XP 1,600
hp 63 (*Pathfinder Roleplaying Game Bestiary* "Troll")

The remains of a pair of second-story men who thought to come through the roof are strewn about the room. Among their leavings are a set of lock picks, a *scroll of dispel magic*, and a gold ring set with an imitation (but excellent quality) ruby worth 60 gp.

Beneath a loose floorboard is a locked treasure chest. The chest is trapped with a poison dart trap that requires a successful DC 12 Perception check to notice and a successful DC 15 Disable Device check to disarm. If the trap is triggered, a hail of darts attacks every target within 5 ft. of the chest.

POISONED DART TRAP CR 1
XP 400
Type mechanical; **Perception** DC 12; **Disable Device** DC 15

Trigger location; **Reset** manual; **Bypass** proper key
Effect +10 ranged (1d4 piercing plus sassone leaf residue); multiple targets (all targets within 5 ft. of the chest)

The chest contains a pile of IOUs and gambling vouchers from the Fortune's Fool and the Blazing Bones.

Part 3: Irtep's Dish and the Minzoa

In this section, the characters find themselves within the Minzoa held inside Irtep's mother's candy dish. The Minzoa is a miniature world where protozoan creatures loom huge in relation to the player characters. Within this forbidden world, the characters seek Irtep for good or ill and try to wrest from him the means to return to their own world.

Basic Features

Light: The Minzoa is lit as if by midday sun all the time, but the light provides little heat and seems to originate from every direction.

Wet: Everything in the Minzoa is moist. A vast lake occupies a broad expanse of the Minzoa, and living bodies of matter float on the lake. Nonmagical equipment of iron and steel rusts quickly if not oiled regularly. Most metal equipment shows a patina of rust after the first day in the Minzoa. Within two weeks, these items become pocked with rust. Within two months, they become brittle; within a year, they are rusted through.

Minzoa Lake: The lake is 50 feet deep across its entirety. The bed of the lake is a clear, crystalline substance that is extremely hard and seemingly unbreakable.

Walls: Player characters traveling to the edge of the Minzoa find themselves facing a crystalline wall 100 feet high that is completely smooth. Normal climbing methods are useless against it; it can be scaled only with a *spider climb* spell or similar means, or it can be flown or

Minzoa

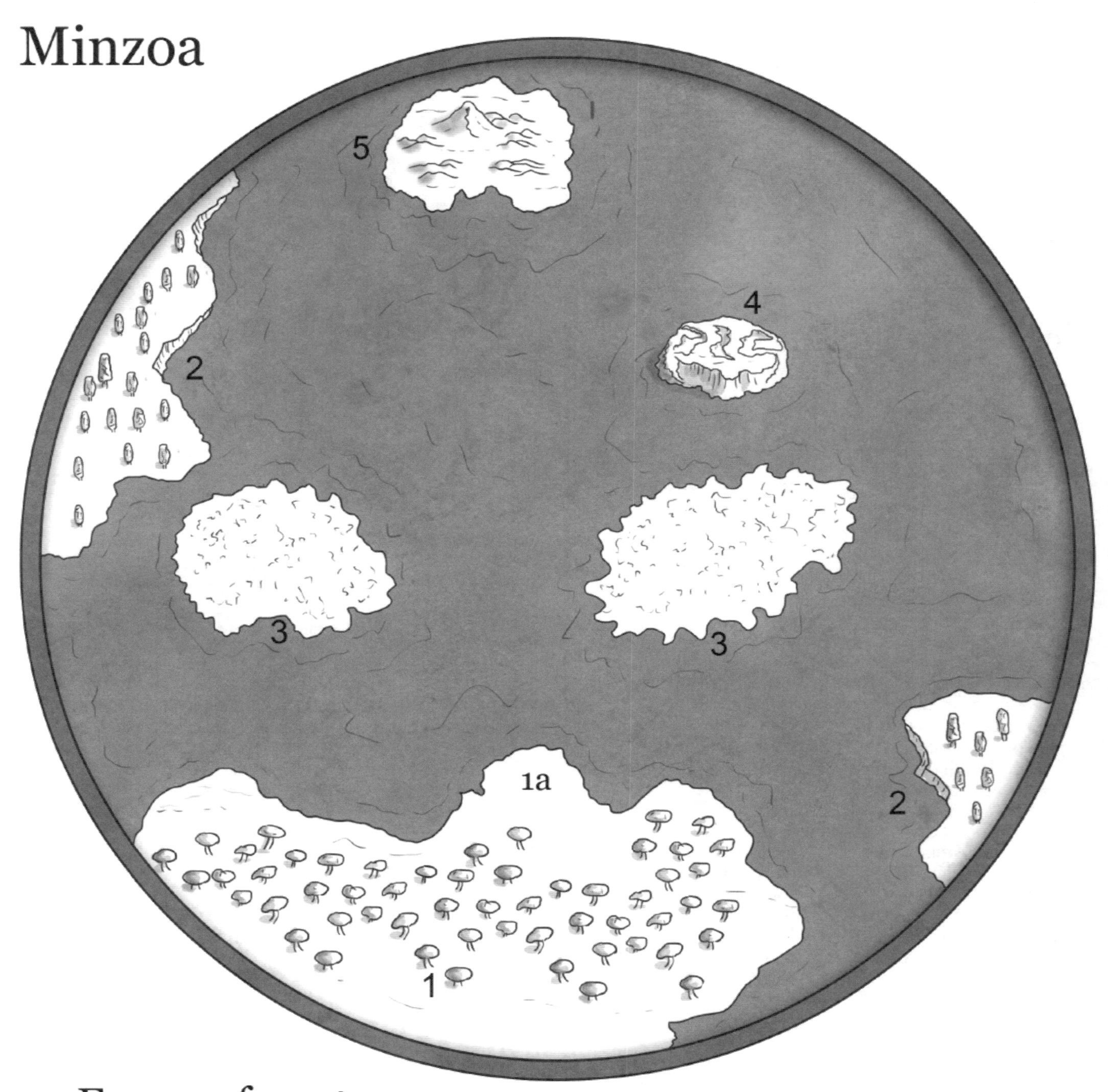

1 = Fungus forest
1a = Abandoned campsite
2 = Island of carnivorous fungi
3 = Islands of floating algae
4 = The Rock
5 = Irtep's Island

levitated over. At the top, a climbing, flying, or levitating character must succeed on a DC 14 Wills ave to avoid being teleported back to the Fungal Forest. Those who make a successful saving throw escape from the Minzoa, but they remain at their microscopic Minzoa size!

Minzoa Lake Random Encounters

Roll for a random encounter for every 10 "miles" traveled on the lake. These creatures are all described in detail in the **Appendix**.

1d12	Encounter
1	Giant Hydrozoa
2	1d4 Giant Nematodes
3	1d4 Giant Tardigrades
4	1d4 Giant Protozoan Orbs
5	1d4 Giant Sporozoan
6	Red Blades Assassin Squad (1d2+1 assassins)
7	Giant Amoeba
8–12	No Encounter

Hydrozoa: This is an encounter with **1 giant hydrozoa**. If the hydrozoa is over the lake, it languidly strikes out with its tentacles as it floats past.

Giant Nematode: This encounter is with **1d4 giant nematodes**. The creatures assume the player characters are food and attack mindlessly (the only way they can).

Giant Tardigrade: This encounter is with **1d4 giant tardigrades**. These great swollen beasts might ignore the characters altogether unless approached too closely or annoyed. If surprised or frightened, they attack.

Giant Protozoan Orb: 1d4 tick-like protozoan orbs smell the player characters and attack.

Giant Sporozoan: If this encounter occurs on water, it is with **1d4 sluglike giant sporozoan** swimming by. If this encounter occurs on land, it is with a single **sporozoan cyst** that bursts open as characters pass.

Red Blades Assassin Squad: These are **1d2+1 Red Blade assassins** who found their way into the tower and through the *sextant*. They float haplessly on a fungus cap they fashioned into a raft. The assassins lost most of their companions to the creatures of the Minzoa, and are terrified and desperate for a means of escape. They are willing to make a truce with the characters in exchange for the greater protection of a group and help in finding a way home. They honor the truce until they find an exit back to the normal world; what they do after that is up to you. The Red Blade assassins are 3rd-level rogues, and use the stat block for the **burglar** in the *Pathfinder Roleplaying Game GameMastery Guide*.

Giant Amoeba: The **amoeba** floats through the Minzoa lake devouring anything in its path.

Stats for these creatures are in the **Appendix**.

Area 1. Fungal Forest

This is the initial landing place of player characters teleported into the Minzoa. The "forest" is composed of massive fungal structures that resemble giant mushroom trees. Most of the fungi is benign, with some exceptions.

The broad caps of the mushroom trees can be eaten raw (bland) or roasted (less bland). Large ones are big enough to hollow out and use as coracles. One large cap can be made into a boat in an hour, and it holds up to four passengers. Other mushroom stalks are easily carved into crude paddles.

A mushroom coracle can navigate the waters of the Minzoa at a rate of 1 to 4 miles per hour; the actual speed equals the number of rowers.

Fungal Forest Random Encounters

Roll for a random encounter once every 10 miles, or every eight hours if characters are stationary. These creatures are all described in detail in the **Appendix**.

1d12	Encounter
1	Spore Cloud
2	Giant Tardigrade
3	Giant Sporozoan Cyst
4	Giant Hydrozoa
5	Shadow Masks Thieves Band (1d4+1 thieves)
6	Giant Protozoan Orb
7	Carnivorous Fungi
8–12	No Encounter

Spore Cloud: Characters disturbed the nearby fungi into releasing a defensive cloud of choking spores. The **spore cloud** is 50 feet in radius. Characters within the spore cloud who fail a DC 15 Fortitude save are overcome by choking and wheezing, and unable to breathe. Such characters take 1d6 points of damage immediately and begin suffocating, and continue suffocating until they get out of the spore cloud.

Shadow Masks Thieves Band: This is a band of **1d4+1 Shadow Mask thieves** who made their way this far in their search for Irtep. The band may attempt to separate and capture individual characters to use as hostages in an attempt to force the entire party into surrendering. Their goal is to find Irtep and get the hell out of the Minzoa, a world they find terrifying in the diversity of its life. Unlike the Red Blades assassins, these NPCs aren't interested in teaming up with the characters except to use them as porters, bait, or meat shields. **Shadow Mask thieves** are 3rd-level rogues, and use the stat block for the **burglar** in the *Pathfinder Roleplaying Game GameMastery Guide*.

Carnivorous Fungi: This is an encounter with a large patch of **carnivorous fungi**. See the **Appendix** for details.

Area 1A. The Ruined Campsite

This ruined campsite was set up by a small band of Shadow Masks who gained access to the Minzoa. Unfortunately, a pod of tardigrades tore them to pieces and devoured them. Nothing remains of their bodies except a few blood smears on the ground and on the trunks of mushroom trees. Amid the wreckage of the camp, however, is a bounty poster showing an image of Irtep. The image is an illusory likeness, so it is entirely accurate. The poster reveals a man with a thin moustache and goatee, and hair that might once have been stylish but has gone a little crazy. The image is complete with a black eye and blood dripping from the left nostril from a recent beating.

Also scattered on the ground are a *+1 rapier*, 3 *potions of cure light wounds*, a *potion of invisibility*, and a torn pouch containing a clay pipe and good tobacco. A short distance from the camp is a site where the thieves worked mushroom caps into boats. Mushroom chips and cuttings are scattered around between the felled trunks of several mushroom trees without caps.

Area 2. Carnivorous Fungi Islands (CR 4+)

Growing along the side of one wall of the dish is a massive colony of **carnivorous fungi**. These areas occupy the equivalent of 100 square miles each. The islands are full of carnivorous fungi; another group of 1d4 is encountered every 100 yards or so, making them all but impassable. Characters who try to explore these areas are attacked continually until they leave.

GIANT CARNIVOROUS FUNGI **CR 4**
XP 1,200
hp 58 (see the **Appendix**)

Area 3. Algae Islands

These two islands are composed of dense colonies of protozoan algae cells. In the Minzoa, the cells are the size of a rhinoceros and are slightly sticky, so that everywhere on the algae islands is considered difficult terrain. The islands are home to hydrozoa, giant tardigrades, and sporozoan cysts. The ground is reasonably solid, and the algae itself can be sliced from the "ground" and eaten as a reasonably nutritious food, although the flavor leaves much to be desired.

Algae Islands Random Encounters

Roll for random encounters once every hour. These creatures are all described in detail in the **Appendix**.

1d12	Encounter
1	Giant Tardigrade
2	Giant Hydrozoa
3	Sporozoan Cyst
4	Dominion Arcane Enforcer
5	Giant Amoeba
6–12	No Encounter

Dominion Arcane Enforcer: This is an encounter with a 5th-level wizard sent to find and capture Irtep and return him to the Dominion for questioning. The enforcer is alone, as creatures of the Minzoa killed his allies. He is desperate to complete his mission and has no reservations about joining forces with the characters (unless they give him one). See the **Appendix** for details.

Area 4. The Rock

This towering, cliff-sided, stony island is no more than a bit of pebble that found its way into Irtep's Dish. It is contested territory in a three-way feud between Shadow Masks and Red Blades. The assassins and their rivals hide within fissures and cracks in the stone, defending themselves against beasts that crawl up the stone from the lake and from one another. Amoebas and nematodes ate their fungus cap boats long ago, stranding them here.

Tully's Fort (CR 7)

Tully's Fort is a fissure in the Rock that **Tully** and his assassins fortified for keeping watch on the Shadow Masks and for protection against the creatures of the Minzoa while the assassins search for a way to escape the Minzoa.

TULLY SMOOTH **CR 4**
XP 1,200
Male human rogue 5
NE Medium humanoid (human)
Init +3; **Perception** +8

AC 18, touch 14, flat-footed 14 (+4 armor, +3 Dex, +1 dodge)
hp 36 (5d8+10)
Fort +3; **Ref** +7; **Will** +1

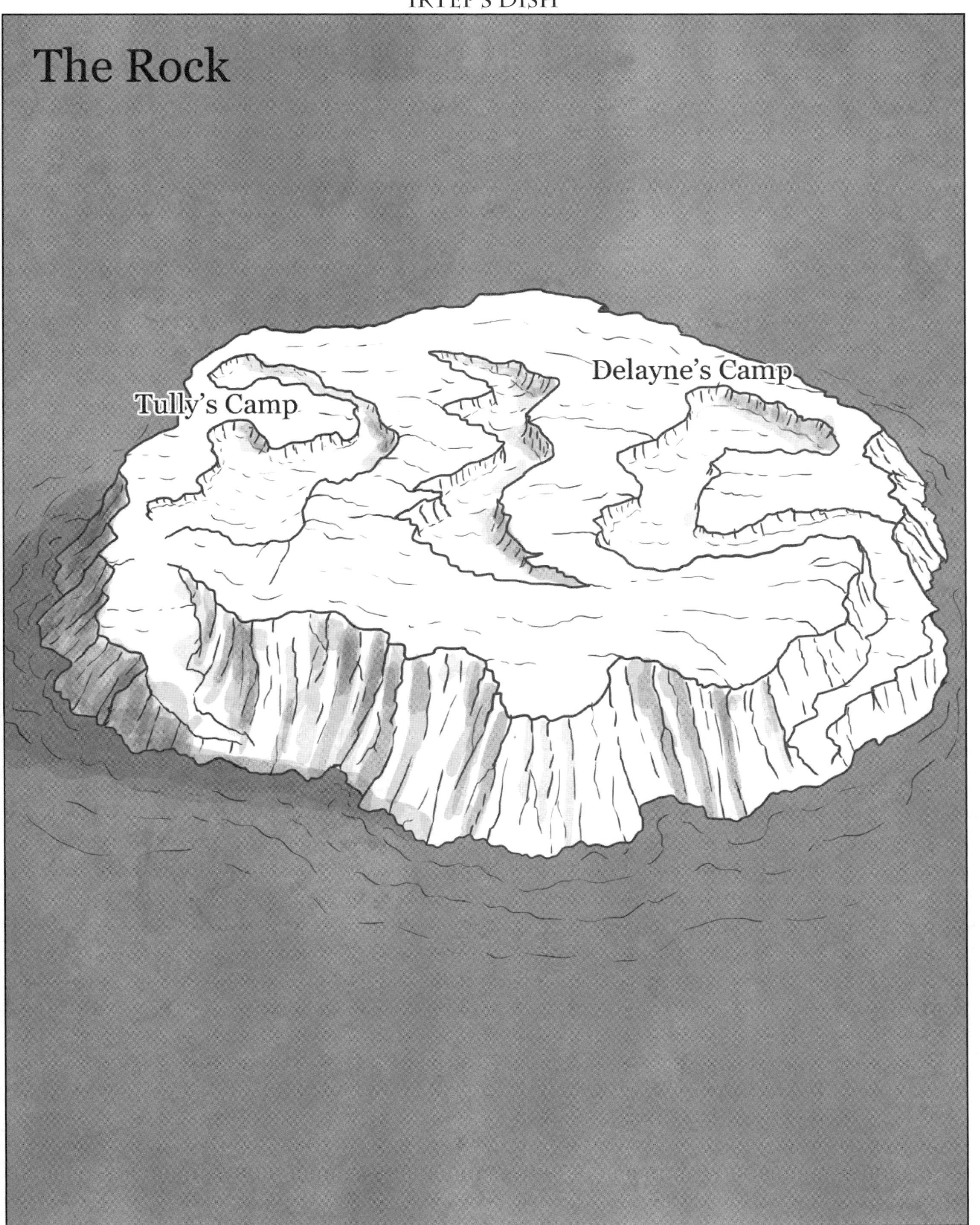
The Rock
Tully's Camp
Delayne's Camp

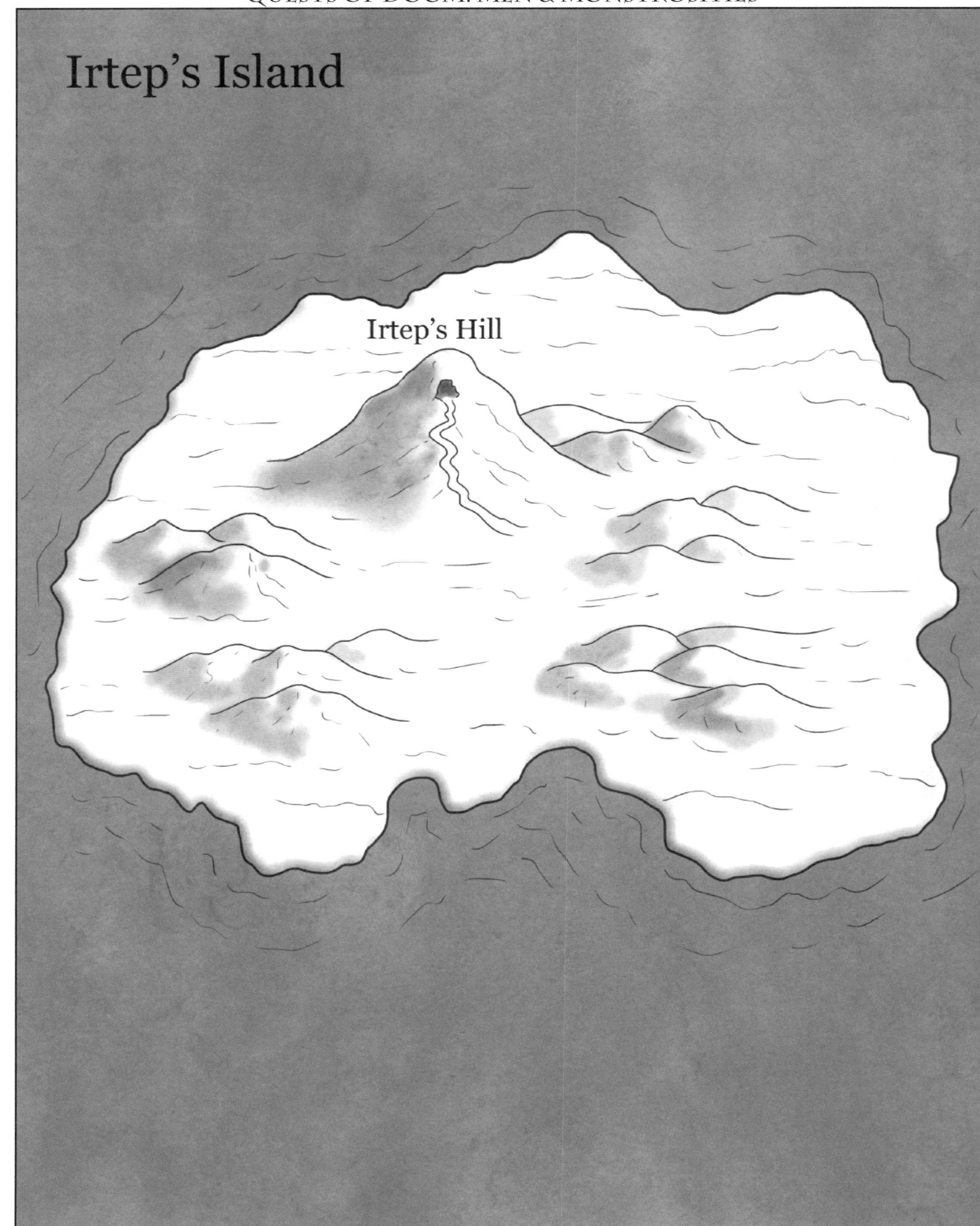
Irtep's Island
Irtep's Hill

Defensive Abilities evasion, trap sense +1, uncanny dodge

Speed 30 ft.
Melee *+1 rapier* +7 (1d6+2/18–20)
Ranged *+1 light crossbow* +7 (1d8+1/19–20)
Special Attacks bleeding attack 3, sneak attack +3d6

Str 12, **Dex** 16, **Con** 14, **Int** 13, **Wis** 11, **Cha** 15
Base Atk +3; **CMB** +4; **CMD** 18
Feats Deadly Aim, Dodge, Mobility, Weapon Finesse
Skills Acrobatics +11, Appraise +9, Bluff +10, Climb +9, Escape Artist +11, Intimidate +10, Perception +8, Sense Motive +8, Sleight of Hand +11, Stealth +11, Swim +9
Languages Common, Elven
SQ rogue talents (fast stealth), trapfinding +2
Combat Gear *potion of invisibility*, 3 vials of greenblood oil; **Other Gear** *+1 studded leather*, *+1 light crossbow*, *+1 rapier*, 30 crossbow bolts, *boots of speed*

RED BLADE ASSASSINS (4) **CR 2**
XP 600
hp 16 (*Pathfinder Roleplaying Game GameMastery Guide*, "Burglar")

Tully is glad to see the player characters arrive, because the Shadow Masks have been assassinating his team slowly but surely. Tully is convinced one of the Shadow Masks must be a shapeshifter. He suggests joining sides to clear out the Shadow Masks and then to find a way out of this "tiny world of horrors" that they find themselves trapped in. If the characters side with Tully and his band, they find Tully and his crew intent on killing Irtep and collecting the bounty that they themselves falsely laid.

Delayne's Fort (CR 7)

Delayne, a doppelganger agent of the Dark Brotherhood and master of the Shadow Masks, is stuck in her makeshift fort with her squad. Delayne tried to infiltrate the enemy camp disguised as an assassin; the ruse worked until recently, but now she suspects that the Red Blades have caught on to the trick and gone on high alert.Delayne and her band of **3 Shadow Mask rogues** now seek only to escape the Minzoa. They need a boat to get across the lake, and strong swords and powerful magic to survive the trip. Delayne offers to cut the characters in on a percentage of whatever they can steal from Irtep's tower. Even as she makes this offer, she knows perfectly well (as the characters probably do, too) that, outside of the laboratory, Irtep is broke.

At this point, Delayne could not care less about the Red Blades, but her murderous nature still drives her to kill them as a defensive measure. If the characters arrived with at least one mushroom boat, she may try to trick the characters into heading over to the Red Blade camp while she steals their boat.

DELAYNE **CR 5**
XP 1,600
Female doppelganger rogue 2 (*Pathfinder Roleplaying Game Bestiary* "Doppelganger")
N Medium monstrous humanoid (shapechanger)
Init +4; **Senses** darkvision 60 ft.; **Perception** +8

AC 20, touch 16, flat-footed 15 (+1 deflection, +4 Dex, +1 dodge, +4 natural)
hp 43 (4d10+8 plus 2d8+4)
Fort +5; **Ref** +11; **Will** +5
Defensive Abilities evasion; **Immune** charm, sleep

Speed 30 ft.
Melee *+1 longsword* +8 (1d8+2/19–20) or *+1 dagger* +7 (1d4+2/19–20) or 2 claws +6 (1d8+1)
Special Attacks sneak attack +1d6
Spell-Like Abilities (CL 18th):
At will—*detect thoughts* (DC 14)

Str 13, **Dex** 18, **Con** 14, **Int** 12, **Wis** 13, **Cha** 15
Base Atk +5; **CMB** +6; **CMD** 22
Feats Deceitful, Dodge, Great Fortitude, Weapon Focus (longsword)[B]
Skills Acrobatics +13, Bluff +17, Diplomacy +11, Disguise +17, Intimidate +9, Perception +8, Sense Motive +8, Stealth +11;
Racial Modifiers +4 Bluff, +4 Disguise, +20 disguise while using change shape ability, +4 bluff while using change shape ability
Languages Common, Gnome
SQ change shape (alter self), mimicry, perfect copy, rogue talent (combat trick; Weapon Focus), trapfinding +1
Combat Gear *scroll of knock*; **Other Gear** *+1 dagger*, *+1 longsword*, *ring of protection +1*

SHADOW MASK HENCHMAN (3) **CR 2**
XP 600
hp 16 (*Pathfinder Roleplaying Game GameMastery Guide*, "Burglar")

Isle of Irtep

A clump of earth and sand smudged into the northern part of the dish serves as Irtep's Lair. Irtep formed a defensive cavern where he hides in relative luxury, assuming nobody will ever find him within the confines of his beloved Minzoa. The cavern atop the "island" affords Irtep a grand view of the area. He can see approaching figures from miles away and prepares any defenses he deems necessary to defend himself from approaching enemies or assassins. Characters might need to get clever to approach the Isle of Irtep safely, such as disguising themselves as creatures of the Minzoa, turning *invisible*, or some other ploy.

Encountering Irtep

If the characters simply press forward on a fungus raft, Irtep sends a magical message that reaches the approaching characters a mile from shore. He demands that they return at once to the "big world" or face the wrath of his minions of the Minzoa. If the characters exclaim that they do not know how to get free of the Minzoa, Irtep offers to send them, so long as they swear never to return. He is not above using a *geas* spell of his own to force this point home.

Irtep is reluctant to negotiate or talk to anyone. If necessary, he uses the *pipes of Minzoa* to summon creatures of the Minzoa to defend his position.

Irtep's Hill

Irtep defends himself from a cave and bungalow crafted at the top of an 80-foot-high hill that affords him an excellent vantage point from which to rain down magic and to summon creatures to fight for him.

The hill has a 40-degree slope, meaning it is steep enough that everywhere on the slope is difficult terrain. A successful DC 10 Acrobatics check is necessary for characters to move and take a combat action on the same turn. Characters must make the roll before attacking if they've already moved, and vice versa. Failure on the roll ends their turn immediately.

Battle

It should be apparent at the onset of any conflict with Irtep that the wizard is not well. He looks gray, shaky, drawn, and emaciated. This is

a far different Irtep from his wanted posters or the portraits in his home. The change came about from ignoring the compulsion of Osgood's *geas* upon him.

If Irtep's summoned creatures are defeated and the wizard appears to be losing the battle, he surrenders. He swears that he will not return to his creditors in Bard's Gate because they mean to kill him. He begs the characters to become his agents and to act on his behalf in the outside world, offering them a way out of the Minzoa in exchange. He is oblivious to how ill he is or how terrible he looks, and he speaks frequently of the desire to see his beloved Michalena again. He would like her brought here so they can start a new life in his "mountaintop bungalow." He admits he has no money, but he could craft scrolls, potions, and magic items for the characters if they bring him the raw materials.

Any attempt at negotiating with Irtep fails if any Red Blades assassins are in the mix. They intend to take Irtep's head and trade it to Big Julie or Tuvio, and to trade any of his magical belongings to the Dominion Arcane for whatever profit they can make.

Avoiding Battle

Because of the *geas* placed on Irtep by Osgood Flumph, Irtep is unable to refuse an offer to engage in a game of chance. If challenged to a wager, he must accept, but he can and will negotiate the stakes. For example, if a burly fighter challenges Irtep to a stone-throwing contest, he accepts the contest but argues that, because the fighter's obviously greater strength gives him an advantage, Irtep should win 5 gp from the characters for every 1 they would win from him, or something similar. He conjures up a gaming table, a deck of cards, or a bag of dice on command. If the characters schmoozed with Michalena Goodeau or allied themselves with Gynnen Valzoe, they are aware of this quirk of Irtep's personality and might be prepared to use this to their advantage against Irtep.

As soon as Irtep plays a game of chance, he is immediately invigorated to his full health, which makes him more demanding about the characters' need to depart from his hidden domain. Characters need to talk themselves out of any dangerous situations they get into with Irtep, or figure out some way to break his *geas*.

Persuading Irtep to Leave

Either through gambling or battle, eventually the characters should bring Irtep to a point where he is willing to talk. Persuading Irtep to leave and return to the outer world is not an easy task. Characters might point out that invaders have already made their way into his home and it is only a matter of time before others such as themselves make contact with him and are less than friendly. Worse, intruders in his tower might inadvertently or intentionally destroy Minzoa in its entirety. It may be time for Irtep to face the consequences of his actions after all and figure out some way to pay back his creditors.

Irtep doesn't want to hear these things. He is quite ill, however, and is beginning to suspect that he needs help. Suggestions that his creditors might be willing to take one last double-or-nothing bet with him have the best shot at winning his confidence. Characters who can talk knowledgeably about Irtep's debts, the people to whom he owes money, and gambling in general hold his attention. Speaking positively about his friendship with Faisal and Gynnen or about Tuvio's respect for him (a bit of exaggeration is helpful here) perks him up. Any mention of Michalena, other than a proclamation that she regrets leaving Irtep and longs for him to take her back, casts the wizard into a deep funk.

In short, Irtep needs to hear that he has a chance to recover his fortune, to reclaim his good reputation, and to win back his lover Michalena, whether or not such things are true. Intimidation doesn't get the characters anywhere unless they knock Irtep unconscious and take him away by force. *Charming* him makes him friendly but won't make him want to leave Minzoa. Removing the *geas* opens his eyes to the real situation and lets him remember that it was Osgood Flumph who enchanted him out of jealousy over Irtep's research and growing power. Irtep is horrified about the betrayal and determined to make amends to those he owes. He immediately begins planning to file a censure with the Dominion Arcane against Osgood for his betrayal, or to take revenge after his own fashion.

However they persuade Irtep to leave Minzoa, he asks the characters to gather near as he withdraws his *passkey*: a pair of green dice that he shakes in his hand while uttering the command phrase, *"Get big, baby!"* With that, characters find themselves back in Irtep's private study on the fifth floor of his tower.

Killing Irtep

If the characters kill Irtep, they can leave his body behind in Minzoa or bring it back to the world where they can deliver it to someone for a bounty or even have him raised. If Irtep stays dead, they need merely deliver the items of interest to his creditors and collect their pay. Or so they hope. See "Conclusions" to determine how to play this series of events. Only Irtep knows the *passkey* and its command phrase to escape from Minzoa. If characters kill the wizard without first discovering that information, and they don't have the means to extract it from the dead wizard, they could be trapped forever.

Part 4: Conclusions

At some point, characters must leave Irtep's Tower. How they leave and what conflicts follow are dependent on whom the characters allied with and the care they take in leaving the tower.

Allies

Regardless of whom the characters allied with before taking the quests of ***Irtep's Dish***, their previous allies are lying in wait for their exit from the tower. Each of the allies has its own agenda. Amid this conflict are the wildcards presented by the guard and the half-orc trackers employed by Big Julie and Tuvio.

When the characters leave the tower, they are immediately confronted by Osgood, Faisal, and Gynnen Valzoe — or all three. The wizards each demand the items that the characters gathered from the tower. At first, they attempt to out-bid one another for the items. If that doesn't work, they try to persuade the characters why they deserve the items. Depending on the characters' actions or reactions, this can lead to a battle between the wizard they side with and the other parties who are angered at being cut out of the deal.

Leaving the Tower

If the characters leave the tower by flying, by swimming, invisibly, or by somehow just sneaking out, they notice that the guards that were so abundant and alert before all seem to be asleep at their posts. From then on, the situation develops according to the guidelines below. Use these examples to adjudicate what happens in your specific situation. Feel free to add additional NPCs if appropriate, such as bartenders and wizard guards at the Wizard's Familiar.

Pipes of Minzoa

Aura moderate conjuration and enchantment; **CL** 7th
Slot none; **Price** 15,000 gp; **Weight** 1 lb.

DESCRIPTION

These pipes of ivory, platinum, silver, and gold are as finely crafted as one could imagine. Three magical songs can be played on these magical pipes. A bard can use each power of the *pipes* one additional time per day.

Summon Minzoan Creature (3/day): The pipes can be played over a vial of plain water to summon a number of creatures from the Minzoa whose total HD equals 12 or less. These creatures obey the summoner's commands and remain for one minute or until destroyed, or until dismissed by the summoner.

Charm Minzoan Creature (1/day): The pipes can be played to charm a single Minzoan creature for a number of days equal to the Charisma bonus of the character playing the *pipes* (minimum 1 day). A charmed creature remains loyal to the character so long as the character or one of its allies doesn't attack the charmed creature. The creature affected can make a DC 15 Will save to negate the effect. The *pipes* are effective on Minzoan creatures even though most are immune to charm effects.

Invisibility to Minzoan Creature (1/day): This song causes all creatures of the Minzoa to ignore the character for up to one hour. This effect is broken if the character or one of its allies attacks an affected creature.

CONSTRUCTION

Requirements Craft Wondrous Item, *charm monster*, *summon monster IV*; **Cost** 7,500 gp

Irtep's Passkey

Irtep's passkey for leaving the Minzoa is a set of six-sided dice given to him by his aged master. When Osgood and Irtep crafted the *sextant of Minzoa*, they tied the dice into the effect. The dice need only be rolled in the palm of the hand while the password (*"Get big, baby!"*) is spoken to reverse the *sextant's* effect.

Confrontation: The Trio

If the characters simply walk out the front door, they find the guards asleep. Once they cross the moat, Osgood, Faisal, and Gynnen confront them. The trio approach at the same time but separately from different directions. Everyone's hands are on wands or weapons, and it's clear none of them trusts each other or are happy to see one another.

If Irtep is Alive

If Irtep is alive but his *geas* has not been broken, he is leery of Osgood and Faisal and appears humiliated in the presence of Gynnen.

Osgood demands Irtep relinquish the magic items to him so he can continue their research. He points out that it would be best if Irtep left town and never came back since his gambling problem has cost him so dearly.

Faisal demands that Irtep give the items to him so that he can turn them over to the Dominion to be destroyed.

Gynnen begs Irtep to leave the wizards to their toys and come with him to get help for his failing health and for his gambling problem. Gynnen accuses Osgood of placing a *geas* on Irtep and claims that he has evidence the scroll was bought from the wizard Manisool.

If the *geas* has not been broken, Irtep gains a new saving throw against it (a DC 14 Will save) as he realizes what Osgood did to him. If he breaks the spell, an angry Irtep attacks Osgood, and Faisal joins in. If the saving throw fails and the characters never received the *scroll of remove curse* from Gynnen, then Gynnen unrolls the scroll to cast the spell now. During this attempt, Osgood attacks him!

The wizards avoid using spells that cause mass destruction to the neighborhood and further raise the ire of the city watch, who arrive 10 rounds after the first spell is cast. Gynnen pleads with the wizards to cease fighting; he joins in the melee only to defend himself or to protect Irtep. Irtep does everything in his power to defeat Osgood, with the assistance of Faisal, though Faisal does not allow Irtep to kill Osgood; he'd rather see Osgood turned over to the Dominion Arcane for a private trial.

The player characters can take any actions they wish during the wizards' and bard's duel, coming in on whichever side they favor or standing aside completely. They'll be ignored while the combatants have each other to worry about.

During the fight, **2 half-orcs** working for Big Julie and **2 half-orcs** working for Tuvio arrive. They use the battle as a distraction while they make a beeline for Irtep. These two teams of leg-breakers are not allied; their separate goals are to capture Irtep and bring him back to their respective masters. They fall to fighting one another as soon as all four close on the wizard.

When the half-orcs make their grab for Irtep, Gynnen steps in to stop them. Player characters are free to take any actions they deem appropriate, including aiding or betraying whichever faction they signed on with at the beginning of the adventure, understanding any consequences that occur from their actions.

As if all this isn't bad enough, members of the city guard begin arriving within 10 rounds. The arriving guards awaken the guards that Osgood and Faisal put to *sleep*, for a total of **14 guards**, **Officer Gralme**, **4 guard dogs**, and the wizard **Finly** on the scene. Killing Lyreguards is a serious crime, of course.

If Irtep is Dead or not with the Party

If Irtep is dead or absent from the party, his former associates still meet the characters as they exit the tower. In this case, Faisal and Osgood demand the *sextant*, the *passkey*, and the *pipes of Minzoa*. If the characters are under contract with one of the wizards, he reminds them openly of their deal. If the players choose to side with Faisal, Osgood attacks Faisal, intending to kill him before he takes custody of Irtep's treasures.

Gynnen is only concerned about the fate of Irtep, not his creations. If the characters tell him that Irtep is dead, the bard is visibly sad and departs.

Shortly after Gynnen leaves, the half-orcs arrive and demand Irtep's treasures as payment to their bosses. It is up to the players and Game Master to determine how this plays out.

Tying Up Loose Ends

It is possible at the end of the adventure that the characters are outlaws in Bard's Gate. They may have made enemies or allies of the Red Blades, Shadow Masks, Dominion Arcane, Big Julie, Tuvio, Faisal, Osgood, or Irtep if he survived.

How the characters move forward after this adventure is something to be decided between the Game Master and players based on their deeds and choices!

If characters rescue Irtep and bring him home to a happy conclusion, he gives them his dish and the *pipes of Minzoa*, as his magic has grown enough to continue his explorations of other tiny worlds. Irtep goes out of his way to make amends with his debtors, paying them off with a cache of scrolls and other treasures he hid in the Minzoa.

In this event, award the characters each an additional 1,000 XP for their hard work. Irtep remains an ally to the characters for the duration of their careers, offering what advice and help he can and thanking them always for saving him anytime their paths cross.

NPCs and Monsters

Stat blocks for NPCs and monsters that can be encountered in multiple locations are listed here. Only new or unique creatures are included. Abbreviated stat blocks are included for monsters and NPCs that are covered in the *Pathfinder Roleplaying Game GameMastery Guide*, the *Pathfinder Roleplaying Game NPC Codex* and *Pathfinder Roleplaying Game Bestiaries*, and GMs are directed to those books for full details on those creatures.

Irtep and His Associates

IRTEP **CR 9**
XP 6,400
Male human wizard 10
CN Medium humanoid (human)
Init +5; **Perception** +16

AC 14, touch 12, flat-footed 13 (+2 armor, +1 deflection, +1 Dex)
hp 37 (10d6)
Fort +5; **Ref** +4; **Will** +9

Speed 35 ft.
Special Attacks hand of the apprentice (7/day)
Spells Prepared (CL 10th; melee touch +5, ranged touch +6):
5th—*cone of cold* (x2, DC 19)
4th—*dimension door, lesser globe of invulnerability, ice storm, stoneskin*
3rd—*dispel magic, fireball* (DC 17), *protection from energy, suggestion* (DC 17)
2nd—*bear's endurance, blur, flaming sphere* (DC 16), *invisibility, web* (DC 16)
1st—*burning hands* (DC 15), *endure elements, magic missile, shocking grasp, sleep* (DC 15)
0 (at will)—*acid splash, dancing lights, prestidigitation, read magic*

Str 10, **Dex** 12, **Con** 11, **Int** 18, **Wis** 15, **Cha** 14
Base Atk +5; **CMB** +5; **CMD** 17
Feats Alertness, Combat Casting, Craft Wand, Craft Wondrous Item, Fleet, Great Fortitude, Improved Initiative, Run, Scribe Scroll
Skills Acrobatics +1 (+5 to jump with a running start), Appraise +12, Knowledge (arcana) +17, Knowledge (dungeoneering) +17, Knowledge (history) +17, Knowledge (Minzoa) +12, Knowledge (nature) +17, Perception +16, Sense Motive +9, Spellcraft +17, Survival +7, Swim +5
Languages Abyssal, Aquan, Common, Giant, Infernal
SQ arcane bond (*wand of lightning bolt* [14 charges]), metamagic mastery (2/day)
Combat Gear 3 *scrolls of charm person, wand of lightning bolt* (14 charges); **Other Gear** *bracers of armor +2 , broom of flying , ring of protection +1 , ring of swimming , pipes of Minzoa*, passkey of minzoa (dice)
Spellbook 0—all; 1st—*burning hands, endure elements, magic missile, shocking grasp, sleep*; 2nd—*bear's endurance, blur, darkvision, flaming sphere, invisibility, web*; 3rd—*dispel magic, displacement, fireball, gaseous form, haste, protection from energy, suggestion*; 4th—*dimension door, ice storm, lesser globe of invulnerability, minor creation, stoneskin*; 5th—*cone of cold*.

FAISAL DHAKEN **CR 6**
XP 2,400
Male human wizard 7
CN Medium humanoid (human)
Init +6; **Perception** +10

AC 15, touch 13, flat-footed 12 (+2 armor, +2 Dex, +1 dodge)
hp 34 (7d6+7)
Fort +3; **Ref** +4; **Will** +8

Speed 30 ft.
Special Attacks hand of the apprentice (6/day)
Spells Prepared (CL 7th; melee touch +2, ranged touch +5);
4th—*greater invisibility*
3rd—*dispel magic*, *lightning bolt* (DC 16), *suggestion* (DC 16)
2nd—*acid arrow*, *fog cloud*, *mirror image*, *web* (DC 15)
1st—*expeditious retreat*, *mage armor*, *magic missile*, *shocking grasp*, *sleep* (DC 14)
0 (at will)—*acid splash*, *daze* (DC 13), *light*, *ray of frost*

Str 8, **Dex** 14, **Con** 12, **Int** 17, **Wis** 13, **Cha** 10
Base Atk +3; **CMB** +2; **CMD** 15
Feats Alertness, Combat Casting, Craft Wondrous Item, Dodge, Improved Initiative, Iron Will, Scribe Scroll
Skills Diplomacy +7, Knowledge (arcana) +13, Knowledge (dungeoneering) +13, Knowledge (local) +13, Perception +10, Sense Motive +10, Spellcraft +13
Languages Common, Elven, Giant, Sylvan
SQ arcane bond (*staff of fire*)
Combat Gear 2 *potions of cure serious wounds*, *staff of fire* (12 charges), *wand of magic missile* (7 charges); **Other Gear** *bracers of armor* +2, gems and jewelry (worth 3,000 gp)

OSGOOD FLUMPH **CR 8**
XP 4,800
Male human wizard 9
NE Medium humanoid (human)
Init +5; **Perception** +8

AC 13, touch 13, flat-footed 11 (+1 deflection, +1 Dex, +1 dodge)
hp 43 (9d6+9)
Fort +4; **Ref** +4; **Will** +7

Speed 30 ft.
Melee *+1 dagger* +5 (1d4+1/19–20)
Special Attacks hand of the apprentice (6/day)
Spells Prepared (CL 9th; melee touch +4, ranged touch +5):
5th—*cone of cold* (DC 18)
4th—*greater invisibility*, *stoneskin*
3rd—*fireball* (DC 16), *fly*, *lightning bolt* (DC 16), *suggestion* (DC 16)
2nd—*blur*, *flaming sphere* (DC 15), *invisibility*, *scare* (DC 15), *web* (DC 15)
1st—*burning hands* (DC 14), *cause fear* (DC 14), *mage armor*, *magic missile*, *shield*
0 (at will)—*acid splash*, *ghost sound* (DC 13), *light*, *mage hand*

Str 10, **Dex** 13, **Con** 12, **Int** 17, **Wis** 12, **Cha** 14
Base Atk +4; **CMB** +4; **CMD** 17
Feats Alertness, Brew Potion, Combat Casting, Craft Wand, Dodge, Improved Initiative, Mobility, Scribe Scroll
Skills Appraise +15, Craft (alchemy) +15, Knowledge (dungeoneering) +15, Knowledge (history) +15, Knowledge (planes) +15, Perception +8, Sense Motive +7, Spellcraft +15
Languages Common, Dwarven, Elven, Giant
SQ arcane bond (*ring of protection +1*), metamagic mastery (1/day)
Combat Gear *brooch of shielding*, *scroll of dispel magic* and *lesser geas*, *wand of lightning bolt* (7 charges); **Other Gear** *+1 dagger*, *bag of holding I*, *boots of levitation*, *ring of protection +1*, gems and jewelry (worth 3,500 gp)

GYNNEN VALZOE **CR 5**
XP 1,600
Male human bard 6
CG Medium humanoid (human)
Init +3; **Perception** +7

AC 19, touch 14, flat-footed 15 (+5 armor, +3 Dex, +1 dodge)
hp 36 (6d8+6)
Fort +3, **Ref** +8, **Will** +6; +4 vs. bardic performance, language-dependent, and sonic

---

Speed 30 ft.
Melee *+1 longsword* +7 (1d8+3/19–20)
Ranged *+1 light crossbow* +8 (1d8+1/19–20)
Special Attacks bardic performance 17 rounds/day (countersong, distraction, fascinate [DC 16], inspire competence +2, inspire courage +2, suggestion [DC 16])
Bard Spells Known (CL 6th; concentration +9):
2nd (4/day)—*hold person* (DC 15), *invisibility*, *mirror image*, *silence* (DC 15)
1st (5/day)—*charm person* (DC 14), *comprehend languages*, *cure light wounds*, *hideous laughter* (DC 14)
0 (at will)—*daze* (DC 13), *detect magic*, *ghost sound* (DC 13), *light*, *mage hand*, *prestidigitation*

Str 14, **Dex** 16, **Con** 12, **Int** 14, **Wis** 12, **Cha** 17
Base Atk +4; **CMB** +6; **CMD** 20
Feats Combat Casting, Dodge, Extra Performance, Mobility
Skills Acrobatics +11, Bluff +12, Knowledge (arcana) +11, Knowledge (history) +11, Knowledge (local) +11, Perception +7, Perform (sing) +12, Perform (wind instruments) +12, Sense Motive +12, Spellcraft +11, Stealth +11, Use Magic Device +12
Languages Common, Dwarven, Elven
SQ bardic knowledge +3, lore master 1/day, versatile performances (sing, wind)
Combat Gear *scroll of remove curse*; **Other Gear** *+1 chain shirt*, *+1 light crossbow*, *+1 longsword*, gems and jewelry (worth 500 gp)

Irtep's Creditors

Fat Julie Broad-Toe

FAT JULIE BROAD-TOE **CR 3**
XP 800
Male halfling rogue (spy) 4 (*Pathfinder Roleplaying Game Advanced Players Guide* "Spy")
NE Small humanoid (halfling)
Init +4; **Perception** +10

AC 17, touch 17, flat-footed 12 (+1 deflection, +4 Dex, +1 dodge, +1 size)
hp 29 (4d8+8)
Fort +4; **Ref** +9; **Will** +3; +2 vs. fear
Defensive Abilities evasion, uncanny dodge

Speed 20 ft.
Melee short sword +8 (1d4–1/19–20)
Ranged shortbow +8 (1d4–1/x3)
Special Attacks sneak attack +2d6

Str 8, **Dex** 18, **Con** 14, **Int** 13, **Wis** 12, **Cha** 10
Base Atk +3; **CMB** +1; **CMD** 17

Feats Dodge, Skill Focus (Stealth), Weapon Finesse
Skills Acrobatics +11 (+7 to jump), Bluff +7 (+9 on opposed rolls to attempt to deceive someone (does not apply to feint attempts or attempts to pass secret messages)), Climb +7, Diplomacy +6, Disable Device +10, Escape Artist +11, Intimidate +7, Knowledge (local) +8, Perception +10, Sense Motive +8, Sleight of Hand +11, Stealth +15; **Racial Modifiers** +2 Acrobatics, +2 Climb, +2 Perception
Languages Common, Elven, Halfling
SQ poison use, rogue talents (fast stealth, finesse rogue)
Combat Gear 2 *potions of cure moderate wounds*, 2 *potions of invisibility*; **Other Gear** 30 arrows, shortbow, short sword, *ring of protection +1*

Fat Julie's Brute Squad

Fat Julie has many half-orcs working for him as all-purpose leg-breakers. The toughest of them are **Choli Bonesnapper**, **Colic**, **Pinkeye**, and **Blister**. Many other orcs work under these bruisers.

CHOLI BONESNAPPER, COLIC, PINKEYE, AND BLISTER — CR 2
XP 600
hp 40 (*Pathfinder Roleplaying Game NPC Codex* "Axe Warrior")

ORC THUGS — CR 1/3
XP 135
hp 6 (*Pathfinder Roleplaying Game Bestiary* "Orc")

Tuvio

TUVIO — CR 4
XP 1,200
Male human rogue (bandit) 5 (*Pathfinder Roleplaying Game Ultimate Combat* "Bandit")
NE Medium humanoid (human)
Init +3; **Perception** +7

AC 19, touch 14, flat-footed 15 (+5 armor, +3 Dex, +1 dodge)
hp 41 (5d8+15)
Fort +3; **Ref** +7; **Will** +0
Defensive Abilities evasion, trap sense +1

Speed 30 ft.
Melee *+1 longsword* +7 (1d8+3/19–20)
Ranged composite shortbow +6 (1d6+2/×3)
Special Attacks sneak attack +3d6

Str 15, **Dex** 16, **Con** 14, **Int** 10, **Wis** 8, **Cha** 12
Base Atk +3; **CMB** +5; **CMD** 19
Feats Dodge, Intimidating Prowess, Martial Weapon Proficiency (longsword), Toughness, Weapon Focus (longsword)
Skills Acrobatics +10, Bluff +9, Diplomacy +9, Escape Artist +10, Intimidate +11, Knowledge (local) +8, Perception +7, Sense Motive +7, Sleight of Hand +10, Stealth +10
Languages Common
SQ ambush, rogue talents (combat trick, fast stealth), trapfinding +2
Combat Gear 2 *potions of cure moderate wounds*, *potion of invisibility*; **Other Gear** *+1 chain shirt*, *+1 longsword*, 20 arrows, composite shortbow (+2 Str)

Ambush (Ex) When able to act in the surprise round, Tuvio can take a move, standard, and swift action.

Tuvio's Torpedoes

Like Fat Julie, Tuvio has half-orcs working for him as musclemen and leg-breakers. The toughest of them are **Fleaface** and **Hogbreath**. Many other orcs work under these two.

FLEAFACE AND HOGBREATH — CR 2
XP 600
hp 40 (*Pathfinder Roleplaying Game NPC Codex* "Axe Warrior")

ORC THUGS — CR 1/3
XP 135
hp 6 (*Pathfinder Roleplaying Game Bestiary* "Orc")

Giant Protozoans

The following are a class of creatures known to inhabit the hidden Minzoa that lies just beyond the sight of men and beasts. Alchemists, scientists, madmen, druids, and dabblers in the arcane arts have long suspected the existence of minute beings, pointing to creatures such as lice and ticks as evidence of a world much smaller than our own. The wizard Irtep found a way to enter this world, where he encountered and categorized the following creatures.

These creatures have a new subtype to differentiate them from normal-sized creatures.

Minzoan Subtype

Minzoan creatures are microorganisms that inhabit a miniature world far too small to be seen or interacted with by normal-sized creatures. They are far smaller Fine in size and have no effect on the larger world except in the manifestation of diseases, some fungus, and natural decay. Hundreds or even thousands of these creatures could exist in a drop of water. Most creatures with the minzoa subtype are oozes, plants, or vermin.

Through the use of powerful magic these creatures can be enlarged as if by summoning to appear in the normal-sized world, and normal-sized creatures can be miniaturized to exist in the Minzoa.

Giant Amoeba

This strange creature is semi-translucent and difficult to see as it swims, looking like little more than ripples in the water.

GIANT AMOEBA — CR 5
XP 1,600
Advanced giant amoeba (*Pathfinder Roleplaying Game Bestiary 2* "Amoeba, Giant")
N Large ooze (aquatic, minzoa)
Init –7; **Senses** blindsight 30 ft.; **Perception** –5

AC 4, touch 2, flat-footed 4 (–7 Dex, +2 natural, –1 size)
hp 63 (6d8+36)
Fort +8; **Ref** –5; **Will** –3
Immune ooze traits

Speed 10 ft., climb 10 ft., swim 20 ft.
Melee slam +10 (1d6+10 plus grab)
Space 10 ft.; **Reach** 10 ft.
Special Attacks constrict (1d6+10)

Str 25, **Dex** -3, **Con** 22, **Int** —, **Wis** 1, **Cha** 1
Base Atk +4; **CMB** +12 (+16 grapple); **CMD** 15 (can't be tripped)
Skills Acrobatics –7 (–15 to jump), Climb +15, Swim +15
SQ amphibious

Environment Water (Minzoa)

Organization Solitary
Treasure None

The Minzoan amoeba is a large creature that could easily fill a 10-foot cube if contained in that shape. The creature is semi-translucent and therefore difficult to see or distinguish from water save for its slightly sticky wet exterior.

Minzoan amoebas live in water and die if they are away from liquid water for more than one hour.

Amoebas are voracious eaters and may even try to devour smaller amoebas. They attack by slamming their body onto their prey.

Giant Carnivorous Fungi

This creature resembles stalks of clear, reed-like staves rising from a pool, thick with slime.

GIANT CARNIVOROUS FUNGI **CR 4**
XP 1,200
N Large plant (minzoa)
Init –2; **Senses** low-light vision; **Perception** –1
Aura pheromones (30 ft.; Fort DC 16)

AC 11, touch 7, flat-footed 11 (–2 Dex, +4 natural, –1 size)
hp 58 (9d8+18)
Fort +8; **Ref** +1; **Will** +2
Immune plant traits

Speed 10 ft., swim 10 ft.
Melee 4 tentacles +7 (1d6+2 plus grab)
Space 10 ft.; **Reach** 10 ft.
Special Attacks constrict (1d6+2)

Str 14, **Dex** 6, **Con** 14, **Int** —, **Wis** 8, **Cha** 3
Base Atk +6; **CMB** +9 (+13 grapple); **CMD** 15 (can't be tripped)

Environment Temperate (Minzoa)
Organization Forest
Treasure None

Pheromones (Ex) The giant carnivorous fungus emits pheromones in a 30-foot radius centered on itself. A living creature within or entering the area must succeed on a DC 16 Fortitude save or be forced to move within reach of the fungus's tentacles (10 feet). After that, it can use a standard to make a new Will save to end the effect. This charm effect lasts for 1 minute or until the creature makes a successful saving throw against the effect.

These plantlike beings thrive in the Minzoa, in areas with plenty of moisture and humidity. They resemble copses of clear, reed-like staves rising from a pool of primordial goop 15 to 30 feet in diameter. Carnivorous fungi feed on other living beings of the Minzoa, trapping them in their sticky strands where they are slowly devoured.

Carnivorous fungi lie in wait for the nearly mindless creatures of the Minzoa to swim or crawl through their primordial goop in search of food. There the creatures become trapped in the fungi's gluey excretions as the reed staves wrap around their prey and squeeze it to death.

Giant Hydrozoa

A slender tube, 10-feet-long, seems to be anchored to the rock beneath it. From its open end extends a swarm of grasping tentacles.

GIANT HYDROZOA **CR 8**
XP 4,800
N Large ooze (aquatic, minzoa)
Init +0; **Senses** blindsight 60 ft.; **Perception** –1

AC 13, touch 9, flat-footed 13 (+4 natural, –1 size)
hp 90 (12d8+36)
Fort +7; **Ref** +4; **Will** +3
DR 5/ piercing or slashing; **Immune** ooze traits

Speed 10 ft., swim 20 ft.
Melee 6 tentacles +10 (1d8+2 plus grab plus paralysis)
Space 10 ft.; **Reach** 10 ft.
Special Attacks constrict (1d8+2), paralysis (1 minute, DC 19)

Str 15, **Dex** 10, **Con** 16, **Int** —, **Wis** 8, **Cha** 3
Base Atk +9; **CMB** +12 (+16 grapple); **CMD** 22 (can't be tripped)

Environment Temperate (Minzoa)
Organization Solitary
Treasure None

Giant Hydrozoa are humongous protozoan creatures brought from the world in miniature by mad science and arcane magic. These horrid creatures appear as a slender tube 10 to 30 feet long. The creature fuses one end of the tube immovably to a floor or to the ground with pseudopods, typically in a watery area such as a lake, stream, river, or shallow sea. The creature uses its tentacles to snatch prey, injecting them with paralytic venom before drawing the meal whole into its maw, where it is digested by powerful acids.

Giant hydrozoa move by drifting with the current or by propelling themselves with a looping, somersaulting-type motion.

Giant Nematode

Lurching up from the boggy ground comes a translucent horror. It resembles a flatworm the size of a man but with flesh that is almost entirely transparent.

GIANT NEMATODE **CR 2**
XP 600
N Medium vermin (aquatic, minzoa)
Init +1; **Senses** darkvision 60 ft.; **Perception** –1

AC 11, touch 11, flat-footed 10 (+1 Dex)
hp 45 (7d8+14)
Fort +7; **Ref** +3; **Will** +1
Defensive Abilities split, transparent; **DR** 5/piercing or slashing

---

Speed 20 ft., swim 30 ft.
Melee bite +5 (1d6 plus 2d6 acid)

Str 10, **Dex** 12, **Con** 15, **Int** —, **Wis** 8, **Cha** 3
Base Atk +5; **CMB** +5; **CMD** 16 (can't be tripped)

Environment Temperate (Minzoa)
Organization Solitary
Treasure None

Split (Ex) If a giant nematode of at least Medium size takes slashing damage, it splits into two identical giant nematodes, each with half the original's current total hit points, rounded down. A giant nematode with 10 or fewer hit points cannot be further split.
Transparent (Ex) The giant nematode is difficult to spot. A creature must succeed on a DC 12 Perception check to spot a giant nematode.

Giant nematodes are man-sized flatworms that inhabit the world in miniature, thanks to arcane magic and the experimentations of mad scientists. These creatures are nearly transparent, making it difficult to spot them until it is too late.

Giant nematodes are always hungry; they are driven entirely by the desire to eat and reproduce. They attack by spearing their frontal portion into their victims, injecting them with an acidic gastric substance, and sucking the creature's liquefied nutrients into their body.

Giant Protozoan Orb

This giant insect looks like a tick with a clear carapace, revealing the strange globular composition of its insides. A wicked-looking hooked jaw extends from beneath its head as it scuttles forward to attack.

GIANT PROTOZOAN ORB **CR 3**
XP 800
N Medium vermin (aquatic, minzoa)
Init +0; **Senses** blindsight 60 ft.; **Perception** –2

AC 11, touch 11, flat-footed 10 (+1 Dex)
hp 39 (6d8+12)
Fort +7; **Ref** +2; **Will** +0
DR 5/piercing or slashing; **Immune** vermin traits

Speed 30 ft. swim
Melee bite +4 (1d8 plus 1d6 acid plus grab)
Special Attacks blood drain

Str 11, **Dex** 10, **Con** 14, **Int** —, **Wis** 6, **Cha** 1
Base Atk +4; **CMB** +4 (+8 grapple); **CMD** 14 (18 or 22 vs. trip)

Environment Salt water (Minzoa)
Organization Solitary
Treasure None

Blood Drain (Ex) A giant protozoan orb drains blood from its victim on each round that it maintains a pin. This blood drain deals 1d6 points of Constitution damage to the target. After a giant protozoan orb drains 9 points of Constitution from a target, it detaches and moves away to digest its meal.

Protozoan orbs are common in brackish waters of the Minzoa. They typically resemble ticks with four or six limbs, but they are 3 to 6 feet across. They have hooked jaws just below the beginnings of their insect-like eye. Their carapace is clear, revealing the juices of their primitive cellular structure within.

Protozoan orbs feast on carrion and vegetable matter, though they are not above attempting to devour small, live prey that crosses their path. Their primary form of travel is by slurping water in through their mouth and jetting it out through their hind end, which gives them a jerky, flitting movement. They are common prey of hydrozoa and giant nematodes.

Giant Sporozoa

Feeding upon the fetid remains of some rotted corpse, this bloblike entity resembles little more than a pile of clear muck from which four thrashing tentacles extend.

GIANT SPOROZOA **CR 4**
XP 1,200
N Medium ooze (aquatic, minzoa)
Init +0; **Senses** blindsight 60 ft.; **Perception** –5

AC 10, touch 10, flat-footed 10
hp 39 (6d8+12)
Fort +4 ; **Ref** +2; **Will** +0
DR 5/piercing or slashing; **Immune** ooze traits

Speed 10 ft., swim 20 ft.
Melee 4 tentacles +5 (1d6+1 plus grab plus disease)

Str 12, **Dex** 10, **Con** 15, **Int** —, **Wis** 6, **Cha** 1
Base Atk +4; **CMB** +5 (+9 grapple); **CMD** 15 (can't be tripped)
SQ amphibious

Environment Temperate (Minzoa)
Organization Solitary or cluster (2-6)
Treasure None

Disease (Ex) *Filth fever*: Bite—injury; *save* Fort DC 15; *onset* 1d3 days; *frequency* 1/day; *effect* 1d3 Dex damage and 1d3 Con damage; *cure* 2 consecutive saves. The save DC is Constitution-based.

These foul creatures of the Minzoa appear as man-sized blobs of gelatinous matter surrounded by four tentacles. The tentacles are used for mobility and to attack. They are typically found near the corpses of creatures that died recently from the sporozoans' disease or in filthy, dead matter, as such corpses are breeding grounds for sporozoans. The creatures hibernate in a hardened cyst until agitated or roused by proximity to other living organisms.

Giant Tardigrade

This strange creature looks like a cross between a hairless bear and a caterpillar. It stands 10 feet tall with a grayish-pink body made of loose folds of thick skin. Its body seems to have segments, and from these protrude four pairs of legs with wickedly clawed tips.

GIANT TARDIGRADE **CR 5**
XP 1,600
N Large vermin (aquatic, minzoa)
Init +0; **Senses** darkvision 60 ft.; **Perception** –1

AC 13, touch 9, flat-footed 13 (+4 natural, –1 size)
hp 65 (10d8+20)
Fort +9; **Ref** +3; **Will** +2
Immune vermin traits; **Resist** cold 5, fire 5

Speed 30 ft., swim 20 ft.
Melee bite +8 (1d8+2), 4 claws +8 (1d6+2)
Space 10 ft.; **Reach** 5 ft.
Special Attacks rend 2 claws (1d8+3)

Str 15, **Dex** 10, **Con** 15, **Int** —, **Wis** 9, **Cha** 6
Base Atk +7; **CMB** +10; **CMD** 20 (32 vs. trip)
SQ amphibious

Environment Any (Minzoa)
Organization Solitary
Treasure Standard

Giant tardigrades, also known as water bears, look like a cross between a hairless bear and a caterpillar. The creatures stand 10 feet tall and weigh 1,400 lbs. The body of the giant tardigrade is a grayish-pink, though some run to gray-green. Their body is slightly segmented and has eight legs, four of which may be used to attack their prey. Their skin is thick and loose after the fashion of the rhinoceros, and sloughs off damage easily, affording them an excellent armor class.

Commonly they are found in water, though they can be found in almost any extreme climate. Giant tardigrades have been brought to the world through a mixture of alchemy, mad science, magic, and the occasional druid gone wrong. Tardigrades are some of the hardiest creatures on the planet. They seem to hardly notice extreme heat or extreme cold. They can lie dormant for years without food or water.

Tardigrades eat almost anything, though they are slow to provoke and hard to anger. When engaged, they attack with their four front claws and their circular maw filled with razor-sharp teeth.

Perils of Ghostwind Pass

By Matt Finch

The Perils of Ghostwind Pass is a Pathfinder Roleplaying Game adventure designed for 4–6 characters of levels 5–7.

"Once upon a time, twin sisters went to slay the Winter Prince, who held the freezing winds like tigers leashed in the Ghostwind Pass ..."

Introduction

Roll 3d6 and add 10. Write that number down. You'll need it later. Perils of Ghostwind Pass is an adventure designed for 4–6 characters of levels 5–7. It is playable at other levels and with different numbers of characters, but the monsters and risks of the adventure may require adjustment by the GM to offer an appropriate challenge to the players. The adventure has two levels of complexity. On one level there is an interesting background story with a mystery to solve that leads to a powerful artifact. It can be left out if desired, leaving a straightforward location-based adventure with a race against time and an evil mastermind.

The adventure is designed to fit anywhere in your campaign world, as long as you have some mountains available. If you're using the **Lost Lands** campaign setting, Ghostwind Pass cuts through the northern reach of the Cretian Mountains, connecting Yolbiac Vale to the Town of Elet.

Background

The Ghostwind is a mountain pass threading a high trail through the taller peaks rising to either side. It is the main pass in the area since it can be traversed (although with difficulty) by wagons. A few smaller trails remain usable later into the winter, but these mule-trails are too rough for wagons, and generally pose other significant dangers such as rockslides or narrow, cliff-side trails. An old stone road winds its way through the pass, a relic of the Hyperborean Empire that has receded from these lands, leaving them unprotected and wild. Although the road is dilapidated and broken, the remains of the work done by its builders still allows the pass to be traversed by wagons, even centuries after the stones were originally set. The road is vital to the merchants and other travelers in the Ghostwind for another reason: As long as it is not covered in snow, it shows travelers the fastest and safest way through a pass that has several dead-end ravines and blind canyons. Without it, a large number of journeyers through the pass would never arrive on the far side of the mountains.

The ravines and canyons of Ghostwind Pass are rich hunting and trapping grounds during the warm seasons, drawing fortune-seekers to the hunting camp around the Abbey of Saint Kathelynn and to the "South Camp" on the far side of the mountains. There is a third settlement in the highlands of the pass, the Manor of the Mountain Queen, but visitors to the pass avoid this fell place. It is said that the Mountain Queen is not human, although no one really knows what she might be.

Twice each year, the Ghostwind blows down the high peaks, hurling snow and sleet before it to bury most of the pass. The weather is violent and murderously cold. Anyone caught in the heights when this maelstrom hits is most likely doomed. Entire caravans have been lost, found at the end of the season where they froze to death after only a day or two of desperate travel back toward the lower altitude. The Ghostwind season lasts 2 months, and during this time the pass is effectively closed off to all passage.

If you intend to run a player character in this adventure, READ NO FURTHER.

GM Notes

The vague rumors about the Mountain Queen's Manor are entirely correct: The Mountain Queen is not human. She is a lamia with innate power over storms and snow who uses these powers to insulate her stone castle from the Ghostwind. Once the Ghostwind falls, she and her monstrous followers rule the high regions of the pass for the 2 months until the murderously cold storms abate. Chief among her clan are her children: the grey saber-tooths and the white weretigers that hunt in the higher regions of the pass. The lamia is long-lived. She knows a great deal about the series of events that took place in the pass 75 years ago when a powerful fey known as the "Winter Prince" was supposedly defeated by the paladin Kathelynn — because she *is* Kathelynn, or at least what is left of her original self (see, "What Really Happened," below). Although the Winter Prince survived, he traded his life for a promise to restrict the supernatural storms in the pass to twice per year. The characters might stumble upon the odd mysteries and contradictions surrounding the defeat of the Winter Prince; it is there to be found, but is not necessary to the adventure.

For adventurers, the most important key to survival in the high region of Ghostwind Pass (other than avoiding frontal assaults on the Mountain Queen's hall) is to understand how the cold weather moves in. During the warm seasons, humans and their kin are able to survive in the pass. Once the Ghostwind season begins, the storms and cold turn the pass into a deathtrap. The only hope for a hunter or a group of adventurers is to fight their way back down to the lower altitudes, out of the deadly weather. No one knows exactly when the Ghostwind will suddenly fill the pass with snow and bitter ice, but the locals are able to make a close estimate. It is up to the characters how long they remain in the pass as the Ghostwind draws closer. If greed delays them too long, there is a good chance they die in the harsh conditions of the Ghostwind, joining the ranks of many other fortune-seekers who thought they could risk "just one more day."

Missions

The adventure assumes that the characters have arrived at the north side of the mountains, beginning the adventure just as they approach the Abbey of St. Kathelynn. The town of Elet lies close behind them to the north, so allow the characters to do any pre-adventure information gathering there, if they choose. They might simply be traveling through the area, soon to learn that the pass offers some interesting possibilities; but less time will be wasted at the game table if the characters start with some kind of objective (which can, of course, change during the course of the adventure). A list of possible missions follows:

- A local baron's son on a hunting expedition into the ravines recently disappeared in the pass. Find out what happened to him and his 3 companions and return them (or their bodies) to the baron. The reward is appreciably larger if the lost nobles are still alive.
- A wizard offers to pay well for the heart of a peryton, and even more for one or more eggs. More than one caravan through the pass has been savaged by perytons, so finding and killing one ought to be easy pickings!
- The characters are hired to guard a small hunting party of a minor noble and his/her courtiers (1d3+3 or so). They are seeking large game such as boars or deer. Unfortunately, the highborn can be very independent minded when it comes to taking advice from members of the lower social orders…
- The characters may have decided to go hunting on their own behalf. A lot of undeserving monsters are out there, wearing some very valuable furs.
- An alchemist hires them to find a particular plant known as the "blood violet." The more sacks of blood violets they can collect, the better.
- The characters are hired to guard a mule train through the pass.
- In the midst of the Ghostwind season, while the storms are blowing, the characters are hired to get an emergency message (or medicine, or a fugitive) through the pass.

Arrival of the Ghostwind

The very first thing to do at the beginning of the adventure is to roll three six-sided dice and add 10 (3d6+10). This is the number of days from the characters' arrival at the Abbey of St. Kathelynn until the Ghostwind blows into the pass. The actual effects of being caught in the Ghostwind are described below in the "Wilderness Map" section.

The players ought to have some idea of the bell-curve probability involved in their race against time (that all-important 3d6+10 days), so it's important that even if you like to give descriptions in character, someone in the abbey should tell the characters something like the following:

> After the Ghostwind blows in, you'll die if you're in the pass. It's just too cold. But you've got some time until then. My rheumatism says the Ghostwind won't blow in for another 10 days plus another three rolls of the dice or so. You never know exactly when, until a couple of days before. Two days of clouds and then the cold.

If you and your gaming group have a more "beer and pretzels" approach to the game, feel free to just tell them that you rolled 3d6+10 days to find out when the Ghostwind blows in, and that you're not telling them the result. They'll figure out that the probability makes a bell curve.

Wilderness Map

The map shows three elevations, each shaded differently. Capital letters offer a rough indication of "risk levels." The numbered locations on the Wilderness Map are all referred to in the Map Key with the letter W for "Wilderness." The elevations and other symbols are all described in more detail below.

Three Elevations

Low Elevation: This is the floor of the pass itself. It is very rough terrain, but passable by mules and horses. Wagons can negotiate the road, but they move slowly. Although this is the lowest elevation in the mountain pass itself, and is low enough for evergreen trees to survive, it is still high, cold, rocky ground. The trees here are sparse and small; most cannot live through the bitter cold of the Ghostwind season.

Middle Elevation: These are high, steep areas, but not quite bad enough to require the use of ropes and other equipment. Lots of the movement in these areas is climbing rather than walking, using hands as well as feet. This contour line also represents the tree line. Trees cannot grow in the middle or highest elevations of the pass.

Highest Elevation: The highest elevation is impassable for the purposes of the adventure. A high-elevation area can be reached with climbing gear (the peryton nest is an example) but it is not possible to move from one high-elevation square to another. Up and down are the only choices here.

Special Movement

Mules and other Mounts: Mules do not increase an expedition's speed; they are no faster than people, but they can carry more. Horses also do not increase speed, and since they are not as surefooted as mules, they double movement cost on the Middle Elevation (see "Movement Cost" below). Only mountain creatures such as giant mountain goats and great cats, or giant mounts such as mammoths and elephants affect movement. Such mounts do not increase the party's speed, but they reduce the toll of moving at speed through the uneven terrain, adding 1 hour to the length of time the characters can move during the day (increase from 8 to 9).

Wagons: Wagons move at "slow" speed on the road at the lowest elevation (see "Movement Speed" below). They can move off the road but have a 10% chance per hex traveled of breaking a wheel. They cannot move into the Middle Elevation at all.

Flying: Flying might appear to be the ideal solution to the perils of the Ghostwind Pass, but it actually affords little benefit. During the Ghostwind, flying and levitation are simply not possible. Even before the Ghostwind arrives, the winds in the pass are quite violent if anyone flies higher than 50 foot flying provides the following benefits and drawbacks:

Flying Speed: Flying speed requires 12 minutes to cross a mile-wide hex on the map. This might seem slow, but the winds are very difficult to handle when airborne.

Benefit: The adventurers cannot be surprised at the beginning of an encounter.

Benefit: If the characters are specifically hunting for animals, roll a second encounter each time you make a normal encounter check. They won't have two encounters, but if the second roll indicates an encounter when the first roll didn't, this means the flying character spots the other possibility at a distance of 1d10x0.1 miles (from a tenth of a mile up to a full mile). Note that the other encounter may have spotted the flying character as well, and if it is intelligent it most definitely reacts in some way once it knows it is being observed from afar.

Higher than 50 ft., Immediate Risk: Every time the character tries to fly higher than 50 foot, there is an immediate 10% chance that a violent gust yanks the character 1d4x100 feet sideways and down in a random direction to smash against the rocky floor of the Pass for 2d6 points of damage.

Higher than 50 ft., Ongoing Risk: Each mile scouted (and if stationary, once per 20 minutes) while a character remains airborne at an altitude above 50 foot, the character has a 10% chance to be blown off course 1d3 miles in a random direction. If a character hits one of the highest-altitude squares while being blown off course, it results in a rapid stop and 4d6 points of damage. As soon as a character reaches this elevation, the feel of the winds alone alerts the character to the risk. (It is a good idea, for purposes of the game, to give the player a fairly good description of the risk and the result of having a character flying in this sort of wind).

Lower than 50 ft., flying fast, Ongoing Risk: A character planning to skim along at an altitude below 50 foot can travel at a movement cost of 0.1 hours per mile, without the risk of blowing off course. However, the low-flying character runs the risk of downdrafts. Once per mile traveled, a low-flying character has a 10% chance of being caught in one of these and smashed to the ground (1d4x100 feet of random sideways movement, and 2d6 points of damage upon landing).

Lower than 50 ft., flying slowly, No Risk: It is safe to remain with the rest of the party at an altitude of less than 50 foot, gaining the benefits of aerial scouting. The character is tossed around in the wind, but not thrown sideways, downward, or off into the distance.

Movement Speed

Overland movement in Ghostwind Pass is considerably slower than the official speed in the Pathfinder Roleplaying Game , reflecting the fact that the characters aren't really "traveling" here. However, in any *combat* on the rocky terrain of the mountain pass, just use the movement rate for "Difficult Terrain" (half speed).

Each hex on the Wilderness Map takes a certain amount of time to cross, depending on its elevation. Crossing the contour lines themselves does not cost extra time; that's accounted for by the different movement rates at the different elevations. A normal speed and a slow speed are given; certain circumstances can reduce the characters' movement rate as described later. Moreover, the characters are normally limited to 8 hours of hiking in a day (see below).

Lowest Elevation: It takes 0.5 hours to cross a hex at normal speed, and 1 hour at slow speed. Movement cost during the Ghostwind is 1.5 hour at normal speed and 2 hours for slowed speed.

Middle Elevation: It takes 1 hour at normal speed to cross a Middle Elevation hex, and 2 hours at slow speed. The characters cannot cross Middle Elevation terrain if they are "force marching" in the 9th or 10th hour of the march. During the Ghostwind, it takes 3 hours at normal speed to cross Middle Elevation terrain, and 4 hours at slowed speed.

Highest Elevation: The High Elevations can be scaled to reach a particular objective such as the peryton nest at **Area W-4**. However, they are impassable for purposes of movement; the characters cannot move from one high-elevation hex to another.

Quick Travel-Rules Summary

1. Determine Movement Rate (normal or slow). If flying, check flying rules.

2. Move into a hex

- **a.** Mark off the time required for a hex at that elevation. *Ghostwind Rules: When 2 hours elapse, each character makes a check on the Ghostwind Effects Table.*
- **b.** Determine Risk Level for that hex (the nearest capital letter at that elevation)
- **c.** Roll for Encounter: Use the table for that Risk Level. *Ghostwind Rules: use the Ghostwind Encounter Table, not the Risk Level Tables.*
- **d.** After 8 hours of movement are marked off, the characters must either make camp or force-march.
- **e.** If they force-march a character may walk more than 8 hours in a day, for each hour of marching beyond 8 hours, a Constitution check (DC 10 plus 2 per extra hour) is required (see *Pathfinder Roleplaying Game Core Rulebook*). If this check fails, the character becomes fatigued. If the character continues and fails an additional check they become exhausted. *Ghostwind Rules: Cannot force-march during Ghostwind.*
- **f.** When they make camp, make one more encounter check for that Risk Level, covering the entire night. Check to see if the Ghostwind is going to hit the next day. *Ghostwind Rules: Use the Ghostwind Encounter Table, not the Risk Level Tables. Make only one more check on the Ghostwind Effects Table for each character.*

Exhaustion and Encumbrance

The characters can hike up to 8 hours per day, spending the remaining time making/breaking camp, cooking dinner and breakfast, resting, and sleeping. It is very, very difficult to travel over rough terrain for 8 hours while carrying supplies. Nevertheless, it is possible for the characters to really push themselves and "force-march" more than 8 hours a day. Forced marching allows the characters to keep going an additional 2 hours (for a total time of 10 hours).

Forced marching is dangerous in treacherous terrain like the Ghostwind Pass. Exhaustion can set in, reducing alertness and making people clumsier than normal. It is much easier to miss your footing or trip over a rock that would have been noticed and avoided earlier in the day. See "Overland Movement" in Chapter 7 of the Pathfinder Roleplaying Game for the rules governing force marches.

If the characters are extremely burdened (not likely, but possible), or slowed by exhaustion, they are moving at "slow" speed — which is not necessarily half speed.

Risk Zones

The Wilderness Map is divided into several "risk zones," denoted by capital letters. Along the same elevation the exact boundaries of the risk zones are unimportant, but the risk zones don't cross the contour lines. Whenever the characters climb up or down past one of the contour lines, they are automatically crossing into the risk zone in the new elevation. Most of the risk zones specifically indicate how dangerous the higher elevations are.

There's another side to risks, of course. As they say, "the greater the risk, the greater the reward." If the characters are hunting for the valuable pelts, they find them in the more dangerous parts of the pass.

Hunting

The valuable hunting — for furs — is handled by the system of encounter checks described below. Whenever the characters enter a new hex, there is a chance for an encounter. If the characters are also hunting for subsistence, use the normal rules for foraging.

Encounter Checks

The short answer: Check for an encounter when characters enter a new hex, and once during the night. If the Ghostwind is blowing, use the special encounter table for the Ghostwind Season.

Note: the *Ghostwind Effect Check* is a different check (made every 2 hours and once at night).

To check for an encounter when the characters enter a new hex (or for the one "nighttime" check), find which Risk Area the characters are closest to (reminder: don't cross contour lines), and roll on the encounter table for that Risk Area. It is fine to be approximate in terms of which risk area the characters are in.

Ghostwind Effect Check

Once the Ghostwind blows in, it becomes so cold that no matter how long the characters try to rest, they cannot gain the benefits of rest.

Each day the characters are in the pass while the Ghostwind is blowing, they may suffer damage and other effects from the supernatural cold and violent storms. For every 2 hours of movement, in addition to the encounter checks, roll for *each character* on the Ghostwind Effects Table (d%). A successful DC 15 Fortitude save gains a +5 on the die roll.

If the characters are fighting their way out of the Pass during the Ghostwind, consider them "out of the pass" if they reach the abbey or the south camp.

Wilderness Travel Tables

Ghostwind Effects Table

Die Roll (d%)	Effect
01–10	Make a saving throw to avoid severe frostbite*
11–15	6 hit points of damage**
16–20	4 hit points of damage**
21–25	2 hit points of damage**
26–00	No adverse effect

*** Randomly determine on 1d6 whether the frostbite is in (1) fingers of left hand, (2) fingers of right hand, (3) toes of left foot, (4) toes of right foot, (5) nose, (6) ear. *Cure serious wounds* or higher can reverse the damage if it is cast before the frostbitten piece falls off (1d6 days). Unless more than one finger is lost on the same hand, missing fingers are not enough of a problem to cause modifiers on die rolls.**
**** Because the characters cannot get rest during the Ghostwind, these hit points are not automatically restored even after a night's sleep.**

Encounter Table During the Ghostwind (use this table in *all* Risk Areas)

Die Roll (d%)	Encounter/Result
1–76	No Encounter
77–78	**White Pudding**
79–80	**Giant Owl**
81–82	**1d4+1 Dire Goats**
83–84	**Dire Wolverine**
85–86	**1d4+1 Ice Elementals**
87–90	**1d3 Giant Weasels**
91–92	**1d2 Polar Bear**
93–94	**Giant Ermine**
95–96	**1d2 Smilodon**
97	**Weretiger**
98–99	**Remorhaz**
00	**Khethro Tulroc the Satyr** (see **Area W-7**)

Encounter Table for Risk Areas A, B, C, D (lower risk)

Die Roll (d%)	Risk Area A Low Elevation Low Risk	Risk Area B Low Elevation Higher Risk	Risk Area C High Elevation Low Risk	Risk Area D High Elevation Low Risk
1–75	No encounter	No encounter	No encounter	No encounter
76–78	**1d4+2 Goats**	**1d4+2 Goats**	**1d4+2 Goats**	**1d4+2 Goats**
79–80	**1d4 Wolves**	**1d6 Wolves**	**1d6+2 Wolves**	**1d6+2 Wolves**
81	**Cave Lion**	**1d3 Cave Lion**	**1d3 Cave Lion**	**1d3 Cave Lion**
82	**Boar**	**1d3 Boars**	**1d4 Dire Goat**	**1d4 Dire Goat**
83	**Wolverine**	**1d2 Wolverines**	**1d3 Wolverines**	**1d3 Wolverines**
84–85	**Bear, Grizzly**	**Bear, Grizzly**	**1d2 Bears, Grizzly**	**1d2 Bears, Grizzly**
86	**Giant Weasel**	**Giant Weasel**	**1d2 Giant Weasels**	**1d2 Giant Weasels**
87–88	**Giant Ermine**	**Giant Ermine**	**1d2 Giant Ermines**	**1d2 Giant Ermines**
89–90	**1d3 Humans (trappers, normal humans)**	**1d4+1 Ogre Hunting Party**	**1d3+1 Minotaur Hunting Party**	**1d2 Perytons or Minotaur Hunting Party if the perytons are dead**
91	**Hawk** overhead (normal)	**Vultures** circle party for 2 hours (normal)	**1d2 Perytons; normal hawk** overhead if perytons are dead	**1d6 Peryton**; normal **hawk** overhead if perytons are dead
92	**1d2 Giant Badgers**	**1d2+1 Giant Badgers**	**Giant Ermine**	**Giant Ermine**
93	**1d4+1 Giant Ants**	**1d6+3 Giant Ants**	**1d12+4 Giant Ants**	**1d12+6 Giant Ants**
94	Slip and fall on rock; 1 character takes 1d4 points of damage.	Slip and fall on rock; 1 character takes 1d4 points of damage.	Trip and slide on rocks; 1 character takes 1d4+1 points of damage from fall and makes a DC 15 Reflex saves against sprained ankle.*	Trip and slide on rocks; 1 character takes 1d4+1 points of damage from fall and makes a DC 20 Reflex save against sprained ankle.*
95	No encounter	No encounter	Rockslide. Each character must make a DC 15 Reflex save or sustain 3d6 points of damage.	Rockslide. Each character must make a DC 15 Reflex save or sustain 3d6 points of damage.
96	**1d2 Giant Stag Beetles**	**1d2 Giant Stag Beetles**	**1d3+1 Giant Stag Beetles**	**1d3+1 Giant Stag Beetles**

Die Roll (d%)	Risk Area A Low Elevation Low Risk	Risk Area B Low Elevation Higher Risk	Risk Area C High Elevation Low Risk	Risk Area D High Elevation Low Risk
97–98	No encounter (squirrels)	**Blood violets** (1d3 sacks' worth)	**Blood violets** (1d3+2 sacks' worth)	**Blood violets** (1d3+2 sacks' worth)
99	No encounter (crickets)	**Troll**	**1d3 Troll**	**1d3 Troll**
00	**Smilodon**	**Smilodon**		

* A sprained ankle causes a delay of 0.5 hour while it is wrapped, and the cursing and swearing abates. The sprain reduces character to half movement (in combat) and the party's wilderness speed to "slow," with the movement penalty lasting 1d100 hours. *Cure serious wounds* higher immediately cures the sprain, and *cure moderate wounds* reduces the duration by 10 hours. Ignore this result for the night encounter check and re-roll.

Encounter Table for Risk Areas E, F, G (higher or specific risk)

Die Roll (d%)	Risk Area E Highest Elevation Very High Risk	Risk Area F Any Elevation Very High	Risk Risk Area G Any Elevation Highest Risk
1–70	No encounter	No encounter	No encounter
71–73	**1d4+2 Goats**	**1d4+2 Goats**	**1d4+2 Goats**
74–75	**1d6+2 Wolves** with **Winter Wolf**	**1d6+2 Wolves** with **2 Winter Wolves**	**1d8+3 Wolves** with **3 Winter Wolves**
76–77	**1d6 Dire Goat**	**1d6+1 Dire Goat**	**1d6+2 Dire Goat**
78	**1d3+1 Dire Wolverine**	**1d4+1 Dire Wolverine**	**1d2 Polar Bear**
79	**Polar Bear**	**1d2 Polar Bear**	**1d2 Polar Bear**
80	**1d4 Giant Weasel**	**1d4 Giant Weasel**	**1d4 Giant Weasel**
81–85	**1d4 Giant Ermine**	**1d4+1 Giant Ermine**	**1d4+2 Giant Ermine**
86	**1d3 Troll**	**White Weretiger** (from the Roster)	**Khethro Tulroc the satyr** (see **Area W-7**)
87–88	**2d10+5 Giant Ants**	**2d10+5 Giant Ants**	**Hill giant** and **2 ogres**, carrying 1d6+3 giant ermine pelts.
89–90	Trip and slide on rocks: 1 character takes 1d4+1 points of damage from fall and makes a DC 15 Reflex save against sprained ankle.*	Trip and slide on rocks: 1 character takes 1d4+1 points of damage from fall and makes a DC 20 Reflex save against sprained ankle.*	Trip and slide on rocks: 1 character takes 1d4+1 points of damage from fall and makes a DC 20 Reflex save against sprained ankle.*
91	Rockslide. Each character must make a DC 15 Reflex save or take 2d6 points of damage.	Rockslide. Each character must make a DC 15 Reflex save or take 3d6 points of damage.	Rockslide. Each character must make a DC 15 Reflex save or take 4d6 points of damage.
92–93	**Blood Violets** (1d6+1 sacks' worth)	**Blood Violets** (1d6+2 sacks' worth)	**Blood Violets** (1d6+3 sacks' worth)
94–95	**1d3 Grizzly Bear**	**1d3 Grizzly Bear**	**1d3 Grizzly Bear**
96–97	**1d4 Ice Elemental, Medium**		**1d4 Ice Elemental, Medium**
98	**1d2 Dire Badger**	**1d2+1 Dire Badger**	**1d2+1 Dire Badger**
99–00	**1 Smilodon**	**1 Smilodon**	**1 Smilodon**

Rumors and Whispers

Before the adventure really begins, the characters have a chance to gather some information in the town to the north. (In the **Lost Lands** campaign setting, this is the town of Elet.) The characters automatically get the "Basic Information" below. Each character (to a maximum of 7 characters) rolls a Knowledge (local) check. This number determines which category of rumor the character hears through investigation (False, Easy, Pretty Good, and Extraordinarily Good). Once the category is determined, roll in that category to see what sort of tidbits the character learns.

Automatic

Basic Information:

1) The mountain pass is blocked twice per year when blizzards called the Ghostwinds blow in.

2) The Abbey of St. Kathelynn is a safe place to rest.

3) There is a druid who lives just by the abbey. Their religious beliefs cause some friction.

Result of 0–5

False Rumors (1d6):

1) The Mountain Queen is a giantess who collects the heads of anyone who casts magic in her mountain pass.

2) Giant Ice-toads built a massive windmill in the heights of the pass and it pulls in the Ghostwind when their human slaves work the treadmills that turn its diamond-edged blades faster and faster.

3) A songbird kept for three days in the pass will lay golden eggs for a week thereafter.

4) Some people say that the Abbot of Saint Kathelynn actually killed the saint.

5) Ice gnomes have built a giant waterwheel at a high elevation near one of the lakes. It is used to catch salmon, but a giant fish with legs has started attacking their settlement.

6) A woman who lives near the abbey is actually a necromancer who curses adventurers by using some sort of rune magic.

Result of 6–12

Easy Rumors (1d6):

1) The higher you go up the walls of the pass, the more dangerous it gets, but the better the hunting.

2) The best hunting in the pass is the giant ermine. Don't use cutting weapons on them, or you drop the value of the pelt.

3) Some kind of powerful artifact can be found in the pass.

4) You better have some magic weapons or silver weapons if you go exploring where you shouldn't go.

5) An abbey of a saint is at the base of the pass. She was sainted only 75 years ago, and they consecrated an old watch-fort to put her bones in. They haven't repaired it very well, if you ask me.

6) Rope yourselves together to cross the river fords, and if you plan on climbing any of the crags, bring spikes, ropes, and grappling hooks. The giant owl eggs are worth a lot, and that's the only way to get them since they nest in the high places. If you get one of the owl eggs back safely, you can buy me a drink.

Result of 13–18

Pretty Good Rumors (1d10):

1) Strange grey saber-toothed cats live in the pass. Avoid them, they're pretty cunning.

2) The abbot of St. Kathelynn's is so old that he remembers the last days of the saint's life.

3) A nest of perytons is on one of the high peaks.

4) An artifact associated with Saint Kathelynn is supposed to be buried with her bones.

5) Saint Kathelynn had a sister you almost never hear about in the stories.

6) Watch out for the Manor of the Mountain Queen. You don't want to go there.

7) If you're going to hunt giant ermines, you should wear the Druid's Mark.

8) They say the Mountain Queen hunts people in the wilderness. If she finds you, you become her slave and are never seen again.

9) The abbey at the base of the pass is kept warm by the Saint. It's the only place the Ghostwinds can't freeze when they blow in.

10) They say the Mountain Queen has a magic pool, and she can see things in it even if they are far away.

Result of 19+

Extraordinarily Good Rumors (1d4):

1) The servant of a fey winter power by the name of Tulroc who lives near the eastern wall of the pass.

2) The Ghostwinds are fey powers called into the pass by a creature named Tulroc.

3) Saint Kathelynn and her twin sister were both famous, but Kathelynn was definitely the one who shone the brightest.

4) The Ghostwinds are fey powers controlled by a creature called the Winter Prince.

What Really Happened

The characters might realize early on that there is something strange about Kathelynn's canonization. The fact of the matter is that the proper authorities of the church, rushing to honor the heroine of the Ghostwind Pass, canonized the wrong person. Not only that, Kathelynn is the one who killed Elys, and she is still alive, no longer a champion of the faith. Cursed and transformed by the gods, her mind twisted to murderous hate, she still lives in the Ghostwind Pass under the name of the Mountain Queen.

Kathelynn and Elys were identical twin sisters and devote warriors. Kathelynn was the famous warrior-priestess, and the quiet sister Elys was her standard-bearer, carrying Kathelynn's red rose banner into battle. The twins could be told apart by their shields: Kathelynn wore her red rose, and Elys' rose was white as snow. The only other difference was a vertical battle scar on Kathelynn's face.

At this time 75 years ago, the Ghostwind Pass had been choked off for many years by a fey lord known as the Winter Prince. His Ghostwinds, like chained hounds, kept the area in a perpetual blizzard, completely impassable. The sister paladins swore an oath to banish the immortal Winter Prince and free the mountain pass from his influence. They and their 5 retainers stopped at the fort just north of the pass (now the abbey), and the sisters went out alone into the snow to pray. They returned bearing the *Staff of the Remorhaz*, a holy artifact dating back to the beginning of history and the wars against forgotten evil gods.

With Kathelynn at the forefront, and Elys bearing the staff and red rose banner, the twins became separated from their followers in the blizzard, and then lost each other, too, coming separately upon the Winter Prince in the midst of his howling Ghostwinds.

First to meet him was Kathelynn, and the prince's sweet words and subtle magic undid Kathelynn's defenses and corrupted her to the service of evil. Then Elys came upon them, and fought the fey lord in single combat. In the great battle, the power of the Winter Prince snapped the *Staff of the Remorhaz*, but he was forced to yield by Elys' prowess in battle. The prince agreed to free the mountain pass from the Ghostwinds except for twice a year. As Elys put her weapon away, though, the Winter Prince gestured to Kathelynn. The prince's newest servant, standing behind Elys, crushed half of her twin sister's skull with her mace. Dying, Elys swung with the last strength in her, and killed the body of the Winter Prince. Laughing, the spirit of the Winter Prince rode his Ghostwinds away to find a new body: victorious, although still bound by the oath he had sworn to Elys. The Ghostwinds would return to the pass only twice a year instead of year-round.

Kathelynn reached out to take the *Staff of the Remorhaz*, for without her twin holding the cold-warding staff, she was freezing in the bitter chill of the high mountain. But the moment she touched the ancient artifact, it took a terrible vengeance upon her for murdering her twin.

She was transformed into a horrible beast with the lower body of a white tiger and her own body from the waist up, a dreadful lamia of the cold mountains. Blinded by the pain of the transformation, she grabbed what she thought was her own shield and ran, still clutching the part of the ancient relic she had taken. When the lamia awoke in the wilderness, fully transformed, she saw what she had left the battle with: the *Eye* from the top of the staff and her sister's white-rose shield.

With the Ghostwinds gone, the five knights found Elys' body where it lay next to the body of the slain Winter Prince, together with Kathelynn's shield and the *Staff of the Remorhaz* fallen nearby. The knights, of course, assumed it was the famous sister, Kathelynn, apparently the victor over the Winter Prince. They brought the body and the broken staff back to the chapel at the base of the pass, where they buried it in secret, concealing it in a grave labeled with another person's name ("Gryffin Winemaker"). Their thinking was simply to hide it from anyone who might try to desecrate it before Kathelynn could be sainted. The result was disaster. Kathelynn, now a lamia, insanely believes that if she can repair the artifact, she can reverse her transformation. Not knowing where the other half could be found and correctly assuming that it was buried with Elys, Kathelynn kidnapped each of the retainers in turn, and tortured them to find out the periapt's location. Each of them died without divulging the secret.

With the retainers all dead, the situation has become a lost secret. No living person knows where St. Elys' body can be found, and only Kathelynn the lamia knows that the wrong saint was consecrated.

Trimming the Background Story

If you want to remove the artifact-and-buried-saint mystery from the adventure to make it simpler, all you have to do is make one change: Make sure that the rose symbols in the Manor of the Mountain Queen are white rather than red (or that they aren't roses, but tigers or some other symbol). As long as that's done, all you have to do is ignore all references to Saint Elys and her burial.

Wilderness Map

You and your companions have traveled up an increasingly poor trail toward the foot of the mountains. You now stand looking across at what definitely appears to be the last ragged gasp of civilization this side of the mountain peaks. A dilapidated-looking drum tower is set on a hill, attached to a sagging wooden stockade that probably encloses a couple of other buildings. A watchtower stands to each side of a wooden gate. A cottage of some kind sits beside the hill, with one or two trees around it.

Area W-1. Abbey of Saint Kathelynn, Druid's Cottage

See the separate map of the abbey grounds.

Area W-2. River Crossing

The river is deep and very fast-flowing, although it is obviously not as full as gets during the early days of the spring thaw. There is a ford here, where the river widens and becomes shallower as it runs over a broad rock shelf. Any person going across the ford on foot must make two successive DC 15 Reflex saves along the way to avoid tripping, falling, and being carried away by the water into the rapids below.

Anyone failing a saving throw has one chance (DC15 Reflex save) to grab hold and stop before being pulled into the rapids. If this chance fails, the character takes 3d6 points of damage before getting to one side of the river or the other (roll randomly to see which bank).

The same risks apply to crossing the river anywhere in the pass.

Area W-3. Tembril Tarn

The water of this lake is, of course, icy cold, and it is very deep. At night, an eerie luminescence rises over the lake, and anyone near the banks hears a soft, muttering, whining voice that does not form words but continues for several minutes, then suddenly cuts off with a low scream. This phenomenon repeats itself over and over until dawn. Spellcasters cannot regain any spell "slots" if the characters are camped within a mile of the banks of the tarn.

Area W-4. Peryton Nest (CR 8)

This is the nest of **4 perytons**, some of which may already have been killed by the time the characters scale the cliff to the nest itself.

The cliff is very steep, 110 feet tall, and the wind whipping around the rock formation makes it impossible to fly to the top. There might be ways around this (players are ingenious). Their solution, if it is to succeed without catastrophe, needs to address all 6 directions in which a flying or levitating character could be violently pitched (forward/back, side/side, up/down). Impacts could range from a bad bump of 1d4 points of damage, up to a massive gust causing 4d6 points of damage if the character hits the stone.

It has to be climbed, which is not tremendously dangerous if the characters have spikes, ropes, and lots of time. However, unless the characters already killed all the perytons—in which case they probably don't know how to find the nest in the first place—they have to climb the cliff under attack from at least 1 peryton and possible as many as 4. The perytons do not hunt in groups of more than 2 unless a human kill is available (possibly a decoy miles away, if the party splits up to leave a human effigy somewhere). If the adventurers manage to decoy some of the perytons away from the nest, roll 1d4+1 to see how many leave (subtract previously killed ones, too). Waiting for a couple of perytons to leave, whether decoyed or just hunting, is a good strategy.

The climb has three stages:

Stage 1: Starts at the ground, hits a difficult area (DC 15 Climb check) at 20 foot, and ends at a secure 6-inch-wide ledge at the 50 feet mark.

Stage 2: Starts at the 6-inch ledge 50 foot, hits a difficult area (DC 15 Climb check) at 80 feet and 90 feet, ends at 100 feet.

Stage 3: Starts at the 100-foot mark, and is a fairly easy scramble to the cliff-top at 110 feet.

All vertical movement is at a speed of 5 feet per minute, and movement is not possible in the same round as a character attacks or takes any other action. The location between the "difficult areas" can be climbed by any unskilled person either using a rope, or driving spikes into the rock along the way; it just takes time and care. Climbing such an area without equipment requires a DC 20 Climb check. A first failed check roll does not indicate that the character falls, it just means that the character is stuck on the rock face and cannot proceed farther without equipment.

If a second check fails (while the character retreats down from being stuck) the character actually falls.

If anyone uses a hammer to drive spikes at an altitude higher than Stage 1 of the climb, it alerts the perytons. They defend their lair savagely, swooping in to attack climbers.

PERYTONS (4) **CR 4**
XP 1,200
hp 42 (*Pathfinder Roleplaying Game Bestiary 2* "Peryton")

Treasure: The perytons actually collect treasure in the nest, although they also threw out one object of considerable information value (the notebook of Jauric Tallbones, see below). In the nest the characters find a scattering of 52 gp, 129 sp, and 533 cp. Two halves of a useless magic wand, as well as a steel scroll case, shiny enough stay in the nest and tough enough to protect its contents of 2 scrolls. One scroll is divine, with the spells *cure light wounds* (x3) and *cure serious wounds*. The other scroll contains the magic-user spells *web, mirror image*, and *gust of wind*. A golden bracelet is worth 100 gp, and a piece of jade carved into the shape of an ugly baby is worth 300 gp (the value of the jade). A necklace of ivory rabbits is worth 500 gp, and a well-chewed quiver contains a *+2 arrow*, 6 broken arrows and 3 normal arrows.

Many bones are on the cliff ledges below the peryton nest, and below the aerie falls a curtain of death's garbage: clothes, empty boots, and bits of hair. One of the more noticeable items is a small leather-bound notebook.

The notebook is the journal of an adventurer named Jauric Tallbones, son of John Tallbones, one of the names in the abbey graveyard. Jauric came to the abbey to learn more about his father, taking notes and collecting information about the ill-fated expedition to the Hall of the Winter Prince.

My father, John Tallbones, told me before his martyrdom how they found Saint Kathelynn and the dying Winter Prince. He spoke of a battle standard with the faceted gem on top broken away. This staff was a holy item with great power, and he said that if I should become a knight, I should seek it. My father used to say, "Find Elys, the sister, and you'll find the Eye of the Othroäta. *It's probably treasure in the Manor of the Mountain Queen now, or sitting in some badger's lair. The other half we buried with Saint Kathelynn of the Red Rose, blessed may be she, but I am sworn never to reveal where the saint's bones are buried, even under torture. All I can say is to look in the griffin's lair, son."*

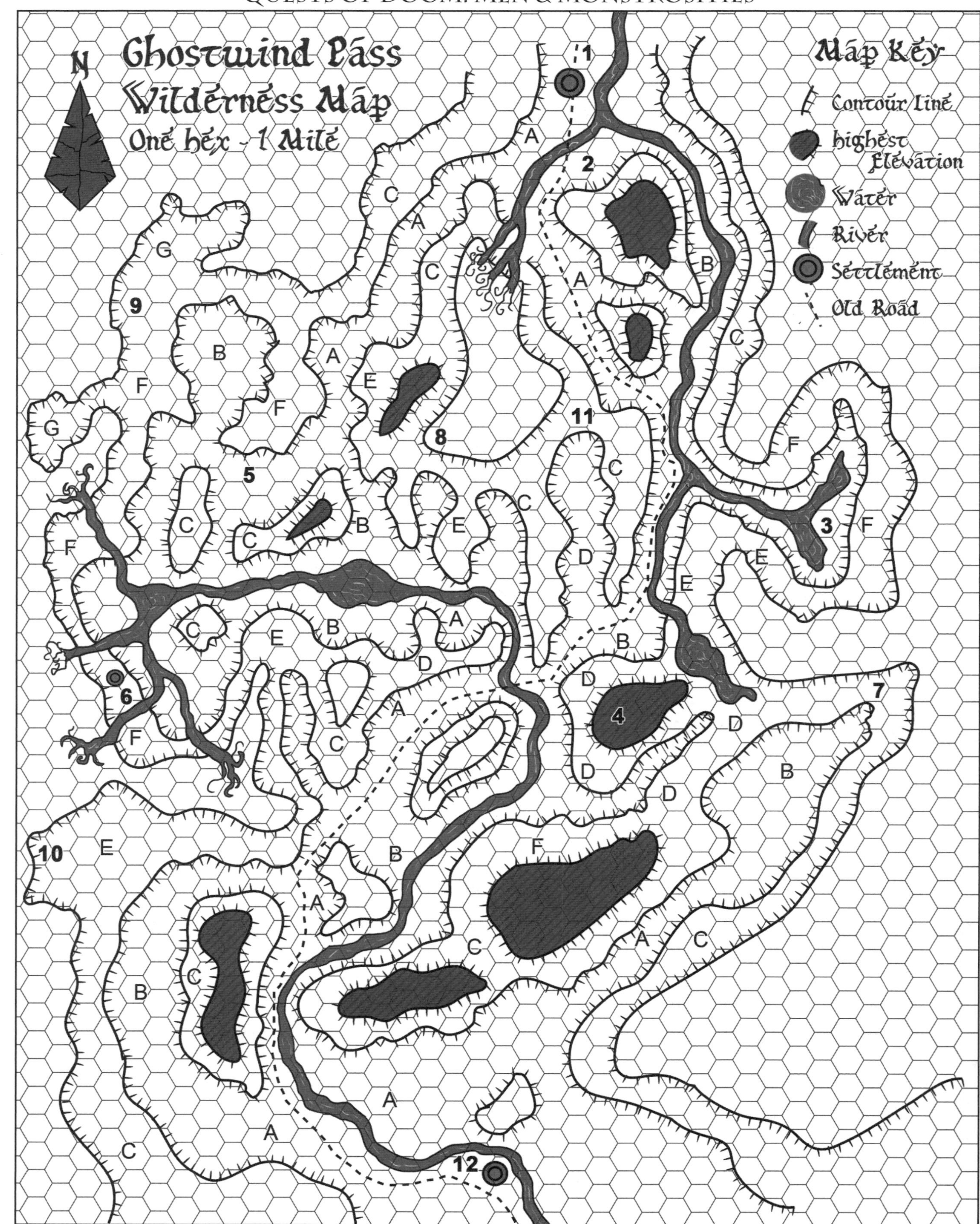
Ghostwind Pass
Wilderness Map
One hex - 1 Mile
N
Map Key
Contour Line
highest Elevation
Water
River
Settlement
Old Road
1
2
3
4
5
6
7
8
9
10
11
12

Area W-5. Shrine of St. Kathelynn

A memorial is here where the battle took place. The ground around the shrine is dug up in several places (by Kathelynn's bugbears, checking to make sure that Elys' bones were not buried at this fairly obvious location). Red roses have been left here in memory of "Saint" Kathelynn. Kathelynn the lamia occasionally collects these to decorate her rooms, appreciating the irony.

Just as the Druidess Lurilune makes an occasional trip to Cenaur Yltair (**Area W-11**), Abbot Godefroy makes a pilgrimage to this site, leaving roses and offering prayers. Any character making a DC 15 Perception check notices what looks like larger animal track around the shrine, a DC 10 Knowledge (nature) check confirms it to be the tracks of a large lion or panther.

Area W-6. Manor of the Mountain Queen

The Mountain Queen is Kathelynn, whose acts transformed her into a lamia with the body of a white saber-toothed tiger (smilodon) and a woman's torso. See the separate map of the Manor of the Mountain Queen (and the map entries with an "H" prefix).

Area W-7. Piper of the Winds (CR 4)

Roll an encounter as normal for this hex, but in addition to whatever else might be here, the area contains a cave, the den of a **satyr** named **Khethro Tulroc**.

Tulroc has a very unusual appearance for a satyr, being the servant of a different power than most satyrs follow. His skin, horns, and hair are bone-white; his only color is in his ice-blue eyes. The satyr carries a set of bone pan-pipes and wears nothing but a belted sporran and cudgel, even in the most biting cold. His behavior is not much different than normal satyrs, although he is quite old and very canny.

Tulroc is a servant of the Winter Prince, and his bone pan-pipes are actually the instrument of luring the Ghostwinds down into the pass. If Tulroc does not play the pipes, the Ghostwinds eventually come looking for him—but with a delay of 1d4+2 days beyond the time they would normally have arrived. However, if the satyr is killed, the Ghostwinds bring some other servants of the Winter Prince to avenge him: a pack of **5 white trolls** with maximum hit points. The trolls pursue their quest for vengeance beyond the heights of the pass. If they are defeated, no further servants of the Winter Prince follow.

Tulroc has full cover among his rocks, and this makes it unlikely that the characters find him if he doesn't want to be found, even if they have a character scouting from the air. He could be enticed into the open if the characters camp here, if there are any females in the group, if they play any music, or if the characters call his name.

The pipes do not call the Ghostwinds unless it is Tulroc playing them; they are not magical.

KHETHRO TULROC THE SATYR **CR 4**
XP 1,200
hp 44 (*Pathfinder Roleplaying Game Bestiary* "Satyr")

WHITE TROLLS (5) **CR 4**
XP 1,200
Ice Troll (*Pathfinder Roleplaying Game Bestiary 2* "Troll, Ice")
CE Large humanoid (cold, giant)
Init +4; **Senses** darkvision 60 ft., low-light vision; **Perception** +9

AC 17, touch 13, flat-footed 13 (+4 Dex, +4 natural, –1 size)
hp 45 (6d8+18); **regeneration** 5 (acid or fire)
Fort +8; **Ref** +8; Will +2
Immuninties cold
Weaknesses vulnerable to fire

Speed 30 ft.
Melee battleaxe +7 (2d6+4), bite +2 (1d6+2), claw +2 (1d4+2) or bite +7 (1d6+4), 2 claws +7 (1d4+4)
Space 10 ft.; **Reach** 10 ft.
Special Attacks rend (2 claws, 1d6+6)

Str 19, **Dex** 18, **Con** 16, **Int** 9, **Wis** 10, **Cha** 7
Base Atk +4; **CMB** +9; **CMD** 23
Feats Intimidating Prowess, Lightning Reflexes, Skill Focus (Perception)
Skills Intimidate +7, Perception +9, Survival +4
Languages Giant

Area W-8. Snowy Owl Nest (CR 7)

A nest of **2 giant owls** is in this cave high up the cliff face. Unless the GM chooses to use a different procedure, the cliff must be scaled in the same way as the one where the perytons make their nest (**Area W-4**). In this case, the owl nest is only 70 feet up the cliff and 2 stages to the climb.

Stage 1: Starts at the ground, hits a difficult area at 30 ft, and ends at a secure foot-wide ledge at the 40-foot mark.

Stage 2: Starts at the ledge (40 ft), hits a difficult area at 50 ft, ends at the cave mouth (70 ft).

At night, 1 of the owls is always out hunting while the other guards the nest. During the day, both owls are here.

GIANT OWLS (2) **CR 5**
XP 1,600
hp 57 (*Pathfinder Roleplaying Game Bestiary 3* "Owl, Giant")

Treasure: There are 3 giant owl eggs in the nest.

Area W-9. Druidic Holy Place (Olir Orphais)

The holy place known as Olir Orphais is a natural rock arch, flickering all over with a faint greenish fire. The flames cannot be extinguished other than by the power of a demigod, at the least. This arch is one of the sacred places Lurilune (**Area A-8**) is sworn to protect and maintain.

Area W-10. Druidic Holy Place (Ambioc Tor)

Ambioc Tor is a naturally formed tower of rock 60 feet tall and 20 feet in diameter. It is a place where the Material Plane lies very close to the Elemental Plane of Earth. Anyone within a quarter mile of the Tor begins to hear a very low-toned, slightly rhythmic music, like several bass drums whose every beat occupies a half minute rather than a half second. This is the living sound of elemental earth, so close that it reverberates into the Material Plane.

Area W-11. Druidic Holy Place (Cenaur Yltair) (CR 6)

Cenaur Yltair is found on a mile-wide saddle of high, rocky land. It is a rock formation shaped like a curving ramp, with its apex 50 feet over the height of the surrounding rocks. If a druid is in the party, with a DC 15 Knowledge (local) check the character might know that according to local druidic tradition, a person is sacrificed here once every 7 years by throwing them off the top after a procession up the ramplike rock formation. These sacrifices are usually criminals already sentenced to death in the town of Elet to the north. The town tends to keep this connection and tradition fairly quiet.

In between the major sacrifices, one of Lurilune's duties is to come to Cenair Yltair once a year to light a bonfire at the top. It is possible that she might recruit the characters, especially if a druid is among them, to come with her as guards and assistants on the bonfire trip to Cenaur Yltair.

Coming too close to the area around Cenaur Yltair without a druid is dangerous: a **will-o'-wisp** guards it (for no apparent reason). The will-o'-wisp can charm people up the formation, causing them to fall over the edge. It darts from behind one rock over to the next, showing its eerie lights to one character after another, trying to enrapture at least one of them into walking up the Yltair (saving throw negates). The will-o'-wisp then leads the way toward (and over) the edge, which ends up giving the other characters a short window of time to attack it. With luck, they manage to kill it before their companions walk off the edge to their doom. The will-o'-wisp leaves the characters alone if they are accompanied by a druid.

WILL-O'-WISP **CR 6**
XP 2,400
hp 40 (*Pathfinder Roleplaying Game Bestiary* "Will-o'-Wisp")

Area W-12. South Camp

The South Camp is a base camp for the hunters and trappers who live to the south of the mountain pass. It is far enough down and sheltered enough from wind, that it is considered "out of the pass" for purposes of escaping the Ghostwind's terrible cold. If the characters are starting the adventure by approaching the pass from the south, they can use Diplomacy skill checks to gather information from the hunters and trappers who are camping here in between their expeditions into the wilderness.

Abbey of Saint Kathelynn

"Saint" Kathelynn was canonized only 75 years ago, but the tower and outbuildings of the fortified monastery are obviously older than that. It was originally an old border fort, which was consecrated to Saint Kathelynn after her "death." Despite the fact that Kathelynn is neither saintly nor dead, the yet-to-be-recognized Saint Elys protects the abbey as her own.

The nature of this protection is warmth and protection from the Ghostwind. If you are running the adventure to include the mystery of Elys and the location of the *Staff of the Remorhaz*, the relative warmth of the abbey is an important clue, DC 20 Perception check, so make sure you stress that *the entire abbey is far warmer than the biting mountain air outside the walls.*

Area A-1. Gates (CR 5)

> Two watchtowers stand with a wooden gate between them, a bowman in each tower. The gate is painted with a red rose, and the towers are crude, providing cover for only one person at a time.

The **2 archers** are the lay brethren Brother Maru and Brother Tenir. They are considered Indifferent towards the PCs as they approach. If the two brethren decide the characters aren't a threat to the abbey, Brother Maru climbs down his ladder and unbar the gates.

The moment the characters step through the gates and into the abbey's curtilage, they feel the biting cold of the mountain air lessen. Although the temperature does not rise to the point of complete warmth, it is definitely above the freezing point. Everyone ascribes the divine warmth to Saint Kathelynn's intervention, since it started only after the abbey was consecrated to her.

ARCHERS (2) **CR 3**
XP 800
Male human fighter 4
LG Medium humanoid (human)
Init +7; **Perception** +5

AC 18, touch 13, flat-footed 15 (+5 armor, +3 Dex)
hp 38 (4d10+8 plus 4)
Fort +6; **Ref** +4; **Will** +2; +1 vs. fear
Defensive Abilities bravery +1

Speed 30 ft.
Melee warhammer +6 (1d8+2)
Ranged composite longbow +7 (1d8+2/x3)

Str 15, **Dex** 16, **Con** 14, **Int** 10, **Wis** 12, **Cha** 8
Base Atk +4; **CMB** +6; **CMD** 19
Feats Alertness[B], Improved Initiative[B], Point-Blank Shot, Precise Shot, Rapid Shot[B], Weapon Focus (longbow)
Skills Acrobatics +1, Climb +4, Diplomacy +2, Perception +5, Survival +6
Languages Common
SQ armor training 1
Gear robes over scale mail, composite longbow (+2 Str), warhammer, quiver with 20 arrows, wooden holy symbol of a rose (unpainted).

Area A-2. Abbey Hall (CR 3)

> This is a stone building with shuttered arrow slits for windows and a steeply pitched slate roof. A painting of a red rose has been added over the top of the door, but the red paint has faded to a delicate shade of pink.

This is the abbey's main hall, containing a storage room, a kitchen, and a dining hall. Stairs lead up to a second floor that has small bedrooms for up to 8 lay brethren. Six of these are occupied by brothers Maru, Tenir, Odoc, Bernart, Ocrip, and Selmus, and the other 2 are empty. The two empty rooms are used as guestrooms if the abbey has visitors. **Brother Odoc**, the abbey's cook (and generally responsible for this entire building), is usually to be found here.

BROTHER ODOC **CR 3**
XP 800
Male human fighter 4
LG Medium humanoid (human)
Init +1; **Perception** +0

AC 18, touch 12, flat-footed 16 (+6 armor, +1 Dex, +1 dodge)
hp 42 (4d10+8 plus 8)
Fort +6; **Ref** +2; **Will** +3; +1 vs. fear
Defensive Abilities bravery +1

Speed 30 ft.
Melee mwk longsword +9 (1d8+3/19–20)
Ranged longbow +5 (1d8/x3)

Str 17, **Dex** 13, **Con** 14, **Int** 12, **Wis** 10, **Cha** 9
Base Atk +4; **CMB** +7; **CMD** 19
Feats Dodge[B], Iron Will[B], Point-Blank Shot, Power Attack, Toughness[B], Weapon Focus (longsword)
Skills Appraise +5, Climb +4, Diplomacy +2, Knowledge

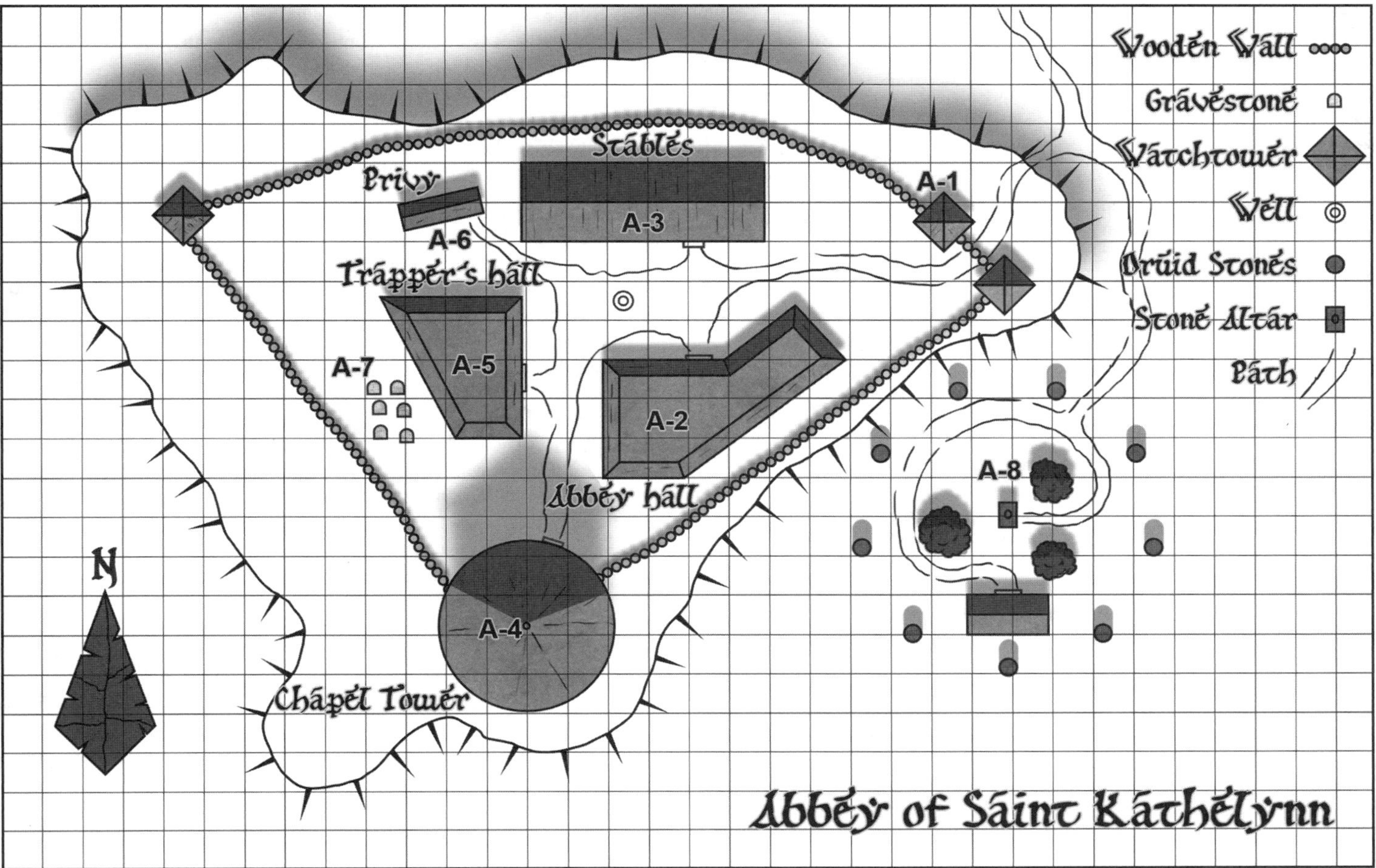

(dungeoneering) +5, Profession (cook) +7, Survival +4, Swim +3
Languages Common, Orc
SQ armor training 1
Gear robes over scale mail, longbow, masterwork longsword, quiver with 20 arrows, wooden holy symbol of a rose (unpainted)

Area A-3. Stable and Barn (CR 2)

> This stone building smells like a stable, and has doors to match. A rudimentary blacksmith's forge stands outside under a canvas shade, not capable of much beside horseshoes.

The stable is used as a barn as well and currently houses 6 mules and 10 goats. **Brother Bernart** is currently here tending the animals, but he doubles as the abbey's blacksmith and goatherd. He is often away from the abbey, guarding the goats as they graze the meager fodder of the foothills north of the pass.

BROTHER BERNART CR 2
XP 600
Male human cleric of Muir 3
LG Medium humanoid (human)
Init –1; **Perception** +2

AC 16, touch 9, flat-footed 16 (+6 armor, –1 Dex, +1 shield)
hp 26 (3d8+6 plus 3)
Fort +5; **Ref** +0; **Will** +7

Speed 20 ft.
Melee warhammer +3 (1d8+1)
Special Attacks channel positive energy 5/day (DC 13, 2d6)
Domain Spell-like Abilities (CL 3th; concentration +5, melee touch +3):
5/day—*touch of law*, *resistant touch* (+1)
Spells Prepared (CL 3rd; concentration +5):
2nd—*aid*, *hold person* (DC 14), *shield other*[D]
1st—*bless*, *endure elements*, *protection from chaos*[D], *shield of faith*
0 (at will)—*create water*, *mending*, *purify food and drink* (DC 12), *resistance*
D Domain spell; **Domains** Law, Protection

Str 12, **Dex** 8, **Con** 14, **Int** 10, **Wis** 15, **Cha** 15
Base Atk +2; **CMB** +3; **CMD** 12
Feats Iron Will, Selective Channeling, Skill Focus (Craft [blacksmith])
Skills Appraise +4, Craft (blacksmith) +4, Diplomacy +6, Knowledge (history) +4, Knowledge (nature) +4, Knowledge (planes) +4, Knowledge (religion) +4, Profession (shepherd) +6, Spellcraft +4
Languages Common
Gear robes over masterwork chainmail, light steel shield, warhammer, longbow, quiver with 20 arrows, wooden holy symbol of a rose (unpainted)

Area A-4. Chapel Tower

> The tower is stone, with a conical roof. The roof is shingled with slates, some of which are missing. A red rose is painted on the door, but the paint seems to be developing small white spots where the red pigment is dropping away.

Fading Roses

The whitening of all the red roses in the abbey, and the brothers' unconscious preference for leaving their wooden holy symbols unpainted, is a symptom of the abbey's mis-consecration to the "red rose" twin, rather than the "white rose" twin. If the characters use any sort of divination spell that requires a vague answer from the higher powers, the answer to the spell might be pointing out the whitening of the abbey's red roses.

In the tower:

The ground floor of the tower obviously serves as the chapel. Along with lots of candles and a small wooden altar, the chapel's central feature is an empty sarcophagus. The wooden lid is propped up vertically beside the stone coffin and bears the painting of an armored woman with the symbol of a red rose on her shield. She has a vertical scar on the left side of her face. A flight of stone stairs leads to the upper stories.

A very old man stands by the sarcophagus, looking at the painting.

This is **Abbot Godefroy**, the 85-year-old man in charge of the abbey. He receives little from his superiors, and less in tithes, so the abbey has gone from being in merely poor repair to being in very poor repair over its 75 years as a religious institution.

If the characters look closely at the painting they notice that the paint of the red rose is flaking very slightly (automatic success if a player announces she is checking the painting for detail). The rest of the picture's paint appears to be fine, although a DC15 Perception check reveals that the paint of the facial scar also seems to be suffering the same problem. If asked about the painting, the abbot admits sheepishly that he painted it himself from memory, decades ago. No doubt he mixed the red paint poorly, he admits; such things happen with pigments.

Abbot Godefroy can provide a great deal of information if the characters have begun to get curious about the *Staff of the Remorhaz* (see "Talking to Abbot Godefroy," below), but if they are just here to hunt monsters or guard caravans, don't push the area's background story on them. They either start looking into the mysteries of the pass or they won't. If they do, they'll be back at the abbey asking questions soon enough. If not, Ghostwind Pass offers plenty of adventure and treasure for those who aren't interested in playing detective.

The second floor contains Abbot Godefroy's bedroom and study, together with bedroom-cells for 2 monks. These are currently empty, since the only ordained brother here is the abbot. The third floor contains 6 more monkish cells and some arrow slits. The tower's conical slate roof can be reached by a trapdoor, but the slates of the roof are in poor condition, and climbing around on them is unsafe, to say the least (make a DC 17 Acrobatics check or fall).

Talking to Abbot Godefroy

If the characters appear to be worthy individuals, or rich ones, Abbot Godefroy offers to grant them a benediction to help them in their endeavors. A generous contribution to the abbey would certainly be appreciated, of course (see "Abbot's Benediction").

If the characters are specifically asking about Saint Kathelynn, or the abbey's history, Abbot Godefroy is happy to talk.

The Story of Saint Kathelynn

The sarcophagus is empty because the bones of St. Kathelynn were buried in secret by her five retainers; the characters are invited to pay respect to their memorials in the graveyard. The sarcophagus awaits the day when the saint's bones are finally returned to their proper place. Anyone who does so, the abbot notes, would be greatly blessed. Not only that, more visitors and pilgrims would also make their way to the abbey to see a real relic.

Godefroy was a 10-year-old boy when the twin paladins Elys and Kathelynn undertook their fatal mission to the heights of the pass, along with five loyal retainers. He remembers seeing the saint and her twin sister, but of course he was not actually on the expedition. He wrote down the story as it was told to him by the five retainers who were there (almost), and provides the characters with a copy if they wish.

Abbot's Benediction

This is also where the characters can receive the Abbot's blessing if they donate money or other valuables to the upkeep of the abbey. In particular, the Abbot wants to repair the tower's roof to avoid having slates fall off and possibly hit someone—also it is beginning to leak a bit. He also wants to replace the wooden wall with a stone curtain wall, but this requires many thousands of gold pieces.

If a character donates 500 gp or more (each), they can receive the Abbot's ordinary benediction. The benediction is a powerful blessing from the greater powers of Law—although it is delivered in the name of "Saint" Kathelynn. The blessing allows the character to call on the saint before attempting a task, and to gain divine favor for the attempt. This boon may be granted twice in a character's lifetime.

Boon

Saint Kathelynn's Benediction: Whenever the PC is required to make an attack roll, ability check, saving throw, or skill check, she can spend they use of his boon as an immediate action to roll twice and take the better result. He must decide to use this ability before he rolls the saving throw and call out the saint's name.

If the character donates 1,000 gp or more, they can receive the Abbot grants a greater benediction—but this "greater benediction" may only be received by a character once in the character's lifetime. They must choose the attempts wisely!

Greater Boon

Saint Kathelynn's Greater Benediction: Whenever the PC is required to make an attack roll, ability check, saving throw, or skill check, she can

Abbot's Note

And so began the Expedition to kill the Winter Prince, led by Kathelynn, who would be the saint, and her twin sister Elys, her standard-bearer. The twins forged ahead, magically protected from the cold by their gem-topped staff, and the five warriors of their retinue became separated from them in the blizzard.

Ahead of them the warriors heard an inhuman scream upon the cold, white winds, and when they made their way forward the harm was done. The body of Sainted Kathelynn lay upon the snow, her skull half crushed. Of Elys, there was no sign at all.

But there also lay dying the body of the Winter Prince, its evil soul already gathering away from the body in a freezing mist. And the Winter Prince laughed from the lips of that dead man, saying, "I am defeated and I keep my bargains. I shall release the Ghostwinds from the mountain pass except twice a year." And then the body of the Winter Prince fell dead, and its misty soul blew away on the wind to wait for the evils it would do in the next winter.

The warriors brought back the body of the Saint, and buried her in secret. Shortly thereafter they all disappeared one by one, leaving no trace. For killing the Winter Prince and thus banishing the Ghostwinds for most of the year, Kathelynn was canonized as a saint. The mystical way in which she called her loyal followers to her, to serve her as knights where they were needed, serves as obvious confirmation of her sainthood.

And so began the Expedition to kill the Winter Prince, led by Kathelynn, who would be the saint, and her twin sister Elys, her standard-bearer. The twins forged ahead, magically protected from the cold by their gem-topped staff, and the five warriors of their retinue became separated from them in the blizzard.

Ahead of them the warriors heard an inhuman scream upon the cold, white winds, and when they made their way forward the harm was done. The body of Sainted Kathelynn lay upon the snow, her skull half crushed. Of Elys, there was no sign at all.

But there also lay dying the body of the Winter Prince, its evil soul already gathering away from the body in a freezing mist. And the Winter Prince laughed from the lips of that dead man, saying, "I am defeated, yet I keep my bargains. I shall release the Ghostwinds from the mountain pass except twice a year." And then the body of the Winter Prince fell dead, and its misty soul blew away on the wind to wait for the evils it would do in the next winter.

The warriors brought back the body of the Saint, and buried her in secret. Shortly thereafter, they disappeared one by one, leaving no trace. For killing the Winter Prince and thus banishing the Ghostwinds for most of the year, Kathelynn was canonized as a saint. The mystical way in which she called her loyal followers to her, to serve her as knights where they were needed, serves as obvious confirmation of her sainthood.

spend they use of his boon as an immediate action to roll three times and take the better result. He must decide to use this ability before he rolls the saving throw and call out the saint's name.

The Abbot and Druidism

The abbot stresses very strongly that a character **cannot** carry *Saint Kathelynn's Benediction* and a *Druid's Mark* at the same time. He is obviously disdainful of the druidic faith, and cautions the characters that they should not trust druids in general or Lurilune in particular. Druidism, he believes, is like an extortion scheme, holding Lawful civilization hostage to the amoral forces of Nature, demanding sacrifices in exchange for good weather and fertile lands. If a druid is in the party who takes offense at this attitude, the abbot quickly shifts into the role of an old man who perhaps rambles too much, that he does not mean to offend, and that he perhaps overstated his opinions. He did *not* overstate his opinion, of course, but he is not a confrontational person. He specifically offers the druid character the Abbot's ordinary benediction with no donation required.

ABBOT GODEFROY **CR 8**
XP 4,800
Male human cleric of Muir 9
LG Medium humanoid (human)
Init +6; **Perception** +4

AC 21, touch 15, flat-footed 18 (+5 armor, +2 deflection, +2 Dex, +1 dodge, +1 natural)
hp 62 (9d8+9 plus 9)
Fort +8; **Ref** +6; **Will** +11
Defensive Abilities aura of protection (9 rounds/day)

Speed 20 ft.
Melee *+1 warhammer* +6/+1 (1d8+1)
Special Attacks channel positive energy 4/day (DC 15, 5d6), holy lance (4 rounds, 1/day)
Domain Spell-Like Abilities (CL 9th; concentration +13, melee touch +5):
7/day—*resistant touch* (+2), *touch of good* (+4)
Spells Prepared (CL 9th; concentration +13)
5th—*dispel evil*[D], *true seeing*
4th—*discern lies* (DC 18), *freedom of movement*, *holy smite*[D] (DC 18), *restoration*
3rd—*dispel magic*, *invisibility purge*, *magic circle against evil*[D], *meld into stone*, *searing light*
2nd—*align weapon (good only)*[D], *hold person* (DC 16), *shield other*, *silence* (DC 16), *sound burst* (DC 16), *zone of truth* (DC 16)
1st—*bless*, *detect evil*, *obscuring mist*, *protection from evil*[D], *ray of sickening** (DC 15), *shield of faith*
0 (at will)—*detect magic*, *purify food and drink* (DC 14), *read magic*, *stabilize*
D Domain spell; **Domains** Good, Protection

Str 8, **Dex** 14, **Con** 13, **Int** 10, **Wis** 18, **Cha** 13
Base Atk +6; **CMB** +5; **CMD** 20
Feats Blind-fight, Combat Casting[B], Dodge, Improved Initiative, Selective Channeling, Vital Strike
Skills Appraise +4, Diplomacy +8, Knowledge (arcana) +8, Knowledge (history) +5, Knowledge (planes) +4, Knowledge (religion) +11, Sense Motive +8, Spellcraft +8
Languages Common
Combat Gear *potion of neutralize poison*, *potion of resist cold 10*; **Other Gear** robes over *+1 chain shirt*, *+1 warhammer*, *amulet of natural armor +1*, *cloak of resistance +1*, *ring of protection +2*, silver holy symbol of a rose (painted), 188 gp
*See *Pathfinder Roleplaying Game Ultimate Magic*

OCRIP AND SELMUS **CR 3**
XP 800
hp 34 (*Pathfinder Roleplaying Game GameMastery Guide* "Guard Officer")

Area A-5. Trappers' Hall.

> This building is stone, with a high, peaked roof and a sign above the door showing a white animal fur, and underneath, the words, "Trappers' Hall."

The Trappers' Hall is a mixture of an inn, tavern, warehouse, and store. There are 10 rooms on the upper floor, 3 of which are occupied by traders, and 2 of which are occupied by trappers recently returned from expeditions into the pass. The traders have offices with one-room vaults containing their furs and other goods. They buy pelts from the trappers throughout the hunting season, then retreat back to the town of Elet when the Ghostwinds blow into the pass. They are mostly interested in purchasing furs from the hunters and trappers, but they also do a brisk business selling them the various goods needed for long expeditions into the wilderness.

Prices offered by the traders are as follows:

Blood violets: 200 gp/sack
Goat meat: 5 gp/goat (150lb)
Giant owl egg: 1000 gp
Giant lynx pelt: No trader purchases these due to the druidic ban on killing or hurting the giant lynxes of the pass.
Giant weasel pelt: 200 gp
Polar bear pelt: 800 gp
Giant ermine pelt: 1000 gp
Saber-tooth pelt: 800 gp
Weretiger pelt: 1000 gp
Wolf pelt: 5 gp
Winter wolf pelt: 500 gp

The Traders

AULOYNE OF ELET **CR 1**
XP 400
hp 13 (*Pathfinder Roleplaying Game GameMastery Guide* "Shopkeep")

To lower Auloyne's selling price by 5% requires a DC 20 Diplomacy check. To raise Auloyne's buying price by 5% requires a DC 20 Diplomacy check.

TADRIC FURMAN **CR 1**
XP 400
hp 13 (*Pathfinder Roleplaying Game GameMastery Guide* "Shopkeep")

To lower Tadric's selling price by 5% requires a DC 15 Diplomacy check. To raise Tadric's buying price by 5% requires a DC 20 Diplomacy check.

PAGANNE OF TROYE **CR 1**
XP 400
hp 13 (*Pathfinder Roleplaying Game GameMastery Guide* "Shopkeep")

To lower Paganne's selling price by 5% requires a DC 20 Diplomacy check. To raise Paganne's buying price by 5% requires a DC 15 Diplomacy check.

The Trappers

LODO THE TRAPPER **CR 3**
XP 800
hp 30 (*Pathfinder Roleplaying Game GameMastery Guide* "Trapper")

Gear leather armor, dagger, shortbow, 20 arrows, smelly

fur-lined sleeping bag, pouch containing 10 garnets (5 gp), various bits of outdoor survival gear.

GHENTRY BADGER **CR 3**
XP 800
hp 30 (*Pathfinder Roleplaying Game GameMastery Guide* "Trapper")

Gear leather armor, dagger, shortbow, 20 arrows, fur-lined sleeping back, pouch containing 34 gp, 3 dice, and a rabbit's foot, flask of whiskey, various bits of outdoor survival gear.

Area A-6. Privies

> This is a rickety wooden building with a half-moon-shaped hole in the door.

The facilities boast wooden seats and an unpleasant smell.

Staff of the Remorhaz (Major Artifact)

STAFF OF THE REMORHAZ (MAJOR ARTIFACT)
Aura overwhelming conjuration and transmutation; **CL** 24th
Slot none; **Weight** 4 lbs.

DESCRIPTION

This staff of pure white wood is a *+3 icy-burst staff*. The six-foot shaft is topped by a multi-faceted gem, the Eye *of Othroäta* and when unbroken grants it full powers on the wielder. The half-artifact or broken version conveys no benefits to a wielder unless it is joined with its other half. It does, however, exert enough magical force that it warms the entire area of the abbey and acts as a *+1 frost staff*.

The *Staff of the Remorhaz* is a holy artifact dating back to the beginning of history and the wars against forgotten evil gods. Despite the vast magical power of the artifact, it is shielded from all detection magic other than the direct intercession of a deity.

Any good-aligned divine caster who holds the staff is granted immunity to cold, although it imparts vulnerability to fire and the holder of the staff suffers double normal damage from any fire-type attack. The staff's powers can be used only by a divine caster and it acts as a *+1 frost staff* to any not able to cast divine spells.

The wielder's hair transforms and becomes snow white for as long as the character holds the artifact, and if the staff is used thrice, the change is permanent.

When used, the staff absorbs coldness from the air surrounding the user in a blast of violent heat; anyone within a 10-ft. radius must make a DC 20 Reflex save or sustain 1d4+4 points of fire damage. Anyone in contact with the artifact is unaffected.

The staff's powers are:

- *comprehend languages* (at will)
- *find traps* (3/day)
- *cone of cold, wall of ice* (2/day)
- *ice storm, polymorph self* (1/day)
- *vision**

*This attribute of the staff is not under the wielder's control. When great evil must be addressed, the wielder may begin having visions about it, as per spell *vision*. This aspect of the staff is neither predictable nor constant.

If anyone who is non-good aligned takes hold of the staff, the artifact defends itself by casting polymorphing the offender into a white lynx with the intelligence of a wild animal (a successful DC 15 Will save prevents the transformation).

DESTRUCTION

The only way to destroy the staff is to bathe it in the still-hot blood of a remorhaz.

From the Northlands Saga, ***NS2: Beyond the Wailing Mountains***

In eons past, many dread gods rose and fell, thrown down by deities of good and their heroic champions. Most of these elder gods were born when the world was young, and were savage and feral, drawing their power from the primordial forces of nature perverted to evil and destruction. Most of these elder gods have long since been destroyed, but a few remain, sleeping away the ages and waiting for the opportunity to rise again.

One such elder god is Althunak, the Lord of Ice and Cold. His is not the natural changing of the season, of the cycle of autumn, winter, and spring, but instead the continual death of a perpetual winter. His cult once flourished when the races of the world were young, but he was challenged and destroyed by some of the earliest heroes to walk the world, or so it was thought.

One of the abominations in Althunak's dread horde was a great remorhaz, Othroäta the Paleworm. When the vanguard of Althunak's army was broken at the Battle of Heshkar, Othroäta was slain by Ulhred the Horned Paladin, who ripped out the beast's great, faceted eye. Spiking the eye on his battle-spear, Uhlred raised it aloft as a battle standard to call his warriors forward. Seeing this, the great ice trolls and giants of the horde's vanguard ceased their advance, the troops behind them halting and milling about in great consternation. Whereupon the warriors in their ranked battalions behind the Horned Paladin gave a great cry of triumph and charged, following Ulhred and his grisly standard to the legendary victory on Heshkar's blood-glutted fields, where Althunak's horde was broken and the evil god himself was thought slain.

This battle standard, the *Eye of the Othroäta* on the spear of the Horned Paladin, is then lost to history for a very long time. It does not reappear until Tourmaj's account of the Second Battle of Aixe, at the darkest and most desperate moment of the battle, in the small wood where the true King lay wounded, defended by his embattled knights. As the snow began to fall, Leothrand the High Priest raised the staff as a battle-standard to rally the remaining forces of the king. The last charge of Leothrand Cold-wielder shattered the half-demon army of the Alabastrian Heresy and brought peace once again to the lands. When Leothrand's body was recovered from the piles of dead, the staff was gone. Thereafter, the Chansons of Ghen describe three more instances after the Second Battle of Aixe when the S*taff of the Remorhaz* was granted to heroes; always clerics, always of lawful alignment, always by an angelic being, always in blizzardlike snow. The only change in detail is that the *Eye of the Othroäta* seems to have hardened into a multi-faceted gem atop the staff.

The staff was most recently held by the paladins Elys and Kathelynn, three quarters of a century ago, when it was broken in half in battle with the Winter Prince. The two parts are assumed to be lost in the Ghostwind Pass where the battle took place.

Area A-7. Graves

This is a very small graveyard with only six headstones. Each headstone bears a name but no inscription, other than a rose carved into the stone below the name.

The names on the gravestones are: Tallow Smith, John of Elet, John Tallbones, Griffin Winemaker, Claude Yellowhair, and Benedict the Bald. None of the graves, except the one for Griffin Winemaker, actually contain bodies; these are memorials for the 5 loyal retainers who disappeared shortly after burying St. Kathelynn's body in a hidden sanctum. Give no hints or helpful die rolls in this area! If the characters are to get hold of a powerful artifact like the staff, or earn the fame that comes from finding a saint's lost bones, they should be allowed to earn it fairly, without help.

The grave carved with the name of Griffin Winemaker contains the lead-shielded bronze casket of St. Elys (a body everyone believes to have belonged to Kathelynn). In the casket along with the true saint's bones is the wooden *Staff of the Remorhaz*. The staff is bereft of its tip, the multi-faceted *Eye of the Othroäta*. Despite the vast magical power of the artifact, it is shielded from all detection magic other than the direct intercession of a deity. This is no magical trinket with a distinct aura: It is ancient power that blends into the power of the earth itself, unable to be distinguished unless a detection spell is cast directly upon it.

Area A-8. Circle of the Druidess (CR 8)

A cottage made of stone and roofed with slates is surrounded by a circle of widely spaced stones, each of them about five feet tall and carved with runes. Green grass grows within the stone circle, and at the center of the field stands a stone altar. A giant lynx, the size of a wolf, sits in the path at the entrance to the strange garden.

Sitting in the path is the druid **Lurilune** in her favorite form of a giant lynx. The cottage at the end of the pathway is her humble abode and has been as long as she has been the druidic custodian of the Ghostwind Pass. Her task here, as she sees it, is fairly simple: She maintains the various small druidic shrines in the pass; makes sure the visiting hunters do not abuse the bounteous hunting in the area; and looks for ways to destroy the Mountain Queen, whom Lurilune considers to be completely outside the natural order. She knows and constantly reminds herself not to seek a direct confrontation with the monstrosity that Kathelynn has become, but if she makes contact with a strong-enough looking group of adventurers she would definitely seek ways to point them toward the lamia. She will not risk herself, the guardian of the pass, by accompanying them, but she gives each of them a *Druidic Mark* if they swear to use it in an attack on the Manor of the Mountain Queen. She does not know the lamia's true identity, simply referring to her as the Mountain Queen, but she does know that the Mountain Queen has the lower body of a white tigress. Having the secretive nature common to many druids, she only shares this information if the characters are definitely on a quest to attack the manor.

The *Druidic Mark* is a pattern that Lurilune traces upon a person's face before they venture into the pass, and most of the hunters would not dream of entering the pass without the mark. To get the *Druidic Mark*, one must make some sort of sacrifice on the altar in the center of Lurilune's green freehold. Only a few types of things are acceptable sacrifices:

Acceptable	Not Accepted
Gems or precious stone (100 gp minimum)	Gold, silver, copper
Gems or precious stone (500 gp minimum)**	
Blood (1 hit points worth)*	Someone else's blood
Blood (5 hit points worth)**	
Pelt of a wolf, wolverine, or giant weasel	Herbivore pelts or a lynx pelt
Heart of a peryton** or pelt of a saber-tooth**	Iron or steel
* A blood sacrifice reduces the character's max hit points by 1 (or 5) points for as long as the character is in the pass. Even a *heal* spell will not return the lost hit points until the character enters the abbey, the south camp, or otherwise leaves the pass into the lowlands. ** These are the "greater sacrifices" described in more detail below.	

A normal sacrifice "allows" the recipient to hunt the giant ermines that live in the pass. Anyone without the mark who kills more than one of the giant ermines immediately suffers from a curse that causes a weakness of the joints (–1 on all attack rolls and damage rolls). Leaving the pass abates the weakness, but it returns if the victim enters the pass a second time without having the curse removed by Lurilune or by a spell. Each additional giant ermine killed without the *Druidic Mark* worsens the curse, which becomes a penalty of –2, then –3, etc.

Making one of the greater sacrifices (5 hit points or a peryton heart) confers a temporary druidic power against death itself. If the bearer of the *Greater Druidic Mark* takes a mortal wound (would be brought to 0 hit points or below), the mark draws upon the natural pattern of sacred sites in the pass to bring the character back to 1 hit point. When this happens, the *Greater Druidic Mark* also disappears from the character's face. The mark disappears if the character leaves the pass, but reappears upon return (until its power is used).

There are some restrictions on the existence of the mark. It disappears permanently if the character bearing the mark sets foot in the chapel tower of the abbey. Similarly, it is not possible to have both *Saint Kathelynn's Benediction* and the *Druidic Mark*. Moreover, the *Druidic Mark* immediately disappears if the character kills one of the giant lynxes in the pass. These are Lurilune's eyes and ears, sacred to the druidic powers of the area.

LURILUNE **CR 8**
XP 4,800
Female human druid (giant lynx shaman) 9 (*Pathfinder Roleplaying Game Advanced Player's Guide* "Lion Shaman")
N Medium humanoid (human)
Init +1; **Perception** +10
Aura predator's grace (15 ft.)

AC 14, touch 11, flat-footed 13 (+2 armor, +1 Dex, +1 natural)
hp 80 (9d8+18 plus 18)
Fort +9; **Ref** +5; **Will** +11; +4 vs. fey and plant-targeted effects

Speed 30 ft.
Melee bite +5 (1d4–1), 2 claws +5 (1d4–1)
Special Attacks rake (2 claws +5, 1d4–1, wild shape 3/day
Spells Prepared (CL 9th; concentration +13):
5th—*beast shape III (animals only)*[D], *stoneskin*
4th—*air walk, cure serious wounds, flame strike* (DC 18),

*summon nature's ally IV (animals only)*D
3rd—*beast shape I (animals only)*D, *call lightning* (DC 17), *call lightning* (DC 17), *speak with plants*, *stone shape*
2nd—*cat's grace*, *flaming sphere* (DC 16), *hold animal*D (DC 16), *hold animal* (DC 16), *resist energy*, *tree shape*
1st—*cure light wounds*, *endure elements*, *hide from animals*, *longstrider*, *magic fang*D, *produce flame*
0 (at will)—*detect magic*, *know direction*, *read magic*, *resistance*
D Domain spell; **Domain** Animal (Fur subdomain)

Str 8, **Dex** 12, **Con** 14, **Int** 10, **Wis** 19, **Cha** 13
Base Atk +6; **CMB** +5 (+7 grapple); **CMD** 16
Feats Blind-fight, Combat Casting, Lunge, Natural Spell, Self-sufficient, Stealthy, ToughnessB
Skills Appraise +1, Climb +3, Diplomacy +2, Fly +5, Handle Animal +6, Heal +15, Knowledge (geography) +4, Knowledge (nature) +10, Linguistics +2, Perception +10, Profession (gardener) +12, Profession (herbalist) +10 , Sense Motive +7, Spellcraft +8, Stealth +5, Survival +15
Languages Aquan, Common, Druidic, Sylvan
SQ animal companion (giant lynx [lion] named Kaivy), giant lynx [lion] wild shape, giant lynx's [lion's] totem transformation, giant lynx's [lion's] totemic summons, nature bond (Fur domain), nature sense, totem transformation (giant lynx's [lion's] natural weapons), trackless step, wild empathy +10, woodland stride
Combat Gear *wand of cure light wounds*; **Other Gear** *amulet of natural armor +1*, *bracers of armor +2*, *cloak of resistance +1*

KAIVY CR —
XP —
Male giant lynx animal companion (*Pathfinder Roleplaying Game Bestiary* "Lion")
N Medium animal
Init +4; **Senses** low-light vision, scent; Perception +7

AC 20, touch 14, flat-footed 16 (+4 Dex, +6 natural)
hp 39 (+12)
Fort +6; **Ref** +9; **Will** +4 (+4 morale bonus vs. Enchantment spells and effects)
Defensive Abilities evasion

Speed 40 ft.
Melee bite +7 (1d8+3), 2 claws +7 (1d4+3)
Special Attacks rake (2 claws +7, 1d4+3)

Str 16, **Dex** 19, **Con** 13, **Int** 2, **Wis** 15, **Cha** 10
Base Atk +4; **CMB** +7; **CMD** 21 (25 vs. trip)
Feats Improved Natural Armor, Improved Natural Attack (bite), Toughness
Tricks Attack, Attack, Come, Defend, Down, Fetch, Heel, Heel, Hunting, Seek, Stay, Track, Track
Skills Acrobatics +8 (+12 to jump), Climb +7, Escape Artist +5, Perception +7, Stealth +8
SQ attack, come, defend, devotion, heel, hunting, stay, track

Treasure: The inside of Lurilune's cottage is carpeted with woven green rugs, and several books are stacked on a writing desk. A bedroom in a back room contains an unnaturally soft mattress stuffed with fragrant grasses, and a wardrobe contains white druidic robes. The books all contain complex astrological charts, weather predictions, records of prophetic bird migrations, and instructions for all kinds of auguries and divinations. All told they are worth 10,000 gp, but if they are sold, eventually the druids find out that one of their own has been robbed, and they begin seeking the thieves (or, perhaps, murderers).

A small chest (unlocked) contains 40 small emeralds (500 gp) in a pouch. If anyone departs the cottage with these emeralds and does not leave one of the stones behind, a **greater earth elemental** is released from imprisonment beneath the stone circle — the precious stones are part of the binding. It attacks ferociously to retrieve the emeralds and thus escape.

GREATER EARTH ELEMENTAL CR 9
XP 6,400
hp 136 (*Pathfinder Roleplaying Game Bestiary* "Elemental, Earth")

Manor of the Mountain Queen

The Mountain Queen's minions are tracked on a monster roster since the battle for the manor most likely involves monsters moving around rather than staying in one place.

Approaching the Manor

A huge manor house is built into the sloping side of a hill, with three levels. The roof is steeply pitched and made of slate shingles.

Being Spotted

A sentry in **Area H-28** keeps watch over the front of the building, waiting for the sort of visitors who walk up to front doors.

The Roof

It is not hard to get onto the roof of the manor, but getting through the heavy slate shingles is virtually impossible to do quietly. A single person on the roof can make a hole large enough for one person as follows:

DC 20 Strength check to physically move the tiles without making noise from dropping any;

DC 25 Dexterity check to get into the gap without dislodging more tiles and creating noise.

If a character succeeds at both checks, then he/she gets inside, possibly in a loft, possibly onto nothing more substantial than one of the roof beams 40 feet above the floor (in the low or middle tiers) or 20 feet above the floor in the top tier.

Unless the characters want to fight a pitched battle with all of the Manor's inhabitants at one time, they will immediately realize that making a hole in the roof is not a way to get in quietly.

Arrow Slits

In the front wall of the manor are 4 arrow slits, two of them high up on the first tier and two of them high up on the second tier. The arrow slits on the second tier have line of sight on anyone on the roof or the bottom tier.

Wandering Monsters

Wandering monsters are only an issue in the manor if the characters try to stop in one place for a long time (or set an ambush). If the characters stay in one place for more than an hour, or set up in a corridor, roll on the following table once every 30 minutes.

Wandering Monsters (if needed)

Roll 1d20	Encoutner
1–10	No Encounter
11–12	**1d2+1 bugbears**
13	**Gaston the Cook (Area H-7)**
14	**1 weretiger** and **1 smilodon**
15	**1d2 smilodon**

Roll 1d20	Encoutner
16	**Glaivorn** (**Area H-13**) and **1d3 bugbears**
17	**Henri Tharnac** and **1 weretiger** (**Area H-17**)
18	**Serz** and **Cloyaun**, human servants (**Area H-18**)
19	**Martin of Becqueril** (**Area H-19**)
20	**1d4+1 weretiger**

All is Not as it Seems

Even if they are being attacked, the weretigers remain human for one or two rounds, trying to convince intruders that the manor is a normal settlement that just happens to have saber-toothed tigers and bugbears wandering around. The charmed slaves and Henri back this up convincingly. Gaston the Cook tries to lie, but it won't be very convincing. The weretigers, of course, try to keep the characters away from Gaston, introduce them to an illusion of Kathelynn, and get them to sleep in one of the guestrooms. If the characters are separated, Kathelynn tries to charm and enslave them one at a time.

Kathelynn may use her ability to create a *major image* of herself as a human, with a different face than her own. She usually only attempts this in the Great Hall where she can regally dismiss the characters before the 10-minute duration of her capacity to maintain the illusion. One of the weretigers always stands near the illusion to open doors for it or prevent it from being touched.

The weretigers are usually in human form, even when they are alone.

Area H-1. Main Gate

> This solid-looking wooden door has a red rose painted on it. A slot through the door at eye level can be opened from within to look at visitors.

During the day, the door stands open, allowing the saber-toothed tigers to come and go as they please. At night, the door is barred (and a bugbear stands watch behind it in the murder hall, see below).

Area H-2. Murder Hall (CR 0 or 2)

This stone room has arrow slits pointing into it from the room beyond (the Covered Court, **Area H-3**), and a stout door that obviously leads into the main part of the manor.

If it is nighttime, describe the bugbear (see below)

As with the main gate, during the day this door is open to the rest of the hall so the cats can go in and out. At night, a **bugbear** stands guard here with a horn to summon reinforcements if the manor comes under attack.

BUGBEAR **CR 2**
XP 600
hp 16 each (*Pathfinder Roleplaying Game Bestiary* "Bugbear")

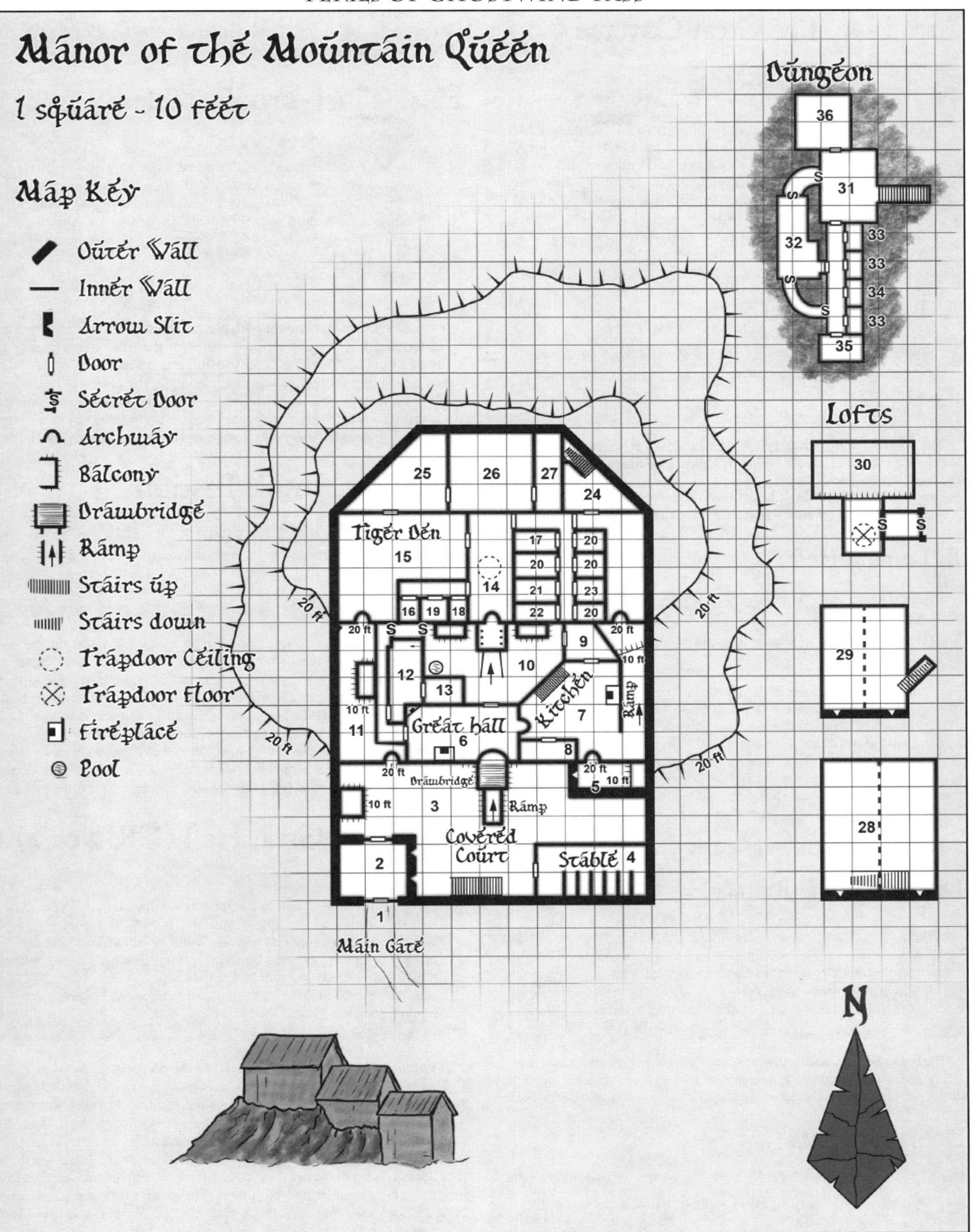
Manor of the Mountain Queen
1 square - 10 feet
Map Key
Outer Wall
Inner Wall
Arrow Slit
Door
Secret Door
Archway
Balcony
Drawbridge
Ramp
Stairs up
Stairs down
Trapdoor Ceiling
Trapdoor Floor
Fireplace
Pool
Dungeon
Lofts
Tiger Den
Great hall
Kitchen
Covered Court
Stable
Drawbridge
Ramp
Main Gate
N

Area H-3. The Great Covered Court

This room comprises almost all of the castle's lowest tier. The ceiling is steeply pitched overhead, supported with wooden beams and stone buttresses. There appears to be a walled-in loft under the center of the roof, surrounded by a cobweblike array of heavy beams and struts. This room has a number of strange features: balconies, arched opening placed high up the wall, a ramp and drawbridge leading to the next tier of the fortified manor, stairs that lead up to the loft area, a wall with arrow slits pointing into the hall rather than outward, and some large double doors. It is a lot to take in at first glance.

A. Balcony (10 ft.)

A sturdy balcony made of stone with no railing is mounted 10 feet above the floor.

The tigers can only manage vertical leaps of 10 feet, so each of the leaping-holes has a balcony 10 feet below it that allows the tigers to clear the upward distance in two jumps. They can pounce downward from the leaping-hole all the way to the floor in a single leap, however. One of the saber-tooths watches the balcony through the leaping-hole (see **Area H-11,** the Tiger Run).

B. Leaping-Hole.

This is an arch-shaped opening in the wall, 20 feet from the floor. This presumably leads up to the second tier of the building.

Several leaping-holes are in the manor; they are designed to let the great cats pounce in and out of a room through a door humanoids can't reach. All of the leaping-holes have an adjacent balcony, as described above, to reduce the required vertical leap. One of the saber-tooths can come blasting down and out of the leaping-holes at full speed for an automatic raking-attack as well as front claws and bite. A quarter ton of fast moving saber-toothed tiger also knocks down anything smaller than a hill giant, and they don't need a to hit roll for the impact (they have to roll to hit normally for the claws and bite, of course).

As described in **A** above, one of the saber-tooths watches the balcony and can pounce directly to it if it sees prey.

Drawbridge and Ramp

A wide stone ramp leads up 20 feet to a spot roughly 10 feet from (and directly across from) one of the high-set archways. A drawbridge spans the gap and can clearly be opened to allow access to the second tier or closed to block the archway.

The drawbridge is usually down, allowing the bugbears and guests to move freely about the manor. If Kathelynn decides that she faces a measurable threat, she has this drawbridge pulled up to block the way into the higher tier.

D. Stairs to Loft

A narrow flight of stone stairs is flush against the south wall.

These stairs are too narrow for anything other than walking single file (and only just wide enough for one of the saber-tooths). They lead to **Area H-28**, a storage loft.

H-4. Tiger-Proof Stable

The large double doors, which seem extremely powerful for internal doors, even in a castle, lead into a closed-in stable. Two mules watch you placidly from inside their stalls, which is unsurprising. The third animal is most definitely unusual, though: it is a chestnut-brown warhorse, the sort that would ordinarily be found in the possession of a knight or noble. The warhorse is obviously much more nervous than the mules.

The design requirements of a stable in a castle where weretigers and saber-toothed tigers roam free are different than the requirements for a normal stable. The mounts only come out when the cats are safely occupied in other rooms, and make a beeline for the outside.

The warhorse belongs to Martin of Becqueril, the son of Baron Jauntir of Becqueril, who is willing to pay a considerable ransom (1,000 gp) for the return of his missing son. Martin has been enthralled by the lamia (see **Area H-19**).

Area H-5. Inside Bastion

This closed-in space can be entered only from one of the high-set holes in the wall. It contains two arrow slits that would allow an archer to loose arrows from inside the room.

If the characters announced their arrival by knocking on the door, or have given the entire manor time to prepare for combat, then Kathelynn the lamia is in this area to watch the characters in the covered courtyard (**Area H-3**). If endangered at all, she leaps out of the room and into the kitchen above (**Area H-7**). She won't necessarily attack; visitors might be bringing messages or interesting news of the outside world.

From here, she might possibly even speak to the characters since the arrow slit conceals the fact that her lower body is that of a white tiger. If she decides that her best course of action is to impersonate a human, she plays the trick here.

Area H-6. Great Hall (CR 2 or 4)

The walls of this room are hung with tapestries depicting saber-toothed tigers stalking and killing humans in the snowy crags and rifts of a mountainous region. Two fireplaces blaze with the crackle of pine wood, and three great wooden tables are set out with embroidered cloths and tableware.

Two confused-looking humans holding mops and buckets seem to have been working in the room.

If applicable, describe the bugbears to the players (see below)

This is the great hall where the denizens of the manor eat their meals and socialize, and also where visitors are brought to meet Kathelynn. There are always **1d2 bugbears** in the hall, if enough are left on the roster, and 2 human slaves. The slaves are **Caurien** and **Jirral**, both of them charmed by the lamia's magic. They won't help the bugbears or the characters if a fight occurs, but if Kathelynn or one of the weretigers is here and gives an order, they follow it. They won't follow the characters or act as lookouts; they have been told to mop the floor, and they aren't going to let themselves be sidetracked from that task.

If the characters check out the ceiling at all, they see a wooden loft running north/south over the eastern half of the room. It has wooden walls and no entrance to it is visible (the stairs to the loft are in the kitchen, **Area H-7**).

BUGBEARS (1d2) **CR 2**
XP 600
hp 16 each (*Pathfinder Roleplaying Game Bestiary* "Bugbear")

CAURIEN AND JIRRAL **CR 1**
XP 400
hp 23 (*Pathfinder Roleplaying Game GameMastery Guide* "Drunkard")

Treasure: The tapestries are worth a total of 100 gp and weigh 500 pounds altogether. The embroidered cloths on the tables are worth a total of 200 gp. The tableware is of no particular value.

Area H-7. Kitchen (CR 1)

This room is obviously the kitchen. A massive fireplace stands almost in the center of the room. Its chimney is a stone column that rises to the roof above. A fat man wearing a chef's hat is chopping vegetables at a large table in the center of the room, apparently preparing the stuffing for a roast goat, which also lies on the table.

In addition to these basics, the room has several entrances and exits:

A flight of stairs leads to a loft overhead.

Doors are in the north and south walls.

An archway in the west wall leads to another room on the same level as the kitchen.

An archway in the south wall drops down to the level below.

An archway in the north wall enters the room 20 feet above floor level. A ramp leads up along the east wall, behind the chimney, and ends 10 feet away from, and 10 feet below, the north archway.

The cook at the table is **Gaston Payis**, a normal human. He is a tremendously good cook; the weretigers kidnapped him from the town of Elet and brought him here specifically to become the manor's cook. Unlike the lamia's other slaves, Gaston is not charmed; the monsters decided it might somehow inhibit his cooking skills. He is utterly terrified of the other denizens of the manor, but he knows he couldn't possibly survive in the wilderness of the Ghostwind Pass long enough to get away. He may be hesitant to help the adventurers — since they might fail — unless it is clear that they are going to succeed in killing the lamia and the weretigers. Because if they fail, what then for Gaston Payis, who betrayed the tigers?

Various kitchen supplies are kept in boxes under the table, including knives, pots, pans, buckets, and the like.

GASTON PAYIS **CR 1**
XP 400
hp 23 (*Pathfinder Roleplaying Game GameMastery Guide* "Drunkard")

Gear club, a butcher knife and 5 gp

Area H-8. Storage Room

This room contains crates and sacks on the floor, and several shelves on the walls contain earthenware pots and wine bottles.

This is the kitchen's storage room. It has flour, sugar, herbs, cheese, and various other ingredients found in kitchens. Most of the wine is poor quality (total 300 gp) with the exception of 5 bottles of Chateau d'Ambre, which can be sold for as much as 200 gp each in a large enough town. One of the crates has a piece of parchment nailed to it, which reads: "For delivery, Henri Tharnac of Elet." (Henri is a merchant who deals with the manor, see **Area H-17**).

Area H-9. Cook's Quarters

This modest room contains a bed, table, chair, and an unlocked wooden cabinet.

This is Gaston the cook's room (see **Area H-7**). Nothing is here to interest the adventurers.

Area H-10. Foyer (CR 7)

This room's largest feature is another ramp-and-drawbridge arrangement like the one on the lower tier. It is on the north wall and obviously leads to the manor's third tier. A balcony is on either side of the drawbridge, 10 feet above the floor, and the ramp/archway are 20 feet above the floor. A wooden-walled loft runs north/south over the middle of the room, but has no visible entrances or exits.

Most of the area is bare stone, but a little island of luxury sits in the eastern part of the room. Three armchairs are grouped around a delicate wooden table on a flower-patterned carpet.

There is also some sort of decorative pool in the western part of the room.

A gentleman is sitting in one of the armchairs, unless the alarm has already been sounded. This is **Claude**, one of Kathelynn's weretiger sons. He wears a black robe and sandals; he looks a bit like a monk, but wears no holy symbol. The robe is what Claude always wears; it keeps him from tearing his clothes when he transforms into a tiger.

If the characters are trying to trick their way in, Claude is not easily fooled and they need to succeed a DC 25 Bluff check because he is usually the one of the three brothers whom Kathelynn sends to the town of Elet on errands such as kidnapping people or dealing with merchants.

Indeed, the flowers on the carpet are red roses, if PCs succeed a DC 20 Perception check. Kathelynn is as obsessed with her heraldic symbols as any knight.

The pool in the western part of the room is not more than 3 inches deep. It has a shallow, concave bottom that appears to be coated in silver making the pool so reflective that it is almost a perfect mirror. This pool is actually a scrying bowl, DC 20 Knowledge (arcane) check to identify, Kathelynn can use to find the location of intruders in her manor, and direct her defenses against them.

If the manor is widely alerted to the presence of armed strangers, the monsters' fighting contingent assembles here (see the roster for details).

CLAUDE (HUMAN FORM) **CR 7**
XP 3,200
Male human natural weretiger ranger 7 (*Pathfinder Roleplaying Game Bestiary 2* "Lycanthrope, Weretiger")
NE Medium humanoid (human, shapechanger)
Init +5; **Senses** low-light vision, scent; Perception +10

AC 17, touch 14, flat-footed 15 (+2 armor, +2 deflection, +1 Dex, +1 dodge, +1 natural)
hp 64 (7d10+14 plus 7)

Fort +7; **Ref** +6; **Will** +4

Speed 30 ft. (20 ft. in armor)
Special Attacks combat style (natural weapon), curse of lycanthropy, favored enemies (elves +2, humans +4)
Ranger Spells Prepared (CL 4th; concentration +4)

Str 18, **Dex** 13, **Con** 14, **Int** 10, **Wis** 10, **Cha** 10
Base Atk +7; **CMB** +11; **CMD** 25
Feats Dodge[B], Endurance, Improved Initiative, Iron Will, Power Attack[B], Rending Claws*, Toughness[B], Weapon Focus (claw)
Skills Acrobatics +5 (+1 to jump), Bluff +7, Climb +10, Diplomacy +5 (+9 to change attitude vs. animals related to lycanthropic form), Intimidate +8, Perception +10, Sense Motive +5, Stealth +8, Survival +9, Swim +5
Languages Common
SQ change forms, favored terrain (cold +2), hunter's bond (companions), lycanthropic empathy, track +3, wild empathy +7, woodland stride
Gear *amulet of natural armor +1*, *bracers of armor +2*, *ring of protection +2*
*See *Pathfinder Roleplaying Game Advanced Player's Guide*

CLAUDE (HYBRID FORM) **CR 7**
XP 3,200
Human natural weretiger ranger 7 (*Pathfinder Roleplaying Game Bestiary 2* "Lycanthrope, Weretiger")
NE Large humanoid (human, shapechanger)
Init +6; **Senses** low-light vision, scent; **Perception** +12

AC 22, touch 14, flat-footed 19 (+2 armor, +2 deflection, +2 Dex, +1 dodge, +6 natural, –1 size)
hp 78 (7d10+28 plus 7)
Fort +9; **Ref** +7; **Will** +6
DR 10/silver

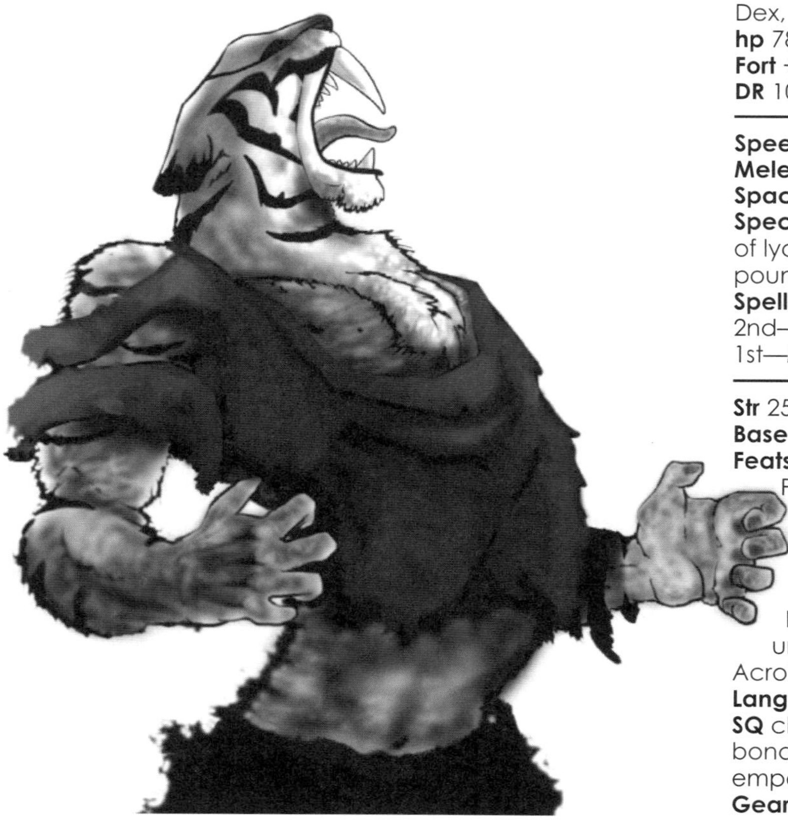

Speed 30 ft.
Melee bite +13 (2d6+7), 2 claws +14 (1d8+7 plus grab)
Space 10 ft.; **Reach** 10 ft.
Special Attacks combat style (natural weapon), curse of lycanthropy, favored enemies (elves +2, humans +4), pounce, rake (2 claws +14, 1d8+7 plus grab)
Spells Prepared (CL 4th; concentration +6):
2nd—*cure light wounds*
1st—*longstrider*, *magic fang*

Str 18/25, **Dex** 13/15, **Con** 14/19, **Int** 10, **Wis** 10/14, **Cha** 10
Base Atk +7; **CMB** +15 (+19 grapple); **CMD** 30
Feats Dodge[B], Endurance, Improved Initiative, Iron Will, Power Attack[B], Rending Claws*, Toughness[B], Weapon Focus (claw)
Skills Acrobatics +13, Bluff +7, Climb +16, Diplomacy +5 (+9 to change attitude vs. animals related to lycanthropic form), Intimidate +8, Perception +12, Sense Motive +7, Stealth +12 (+16 in undergrowth), Survival +11, Swim +11; **Racial Modifiers** +4 Acrobatics, +4 Stealth in undergrowth
Languages Common
SQ change forms, favored terrain (cold +2), hunter's bond (companions), lycanthropic empathy, track +3, wild empathy +7, woodland stride
Gear *amulet of natural armor +1*, *bracers of armor +2*, *ring of protection +2*
*See *Pathfinder Roleplaying Game Advanced Player's Guide*

CLAUDE (TIGER FORM) **CR 7**
XP 3,200
Male human natural weretiger ranger 7 (*Pathfinder Roleplaying Game Bestiary 2* "Lycanthrope, Weretiger")
NE Large humanoid (human, shapechanger)
Init +6; **Senses** low-light vision, scent; Perception +12

AC 22, touch 14, flat-footed 19 (+2 armor, +2 deflection, +2 Dex, +1 dodge, +6 natural, –1 size)
hp 78 (7d10+28 plus 7)
Fort +9, **Ref** +7, **Will** +6
DR 10/silver

Speed 40 ft.
Melee bite +13 (2d6+7), 2 claws +14 (1d8+7 plus grab)
Space 10 ft.; **Reach** 10 ft.
Special Attacks combat style (natural weapon), curse of lycanthropy, favored enemies (elves +2, humans +4), pounce, rake (2 claws +14, 1d8+7 plus grab)
Spells Prepared (CL 4th; concentration +6):
2nd—*cure light wounds*
1st—*longstrider*, *magic fang*

Str 25, **Dex** 15, **Con** 19, **Int** 10, **Wis** 14, **Cha** 10
Base Atk +7; **CMB** +15 (+19 grapple); **CMD** 30
Feats Dodge[B], Endurance, Improved Initiative, Iron Will, Power Attack[B], Rending Claws*, Toughness[B], Weapon Focus (claw)
Skills Acrobatics +13 (+17 to jump), Bluff +7, Climb +16, Diplomacy +5 (+9 to change attitude vs. animals related to lycanthropic form), Intimidate +8, Perception +12, Sense Motive +7, Stealth +12 (+16 in undergrowth), Survival +11, Swim +11; **Racial Modifiers** +4 Acrobatics, +4 Stealth in undergrowth
Languages Common
SQ change forms, favored terrain (cold +2), hunter's bond (companions), lycanthropic empathy, track +3, wild empathy +7, woodland stride
Gear *amulet of natural armor +1*, *bracers of armor +2*, *ring of*

protection +2
**See Pathfinder Roleplaying Game Advanced Player's Guide*

Area H-11. Tiger Run (CR 5)

The south end of this hallway has a jumping-hole leading down to the manor's lowest tier, and the north end has a jumping-hole 20 feet up the wall leading to the top tier, with a balcony below it.

Unless the saber-tooths are all killed by the time the characters get here, one of the **smilodon** is sitting here watching the leaping-hole, like a cat outside a mouse hole.

SMILODON CR 5
XP 1,600
The Tome of Horrors Complete 692
N Medium animal
Init +2; **Senses** low-light vision; **Perception** +9

AC 15, touch 12, flat-footed 13 (+2 Dex, +3 natural)
hp 51 (6d8+24)
Fort +9; **Ref** +7; **Will** +3

Speed 40 ft.
Melee bite +10 (1d8+6 plus grab plus bleed), 2 claws +10 (1d4+6 plus grab)
Special Attacks bleed (1d3), pounce, rake (2 claws +10, 1d4+6)

Str 23, **Dex** 15, **Con** 19, **Int** 2, **Wis** 12, **Cha** 6
Base Atk +4; **CMB** +10 (+14 grapple); **CMD** 22 (26 vs. trip)
Feats Power Attack, Run, Skill Focus (Perception)
Skills Acrobatics +10 (+14 jump), Perception +9, Stealth +11 (+15 in heavy undergrowth or tall grass), Swim +10;
Racial Modifiers +4 Acrobatics, +4 Stealth (+8 in heavy undergrowth or tall grass)

Area H-12. Bugbear Quarters (CR 8)

Ten very big beds are topped with shaggy sleeping furs in this rather rancid-smelling room. A substantial wooden table is in the middle of the room, looking like it has taken a beating and been repaired several times. A door is in the far wall, with a knife sticking in it.

This is the room where the manor's bugbears sleep. If the characters get this far, assume that all of the **bugbears** (with the exception of the ones that have set locations on the map key) are here.

A burlap sack is underneath each of the beds, but these are used for non-valuables, and the characters find nothing in them but dirty clothes, bones, and the occasional mouse.

BUGBEAR (10) CR 2
XP 600
hp 16 each (*Pathfinder Roleplaying Game Bestiary* "Bugbear")

Development: If any combat happens in this room, Glaivorn the Overseer (**Area H-13**) joins the fight in 1d3 rounds.

Treasure: Other than what they carry in their pouches, all of the bugbears keep their treasure in Glaivorn's chest in individual bags.

Area H-13. Bugbear Overseer (CR 5)

This room is a bedroom with a table, bed, sturdy chair, and a wicker basket filled with clothes. A large, padlocked wooden chest is in the northeast corner of the room, with a smaller iron box beside it.

This room belongs to **Glaivorn**, the bugbear who oversees all menial work done in the manor. He wears a black tunic embroidered with Kathelynn's red rose symbol.

GLAIVORN, BUGBEAR LEADER CR 5
XP 1,600
Male bugbear barbarian 3 (*Pathfinder Roleplaying Game Bestiary* "Bugbear")
CE Medium humanoid (goblinoid)
Init +0; **Senses** darkvision 60 ft., scent; **Perception** +7

AC 22, touch 11, flat-footed 22 (+7 armor, +1 deflection, +4 natural)
hp 50 (3d8+9 plus 3d12+9)
Fort +8; **Ref** +5; **Will** +4
Defensive Abilities trap sense +1, uncanny dodge

Speed 30 ft.
Melee *+1 greataxe* +12 (1d12+8/×3)
Special Attacks rage (11 rounds/day), rage power (swift foot +5 ft)

Str 20, **Dex** 10, **Con** 17, **Int** 12, **Wis** 13, **Cha** 8
Base Atk +5; **CMB** +10; **CMD** 21
Feats; Improved Natural Armor, Power Attack[B], Weapon Focus (greataxe)
Skills Acrobatics +3, Climb +5, Heal +5, Intimidate +12, Perception +7, Sense Motive +3, Stealth +9, Survival +8;
Racial Modifiers +4 Intimidate, +4 Stealth
Languages Common, Goblin, Infernal
SQ fast movement
Combat Gear *potion of cure moderate wounds, potion of haste*; **Other Gear** *+1 chainmail, +1 greataxe, cloak of resistance +1, ring of protection +1*, key to iron box in **Area H-13**, 33 gp

The large wooden chest contains 10 leather bags, each containing the treasure of one of the bugbears.

Bag #1: 15 gp, gold earring with pearl (100 gp), 2 dwarf-bone dice
Bag #2: 22 gp, 28 sp, 119 cp, cat skull with "bad kitty" written on it in Goblin, iron ring with quartz stone (1sp).
Bag #3: 169 gp and a hand mirror (10 gp)
Bag #4: 56 gp, 260 sp, 2 cp, and a set of ivory false teeth (25 gp)
Bag #5: 9 gp, 28 sp, bracelet of wooden thorns (worthless), someone's finger bone, crushed-velvet hat (1 gp) with broken feather, polished obsidian fish (50 gp)
Bag #6: large sewing needle, thread, pincers, thumbscrews, and a large piece of amber containing a preserved lizard (200 gp)
Bag #7: 16 gp, 189 sp, 295 cp, 1 wad of chewing tobacco (1 cp)
Bag #8: 6 gp, 505 sp, 2 rolled-up ermine furs (normal-size and lower quality, at 100 gp each)
Bag #9: 35 gp, 69 sp, 12 cp
Bag #10: 8 gp, wax candle (1 sp)

Glaivorn's own treasure is in the smaller iron box. It is locked (DC 30 Disable Device, or Glaivorn has a key) and has a poison needle **trap** on the catch.

POISON NEEDLE TRAP **CR 8**
XP 4,800
Type mechanical; **Perception** DC 30; **Disable Device** DC 23

Trigger touch **Reset** repair
Effect Atk +15 melee (2d4+2 damage plus poison [blue whinnis]).
Blue Whinnis Poison—Type poison, injury; **Save** Fortitude DC 14; **Frequency** 1/round for 2 rounds;
Initial Effect 1 Con damage; **Secondary Effect** unconsciousness for 1d3 hours; **Cure** 1 save

Treasure: The box contains 10 gp, 16 sp, 31 cp, and a silver brooch inlaid with jade and garnet (300 gp).

Area H-14. Central Hall

This broad stone hallway is accessed by one of the odd ramp-and-drawbridge arrangements, and has doors on the west and east walls.

What is not apparent in this room is the concealed trapdoor in the ceiling (DC 25 Perception check). If Kathelynn is cornered in her rooms and tries to circle around the characters through her escape loft (**Area H-30** is above the trapdoor), this is where she jumps down.

Area H-15. Tiger Den (CR 5)

This large room contains boulders, apparently brought into the manor from the outside. They range from 4–6 feet in diameter. The remains of a goat, not much more than bones, are widely scattered about, and fresh blood is splashed on one of the larger rocks. A door is in the room's north wall.

This is the playroom for Kathelynn's grey saber-toothed tigers, which, along with the weretigers, she refers to as her "children." If the characters reach this room, assume that all the saber-toothed tigers remaining on the roster are in here.

The door in the north wall is locked and PCs must succeed on a DC 20 Disable Device to unlock.

SMILODON **CR 5**
XP 1,600
hp 51 (See **Area H-11**)

Area H-16. Weretiger Room (Thibault) (CR 7)

This room is luxuriously furnished, with a velvet-draped feather bed, a locked iron chest, several thick rugs covering the floor, and woolen tapestries on the walls.

Thibault (*Ti*-bawlt) is Kathelynn's youngest son, a white weretiger. Unless the characters launched a frontal assault on the manor, they most likely encounter Thibault first in his human form. He is a tall and handsome man with a long ponytail, long mustaches, and bushy eyebrows, all extremely blond. His yellow eyes are a bit disconcerting, but they have normal, round pupils rather than a cat's.

THIBAULT (HUMAN FORM) **CR 7**
XP 3,200
Male human natural weretiger fighter 7 (*Pathfinder Roleplaying Game Bestiary* 2 "Lycanthrope, Weretiger")
NE Medium humanoid (human, shapechanger)
Init +7; **Senses** low-light vision, scent; **Perception** +6

AC 15, touch 14, flat-footed 11 (+1 armor, +3 Dex, +1 dodge)
hp 57 (7d10+7 plus 7)
Fort +6; **Ref** +5; **Will** +4 (+6 vs. fear)
Defenisve Abilities bravery +2

Speed 30 ft.
Special Attacks curse of lycanthropy, weapon training (natural +1)

Str 14, **Dex** 17, **Con** 12, **Int** 10, **Wis** 11, **Cha** 11
Base Atk +7; **CMB** +9; **CMD** 23
Feats Blind-fight[B], Dodge[B], Improved Initiative[B], Iron Will[B], Lunge, Mobility, Power Attack, Rending Claws*, Weapon Focus (claw)
Skills Acrobatics +6, Diplomacy +0 (+4 to change attitude vs. animals related to lycanthropic form), Intimidate +5, Perception +6, Sense Motive +4, Stealth +13, Survival +4
Languages Common
SQ armor training 2, change forms, lycanthropic empathy
Combat Gear *potion of rage*; **Other Gear** *bracers of armor +1*, *cloak of elvenkind*, *dire collar*, locked box key, 250 gp
*See *Pathfinder Roleplaying Game Advanced Player's Guide*

THIBAULT (HYBRID FORM) **CR 7**
XP 3,200
Male human natural weretiger fighter 7 (*Pathfinder Roleplaying Game Bestiary* 2 "Lycanthrope, Weretiger")
NE Large humanoid (human, shapechanger)
Init +7; **Senses** low-light vision, scent; **Perception** +8

AC 19, touch 13, flat-footed 15 (+1 armor, +3 Dex, +1 dodge, +5 natural, -1 size)
hp 78 (7d10+28 plus 7)
Fort +9; **Ref** +5; **Will** +6 (+8 vs. fear)
DR 10/silver
Defenisve Abilities bravery +2

Speed 30 ft.
Melee bite +14 (2d6+8), 2 claws +15 (1d8+10 plus grab)
Space 10 ft.; **Reach** 10 ft.
Special Attacks curse of lycanthropy, pounce, rake (2 claws +15, 1d8+8 plus grab), weapon training (natural +1)

Str 14/25, **Dex** 17, **Con** 12/19, **Int** 10, **Wis** 11/14, **Cha** 11
Base Atk +7; **CMB** +15 (+19 grapple); **CMD** 29
Feats Blind-fight[B], Dodge[B], Improved Initiative[B], Iron Will[B], Lunge, Mobility, Power Attack, Rending Claws*, Weapon Focus (claw)
Skills Acrobatics +10, Intimidate +5, Perception +8, Sense Motive +6, Stealth +13 (+17 in undergrowth), Survival +6;
Racial Modifiers +4 Acrobatics, +4 Stealth in undergrowth
Languages Common
SQ armor training 2, change forms, lycanthropic empathy
Combat Gear *potion of rage*; **Other Gear** *bracers of armor*

+1, *cloak of elvenkind*, *dire collar*, locked box key, 250 gp
*See *Pathfinder Roleplaying Game Advanced Player's Guide*

THIBAULT (TIGER FORM) **CR 7**
XP 3,200
Male human natural weretiger fighter 7 (*Pathfinder Roleplaying Game Bestiary 2* "Lycanthrope, Weretiger")
NE Large humanoid (human, shapechanger)
Init +7; **Senses** low-light vision, scent; **Perception** +8

AC 19, touch 13, flat-footed 15 (+1 armor, +3 Dex, +1 dodge, +5 natural, -1 size)
hp 78 (7d10+28 plus 7)
Fort +9; **Ref** +5; **Will** +6 (+8 vs. fear)
DR 10/silver
Defenisve Abilities bravery +2

Speed 40 ft.
Melee bite +14 (2d6+8), 2 claws +15 (1d8+10 plus grab)
Space 10 ft.; **Reach** 10 ft.
Special Attacks curse of lycanthropy, pounce, rake (2 claws +15, 1d8+10 plus grab), weapon training (natural +1)

Str 25, **Dex** 17, **Con** 19, **Int** 10, **Wis** 14, **Cha** 11
Base Atk +7; **CMB** +15 (+19 grapple); **CMD** 29
Feats Blind-fight[B], Dodge[B], Improved Initiative[B], Iron Will[B], Lunge, Mobility, Power Attack, Rending Claws*, Weapon Focus (claw)
Skills Acrobatics +10 (+14 to jump), Diplomacy +0 (+4 to change attitude vs. animals related to lycanthropic form), Intimidate +5, Perception +8, Sense Motive +6, Stealth +13 (+17 in undergrowth), Survival +6;
Racial Modifiers +4 Acrobatics, +4 Stealth in undergrowth
Languages Common
SQ armor training 2, change forms, lycanthropic empathy
Combat Gear *potion of rage*; **Other Gear** *bracers of armor +1*, *cloak of elvenkind*, *dire collar*, locked box key, 250 gp
*See *Pathfinder Roleplaying Game Advanced Player's Guide*

Treasure: The velvet bedclothes are worth 200 gp, and the rugs (weighing 300 pounds in total) are worth 200 gp. The locked iron box (DC 30 Disable Device) contains a leather bag with a drawstring, with 56 gp, 229 sp, 3 pearls (300 gp).

Area H-17. Guestroom (Henri Tharnac) (CR 5)

> This room contains a featherbed with a quilt. There is a nightstand with a candlestick on it, and a backpack on the floor. A man sits at a small writing desk.

This man is **Henri Tharnac**, a merchant from Elet. He visits the manor when it is not snowed in to deliver supplies and to take orders for the next delivery. Henri is quite aware of his customers' monstrous nature, but he allows himself to assume that they do not actually kill people. After all, he delivers large quantities of salted meat and even drives small herds of goats here.

HENRI THARNAC **CR 5**
XP 1,600
hp 31 (*Pathfinder Roleplaying Game GameMastery Guide* "Traveling Merchant")

Area H-18. Slaves' Quarters (CR 8)

> Two humans are asleep on straw pallets in this room, which contains two empty pallets as well. The people are dressed in clothing that was once of extremely fine quality but is now stained and torn.

Four of the lamia's human slaves share this room as their sleeping quarters. Two of them, Caurien and Jirral, are in the Great Hall (**Area H-6**). The other two, **Serz** and **Cloyaun**, are the ones currently in the room. Serz and Cloyaun were originally courtiers in the service of Martin of Becqueril, but, like Martin, they are now under the lamia's spell and are her willing servants. They have been put to cleaning and other menial tasks, but they bear no resentment at all. Serz is quite pudgy, but Cloyaun looks like he is half-starved. They actually receive different quantities of food; Serz is being fattened up for slaughter.

SERZ **CR 5**
XP 1,600
hp 30 (*Pathfinder Roleplaying Game GameMastery Guide* "Minstrel")

CLOYAUN **CR 7**
XP 3,200
hp 80 (*Pathfinder Roleplaying Game GameMastery Guide* "Sellsword")

Area H-19. Martin's Guestroom (CR 8)

> This room is furnished with a cot, a wooden chest, and a small writing table. A peg on the wall holds an expensive green cloak of boiled wool, trimmed with what looks like fox fur.
> A dreamy-eyed man sits at the table, clad in the fine clothes of a nobleman.

This room belongs to the Mountain Queen's "guest," **Martin of Becqueril**. Martin is the heir to a barony and was hunting with three of his courtiers in the pass when Kathelynn came upon them. Returning with the weretigers, she made short work of kidnapping all of them and returning to the manor with the unfortunate captives, DC 25 Knowledge (local) or DC 20 Knowledge (nobility) to have heard rumors of this kidnapping. One of the courtiers is now dead and eaten; the other three, including Martin, are alive but have been drained of all their wisdom and are Kathelynn's slaves.

It is not readily apparent that Martin has been mentally emptied out. He tends to be excitable and babble on about nothing, unless Kathelynn is nearby, in which case he immediately becomes completely alert, hanging on her every word. A substantial reward is offered for his return, which is paid by the Baron of Becqueril, and the next mission offered to the characters might be to help get Martin back to his former mental condition (which was never particularly remarkable, but at least involved free will).

MARTIN OF BECQUERIL **CR 8**
XP 4,800
hp 60 (*Pathfinder Roleplaying Game GameMastery Guide* "Noble")

Area H-20. Empty Guestrooms

> This room contains a comfortable featherbed and a wooden chest. A thick wool carpet covers the floor, and the walls are hung with heavy tapestries for warmth.

These rooms are given to Kathelynn's guests. The locks work properly, and the guest is given the key. Even if the door is locked from the outside (using another key), the guest can unlock it again from the inside.

Area H-21. Treacherous Guestroom

> This room contains a comfortable featherbed and a wooden chest. A thick wool carpet covers the floor, and the walls are hung with heavy tapestries for warmth.

This room is given to guests that might cause problems in some way, or guests that need to be gotten rid of. As with the other guestrooms, the guest is given a key. However, the lock in this door is unusual; it can be locked from the outside with a different key, and if this is done, the guest key cannot unlock it from the inside. Thus, a guest can be neatly confined in the room while any companions are dealt with. The door itself appears to be made of wood, but it is in fact wood panels covering an iron door (hardness 10, hp 60, Break DC 30).

Area H-22. The Unpleasant Minstrel (CR 7)

> This room contains a bed, a chest, a small table, and a chair. A lute and a small set of bagpipes hang on wall pegs.
> A man dressed in a multicolored tunic is reading through several parchment sheets that appear to be musical notations.

The manor's minstrel, **Cap Jongleur**, lives in this room for the time being. He is not charmed by the lamia, nor does he have any particular problem living with a clan of psychotic monsters. He is confident that if he ever needs to escape, it will make a great story to turn into a ballad. It doesn't occur to him that he might not survive to the end of the ballad.

CAP JONGLEUR CR 7
XP 3,200
Male human skald (spell warrior) 8 (*Pathfinder Roleplaying Game Advanced Class Guide* "Skald")
CE Medium humanoid (human)
Init +2; **Perception** +10
Aura evil

AC 18, touch 13, flat-footed 16 (+5 armor, +1 deflection, +2 Dex)
hp 47 (8d8 plus 8)
Fort +6; **Ref** +6; **Will** +5; +4 vs. bardic performance, language-dependent, and sonic
Defensive Abilities improved uncanny dodge

Speed 30 ft.
Melee *+1 spiked gauntlet* +7/+2 (1d4+3) and *+1 spiked gauntlet* +7 (1d4+3)
Special Attacks rage powers (animal fury, scent), raging song 20 rounds/day (move action; enhance weapons, song of marching, song of strength)
Spells Known (CL 8th; concentration +11):
3rd (3/day)—*dispel magic, gaseous form, see invisibility*
2nd (5/day)—*blindness/deafness* (DC 15), *blur, detect thoughts* (DC 15), *hold person* (DC 15)
1st (5/day)—*cause fear* (DC 14), *charm person* (DC 14), *cure light wounds, ear-piercing scream** (DC 14), *grease*
0 (at will)—*detect magic, light, mage hand, message, read magic, resistance*

Str 15, **Dex** 15, **Con** 10, **Int** 12, **Wis** 8, **Cha** 16
Base Atk +6; **CMB** +8; **CMD** 21
Feats Combat Casting, Double Slice[B], Eschew Materials, Improved Counterspell, Lightning Reflexes, Two-weapon Fighting[B]
Skills Acrobatics +10, Appraise +6, Knowledge (arcana) +15, Perception +10, Perform (oratory) +11, Perform (sing) +14, Spellcraft +8, Stealth +10, Swim +6
Languages Common, Infernal
SQ bardic knowledge +4, greater counterspell, lore master 1/day, rage powers, versatile performances (oratory, sing)
Gear *+1 mithral shirt, +1 spiked gauntlet, +1 spiked gauntlet, ring of protection +1*
*See *Pathfinder Roleplaying Game Ultimate Magic*

Treasure: Lute, bagpipes, chest containing 3 sets of clothes, lady's handkerchief (a favor from his days singing in Elet), another lady's handkerchief, embroidered with a red rose (a token from Kathelynn), a golden bracelet (50 gp), a belt pouch containing 25 gp, and a backpack containing 5 days' rations, a winter cloak, fur-lined boots, a half-gallon waterskin (full), and a short sword.

Area H-23. Empty Guestroom

> This room contains a comfortable featherbed and a wooden chest. A thick wool carpet covers the floor, and the walls are hung with heavy tapestries for warmth.

This was the guestroom assigned to a huntsman named Ormant Ulute who was recently killed, cooked, and served to the monsters and Kathelynn's charmed slaves (Martin, etc.). Ormant happened upon Cap Jongleur (**Area H-22**) playing bagpipes by a nearby mountain stream, and Cap invited him back to the manor for dinner. Kathelynn was so amused by the prank that she gave the minstrel a token of affection, deciding to keep him alive for at least another month. Ormant, on the other hand, was served for dinner after a couple of days as an honored guest.

Ormant suspected something was not quite right in the manor and wrote a note, which he hid under the mattress along with a *+1 dagger* (hoping that the next person to sleep in the bed would feel the dagger and find the hidden note).

The note reads:

"I fear I have fallen in among monsters. Do not trust the singer. Run. Have the abbot sing prayers for me, if you find this and live. Signed, Ormant Ulute."

Area H-24. Stairs to Dungeon

> A stone staircase leads down.

This staircase leads to the cellars (**Areas H-31** through **H-36**), first arriving in **Area H-31**, the dungeon cellar.

Area H-25. Lamia's Antechamber

The walls of this room are bare stone with only two decorations. The first is a suit of armor carrying a shield in one corner. The second is a large basin in the center of the room, mounted on a 4-foot stone pedestal.

The suit of armor is *+1 full plate mail*, and the shield bears the sigil of a red rose. The red paint on the rose is still wet, and remains so until it is removed, leaving a white rose beneath. This is the *Shield of St. Elys*, which Kathelynn grabbed by accident when she fled the scene of her sister's murder

Shield of St. Elys

SHIELD OF ST. ELYS
Aura moderate evocation; **CL** 6th
Slot shield; **Price** 5,580 gp; **Weight** 15 lbs.

DESCRIPTION

This +1 *champion* heavy steel shield is has a large central white rose. Once per day the user of this shield may empower his attack and make a single melee attack at your highest base attack bonus that deals additional damage. Roll the weapon's damage dice for the attack twice and add the results together before adding bonuses from Strength, weapon abilities (such as *flaming*), precision-based damage, and other damage bonuses. These extra weapon damage dice are not multiplied on a critical hit, but are added to the total.

CONSTRUCTION

Requirements Craft Magic Arms and Armor, Vital Strike, *bless, protection from evil*; **Cost** 2,875 gp

The basin contains water, and its bottom is coated with silver, making it highly reflective. This is Kathelynn's scrying basin. It is not inherently magical, but it provides a place for the lamia to "see" what her magic reveals.

Area H-26. Lamia's Bedchamber (CR 9)

The walls of this room are lurid with blood-red tapestries, and the floor is painted red as well. A four-poster bed is against the southern wall, with closed curtains that look uncomfortably like crimson-dyed human skins stitched together. A high loft is placed above and just to the south of the room, but no ladder or stair leads up to it. The strangest feature of the room, though, is the east wall, which is entirely covered by a blooming rosebush: tangled thorns, red flowers, and green leaves grow more than a foot deep all the way to the ceiling. A door leads through this hedge, but at first glance it looks as if it is covered in thorns as well.

A window in the north wall looks out over the mountainous scenery behind the manor.

This is the lamia's bedchamber. If the manor is taken entirely by surprise, she is found here. It is also the room to which she flees if a battle is going badly, because the loft has a secret exit from the roof (see **Area H-30**, the Escape Loft).

Kathelynn has the torso of a human female, but the lower body of a white tiger. Her face looks human, although her canine teeth are quite long and the irises of her eyes are a golden color. She has a vertical scar on the left side of her face. If the characters have seen the painting of St. Kathelynn in the abbey's chapel, the resemblance is remarkable (DC 10 Perception check).

The rosebush over the east wall is real, although it is created by magic. The thorns drip with poison (**Type** poison (injury); **Save** Fortitude DC 15, **Frequency** 1/round for 6 rounds; **Effect** 1d4 Con damage; **Cure** 1 save), and the thick branches regenerate almost instantly. See the preface to **Area H-27** for more information about the rosebush.

There is no window in the north wall, as the characters might know if they scouted the outside of the manor. It is an illusion permanently (DC 15 Will save) placed to conceal a niche in the wall that contains a key. Anyone touching the window immediately detects the illusion, although it does not disappear when detected. If the character feels around behind the "window," the niche is found easily, and the key recovered.

KATHELYNN **CR 9**
XP 6,400
Female lamia antipaladin 6 (*Pathfinder Roleplaying Game Bestiary* "Lamia"; *Pathfinder Roleplaying Game Advanced Player's Guide* "Antipaladin")
CE Large monstrous humanoid
Init +3; **Senses** darkvision 60 ft.; **Perception** +15

AC 21, touch 13, flat-footed 18 (+1 deflection, +2 Dex, +1 dodge, +8 natural, –1 size)
hp 146 (9d10+36 plus 6d10+24 plus 6)
Fort +14; **Ref** +10; **Will** +14
Immune disease; **Resist** cold 20

Speed 60 ft.
Melee *+1 heavy mace* +21/+16/+11 (1d8+6) or 2 claws +19 (1d4+5)
Space 10 ft.; **Reach** 5 ft.
Special Attacks channel negative energy 3/day (DC 17, 3d6), smite good
Spell-Like Abilities (CL 9th; concentration +13):
At will— *disguise self, ventriloquism* (DC 15)
3/day—*charm monster* (DC 17), *major image* (DC 17), *mirror image, suggestion* (DC 16)
1/day—*deep slumber* (DC 16)
Spell-Like Abilities (CL 3rd; concentration +7):
At will—*detect good*
Spells Prepared (CL 3rd; concentration +7):
1st—*murderous command** (DC 15), *savage maw***

Str 20, **Dex** 14, **Con** 18, **Int** 17, **Wis** 17, **Cha** 18
Base Atk +15; **CMB** +21; **CMD** 35 (39 vs. trip)
Feats Blind-Fight, Dodge, Great Fortitude[B], Iron Will, Mobility, Spring Attack, Warrior Priest[B*], Weapon Focus (heavy mace)[B]
Skills Acrobatics +4 (+16 to jump), Appraise +10, Bluff +15, Climb +10, Diplomacy +8, Disguise +12, Handle Animal +10, Heal +5, Intimidate +14, Knowledge (arcana) +8, Knowledge (dungeoneering) +4, Knowledge (local) +4, Knowledge (planes) +6, Knowledge (religion) +12, Perception +15, Sense Motive +11, Spellcraft +15, Stealth +15, Survival +12, Swim +10; **Racial Modifiers** +4 Bluff, +4 Stealth
Languages Abyssal, Celestial, Common, Infernal
SQ aura of cowardice, aura of evil, channel negative energy, cruelties (cruelty [dazed], cruelty [shaken]), fiendish boon (fiendish boon [weapon]), touch of corruption, unholy resilience, wisdom drain
Combat Gear *potion of cure moderate wounds, potion of spider climb*; **Other Gear** *+1 heavy mace, amulet of natural armor +1, ring of protection +1*, the *Eye of Othroäta* (a very large, multi-faceted gem worn around Kathelynn's neck on a detachable gold chain), jewelry (worth 500 gp), drinking horn, pouch containing 30 gp and the key to **Area H-25**.
*See *Pathfinder Roleplaying Game Ultimate Magic*
**See *Pathfinder Roleplaying Game Advanced Race Guide*

Treasure: The lamia does not keep her treasure in this room, but a longbow and an "escape kit" are in a leather bag next to the bed. The backpack contains a longbow and quiver with 20 arrows, a heavy winter coat, a waterskin, rations for 5 days, a pouch with 30 gp and 3 emeralds worth 1,000 gp each

The full description of the Staff of the Remorhaz if the top piece is connected to the shaft is listed in area **A-7 Graves**

Eye of Othroäta (Major Artifact)

Aura overwhelming abjuration; **CL** 24th
Slot neck; **Weight** 1 lb.

DESCRIPTION

This multi-faceted gem has an array of shifting colors when gazed upon. It currently dangles on a golden chain, but has a small clasp at its bottom that enables it to be fitted to the shaft of a staff. When worn as a necklace or secured on a staff it continually grants the user to gain cold resistance 20.

If the Eye *of Othroäta* is secured to the other half of its artifact *Staff of the Remorhaz* it grants it full powers on the wielder.

DESTRUCTION

The only way to destroy the eye is to bathe it in the still-hot blood of a remorhaz.

Area H-27. Treasure Room (CR 6)

This iron door (hardness 10, hp 60, break DC 30) to the treasure room is powerfully protected with magic wards (Resist all energy types 20), the source of the rosebush that covers the entire wall. The door has no latch or knob; its only feature is a bas-relief rose carved in the middle of it. Rose branches, covered in inch-long thorns, radiate outward from the carving and then thicken to cover the wall. It is not visible from here, but the vinelike branches penetrate the walls at the corners and top, forming this wall and a cage around the interior of the room.

The rose has a round hole in the middle, an inch in diameter, creating a tunnel that goes about 2 inches into the door, and ends in a small round chamber with a hole in the bottom (thus, an item less than an inch across can be pushed into the chamber, and would then drop through the hole). The *Eye of Othroäta*, currently worn around Kathelynn's neck on a detachable gold chain, must be pushed in here to drop into the treasure room on the other side. The *Eye* cannot be dropped in on a string and fished back out; it must be dropped all the way through the door.

Once the *Eye* is dropped through the door, five keyholes open in the door around the rose. The key to these locks (all 5 of them) is the one hidden behind the illusory window in **Area H-26**.

When one of the locks is unlocked and the key removed from the keyhole, the key suddenly reshapes itself. The new shape fits one of the remaining keyholes (the order is not important).

Once the five locks are turned, the thorns covering the door recede into the rosebushes for 10 minutes. At the end of this time, the door slams shut and the roses instantly grow over it again (if it was spiked open, the door takes 2 minutes before it bends the spike and closes all the way).

> The walls of this room are entirely covered by thorns, roses, and leaves; entering it is like walking into a cave of flowers. The room contains 2 treasure chests and five large sacks.

The *Eye of Othroäta*, dropped through a channel in the door, sits on the threshold just inside the room. As soon as the characters walk into the room (after, say, 30 seconds), they smell the overpoweringly cloying scent of the roses. Anyone breathing the smell must make a DC 20 Fortitude save or fall asleep permanently. This magical sleep is profound; it can be removed only by a kiss or by a *remove curse* spell.

All of the sacks are full of human skulls, grisly trophies of Kathelynn's meals. There are 183 skulls, all people she has eaten over the last 75 years.

Treasure Chest #1: The chest is locked (DC 30 Disable Device) and is covered in thorns (all of which are coated in Black Lotus Extract (**Type** poison (contact); **Save** Fortitude DC 20 **Onset** 1 minute; **Frequency** 1/round for 6 rounds **Effect** 1d6 Con damage; **Cure** 2 consecutive saves). Unlocking the chest requires that the PC make a DC 15 Dex check or accidentally get stuck with a thorn while working on the lock. Smashing the chest causes thorns to fly in all directions, Atk +15 melee (1d4+2 damage plus poison [black lotus extract]) hitting everyone within 20 feet. The chest contains 3,205 gp, 6,730 sp, 4,053 cp, 25 lead tokens (worthless), 2 polished wooden disks (rare wood worth 10 gp each), and 3 electrum pieces (worth half a gold piece).

Treasure Chest #2: The chest is **trapped** and locked in the same way as the first chest. It contains a scroll (*protection from normal missiles, hallucinatory terrain, remove curse,* and *wall of stone*), a giant ermine pelt (1,000 gp), a *potion of plant control,* a *potion of growth,* a *potion of invisibility,* and a *potion of gaseous form.*

SYMBOL OF PAIN TRAP **CR 6**
XP 2,400
Type magic; **Perception** DC 30; **Disable Device** DC 30

Trigger location; **Duration** 90 minutes; **Reset** none
EFFECTS Spell effect (*symbol of pain*, CL 9th, DC 19 Fortitude save negates); multiple targets (all targets in a 30-ft.-radius burst).

If the characters are all inside the room when the door closes itself again after 10 minutes, they may be in serious trouble. If a character is within 5 feet of the door and immediately dives for it, DC25 Reflex save to see if the door can be stopped from closing. The roses instantly grow to cover the door, preventing it from being opened again. Since the inside of the door has an ordinary doorknob, opening it is a simple matter of making the roses recede from the door, but they regenerate so fast that it is impossible to just cut them back. If the characters look at the door closely, they see that the roses do not grow near any of the metal (DC 20 Perception check). A wide space is clear around each of the hinges and around the doorknob. Experimenting further reveals that the branches actually move a bit away from iron; they don't like it.

It is possible to start in the middle of the door with some metal (first sword points, then plates of armor) and slowly create a perimeter of metal to push back the thorns. Alternatively, the characters could cut away branches and then block them with metal from regenerating back over the door.

If the roses can be cleared away like this, a group of trapped adventures can clear off the door, turn the knob, open the door, and walk out.

Area H-28. Storage Loft (CR 2)

> This is an airy wooden loft underneath the sharply pitched roof of slate tiles overhead. The front of the loft is the manor's front wall, which is pierced with two arrow slits.
> Several barrels are lined up along the side walls, and thirty chicken coops are stacked against the north wall.

During the daytime, a sentry is in this room (a **bugbear**) and may spot the characters' approach if they head directly for the manor's front gate.

The barrels mostly contain salted meat, although 3 of them contain ale (these are worth 100 gp each, but they are very heavy). Many of the barrels bear a mark with the merchant's initials, "H.T." This is the mark of

Henri Tharnac, a merchant who knowingly deals with the monsters of the manor (see **Area H-17**).

The chickens are ordinary chickens.

BUGBEAR **CR 2**
XP 600
hp 16 each (*Pathfinder Roleplaying Game Bestiary* "Bugbear")

Area H-29. Storage Loft

> Boxes and crates are stacked in here, along with cords of firewood, rope, and 3 statues.

The statues are all of a woman wearing armor with a rose on her shield and a vertical scar on the left side of her face. These are shrines of St. Kathelynn that the lamia has ordered stolen over the years.

The contents of the storage loft are diverse. Virtually anything required to run a wilderness freehold can be found in this loft, at least in small quantities.

Area H-30. Escape Loft (CR 7)

> This loft overlooks the bedroom below. It contains a wooden log supported on sturdy trestles, and a large round cushion 5 feet in diameter, lying on the floor. The center of it is indented slightly.

Unless they fly down to reinforce Kathelynn in combat, **2 giant white owls** are here on the perch. They are very intelligent and can speak the common tongue. However, they are very loyal to the lamia and attack anyone they consider a threat to her.

This room has 2 hidden exits (DC 25 Perception check), and if Kathelynn needs to escape or double back around the characters, this loft provides the opportunity. A secret exit (leading to a secret door in the roof) is located in the loft's eastern wall, and a trapdoor is in the floor (under the cushion) that leads to **Area H-14**.

The cushion is a cat bed for the lamia when she chooses not to use the human-type bed in the room below. It also does a good job of concealing the trapdoor beneath.

GIANT OWLS (2) **CR 5**
XP 1,600
hp 57 (*Pathfinder Roleplaying Game Bestiary 3* "Owl, Giant")

Treasure: Nothing valuable is in the room.

Area H-31. Dungeon Cellar

> This is a low-ceilinged cellar with doors in the north and south walls. It smells bad down here.

Although it looks innocuous, this room is the entrance to the dungeons beneath the manor. Both of the doors are locked (DC 25 Disable Device check needed to unlock doors).

Area H-32. Jailer's Room (CR 7)

> This chamber is decorated with at least 50 shields of all shapes and sizes hung on the walls. A comfortable-looking bed stands against the western wall, and a set of keys hangs on a peg next to the bed.

This bedroom belongs to **Pierre the Weretiger**, one of Kathelynn's sons. If the manor has not been completely alerted, Pierre is here. He is the last to hear of any assault, and deep enough underground not to hear the clamor of battle.

The shield collection is not worth more than any other collection of battered-up shields.

The keys open the cells (**Areas H-33** through **H-35**) and the door to **Area H-36**.

PIERRE (HUMAN FORM) **CR 7**
XP 3,200
Male human natural weretiger slayer 7 (*Pathfinder Roleplaying Game Bestiary 2* "Lycanthrope, Weretiger" *Pathfinder Roleplaying Game Advanced Class Guide* "Slayer")
NE Medium humanoid (human, shapechanger)
Init +5; **Senses** low-light vision, scent; **Perception** +10

AC 15, touch 12, flat-footed 13 (+2 armor, +1 Dex, +1 dodge, +1 natural)
hp 71 (7d10+14 plus 14)
Fort +8; **Ref** +7; **Will** +5

Speed 30 ft.
Special Attacks curse of lycanthropy, sneak attack +2d6 +2 bleed, studied target +2 (2nd, swift action)

Str 17, **Dex** 13, **Con** 14, **Int** 10, **Wis** 11, **Cha** 10
Base Atk +7; **CMB** +10; **CMD** 22
Feats Dodge, Improved Initiative[B], Iron Will, Power Attack, Toughness, Weapon Focus (claw)
Skills Acrobatics +10, Bluff +9, Climb +10, Diplomacy +4 (+8 to change attitude vs. animals related to lycanthropic form), Intimidate +7, Perception +10, Sense Motive +9, Stealth +10, Survival +9
Languages Common
SQ change forms, lycanthropic empathy, slayer talents (bleeding attack +2, combat trick, fast stealth), stalker, track +3
Combat Gear *potion of bull's strength, potion of cure moderate wounds*; **Other Gear** *amulet of natural armor +1, bracers of armor +2, cloak of resistance +1*, pouch with a ruby 300 gp

PIERRE (HYBRID FORM) **CR 7**
XP 3,200
Male human natural weretiger slayer 7 (*Pathfinder Roleplaying Game Bestiary 2* "Lycantrhope, Weretiger" *Pathfinder Roleplaying Game Advanced Class Guide* "Slayer")
NE Large humanoid (human, shapeshifter)
Init +6; **Senses** low-light vision, scent; **Perception** +12

AC 20, touch 12, flat-footed 17 (+2 armor, +2 Dex, +1 dodge, +6 natural, –1 size)
hp 78 (7d10+28 plus 14)
Fort +10; **Ref** +8; **Will** +7
DR 10/silver

Speed 30 ft.

Melee mwk longsword +9 (1d8+3/19–20)
Ranged longbow +5 (1d8/x3)
Melee bite +13 (2d6+7), 2 claws +14 (1d8+7 plus grab)
Space 10 ft.; **Reach** 10 ft.
Special Attacks curse of lycanthropy, pounce, rake (2 claws +14, 1d8+7 plus grab), sneak attack +2d6 +2 bleed, studied target +2 (2nd, swift action)

Str 25, **Dex** 15, **Con** 19, **Int** 10, **Wis** 11/14, **Cha** 10
Base Atk +7; **CMB** +15 (+19 grapple); **CMD** 28
Feats Dodge, Improved Initiative[B], Iron Will, Power Attack, Toughness, Weapon Focus (claw)
Skills Acrobatics +15, Bluff +9, Climb +14, Diplomacy +5 (+9 to change attitude vs. animals related to lycanthropic form), Intimidate +7, Perception +12, Sense Motive +1, Stealth +11 (+15 in undergrowth), Survival +11; **Racial Modifiers** +4 Acrobatics, +4 Stealth in undergrowth
Languages Common
SQ change forms, lycanthropic empathy, slayer talents (bleeding attack +2, combat trick, fast stealth), stalker, track +3
Combat Gear *potion of bull's strength*, *potion of cure moderate wounds*; **Other Gear** *amulet of natural armor +1*, *bracers of armor +2*, *cloak of resistance +1*, pouch with a ruby 300 gp

PIERRE (TIGER FORM) CR 7
XP 3,200
Male human natural weretiger slayer 7 (*Pathfinder Roleplaying Game Bestiary 2* "Lycanthrope, Weretiger", *Pathfinder Roleplaying Game Advanced Class Guide* "Slayer")
NE Large humanoid (human, shapechanger)
Init +6; **Senses** low-light vision, scent; **Perception** +12

AC 20, touch 12, flat-footed 17 (+2 armor, +2 Dex, +1 dodge, +6 natural, -1 size)
hp 85 (7d10+42)
Fort +10, **Ref** +8, **Will** +7
DR 10/silver

Speed 40 ft.
Melee bite +13 (2d6+7), 2 claws +14 (1d8+7 plus grab)
Space 10 ft.; **Reach** 10 ft.
Special Attacks curse of lycanthropy, pounce, rake (2 claws +14, 1d8+7 plus grab), sneak attack +2d6 +2 bleed, studied target +2 (2nd, swift action)

Str 25, **Dex** 15, **Con** 19, **Int** 10, **Wis** 14, **Cha** 10
Base Atk +7; **CMB** +15 (+19 grapple); **CMD** 28
Feats Dodge, Improved Initiative[B], Iron Will, Power Attack, Toughness, Weapon Focus (claw)
Skills Acrobatics +15 (+19 to jump), Bluff +9, Climb +14, Diplomacy +4 (+8 to change attitude vs. animals related to lycanthropic form), Intimidate +7, Perception +12, Sense Motive +11, Stealth +11 (+15 in undergrowth), Survival +11; **Racial Modifiers** +4 Acrobatics, +4 Stealth in undergrowth
Languages Common
SQ change forms, lycanthropic empathy, slayer talents (bleeding attack +2, combat trick, fast stealth), stalker, track +3
Combat Gear *potion of bull's strength*, *potion of cure moderate wounds*; **Other Gear** *amulet of natural armor +1*, *bracers of armor +2*, *cloak of resistance +1*, pouch with a ruby 300 gp

Area H-33. Unoccupied Cell

> The door of the cell is wood with iron bindings and a padlocked bolt. A small, barred window in the door is 6 inches by 3 inches.
> This stone cell is apparently empty.

Yes, it is definitely empty.

Area H-34. Cell (CR 5)

> The door of the cell is wood with iron bindings and a locked bolt which can easily be unlocked from the outside. A small, barred window in the door is 6 inches by 3 inches.
> A person in rags sits in the back of the cell directly across from the door, head bowed so that long hair covers the face.

This prisoner has been tortured and is now blind. He introduces himself as **Mad Andre** and asks if the characters have any food or water with them. Andre is a mystic who has visions of a "Saint Elys," and began preaching about her in the town of Elet, north of the Ghostwind Pass, calling her the Snow Maiden. Word of thi s preacher came to Kathelynn's ears, and she immediately sent the weretigers Claude and Thibault to kidnap him and bring him to the manor. Mad Andre really is having visions of Elys, but although he knows her name and that she is associated with winds and snow, he doesn't know much more about her. Her symbol is a rose, white as snow, and she has difficulty talking to him because she is still far away, but she gradually draws nearer as more people hear Andre talk of her. She says that her bones are hidden "beyond the reach of the Ghostwind, but in the Ghostwind's reach," but Andre doesn't know what this means. If the characters ask, he can tell them that what the "tigers" wanted to know was the location of Elys' bones.

MAD ANDRE CR 5
XP 1,600
Male human oracle (seer) 6 (*Pathfinder Roleplaying Game Advanced Player's Guide* "Oracle" *Pathfinder Roleplaying Game Ultimate Magic* "Seer")
NG Medium humanoid (human)
Init –1; **Senses** [permanently blinded] darkvision 60 ft.; **Perception** +6

AC 9, touch 9, flat-footed 9 (–1 Dex)
hp 36 (6d8+6)
Fort +3; **Ref** +1; **Will** +7

Speed 30 ft.
Spells Known (CL 6th; concentration +9):
3rd (4/day)—*clairaudience/clairvoyance*, *cure serious wounds*, *speak with dead* (DC 16)
2nd (6/day)—*cure moderate wounds*, *cure moderate wounds*, *detect thoughts* (DC 15), *whispering lore**
1st (7/day)—*comprehend languages*, *cure light wounds*, *cure light wounds*, *deathwatch*, *detect undead*, *shield of faith*
0 (at will)—*detect magic*, *guidance*, *mending*, *purify food and drink* (DC 13), *read magic*, *resistance*, *stabilize*
Mystery Life

Str 10, **Dex** 9, **Con** 13, **Int** 12, **Wis** 15, **Cha** 16
Base Atk +4; **CMB** +4; **CMD** 13
Feats Alertness[B], Blind-fight, Combat Casting, Craft Wondrous Item
Skills Appraise +5, Bluff +8, Climb +1, Craft (jewelry) +5,

Diplomacy +8, Handle Animal +7, Heal +6, Knowledge (history) +6, Knowledge (nature) +7, Knowledge (planes) +6, Knowledge (religion) +8, Linguistics +2, Perception +6, Profession (fortune-teller) +6, Profession (soothsayer) +7, Sense Motive +8, Spellcraft +10, Stealth +0, Survival +6, Swim +1
Languages Celestial, Common, Sylvan
SQ oracle's curse (clouded vision), revelations (gift of prophecy, natural divination)
**Pathfinder Roleplaying Game Advanced Race Guide*

Area H-35. Communal Dungeon Cell

> The door here is a barred gate, like a cage wall, secured with a padlock. The inside is a noisome cell containing four people.

The four people in the cell are all normal humans, trappers and hunters captured by the lamia or the weretigers. Their names are **Yaric**, **Otho**, **Kevrix**, and **Winfril**. Winfril is female, the others are all males. Otho has been wounded by one of the weretigers and infected with lycanthropy. However, he does not transform for the first time until he stands under the night sky when the moon is full. Thereafter, he is able to change form at will.

The barred gate (hardness 5, hp 20, Break DC 30) has a lock can be opened with a DC 25 Disable Device check. No reward is offered for any of these prisoners, but—with the exception of Otho—they eventually get a giant ermine pelt to the characters (they are, after all, hunters).

TRAPPERS (5) CR 3
XP 800
hp 30 (*Pathfinder Roleplaying Game GameMastery Guide* "Trapper")

Gear none have any equipment

Area H-36. Five Skeletons

> Five skeletons hang by rusty manacles on the walls of this room.

These are the bodies of the five loyal retainers who buried Elys' body, thinking it belonged to Kathelynn. This room is where they met their demise one after the other, refusing to the bitter end to disclose the body's whereabouts. If a Lawfully-aligned cleric enters the room, the ghostly shape of a woman in chainmail, resembling all the images of Kathelynn but without a scar, appears in the middle of the room. She seems to be trying to speak, but the words are faint, inaudible. She gestures to the skeletons, and you can hear the words, "Must bury [something something] at the Abbey [something something] warm [something] protect." She gestures again at the skeletons, then fades into the air.

The characters have just had a direct encounter with St. Elys. If the five skeletons are brought to the abbey and buried in their appropriate graves (as best can be determined), every Lawful cleric in the party gains one level of experience, or 1,500 XP, whichever is greater. Each other member of the party gains 1,000 XP.

State of Alert

If the manor is alerted, most of the fighting monsters head for **Area H-10** to assemble under Kathelynn's leadership and to counterattack. Kathelynn uses the scrying pool in that room to find the characters and direct the counterattack accordingly. Noncombatants (the "Free Individuals" and the "Charmed Slaves" other than Martin) remain where they are. The giant owls and the saber-toothed at **Area H-11** remain in place. From that point on, the monsters respond as their leaders indicate. The manor is designed to allow lots of tactical mobility.

Concluding the Adventure

If the only focus of the adventure has been hunting and monster-fighting, it either concludes with the characters leaving before the Ghostwind ("Better part of valor") or getting caught in it ("Just one more"). Thereafter, the main focus is to sell the furs and move on to other adventures.

If the characters solved the mysteries of the pass and restored St. Elys' bones to the abbey's chapel, they are rewarded by possession of the *Staff of the Remorhaz*. It seems obvious to all that anyone who can find and safely carry the artifact is its chosen holder.

Since the Ghostwind Pass is a large area, it can easily be used for further adventuring. If the characters joined the two pieces of the *Staff of the Remorhaz*, and the artifact is in their possession, it provides its wielder with fragmented information about other quests, if the characters are inclined to become roving defenders of justice.

Monster Roster

BUGBEAR **CR 2**
XP 600
hp 16 each (*Pathfinder Roleplaying Game Bestiary* "Bugbear")

DIRE GOAT **CR 3**
XP 800
The Tome of Horrors Complete 719
N Medium animal
Init +1; **Senses** low-light vision, scent; **Perception** +10

AC 16, touch 11, flat–footed 15 (+1 Dex, +5 natural)
hp 30 (4d8+12)
Fort +9; **Ref** +5; **Will** +2

Speed 50 ft.
Melee head butt +7 (1d6+6)
Special Attacks trample (1d6+6, DC 16)

Str 18, **Dex** 12, **Con** 16, **Int** 2, **Wis** 12, **Cha** 8
Base Atk +3; **CMB** +7; **CMD** 18 (22 vs. trip)
Feats Alertness, Great Fortitude
Skills Perception +10, Sense Motive +3

DIRE WOLVERINE **CR 4**
XP 1,200
hp 42 (*Pathfinder Roleplaying Game Bestiary* "Wolverine, Dire")

GIANT ERMINE

Giant ermines are a variety of giant weasels for all intents and purposes, but their pelts are extraordinarily valuable (1000 gp). If the ermine is damaged in combat by a cutting weapon, its value is reduced by one-half (each time the cutting weapon hits). See the entry for "Giant Weasel."

GIANT OWL **CR 5**
XP 1,600
hp 57 (*Pathfinder Roleplaying Game Bestiary 3* "Owl, Giant")

GIANT WEASEL **CR 1**
XP 400
hp 9 (*Pathfinder Roleplaying Game Bestiary 4* "Weasel, Giant")

Giant weasel pelts sell for 1d6x100 gp each.

Giant ermines are a variety of giant weasels for all intents and purposes, but their pelts are extraordinarily valuable. If the ermine is damaged in combat by a cutting weapon, its value is reduced by one-half (each time the cutting weapon hits). Giant ermines are less aggressive than giant weasels, and won't fight unless cornered. The pelt of a giant ermine is worth 1d4x1000 gp.

MEDIUM ICE ELEMENTAL **CR 3**
XP 800
hp 30 (*Pathfinder Roleplaying Game Bestiary 2* "Elemental, Ice")

LAMIA **CR 6**
XP 2,400
hp 67 (*Pathfinder Roleplaying Game Bestiary* "Lamia")

POLAR BEAR **CR 5**
XP 1,600
hp 52 (*Pathfinder Roleplaying Game Bestiary* "Bear, Polar")

WHITE PUDDING **CR 6**
XP 2,400
The Tome of Horrors Complete 487
N Huge ooze
Init –5; **Senses** blindsight 60 ft.; **Perception** –5

AC 3, touch 3, flat-footed 3 (–5 Dex, –2 size)
hp 94 (9d8+54)
Fort +8; **Ref** –2; **Will** –2
Defensive Abilities split (piercing and slashing, 10 hp);
Immune ooze traits; **Resist** cold 5

Speed 20 ft., climb 20 ft.
Melee slam +7 (2d6+4 plus 2d6 acid plus grab)
Space 15 ft.; **Reach** 10 ft.
Special Attacks constrict (2d6+4 plus 2d6 acid), corrosion

Str 17, **Dex** 1, **Con** 21, **Int** —, **Wis** 1, **Cha** 1
Base Atk +6; **CMB** +11 (+15 grapple); **CMD** 16 (26 vs. bull rush, can't be tripped)
Skills Climb +11
SQ camouflage, suction

Acid (Ex) A white pudding secretes a digestive acid that dissolves organic material quickly, but does not affect metal or stone. Any melee hit or constriction attack deals acid damage, and the opponent's clothing and armor (non-metal only) take the same amount of damage unless they succeed on DC 19 Reflex saves. A wooden weapon that strikes a white pudding takes 2d6 acid damage unless it succeeds on a DC 19 Reflex save. If a white pudding remains in contact with a wooden object for 1 full round, it inflicts 19 points of damage (no save) to the object. The save DCs are Constitution-based.
Camouflage (Ex) Since a white pudding looks like normal ice and snow when at rest, it takes a DC 20 Perception check to notice it before it attacks. Anyone with ranks in Survival or Knowledge (nature) can use one of those skills instead of Perception to notice the white pudding. Dwarves can use stonecunning to notice a subterranean-dwelling white pudding.
Corrosion (Ex) An opponent that is being constricted by a white pudding suffers a –4 penalty on Reflex saves made to resist acid damage applying to clothing and armor.
Suction (Ex) The white pudding can create powerful suction against any surfaces as it climbs, allowing it to cling to inverted surfaces with ease. A white pudding can establish or release suction as a swift action, and as long as it is using suction, it moves at half speed. Because of the suction, a white pudding's CMD score gets a +10 circumstance bonus to resist bull rush, awesome blows, and other attacks and effects that attempt to physically move it from its location.

Vampires & Liches

Hearken closer and have fear, for in your hands are four adventures from the pit of your deepest nightmares. These fantasy adventures of the macabre are sure to challenge your adventurers to the fullest extent of their abilities. Each dungeon ultimately hides a covetous prize: the *Hollow Blade*, the *Tome of Mind and Body*, and the *Elemental Belt*.

In ***Vampires and Liches***, the party comes face to face with the most powerful of all the undead. Unknown to many, the headquarters of a widespread murder and slave syndicate lies hidden beneath the ruins of an ancient city in the **Sewers of the Underguild**, where Sangre commands his legions with the power of the *Hollow Blade*. Deep in a desert waste awaits a lost oasis and **The Pyramid of Amra**, where the iron-clawed vampire C'nosretep rules in the name of his fell god, Set. Finally, the party travels to the fabled **Isle of Eliphaz**, where the mighty lich Athransma guards a powerful secret, unable to unlock its true power.

The adventures in this module range in difficulty to challenge parties of levels 11 to 13 and higher, depending on the numbers and composition of character classes in your adventuring group. While none of the adventures in this module could be considered "easy," the **Sewers of the Underguild** may be considered the least strenuous of the three. The **Pyramid of Amra** escalates the difficulty, culminating in the insidious dangers posed by a pair of deceptive liches and a godlike elemental in the **Isle of Eliphaz**.

Although the adventures offer challenges and great prizes for rogue, monk, and druid characters, the knowledge and skills of all members of the party are needed for the group to survive. Be for-warned, the encounters herein do scar, and indeed kill. But as cruel C'nosretep shall learn when the truth is brought to him at last by a party of intrepid adventurers, no one individual may persevere alone. Then again, C'nosretep may very well feast upon the blood of all. It is up to your adventurers to find out!

The adventures in ***Vampires and Liches*** are designed to take place in far-off locales, where the lairs themselves are every bit as difficult to find as the treasures they guard. Finding the hidden entrance to the **Sewers of the Underguild** should not be a simple matter of leaving the local pub, taking a left at Green Hill Road, and walking till sundown. Suggested locations for each of the nefarious lairs presented here are given at the introduction of each lair as a guide for the GM.

Sewers of the Underguild

By Casey W. Christofferson and Bill Webb

Introduction

Sewers of the Underguild is an adventure designed for characters of at least 11th level. Hidden within its narrow passages and filth-filled channels is a guild of vampiric rogues, led by their master Sangre and his aide, Ankoz. Deadly traps abound, requiring the services of a rogue with at least 7 ranks in Disable Device and Perception. Due to the high likelihood of desperate combat with numerous vampiric and monstrous opponents, it is suggested that a cleric and at least two fighters be prepared to beat back the many watchdog monsters the guild employs. You can hide the locales in **Sewers of the Underguild** in any ruin or location that fits your campaign purposes. A thriving metropolis that just happens to have a large crime and vampire problem would fit the bill nicely. In the **Lost Lands** campaign setting of **Frog God Games**, the Underguild is located in the sewers beneath the ruins of Curgantium, the ancient imperial capital of the lost Hyperborean Empire. Located at the edge of the modern Kingdom of Foere, the Underguild still finds itself located centrally enough to pull the strings of its weblike network running throughout the former lands of the Hyperborian Empire.

Dungeon Features

Doors: Bronze bound hardwood: 2 in. thick; hardness 5; hp 20; Break DC 25; Disable Device DC 25.

Secret Doors: All secret doors are delicately carved and unless otherwise noted require a DC 25 Perception check to locate, and are locked requiring a DC 25 Disable Device check to open.

Sewer Pipes: All sewer pipes are slippery and filled with fast-moving water. The pipes are 5 feet in diameter and made of glazed ceramic. The sewer pipes rest at an average 34-degree downward slope and are 1/2 to 3/4 filled with raw sewage. Individuals falling into or purposefully leaping into one of the sewage pipes are whisked towards the central sewer drains at a rate of 20 feet per round. Swimming within the pipes requires a DC 15 Swim check to tread water to keep from going farther down the pipe, and a DC 20 Swim check to make positive movement out of the pipe. Individuals of Large size or larger may make a DC 25 Strength check to stop themselves in the pipe and a DC 25 Climb check at every 10-foot section to climb out of the pipe.

Methane Gas Dangers: Spells involving fire, such as *burning hands*, *wall of fire*, and *fireball* have a 15% chance of igniting pooled methane gas within the sewers. A roll of 15% or less indicates that the spell sets off the methane gas, which in the event of a *fireball* means instantaneous eruption at the point of origin of the spell, affording the caster no saving throw against the spell. In the case of *burning hands*, the spell acts normally for purposes of harming the target, however the caster takes damage equal to that taken by the target of the spell. Likewise, a successful use of any spell with the fire descriptor has a 15% chance of dealing 2d6 points of additional damage as it ignites pooled gasses in that area of the dungeon. When the PCs enter a new room or corridor while carrying a torch or other open flame there is the same chance that a small pocket of gas ignites. This deals 2d6 fire damage in a 10 foot radius spread centered on the flame-bearer.

Legend of the Underguild

The site known as the Sewers of the Underguild is the stronghold of the infamous Underguild, an organized crime syndicate ruled by Sangre, the Hand of Death. From within its sewer stronghold, the Underguild has stretched out its clawed fingers into the highest offices of power in the lands. The Underguild traffics not only in stolen merchandise, but also in slaves and information. Their operators, being vampires, have the innate ability to gather documents both arcane and mundane without leaving the slightest trace. Few have attempted to withstand the full might of the Underguild. Their sewer stronghold, hidden in a remote location of the world, is so difficult to find as to create an epic in and of itself.

Legends tell of the exploits of the Hand of Death, and how he has acquired an ancient weapon of truly wondrous power. This thin, frail-looking short sword, known as the *Hollow Blade*, is forged from equal parts of positive and negative energy, allowing the guildmaster the ability to walk amongst the living in broad daylight. The *Hollow Blade* itself is worth a king's ransom to those of the roguish profession, for though it grants the undead the ability to move about in daylight as the living, it also grants the ability to cleave the undead as if they were living flesh.

The *Hollow Blade* is a new magic weapon that gives undead a taste of life, and in the hands of a rogue becomes a deadly tool for the destruction of the undead. This fierce short sword is in the possession of Sangre himself. Sangre guards the sword jealously, even from members of his own guild who would seek to wrest it from his hand. Taking this weapon from Sangre is no easy task.

Locating the Sewers

The ruined city where the Sewers of the Underguild are located should take the party some time to track down. The Underguild itself is a highly secretive organization with its fangs sunk deep into the pulse of nearly every major city, yet few know of its actual existence. Perhaps rumors and a hidden map found within the crypt of a previously defeated vampire lead to the Sewers. Quite possibly this vampire has ties to a major organized crime syndicate in the PCs' base city, thus setting the wheels of the plot in motion. However you choose to convey the PCs to the adventure's launching point, they are assumed to have uncovered the secret base of the Underguild and need but find the entrance and proceed either to glory or to doom.

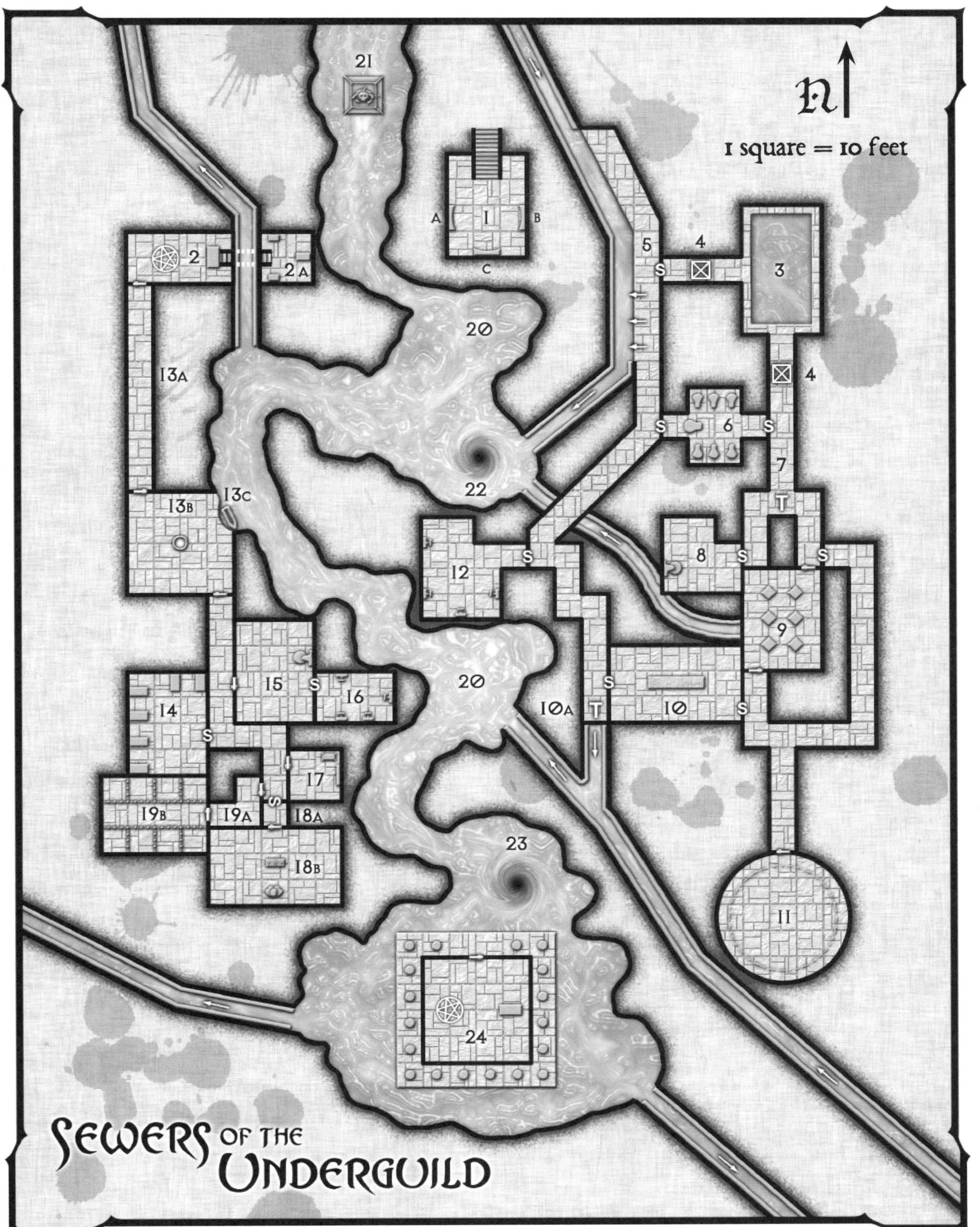

N
1 square = 10 feet
21
1
A
B
C
2
2A
3
4
4
5
6
7
8
9
10
10A
11
12
13A
13B
13C
14
15
16
17
18A
18B
19A
19B
20
20
22
23
24
Sewers of the Underguild

Keyed Locations

Refer to the Sewers of the Underguild Map.

1: The Entryway and the Silver Skull Seal of the Underguild (CR 13)

Hidden beneath the fountain is a stone staircase that leads down to this chamber, roughly 40 feet below the surface. Engraved in the center of the floor is the symbol of a silver inlayed skull, pierced crossways with two knives. The canine teeth of the skull are elongated and blackened.

Three archways filled with swirling mist of orange, green, and yellow are found in the eastern, western, and southern walls, respectively.

Living beings that cross over or otherwise touch the silver skull emblem on the floor set off an *alarm* spell that immediately alerts all vampires within the sewers, unless the PCs pour a sacrifice of fresh blood upon the fangs of the skull within two rounds of entering the chamber. Anyone succeeding on a DC 20 Perception check on the silvered skull notes the dried blood that looks like tarnish from a distance. A rogue succeeding on a DC 34 Perception check or a spellcaster using *detect magic* notes a magical trap; as the PCs search the room, a *wall of stone* spell seals off the staircase leading to the surface. A few words of arcane nature are heard in whispered tones as the spell is activated. Anyone in or near the area who succeeds on a DC 25 Spellcraft check realizes that a *wall of stone* is in the making and has just enough time to attempt a counterspell, requiring a DC 23 caster level check if using *dispel magic*. The second effect of the silver skull triggers a **pressure-sensitive plate** that causes the ceiling to close down up on the PCs in 2 rounds.

CRUSHING CEILING TRAP **CR 13**
XP 19,200
Type mechanical; **Perception** DC 20; **Disable Device** 30*

Trigger location; **Reset** manual; **Bypass** pour blood on the silver skull (Perception DC 30)
Effect crushing ceiling (12d6 bludgeoning); onset delay (2 rounds); never miss; multiple targets (all targets in the room)
*This trap cannot be disabled from within this room, as it is hydraulic trap only disabled when the hydraulic pumps are turned off in areas **12: Eastern Pump Room** and **16:Western Pump Room**. A successful Disable Device only reveals that the trap cannot be disabled from here, only bypassed.

1A: Archway of Orange Swirling Mist (CR 11)

This archway is filled with a glowing and swirling orange mist. Surrounding its doorframe are several silver skulls embedded in the wall, their eye sockets filled with pure amber. Attempts to detect and determine magical effects indicate that the door acts similarly to a *dimension door* spell, and that there is powerful abjuration magic tied into the mists. Individuals entering this swirling portal are teleported bodily and with all of their possessions to **Area 2**.

Attempting to dislodge the glowing petrified amber from the doorframe sets off the **heightened *lighting bolt* trap**, resulting in a shocking blast that strikes the offender and anyone standing in a straight line behind him.

HEIGHTENED *LIGHTNING BOLT* TRAP **CR 11**
XP 9,600
Type magic; **Perception** DC 34; **Disable Device** DC 34

Trigger touch; **Reset** automatic
Effect spell effect (heightened *lightning bolt* [9th-level], 9d6 electricity damage, DC 23 Ref half); multiple targets (all targets in a 30 ft. line)

1B: Archway of Yellow Swirling Mist (CR 7)

This archway of yellow swirling mist looks as unappealing as stepping into a cloud of mustard gas; sickly vapors of brimstone and offal increase as one takes each step closer to the archway. A series of cow skulls, cast in bronze, surrounds the doorframe of this archway, the skulls' eyes glowing like pure sapphires. Stepping through the portal instantly teleports the individual and all of their belongings to **Area 11**. Touching the cow skulls triggers a **maximized widened *fireball* trap** centered on the PC touching the skull; unless gifted with spell resistance, this individual receives no saving throw, however all other persons in the room may roll normally.

MAXIMIZED WIDENED *FIREBALL* TRAP **CR 7**
XP 3,200
Type mechanical; **Perception** DC 28; **Disable Device** DC 28

Trigger touch; **Reset** none
Effect spell effect (maximized widened *fireball*, 30 fire damage, DC 14 Ref half); multiple targets (all targets in a 40-ft. radius spread)

1C: Archway of Green Swirling Mist (CR 7)

Similar to the yellow and orange mists of the first two archways, this archway is filled with foul-looking, pea-green mist. The mist chokes the air around it with a brackish stench of salt and brine. The edges of the archway are carved in the shape of large lizards, with eyes as black as jet yet seeming to have a strange aura about them.

Attempting to pry the jet eye stones from the lizards triggers the ***fear* trap**. PCs crossing into the foul green mist are teleported instantly to the bottom of the saltwater pool in **Area 3**.

***FEAR* TRAP** **CR 7**
XP 3,200
Type magic; **Perception** DC 29; **Disable Device** DC 29

Trigger touch; **Reset** automatic
Effect spell effect (*fear*, 30 ft. cone, DC 16 Will negates)

2: Chamber of Ankoz (CR 14)

A large inlaid black onyx pentagram dominates the center of this chamber. An altar lays at the far end of the room, upon which stands the dark figure of **Ankoz the Lich**.

ANKOZ **CR 13**
XP 25,600
Male human lich wizard 12 (*Pathfinder Roleplaying Game Bestiary* "Lich")
CE Medium undead (augmented humanoid, human)
Init +3; **Senses** darkvision 60 ft.; **Perception** +21
Aura fear aura (DC 19)

AC 24, touch 16, flat-footed 21 (+3 armor, +3 Dex, +3 deflection, +5 natural)
hp 92 (12d6+36 plus 12)
Fort +7; **Ref** +7; **Will** +12; +4 vs. channeled energy
Defensive Abilities channel resistance +4, rejuvenation; **DR** 15/bludgeoning and magic; **Immune** cold, electricity, polymorph, undead traits

---

Speed 30 ft.
Melee touch +6 (1d8+6)
Special Attacks metamagic mastery (3/day), paralyzing touch 1d8+6 (DC 19), hand of the apprentice 8/day (ranged touch +11)
Spells Prepared (CL 12th; melee touch +6):

6th—*acid fog, contingency*
5th—*cone of cold* (DC 20), *teleport, transmute mud to rock* (DC 20), *wall of stone* (DC 21)
4th—*bestow curse* (DC 19), *dimensional anchor, fear* (DC 19), *lesser globe of invulnerability*
3rd—*blink, fireball* (DC 18), *haste, hold person* (DC 18), *invisibility sphere*
2nd—*blindness/deafness* (DC 17), *invisibility* (x2), *minor image* (DC 17), *web* (DC 18)
1st—*burning hands* (DC 16), *chill touch* (DC 16), *feather fall* (DC 16), *magic missile, obscuring mist, summon monster I*
0 (at will)—*daze* (DC 15), *detect magic, flare* (DC 15), *ray of frost*
Specialist School Universalist

Str 10, **Dex** 16, **Con** —, **Int** 21, **Wis** 19, **Cha** 16
Base Atk +6; **CMB** +6; **CMD** 22
Feats Craft Magic Arms & Armor, Craft Staff, Enlarge Spell, Forge Ring, Heighten Spell, Maximize Spell, Quicken Spell, Scribe Scroll, Spell Focus (conjuration), Spell Penetration
Skills Craft (alchemy) +20, Craft (woodworking) +20, Fly +12, Intimidate +18, Knowledge (arcana) +20, Knowledge (religion) +20, Perception +21, Sense Motive +21, Spellcraft +20, Stealth +20; **Racial Modifiers** +8 Perception, +8 Sense Motive, +8 Stealth
Languages Abyssal, Common, Draconic, Elven, Goblin, Undercommon
SQ arcane bond (object [*ring of protection* +3] [1/day])
Combat Gear *staff of fire* (30 charges); **Other Gear** *bracers of armor +3, ring of protection +3*

Tactics: Unless the PCs enter the lair of Ankoz through the door from **Area 13A**, or by some means of teleportation other than coming through the orange swirling mist, he has cast *haste* and has placed *lesser globe of invulnerability* and *mirror image* upon himself by the time the PCs enter the chamber. In combat, Ankoz starts off with *cone of cold*, followed by *acid fog*. Unless held with a *dimensional anchor*, Ankoz's *contingency* spell, triggered if he gets to less than 1/4 of his hit points, *teleports* him to **Area 24**. There he waits, healing and plotting revenge. Ankoz's phylactery is a gold tube into which he has placed rolled scrolls containing the texts of the rituals he used to transform himself into a lich. This gold tube is concealed within his desiccated thigh and can only be discovered if his body is thoroughly searched — requiring a DC 30 Perception check or the breaking of every bone in Ankoz's body to discover. The tube is worth 10,000 gp to the right collector.

Ankoz keeps his spell books hidden in the chamber beneath the dark altar. Anyone succeeding on a DC 20 Perception check discovers that a trigger device within the carved hieroglyphics causes the entire altar to split open, revealing a staircase leading down to a burial chamber. The trigger device is well hidden; failure to disarm the **hidden trap** fills the room with deadly burnt othur fumes.

POISON GAS TRAP **CR 10**
XP 9,600
Type mechanical; **Perception** DC 25; **Disable Device** DC 25

Trigger touch; **Reset** none
Effect poison gas (burnt othur fumes); never miss; onset delay (1 round); multiple targets (all targets in the room)

2A: Burial Chamber

This chamber hidden below the false altar of Ankoz holds the true dark altar, completely covered in gold leaf and encrusted with gems and jewels. The lid itself weighs nearly 400 pounds, with a market value of nearly 4,000 gp in semi-precious gemstones and gold. Lining the walls of this chamber are shelves of books and moldering tomes, as well as rows of scroll cases.

Treasure: Ankoz's spellbooks*, 2 flasks of alchemist's fire, 5 flasks of acid, 1 *potion of cat's grace*, 1 *potion of nondetection*, *arcane scroll* of 2 spells (*haste* and *cone of cold*). A workbench holds a set of masterwork jewelry making tools. Another table is covered with expensive beakers and jars, likely valued over 1,200 gp in alchemical equipment.

*Ankoz's spellbooks contain all of his known spells, and a fair selection of additional spells. These additional spells are left to the GM to decide upon, pursuant to their campaign needs and desire. This is an excellent opportunity to introduce a few new choice spells; perhaps something long lost to all the active arcane archives in the land.

3: Crocodiles in the Pool (CR 10)

The salty smell of briny yet foul water fills the air of this room. An archway to the south heads down a corridor as does a second archway to the west. A narrow walkway along the edge of this room surrounds a pool nearly as wide and long as the room itself, murky and at least 12 feet deep. Lurking in the depths of the pool are **3 vampire crocodiles**. The vampires of the Underguild have groomed these sewer crocs to crave the blood of humanoids.

Note: There is a chance that one or more of the PCs might be teleported into the pool. Submerged PCs are allowed a DC 15 Reflex save to determine if they had their breath held before appearing at the bottom of the pool. Roll initiative immediately, as well as Perception checks against the crocodile's submerged Stealth check to determine who gets to take an action before the crocodiles strike. Have the PCs roll DC 15 Swim checks for any move actions they wish to take while at the bottom of the pool. A ladder stands in the southern end of the pool, requiring a DC 24 Perception check to notice; a DC 10 Climb check (thanks to the slick concentrations of algae and filth) allows those in heavy armor to escape the murky saltwater pool.

VAMPIRE CROCODILE **CR 6**
XP 2,400
Advanced vampiric crocodile (*Pathfinder Roleplaying Game Bestiary* "Crocodile", "Vampire")
NE Large undead (augmented animal)
Init +7; **Senses** darkvision 60 ft., low-light vision; **Perception** +20

AC 23, touch 13, flat-footed 19 (+3 Dex, +1 dodge, +10 natural, –1 size)
hp 27 (5d8 plus 5); fast healing 5
Fort +4, **Ref** +9, **Will** +3
Defensive Abilities channel resistance +4; **DR** 10/magic and silver; **Immune** undead traits; **Resist** cold 10, electricity 10
Weaknesses vampire weaknesses

Speed 20 ft., swim 30 ft.; sprint
Melee bite +10 (1d8+7 plus grab), slam +9 (1d6+7), tail slap +4 (1d12+3)
Space 10 ft.; **Reach** 5 ft.
Special Attacks blood drain, children of the night, create spawn, death roll, dominate (DC 12), energy drain (2 levels, DC 12)

Str 25, **Dex** 16, **Con** —, **Int** 3, **Wis** 14, **Cha** 10
Base Atk +3; **CMB** +11 (+15 grapple); **CMD** 25 (29 vs. trip)
Feats Alertness[B], Combat Reflexes[B], Dodge[B], Improved Initiative[B], Lightning Reflexes[B], Skill Focus (Perception), Skill Focus (Stealth), Toughness[B], Weapon Focus (bite)
Skills Bluff +8, Perception +20, Sense Motive +12, Stealth +16 (+24 in water), Swim +15; **Racial Modifiers** +8 Bluff, +8 Perception, +8 Sense Motive, +8 Stealth, +8 Stealth in water
SQ change shape, gaseous form, hold breath, shadowless, spider climb

Death Roll (Ex) When grappling a foe of its size or smaller, a vampire crocodile can perform a death roll upon making a successful grapple check. As it clings to its foe, it tucks in

its legs and rolls rapidly, twisting and wrenching its victim. The vampire crocodile inflicts its bite damage and knocks the creature prone. If successful, the vampire crocodile maintains its grapple.
Hold Breath (Ex) A vampire crocodile can hold its breath for a number of rounds equal to 4 times its Constitution score before it risks drowning. Of course, being vampires, these crocodiles don't need to worry about that…
Sprint (Ex) Once per minute a vampire crocodile may sprint, increasing its land speed to 40 feet for 1 round.

4: Pudding in the Pits! (CR 8)

Approximately 20 feet down the western and southern corridors from **Area 3** are a pair of **covered pit traps**, each 40 feet deep by 10 feet across. Each pit contains a **black pudding**. The black pudding is covered in a *permanent image* that gives the appearance of each pit containing a pile of gold, coins, and fine-looking weapons amongst skeletal remains.

CAMOUFLAGED PIT TRAP (40 FT. DEEP) CR 3
XP 800
Type mechanical; **Perception** DC 20; **Disable Device** DC 20

Trigger location; **Reset** manual
Effect 40-ft.-deep pit (4d6 falling damage); DC 20 Reflex avoids; multiple targets (all targets in a 10-ft. square area); contains a black pudding.

BLACK PUDDING CR 7
XP 3,200
hp 105 (*Pathfinder Roleplaying Game Bestiary* "Black Pudding")

5: The Dumper (CR 5)

Beyond the secret door outside the western entrance to **Area 3** is a 10-foot-wide walkway that runs north and south along an opened section of sewer pipe. The opened section runs roughly north and south for about 90 feet, with a strong current pouring from some unknown source to the north before emptying into a circular tube to the south.

Weight of over 600 pounds placed on the 30-foot section of stone deck just to the south of the secret door to **Area 3** triggers a **tilting floor trap** that dumps all individuals standing on this section of platform into the opened sewer. Individuals failing their saving throw are immediately sucked down one of the many sewer pipes and flung towards **Area 22**.

TILTING FLOOR TRAP CR 5
XP 1,600
Type mechanical; **Perception** DC 20; **Disable Device** DC 20

Trigger location; **Reset** automatic (instant; counter-weighted)
Effect slide into sewers and swept to **Area 22** (DC 20 Reflex avoids)

6: Hidden Crypt of the Crocodiles (CR 8–11)

Within this chamber are 7 crocodile-sized burial jars. Atop each of the jars is a golden crocodile head encrusted in semi-precious gems. One jar is much larger than the others, being nearly twice the size of the rest. The purpose for this jar is immediately apparent; a very large crocodile with glowing red eyes snaps its jaws at the PCs, inviting them to lunch. This creature is the great **Bloodtooth!**

Any vampiric crocodiles turned to gaseous form in **Area 3** return here to their large burial jars to fast heal.

Note: If the PCs rest at any time after defeating the crocodiles in **Area 3** without making sure they are totally destroyed, they find an additional **3 vampiric crocodiles** in this area along with the mighty Bloodtooth.

BLOODTOOTH CR 8
XP 4,800
Advanced vampiric dire crocodile (*Pathfinder Roleplaying Game Bestiary* "Crocodile, Dire", "Vampire")
NE Huge undead (augmented animal)
Init +6; **Senses** darkvision 60 ft., low-light vision; **Perception** +21

AC 24, touch 11, flat-footed 21 (+2 Dex, +1 dodge, +13 natural, –2 size)
hp 38 (7d8 plus 7); fast healing 5
Fort +5; **Ref** +9; **Will** +4
Defensive Abilities channel resistance +4; **DR** 10/magic and silver; **Immune** undead traits; **Resist** cold 10, electricity 10
Weaknesses vampire weaknesses

Speed 20 ft., swim 30 ft.; sprint
Melee bite +16 (2d6+12 plus grab plus energy drain), slam +15 (2d6+12), tail slap +10 (3d6+6)
Space 15 ft.; **Reach** 10 ft.
Special Attacks blood drain, children of the night (1/day), create spawn, death roll, dominate (DC 13), energy drain (2 levels, DC 13)

Str 34, **Dex** 14, **Con** —, **Int** 3, **Wis** 14, **Cha** 10
Base Atk +5; **CMB** +19 (+23 grapple); **CMD** 32 (36 vs. trip)
Feats Alertness[B], Combat Reflexes[B], Dodge[B], Improved Initiative[B], Lightning Reflexes[B], Power Attack, Skill Focus (Perception), Skill Focus (Stealth), Toughness[B], Weapon Focus (bite)
Skills Bluff +8, Perception +21, Sense Motive +12, Stealth +12 (+20 in water), Swim +20; **Racial Modifiers** +8 Bluff, +8 Perception, +8 Sense Motive, +8 Stealth, +8 Stealth in water
SQ gaseous form, hold breath, shadowless, spider climb

Death Roll (Ex) When grappling a foe of its size or smaller, Bloodtooth can perform a death roll upon making a successful grapple check. As he clings to his foe, he tucks in his legs and rolls rapidly, twisting and wrenching his victim. Bloodtooth inflicts his bite damage and knocks the creature prone. If successful, Bloodtooth maintains his grapple.
Hold Breath (Ex) Bloodtooth can hold his breath for a number of rounds equal to 4 times his Constitution score before it risks drowning. Of course, being a vampire, Bloodtooth doesn't need to worry about that…
Sprint (Ex) Once per minute Bloodtooth may sprint, increasing his land speed to 40 feet for 1 round.

VAMPIRE CROCODILES (3) CR 6
XP 2,400
hp 17 (see **Area 3**)

Treasure: As the head caps of the crocodile jars are coated in semi-precious gems, each jar is worth 1,000 gp as an ancient antiquity, though they weigh nearly 80 lbs. apiece. The jeweled heads are worth 500 gp each and weigh approximately 15 lbs.

7: Forked Pathway (CR 9)

The corridor leading south from the crocodile lair has two branching pathways, each leading south. A decorative mosaic of fine-cut glass and enamel forms diamond patterns along the floor, walls, and ceiling of this corridor. A deadly and extremely well hidden **impaling trap** awaits those who do not notice the switch to turn it off. The cunningly hidden wooden stakes spring out at a length of 10 feet from the floor, ceiling, and the facing southern wall. This trap is set here as a test for new recruits to the Underguild.

IMPALING STAKES TRAP **CR 9**
XP 6,400
Type mechanical; **Perception** DC 20; **Disable Device** DC 20

Trigger location; **Reset** manual; **Bypass** hidden switch (Perception DC 30)
Effect Atk +15 melee (2d4 stakes for 1d4+5 points of damage each); multiple targets (all creatures standing on the 10 ft. square of the trap area)

8: Fountains of Blood, Passage of Innocence (CR 13)

A large wolf's-head fountain dominates the western wall of this dank chamber. Thick red blood pours from its jaws into a man-sized stone bowl at its feet. As the PCs enter the chamber of the fountain, **4 vampires** leap from hiding, hissing and calling to the PCs to join them in un-life and bow to the master of the Underguild as they have done. Assume the vampires took 10 on their Stealth checks to hide, and give the PCs Perception checks to avoid surprise.

Tactics: Each of the Underguild members has its own tactics and own motivations against the PCs. Although they fight in concert against the PCs, a few may have other plans for the group, as they too seek the *Hollow Blade* and would claim it if they could defeat the Hand of Death and claim mastership of the Underguild.

JANDILAR THE SAFE CRACKER **CR 9**
XP 6,400
Male half-elf vampire rogue 8 (*Pathfinder Roleplaying Game Bestiary* "Vampire")
CE Medium undead (augmented humanoid, elf)
Init +10; **Senses** darkvision 60 ft., low-light vision; **Perception** +21

AC 27, touch 16, flat-footed 21 (+5 armor, +5 Dex, +1 dodge, +6 natural)
hp 79 (8d8+24 plus 16); fast healing 5
Fort +5; **Ref** +14; **Will** +4; +2 vs. enchantments, +2 vs. traps
Defensive Abilities channel resistance +4, evasion, uncanny dodge, trap sense; **DR** 10/magic and silver; **Immune** magic sleep, undead traits; **Resist** cold 10, electricity 10, elven immunities
Weaknesses vampire weaknesses

Speed 30 ft.
Melee slam +13 (1d4+6 plus energy drain)
Special Attacks blood drain, children of the night, create spawn, dominate (DC 17), energy drain (2 levels, DC 17), rogue talents (bleeding attack +4, combat trick, finesse rogue), sneak attack +4d6

Str 18, **Dex** 22, **Con** —, **Int** 13, **Wis** 14, **Cha** 17
Base Atk +6; **CMB** +10; **CMD** 26
Feats Alertness^B^, Combat Expertise, Combat Reflexes^B^, Dodge^B^, Improved Initiative^B^, Lightning Reflexes^B^, Mobility, Power Attack, Skill Focus (Disable Device), Spring Attack, Toughness^B^, Weapon Finesse, Weapon Focus (slam)
Skills Acrobatics +22 (+27 to make high or long jumps), Bluff +18, Climb +11, Disable Device +24, Disguise +14, Escape Artist +17, Intimidate +10, Perception +21 (+25 to locate traps), Sense Motive +19, Sleight of Hand +17, Stealth +25, Use Magic Device +10; **Racial Modifiers** +8 Bluff, +10 Perception, +8 Sense Motive, +8 Stealth
Languages Common, Elven, Orc
SQ change shape (dire bat or wolf, *beast shape II*), elf blood, gaseous form, rogue talents (fast stealth), shadowless, spider climb, trapfinding +4
Combat Gear *brooch of shielding* (101 uses); **Other Gear** +2 *studded leather armor, boots of elvenkind, ring of jumping*

Description and Tactics: Jandilar is sly and sneaky. Being an assassin in all but training, one of his favorite tricks is to dominate an individual into breathing a portion of him (usually an arm) into their lungs while he is in gaseous form, reverting into solid form while within the victim, exploding their body, killing them instantly. Only dominated victims can be attacked in his manner; others simply limit their breathing and exhale or cough forcefully when needed, preventing Jandilar's entry. Dominated individuals are permitted a DC 15 Will save to avoid breathing him in as this certainly constitutes an action against their nature. If this save fails, a successful DC 17 Fortitude save forces the solidifying matter out of the body. The victim still sustains 3d6 points of damage from this attack.

Jandilar no longer uses weapons, preferring to create spawn or kill his victims out right. As an aside, Jandilar hates the Hand of Death and covets the *Hollow Blade* for its ability to allow vampires to walk amongst the living, almost unseen. If the PCs seem to take the upper hand and succeed in destroying other guild members, he may attempt to make a deal and clear the way for them in return for the sword. Of course he has no intentions of staying true to the deal, unless of course the PCs are about to kill him.

MEMZE THE LAME **CR 9**
XP 6,400
Male human vampire rogue 3/wizard 5 (*Pathfinder Roleplaying Game Bestiary* "Vampire")
CE Medium undead (augmented humanoid, human)
Init +8; **Senses** darkvision 60 ft.; **Perception** +22

AC 21, touch 15, flat-footed 16 (+4 Dex, +1 dodge, +6 natural)
hp 71 (3d8+9 plus 5d6+15 plus 13); fast healing 5
Fort +7; **Ref** +10; **Will** +7; t+1 vs. traps
Defensive Abilities channel resistance +4, evasion, trap sense; **DR** 10/magic and silver; **Immune** undead traits; **Resist** cold 10, electricity 10
Weaknesses vampire weaknesses

Speed 30 ft.
Melee slam +8 (1d4+4 plus energy drain)
Special Attacks blood drain, children of the night, create spawn, dominate (DC 17), energy drain (2 levels, DC 17), hand of the apprentice 7/day (+8), rogue talents (finesse rogue), sneak attack +2d6
Spells Prepared (CL 5th; ranged touch +8):
3rd—*blink, haste*
2nd—*darkness, web* (DC 16), *summon swarm*
1st—*chill touch* (DC 15), *magic missile* (x2), *ray of enfeeblement* (DC 15)
0 (at will)—*daze* (DC 14), *flare* (DC 14), *ghost sound* (DC 14), *ray of frost*
Specialist School Universalist

Str 17, **Dex** 18, **Con** —, **Int** 18, **Wis** 15, **Cha** 16
Base Atk +4; **CMB** +7; **CMD** 22
Feats Alertness^B^, Combat Casting, Combat Reflexes^B^, Dodge^B^, Great Fortitude, Improved Initiative^B^, Lightning Reflexes^B^, Maximize Spell, Quicken Spell, Scribe Scroll, Silent Spell, Still Spell, Toughness^B^, Weapon Finesse
Skills Acrobatics +14, Bluff +21, Climb +9, Disable Device

+15, Escape Artist +14, Intimidate +9, Knowledge (arcana) +14, Perception +22 (+23 to locate traps), Sense Motive +22, Sleight of Hand +14, Spellcraft +14, Stealth +20; **Racial Modifiers** +8 Bluff, +8 Perception, +8 Sense Motive, +8 Stealth
Languages Common, Draconic, Elven, Goblin, Orc
SQ arcane bonds (object [*wand of lightning bolt*] [1/day]), change shape (dire bat or wolf, *beast shape II*), gaseous form, shadowless, spider climb, trapfinding +1
Combat Gear *scroll of charm monster* (CL 6th), *wand of lightning bolt* (20 charges)

Description and Tactics: Memze was the apprentice to Ankoz in life, and was turned into a vampire before gaining enough power to threaten his master. Memze, known as the Lame because of the limp he bears from a spine twisted from birth, is jaded and decadent to the extreme. His perversity knows no limits, and he personally drains dozens of slaves at a time in orgies of blood and pain. Memze uses his magic power to remain hidden in combat as long as possible, sneak attacking with ranged touch attack spells before closing in on those left standing.

F'HUGE KNEEBREAKER (RAGING) CR 8
XP 4,800
Male ogre vampire barbarian 2/rogue 2 (*Pathfinder Roleplaying Game Bestiary* "Ogre", Vampire")
CE Large undead (augmented humanoid, giant)
Init +5; **Senses** darkvision 60 ft., low-light vision; **Perception** +16

AC 28, touch 9, flat-footed 26 (+8 armor, +1 Dex, +1 dodge, +11 natural, –1 size)
hp 50 (4d8 plus 2d12 plus 2d8 plus 10); fast healing 5
Fort +7, **Ref** +7, **Will** +6
Defensive Abilities channel resistance +4, uncanny dodge; **DR** 10/magic, 10/silver; **Immune** undead traits; **Resist** cold 10, electricity 10
Weaknesses vampire weaknesses

Speed 35 ft.
Melee +2 *spiked chain* +19/+14 (2d6+18) or slam +16 (1d6+16)
Space 10 ft.; **Reach** 10 ft.
Special Attacks blood drain, children of the night, create spawn, dominate (DC 14), energy drain (2 levels, DC 14), rage (4 rounds/day), rage powers (powerful blow +1), rogue talents (combat trick), sneak attack +1d6

Str 32, **Dex** 13, **Con** —, **Int** 8, **Wis** 12, **Cha** 11
Base Atk +6; **CMB** +18; **CMD** 28
Feats Alertness, Combat Reflexes, Dodge, Exotic Weapon Proficiency (spiked chain), Improved Initiative, Iron Will, Lightning Reflexes, Power Attack, Toughness, Weapon Focus (spiked chain)
Skills Acrobatics +4, Bluff +12, Climb +13, Craft (woodcarving) +4, Diplomacy +4, Disguise +5, Escape Artist +4, Intimidate +8, Perception +16 (+17 to locate traps), Sense Motive +11, Stealth +8; **Racial Modifiers** +8 Bluff, +8 Perception, +8 Sense Motive, +8 Stealth
Languages Giant
SQ change shape (dire bat or wolf, *beast shape II*), fast movement, gaseous form, shadowless, spider climb, trapfinding +1
Gear +2 *breastplate*, +2 *spiked chain*

Note F'Huge has the following abilities when not raging: **AC** 30, **Will** +4, **Melee** +2 *spiked chain* +17/+12 (2d6+15) or slam +14 (1d6+13), **Str** 28, Climb +11, Swim +6

Description and Tactics: This hulking brute, despite being a vampire, still relies on brawn and intimidation to defeat his enemies. F'Huge uses his spiked chain to attempt to disarm dangerous opponents like paladins and clerics. He trips his opponents before stepping forward to slam them into submission. He then pins and sucks the blood from PCs deemed near death . He enjoys physical combat to such a degree that he rarely thinks to dominate opponents. An ogre to the last, F'Huge prefers beating the blood out of his victims over tricking it out of them.

HETHEL, THE ACOLYTE OF THANATOS CR 9
XP 6,400
Female elf vampire cleric of Thanatos 6/rogue 8 (*Pathfinder Roleplaying Game Bestiary* "Vampire")
CE Medium undead (augmented humanoid, elf)
Init +9; **Senses** darkvision 60 ft., low-light vision; **Perception** +16

AC 33, touch 15, flat-footed 28 (+8 armor, +4 Dex, +1 dodge, +6 natural, +4 shield)
hp 61 (6d8+6 plus 2d8+2 plus 14); fast healing 5
Fort +6; **Ref** +12; **Will** +9; +2 vs. enchantments
Defensive Abilities channel resistance +4, evasion; **DR** 10/magic and silver; **Immune** magic sleep, undead traits; **Resist** cold 10, electricity 10, elven immunities
Weaknesses vampire weaknesses

Speed 30 ft.
Melee slam +8 (1d4+4 plus energy drain)
Special Attacks blood drain, children of the night, channel energy 4/day (3d6, DC 14), create spawn, dominate (DC 15), energy drain (2 levels, DC 15), rogue talents (combat trick), sneak attack +1d6
Domain Spell-Like Abilities (CL 6th; melee touch +8):
7/day—*bleeding touch, touch of chaos*
Spells Prepared (CL 6th):
3rd—*animate dead*[D], *deeper darkness, dispel magic, magic circle against good*
2nd—*bull's strength, death knell* (DC 16)[D], *desecrate, hold person* (DC 16), *shatter* (DC 16)
1st—*bless, divine favor, doom* (DC 15), *protection from law*[D], *sanctuary* (DC 15)
0 (at will)—*create water, detect magic, resistance, virtue*
D Domain spells **Domains** Chaos, Death

Str 17, **Dex** 21, **Con** —, **Int** 9, **Wis** 18, **Cha** 13
Base Atk +5; **CMB** +8; **CMD** 23
Feats Alertness[B], Blind-Fight, Combat Casting, Combat Reflexes[B], Command Undead, Craft Wand, Dodge[B], Improved Initiative[B], Lightning Reflexes[B], Mobility, Toughness[B]
Skills Acrobatics +8, Bluff +9, Craft (sculpture) +5, Knowledge (religion) +8, Perception +16 (+17 to locate traps), Sense Motive +14, Spellcraft +6 (+8 to determine the properties of a magic item), Stealth +17; **Racial Modifiers** +8 Bluff, +10 Perception, +8 Sense Motive, +8 Stealth
Languages Common, Elven
SQ aura, change shape (dire bat or wolf, *beast shape II*), elven magic, gaseous form, shadowless, spider climb, spontaneous casting, trapfinding +1
Gear +2 *mithral chainmail*, +2 *heavy steel shield*

Description and Tactics: Beautiful and full of hate, Hethel is the servant of Ykthool, high Priest of Thanatos. She is the servant of the Fountains of Blood, guarding the passage from the eastern side of the sewer complex to the western areas by means of this special teleportation device. Hethel fights until turned to gaseous form, and then seeps to **Area 14** to regenerate and reform a new hunting party. In combat Hethel uses the *sanctuary* spell to build her allies with *bless*, *desecrate* and *deeper darkness*, then using remaining spells of *bull's strength*, and *divine favor* before moving in for hand-to-hand fighting.

The Fountain of Blood

This 6-foot-wide stone bowl of blood dominating the back wall of the chamber emanates a powerful magical aura. The bowl detects as evil and magical. If the PCs use *detect magic*, a successful DC 25 Knowledge (arcana) check tells them that it radiates strong transmutation and necromancy magic. Searching the bowl with a DC 20 Perception check reveals an ancient script. A DC 25 Linguistics check reveals the following words.

> *"Through the blood of ancients the passage revealed, darkened path of nightmares wield."*

Entering the fountain instantly teleports individuals via *dimension door* to **Area 15**. All individual passing through the fountain must succeed on a Fort save (DC 14) or be transformed instantly into a vampire. Characters of 4th level or lower become vampire spawn.

Paladins or clerics of lawful good alignment who pass through the pool of blood without first casting *bless* on the blood fountain or themselves suffer a –2 profane penalty to all rolls (no save) for the duration of their stay within the Sewers of the Underguild.

9: False Crypt Room (CR 8)

This room contains six stone crypts, their lids etched with writing in an ancient tongue. Characters that succeed on a DC 25 Linguistics check easily translate the writing on each crypt. The crypts bear strange descriptions of their supposed inhabitants, all of it bad poetry of the sort to make bards shudder and wince.

A. *Here lies Manco the Moneyed one, man he had a honey tongue, work he never labored long, in living death does he grow strong.*

B. *Before you rests Syther Cross, upon a job a hand he lost, but pimp he could with just one hand, now the blood he does drink all warm and neat, of restless harlots on the streets.*

C. *Here is the tomb of the malicious F'Huge, he is bold as he is huge, fear his might and beware his girth, this tomb filled with his charnel earth.*

D. *Jandilar is a sneaky sort, within his tomb is a fair retort, seek within and you may find, what is hidden a rogue's delight.*

E. *Hethel is an evil bitch, tortured slave a favorite dish, strange is her priestly mood, a vampire who often cooks her food.'*

F. *Memze is a guild mage, drinks blood cold which is quite strange, buried here or not with wit, surprise! You're in a room of...* (and the last word is obscured by some sort of brown substance…)

If the characters succeed on a DC 25 Perception check within the first two rounds of entering the chamber, they note that the entire room is one huge and well-concealed **flooding room trap**. After two rounds the room begins to flood with raw sewage from **Area 20**, as stone blocks roll into place, sealing the room. The room fills completely within 4 rounds. After 8 rounds, everything within the room is flushed down a sewer pipe into **Area 20**. Opening the crypts reveals that each is completely empty and has apparently never been used. Tampering with the crypts sets the trap off instantly.

FLOODING SEWER TRAP **CR 8**
XP 4,800
Type mechanical; **Perception** DC 20; **Disable Device** DC 25

Trigger location; **Reset** manual
Effect room floods with sewage (room floods in 4 rounds; see the "Environment, Drowning" section of Chapter 13 of the *Pathfinder Roleplaying Game Core Rulebook*); onset delay (2 rounds); never miss; eight rounds after the room floods, individuals are flushed down a flooded sewer tube.

10: The Board Room (CR 13+)

The PCs can only reach the boardroom through secret doors in the eastern and western walls. The secret doors are hidden behind life-sized portraits of wealthy, rakish individuals, surrounded by women and riches. The locked secret door in the western wall opens into **Area 10A**. Dominating the center of the room is a wide hardwood table with a polished top, which appears to be carved from a single slab of marble. Paintings of exquisite quality line the walls, and the room appears to be lit with a continuous yet dim light source.

Hiding within this room to either side of the opened doorway and under the table, using it as cover, are **4 vampire spawn** and a **Manco Money Tongue**. Leaning back upon a chair facing the group with a sneer on his cruel black lips, revealing his gleaming white fangs as the PCs enter, is **Syther Cross**. He has a rather wicked-looking scythe lying across his lap. He invites the PCs into the room with a gracious flourish of his silk-sleeved shirt and his wide brimmed and feathered hat.

> "Welcome, adventurers, we admit to being amazed that you have made it this far into the Underguild compound. Surely you are a dangerous band, and likely we could use you in our operations. If you would consider joining us in our enterprises, we can assure that your conversion will be as painless as we can make it. I like your style, living ones, and I have a proposition to make…"

Syther Cross parleys with the PCs as long as possible, allowing other spawn and guild members that still survive to move in and surround the party. An additional **2d6 spawn** and **1d2 guild members** arrive upon the scene in 6 rounds to join the vampires in the Board Room. These additional vampires may be selected from survivors within the complex at the GM's discretion.

SYTHER CROSS **CR 11**
XP 12,800
Male human vampire fighter 5/rogue 5 (*Pathfinder Roleplaying Game Bestiary* "Vampire")
CE Medium undead (augmented humanoid, human)
Init +9; **Senses** darkvision 60 ft.; **Perception** +22

AC 28, touch 16, flat-footed 22 (+6 armor, +5 Dex, +1 dodge, +6 natural)
hp 83 (5d10+5 plus 5d8+5 plus 15); fast healing 5
Fort +6; **Ref** +12; **Will** +4; +1 vs. fear, +4 vs. hot or cold environments and to resist damage from suffocation, +1 vs. traps
Defensive Abilities bravery +1, channel resistance +4, evasion, trap sense, uncanny dodge; **DR** 10/magic and silver; **Immune** undead traits; **Resist** cold 10, electricity 10
Weaknesses vampire weaknesses

Speed 30 ft.
Melee +2 *scythe* +17/+12 (2d4+12/x4) or slam +13 (1d4+7 plus energy drain) or unarmed strike +13/+8 (1d3+5 plus energy drain)
Special Attacks blood drain, children of the night, create spawn, dominate (DC 16), energy drain (2 levels, DC 16), rogue talents (bleeding attack +3, combat trick), sneak attack +3d6, stunning fist 2/day (DC 17), weapon training abilities (heavy blades +1)

Str 21, **Dex** 20, **Con** —, **Int** 13, **Wis** 15, **Cha** 12
Base Atk +8; **CMB** +13; **CMD** 29
Feats Alertness[B], Cleave, Combat Reflexes[B], Dodge[B], Endurance, Great Cleave, Improved Initiative[B], Improved Unarmed Strike, Lightning Reflexes[B], Mobility, Power Attack, Spring Attack, Stunning Fist, Toughness[B], Weapon Focus

(scythe), Weapon Specialization (scythe)
Skills Acrobatics +15, Bluff +19, Climb +15, Diplomacy +11, Disable Device +17, Escape Artist +15, Intimidate +11, Perception +22 (+24 to locate traps), Ride +15, Sense Motive +12, Stealth +13, Swim +10 (+14 to resist nonlethal damage from exhaustion), Use Magic Device +9; **Racial Modifiers** +8 Bluff, +8 Perception, +8 Sense Motive, +8 Stealth
Languages Abyssal, Common
SQ change shape (dire bat or wolf, *beast shape II*), gaseous form, shadowless, spider climb, trapfinding +2
Gear *+4 leather armor*, *+2 scythe*, jewelry (2,000 gp)

Description and Tactics: Syther offers directions to the lair of the Hand of Death, and suggests that if the PCs take down the guildmaster and his lieutenant Ankoz, that he will see the party richly rewarded with 50,000 gold pieces worth of precious booty taken from the lands listed upon the maps surrounding them in the Board Room. Syther Cross seeks to take the *Hollow Blade* for himself and establish control of the Underguild, placing it under newer and younger management: Syther has only been a vampire for about 30 years and he grows impatient with what he considers the tired and somewhat overly cautious machinations of the Underguild.

If the parley disintegrates into combat (i.e., the PCs attack Syther), he tries to tumble to safety using his Acrobatics skill, and then use his tumbling abilities to attack spell casters and priests. He also tries to dominate fighter types.

MANCO MONEY TONGUE **CR 7**
XP 3,200
Male halfling vampire rogue 6 (*Pathfinder Roleplaying Game Bestiary* "Vampire")
NE Small undead (augmented humanoid, halfling)
Init +9; **Senses** darkvision 60 ft.; **Perception** +23

AC 27, touch 17, flat-footed 21 (+4 armor, +5 Dex, +1 dodge, +6 natural, +1 size)
hp 42 (6d8+6 plus 6); fast healing 5
Fort +4; **Ref** +13; **Will** +6; +2 vs. fear, +2 vs. traps
Defensive Abilities channel resistance +4, evasion, trap sense, uncanny dodge; **DR** 10/magic and silver; **Immune** undead traits; **Resist** cold 10, electricity 10
Weaknesses vampire weaknesses

Speed 20 ft.
Melee *+1 sickle* +9 (1d4+4) or *+3 dagger* +11 (1d3+6/19–20) or slam +8 (1d3+4 plus energy drain)
Special Attacks blood drain, children of the night, create spawn, dominate (DC 14), energy drain (2 levels, DC 14), rogue talents (bleeding attack +3), sneak attack +3d6

Str 16, **Dex** 21, **Con** —, **Int** 13, **Wis** 16, **Cha** 13
Base Atk +4; **CMB** +6; **CMD** 22
Feats Alertness[B], Blind-Fight, Childlike, Combat Reflexes[B], Dodge[B], Improved Initiative[B], Lightning Reflexes[B], Skill Focus (Perception), Toughness[B]
Skills Acrobatics +16 (+12 jump), Appraise +7, Bluff +18, Climb +5, Craft (traps) +10, Disable Device +17, Escape Artist +14, Intimidate +7, Perception +23 (+26 to locate traps), Sense Motive +20, Sleight of Hand +14, Stealth +26, Use Magic Device +10; **Racial Modifiers** +2 Acrobatics, +8 Bluff, +2 Climb, +10 Perception, +8 Sense Motive, +8 Stealth
Languages Abyssal, Common, Halfling
SQ change shape (dire bat or wolf, *beast shape II*), fearless, gaseous form, rogue talents (fast stealth, trap spotter), shadowless, spider climb, trapfinding +3
Gear mithral chain shirt, *+1 sickle*, 3 *+3 daggers*, 100 pp

Description and Tactics: Manco is devious and diabolical, often pretending to be a human child to pull his scams over unsuspecting marks. He uses his small size and great Stealth skill to the utmost, pouncing upon his victims when they least expect it. Manco and Syther's hidden spawn move in to assault the party, edging in for surprise in the event that their Stealth rolls succeed against any Perception checks the party takes. Manco tries to remain hidden at all times. If the fight goes badly for his side he changes to bat form and moves to **Area 19B**.

VAMPIRE SPAWN (4) **CR 4**
XP 1,200
Pathfinder Roleplaying Game Bestiary "Vampire"
LE Medium undead
Init +1; **Senses** darkvision 60 ft.; **Perception** +11

AC 15, touch 11, flat-footed 14 (+1 Dex, +4 natural)
hp 26 (4d8+8); fast healing 2
Fort +3; **Ref** +2; **Will** +5
Defensive Abilities channel resistance +2; **DR** 5/silver; **Immune** undead traits; **Resist** cold 10, electricity 10
Weaknesses vampire weaknesses

Speed 30 ft.
Melee slam +4 (1d4+1 plus energy drain)
Special Attacks blood drain, dominate (DC 14), energy drain (1 level, DC 14)

Str 12, **Dex** 12, **Con** —, **Int** 11, **Wis** 13, **Cha** 15
Base Atk +3; **CMB** +4; **CMD** 15
Feats Blind-Fight, Skill Focus (Perception)
Skills Intimidate +9, Knowledge (religion) +7, Perception +11, Stealth +16; **Racial Modifiers** +8 Stealth
Languages Common
SQ gaseous form, resurrection vulnerability, shadowless, spider climb

Tactics: Unless utterly destroyed by a cleric, the vampires assume gaseous form when close to defeat and move to their coffins to reform and fight again, now armed with a better understanding of the PCs' tactics.

Additional Room Details: Amidst the fine paintings are wall maps detailing various cities and empires of the civilized lands, as well as the names of Underguild operators in these territories. You (the GM) could use such maps to introduce new campaigns. The paintings on the walls are of great value to collectors, three of which are considered lost treasures of the art world. Any characters that succeed on a DC 25 skill check using skills such as Appraise, Knowledge (history), or the like know something of the nature of each. Characters succeeding on a DC 25 Appraise check can give a near exact estimate of their worth.

Treasure: Three of the paintings are high art, detailed below.

- ***Only by Sunrise*** by Umberto, a famous painter who weaves illusions into his paintings. The painting shows the majestic sunrise over the jeweled cityscape of Bard's Gate. The command word "Cyrillia" is hidden in the painting amongst the crenellations of the Keep. This painting is a particular favorite of Sangre, the Hand of Death, who views the illusion when holding the *Hollow Blade*, as if he were alive. **Value:** 10,000 gp.
- ***Cult of Wights***, the artist unknown but attributed to T. F. Arcevol, a notorious necromancer. This cult piece has great value to a specialized group of collectors who enjoy gruesome art. The painting, horrific in its ultra-realism and delicate brush stroke, features a pack of wights feasting on chained sacrifices as cultists in the black robes of Orcus observe. The painting has been copied many times, though this piece is the original. **Value:** 1,000 gp, to the proper collector the painting could net as much as 6,000 gp.
- ***Queen of Parnuble***, artist unknown. The painting features Tuiliar the Elven Queen of arboreal Parnuble. The theft of this painting is considered one of Sangre's first great heists. The painting eventually found its way to the Museo, in Reme, where it was stolen while on loan from the royal family of Parnuble. Its theft caused quite a scandal and the elves of Parnuble excised a great tax upon Reme to punish the great port city for not protecting their property. **Value:** 6,000 gp.

Other paintings are of excellent quality, but none are as famous as the first three.

Value: 1,200 gp, 750 gp, 900 gp, 500 gp, wall maps with notes are of unlimited value to authorities, vampire hunters, and underworld groups seeking to eliminate spies within their midst.

10A. Tilting Floor Trap (CR 5)

The secret door in the western wall opens into a corridor that runs north and south. The southern section of corridor ends after 10 feet in a collapsed wall, crudely beamed and buttressed with planks of wood. Anyone succeeding on a DC 15 Perception check notices flecks of gold glinting amongst the broken stones. The "gold" is in fact iron pyrite — fool's gold. A DC 15 Appraise check determines its worthlessness. The entire 10-foot section is a **tilting floor trap**. Individuals stepping onto this section for as long as one round are dropped down a chute and thrown into a sewer pipe draining into **Area 20**.

TILTING FLOOR TRAP **CR 5**
XP 1,600
Type mechanical; **Perception** DC 20; **Disable Device** DC 20

Trigger location; **Reset** automatic (instant; counter-weighted)
Effect slide into sewers and swept to **Area 22** (DC 20 Reflex avoids); onset delay (1 round)

11: Prison Chamber of Go'Loke (CR 14)

A circular chamber 50 feet in diameter is inscribed with silver runes that glow with an unnatural green light. Sitting in the center of the circle is a large figure with two huge pincers and a pair of clawed hands sprouting from its chest. Sitting cross-legged before him is a muscular figure with a deathly pallor. The many-armed beast emanates an unholy aura as he turns his horned head to the party, shaking a set of dice in one of his clawed hands.

The demon is **Go'Loke**, a glabrezu. The guild summoned him here 200 years ago as further protection for its lair. At that time Ankoz crafted a permanent *magic circle against evil* etched in silver to lock the demon within the chamber. Once the *circle* was set in place, treasure seekers entering the archway of **Swirling Yellow Mist** in **Area 1** would have an interesting welcome to the guild stronghold. Go'Loke has had little to entertain himself with all these years except for a set of dice left behind as some cruel joke by Ankoz. Go'Loke has spent the last 10 years throwing bones with **Jo'Mena, his ghoul**, whom he treats like a dog most of the time and never lets win at dice.

Jo'Mena was a spoiled chieftain's son of the Bu'ulamin tribe. His mother was a half-hag. Jo'Mena had a penchant for taking things that were not his. He thought fit to sneak into the ruin and find the secret entrance to the Underguild's infamous sewers. That was 10 years ago. Finding the fountain above the sewer entrance, he flipped the switch and descended the staircase, entering the room of swirling archways. Entering the Swirling Yellow Archway he found himself face to face with Go'Loke, who offered him a game of chance, the pile of treasure he had collected from 180 years of dead adventurers for Jo'Mena's soul. Of course Jo'Mena bet his soul and lost, being transformed almost instantly into the pitiful ghoul that he is today.

Note: Anyone of good alignment may open the northern door to this chamber. Doing so, however, breaks the circle that has kept Go'Loke prisoner all this time. Should this happen, Go'Loke attacks the PCs, hoping to kill them and track down Ankoz, seeking to get his revenge. Should a PC enter from **Area 1C** into the chamber, Go'Loke immediately attacks the party.

GO'LOKE the GLABREZU **CR 13**
XP 25,600
hp 186 (*Pathfinder Roleplaying Game Bestiary* "Demon, Glabrezu")

JO'MENA the GHOUL **CR 1**
XP 400
hp 13 (*Pathfinder Roleplaying Game Bestiary* "Ghoul")
Gear *gauntlet of rust*

Tactics: Go'Loke rattles the dice in his hand pointing to the party members and naming them off by number of the individual he is going to kill, calling out such things as "come on baby, come on seven, seven come eleven, daddy needs a new soul!" as Jo'Mena cowers in the corner trying to avoid combat. If approached, Jo'Mena feebly lashes out with the *gauntlet of rust*, and his paralyzing attack. If the northern doorway is opened before combat or during by a character of good alignment, Go'Loke fights until he is nearly destroyed before escaping via *greater teleport*. He stays away long enough to heal up and come back to gain his revenge upon Ankoz for his centuries of imprisonment.

Treasure: An inventory of the chamber reveals the following items that Go'Loke has hoarded over the years of his imprisonment. 6,526 gp, 15 gems worth 600 gp (x2), 500 gp, 400 gp (x2), 200 gp (x3), 125 gp (x3), and 50 gp (x4), respectively.

12: Eastern Pump House (CR 10)

The secret door in the eastern wall of the Pump House reveals a damp chamber filled with many leaking pipes, as well as highly advanced ancient technological marvels that are part of the nerve center for the sewer and aqueduct system of Curgantium and its massive hydraulics. Any character that succeeds on a DC 22 Perception check finds four large bronze wheels mounted in the walls, two in the west, and one in the south and one in the eastern wall.

Hidden amongst the maze of pipes along the ceiling are **6 vampire spawn,** who have been assigned by Sangre to guard this pump room from intruders.

VAMPIRE SPAWN (6) **CR 4**
XP 1,200
hp 26 (See **Area 10**, *Pathfinder Roleplaying Game Bestiary* "Vampire")

The Bronze Pump Wheels

The four bronze pump wheels control the flow of water and sewage to the sewers, as well as the hydraulic controls of several of the mechanical traps within the dungeon. If any of the pump wheels are turned clockwise, the sewage levels remain unchanged in **Area 20**; however the strength of the current drops by 1/8th relative to the number of pumps turned off.

Pump Wheel A

Turning this pump clockwise until it stops shuts off the hydraulic pressure to the covered pit traps in **Area 4**. A DC 24 Perception check reveals that there is a sound of decreasing water pressure as the wheel is turned. Turning this pump counter-clockwise until it stops increases the sewage depth in **Area 20** by 2 feet.

Pump Wheel B

Turning the pump clockwise until it stops turning shuts off hydraulic pressure to the impaling trap in **Area 7**, automatically disarming the trap. A DC 22 Perception check reveals that there is a sound of decreasing water pressure as the wheel is turned. Turning the pump counter-clockwise increases the sewage depth in **Area 20** by 4 feet, and doubles the strength of the whirlpool in **Area 22**.

Pump Wheel C

Turning this pump wheel clockwise until it stops turning shuts off the hydraulic pressure to the trap in **Area 9**; as before, anyone succeeding on a DC 22 Perception check notices a significant reduction in ambient water pressure noise. Turning the bronze wheel counter-clockwise results in an increased volume of sewage pumping into **Area 20**, raising its original depth by 8 feet and filling hallways outside **Areas 5, 12,** and **13** to a depth of 3 feet. If the door to **Area 12** has not been closed by the party after entering the chamber, the foul waters begin to spill into this room and other opened rooms at this time. The 3-foot-deep wave of sewage reduces movement rates by 1/4, requiring characters to succeed on a DC 10 Reflex save to avoid falling and being dragged by the currents of the waters into the whirlpools in **Area 22** and **Area 23**.

Pump Wheel D

Turning this pump clockwise turns off the tilting floor traps in **Areas 5** and **10B**; there is a resounding clank at this time as if something large is unlocking off to the north. Turning the wheel counter-clockwise fills **Area 20** almost to the ceiling with sewage, filling the hallways and opened rooms with a 7-foot-high surge of raw waste, and quadrupling the strength of the whirlpool in **Area 22**.

Filling the sewers in this fashion releases Methaloggot from her imprisonment in **Area 21**. Anyone succeeding on a DC 22 Perception check hears her roar through the murky sewage that now fills the dungeon.

13A: The Never-Ending Corridor

The bronze bound door in the northwestern corner of **Area 13A** is protected by an *arcane lock* spell. The door opens to reveal a dark corridor of polished black diorite, approximately 80 feet deep, with a similar door upon the far end of the corridor. As soon as the PCs have traveled 40 feet down the corridor, allow them DC 15 Perception checks to notice that they are still 80 feet from the door. Turning around to look the other way, they find that they are 80 feet from the door they exited as well. Continuing to move forward down the hall increases this distance away by a proportionate distance to that which the party moves; in other words, if the party moves 10 feet, the door appears 10 feet farther away.

This corridor is shielded against transmutation, to a dangerous and possibly deadly effect. Should PCs attempt to cast *dimension door*, *teleport*, or *plane shift* to escape the corridor, roll 1d6 to let fate determine the result:

Roll	Result
1–2	Caster is *teleported* to **Area 21** to become a snack for Methaloggot.
3	*Teleported* to **Area 11**, to become the demon's new craps partner.
4	*Teleported* into the whirlpool in **Area 23**.
5	*Teleported* to an empty locked burial vault in **Area 14**.
6	*Teleported* to the **Fountain Entrance to the Underguild**.

13B: Hotchka the Medusa (CR 14)

This chamber is missing a large chunk of wall in the northwestern corner of the room. It has locked bronze bound doors in the northwest and southeastern corners. A trio of humanoid figures sits near a flaming bronze brazier. As the tallest of the figures turns to face the party, her eyes glow a demonic blue as she reaches for an arrow from her quiver. A pair of statues reflects the dancing fire glow of the brazier as the woman draws her bow, her hair waving like a nest of snakes.

This area chamber is the lair of **Hotchka**, a medusa whom Sangre transformed to the unliving nearly a hundred years ago. **Cainbry**, a human vampire rogue, and **Phryc** the Unloved, a half-orc guild enforcer, join Hotchka in her lair.

HOTCHKA **CR 12**
XP 19,200
Female medusa vampire rogue 4 (*Pathfinder Roleplaying Game Bestiary* "Medusa", Vampire")
CE Medium undead (augmented monstrous humanoid)
Init +12; **Senses** all-around vision, darkvision 60 ft.; **Perception** +33

AC 28, touch 19, flat-footed 19 (+8 Dex, +1 dodge, +9 natural)
hp 138 (8d8+40 plus 4d8+20 plus 16); fast healing 5
Fort +11; **Ref** +23; **Will** +14; +1 vs. traps
Defensive Abilities channel resistance +4, evasion, trap sense, uncanny dodge; **DR** 10/magic and silver; **Immune** undead traits; **Resist** cold 10, electricity 10
Weaknesses vampire weaknesses

Speed 30 ft.
Melee bite +19 (1d4+4) or slam +19 (1d4+4 plus energy drain)
Ranged *+1 composite longbow* +20/+15/+10 (1d8+5/x3)
Special Attacks blood drain, children of the night, create spawn, dominate (DC 21), energy drain (2 levels, DC 21), petrifying gaze (30 ft., DC 19), poison, rogue talents (bleeding attack +2, combat trick), sneak attack +2d6

Str 19, **Dex** 26, **Con** —, **Int** 20, **Wis** 19, **Cha** 20
Base Atk +11; **CMB** +15; **CMD** 34
Feats Alertness[B], Combat Reflexes[B], Dodge[B], Far Shot, Improved Initiative[B], Lightning Reflexes[B], Point-Blank Shot, Precise Shot, Rapid Shot, Toughness[B], Weapon Finesse
Skills Acrobatics +21, Bluff +26, Craft (carpentry) +14, Diplomacy +18, Disguise +16, Escape Artist +21, Intimidate +18, Linguistics +18, Perception +33 (+35 to locate traps), Sense Motive +29, Sleight of Hand +21, Stealth +29, Use Magic Device +18; **Racial Modifiers** +8 Bluff, +12 Perception, +8 Sense Motive, +8 Stealth
Languages Common
SQ change shape (dire bat or wolf, *beast shape II*), gaseous form, shadowless, spider climb, trapfinding +2
Gear *+1 composite longbow* (Str +4), 50 *+3 arrows*, *cloak of resistance +3*

CAINBRY **CR 7**
XP 3,200
Male human vampire rogue 6 (*Pathfinder Roleplaying Game Bestiary* "Vampire")
CE Medium undead (augmented humanoid, human)
Init +8; **Senses** darkvision 60 ft.; **Perception** +21

AC 25, touch 15, flat-footed 20 (+4 armor, +4 Dex, +1 dodge, +6 natural)
hp 60 (6d8+18 plus 12); fast healing 5
Fort +7; **Ref** +11; **Will** +4; +2 vs. traps
Defensive Abilities channel resistance +4, evasion, trap sense, uncanny dodge; **DR** 10/magic and silver; **Immune** undead traits; **Resist** cold 10, electricity 10
Weaknesses vampire weaknesses

Speed 30 ft.
Melee slam +8 (1d4+3 plus energy drain)
Ranged sling +8 (1d4+2)
Special Attacks blood drain, children of the night, create spawn, dominate (DC 16), energy drain (2 levels, DC 16), rogue talents (bleeding attack +3, combat trick), sneak attack +3d6

Str 14, **Dex** 19, **Con** —, **Int** 13, **Wis** 14, **Cha** 16
Base Atk +4; **CMB** +6; **CMD** 21
Feats Alertness[B], Combat Reflexes[B], Dodge[B], Great Fortitude, Improved Initiative[B], Lightning Reflexes[B], Mobility, Point-Blank Shot, Power Attack, Toughness[B], Weapon Finesse
Skills Acrobatics +13, Bluff +20, Climb +11, Diplomacy +12, Escape Artist +13, Intimidate +12, Perception +21 (+24 to locate traps), Sense Motive +21, Sleight of Hand +13, Stealth +21; **Racial Modifiers** +8 Bluff, +8 Perception, +8 Sense Motive, +8 Stealth
Languages Abyssal, Common
SQ change shape (dire bat or wolf, *beast shape II*), gaseous form, rogue talents (fast stealth), shadowless, spider climb, trapfinding +3
Combat Gear 4 thunderstones; **Other Gear** *+2 leather armor*, sling, 50 *+3 sling bullets*

PHRYC **CR 8**
XP 4,800
Male half-orc vampire fighter 4/rogue 3 (*Pathfinder Roleplaying Game Bestiary* "Vampire")
CE Medium undead (augmented humanoid, orc)
Init +8; **Senses** darkvision 60 ft.; **Perception** +20

AC 28, touch 12, flat-footed 26 (+10 armor, +1 Dex, +1 dodge, +6 natural)
hp 57 (4d10+4 plus 3d8+3 plus 11); fast healing 5
Fort +6; **Ref** +10; **Will** +4; +1 vs. fear, +1 vs. traps
Defensive Abilities bravery +1, channel resistance +4, orc ferocity, trap sense; **DR** 10/magic and silver; **Immune** undead traits; **Resist** cold 10, electricity 10
Weaknesses vampire weaknesses

Speed 30 ft.
Melee slam +11 (1d4+7 plus energy drain)
Special Attacks blood drain, children of the night, create spawn, dominate (DC 14), energy drain (2 levels, DC 14), rogue talents (combat trick), sneak attack +2d6

Str 20, **Dex** 18, **Con** —, **Int** 12, **Wis** 15, **Cha** 12
Base Atk +6; **CMB** +11; **CMD** 23
Feats Alertness[B], Blind-Fight, Cleave, Combat Reflexes[B], Dodge[B], Great Cleave, Improved Initiative[B], Lightning Reflexes[B], Mobility, Mounted Combat, Power Attack, Ride-by Attack, Toughness[B], Weapon Focus (longsword)
Skills Acrobatics +7 (+12 to jump), Appraise +9, Bluff +9, Craft (alchemy) +9, Handle Animal +8, Intimidate +3, Perception +20 (+21 to locate traps), Ride +7, Sense Motive +12, Stealth +20, Swim +8; **Racial Modifiers** +8 Bluff, +2 Intimidate, +8 Perception, +8 Sense Motive, +8 Stealth
Languages Abyssal, Common, Orc
SQ change shape (dire bat or wolf, *beast shape II*), gaseous form, shadowless, spider climb, trapfinding +1
Gear *+2 shadow half-plate, boots of striding and springing*

Tactics: Hotchka immediately attempts to catch the gaze of the PCs as they open the door, using her gaze to turn the intruders to stone. Phryc and Cainbry tumble out of sight and immediately attempt to hide, waiting to sneak attack whoever enters the chamber as Hotchka tries to turn foes to stone while firing her mighty bow at lightly armored targets.

13C: Sewer Skiff

The break in the northeastern wall opens into **Area 20**. The stench rising from this river of fouled water and ancient sewage causes all who smell it to succeed on a DC 15 Fortitude save or be sickened for the remainder of their time in the Sewers of the Underguild.

A finely crafted boat of unknown metal lies submerged in the mire of sewage, tied off to a fine copper chain looped through a bronze ring set in the hard ancient stone. Anyone succeeding on a DC 22 Strength check can pull the boat to the surface, where it becomes instantly clean and free of any foulness. The boat has a pair of oars made of the same unknown material, and it can be used to navigate the river of raw sewage in **Area 20**. The boat holds up to 6 passengers and their gear. It is an ancient craftsmanship and building material that allows it to bear weight in excess of 2,400 pounds without sinking. The odd metal of which it is made acts as though it had a permanent *prestidigitation* spell cast on it, keeping it perpetually clean and shiny. This is not a magical effect, however, and cannot be detected with *detect magic*.

THE SEWER SKIFF
Large water vehicle (*Pathfinder Roleplaying Game Ultimate Combat* "Vehicles")
Squares 3 (5 ft. by 15 ft.); **Cost** 1,000 gp

AC 9; **hardness** 10
hp 60 (29)
Base Save +0

Maximum Speed 30 ft.; **Acceleration** 10 ft.
CMB +1; **CMD** 11
Ramming Damage 1d8

This small water vehicle is primarily used to disembark from larger ships or to traverse small areas of water—perhaps ferrying a few passengers across a stream or small lake. The sewer skiff can carry 2,400 pounds of cargo or 6 passengers.
Propulsion current (water) or muscle (pushed; 1 or 2 Medium rowers; one is the driver)
Driving Check Survival
Forward Facing boat's forward
Driving Device oars
Driving Space the center square of the skiff
Decks 1

14: Crypts of the Underguild (CR variable)

A locked secret door leads into this hidden chamber, lined from floor to ceiling on the northern and western walls with bronze plated burial vaults. Several pairs of glowing blood red eyes peer out of the darkness.

Suddenly, **4 vampire spawn** slink out of the darkness, their blackened lips parting to reveal gleaming white canine teeth, razor sharp and longing for blood.

Guarding the crypt room are the vampire spawn along with any full vampires previously encountered who have regenerated sufficiently to fight off intruders. These vampires do not include Ankoz or Ykthool.

VAMPIRE SPAWN (4) CR 4
XP 1,200
hp 26 (See **Area 10**)

Tactics: The vampires use any and every means at their disposal to protect the burial vaults, including remaining spells, potions, scrolls and charges on wands, or other magic items that they may have.

Note: Previously defeated vampires who have not healed within their vault to at least 1 hit point are within their vault, helpless.

Additional Room Information: The vampires' vaults are closed and locked with a bronze plate scribed with the name and epitaph of each of the undead. The vaults are 2 feet tall and 4 feet wide, comprising 6 columns of bronze plated vaults. Each column is has 5 vaults, making a total of 30 vaults for vampires and their spawn. Personal possessions and treasure of each vampire are found within the vaults. Each vault has a spring-loaded bed with finely crafted wheels, its "slab" pulling out in a similar fashion to a modern morgue vault.

Locked Bronze Vaults: Disable Device DC 28; Break DC 28.

Treasure: Guild members' personal items from descriptions are found within their respective vaults, for example, Memze the Lame's *amulet of natural armor +3*, *arcane scroll* of 2 spells (*deeper darkness* x2), a *wand of lightning bolt* (CL 5th, 20 charges), are found within his vault, in the event that he is reduced to negative hit points and was forced into his vault for healing.

Additional Treasure: 2,669 gp; *potion of disguise self*, a *cursed potion of owl's wisdom* (reduces Wisdom by –4 for 3 hours), a *potion of cat's grace*, and a *cloak of arachnida* (limited, functions only at night; 2/3 value).

15: Western Blood Fountain and Vampiric Ooze (CR 8)

The eastern wall of the room is dominated by a large wolf's headed fountain, dripping thick red blood from its jaws into a 6-foot-diameter stone bowl at its feet. Written in glowing runes of Celestial origin but in the Abyssal language are the following words:

> *"Wield me on the nightmare's path through the innocence of blood."*

Characters succeeding on a DC 24 Linguistics check can translate this message easily if they don't know the languages.

As the last party member steps from the fountain, the blood within it begins to gurgle and congeal with a gelatinous thickness, pouring onto the floor with a sickly slurping noise as it lashes out. An amalgam of all the party's hate, pain, greed, fears and jealousy, the **vampiric ooze** lashes its pseudopods at the nearest party member to it with a vicious slam attack. As the party turns to face the new horror, they see momentarily within the rippling of its syrupy surface a reflection of their own darkness.

VAMPIRIC OOZE CR 8
XP 4,800
The Tome of Horrors Complete 463
CE Large undead (augmented ooze)
Init –1; **Senses** blindsight 60 ft.; **Perception** +3

AC 4, touch 4, flat-footed 4 (–5 Dex, –1size)
hp 52 (12d8–12 plus 12)
Fort +2, **Ref** –2, **Will** +1
Defensive Abilities split (cold and electricity, 10 hp); **Immune** cold, electricity, ooze traits, undead traits
Weaknesses sunlight vulnerability

Speed 10 ft., climb 10 ft.
Melee slam +10 (2d4+3 plus energy drain and grab)
Space 10 ft.; **Reach** 5 ft.
Special Attacks constrict (2d4+3), create spawn, energy drain (1 level, DC 14)

Str 15, **Dex** 1, **Con** —, **Int** —, **Wis** 1, **Cha** 8
Base Atk +9; **CMB** +12 (+16 to grapple); **CMD** 17 (can't be tripped)
Feats Improved Inititiative[B], Toughness[B]
Skills Climb +10, Perception +3;
Racial Modifiers +8 Perception

Environment underground
Organization solitary or pack (vampiric ooze plus 2–4 zombies)
Treasure none

Create Spawn (Su) Any humanoid slain by a vampiric ooze becomes a zombie in 1d4 rounds. Spawn are under the command of the vampiric ooze that created them and remain enslaved until its death. They do not possess any of the abilities they had in life.
Sunlight Vulnerability (Ex) Exposing a vampiric ooze to direct sunlight staggers it on the first round, and it is destroyed utterly in the next round if it cannot escape.

Tactics: The vampiric ooze attacks the same target until it has absorbed the life force of that target before moving on. If the creature splits while attacked, both split halves attack the same target.

After the vampiric ooze in the fountain is defeated, the blood pouring from the fountain transforms to pure clean water, completely potable and crystal clear. The fountain when re-entered *teleports* individuals instantly to **Area 8** and vice versa with no further difficulties.

Searching the room with a successful DC 24 Perception check reveals a **secret door** behind the blood fountain, which leads to **Area 16.**

16: Western Pump Room

The secret door from **Area 15** leads to the second pump room of the ancient sewer system. Large pipes of bronze and ceramic run along the ceilings and up the walls, which are fitted with four bronze pump wheels. Unlike the pump wheels in **Area 8**, these bronze pump wheels, when cranked simultaneously clockwise, remove the stone block in **Area 1**, as long as the pumps in **Area 12** have been shut off. This creates an exit to the Sewers of the Underguild. The secondary effect of shutting off the pumps is to turn off the whirlpools in **Area 22** and **23**, and lowering the sewer level to a depth of 4 feet. Cranking any of the pump wheels counter-clockwise has no other effect.

17: Ykthool's Cloister (CR 8)

Behind the locked door is a richly appointed chamber with polished hardwood paneling and silk wall hangings. A canopied four-poster coffin rests elegantly in the northeastern corner of the chamber. An ornate mirror with a frame of solid gold faces the door. Holy symbols featuring a skull pierced with a bident, also made of solid gold hang upon the walls, along with unusually realistic paintings of men and women of all races just as death takes them, their pale, drawn faces holding the last vestiges of life.

Ykthool spends most of his time within the shrine of Thanatos, **Area**

18B. Ykthool has little fear of losing this coffin to any enemies foolish enough to penetrate this far into the Underguild's lair.

The mirror facing the door is a foul and deadly trick given as gift from Thanatos to one who remembers the old ways. See **New Magic Items** at the end of this adventure for details on the *mirror of abysmal damnation*.

The **locked and trapped coffin** in the northeastern corner of the chamber is the resting place of Ykthool, vampire priest of Thanatos. Touching the coffin in any way releases the ***blade barrier* trap** unless a prayer to Thanatos is intoned.

***BLADE BARRIER* TRAP** **CR 8**
XP 6,400
Type magic; **Perception** DC 31; **Disable Device** DC 31

Trigger touch; **Reset** none; **Bypass** prayer to Thanatos
Effect spell effect (*blade barrier*, 10d6 damage; DC 19 Reflex half or negates); multiple targets (all targets in a 10-ft. radius around the coffin)

Note: Casting *bless* upon the coffin or pouring holy water into it after removing the graveyard dirt denies Ykthool his resting place, requiring him to return to the **Area 14: Crypts of the Underguild**, or some other location to rest until healed.

Treasure: The silk-lined coffin is stitched with 50 diamonds, valued at 100 gp each. *A bag of holding (type I)* contains a *scroll of slay living* (CL 10th). Tearing out the silk lining of the coffin reveals 20 lbs. of graveyard dirt, valued as a spell component to necromancers and certain sects of priests. The four silk wall hangings are valued at 200 gp each, and the two paintings could gain 200 gp each from a collector. Last, but not least, is the *mirror of abyssal damnation*.

18A: Entrance to Shrine of Thanatos (CR 6)

The secret door opens onto corridor with an elaborately carved ebon wood door in the southern wall. A symbol of a silver skull with two daggers driven through it in an "X" pattern is inlaid upon the floor. The floor beyond the locked secret door that leads to the shrine of Thanatos is trapped to trigger an ***enervation* trap** on any living beings that cross the threshold.

***ENERVATION* TRAP** **CR 6**
XP 2,400
Type magic; **Perception** DC 29; **Disable Device** DC 29

Trigger location; **Reset** automatic
Effect spell effect (*enervation*, Atk +10 ranged touch [1d4 negative levels])

18B: Shrine of Thanatos (CR 13)

Directly across from the door is a black altar engraved with skulls of silver, with a white silk cloth set over it, bearing a bowl and candelabra of pure platinum and a skull of deepest black. Behind the altar stands an 11-foot-tall statue in dark gray marble of a beautiful and cruel woman, perhaps an elf. In the statue's right hand is a solid iron bident, its two forked prongs a foul black. An obsidian skull resting on the floor reflects a glinting and malevolent light within the dimly lit room. A large silver pentagram with a silver skull decorates the floor in the center of the room, and the low sounds of chanting can be heard from somewhere within the chamber.

Ykthool began preparing his defensive spells as the PCs enter the chamber, likely having heard them fiddle with the traps outside the door to the Shrine, cloaking himself in *sanctuary* as he prepares his strongest powers.

As soon as the threshold of the chamber is crossed by a living being, the **Statue of Thanatos** animates and attacks. The statue is a gift to Ykthool from Orcus in his guise as Thanatos the Fallen, deliverer of the dead. Orcus appreciates a high priest who remembers the old ways.

YKTHOOL **CR 11**
XP 12,800
Male human vampire cleric of Thanatos 8 (*Pathfinder Roleplaying Game Bestiary* "Vampire")
CE Medium undead (augmented humanoid, human)
Init +7; **Senses** darkvision 60 ft.; **Perception** +17

AC 31, touch 13, flat-footed 28 (+8 armor, +2 Dex, +1 dodge, +6 natural, +4 shield)
hp 118 (10d8+50 plus 20); fast healing 5
Fort +12; **Ref** +8; **Will** +12
Defensive Abilities channel resistance +4, death's embrace; **DR** 10/magic and silver; **Immune** undead traits; **Resist** cold 10, electricity 10
Weaknesses vampire weaknesses

Speed 20 ft.
Melee slam +11 (1d4+6 plus energy drain)
Special Attacks aura of destruction (+5, 10 rounds/day), blood drain, children of the night, channel energy 10/day (5d6, DC 20), create spawn, destructive smite 8/day (+5 dmg), dominate (DC 20), energy drain (2 levels, DC 20)
Domain Spell-Like Abilities (CL 10th; melee touch +11):
8/day—*bleeding touch*
Spells Prepared (CL 10th; melee touch +11, ranged touch +10):
5th—*plane shift* (DC 20), *slay living* (DC 20)[D], *slay living* (DC 20), *summon monster V*
4th—*freedom of movement, inflict critical wounds* (DC 19)[D], *lesser planar ally, poison* (DC 19), *summon monster IV*
3rd—*animate dead*[D], *animate dead, contagion* (DC 18), *deeper darkness, protection from energy*
2nd—*bull's strength, death knell* (DC 17)[D], *desecrate, darkness, hold person* (x2) (DC 17)
1st—*bane* (DC 16), *command* (DC 16), *divine favor, doom* (DC 16), *shield of faith, summon monster I, true strike*[D]
0 (at will)—*detect magic, detect poison, mending, virtue*
D Domain spells **Domains** Death, Destruction

Str 18, **Dex** 16, **Con** —, **Int** 13, **Wis** 20, **Cha** 20
Base Atk +7; **CMB** +11; **CMD** 24
Feats Alertness[B], Combat Reflexes[B], Command Undead, Dodge[B], Empower Spell, Extra Channel, Improved Initiative[B], Leadership, Lightning Reflexes[B], Maximize Spell, Quicken Spell, Toughness[B]
Skills Bluff +13, Diplomacy +15, Heal +9, Knowledge (religion) +12, Perception +17, Profession (scribe) +15, Sense Motive +25, Spellcraft +12, Stealth +6; **Racial Modifiers** +8 Bluff, +8 Perception, +8 Sense Motive, +8 Stealth
Languages Abyssal, Common
SQ aura, change shape (dire bat or wolf, *beast shape II*), gaseous form, shadowless, spider climb, spontaneous casting
Gear +2 *chainmail*, +2 *heavy steel shield*

STATUE OF THANATOS (STONE GOLEM) **CR 11**
XP 12,800
hp 107 (*Pathfinder Roleplaying Game Bestiary* "Golem, Stone")

Tactics: Ykthool remains hidden, using his *sanctuary* spell to further build his defenses. By the time the party enters, he has cast *bull's strength*, *divine favor*, *shield of faith*, *protection from energy [fire]*, *freedom of movement*, and *desecrate*, waiting for the party to become occupied with the stone golem before casting *slay living* on the party's cleric, paladin, or wizard. When reduced to 0 hit points, Ykthool dissolves to gaseous form.

Hidden carefully in Abyssal script within the silver pentagram on the floor are words. Characters succeeding on a DC 20 Perception check find these hidden words, and if they succeed on a DC 25 Linguistics check, they can translate the message.

> *"Through the blood of mortal sacrificed is the invitation made, to the master of Underguild, in Death's fine name, let the living blood be paid."*

A character of good alignment filling the platinum bowl atop the altar with blood *teleports* all living beings within the shrine of Thanatos to **Area 24**, with no saving throw.

Treasure: Sitting atop the altar is the platinum sacrificial bowl valued at 4, 000 gp, four platinum candle sticks of 100 gp value each, Four black *candles of evocation* (*chaotic evil*), and a *darkskull*.

19: Slave Chambers of the Underguild

Beyond this locked door lies the passage to the poor souls who serve as blood slaves of the Underguild.

19A: The Trapped Prison Entrance (CR 10)

An L-shaped corridor lined with torches lit with *continual flame* turns southwest to another locked door after a distance of 30 feet. The corridor is trapped with a **crushing wall trap** that triggers as travelers cross the elbow curve, its disarming device located in a wall sconce containing a guttering torch.

CRUSHING WALL TRAP CR 10
XP 9,600
Type mechanical; **Perception** DC 20; **Disable Device** DC 25

Trigger location; **Reset** manual
Effect crushing walls (10d6 damage); onset delay (2 rounds); never miss; multiple targets (all targets in a 20-ft. by 10-ft space)

19B: The Slave Cages.

Eight iron-barred cells contain the unfortunate blood slaves of the Underguild, charmed and drawn, their necks and arms and thighs covered in fang marks and bruises from their nightly bleeding and seduction. Each of the 8 prisoners, **2 elves** and **6 humans**, were selected for their beauty and vitality to serve the Underguild. The slaves are under the effect of a *charm monster* spell placed upon them by Ankoz, and are thus docile and unwilling to leave their cells. A successful *dispel magic* or *break enchantment* removes the charm. One of the prisoners, **Ayissa** an elf sorcerer, is willing to join the party if rescued, healed, and outfitted for war against the Underguild. If her offer goes unheeded, she merely *teleports* to her home. If Manco's team was defeated in a fight with Syther, he comes here and attempts to charm Ayissa into telling the party he is her little brother and must also be "rescued" by the party.

AYISSA* CR 9
XP 6,400
Female elf sorcerer 10
NG Medium humanoid (elf)
Init +1; **Senses** low-light vision; **Perception** –4

AC 11, touch 11, flat-footed 10 (+1 Dex)
hp 47 (10d6+50)
Fort –1; **Ref** –4; **Will** –1; +2 vs. enchantments, +2 luck bonus during surprise round or when unaware of an attack
Immune magic sleep; **Resist** elven immunities

Speed 30 ft.
Bloodline Spell-Like Ability (CL 10th; melee touch –5):
7/day—*touch of destiny*
Spells Known (CL 10th; melee touch –5, ranged touch –2):
5th (3/day)—*teleport*
4th (6/day)—*beast shape II, fire shield, freedom of movement*
3rd (7/day)—*blink, clairaudience/clairvoyance, fireball* (DC 17), *protection from energy*
2nd (7/day)—*acid arrow, blur, levitate, mirror image, see invisibility*
1st (7/day)—*alarm, burning hands* (DC 15), *charm person* (DC 15), *chill touch* (DC 15), *feather fall* (DC 15), *magic missile*
0 (at will)—*dancing lights, detect magic, detect poison, ghost sound* (DC 14), *light, mage hand, prestidigitation* (DC 14), *ray of frost, read magic*
Bloodline Destined

Str 7, **Dex** 12, **Con** 18, **Int** 12, **Wis** 10, **Cha** 19
Base Atk +5; **CMB** –5; **CMD** 6
Feats Alertness, Combat Casting, Craft Rod, Enlarge Spell, Eschew Materials, Leadership, Maximize Spell
Skills Acrobatics –7, Appraise –7, Bluff +5, Climb –10, Craft (alchemy) +2, Diplomacy –4, Disguise –4, Escape Artist –7, Fly –3, Heal –8, Intimidate +0, Knowledge (arcana) +0, Perception –4, Ride –7, Sense Motive –6, Spellcraft +2 (+4 to determine the properties of a magic item), Stealth –7, Survival –8, Swim –10, Use Magic Device +5; **Racial Modifiers** +2 Perception
Languages Common, Draconic, Elven
SQ fated, it was meant to be (1/day)
*Ayissa is currently suffering 8 negative levels from the vampires' attacks on her. She has a –8 penalty on all ability checks, attack rolls, combat maneuver checks, Combat Maneuver Defense, saving throws, and skill checks. In addition, her current and total hit points are reduced by 40. She is also treated as 2nd-level for the purpose of level-dependent variables (such as spellcasting).

The Brotherhood of Skulls, a pirate band led by the notorious Captain Cho Sun, took Ayissa prisoner and sold her into slavery. Her beauty and strength have captivated both Ankoz and Sangre, causing a minor rift between the two. Ayissa alludes to wild blood orgies that take place within the master's chamber where the guild members gather for their feast. She tells the party that the slaves are gathered every other night from their prison and led to a Shrine of Thanatos, where one of their numbers blood is used to fill a bowl of platinum teleporting them all instantly to the chamber of the one known as the Hand of Death, whom she has overheard Ankoz refer to as Sangre.

20. The Sewer Cavern

This vast, twisting cavern is truly a river of raw filth. The cavern has a ceiling 40 feet high, with the river of filth averaging 20 feet in depth. Stretching nearly 400 feet from the **Area 21** the cavern averages 30 feet in width, until it reaches its widest part surrounding **Area 24** where the cavern is approximately 120 feet wide by 70 feet.

River of Filth

Individuals falling into the river of filth must succeed on a DC 20 Swim check to keep their head above the putrid water in this dangerous current. Anyone falling into the current near **Area 22** moves at a rate of 20 feet per round, accelerating by 10 feet per round the closer they get to the whirlpool. Furthermore, individuals falling into the river of filth must succeed on a DC 12 Fortitude save or become infected with filth fever. If they fall into the pool below **Area 13A**, characters must continue to make Swim checks each round as they are drawn towards **Area 23**. Anyone failing their Swim check by more than 5 goes under water and begins to drown. See the "Environment, Drowning" section of Chapter 13 of the *Pathfinder Roleplaying Game Core Rulebook* for details on drowning.

21: Altar of Filth (CR 14)

At the far northern end of the cavern, a cyclopean altar of pure foulness rises 10 foot above the putrid waters. The carved visage of a froglike face stares out at all viewers, its wide mouth open with a great fountain of filth pouring from it. The filth bathes a large reptilian figure, bound with a collar and chains of pure adamantine, most of its great bulk hidden beneath the foul waters of the underground river. The serpent's yellow eyes stare menacingly at all who approach.

This is the prison of **Methaloggot the Fouler**, an old black dragon.

Methaloggot has been chained here for 300 years. Lured to the Sewers of the Underguild with the scent of easy money in her nostrils, Methaloggot had no idea of the surprise the Underguild had in store for her. After falling for a sinister trap of treasure and glittering gemstones atop the ancient stone platform, the dragon realized her folly. Ankoz and Ykthool blasted the young dragon with magic as Sangre slipped the adamantine noose about her horned head unseen. He then sliced her wings from her back with the *Hollow Blade*. Then, casting a great and powerful ritual, Ankoz consecrated the altar in the name of Tsathogga, and Ykthool blessed it in the name of Thanatos.

METHALOGGOT **CR 14**
XP 38,400
Female old black dragon (*Pathfinder Roleplaying Game Bestiary* "Chromatic Dragon, Black")
CE Huge dragon (water)
Init +4; **Senses** dragon senses; **Perception** +29
Aura frightful presence (240 ft., DC 22, 5d6 rds)

AC 32, touch 8, flat-footed 32 (+24 natural, –2 size)
hp 225 (18d12+108)
Fort +17; **Ref** +11; **Will** +15
DR 10/magic; **Immune** acid, paralysis, sleep; **SR** 25

Speed 60 ft., fly 200 ft. (poor), swim 60 ft.
Melee bite +26 (2d8+13 plus 2d6 acid), 2 claws +25 (2d6+9), tail slap +23 (2d6+13)
Space 15 ft.; **Reach** 10 ft.
Special Attacks breath weapon (100 ft line, 16d6 acid, every 1d4 rds, Ref DC 25 half)
Spell-Like Abilities (CL 18th):
Constant—*speak with animals* (reptiles only)
At will— *darkness* (80 ft. radius), *plant growth*
1/day—*corrupt water*
Spells Known (CL 7th):
3rd (5/day)—*dispel magic, slow* (DC 16)
2nd (7/day)—*glitterdust* (DC 15), *invisibility, summon swarm*
1st (7/day)—*alarm, mage armor, magic missile, obscuring mist, true strike*
0 (at will)—*dancing lights, detect magic, light, mage hand, mending, message, read magic*

Str 29, **Dex** 10, **Con** 23, **Int** 16, **Wis** 19, **Cha** 16
Base Atk +18; **CMB** +29; **CMD** 39 (43 vs. trip)
Feats Alertness, Combat Expertise, Improved Initiative, Improved Vital Strike, Multiattack, Power Attack, Skill Focus (Stealth), Vital Strike, Weapon Focus (bite)
Skills Fly +13, Handle Animal +21, Intimidate +24, Knowledge (arcana) +24, Knowledge (history) +24, Perception +29, Sense Motive +6, Spellcraft +24, Stealth +19, Swim +38

Languages Common, Draconic, Giant, Orc
SQ swamp stride, water breathing

Tactics: Methaloggot uses any spells and tactics that increase her armor class and create havoc amongst the PCs. Often using her *darkness* ability she sets the battleground so her opponents are at the greatest disadvantage while her blindsight permits her to continue to effectively combat her enemies. Methaloggot, having no wings, receives no wing buffet attack.

Altar of Filth (CR 5)

The Altar of Filth generates an aura of absolute evil. Even touching the altar with one's flesh requires the individual to succeed on a DC 14 Fortitude save or become infected with the disease slimy doom. The altar can only be destroyed by first casting *clean*, *bless*, and *create water* over the altar, followed by simultaneously casting *remove curse* and *dispel magic* upon the altar with a targeted *dispel* of DC 23. Once this is done, the face of Tsathogga shatters and breaks from the altar, and pure water begins to pour from the pipe where his mouth once was. A character succeeding on a DC 27 Knowledge (arcana) check understands the exact process by which the altar may be destroyed, with the *legend lore* spell being the only other method of discovering this truly arcane secret.

22. The Big Flush (CR 5)

The northern whirlpool pulls all who come within 30 feet of it into its crushing grasp. A DC 30 Swim check is required to escape from its clutches; those failing are swallowed by the whirlpool on the following round, taking 6d6 points of crushing damage per round as they are sucked under the foul waters to be spewed out in **Area 23**, 4 rounds later. Individuals thus trapped are allowed a DC 20 Constitution check to hold their breath or begin to drown. See the "Environment, Drowning" section of Chapter 13 of the *Pathfinder Roleplaying Game Core Rulebook*. The spell *water breathing* protects individuals from drowning, though only magic that offers damage reduction grants any protection from the crushing force of the whirlpool. Concentration checks within the whirlpool are at a base DC of 20 for the purposes of spell casting while caught in the throes of the crushing water.

23. The Southern Whirlpool (CR 5)

This swirling morass of foul water lies before **Area 24**. Individuals sucked through **Area 22** are vomited forth from the whirlpool here. This whirlpool pushes all things in the vicinity of it towards the walls of the chamber or sends them hurling towards the stone platform where Sangre's Tomb lies, causing an additional 3d6 points of damage. Anyone succeeding on a DC 25 Swim check escapes the power of the whirlpool, allowing the individual to swim to the relative safety of the exterior of Sangre's Tomb. Anyone succeeding on a DC 20 Swim check remains above the surface of the sewage, while others are sucked into one of the 2 sewer pipes draining from the lower end of the cavern at a rate of 20 feet per round. They are eventually swept from the Sewers of the Underguild and deposited 5 miles from the dungeon along a lost waterway.

24. Tomb of Sangre (CR 16 or 18)

The exterior of the Tomb of Sangre looks much like a 60-foot-by-60-foot Greek temple with a solid bronze door set in the center of the northern face of the tomb. The tomb is surrounded by columns carved in the shape of robed and hooded figures, each with a short sword held across its chest. The solid bronze door is cast in bas-relief with demonic images that stand astride hoards of treasure.

The door is sealed with an *arcane lock* spell, and guarded by a ***disintegrate* trap** that triggers on any living being who touches or attempts to *knock* or *dispel* the *arcane lock.*

***DISINTEGRATE* TRAP** **CR 8**
XP 4,800
Type magic; **Perception** DC 31; **Disable Device** DC 31

Trigger touch; **Reset** none; **Bypass** being undead
Effect spell effect (*disintegrate*, Atk +12 ranged touch [22d6 damage])

The interior of the Tomb of Sangre is richly appointed with large pillows, expensive woven rugs, tapestries, and urns full of jewels. A silver pentagram occupies a 10-foot section of the western end of the chamber, and an ornate coffin sits in the eastern side of the chamber. Carved from ivory and gold, the coffin looks valuable beyond reckoning. The room is dimly lit with torches of *continual flame*, casting shadows throughout the chamber.

If Ankoz has survived, he has taken advantage of any healing (*inflict* spells, in this case) Ykthool saw fit to bestow upon him. Ankoz has also placed a *major image* of himself between the entrance and the coffin while hides invisibly at the southern end of the room, preparing whatever magic he has remaining before switching to his staff. Sangre bides his time in silence; he waits for the PCs to explore the chamber, and as they split up begins his attacks.

SANGRE **CR 15**
XP 51,200
Male human vampire ranger 1/rogue 13 (*Pathfinder Roleplaying Game Bestiary* "Vampire")
CE Medium undead (augmented humanoid, human)
Init +9; **Senses** darkvision 60 ft.; **Perception** +29

AC 33, touch 20, flat-footed 27 (+7 armor, +4 deflection, +5 Dex, +1 dodge, +6 natural)
hp 136 (1d10+3 plus 13d8+39 plus 27); fast healing 5
Fort +12; **Ref** +20; **Will** +10; +4 vs. traps
Defensive Abilities channel resistance +4, evasion, uncanny dodge, trap sense; **DR** 10/magic and silver; **Immune** undead traits; **Resist** cold 10, electricity 10
Weaknesses vampire weaknesses

Speed 40 ft.
Melee *Hollow Blade* +19/+14 (1d6+5/19–20), or slam +15 (1d4+3 plus energy drain) or unarmed strike +15/+10 (1d3+2 plus energy drain)
Special Attacks blood drain, children of the night, create spawn, dominate (DC 20), energy drain (2 levels, DC 20), favored enemy (humans +2), rogue talents (bleeding attack +7, crippling strike, finesse rogue, opportunist [1/round]), sneak attack +7d6

Str 14, **Dex** 20, **Con** —, **Int** 12, **Wis** 17, **Cha** 16
Base Atk +10; **CMB** +12; **CMD** 32
Feats Alertness[B], Combat Reflexes[B], Critical Focus, Dodge[B], Far Shot, Improved Initiative[B], Improved Unarmed Strike, Lightning Reflexes[B], Mobility, Point-Blank Shot, Rapid Shot, Spring Attack, Toughness[B], Weapon Finesse, Weapon Focus (short sword)
Skills Acrobatics +20 (+29 to jump), Appraise +12, Bluff +25 (+27 vs. humans), Climb +16, Craft (woodworking) +15, Escape Artist +19, Intimidate +17, Perception +29 (+35 to locate traps, +31 vs. humans), Sense Motive +29 (+31 vs. humans), Sleight of Hand +19, Stealth +32, Survival +17 (+19 vs. humans, +18 to track), Swim +13; **Racial Modifiers** +8 Bluff, +8 Perception, +8 Sense Motive, +8 Stealth
Languages Abyssal, Common
SQ change shape (dire bat or wolf, *beast shape II*), gaseous form, rogue talents (fast stealth, ledge walker), shadowless, spider climb, track, trapfinding +6, wild empathy +4
Combat Gear *brooch of shielding* (20 uses), *potion of haste, potion of invisibility, major ring of spell storing (inflict moderate wounds* x2, CL 10th*)*; **Other Gear** *+4 shadow studded leather armor, the Hollow Blade, boots of striding and springing, cloak of resistance +3, ring of protection +4*

Tactics: Sangre, and Ankoz if he still lives, fight with all the skill and experience they possess. Sangre uses his *boots of striding and springing* to move swiftly through the room, often tumbling into melee to gain the advantage of sneak attack, even if he is spotted by a foe. Sangre, however, has a special problem with the party at this moment. If they have delved this far into his lair, the core of the Underguild has now been vanquished. With this in mind, Sangre uses the *Hollow Blade* to wreak as much havoc upon his foes as he can. If given the opportunity, Sangre seeks to spawn the entire party into his new servants and members of the Underguild; failing that he merely destroys them all. When reduced to 0 hit points Sangre transforms into *gaseous form*. fleeing to his coffin.

The coffin belongs to Sangre. Ankoz's *contingency* spell teleports him to this chamber so he can recuperate. Lying about the room are the riches of the Underguild. Hidden amongst the items is a scroll that, when read aloud, teleports the party back to **Area 1**. The *wall of stone* is still present blocking the escape route, though the trap should hopefully be disarmed at this point. If not, consult the rules on teleportation errors in the *Pathfinder Roleplaying Game Core Rulebook*.

Treasure: 26,742 gp, 5 diamonds (1,000 gp) each, 7 rubies (750 gp) each, 12 sapphires (500 gp) each, 10 emeralds (250 gp) each, *potion of mage armor*, *potion of aid*, *headband of vast intelligence +4*, *+1 icy burst siangham*, *+3 composite longbow* (+1 Str), divine *scroll of cure serious wounds* and *cause critical wounds*, *+2 heavy steel shield*, *gloves of swimming and climbing*, a fur cloak worth 350 gp, gold death mask (250 gp), fire opal pendant 1,759 gp, gold efreeti comb with emerald eyes 375 gp, silver harp inlaid with rubies crafted by Fathilir worth 3,450 gp, ivory statue valued at 320 gp, gold ring worth 220 gp, silver plated steel longsword with jet jewel in hilt 402 gp, and a small jewelry box made of ivory with platinum frame 678 gp. See **New Magic Items** at the end of this adventure for information on the *Hollow Blade*. of the Underguild.

New Magic Items

The Hollow Blade

Aura strong abjuration and necromancy; **CL** 14th
Slot none; **Price** 47,510 gp; **Weight** 2 lbs.

DESCRIPTION

The Hollow Blade is an intelligent +3 undead bane short sword with the following abilities:

- The Hollow Blade has Int 14, Wis 14, Cha 14; AL N; Ego 15. The Hollow Blade communicates through telepathy with its bearer.
- In the hands of any class other than rogue, it acts as a +1 short sword. It seeks to be owned by a rogue, either through telepathic contact or force of will. Any non-rogue who possesses the Hollow Blade must succeed on a Will save once per day (DC 15) or act carelessly with it, leaving it lying about, or displaying it in such a way that it may be easily stolen.
- As it is forged from equal parts of positive and negative energy, the Hollow Blade causes its wielder to feel charged with life energy. Therefore, in the hands of an undead creature, the undead gains immunity to channeling. It also eliminates other undead weaknesses when wielded, such as the vulnerability to cure spells, sunlight powerlessness, and vulnerability to daylight. The last ability allows vampires to walk abroad in daylight for up to 4 hours per day.
- The bearer of the blade may cast death ward as the spell once per day as the negative energies within the blade make the bearer temporarily immune to this form of attack.

CONSTRUCTION

Requirements Craft Magic Arms and Armor, death ward, summon monster I, the creator must be able to channel positive or negative energy; Cost 23,910 gp

Mirror of Abyssal Damnation

Aura strong conjuration and necromancy; **CL** 18th
Slot none; **Price** 200,000 gp; **Weight** 50 lb.

DESCRIPTION

Individuals gazing into a mirror of abyssal damnation must succeed on a DC 20 Will Save or have their soul sucked into the Abyss, lost and wandering among hordes of demons. These individuals are instantly replaced with chaotic evil clones of themselves, bearing arms and equipment that are exact duplicates of that which their other form bore. Individuals who are already of chaotic evil alignment are immune to the mirror's effect. Destroying the mirror causes the individual thus trapped in the Abyss to be lost forever. Nothing short of a wish spell is able to bring them back. Killing the clone of the switched character allows the trapped individual a second DC 20 Will save to find his way back to the mirror portal and escape.

CONSTRUCTION

Requirements Craft Wondrous Item, *clone*, *plane shift*; **Cost** 100,000 gp

The Pyramid of Amra

By Casey W. Christofferson and Bill Webb

The Pyramid of Amra is a challenging adventure designed for characters of 12th level. It is suggested that the PCs include at least one monk, and one rogue with at least 9 ranks each of Perception, Disable Device, and Linguistics. Due to the nature and numbers of undead enemies (vampires) it is recommended that a cleric with the ability to cast *raise dead* and *restoration* be on hand to aid the PCs. The PCs should be rounded out with a wizard or sorcerer and a pair of front-line fighters. In this adventure, the PCs travel to the Pyramid of Amra and the ancient Monastery of Night, where they face one of the most dangerous of opponents they are likely to meet, C'nosretep the Champion of Set.

Legend of the Pyramid of Amra, and the Monastery of Light

For several millennia the monks of the Monastery of Light trained in the deepest mysteries of meditation and unarmed combat. Their master, Ozykathalin, was said to have penned the sacred *Tome of Mind and Body*, a tome containing many of the most cunning and devastating of all martial arts maneuvers. Their reign ended nearly a century ago, when C'nosretep, the Iron Fist of Set, deposed Ozykathalin and placed himself upon the Lotus Throne.

Now reigning supreme within the Step Pyramid of Amra, C'nosretep sits in sole possession of the *Tome of Mind and Body*, much of which he has re-written or embellished. Surrounding himself with fell followers the Champion of Set now presides over pilgrimages of worshippers and slaves who trek across the desert wastes by the thousands. These foolish pilgrims come to witness the power of the Iron Fist of Set. Many hope to gain immortality, if first they can impress C'nosretep with their skills at unarmed combat.

Getting to the Step Pyramid of Amra

The Step Pyramid of Amra should be contained in a deep desert location with an "ancient world" flavor. In the **Lost Lands** of **Frog God Games**, the Pyramid of Amra is located at a remote oasis in the desert land of Khemit, although any desert location will do. The journey should be half of the challenge, fraught with dangers both natural and monstrous, with hints as to the actual location of the Pyramid and the hidden oasis of Amra sprinkled throughout.

Characters could possibly have heard tales of the pyramid and the *Tome of Mind and Body*. The *Tome* itself is treasured by monastic orders throughout the world for its ancient techniques. Through careful study of its venerable pages, students of the *Tome* learn the secrets of a completely unique new martial arts move, usable only by the most experienced of masters.

Alternately, a monk's sect may have sent him questing for the *Tome of Mind and Body* to return to their cloister for further research by the Grandmasters. For whatever the reason, the PCs should be motivated to face any obstacle, although they should not be given the whole story. Best to keep secret some of the lore provided on these pages and let them plan and prepare for the worst on their own.

The Pyramid of Amra sits on a small island in the middle of a lake within a desert oasis. On the shore of the lake sits the Palace of Celestial Flowers.

Palace of Celestial Flowers and Monastery of Night

A large walled structure amid gently swaying palm trees sits exposed to the sands. Almost hidden beyond the tall date palms lies a silvery lake amidst the desert. The point of a pyramid rises above the greenery like a yellowed claw, its very top covered in red gold leaf.

The top of the pyramid is in fact the Pyramid of Amra. However, as mentioned above, it sits on an island in the middle of a lake. Before the characters, and on the shore of the lake, is the Palace of Celestial Flowers, which may be explored before the PCs access the Pyramid and in fact provides the means for the players to get to the island — a secret passage and a boat. Some PCs possessing magical means of transport may wish to simply bypass the Palace. See below.

Bypassing the Palace

PCs could, if they have the means, simply swim, fly, or use a boat to reach the island containing the Pyramid or use some other means to bypass the Palace. However, once in the Pyramid, there are several areas where the *amulet of the lotus master* —which can only be obtained within the Palace — benefits them. It is for your players to decide how they wish to proceed. The adventure can be completed even if the Palace is never entered.

1: Palace of Celestial Flowers

A fine bronze double doors cast with images of a great and mighty god surrounded with rays of sunlight and showering lotus blossoms upon a single child grace the front of this majestic edifice. Beyond the locked bronze double doors is an entrance chamber that must have once been an awesome sight but is now degraded with filth. Torn tapestries flutter in the wind ominously. The PCs nostrils fill with the smell of old death and an uneasy decay. A second set of locked double doors beyond the first open into **Area 8, Great Hall of the Brotherhood of the Fallen Star**.

Bronze Double Doors: hardness 10; hp 60; Break DC 25; Disable Device DC 25.

2: Great Hall of the Brotherhood of the Fallen Star (CR 16 in the day or 18 at night)

As the PCs enter from beyond the locked entrance portals, they can see a great amount of dust and darkness beyond. This was once a place of great majesty and serenity. Ornately carved wooden pillars featuring great battles between celestial and infernal forces stare ominously at the PCs as the breeze from the outside wafts into the room, creating a slight fog of dust. Braziers suddenly light from the corners of the room and the party see a figure sitting atop a throne before you, beckoning them to approach.

The Great Hall has a domed ceiling that rises about 40 feet above the floor, and is lined with eight massive carved pillars. There are doors in the northeastern and northwestern walls leading to **Areas 3, 4, 6** and **7**. There is a flaming brazier in the southeast and southwestern corners of the room that cast a strange and eerie light. The GM should play up this spooky effect prior to the ambush of the PCs.

If The PCs Enter During The Day

If the PCs enter the throne chamber during the daylight hours, they are faced with **Relthren Surret** masked in the guise of C'nosretep, and a pack of **3 doppelganger monks** and **3 asswere monks** hiding atop the invisible bridge in **Area 14**, waiting to pounce upon the PCs. If the battle begins to go against the doppelgangers, they all change shape into C'nosretep. Relthren Surret enters the combat if he is threatened or if things are going badly for his allies. In the confusion, Relthren shape-changes into one of the weakest PCs and attacks that individual until Relthren has lost 30% of his total hit points, at which point he attempts to flee to safety. The asswere monks begin the fight in hybrid form.

RELTHREN SURRET **CR 12**
XP 19,200
Male doppleganger monk 10 (*Pathfinder Roleplaying Game Bestiary* "Doppleganger")
LE Medium monstrous humanoid (shapechanger)
Init +1; **Senses** darkvision 60 ft.; **Perception** +11

AC 23, touch 19, flat-footed 21 (+3 deflection, +1 Dex, +1 dodge, +4 natural, +4 monk)
hp 91 (4d10+4 plus 10d8+10 plus 10)
Fort +11; **Ref** +12; **Will** +13; +2 vs. enchantment spells and effects
Defensive Abilities evasion, improved evasion; **Immune** charm, disease, sleep

---

Speed 60 ft.
Melee 2 claws +15 (1d8+4) or unarmed strike +15/+10/+5 (1d10+4)
Special Attacks flurry of blows +8/+8/+3/+3, ki strike (cold iron/silver, lawful, magic), stunning fist 11/day (DC 19)
Spell-Like Abilities (CL 18th):
At will—*detect thoughts* (DC 13)

Str 18, **Dex** 13, **Con** 12, **Int** 13, **Wis** 14, **Cha** 13
Base Atk +11; **CMB** +18; **CMD** 34
Feats Alertness, Cleave, Combat Expertise, Deflect Arrows, Dodge, Great Fortitude, Improved Unarmed Strike, Mobility, Power Attack, Spring Attack, Stunning Fist, Whirlwind Attack
Skills Acrobatics +14 (+41 jump), Bluff +9, Climb +22, Diplomacy +4, Disguise +9, Escape Artist +14, Intimidate +14, Perception +11, Sense Motive +11, Stealth +15; **Racial Modifiers** +4 Bluff, +4 Disguise, +20 Disguise while using change shape ability, +4 Bluff while using change shape ability
Languages Common
SQ AC bonus, change shape (*alter self*), fast movement, high jump, ki defense, ki pool (7), maneuver training, mimicry, perfect copy, purity of body, slow fall (50 ft.), wholeness of body
Combat Gear 3 *potions of cure moderate wounds*, 2 *potions of invisibility*; **Other Gear** *belt of giant strength +2*, *ring of protection +3*, *masque of the monkey* (see **New Magic Items** at the end of this adventure for more information)

DOPPELGANGER MONKS (3) **CR 8**
XP 4,800
Male doppleganger monk 6 (*Pathfinder Roleplaying Game Bestiary* "Doppleganger")
LE Medium monstrous humanoid (shapechanger)
Init +5; **Senses** darkvision 60 ft.; **Perception** +11

AC 19, touch 15, flat-footed 17 (+1 Dex, +1 dodge, +3 monk, +4 natural)
hp 65 (4d10+4 plus 6d8+10 plus 6)
Fort +9; **Ref** +10; **Will** +11; +2 vs. enchantment spells and effects
Defensive Abilities evasion; **Immune** charm, disease, sleep

---

Speed 50 ft.
Melee 2 claws +12 (1d8+4), or unarmed strike +12/+7 (1d8+4)
Special Attacks flurry of blows +4/+4/–1, ki strike (magic), stunning fist 7/day (DC 17)
Spell-Like Abilities (CL 18th):
At will— *detect thoughts* (DC 14)

Str 18, **Dex** 13, **Con** 13, **Int** 13, **Wis** 15, **Cha** 14
Base Atk +8; **CMB** +14 (+16 trip); **CMD** 27 (29 vs. trip)
Feats Deflect Arrows, Dodge, Great Fortitude, Improved Initiative, Improved Trip, Improved Unarmed Strike, Mobility, Spring Attack, Stunning Fist
Skills Bluff +12, Diplomacy +8, Disguise +12, Escape Artist +10, Intimidate +7, Perception +11, Sense Motive +11, Stealth +10,

Swim +13; **Racial Modifiers** +4 Bluff, +4 Disguise, +20 disguise while using change shape ability, +4 bluff while using change shape ability
Languages Common
SQ AC bonus, change shape, fast movement, high jump, ki defense, ki pool (5), maneuver training, mimicry, perfect copy, purity of body, slow fall (30 ft.)

ASSWERE MONKS (HYBRID FORM) (3) CR 12
XP 19,200
Male asswere monk 9 (*The Tome of Horrors Complete* 739)
LE Medium magical beast (human, shapechanger)
Init +5; **Senses** darkvision 60 ft., low-light vision, scent; **Perception** +10

AC 16, touch 14, flat-footed 15 (+1 Dex, +3 monk, +2 natural)
hp 75 (3d10+3 plus 9d8+9 plus 9)
Fort +10; **Ref** +10; **Will** +10; +2 vs. enchantment spells and effects, +4 vs. hot or cold environments and to resist damage from suffocation
Defensive Abilities evasion, improved evasion; **DR** 10/cold iron; **Immune** disease

Speed 60 ft.
Melee bite +12 (1d3+4) or unarmed strike +11/+6 (1d10+3)
Special Attacks bray, flurry of blows +7/+7/+2/+2, ki strike (cold iron/silver, magic), stunning fist should be 9/day (DC 17)

Str 16, **Dex** 13, **Con** 12, **Int** 12, **Wis** 13, **Cha** 12
Base Atk +8; **CMB** +14 (+16 trip); **CMD** 25 (31 vs. trip)
Feats Blind-Fight, Deflect Arrows, Endurance, Improved Initiative, Improved Trip, Improved Unarmed Strike, Iron Will, Mobility, Skill Focus (Perception), Stunning Fist, Weapon Focus (bite)
Skills Acrobatics +14 (+35 jump), Climb +16, Disguise +6 (+14 in animal form), Escape Artist +14, Perception +10, Stealth +14, Swim +15 (+19 to resist nonlethal damage from exhaustion)
Languages Common
SQ AC bonus, alternate form, fast movement, high jump, ki defense, ki pool (5), maneuver training, purity of body, slow fall (40 ft.), wholeness of body

Bray (Su): An asswere can loose a loud bray as a standard action. All creatures within 30 feet that hear it must succeed on a DC 12 Will save or be affected as by a *confusion* spell for 1d4+3 rounds (caster level 3rd). This is a sonic, mind–affecting effect. A creature that successfully saves cannot be affected again by the same asswere's confusion ability for one day. The save DC is Charisma–based.

Relthren Surret is C'nosretep's chief lieutenant, and is in charge of guarding the vampires during the daylight hours. He and his doppelgangers are skilled monks, bound in service to C'nosretep by their god Set.

If The PCs Enter During The Night

They instead face **C'nosretep** himself! He does not wish to fight with the PCs at the moment, but converses with them instead to assess their intelligence and ability to resist his powerful of charms. Secretly he has **6 vampire spawn** hiding atop the invisible bridge in **Area 14**, waiting to pounce upon the PCs. C'nosretep dominates the strongest warrior or rogue and instructs them to slay the weakest PCs while he parleys with a monk or paladin. He is arrogant and boastful of his powers and thanks them for coming to join the eternal army of undead that he is building here at the oasis. As soon as the trap is ready to be sprung, or as soon as anyone attempts to cast a spell or attack C'nosretep in any way, he attacks that individual mercilessly for one round before using his great speed and powers to turn to vapor and retreat to a random room within the Palace or Pyramid. Most likely C'nosretep's subsequent ambushes are sprung within a room or chamber the PCs have recently passed through and cleared of traps and monsters as they backtrack through the palace. C'nosretep never fights to negative hit points, and only fights to the death when defending his sarcophagus or the *Tome of Mind and Body*.

C'NOSRETEP CR 17
XP 102,400
hp 139 (See **Area U–12**)

VAMPIRE SPAWN (6) CR 4
XP 1,200
Pathfinder Roleplaying Game Bestiary "Vampire"
LE Medium undead
Init +1; **Senses** darkvision 60 ft.; **Perception** +11

AC 15, touch 11, flat-footed 14 (+1 Dex, +4 natural)
hp 26 (4d8+8); fast healing 2
Fort +3; **Ref** +2; **Will** +5
Defensive Abilities channel resistance +2; **DR** 5/silver; **Immune** undead traits; **Resist** cold 10, electricity 10
Weaknesses vampire weaknesses

Speed 30 ft.
Melee slam +4 (1d4+1 plus energy drain)
Special Attacks blood drain, dominate (DC 14), energy drain (1 level, DC 14)

Str 12, **Dex** 12, **Con** —, **Int** 11, **Wis** 13, **Cha** 15
Base Atk +3; **CMB** +4; **CMD** 15
Feats Blind-Fight, Skill Focus (Perception)
Skills Intimidate +9, Knowledge (religion) +7, Perception +11, Stealth +16; **Racial Modifiers** +8 Stealth
Languages Common
SQ gaseous form, resurrection vulnerability, shadowless, spider climb

Searching the Throne

Anyone succeeding on a DC 25 Perception check discovers that the sliding plate beneath the seat of the dragon-footed Throne of the Lotus Master that has an inlay the exact size and shape of the *amulet of the lotus master*. Placing the completed amulet into the depression opens a secret staircase in the floor below the throne that leads to **Area P1** of the Pyramid of Amra.

3: Purification of Body

This chamber was once used to purify the body through massage, steam baths, plunge pools, and the like, though it is now fouled. There is some sign that horrible death once visited this room. The walls are chipped and cracked in places, and broken weapons lie in disarray around the room. The shattered remains of several urns, ewers, and basins crack and break under the PCs' feet. An unlocked door in the northwest corner of the room opens to reveal a staircase leading to **Area 9**.

Treasure: Anyone succeeding on a DC 30 Perception check uncovers the skeleton of a slain monk, lodged into a hole in the floor that once released natural steam. Upon his person are 200 pp, *+1 shocking burst gauntlet*, and a *+3 dagger*.

4: Meditation Chamber (CR 8)

This is a simple room with pure black walls and no visible markings whatsoever. The door to the room, when closed, perfectly blends with the wall to make it appear as if there is no door at all. A white star-like shape dominates the center of the floor. An unlocked door in the eastern wall leads to **Area 5**.

Hiding in this chamber are **4 vampire spawn** of C'nosretep, hanging from the ceiling and walls and waiting to drop like spiders on unsuspecting PCs.

VAMPIRE SPAWN (4) **CR 4**
XP 1,200
hp 26 (see **Area 2**)

Tactics: The spawn first attempt to dominate any barbarians or rogues in the group, inducing them to slay any clerics before entering melee. They use their great speed and agility to their advantage, striking at lightly armored individuals such as wizards and rogues first before moving on to the fighters.

Note: A monk of lawful good alignment spending 3 solid rounds contemplating the white star in the center of the chamber gains a +3 competence bonus on his next attack or the next use of his Acrobatics or Climb skill.

5: Barge of the Darkstar (CR 7)

This chamber has a door in the center of the north, east, and west walls. A large funerary barge made of black wood and inlaid with silver celestial symbols and images dominates the room. The barge is 25 feet long and about 5 feet wide, with a paddle and a sarcophagus attached across its center. If the sarcophagus were to be removed, it would make room to seat about 7 individuals. There are two intact oars in oarlocks at the front and back of the barge. Anyone succeeding on a DC 20 Profession (sailor) check can easily discern that this barge is water-worthy and narrow enough to fit through the door at the end of the hall. The boat is very heavy and would require at a combined DC 25 Strength check to move it out of the room. The sarcophagus on the barge emanates a powerful ***fear aura***.

***FEAR* TRAP** **CR 7**
XP 3,200
Type magic; **Perception** DC 29; **Disable Device** DC 29

Trigger proximity; **Reset** automatic (effectively permanent unless disabled)
Effect spell effect (*fear*, DC 16 Will resists); multiple targets (all targets within 10 ft. of the sarcophagus)
Note: Anyone who fails the Will save is forever afraid of the barge. Only a successful *remove curse* breaks this compulsive fear.

Treasure: The funerary barge is very valuable; it would be worth 30,000 gp to a collector due to the ebony and mahogany hardwoods of its construction. The boat, although extremely heavy, actually sails as a masterwork item, giving a +2 circumstance bonus to any Profession (sailor) checks.

BARGE OF THE DARKSTAR
Huge water vehicle (*Pathfinder Roleplaying Game Ultimate Combat* "Vehicles")
Squares 5 (5 ft. by 25 ft.); **Cost** 30,000 gp

AC 8; **hardness** 5
hp 75 (37)
Base Save +2

Maximum Speed 60 ft. (current) or 30 ft. (muscle);
Acceleration 15 ft. (muscle) or 30 ft. (current)
CMB +2; **CMD** 12
Ramming Damage 2d8

This long, flat-bottomed ship has a few oars to supplement its single mast with a square sail. It can make both sea and river voyages. The barge can carry 5 tons of cargo or 7 fully-equipped soldiers.

Propulsion current (air; 5 squares of sails, hp 20), current (water), or muscle (pushed; 8 Medium rowers)
Driving Check Diplomacy or Intimidate while rowed, or Profession (sailor) or Knowledge (nature) +10 to the DC when sail is used
Forward Facing ship's forward
Driving Device rudder
Driving Space the two middle rear squares of the barge
Crew 8
Decks 1

6: Meditation chamber (CR 12)

This is a second meditation chamber, similar to **Area 10**, except this one is completely white and the star symbol on the floor is completely black.

Hiding within this chamber, blending completely with the white of the walls, are **4 doppelganger monks**.

DOPPLEGANGER MONKS (4) **CR 8**
XP 4,800
hp 65 (see **Area 2**, *Pathfinder Roleplaying Game Bestiary*, "Doppleganger")

Tactics: The doppelganger monks wait for a moment while the PCs examine the black star in the center of the floor, then they strike out from the walls with concealment. All attack a lightly armored target at the same time, and all transform into this target on the following round to add chaos and confusion to their assault. If the doppelgangers suddenly begin to take casualties, they attempt to flee and fight again another day.

Note: A monk of lawful evil alignment spending 3 rounds contemplating the white star in the center of the chamber gains a +3 competence bonus on his next attack, or the next use of his Acrobatics or Climb skill.

7: Massage chamber (CR 13)

Several tables line the walls of this room, along with small-wheeled carts containing bottles of various oils, unguents, mud, and herbal wraps. Artwork inlaid in enamel upon the walls depicts monks practicing the art of massage upon one another to work out the soreness of intense physical and mental training. Waiting within the room are **2 invisible clay golems**. An unlocked door in the northeastern corner of the chamber opens to a staircase leading upwards to **Area 13**.

INVISIBLE CLAY GOLEMS (2) **CR 11**
XP 12,800
hp 101 (*Pathfinder Roleplaying Game Bestiary* "Golem, Clay")
Defensive Abilities invisibility

Invisibility (Su) An invisible clay golem remains invisible even when it attacks. This ability is constant, but the clay golem can suppress or resume it as a free action.

Tactics: The golems grab the first person(s) entering the room, slamming them onto the table and begin giving them a serious massage. These golems were specially created to be invisible masseurs. In the long years since their creation, however, the elemental spirits that animate them have gone quite mad. They spare no ounce of their strength when giving a massage, which usually reduces to putty the unfortunate person in their care. If attacked, they respond in kind.

Treasure: There are enough herbal wraps and oils are to make up 3 masterwork healers kits.

8: Rear Gatehouse

The door from **Area 11** enters into gatehouse a with a 10-ft.-wide iron portcullis at the far end. Doorways to the left and right of the room lead up staircases to each of the guard towers. It is dark and cobwebbed in the gatehouse area and looks as if it has not seen a living soul in centuries. The closed iron portcullis leads to the stone quay, where rowboats were once taken by the faithful brothers to work the grounds of the renamed Monastery of Night.

Portcullis: hardness 10, hp 60, Break DC 28.

8a: Left Gatehouse (CR 9)

A lever on the second floor of the gatehouse must be switched to set the mechanism to lift the portcullis. It is guarded by **4 wraiths** — former monks killed by C'nosretep.

WRAITHS (4) **CR 5**
XP 1,600
hp 47 (*Pathfinder Roleplaying Game Bestiary* "Wraith")

These wraiths are vengeful and spiteful, but if they are confronted by an individual bearing the *amulet of the lotus master* they back away and allow the lever to be switched without a fight. They bow before the PCs and say:

> "Slay the beast and free us in the name of the true master, so that we may become one with enlightenment and fade from view."

If attacked, they seek out paladins and clerics first, attempting to eliminate them before moving on to other targets. They use darkness and fade into walls and floors to maximize their effectiveness, gaining total concealment.

8b: Right Gatehouse

This gatehouse is dust-filled and devoid of valuables, as if it has been stripped for other uses.

9: Training Room (CR 8 at night or CR 14 during the day)

Padded walls and bamboo mats decorate this darkened room. Within the room are several wooden training dummies that stand in the four corners, motionless and covered with dust.

By night, **4 vampire spawn** take up residence within this chamber; during daylight hours it is occupied by **2 asswere monks** who spar with one another to keep boredom at bay. They attack intruders who enter the chamber.

VAMPIRE SPAWN (4) **CR 4**
XP 1,200
hp 26 (see **Area 2**)

ASSWERE MONKS (2) **CR 12**
XP 19,200
hp 75 (see **Area 2**)

10: Bed Chamber of the Light Master (CR 7)

An ornately carved door features the holy symbol of Arden carved into its paneling. The symbol is shining brightly, and the PCs must take a moment to let their eyes adjust to the light.

The door requires a DC 25 Disable Device check to open. Once unlocked, the door swings open to reveal a small room holding the dusty belongings of the former Master of the Lightstar. His belongings have been left undisturbed for centuries, as the holy symbol carved into his door has a permanent 6th-level *daylight* spell worked into it. C'nosretep and his vampire minions keep away from this area, and C'nosretep sees no reason to send his doppelganger and asswere monks here to see what's in the room.

The interior is covered in a thick layer of dust. There is a small mat on the floor with a wooden neck-board, a sconce, brass incense burner on a brass chain, and a small strange-looking box about 6 inches by 6 inches. The sides of the box have numerals in a strange language, with 9 numerals and 10 spaces upon the top of the box arranged in a square of 3 by 3 with an additional location connected on one of the sides. Next to the 9 numerals and the empty space there appears to be some sort of button that does nothing if depressed when the box is first found and the numerals are in their original scrambled position. Anyone succeeding on a DC 25 Linguistics check can determine that the numerals are in the Celestial tongue. (This knowledge is automatic if a PC already knows that language). The numerals on the top of the box, 1–9, are all scrambled but the number 15 is repeated six times along two sides of the perimeter of the box.

The box number panels slide if they are oiled and maybe reconfigured into any combination of numbers from 1 through 9.

When all of the numbers are slid so they equal 15 across the bottom, side, and each diagonal of the box and the button is pushed, the box opens to reveal an amulet with a large clear gemstone of unknown origin on a golden chain. If the numbers are arranged in any other combination and the button is depressed, keen adamantine blades shoot out in all directions.

A possible solution to this puzzle looks like this:

8	1	6
3	5	7
4	9	2

ADAMANTINE BLADE TRAP **CR 7**
XP 3,200
Type mechanical; **Perception** DC 30; **Disable Device** n/a*

Trigger touch; **Reset** automatic
Effect 4d6 points of damage and 1d2 Dex drain (DC 25 Reflex avoids)
***Note** This device can't be disabled; only solving the puzzle can open it.

Treasure: The amulet within the box, the *amulet of the lightstar* seems to exude a sense of power and glows with a bright light when held clasped in the hand. See **New Magic Items** at the end of this adventure for details.

11: Chamber of the Lotus (CR 8)

This is a large cross-shaped chamber with a beautifully rendered lotus flower mosaic in the center of the floor. The flower appears to change colors depending on the angle at which it is viewed. This room was once the private meditation chamber of the Master of the Lotus.

Blue Lotus

A failed Fortitude save against the blue lotus blossom gas has one of the following effects. Roll 1d4.

Roll	Hallucination
1	The hallucination is such that those who fail their Fortitude save see a party member as a spectre attempting to kill them.
2	Hallucination causes individual to see the person next to them as a very comely member of the opposite sex and fills them with a desire to "be with them." If the target of this desire spurns their sudden advances, the individual hallucinating begins to *rage* as the spell in their lust.
3	Those failing their saving throw are filled with despair and are unable to take action while under the influence of the lotus gas. They curl up in a small ball on the floor and begin to clutch themselves and cry.
4	Failed saving throw results in tranquil vision lasting 1d4+1 hours. The individual thus affected sits upon the floor and sees things going on about the monastery as they did before C'nosretep's conquest. This vision gives a glimpse of the master of the Lightstar and a hint as to how to reach his chamber.

A **trapped secret door** is in the center of the northern wall. Placing the *shimmering lotus flower* from the upper balcony into the center of the petals opens the door to **Area 16** automatically.

Secret Door: 4 in. thick; hardness 8; hp 60; **Perception** DC 30; Disable Device DC 30.

BLUE LOTUS BLOSSOM GAS TRAP **CR 8**
Type mechanical; **Perception** DC 25; **Disable Device** DC 20

Trigger location; **Reset** repair
Effect poison gas (insanity mist); never miss; onset delay (1 round); multiple targets (all targets in the room)
***Note:** Attempting to open the door without the proper key or command word fills the room with potent blue lotus blossom gas (similar to insanity mist, but with a hallucinogenic compound; see the side bar). A successful disable device roll merely delays the release of the gas for 1d4 rounds.

12: Bed Chamber of the Dark Master (CR 9)

A stout locked door bearing signs of shadow and darkness requires a Disable Device check (DC 20) to open. This room has a strange sense of dread within it. Dusty and dark, the room seems to dim all light sources. A low growling can be heard from the corners.

Guarding this room from intruders are **5 shadows**, which move to attack from the darkness. They instantly concentrate their attacks first on the party's cleric, followed by paladins.

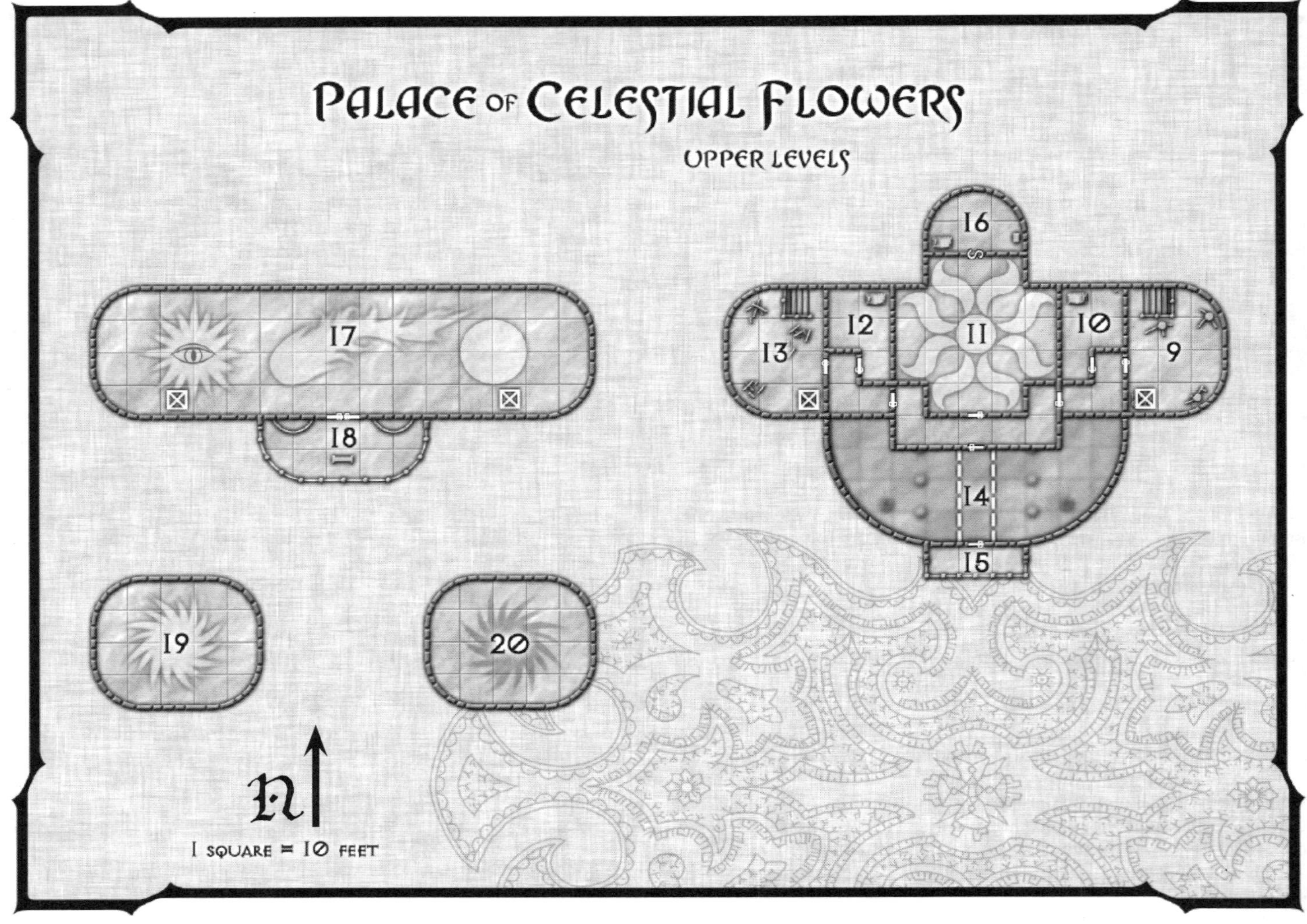

SHADOWS (5) **CR 3**
XP 800
hp 19 (*Pathfinder Roleplaying Game Bestiary* "Shadow")

Any character that succeeds on a DC 16 Perception check finds a small chest. It is **trapped** (see below), and within is a dark amulet that seems to absorb all light.

POISON NEEDLE TRAP **CR 6**
XP 2,400
Type mechanical; **Perception** DC 22; **Disable Device** DC 20

Trigger touch; **Reset** manual
Effect Atk +8 ranged (1, plus deathblade poison)

Treasure: *amulet of the darkstar*. See **New Magic Items** at the end of this adventure for details.

13: Smashed Training Room

Within this room are the remains of several practice dummies, all shattered and broken beyond repair. A set of stairs in the northwest of the room leads downwards to the first floor.

Anyone succeeding on a DC 20 Perception check notices a **trapdoor** in the ceiling to the southwest of the room. The trapdoor may be hooked with a 10-foot pole. Pulling down the trapdoor opens a wooden ladder staircase that leads to the floor above and **Area 17**.

14: Locked Door and Invisible Bridge (CR 9, or 0)

The locked door is not trapped but it requires a DC 25 Disable Device check to unlock and open. Behind the locked door is a walkway through the center of the palace. It leads to the lower balcony. The walkway is permanently invisible. Characters attempting to cross the invisible walkway must succeed on a DC 14 Acrobatics check to cross the walkway with no chance of falling. Those failing the check must succeed on a DC 20 Reflex save or fall 20 ft. to the Great Hall, taking 2d6 damage.

If the **6 vampire spawn** that were waiting to ambush the PCs earlier have not yet done so, they are waiting here to attack. The vampire spawn hang from the walls in shadows or they use their *spider climb* ability to attack with stealth and surprise.

VAMPIRE SPAWN (6) **CR 4**
XP 1,200
hp 26 (see **Area 2**)

15: Lower Balcony

A balcony juts out from the lower portion of the dome of the Palace of Celestial Flowers. It was once used by the Master of the Lotus to address the disciples as they went through exercises in the courtyard. Now it serves as a lookout spot during the nighttime hours for vampire spawn that serve C'nosretep.

16: Sanctuary of the Master of the Lotus

This chamber served as the private sanctum of the Master of the Lotus. It is a simple room devoid of most comfort items one would associate with a great leader. Instead it merely contains a dry rotted sleeping mat, meditation rug, neck board, several scroll cases, manuals of various sorts, dried writing inks, reed brushes and a small locked chest.

The chest has an intricate lock requiring a DC 28 Disable Device check to open.

Within the chest is an amulet made in the shape of a lotus blossom with an odd piece of engraving upon the back. There is a diary within the chest as well, and diagrams showing an individual grasping the *amulet of the darkstar* in one hand the *amulet of the lightstar* in the other with the *medallion of the lotus* about their neck, all while under a curtain of stars. A perfect lotus flower is at his feet.

Treasure: The amulet is the *medallion of the lotus*, which is currently incomplete. It is missing the rose diamond that is the centerpiece of the item. The medallion does not function to open the secret passage beneath the Lotus Throne without this central diamond. One of the books is the *History of the Monastery of Light*, by Ozykathalin, worth 5,000 gp to a collector that understands its value.

17: Third Floor Dome and Chamber of Celestial Light and Darkness

Two features stand out as most impressive about this chamber, the first being the intricate mosaic patterns of a comet, moon, and a sun with an all-seeing eye in the center of it. The second impressive feature of this chamber is the domed ceiling that reflects the light with diamonds. The diamonds are set in the ceiling so as to appear as the sky and constellations of over 4,000 years ago. Characters who succeed on a DC 26 Knowledge (nature) check recognize the difference in the stars from then and now. At the GM's discretion, other skills might also impart this information, such as Profession (astrologer) or Profession (astronomer).

Any character succeeding on a DC 24 Perception check on the mosaic discovers ancient writing in a lost language upon the floor. Anyone succeeding on a DC 28 Linguistics check or casting *comprehend languages* can read the words. The word hidden within the sun and eye is *"Solaris."* Hidden within the moon is the word *"Eclipsis."* The word hidden within the comet is *"Ozykathalin."* If a character succeeds on a DC 30 Knowledge (history) check, she recalls that this last word is also the traditional name of each Master of the Lotus that is born into the Order.

The center of each mosaic acts as a teleportation disk if the following requirements are met: Holding the *amulet of the darkstar* in one's hand while standing over the moon and reciting the word *"Eclipsis"* teleports the user and anyone within 10 ft. of her to **Area 20**. Holding the *amulet of the lightstar* in one's hand while standing upon the mosaic of the sun and repeating the word *"Solaris"* instantly teleports the individual and anyone within 10 ft. of her to **Area 29**.

Standing over the comet with the *amulet of the darkstar*, *amulet of the lightstar*, *medallion of the lotus*, and one of the *shimmering lotus blossoms* causes the room to be bathed in a golden light. Should the PCs complete these actions, uttering the name of Ozykathalin, the *shimmering lotus* rises up into the air above their heads and the room is bathed in a golden light. As the PCs watch, the *shimmering lotus* begins to spin and prismatic rays spray about the room. Spinning ever faster, the lotus blossom begins to transform until a beautiful rose diamond appears where the flower once was. The perfect diamond slowly drops from the ceiling and fuses with the medallion about the neck of the PC who completed the ritual with a brilliant flash of white light.

Treasure: The *medallion of the lotus master*. See **New Magic Item** at the end of this adventure for details. The *medallion* is also the key to triggering the secret trapdoor hidden beneath the seat of the Throne of Lotus Master in **Area 8**.

18: Upper Balcony

This upper balcony has two planters that are overgrown and filled with weeds. A stone bench overlooks the courtyard and gives a view of the desert beyond the oasis when not blocked by clouds of sand. Growing amongst the weeds in a pool of disgusting looking water is a *shimmering lotus flower*. A character succeeding on a DC 15 Perception check locates these strange flowers.

Treasure: Each planter contains one *shimmering lotus flower*. See **New Magic Items** at the end of this adventure for details.

19: Dome of the Lightstar

This chamber has no windows or doors and can only be accessed by using the *amulet of the lightstar*. The room has a beautiful golden dome lined with diamonds. There is a floor mosaic featuring a brilliant shining sun. As the adventurers enter the room the *amulet of the lightstar* glows brightly and the shimmering form of Master Seung appears. The apparition smiles to the adventurers and begins to speak.

> "Master Seung, called Solaris I am and you have called me across the depths of time and space; long has the time been since I have had fortune to send my form into this place. Cursed is the One who betrayed the Order of Stars. Blessed be those that seek enlightenment that would heal his harms. Through the Halls of Night to walk where bloodless fiends do hide and stalk. Seek you there the candles' flames and light them in Lotus Masters Name. Place them at the points of the celestial eye and closer to the ground will be the sky."

After reciting his oracle, the spirit of the Master of the Lightstar dissipates into nothingness and the PCs is teleported back to the Chamber of Celestial Light and Darkness.

20: Dome of the Darkstar (CR 16)

Upon teleporting into this chamber the PCs are filled with a sense of dread. The room is cold as ice and seems to drain the light from all light sources. **Mi'Tang the nightwalker** dwells here. Mi'Tang arrogantly taunts the PCs as they arrive in his prison.

> "At last fools have gathered the darkstar, and I, Mi'Tang shall once again bring death to the land of the living!"

He then attacks, shattering magical weapons and killing whoever he can.

MI'TANG the NIGHTWALKER **CR 16**
XP 76,800
hp 241 (*Pathfinder Roleplaying Game Bestiary 2* "Nightshade, Nightwalker")

A character succeeding on a DC 30 Knowledge (history) check can provide some insight into the life of Mi'Tang, prefect of the House of Dragon, and Master of the Darkstar.

Mi'Tang was a rival of C'nosretep in life. Equal in nearly every way to C'nosretep, he was master of the darker sects of the Monastic order. When C'nosretep brought his armies to the Monastery of Light, Mi'Tang instructed his own personal minions to stand down and fight only if attacked. Mi'Tang figured that C'nosretep and his allies would grind themselves down fighting Master Seung and others faithful to Ozykathalin. Mi'Tang would then instruct his disciples to strike down the survivors of the battle and take his place as master of the oasis of Amra.

Failing in his scheme, Mi'Tang was slain by C'nosretep. Set returned Mi'Tang to this realm as a nightwalker, imprisoned in the Dome of the Darkstar until such time as the *amulet of the darkstar* is returned to him. As a further insult, Set turned many of Mi'Tang's most loyal disciples into non-corporeal undead. They lurk now on the fringes of the Monastery and Pyramid, forever reminded of their failure, and inferiority to his chosen champion.

Mi'Tang loathes and despises C'nosretep with half of a millennium's worth of hatred. This may be to the PCs advantage, for Mi'Tang has complete control of non-corporeal undead within the monastery and pyramid of Amra once he is freed from the Dome of the Darkstar. Mi'Tang can be bargained with, if his rage can be abated. Clever PCs could suggest that Mi'Tang and his minions take out the assweres and doppelgangers within the monastery and pyramid. This would leave the party to handle

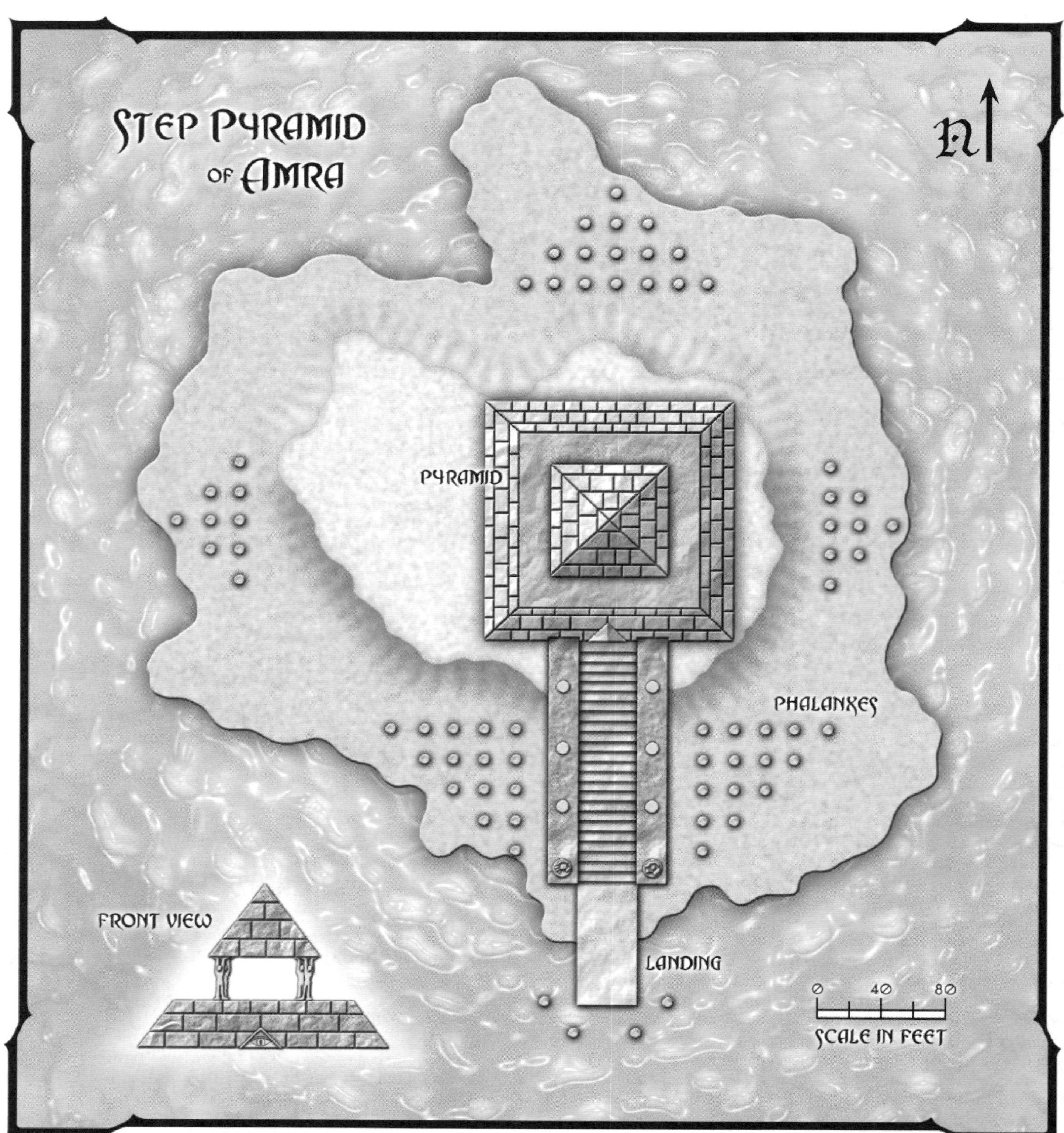

the vampires that he and his ilk are all but powerless to harm.

Tactics: Mi'Tang taunts and berates the PCs, summoning a specter and directing it to attack clerics as he strikes out at the PC grasping the *amulet of the darkstar*. Mi'Tang typically Power Attacks, attempting to slay his foe quickly and snatch up the *amulet*. Mi'Tang has been trapped within the Dome of the Darkstar for about 500 years and is thrilled that he may have the opportunity to escape this chamber with the stone.

If defeated, Mi'Tang cries out before fading from existence:

> "I am Mi'Tang the mighty! How dare you slay… me?"

Treasure: If the players are able to defeat Mi'Tang they find some of his former belongings with a successful DC 16 Perception check.

An unlocked chest contains 4,000 gp and a *ring of mind shielding*. A *+4 defending quarterstaff* lies on the floor of the chamber.

The Isle of the Pyramid

The Pyramid of Amra rests upon a solitary island in the center of the mountain's crater. A lake of pure blue water surrounds this island and strange mists cover its view most of the time. The Step Pyramid structure sits upon a plateau in the center of the island, the lower half made of cyclopean blocks, the upper half held suspended by four stone statues. The faces appear to have been re-carved and set with different stone to take the likenesses of a snake, an ass, an insect, and a crocodile. Below the plateau, shrouded in mist of the lower island, stand phalanxes of terracotta monks staring out from the cardinal points of the Pyramid.

The PCs may reach this island by the secret passage under the throne at **Area 2** in the Palace. If so, they begin at **Area P-1**. If the PCs reach the island by using the barge from **Area 5** or by other above-ground means, they encounter the island detailed in the map above and may proceed to the above-ground entrance to the Pyramid at **Area U-1**.

The PCs may have tried to bypass the Palace, as detailed above, and may simply fly or use other means of transport to the island. They will quickly discover, however, that they lack the *amulet of the lotus master*, and thus will need to investigate the Palace despite their intent to bypass it.

Pyramid of Amra: Lower Chambers

P-1: Entrance from the Throne of Lotus Master

A long subterranean pathway leads from the tunnel beneath the Throne of the Lotus Master onwards and up several flights of carved and little used stone stairs until finally you reaching the base of what must be the lower pyramid. Ancient hieroglyphics along the walls feature the great heroes of the Brotherhood, as they are interred respectfully for all time.

P-2: Trapped hallway (CR 9)

This small hallway is covered from floor to ceiling in gold leaf bas-relief of the ancients instructing their human subjects in the proper preparation of the dead for transportation into the afterlife. The images show mummification techniques and herbal knowledge.

A **trapped pressure plate** closes the secret door to **Area 1** and ceramic nozzles in the ceiling spray the gold lined hallway with acid. A trigger mechanism located on the bas-relief disarms the trap, draining the acid through hidden holes in the floor to some unknown repository below the hallway.

ACID BATH TRAP **CR 9**
XP 2,400
Type mechanical; **Perception** DC 25; **Disable Device** DC 25

Trigger location; **Reset** manual
Effect room sprayed with acid (2d6 acid per round for 4 rounds); never miss; onset delay (2 rounds); multiple targets (all targets in a 10-ft.-by-20-ft. room)

P-3: Tomb of Skulls (CR 8)

Hundreds upon hundreds of skulls stare out at you from blank black sockets as you open the stone slab that seals this chamber. Behind each skull is a set of canopic jars containing the innards of the monk whose skull is displayed with care within the niche. Dark figures — **8 vargouilles** — suddenly from the corners into the air as the PCs advance.

VARGOUILLES (8) **CR 2**
XP 600
hp 19 (*Pathfinder Roleplaying Game Bestiary* "Vargouille")

Tactics: The **vargouilles** shriek repeatedly to dishearten the PCs and hopefully catch someone with their paralytic moan.

P-4. Mausoleum of the Thirsting Ones (CR 10)

This roughly rectangular room is lined with nine sarcophagi. If the PCs explore this area during daylight hours (if the GM is feeling particularly kind to the player characters) the **8 vampire spawn** that hide throughout the Palace and Mausoleum are found resting here. Vampire spawn encountered and destroyed in the palace should be taken from the numbers in this area of the dungeon. Hidden behind the eighth sarcophagus is the secret entrance to **Area 6**.

VAMPIRE SPAWN (8) **CR 4**
XP 1,200
hp 26 (see **Area 2**)

Tactics: If the PCs enter this room during the daylight hours **1d4 vampire spawn** are already awakened in the chamber, as they need little sleep. The others are resting or regenerating in their sarcophagus. If the encounter occurs at night, subtract the number of vampire spawn already defeated from the number originally found within the room. These remaining vampires hide within the chamber as they hear the PCs approach, usually *spider climbing* along the ceiling or next to their sarcophagus waiting to spring a trap. They target priests and spellcasters first, rogues and bards second, saving up for the fighters last. They gang attack, seeking to drain as many levels from these casters as they can. If Nestrij has been encountered and forced to flee she organizes the spawn that are within this chamber. Several attempts should be made to dominate PC's so that they can be turned against their allies and eventually fed upon.

Treasure: Hidden in the crypts are 10,174 sp, 4948 gp, and a *wand of mirror image* (20 charges).

P-5: Chamber of the Hand (CR 8)

A mosaic of a large hand dominates this chamber within the heart of the Lower Pyramid.

Tomb of C'Nosretep
Chamber of the Book
Upper Chambers
Lower Chambers
Pyramid of Amra
1 square = 10 feet
U10
U12
U11
C
B
A
I4
I3
U5
U8
U4
U3
U6
U2
U9
U7
U1
P4
P6
P5
P2
P3
P1
N

Anyone succeeding on a DC 20 Perception check recognizes a depression in the palm of the hand that is the exact shape and size of one of the *amulet of lotus master*. Placing the sacred amulet into the palm depression causes a great rumbling and grinding sound to begin. The floor begins to rise, moving the hand upwards towards the ceiling. Players have two rounds to either get out of the room or get onto the palm and ride it up to **Area 4, the Upper Chambers.** Those remaining within the room but not standing upon the hand must succeed on a DC 20 Reflex save or be crushed against the ceiling for 6d6 points of damage.

CRUSHING CEILING TRAP **CR 8**
XP 4,800
Type mechanical; **Perception** DC 15; **Disable Device** n/a

---

Trigger location; **Reset** automatic
Effect rising floor (6d6 crushing damage); never miss; onset delay (2 rounds); multiple targets (all targets in a 20-ft.-by-20-ft. room)

As the players place the disk within the center of the palm, after much complex grinding and turning of gears that have not moved in centuries, the palm they stand upon turns in a spiral ever upwards looking as if they will be crushed against the ceiling. Just at the last moment a circular opening twists above their heads; they are now in a new chamber. The mosaic below the party's feet is now of a different pattern, the hand has become a great celestial eye, and the Amulet of Lotus Master a strange glowing iris within its center.

P-6. False Crypt of C'nosretep (CR 15)

This chamber is filled with the dust of a millennium. Its dark diorite walls reflect little light. At one end of the chamber is a 9-foot long sarcophagus, also of dark diorite stone. The top is carved in the likeness of C'nosretep, grasping a lotus within his hands and wearing a headband with a serpent upon his brow.

Touching or searching the diorite sarcophagus sets off the ***teleport* trap**.

***TELEPORT* TRAP** **CR 7**
XP 3,200
Type magic; **Perception** DC 30; **Disable Device** DC 30

Trigger touch; **Reset** automatic
Effect *teleported* into the sarcophagus (DC 23 Will avoids)

Sealed within this sarcophagus is **Eshtartha, a lich cleric** and former advisor and lover of C'nosretep. He wanted her to join him in eternity as a vampire, but she defied him and instead transformed herself into a lich to increase her powers as a spellcaster. For her audacity, C'nosretep tricked her and caused her to set off the *teleport* trap, forever imprisoning her.

The first character to be teleported into the sarcophagus actually trades places with Eshtartha. The same happens if others touch the sarcophagus; the one who touched the stone is teleported in as the previous occupant is teleported out.

Victims inside the sarcophagus are affected by a *temporal stasis* spell. Unless somehow released from the sarcophagus they are trapped inside forever — awake and aware of the passage of time, but unable to take any action other than to lie there and stare at the sealed lid above them.

Sarcophagus: The sarcophagus has a hardness of 8 and 60 hp. The only way to free anyone trapped inside without taking their place is to break it open.

ESHTARTHA **CR 14**
XP 38,400
Female human lich cleric of Set 13 (*Pathfinder Roleplaying Game Bestiary* "Lich")
LE Medium undead (augmented human)
Init +2; **Senses** darkvision 60 ft.; **Perception** +17
Aura evil, fear aura (DC 18)

AC 17, touch 12, flat-footed 15 (+2 Dex, +5 natural)
hp 101 (13d8+26 plus 13)
Fort +10; **Ref** +6; **Will** +13; +4 vs. channeled energy
Defensive Abilities channel resistance +4, rejuvenation, remote viewing; **DR** 15/bludgeoning and magic; **Immune** cold, electricity, polymorph, undead traits

---

Speed 30 ft.
Melee touch +11 (1d8+6 plus paralysis; DC 18)
Special Attacks channel energy 7/day (7d6, DC 18), lore keeper, paralyzing touch, scythe of evil, touch of evil
Domain Spell-Like Abilities (CL 13th; melee touch +11):
At will—*lore keeper*
13 rounds/day—*remote viewing*
8/day—*touch of evil*
Spells Prepared (CL 13th):
7th—*destruction* (DC 22), *legend lore*[D]
6th—*blade barrier* (x2) (DC 21), *create undead*[D]
5th—*flame strike* (x2) (DC 20), *greater command* (DC 20), *summon monster V*, *true seeing*[D]
4th—*death ward, dimensional anchor, divine power, greater magic weapon, restoration, unholy blight* (DC 19)[D]
3rd—*bestow curse* (DC 18), *contagion* (DC 18), *magic circle against good*[D], *magic vestment, summon monster III* (x2)
2nd—*align weapon*[D], *darkness, desecrate, enthrall* (DC 17), *hold person* (DC 17), *resist energy*
1st—*bane* (DC 16), *cause fear* (DC 16), *command* (DC 16), *detect good, doom* (DC 16), *endure elements, protection from good*[D]
0 (at will)—*detect magic, guidance, resistance, virtue*
D Domain spells **Domains** Evil, Knowledge

Str 14, **Dex** 14, **Con** —, **Int** 12, **Wis** 20, **Cha** 14
Base Atk +9; **CMB** +11; **CMD** 23
Feats Combat Casting, Command Undead, Craft Wondrous Item, Extra Channel, Heighten Spell, Improved Critical (heavy mace), Maximize Spell, Power Attack
Skills Diplomacy +13, Intimidate +13, Knowledge (arcana) +12, Knowledge (history) +13, Knowledge (religion) +13, Perception +17, Sense Motive +13, Spellcraft +13, Stealth +10; **Racial Modifiers** +8 Perception, +8 Sense Motive, +8 Stealth
Languages Common, Infernal

Tactics: The only thought in the mind of Eshtartha is for revenge against C'nosretep. To this end, as she appears before the PCs, she raises her hands and begs them not to attack her. If they press the attack she has no choice but to defend herself, but her only goal in combat is protect herself and flee. She uses the divine spells at her disposal to affect her escape. Should the PCs listen to her, she tells them the sad tale of a love betrayed and countless years of imprisonment. Then, much to the surprise of the PCs, she asks if she might join them as they venture further into the Pyramid so that she may help them defeat C'nosretep. Should they agree, they have gained a somewhat unusual ally, but an ally nonetheless. Although she is truly evil through and through, Eshtartha keeps promise to help the PCs against C'nosretep and the other dangers in the remainder of the Pyramid. After the adventure, should Eshtartha survive, she parts company with the PCs, but promises to remain their ally should they desire such.

Treasure: Hidden within the diorite sarcophagus are a 1,000 gp ruby necklace and a *staff of defense* (*30 charges*).

Pyramid of Amra: Upper Chambers

U-1: Portal of the Eye and First Test, "The Test of Hospitality" (CR 7)

Dominating this room is a 10-foot-wide by 10-foot-tall arched doorway inlaid with an eye set into the center of a triangle. Inscribed upon the Portal of the Eye are words in a long forgotten script.

Characters that succeed on a DC 25 Linguistics check comprehend these words.

> *"When come unbidden to our rest, politic and manners serve you best. In order to proceed thus shall be the first test. Where rings of metal doth fail the fist may do; thus shall this wisdom then guide you."*

Stone Door of the Echo: 4 in thick; hardness 6; hp 30; Break DC 25.

To open the door requires a simple knock loud enough to cause an echo, which is simply done, as the door is hollow. Should there be more than one knock or a knock that is loud, i.e. pounding on the door or trying to break it down, the small ***glyph*** placed upon the ceiling activates.

***GREATER GLYPH OF WARDING* TRAP** **CR 7**
XP 3,200
Type magic; **Perception** 31; **Disable Device** 31

Trigger spell; **Reset** none; **Bypass** knock politely
Effect spell effect (*greater glyph of warding [bestow curse, –6 to Charisma]*, DC 21 Will resists); boils and sores erupt from the victim's skin, their attitude sours, and they become belligerent.

Successfully disabling or bypassing the trapped door reveals a hieroglyphic lined chamber depicting various aspects of hospitality and preparation for the afterlife to the recently deceased.

U-2: The Second Test: Test of Friendship (CR 7)

Runes upon this door, when deciphered, pose the basic question to those who would pass its lapis portal. Characters must succeed on a DC 20 Linguistics check to read them.

> *"What is the greatest treasure that anyone could have?"*

Answering the word "**friendship**" automatically disables the **trap** and the great lapis slab slides open revealing the third test. Uttering any other word triggers the *greater glyph of warding*.

***GREATER GLYPH OF WARDING* TRAP** **CR 7**
XP 3,200
Type magic; **Perception** DC 31; **Disable** Device DC 31

Trigger spell; **Reset** none; **Bypass** code word (friendship)
Effect spell effect (*greater glyph of warding [bestow curse, paranoia]*, DC 21 Will resists); the character who first says any word but "friendship" is cursed with paranoia (See the "Sanity and Madness, Paranoia" section in Chapter 8 of the *Pathfinder Roleplaying Game GameMastery Guide*)

U-3. The Final Test, Test of Bravery (CR 7)

The letters on this door bear a chilling threat. Characters must succeed on a DC 15 Linguistics check to read them.

> *"No more riddles are there here for you and I. Succor your courage and prepare to die."*

Upon reading these words, a ***symbol of fear*** is triggered.

***SYMBOL OF FEAR* TRAP** **CR 7**
XP 3,200
Type magic; **Perception** DC 31; **Disable Device** DC 31

Trigger spell; **Reset** none
Effect spell (*symbol of fear*, DC 21 Will save resists, panicked 13 rounds)

Characters not driven away need only press their palm against the door and it opens at a touch revealing **Area U–4: The Chamber of the Eye** beyond.

U-4: Chamber of the Eye

As the PCs enter this large chamber it seems to pulsate with some unknown power that bears down upon them like a stack of bricks. The feeling continues as they linger, as if someone were continually adding another brick and yet another brick to the stack. After a few moments this sensation subsides.

At the center of the room is a large mosaic image of an eye in the center of a pyramid. The pupils are slits like those of snakes and there is a golden sconce imbedded in each of the three corners of the triangle surrounding the eye.

If the PCs entered the chamber through the front portals, something appears to be missing from the center of the eye where the iris would normally be.

There are secret doors hidden in the center of the eastern and western walls, requiring DC 24 Perception checks to locate. They are not trapped and lead into the maze beyond. The sconces at the points of the pyramid are the keys to lowering the upper pyramid and proceeding to the lair of C'nosretep and the Chamber of the Book. Close examination of each sconce at the points of the triangle reveals these barely noticeable runes.

Anyone succeeding on a DC 20 Decipher script check may read the following:

> *"Gathered by the candle flame, bring down the sky but not for shame, as beyond the sky lie riches true, the master buried in his tomb, Faithfully guards forever in spirit form, the Tome of Mind and Body borne to us in the worlds fond spring, golden words of Arden ring the truth which all devout should know, For the Wise do see their powers grow. Seek its knowledge you who are Brave, to your weakness be not slaves."*

U-5: Chamber of the Monkey (CR 9)

Once the burial place of all members of the House of the Monkey, this chamber now houses the **Cie Tzu**, an advanced specter and former master. This room has been influenced by powerful evil forces, and Cie Tzu enjoys the benefits of a permanent *protection from good* spell.

CIE TZU, ADVANCED SPECTRE **CR 9**
XP 6,400
Advanced spectre (*Pathfinder Roleplaying Game Bestiary* "Spectre")
LE Medium undead (incorporeal)
Init +7; **Senses** darkvision 60 ft.; **Perception** +22
Aura unnatural aura

AC 16, touch 16, flat-footed 13 (+3 deflection, +3 Dex); +2 deflection vs. good opponents
hp 75 (10d8+30)
Fort +6; **Ref** +6; **Will** +10
Defensive Abilities channel resistance +2, incorporeal; **Immune** undead traits
Weaknesses resurrection vulnerability, sunlight powerlessness

---

Speed fly 80 ft. (perfect)
Melee incorporeal touch +11 (energy drain)
Special Attacks create spawn, energy drain (2 levels, DC 18)

Str —, **Dex** 16, **Con** —, **Int** 14, **Wis** 16, **Cha** 16
Base Atk +7; **CMB** +10; **CMD** 23
Feats Blind-Fight, Combat Reflexes, Improved Initiative, Skill Focus (Perception), Weapon Focus (melee touch attack)
Skills Fly +15, Intimidate +16, Knowledge (history) +12, Knowledge (religion) +14, Perception +22, Stealth +16, Survival +13

Create Spawn (Su) Any humanoids slain by a spectre become spectres themselves in 1d4 rounds. Spawn so created are less powerful than typical spectres, and suffer a –2 penalty on all d20 rolls and checks, receive –2 hp per HD, and only drain one level on a touch. Spawn are under the command of the spectre that created them and remain enslaved until its death, at which point they lose their spawn penalties and become full-fledged and free-willed spectres. They do not possess any of the abilities they had in life.
Resurrection Vulnerability (Su) A *raise dead* or similar spell cast on a spectre destroys it (Will negates). Using the spell in this way does not require a material component.
Sunlight Powerlessness (Ex) Spectres are powerless in natural sunlight (not merely a *daylight* spell) and flee from it. A spectre caught in sunlight cannot attack and is staggered.
Unnatural Aura (Su) Animals, whether wild or domesticated, can sense the unnatural presence of a spectre at a distance of 30 feet. They do not willingly approach nearer than that and panic if forced to do so unless a master succeeds at a DC 25 Handle Animal, Ride, or wild empathy check. A panicked animal remains so as long as it is within 30 feet of the spectre.

Tactics: As the PCs enter, Cie Tzu sinks beneath the floor and to rise up behind the PCs, striking out against clerics and spellcasters.

Treasure: A DC 20 Perception check of Cie Tzu's crypt uncovers a *staff of frost* (*49 charges*).

U-6. Mausoleum of the Wind (CR 17)

Stepping beyond the locked stone doorway is a square chamber with a 15 foot high ceiling. Suspended in the air in the center of the room is a blue candle with a brilliant glowing flame.

1st trap: Stepping into the chamber causes the entire floor, a *wall of stone*, to be dispelled. In its place is a very deep pit with a 6-inch wide ledge that runs around the edges of the chamber.

PIT TRAP (150 FT. DEEP) **CR 5**
XP 1,600
Type mechanical; **Perception** DC 20; **Disable Device** DC 20

Trigger touch; **Reset** none
Effect 150 ft. deep pit (15d6 falling damage, DC 20 Reflex avoids)

Characters must succeed on a DC 15 Acrobatics check to walk along the ledge without falling into the pit. A brave character can attempt to jumping the distance and grab the candle with a successful DC 40 Acrobatics check followed by an attack roll against AC 9 to grab the candle (AC 5 base +4 for a Fine object), and another DC 25 Acrobatics check to land safely upon the opposite ledge. Using a lasso to rope the candle requires a successful ranged attack roll against AC 9 to loop the rope around the candle. If the lasso attempt fails, roll 1d6; on a roll of 1 or 2, the candle falls down into the pit. Alternately, a spellcaster can simply use *mage hand* or similar spells to grab the candle and pull it safely to the side. Using spells such as *levitating* or *fly* also allows the easiest access to the candle.

2nd trap: Once the PCs have the candle, they have 1 round to leave the chamber before the door suddenly closes. Anyone standing in the doorway might be crushed as the heavy door slams shut.

SLAMMING DOOR TRAP **CR 1**
XP 400
Type mechanical; **Perception** DC 20; **Disable Device** DC 20

Trigger location; **Reset** none
Effect slamming stone door (4d6 damage, DC 20 Reflex avoids); onset delay (1 round)

3rd trap: As the door slams down, the ledge slides into the wall and disappears. Anyone standing on the ledge falls into the pit. Since there is no ledge and nothing to grab onto, characters incapable of avoiding gravity are allowed no Reflex save.

PIT TRAP (200 FT. DEEP) **CR 16**
XP 76,800
Type mechanical; **Perception** DC 20; **Disable Device** DC 20

Trigger touch; **Reset** none
Effect 200 ft. deep pit (20d6 falling damage); never miss;

Quest Candles: Candle of the Wise, Candle of the Faithful, and Candle of Bravery

These three candles are the three marks of success at the challenges presented. They have no further magical abilities other than as necessary components to access the later stage of this adventure.

onset delay (1 round); multiple targets (all targets on the ledge when it disappears)

Treasure: *candle of the wise*

U-7: Chamber of the Dragon (CR 7)

Beyond the locked secret stone portal is a single white candle floating 6 feet above a raised dais in the center of the chamber. Coiled around the dais is a **giant vampire constrictor snake**, its scales rasping dully against the stone as it turns its slitted eyes to face the PCs.

GIANT VAMPIRE CONSTRICTOR SNAKE **CR 7**
XP 3,200
Pathfinder Roleplaying Game Bestiary "Snake, Constrictor", "Vampire"
NE Huge undead (augmented animal)
Init +7; **Senses** darkvision 60 ft., low-light vision, scent; **Perception** +24

AC 25, touch 12, flat-footed 21 (+3 Dex, +1 dodge, –2 size, +13 natural)
hp 33 (6d8 plus 6); fast healing 5
Fort +5, **Ref** +10, **Will** +4
Defensive Abilities channel resistance +4; **DR** 10/magic and silver; **Immune** undead traits; **Resist** cold 10, electricity 10
Weaknesses vampire weaknesses

Speed 20 ft., climb 20 ft., swim 20 ft.
Melee bite +16 (1d8+14 plus grab), slam +16 (3d6+14)
Space 15 ft.; **Reach** 15 ft.
Special Attacks blood drain, children of the night, constrict (1d8+14), create spawn, dominate (DC 13), energy drain (2 levels, DC 13)

Str 39, **Dex** 17, **Con** —, **Int** 3, **Wis** 14, **Cha** 10
Base Atk +4; **CMB** +20 (+24 grapple); **CMD** 34 (can't be tripped)
Feats Alertness[B], Combat Reflexes[B], Dodge[B], Improved Initiative[B], Lightning Reflexes[B], Power Attack, Skill Focus (Perception), Toughness[B]
Skills Acrobatics +16 (+12 jump), Bluff +8, Climb +22, Perception +24, Sense Motive +12, Stealth +12, Swim +22; **Racial Modifiers** +8 Acrobatics, +8 Bluff, +12 Perception, +8 Sense Motive, +12 Stealth
SQ change shape, gaseous form, hero points, shadowless, spider climb

Tactics: The vampiric giant constrictor attempts to dominate the first person entering the room, using them as both shield and ally as it bites as many individuals as it can with its jaws, placing them in its crushing coils and draining them of life every round.

Note: The chamber is shielded against transmutation magic. Therefore spells such as *mage hand* have no effect in this chamber.

Treasure: *candle of the faithful*

U-8: Library of the Ancients (CR 13)

This hidden chamber contains rack upon rack of scrolls and tomes from around the world gathered in times of peace by the Brotherhood of Light. Now the dusty library is administrated by the Brotherhood of Set, who fear that destroying the arcane knowledge held within these tomes may bring other powers into play.

A strangely beautiful being with the head of an ass turns towards the PCs as they enter and begins chanting in an arcane tongue.

RHYLON **CR 13**
XP 25,600
Male asswere sorcerer 10 (*The Tome of Horrors Complete* 739)
LE Medium magical beast (human, shapechanger)
Init +1; **Senses** darkvision 60 ft., low-light vision, scent; **Perception** +13

AC 13, touch 11, flat-footed 12 (+1 Dex, +2 natural)
hp 71 (3d10+3 plus 10d6+10 plus 10)
Fort +7; **Ref** +7; **Will** +12; +4 vs. poison, +4 vs. hot or cold environments and to resist damage from suffocation
DR 10/cold iron; **Resist** fire 10, infernal resistances

Speed 30 ft.
Melee *+3 longspear* +13/+8 (1d8+7/x3), bite +10 (1d3+4)
Special Attacks bray, hellfire 1/day (10d6 fire, 10 ft. square, good creatures shaken 10 rounds, DC 17)
Bloodline Spell-Like Abilities (CL 10th; melee touch +10): 5/day—*corrupting touch* (5 rounds/day)
Spells Known (CL 10th; ranged touch +8):
4th (5/day)—*charm monster* (DC 18), *greater invisibility, stoneskin*
3rd (6/day)—*gaseous form, haste, stinking cloud* (DC 15), *suggestion* (DC 15)
2nd (7/day)—*acid arrow, glitterdust* (DC 14), *scorching ray, see invisibility, web* (DC 14)
1st (7/day)—*grease* (DC 13), *mage armor, magic weapon, protection from good* (x2), *shield*
0 (at will)—*daze* (DC 12), *detect magic, flare* (DC 12), *ghost sound* (DC 12), *light, open/close* (DC 12), *ray of frost, resistance, read magic*
Bloodline Infernal

Str 16, **Dex** 13, **Con** 12, **Int** 12, **Wis** 14, **Cha** 14
Base Atk +7; **CMB** +10; **CMD** 21 (25 vs. trip)
Feats Alertness, Blind-Fight, Brew Potion, Combat Casting, Craft Magic Arms & Armor, Endurance, Eschew Materials, Iron Will, Skill Focus (Perception)
Skills Acrobatics +11, Diplomacy +6, Disguise +12 (+20 in animal form), Intimidate +7, Knowledge (arcana) +11, Perception +13, Profession (librarian) +8, Sense Motive +4, Spellcraft +12, Stealth +5
Languages Common
SQ alternate form
Combat Gear *scroll of control water, scroll of dispel magic, scroll of fire shield, scroll of legend lore, scroll of prismatic spray, scroll of protection from arrows, scroll of shadow greater conjuration, scroll of stone to flesh,* 3 vials of *universal solvent*; **Other Gear** *+3 longspear*

Bray (Su): An asswere can loose a loud bray as a standard action. All creatures within 30 feet that hear it must succeed on a DC 12 Will save or be affected as by a *confusion* spell for 1d4+3 rounds (caster level 3rd). This is a sonic, mind–affecting effect. A creature that successfully saves cannot be affected again by the same asswere's confusion ability for one day. The save DC is Charisma–based.

Rhylon is the only truly living being allowed in the Pyramid of Amra. He is keeper of the tomes and scrolls within this great repository, and spends many long hours here examining their wealth of knowledge that could increase his arcane power.

Tactics: Rhylon despises humans and humanoids, and never assumes his humanoid form — he considers it weak and ugly. He undoubtedly has knowledge of the PCs thanks to their destruction of doors and setting off traps throughout the Pyramid, and the loud grating noise of the Hand rising from the bowels of the structure. As the PCs fumble with the door he covers himself in defensive spells. His defensive spells include those found on his scrolls, such as *fire shield*, and *protection from arrows*. Rhylon casts *grease* on the floor before the doorway and then uses his scroll of *prismatic spray* on the PCs as they open the door. He next burns through his attack spells as quickly as he can. If hard pressed in combat and he feels that he should die he attempts to flee using whatever means necessary and available to insure his survival.

Treasure: The shelves are lined with various books.

- 18 of the books contain historical and genealogical data that would be of value to loremasters and sages. These books are valued at 3d6 x 100 gp each.
- One of the books is a *vacuous grimoire*.
- One of the books is a *manual of bodily health +3*.
- One of the books is a treatise on demonology and summoning by the noted summoner Yelseila Warcret. It includes the following spells: *contact other plane*, *dimensional anchor*, *dismissal*, *lesser planar binding*, *planar binding*, and *gate*. Each of these spells has a +15% chance of arcane spell failure on the first casting, as Yelseila was quite mad and his spidery scrawl is suspect at best. The tome includes the true names of 6 outsiders who may be contacted with the spells in this book. Each hour spent dabbling in the deep mysteries compiled in this tome incurs a 1% per hour cumulative chance of the reader going completely insane, no saving throw. The names of these outsiders are left to the GM's discretion.
- One book contains a *headband of mental prowess +4 (Wisdom and Charisma)* in a hollow space carved into the pages. This *headband* only grants its benefit to good-aligned divine spellcasters. This limitation reduces its value from 40,000 gp to 12,000 gp.
- One is a *book of noble accomplishments*. See **New Magic Items** at the end of this adventure for details.

U-9: Chamber of the Hands (CR 10)

A secret door opens into this chamber. At the far end of the chamber is a 10-foot wide dais. Over the dais, 6 feet in the air, floats a single glowing candle.

Twenty feet beyond the entrance to this chamber is a **hidden pressure plate** which when triggered releases a thin layer of *sovereign glue* across the 40-foot section of floor that lies before the altar. One round later a ceramic sprayer drops from the ceiling and begins spraying acid throughout the entire 40 foot area in front of the dais.

***SOVEREIGN GLUE* TRAP** **CR 6**
XP 2,400
Type mechanical; **Perception** DC 27; **Disable Device** DC 27

Trigger location; **Reset** none
Effect *sovereign glue* (DC 23 Reflex avoids); multiple targets (all targets on the floor in a 40 ft. area); triggers acid sprayers; **Note:** *sovereign glue* instantly binds any two objects together permanently. Thus, boots, shoes, and feet are bound to the floor instantly. Objects thus joined can only be unbound by application of *universal solvent*.

ACID SPRAY TRAP **CR 9**
XP 6,400
Type mechanical; **Perception** DC 20; **Disable Device** DC 20

Trigger *sovereign glue* **trap**; Reset none
Effect acid spray (2d6 acid damage per round for 5 rounds); never miss; onset delay (1 round); multiple targets (all targets captured by the *sovereign glue*)

Note: The chamber is shielded against transmutation magic, excluding the magic that it took to make the *sovereign glue*. Therefore spells such as *mage hand* have no effect in this chamber.

Treasure: *candle of bravery*.

U-10. Upper Chamber of the Eye (CR 15)

Once the PCs have placed the three candles into the sconces at the points of the pyramid symbol in the center of **Chamber 4: Lower Chamber of the Eye**, as the candlelight fills the room a grating of stone and metal starts its low rumblings within the deep recesses of the pyramid. The very floor the PCs stand upon feels as if it is rising to crush you against the dusty limestone ceiling. The ceiling vanishes before their eyes in a flash, as the top portion of the Step Pyramid of Amra descends to meet the lower portion, sealing off this chamber with a new roof of glimmering blue enameled stone, which replaces the one that stood before. Four stone statues now occupy the corners of the chamber, their megalithic hands against the roof as if their very eminence supports the starred sky above.

The new chamber is a perfect square that appears to have no entrances and exits. If the PCs have left the *amulet of the lotus master* within the depression in the center of the eye, the room is bathed with a shimmering light, an orb forming in the center of the room just above the PCs. The image of a gentle looking man of great grace and indeterminate age gazes at the group with a pure benevolence and begins to speak:

> "Know that I am Ozykathalin, first and last Master of the Lotus within this ancient and holy place. I am he who knew the voice of Arden; I am he who strides in the realms of light, purest of all energy forever alive beyond the Gates of Wisdom. Wise too are you who have discovered the secrets of this place, but one secret still you do seek. To gain it, you must defeat he who was the betrayer. Know you that C'nosretep's worst betrayal was not to those who nurtured him, but to his own soul. Lost in his self-hatred, he did not realize the gifts that friendship and brotherhood offer. As allies you have gained much and risked much in your sojourn thus far, and to those who risk all for one another and their faith are granted the greatest of treasures. I grant you one boon before I make the way open to you. Ask of me what you will, and should it be within the powers of light to grant this thing, it is yours. Ozykathalin has spoken."

Ozykathalin grants the PCs one *limited wish*, before lifting his hands to reveal a shimmering staircase that leads to a hidden chamber amongst the "stars", **U-11 A.** The shimmering stairs are made of insubstantial light, but are easily climbed.

Note: If the PCs did not place the *amulet of lotus master* within the eye in the center of the triangle before placing the candles at each point of the triangle, the floor still rises, and the ceiling descends as before. However, much to the dismay of the PCs, the **4 statues** that once supported the upper portion of the Step Pyramid animate and attack.

STONE GOLEMS (4) **CR 11**
XP 12,800
hp 107 (*Pathfinder Roleplaying Game Bestiary* "Golem, Stone")

After defeating the stone golems allow the PCs to search the chamber. Searching along the ceiling (Perception DC 24) notes a secret panel about 20 feet above the floor of the chamber. Beyond the secret panel is **Area 11A: Stairway into Darkness**. The distance to the secret panel must somehow be navigated either by jumping, climbing, flying, or some other magical means.

U-11: Three Final Tests

U-11A: Stairway into Darkness

This ten foot long, five foot wide stairway is shrouded in deepest blackness.

The stairway is bathed in a *deeper darkness* spell. Only a *daylight* spell can negate the darkness, which in turn dispels the *daylight* spell as well. A DC 24 *dispel magic* also cancels the *deeper darkness*.

U-11B: First Stone Door (CR 9)

At the top of the stairs is a stone door set onto a 5 foot wide stone platform. The door is 6 feet tall and is carved with the likeness of a youthful man of great physical build, kneeling before the dark god Set. Set towers over the man with his arm outstretched. The man grasps Set's wrist in both of his smaller hands, and appears to be drinking blood from the wrist of the god. Anyone touching the door triggers a ***flesh to stone* trap**.

***FLESH TO STONE* TRAP** **CR 8**
XP 9,600
Type magic; **Perception** DC 31; **Disable Device** DC 31

Trigger touch; **Reset** automatic
Effect spell effect (*flesh to stone*, DC 19 Fortitude resists); sets off slide trap; petrified party member has hardness 8 and 60 hp.

SLIDE TRAP **CR 4**
XP 1,200
Type mechanical; **Perception** DC 25; **Disable Device** DC 25

Trigger *flesh to stone* trap; **Reset** automatic
Effect stairs become a ramp (2d6 falling damage; DC 20 Reflex save avoids); multiple targets (all targets in a 5-ft. by 10-ft. space)

Note: This door trap has two effects. First, anyone touching the door sets off the *flesh to stone* trap. The staircase then converts to a sliding ramp as the stone door begins to slide forward across the landing. The door pushes anyone or anything upon the platform down the ramp. Anyone tumbling down the ramp takes 2d6 points of damage; one character (chosen randomly) takes an additional 3d6 points of damage as the petrified party member collapses atop them. The petrified character also takes 3d6 points of damage; if the character takes damage while petrified, he or she may be missing a finger or a hand when restored to flesh. If the petrified character is reduced to 0 hp from the fall, hopefully the other PCs remembered to take hair and skin samples of the victim before the adventure and have available a handy *scroll of resurrection*!

U-11C: Second Door (CR 8)

This door features the carved image of Set, with C'nosretep sitting upon his lap, re-writing the *Tome of Mind and Body* with a raven quill feather in his hand.

This door is sealed with an *arcane lock*, and **trapped with *greater dispel magic***. The *greater dispel magic* is retributively set to go off the second a *knock* spell is cast. The intent of this trap is to remove any magical effects the PCs have cast in the process of preparing themselves for the final showdown with C'nosretep. The *knock* spell opens the door successfully.

***GREATER DISPEL MAGIC* TRAP** **CR 8**
XP 4,800
Type magic; **Perception** DC 31; **Disable Device** 31

Trigger *knock* spell; **Reset** none
Effect spell effect (*greater dispel magic*, dispel check at 1d20+15); multiple targets (all targets within a 30 ft. radius)

U-12: Tomb of C'nosretep (CR 17)

The second door opens into a chamber shrouded in magical darkness and filled with a great aura of evil. A quiet, reserved chuckle reverberates off of the low ceiling.

A *deeper darkness* permanently wrought within this room by Minions of Set negates the power of any *daylight* spells, instead rendering a murky dimness within the chamber. The twilight gloom reveals a golden sarcophagus set against the middle of the western wall. The unholy symbol of Set, carved into the sarcophagus acts to both *desecrate*, and *unhallow* the chamber, giving C'nosretep enhanced abilities here and reducing the DC to resist positive energy channeling by 4. The spell effect tied to the *unhallow* effect is *deeper darkness*. A narrow stone staircase in the southwestern corner of the chamber leads upwards into the darkness beyond.

As the utter darkness is swept away, C'nosretep stands to greet the PCs, stripped to the waist. His lips pulled back in a deadly smile to reveal his gleaming white fangs, his head shaved but for a long braid down his back. His pale, bluish skin ripples with muscle and a deep inner strength. A cruel voice calls to the PCs as they enter the chamber.

> "So champions, you seek to take the book from C'nosretep? Very well, let your screams reverberate from the Pyramid of Amra for all time. Know as your souls howl towards hell that it was the Champion of Set who sent you on your path. Just as I defeated Ozykathalin, so too shall your blood slake my undying thirst!"

C'NOSRETEP **CR 17**
XP 102,400
Male human vampire monk 16 (Pathfinder Roleplaying Game Bestiary "Vampire")
LE Medium undead (augmented humanoid, human)
Init +8; **Senses** darkvision 60 ft.; **Perception** +33

AC 37, touch 28, flat-footed 32 (+3 armor, +4 Dex, +3 deflection, +1 dodge, +10 monk, +6 natural); +2 deflection vs. good opponents (from *unhallow*, but doesn't stack with the bonus from his *ring*)
hp 139 (171) (16d8+32 plus 32 plus 32 [from *desecrate*]); fast healing 5
Fort +12 (+14/+16); **Ref** +16 (+18/+20); **Will** +17 (+19/+21); +2 vs. enchantment spells and effects, +4 vs. channeled energy, +2 profane bonus on all saves (from *desecrate*, shown in parentheses), +2 resistance bonus on all saves vs. good opponents (from *unhallow*, shown in parentheses)
Defensive Abilities channel resistance +4, evasion, improved evasion; **DR** 10/magic and silver; **Immune** undead traits; **Resist** cold 10, electricity 10; **SR** 26
Weaknesses vampire weaknesses

Speed 80 ft.
Melee slam +16 (+18) (1d4+6 [+8] plus energy drain) or unarmed strike +16/+11/+6 (+18/+13/+8) (2d10+4 [+6]) (attack bonus in parentheses and damage bonus in brackets include bonuses from *desecrate*)
Special Attacks blood drain, children of the night, create spawn, dominate (DC 20), energy drain (2 levels, DC 20), flurry of blows +14/+14/+9/+9/+4/+4/–1, ki strike (adamantine, cold iron/silver, lawful, magic), quivering palm 1/day (DC 23), stunning fist 17/day (DC 23)

Str 18, **Dex** 18, **Con** —, **Int** 16, **Wis** 20, **Cha** 15
Base Atk +12; **CMB** +20 (+22 trip); **CMD** 44 (46 vs. trip)
Feats Alertness[B], Cleave, Combat Expertise, Combat Reflexes[B], Deflect Arrows, Dodge[B], Great Cleave, Improved Initiative[B], Improved Trip, Improved Unarmed Strike, Iron Will, Lightning Reflexes[B], Mobility, Power Attack, Run, Scorpion Style, Spring Attack, Step Up, Stunning Fist, Toughness[B], Whirlwind Attack
Skills Acrobatics +23 (+63 jump), Bluff +10, Climb +23,

Escape Artist +23, Intimidate +21, Knowledge (arcana) +16, Knowledge (history) +13, Knowledge (religion) +13, Perception +33, Sense Motive +26, Stealth +31; **Racial Modifiers** +8 Bluff, +8 Perception, +8 Sense Motive, +8 Stealth
Languages Aklo, Celestial, Common, Infernal
SQ abundant step, AC bonus, change shape (dire bat or wolf, *beast shape II*), diamond body, fast movement, gaseous form, high jump, ki defense, ki pool (13), maneuver training, purity of body, shadowless, slow fall (80 ft.), spider climb, wholeness of body
Combat Gear *brooch of shielding* (101 uses); **Other Gear** *bracers of armor +3, monk's robe, ring of protection +3*

Note The AC, attack, damage, and saving throw bonuses in parentheses are supplied by the *desecrate* and *unhallow* effects in play in this room. If the seal of Set on the sarcophagus is destroyed, use the lesser values.

Tactics: C'nosretep seeks to dominate the strongest fighter or rogue in the party before unleashing a series of violent blows against a paladin or other fighter type, attempting to stun and spawn them as quickly as possible for use against the PCs later in the fight. He then turns on a PC cleric using the quivering palm attack in an attempt to outright kill the individual most dangerous to him. C'nosretep has very high spell resistance and therefore considers arcane spellcasters little more than a nuisance to him attacking other fighters, monks, and rogues on subsequent rounds, saving the spellcasters for "a light snack." After he has defeated the PCs, he sends his dominated slave to stand in the corner as he drains them of their life's blood, spawning them as a vampire and new guardian to the Monastery and Pyramid to replace the ones the PCs have destroyed. At any point where C'nosretep takes a large amount of damage, he uses the Touch of Life and Death to drain his opponent of hit points, healing himself in the process. If C'nosretep is defeated, he howls in rage and throws his fists in the air. He turns to vapor and flows into his nearby sarcophagus in a vain attempt to heal.

Sarcophagus of C'nosretep: This stone sarcophagus, covered in semiprecious jewels and gold leaf, has the seal of Set placed upon its jeweled lid. The seal acts to *desecrate* and *unhallow* the area, as well as filling a 60-foot radius with *deeper darkness*, granting C'nosretep even greater strength with which to combat his foes. Destroying the seal dispels the *deeper darkness*, *unhallow*, and *desecrate* effects within the chamber. If this happens C'nosretep becomes visibly weaker. The seal itself may be dispelled for 1d4 rounds if a *dispel magic* check against a 20th level caster is successful. Allow characters a DC 20 Perception check to notice the pulsing black stone seal carved in the shape of an asp atop the sarcophagus.

The Seal of Set: hardness 10; hp 30.

The sarcophagus itself is very heavy and tough (hardness 10, hp 90, Break DC 30). A DC 30 Strength check is required to slide the lid aside. Within the sarcophagus are the following items as well as C'nosretep's body if he was reduced to less than 0 hit points in the battle.

Treasure: Approximately 2,000 gp worth of precious gems and gold encrusts the lid of the sarcophagus. Within it is a solid gold funeral mask of the first Master of the Lotus, valued at 5,000 gp, as well as the items found upon C'nosretep's person.

U-13: Final Test of Wisdom (CR 11)

A plain stone door stands at the top of the staircase.

Nearly invisible hieroglyphics upon the door (DC 25 Perception to find, DC 25 Linguistics to decipher) reveal these hidden words.

> *"The Words of Arden lie beyond this door, ancient tome of the wisdom bound in stone, to win it you must thwart this poem. A Monkey has it, and so does a Cat. The Merchant often has his finger on it; Judges and Monks seek to perfect the art of it."*

The answer to the riddle is "**balance**." If answered correctly the stone slab slides away revealing a chamber beyond. Answering the riddle incorrectly sets off a **crushing ceiling trap**, unless already detected and disarmed. The ceiling descends in 1 round, filling the landing and the staircase.

CRUSHING CEILING TRAP **CR 11**
XP 12,800
Type mechanical; **Perception** DC 20; **Disable Device** DC 20

Trigger location; **Reset** automatic; **Bypass** code word (balance)
Effect crushing ceiling (13d6 damage); never miss; onset delay (1 round); multiple targets (all targets in a 5-ft. by 20-ft. space)

U-14: Chamber of the Book

Sitting atop a stone pedestal in the center of this tiny room is the *Tome of Mind and Body*. See **New Magic Items** at the end of this adventure for details.

New Magic Items

Amulet of the Darkstar

Aura moderate evocation and transmutation; **CL** 6th
Slot neck; **Price** 56,400 gp; **Wight** 1/2 lb.

DESCRIPTION

When grasped or worn, the amulet's user can see perfectly in darkness of any kind, even that created by a deeper darkness spell, as if he had the see in darkness ability of devils. Once per day, the amulet can be used to cast deeper darkness when the command word "Necrodarkanum" is spoken. This command word may be learned through use of a legend lore spell, a DC 30 Knowledge (arcana) check.

CREATION

Requirements Craft Wondrous Item, *darkvison*, *deeper darkness*; **Cost** 28,200 gp

Amulet of the Lightstar

Aura moderate evocation; **CL** 6th
Slot neck; **Price** 43,114 gp; **Weight** 1/2 lb.

DESCRIPTION

Twice per day the amulet of the lightstar allows the bearer to cast searing light. Once per day the wearer can cast daylight.

CONSTRUCTION

Requirements Craft Wondrous Item, *daylight*, *searing light*; **Cost** 21,557 gp

Book of Noble Accomplishments (Minor Artifact)

Aura moderate evocation; **CL** 18th
Slot none; **Weight** 4 lb.

DESCRIPTION

This valuable tome is a boon to divine spellcasters of any good alignment and ruin to any evil divine spellcaster that look upon its pages. Studying this volume for at least 40 hours (no more than 8 hours per day) imparts effects upon the reader. For those divine spellcasters of a good alignment (LG, NG, CG), it imparts a gain of XP enough to boost the reader to the beginning of the next level of experience (which must be taken as a level in divine spellcaster) as well as a +1 inherent boost to both Wisdom and Charisma. Divine spellcasters of evil alignment (LE, NE, CE) lose enough XP to demote them to the mid-point of the previous level. Neutrally aligned divine casters loose 1d8 x 1,000 XP; however, they gain a new view on the cosmos, enjoying a +1 inherent bonus to their Wisdom in the process and unless a Will save (DC 18) is made, a conversion to good is made (LN becoming LG, N becoming NG, and CN becoming CG). Those without divine spellcasting ability are unaffected.

This tome cannot be distinguished from any other magical libram or book until the writings contained within are studied. Once fully pursued, this remarkable work vanishes into thin air. Those affected by it may never again benefit or be harmed by examining a similar book.

DESTRUCTION

If the life's blood of a good-aligned divine spellcaster is spilled upon the book during a sacrificial ritual by an evil-aligned divine spellcaster, the book bursts into flame and is irretrievably reduced to sodden ashes.

Masque of the Monkey

Aura faint transmutation; **CL** 5th
Slot head; **Price** 5,000 gp; **Weight** 1 lb.

DESCRIPTION

A masque of the monkey is a wooden mask carved in the likeness of a shrieking spider monkey. The individual donning the mask gains a +5 competence bonus on Acrobatics and Climb checks.

CONSTRUCTION

Requirements Craft Wondrous Item, *spider climb*; **Cost** 2,500 gp

Medallion of the Lotus Master

Aura strong abjuration and transmutation; **CL** 12th
Slot neck; **Price** 48,000 gp; **Weight** 1/2 lb.

DESCRIPTION

This item acts as an amulet of natural armor +4, and grants an additional +2 deflection bonus to AC.

CONSTRUCTION

Requirements Craft Wondrous Item, *barkskin*, *shield of faith*; **Cost** 24,000 gp

Shimmering Lotus Flower

Aura faint enchantment; **CL** 3rd
Slot neck; **Price** 6,000 gp; **Weight** —

DESCRIPTION

This item is pinned to the collar and worn like a brooch. It grants the wearer the effect of a bless spell as long as it is worn.

Requirements Craft Wondrous Item, *bless*; **Cost** 3,000 gp

Tome of Mind and Body (Minor Artifact)

Aura strong evocation and necromancy (if miracle is used); **CL** 17th
Slot none; **Weight** 5 lb.

DESCRIPTION

The Tome of Mind and Body is a powerful magical text usable only by monks. Studying its pages for a month grants the following special benefits to the user.

- A permanent increase of +2 inherent bonus to Strength, +2 inherent bonus to Dexterity, and inherent bonus to +2 Wisdom.
- The student gains knowledge of the secret Touch of Life and Death. This new ability grants the monk the ability to use an unarmed touch attack that acts similarly to the spell vampiric touch, using the character's monk levels as her caster level. This attack must be declared before the die is rolled. A miss means that the use of the ability is wasted. The monk can either gain the damage done as temporary hit points as per the vampiric touch spell, or she can store any portion of the hit points thus gained and grant them as temporary hit points to a comrade. This special ability is useable once per day per 3 levels of monk (minimum 1).
- Due to C'nosretep's twisting of the words contained in the text, a monk reading the tome must succeed on a DC 25 Will save or have his alignment permanently changed to chaotic evil, forever losing the ability to continue his studies as a monk. Only a wish or miracle spell cast upon the individual can change his alignment back again.

The Tome of Mind and Body may be studied only once in a monk's lifetime, as further study grants no more special powers or ability increases. Once completed, the book loses its powers to grant special benefits to any other monk for one full year, at which time another monk may study its ancient lore.

DESTRUCTION

The tome is destroyed if a new Ozykathalin rises as Master of the Lotus and touches the book with the petal of a fresh lotus blossom. This any Ozykathalin will do in order to eradicate the corrupted book and then set out to pen a new, unsullied copy.

The Isle of Eliphaz

By Casey W. Christofferson and Bill Webb

Introduction

The Isle of Eliphaz is an adventure for characters of at least 14th level. In the course of the adventure, the PCs face the powerful lich Athransma in the hidden Maze of Ancients. Careful searching and sharp wits help the PCs avoid being led astray by the devices of Athransma in his goal to awaken the primal Eliphaz. The group should include a rogue with at least 9 ranks of Disable Device and Perception. The party should also include a druid, a wizard, and at least two characters with skill in combat. Under no circumstances should any adventuring group set out without a cleric.

Island of Eliphaz Keyed Locations

A: A Mysterious Island at Sea

It is said among sages and treasure-hunters that on the Isle of Eliphaz, located in the Crescent Sea nearly 200 miles off the coast of the Grand Duchy of Reme, the false tomb of an ancient wizard lies buried. Local legend flies as far as Bard's Gate that a great evil god lies in a slumber on the isle, waiting to be awakened by some poor unfortunate souls. Indeed, it is said by all that this is an island to be feared, and no local sailors ever agree to an attempt to reach its shores.

The island is small and rocky, with only two places available for egress by ship. The beaches of this island are nondescript, though the rocks in the channels leading to them are treacherous. These passages are so vicious that any ship with a draft of greater than six feet has an 80% chance of running aground, with half that chance of inflicting so much damage to the ship that it begins to sink. At best, a successful DC 20 Profession (sailor) check cuts these probabilities in half.

The island itself is a typical one for this region, with coniferous trees, sea birds, and thick undergrowths of brush. This land is curious in the fact that no magic of any sort functions on or around it. In fact, anyone approaching the island within 50 feet has all active magic nullified — a potentially lethal hazard for anyone attempting to reach the island by air. This effect is the result of a permanent *antimagic field* cast on the island by the evil wizard prior to the time of his demise.

B: Crater of Eliphaz

Once on the island a quick search by the PCs discovers a low volcanic cone within the center. Characters succeeding on a DC 15 Climb check can reach the edge of the cone. There, they spy a small tower with a single door and no windows sitting atop the volcano's cooled cone in the very center of the crater. A second DC 15 Climb check allows the characters progress down the slope to the crater itself. A failed climb check results in the character falling and taking 4d6 points of damage from sharp rocks and the distance of the fall.

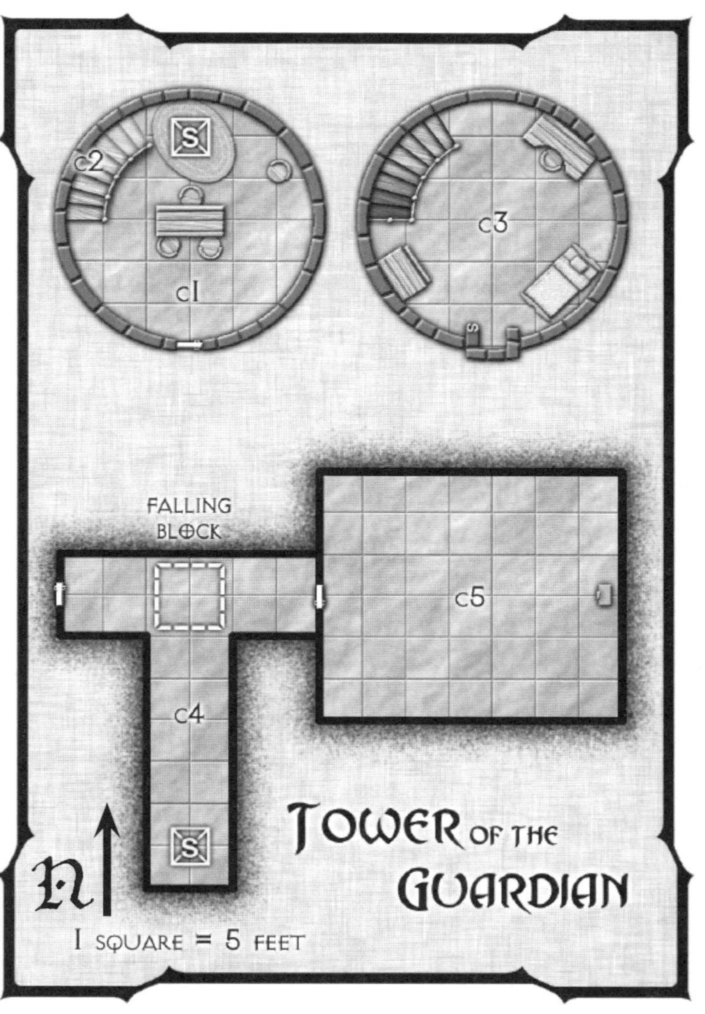

C: The Tower of the Guardian

The tower is made of dark stone, the door of fine wood. Strangely enough, the door is unlocked.

C1: Bottom Floor (CR 4)

Once inside the tower, the intruders discover some old furniture: a table, four chairs, and an old wooden staircase leading up. Hidden in the table, revealed only by a DC 20 Perception check, is a note from the wizard and a *deck of many things*. The *deck* is special, and anyone drawing a card has double the normal chance of drawing a negative one. When a character draws a card, if the card is a good result, ignore it and have them draw again. If the second card is a bad result, apply those results. If this second card is a good result, apply the results. The deck does not function until the *antimagic field* is turned off, of course. The note is a challenge from the wizard to:

"Trust Lady Luck in your quest for my tomb."

In the floor of this level is a **secret trapdoor**, which can be found with a successful DC 25 Perception check. The trapdoor leads to **C4: Passage to the False Crypts,** the dungeon below the tower.

There is nothing of value in this level of the tower, but on the fifth round after it is entered, a **gray ooze** attacks from above. It is nearly impossible to detect due to its color, and unless a successful DC 15 Perception check is made, it surprises the characters.

GRAY OOZE **CR 4**
XP 1,200
hp 50 (*Pathfinder Roleplaying Game Bestiary* "Gray Ooze")

C2: Rickety Stairs

The stairs, which are old and rickety but can easily support the PCs, lead up to the second level.

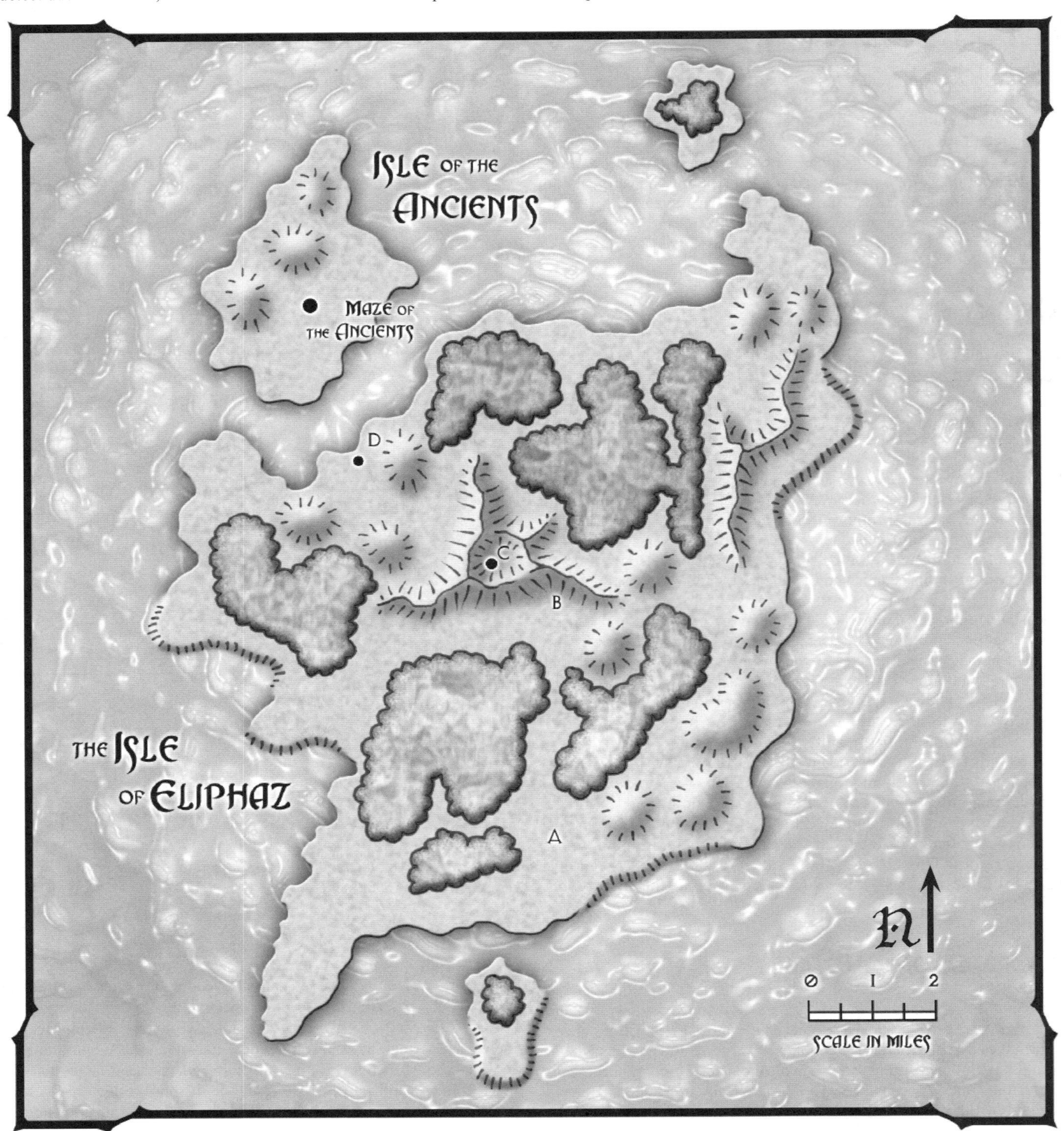

C3: Second Floor (CR 1/4+)

The second level of the tower is not a very nice place to be. All that it contains is the old bedroom furniture of the wizard, a couple of useless papers, scrolls, books, a fireplace, and a golden statue of a cat; about 18 inches tall. This is a really mean **guardian familiar** named Natasha. She circles and hisses, and when gets within 15 feet of an opponent, she attacks. She is particularly nasty since she has damage reduction and all magic weapons temporarily lose their enhancement on the island due to the *antimagic field*. See the **New Monsters** at the end of this adventure for details on the guardian familiar.

Secret Panel and Locked Box: In the fireplace is a secret panel, which the characters discover with a successful DC 30 Perception check. Inside is a locked box requiring a DC 25 Disable Device check to open. Within the box there is a key and two keyholes. The key appears to fit both of the keyholes. The left hole lowers the *antimagic field* surrounding the island. The right triggers a *mage's disjunction* which goes off in the tower, probably destroying most of the PCs' magic. Natasha must succeed on a DC 20 Fortitude save or be destroyed by the latter effect as well.

Athransma has found it necessary in his studies of the Ancients to craft this box. He intended for it to dampen all magic upon the island in the event that one of his experiments went awry within the Maze of Ancients. In addition, it was his hope that treasure hunters and looters would be put off at the immediate loss of their powers upon stepping onto the shore. Much to the chagrin of Athransma, the spells on the box, although powerful, are not strong enough to overcome the bindings that the Ancients placed upon the elemental god. Athransma had hoped his little box of tricks would work. Athransma added the second keyhole purely out of spite.

C4: Passage to the False Crypts (CR 7)

The trapdoor in **Area C1: Bottom Floor** leads down to a T-intersection of 10-foot by 10-foot tunnels. At the end of each tunnel is a door. To the left are a **false trapped door** and a pressure plate that releases a stone block that falls in the third 10-foot section of the hall (see below). The center passage leads to a door with a *nondetection* spell cast on it, a **poison needle trap** on the handle (see below), and an *arcane lock* cast at 14th level. Behind this door is a small pentagram inscribed on the floor. This symbol has a *magic aura* cast upon it, but has no other function.

FALSE DOOR TRAP **CR 5**
XP 1,600
Type mechanical; **Perception** DC 20; **Disable Device** DC 25

Trigger location; **Reset** none
Effect falling stone block (6d6 damage; DC 18 Reflex half); multiple targets (all targets in a 10-ft. square)

POISON NEEDLE TRAP **CR 5**
XP 1,600
Type mechanical; **Perception** DC 20; **Disable Device** DC 20

Trigger touch; **Reset** manual
Effect poison needle (Large scorpion venom); never miss; onset delay (1 round)

C5: The False Tomb (CR 10)

The right passage leads to the first false tomb. When the door is opened, a *magic mouth* spell triggers evil laughter and the voice of the wizard screams:

> "Now prepare to die the most painful of all deaths!"

The room then fills with a *fireball* spell. The *fireball* is actually an illusion generated by *shadow evocation*.

***SHADOW EVOCATION* TRAP** **CR 6**
XP 2,400
Type magic; **Perception** DC 30; **Disable Device** DC 30

Trigger location; **Reset** automatic
Effect spell effect (*shadow evocation [fireball]*; 4d6 fire damage; DC 22 Will save for 1/5 damage); multiple targets (all targets in a 20 ft. radius spread)

Once the *shadow evocation* is dispelled or overcome, the room can be entered and its contents examined.

The room contains a large golden calf, a tomb, and a bronze chest. Three rounds after the room is entered, the golden calf reveals its true nature, metamorphosing into a **gorgon**. It attacks immediately, breathing at anyone within range.

GORGON **CR 8**
XP 4,800
hp 100 (*Pathfinder Roleplaying Game Bestiary* "Gorgon")

Tactics: Moo! Charge, breathe, charge, breathe, charge, etc.

The chest is unlocked and contains a pile of gold (in reality a patch of **yellow mold** covered in a *permanent illusion*), and potion bottle wrapped with a note written on leather. The note is from the wizard.

YELLOW MOLD **CR 6**
XP 2,400 (*Pathfinder Roleplaying Game Core Rulebook,*

"Environments")

If disturbed, a 5-foot square of this mold bursts forth with a cloud of poisonous spores. All within 10 feet of the mold must make a DC 15 Fortitude save or take 1d3 points of Constitution damage. Another DC 15 Fortitude save is required once per round for the next 5 rounds, to avoid taking 1d3 points of Constitution damage each round. A successful Fortitude save ends this effect. Fire destroys yellow mold, and sunlight renders it dormant.

Above the chest is a moldering tapestry depicting an island nearby. The island on the tapestry reveals the true location of the wizard's tomb, and was left here by mistake. If the ancient writing on the tapestry is deciphered, requiring a DC 25 Linguistics check, the location of the new island can be found by the following means: The new island is known as the Island of the Ancients. If characters compare this map to the zodiacal symbols found on the dolmen of the pierced stone along the northern banks of the Isle of Eliphaz, they find that the hole in the center of the disk there points directly to the island's location. It lies just off the shore of the Isle of Eliphaz, beneath the waves. See **Area D: Dolmen of the Pierced Stone** for further details on raising the Isle of The Ancients.

Treasure: The bottle is marked "*potion of stone-flesh, 1 dose*," but is in reality a dose of extremely powerful acid. Anyone or anything onto which this is poured takes 10d6 acid damage. The note reads:

> *"Fools! You have failed in your grave-robbing ways to find my tomb, for it is far away, and this is just a hoax. Now, you idiots must decide which of your stony comrades you will save, for in ten minutes, all of the statues will turn to dust. Go home and become shopkeepers, for you are failures as grave robbers. Lick your wounds and rejoice that I have allowed you live, for I could have chosen not to do so."*

The note is signed, *Athransma the Merciful*.

The coffin is made of common stone, and contains a skeleton holding a wooden staff and adorned in fake jewelry. If an *identify* spell is cast upon the robe he wears, it reveals itself as being a *robe of the arch-magi*. The robe is actually a *poisonous cloak*. The only real piece of treasure is a fully charged *gem of seeing*.

D: Dolmen of the Pierced Stone

This dolmen on the north shore of the island comprises several standing stones carved with various arcane or zodiacal symbols, as well as symbols easily recognized runes of both earth and water. A stone disk stands balanced upon an altar of large stones. The center of the disk has a hole in it approximately the size of a fist. A character that succeeds on a DC 25 Linguistics check reads the following passage.

> "Into the eye of the disk do place that which makes secret things revealed, thus does the light then find Isle of The Ancients divined."

Placing the *gem of seeing* into the hole in the center of the disk causes a great beam of light to flare forth from the disk. The disk itself swivels on its altar pointing a short distance into the ocean. The water begins to boil as the beam strikes it, and the island of Eliphaz rumbles and shakes beneath the player's feet. After a few moments a second island rises from the waves not far from the shore of the first island. The second island is shrouded in a silvery mist as steam billows from the seawater. The *gem of seeing* is completely consumed in the process of raising the **Isle of the Ancients**.

Isle of the Ancients

This small island just off the coast of the Isle of Eliphaz is shrouded in steaming mist generated from the Dolmen of the Pierced Stone. Walking upon the island is treacherous as the entire island is concealed as by an Enlarged *fog cloud* spell. Furthermore the footing is very slippery from a rank-smelling muck of ankle deep silt, which has coated the island during its years of submersion beneath the waves. The island counts as difficult terrain, and movement across the island is reduced to 1/4. Any character moving at a higher speed or jumping must succeed on a DC 15 Acrobatics check or fall prone into the mud and seaweed.

Entrance to the Maze of Ancients (CR 8)

Two huge pillars carved with images weathered and covered in thick barnacles dominate the entrance; whatever symbolism the carvers of these pillars left behind has been lost to the ravages of the sea. Between the two pillars sits a low shrine-like structure carved of the same materials as the weathered pillars. A tight-fitting door sits in the center of the southern wall of the shrine.

When the characters clear away the muck and seaweed, they reveal a finely crafted bronze door. Bright green with the patina of age and salt water, the door is inscribed with an *arcane mark* which reads the following passage if *detect magic* is cast:

> *"So have you found the entrance to my tomb! Know that through the Maze of Ancients you must pass. Be warned: their evil is greater than my own. Tread here and breathe your last, for Athransma the Merciful am I. Turn back thieves or surely die!"*

The door to the Maze of Ancients is **trapped** with a *black tentacles* spell that triggers the moment the door is touched. An *arcane lock* spell also seals the door. Casting *knock* on the door may open it, however it still triggers the trap, which may only be disarmed by a high level rogue or some form of *dispel magic*.

***BLACK TENTACLES* TRAP** **CR 8**
XP 4,800
Type magic; **Perception** DC 29; **Disable Device** DC 29

Trigger touch; **Reset** none
Effect spell effect (*black tentacles*; CMB +10, 1d6+4 damage per round for 5 rounds); multiple targets (all targets in a 20-ft. radius spread)
Once the PCs open the door, they see a stone staircase descending hundreds of feet deep into the heart of the island ending at **Area M1**.

M1: Portal of the Ancients

At the end of the hallway is the **Portal of the Ancients**. The Portal of the Ancients is 30 feet tall by 20 feet wide and engraved with ancient celestial holy symbols that some unknown hand scarred and desecrated long ago. The engravings once featured law and celestial power being brought to bear against the elemental chaos of a primeval world, forging it and shaping it into a semblance of order. Casting *detect magic* reveals a strong *antimagic field* within, possibly shielding against certain transmutation spells.

Writing upon the portal is in an ancient tongue, decipherable with *comprehend languages*, or a DC 26 Linguistics check:

Maze of the Ancients
1 square = 10 feet
N
CHASM
CHASM
1
2
3
4
5
6
7
8
9
10
11
A
B
C
D
E
F

"So did they who came instruct in all manner of goodness and power over chaos, thus here did we build for them a remembrance of what was left behind, eternally restful by device. Thus through this door may those with wisdom glean their sage advice. Bringers of chaos and hatred enter not into their sacred womb for thus trapped forever find their doom. Those who bring with them nature's gift, welcome be and not bereft for close you are to a power true, within Letek're stones lies the answer sought by you. Only one with true balance may complete the task, setting the bound god upon the path of natural order at last."

2. The Trapezoidal Conflagration (CR 11)

This room is filled with 10 doors, three of which lead into the maze itself, one that leads to the bottomless bowels of the mountain, and the other 6 doors being false doors that are actually part of the wall. Searching for which doors lead out into the maze and which doors lead nowhere or do nothing at all should be an interesting challenge for the players.

A Perception check is required for each of the six doors. A successful DC 30 Perception check reveals that two of the doors, door **C** and door **D** are false doors, merely carved into the stone to look like regular doorways.

A: Door of the Narrow Path

SPEAR TRAP **CR 2**
XP 600
Type mechanical; **Perception** DC 20; **Disable Device** DC 20

Trigger location; **Reset** automatic
Effect Atk +12 ranged (1d8/x3 crit, rang 200 ft.)

B: False Door.

The door is locked (DC 20 Disable Device), but when opened reveals only a stone wall.

C: Door of the Far Path

Trapped but not locked, this door allows passage into the maze.

HAIL OF POISONED NEEDLES TRAP **CR 5**
XP 1,600
Type mechanical; **Perception** DC 25; **Disable Device** DC 25

Trigger location; **Reset** none
Effect Atk +20 ranged (1d4 plus bloodroot poison)

D: False Door

The door is locked (DC 20 Disable Device), but when opened reveals only a stone wall.

E: Door of the Dark Path

Trapped and locked (DC 20 Disable Device), when opened, a stone wall is revealed and the floor section immediately in front of the door tilts, casting the opener into the trackless void from which there is no escape.

TILTING FLOOR TRAP **CR 10**
XP 9,600
Type mechanical; **Perception** DC 20; **Disable Device** DC 20

Trigger location; **Reset** automatic
Effect tilting floor (DC 15 Reflex avoids); **Note:** Failing the saving throw means the character has been cast into the trackless void beneath the Maze of Ancients.

Maze of the Ancients

This area below the Isle of Ancients is the lair of several intellect devourers and the tomb of Athransma the Lich. The Maze of Ancients is so named for the bodies of ancient outsiders, encased in pillars of pure energy.

Maze Features

The maze itself comprises an area of 10-foot wide pathways that twist over a deep chasm which apparently falls off to nothingness. An additional magic field, functioning regardless of the stasis of the *antimagic field* — one in place due to the presence of the Ancients — renders all magical levitation, flying, *dimension door*, or *teleport* ineffective. *Wings of flying*, *boots of levitation*, and spells such as *wind walk* do not work normally within the maze. The spells work normally on the pathway itself, however they do not work to move across path from one section of maze to the next. This field is only in effect on the actual path itself, and does not impede magic in any of the various chambers located within the maze unless otherwise noted. Should all the Ancients be either destroyed or released, should Eliphaz be released from his confinement, or should all three *Letek're stones* be brought together, this effect is eliminated. Individuals falling off of the side of the maze must succeed on a DC 20 Reflex check to catch the edge of the pathway. Should the character fall beyond 100 feet without being rescued somehow, they are effectively dead.

Locked Stone Doors: Hardness 10; hp 60; Break DC 28, Disable Device DC 25. Unless otherwise noted all of the doors in the maze of the Ancients are locked stone.

F: Door of the Den

An *arcane lock* protects this door; when opened, it releases the barghests from **Area 6: Den of the Barghests**.

3. The Maze of the Ancients.

The stone pathway is ten feet wide. It is all that exists between the characters and oblivion. In the near darkness they can see other parts of the path about 10 ft. away in several different directions.

The magical effect of the Ancients prevents magical flying and *levitating* or *air walking* effects to merely cross directly through the maze, anyone attempting such an action find that their spell has failed. The chasm below the pathway is effectively bottomless. Of course fast thinking, ropes, bungee jumping off the side and catching a falling comrade are interesting game possibilities.

4: Pillar of the Ancients

Here, seemingly suspended in the air within a pillar of pure light energy, is a wizened and hairless figure sitting in the crouched lotus position. His four fingertips are pressed together in a contemplative state, and beautiful wings like mother of pearl are folded behind him. There is a strong aura of good and justice emanating from the glowing image though it does not move or even breathe. The ancient winged figure is dressed in a simple robe and his oversized eyes are closed. At the base of the pillar of energy the PCs note strange writing of an unknown language glowing along the side of a metallic disk upon which the Ancient sits.

The language upon the base of the pillar is Druidic, therefore it is quite possible that it is unknown to many of the PCs and would require a DC 30 Linguistics check to uncover its true meaning without a druid present. The words upon the pillar read:

> *"Guardians here for eternity our sacrifice keeps primal beast beneath, trapped here with us by our leave. So disks of stone in Nature's hand thus with a sense of balance stand. Force of will upon a knotted brow rebukes the mountain god for once and all."*

The two remaining pillars of the Ancients cannot be moved by any force, or entered without a complex ritual that involves dampening the energy field that is generated around them using the pedestals in **Area 9**.

A druid channeling elemental energy through the Pillar of Ancients using that pillar's corresponding *Letek're stone* generates the following effect: The pillar fills the Ancient with energy as the pillar itself dissipates, releasing the astral deva from his self-imposed slumber. Dissolving the pillar of light has the secondary effect of breaking one of the two remaining seals that bind Eliphaz beneath the main islands volcanic cone.

Ancient (Astral Deva)

The Deva greets the PCs addressing the druid of the group.

> "Ten thousand of your years have we bound ourselves to this place. In doing, we bound the one called Eliphaz to the island of his name. Great was his power for destruction, and hatred did he have for all manner of green life, and the life which bleeds precious red blood, for his is a heart of burning fire, and a mind of wrath. Sad am I that one of the three has been lost to this place. For now, with only two who remain, sworn to defend your world against the elemental. I fear we are not strong enough to save precious mortal lives from his burning vengeance. Unless…"

The deva suggests that within the bound crater of Eliphaz the *elemental belt* lies hidden. If the other Ancient is freed from the Pillar of the Ancient, the deva acts as a diversion allowing the PCs time to slip within the mouth of the volcano and grab the *elemental belt*, allowing them one chance to send Eliphaz to rest forever. Should the PCs agree to this course of action, the deva summons his mace to his hand and vanishes to stand watch over the rim of the crater waiting for Eliphaz to rise.

5. Pillar of the Ancient

As with **Area 4**, this Ancient is also in a state of meditation within the pillar of light that is so deep no mortal power, not even a *wish* spell can remove them from it. An aura of good and law exudes from the pillar in a 40-ft. radius that causes individuals of chaotic and or evil alignments to become uncomfortable. Athransma appears immune to this effect. The light from the pillar is as bright as daylight in a 20-ft. radius from the pillar itself.

Ancient (Astral Deva)

The Druidic writing on the around the base of this disk reads:

> *"When angels again absorb their light, the slumbering one shall rise. Turned from nature in his wrath did the fiery god despise every living thing upon which he set his burning eyes: A word of pause to nature's servants who would bring down the pillars of light, our strength was not enough before to win that brutal fight. Is your faith in earth now great enough to set the balance right?'*

Note: A druid, and only a druid, using the correct *Letek're stone* may dissolve the power of the pillar of light. If this deva is the first one freed, use the description in **Area 4**. If this deva is the second one freed by the players, the pillar of light dissipates as before, filling the Ancient with light and recharging his powers. It looks to the PCs and says:

> "We must hurry to my ally's aid. The beast rouses from slumber, and the *elemental belt* must be gained. We shall hold it away from you as long as we can."

It then summons its mace to its hand and teleports to the rim of the volcano as a rumble shakes the Maze of Ancients. See **Final Confrontation** section for information on how to run the end of this adventure.

6: Barghest Lair (CR 11)

This chamber was once a place of divine meditation within the presence of the Ancients. Held here in temporal stasis are 10 barghests. When door **F** in **Area 2: The Trapezoidal Conflagration** is opened, they are released from their rest and allowing them to hunt freely within the maze. If this door is opened first, these beasts are also released, confronting the PCs with a pack of dangerous, snarling beasts. This chamber once held the desecrated *Letek're stone*, and was plundered by Tlip Lopodi and his intellect devourers.

BARGHESTS (10) CR 4
XP 1,200
hp 45 (*Pathfinder Roleplaying Game Bestiary* "Barghest")

7: Shrine of the Ancients (CR 5)

This sacred shrine of the Ancients can only be reached by somehow crossing the 10 foot wide abyss from the pathway to the Shrine. Players are likely to invent any number of ingenious methods by which their characters can cross the gap. They may simply leap across—requiring an Acrobatics check that carries them at least 10 feet — or attempt some other means of passage. Only Small characters are light enough to try to walking or shimmying across a pole, as poles are not strong enough to carry the weight of larger characters. If a daring Small character attempts walk across a pole, they must succeed on a DC 20 Acrobatics check; shimmying across requires only a DC 5 Strength check. Remember that flying, levitation, and other magical means of defying gravity do not work within the Maze.

The door to the shrine of the Ancients is trapped with a **falling floor stones trap**.

FALLING FLOOR STONES TRAP CR 5
XP 1,600
Type mechanical; **Perception** DC 25; **Disable Device** DC 17

Trigger location; **Reset** none
Effect stones drop out of the floor (Reflex Save (DC 15); multiple targets (all targets in the room)
Note: Characters that fail the Reflex save, who are not tied to another character or have taken some other similar action, are dead if they fall into the void. When the trap is triggered the floor stones begin to fall away from the floor in a spiral pattern from the center of the 10-foot square in front of the door.

The Shrine of the Ancients, as it was once known, lies behind a door of solid stone. A Heightened lawful good *forbiddance* spell wards the door, and characters must succeed on a DC 25 Will save or be unable to enter the chamber by any means. The door pushes easily aside to anyone of lawful good alignment.

Within the shrine are carvings of a great battle between angelic beings and a gargantuan elemental of stone and fire. The carvings tell the tale of a titanic struggle. The three angelic beings are depicted hurling the elemental into the midst of a small island, creating a massive crater. There the angelic beings set to binding the creatures' arms and feet with chains forged from the elements of air and water.

Floating in the center of the room within a shaft of light is a small disk of purest milky jade, with a hole pierced in its center. Very fine writing in the druidic tongue translates exactly to what is written upon the base of the pillar of light in **Area 5**.

Treasure: *Letek're* (LA 'Teck 'Ray) *stone*. See the **New Magic Item** at the end of this adventure for details.

8: Corrupted Pillar of the Ancients

This light pillar is of a less peaceful and more menacing hue than the others, and there is no Ancient within the light that is present. The runes that would be in the stone below have been desecrated.

9: Laboratory of the Lich

In the center of the maze is this odd wedge-shaped construction that appears to be crafted completely from an otherworldly greenish metallic substance. The circular doorway is completely crafted from metal and appears to pulse as you approach. Symbols similar to others found throughout the Monastery and Mausoleum complex adorn the door in a swirling pattern. The door is held with an *arcane lock* (CL 20th). Within the metallic looking building is a single room that seemed to once have been a place of meditation and enrichment for the Ancients that was stripped and desecrated and is now the laboratory of Athransma. Bubbling cauldrons and beakers line the walls of the chamber. Three curious pedestals, pulsing with an unholy arcane light, stand near the back of the triangular room.

Two of the three curiously carved pedestals are empty. The third contains a small disk seemingly carved of jade about a hands-breadth across which floats and gives off a malignant aura. This is one of the three *Letek're stones*, one that has been cursed and warped by the foul magic of Athransma. In using of this stone, Athransma was able to force movement from the god of the island. This resulted in the destruction of the third pillar of light and the death of the Ancient contained therein. With these dark pedestals and the *Letek're stones*, Athransma believes he can actually rouse the god of the island from his slumber. If he succeeds, he plans to use the great elemental as a weapon with which to conquer the world. From there, his goals include placing himself in a position to challenge the gods themselves and join the ranks of the deities. His problem thus far has been the presence of the Ancients themselves, and the divine warding over **Area 7**, which forbids him entrance into the chamber which contains the last two stones. He has found the language of this *Letek're stone* undecipherable even with his magic, not knowing that it is in the lost script of the druids. In his arrogance, Athransma never bothered to study this simple language of the humble servants of nature.

Treasure: Tainted *Letek're stone* worth 2,000 gp due to its impurity, 6 vials of alchemist fire, 2 potions of *gaseous form* (CL 5th), 2 *potions invisibility* (CL 5th), *2 vials of poison*, detect as *cure serious wounds* (CL 5th)

10: Lair of the Intellect Devourers (CR 13)

A curious looking door made of solid stone of an unknown origin stands at the end of this section of the Maze.

Behind this locked stone portal is an odd shaped chamber that appears to be only twenty feet deep and thirty feet wide at its widest segment, but is in actuality double that size due to dimensional warping of space. The room is adorned with strange iconography of an almost alien design as well as four high backed chairs surrounding a swirling pool of brackish liquid.

Tlip Lopodi and three of his kin are servants of Athransma who have joined in the curious research of the Ancients. It is seldom that their kind are allowed such close scrutiny of celestial powers, the intellect devourers eagerly absorb any knowledge they can for use against these powers of good.

TLIP LOPODI **CR 10**
XP 9,600
Male intellect devourer wizard 3 (*Pathfinder Roleplaying Game* "Intellect Devourer")
CE Small aberration
Init +10; **Senses** blindsight 60 ft., darkvision 60 ft., *detect magic*; **Perception** +24

AC 23, touch 18, flat-footed 16 (+6 Dex, +1 dodge, +5 natural, +1 size)
hp 115 (8d8+40 plus 3d6+15 plus 14)
Fort +8; **Ref** +9; **Will** +16
DR 10/adamantine and magic; **Immune** fire, mind-affecting effects; **Resist** cold 20, electricity 20, sonic 20; **SR** 23
Weaknesses vulnerable to *protection from evil*

Speed 40 ft.
Melee 4 claws +14 (1d4+1)
Special Attacks body thief, sneak attack +3d6, hand of the apprentice 7/day (ranged touch +11)
Spell-Like Abilities (CL 8th; melee touch +9):
Constant—*detect magic*
At will—*confusion* (DC 17, single target only), *daze monster* (DC 15, no HD limit), *inflict serious wounds* (DC 16), *invisibility*, *reduce size* (as reduce person but self only)
3/day—*cure moderate wounds*, *globe of invulnerability*
Spells Prepared (CL 3rd; melee touch +9, ranged touch +14):
2nd—*darkness*, *fog cloud*
1st—*magic missile*, *ray of enfeeblement* (DC 15), *shocking grasp*
0 (at will)—*acid splash*, *daze* (DC 14), *flare* (DC 14), *mage hand*
Specialist School Universalist

Str 12, **Dex** 23, **Con** 21, **Int** 19, **Wis** 21 (17), **Cha** 17
Base Atk +7; **CMB** +7; **CMD** 24 (28 vs. trip)
Feats Combat Casting, Dodge, Improved Initiative, Iron Will, Scribe Scroll, Toughness, Weapon Finesse
Skills Acrobatics +10 (+14 jump), Bluff +19, Disguise +11, Escape Artist +10, Intimidate +10, Knowledge (arcana) +11, Knowledge (dungeoneering) +11, Knowledge (local) +15, Knowledge (nature) +11, Knowledge (planes) +11, Perception +24, Sense Motive +13, Spellcraft +11, Stealth +29, Use Magic Device +11; **Racial Modifiers** +8 Bluff, +8 Perception, +8 Stealth
Languages Undercommon (cannot speak); telepathy 100 ft.
SQ arcane bond (object [amulet] [1/day])
Gear arcane bond amulet, *headband of inspired wisdom +4*

Body Thief (Su) As a full-round action that provokes an attack of opportunity, an intellect devourer can reduce its size, crawl into the mouth of a helpless or dead creature, and burrow into the victim's skull to devour its brain. This is a coup de grace attempt that inflicts 8d4+3d6+8 points of damage. If the victim is slain (or already dead), the intellect devourer usurps control of the body and may use it as its own, as if it controlled the target via a *dominate* *monster* spell. The intellect devourer has full access to all of the host's defensive and offensive abilities save for spellcasting and spell-like abilities (although the intellect devourer can still use its own spell-like abilities). A host body may not have been dead for longer than 1 day for this ability to function, and even successfully inhabited bodies decay to uselessness in 7 days (unless this time is extended via *gentle repose*). As long as the intellect devourer occupies the body, it knows (and can speak) the languages known by the victim and basic information about the victim's identity and personality, yet has none of the victim's specific memories or knowledge. Damage done to a host body does not harm the intellect devourer, and if the host body is slain, the intellect devourer emerges and is dazed for 1 round. *Raise dead* cannot restore a victim of body theft, but *resurrection* or more powerful magic can.

Vulnerable to *Protection from Evil* (Ex) An intellect devourer is treated as a summoned creature for the purpose of determining how it is affected by a *protection from evil* spell.

INTELLECT DEVOURERS (3) **CR 8**
XP 4,800
hp 84 (*Pathfinder Roleplaying Game Bestiary* "Intellect Devourer")

Tactics: The intellect devourers spy on the PCs through their scrying pool. As PCs approach the door to their lair, they spring their trap. They first use *invisibility* to move from their chamber to face the PCs from the front and the rear; they aim their *daze monster* and *confusion* so that PCs are caught in the wash of their multiple mind-numbing force. As the PCs reel from the mental attack, the intellect devourers' use *daze monster* again, seeking to catch everyone who survived the first blast. Two of the intellect devourers then use *invisibility* to move next to PCs who are farthest from the rest of the group and begin attempting sneak attacks.

Treasure: Amongst the silks and lacquered boxes of the intellect devourers' chamber are three metal coffers containing the following potions; *potion of cure serious wounds* (CL 6th), *potion of enlarge* (CL 5th), the 6 lacquered boxes are worth 200 gp each. Hanging silks of exquisite craftsmanship are valued at 200 gp each.

11: Tomb of Athransma (CR 21)

The PCs can only open these adamantine doors with the key that is found in magical box from **Area C3**. Casting *detect magic* upon the door reveals these words scribed with *arcane mark.*

> *"Fools you are to have come this far. Know thou that you have been warned Athransma's mercy goes only so far. Enter and be destroyed says the cat to the mouse when he has tired of his toys."*

Beyond the huge adamantine doors lies a chamber of opulence and rot. The dust of centuries clings to what must have once been finely crafted hangings of crushed velvet. The floor is inlaid with a summoner's pentagram exquisitely set with silver and platinum. Paintings with images long since worn away lie in piles with urns of gems and precious coins from antiquity, all finely covered in a film of dust. A large stone dais stands in the center of the chamber dominating the room, its stone slab swirling with arcane markings over every inch. There standing in his glorious rot with a bejeweled crown upon his skull is the face of evil personified: the lich Athransma. A black fire glows from the empty sockets of his eyes as he grasps his staff tightly in his right hand and an opened book in his left. Athransma's grating voice is filled with a millennium of dust from the grave as he hisses his incantations, interwoven with taunts against the PCs for disturbing his tomb.

> "Now grave robbers, there is this question. Do I slay you now and be forever done with you and your meddling, or do I respect such power for having survived thus far and send you on a task for me, sparing your lives in return? Merciful it is said I be, so a merciful fate I offer. In your quest to plunder my tomb, I offer a chance for you now to choose you own doom!"

If the PCs answer that they wish to be spared, Athransma directs them to **Area 7**, hoping that the PCs find a way where powerful liches and intellect devourers have failed, or are destroyed in the effort — which would suit Athransma just fine.

ATHRANSMA **CR 21**
XP 409,600
Male human lich wizard 20 (*Pathfinder Roleplaying Game Bestiary* "Lich")
CE Medium undead (augmented humanoid, human)
Init +1; **Senses** darkvision 60 ft.; **Perception** +34
Aura fear aura (DC 22)

AC 27, touch 16, flat-footed 26 (+6 armor, +1 Dex, +3 deflection, +5 natural)
hp 152 (20d6+40 plus 40)
Fort +13; **Ref** +12; **Will** +20; +4 vs. channeled energy
Defensive Abilities channel resistance +4, rejuvenation;
DR 15/bludgeoning and magic; **Immune** cold, electricity, polymorph, undead traits; **Resist** fire 10

Speed 30 ft.
Melee *staff of power* +12/+7 (1d6+2), or touch +10 (1d8+10 plus paralysis; DC 22)
Ranged mwk light crossbow +12/+7 (1d8/19–20)

Special Attacks metamagic mastery (7/day), paralyzing touch, hand of the apprentice 9/day (ranged touch +16)

Spells Prepared (CL 20th; melee touch +10, ranged touch +11):
9th—*imprisonment* (DC 25), *power word kill* (x2), *wail of the banshee* (DC 25)
8th—*horrid wilting* (DC 24), *incendiary cloud* (DC 24), *power word stun, trap the soul* (DC 24)
7th—*finger of death* (DC 23), *forcecage* (DC 23), *greater teleport, spell turning*
6th—*antimagic field, chain lightning* (x2) (DC 22), *circle of death* (DC 22), *mass suggestion* (DC 22)
5th—*cone of cold* (x2) (DC 21), *dominate person* (x2) (DC 21), *wall of stone* (DC 21)
4th—*beast shape II, enervation* (x2), *fire shield, ice storm*
3rd—*blink, fly, hold person* (DC 19), *lightning bolt* (DC 19), *magic circle against good*
2nd—*blindness/deafness* (x2) (DC 18), *darkness, resist energy, web* (x2) (DC 18)
1st—*burning hands* (x2) (DC 17), *magic missile* (x2), *ray of enfeeblement* (DC 17), *shocking grasp*
0 (at will)—*dancing lights, daze* (DC 16), *flare* (DC 16), *resistance*
Specialist School Universalist

Str 11, **Dex** 12, **Con** —, **Int** 23, **Wis** 16, **Cha** 14
Base Atk +10; **CMB** +10; **CMD** 26
Feats Brew Potion, Combat Casting, Craft Rod, Craft Wand, Craft Wondrous Item, Empower Spell, Enlarge Spell, Extend Spell, Leadership, Maximize Spell, Quicken Spell, Scribe Scroll, Silent Spell, Spell Mastery (*finger of death, greater dispel magic, incendiary cloud, lightning bolt, magic missile, power word kill*), Still Spell, Toughness
Skills Craft (alchemy) +29, Fly +24, Intimidate +25, Knowledge (arcana) +29, Perception +34, Profession (herbalist) +26, Sense Motive +34, Spellcraft +29, Stealth +32; **Racial Modifiers** +8 Perception, +8 Sense Motive, +8 Stealth
SQ arcane bond (object [*staff of power*] [1/day])
Combat Gear *rod of absorption* (50 spell levels), *scroll of planar binding, shapechange, maze*, 2 *scrolls of teleport, staff of power, wand of fireball* (22 charges); **Other Gear** *staff of power* (32 charges), masterwork light crossbow, 20 masterwork crossbow bolts, *bracers of armor +6, cloak of resistance +3, ring of minor fire resistance, ring of protection +3*, belt pouch, 3 black pearls (500 gp ea.), 400 gp
Spellbook: 0—all; 1st—*burning hands, cause fear, chill touch, comprehend languages, feather fall, mage armor, magic missile, ray of enfeeblement, shocking grasp, true strike*; 2nd—*arcane lock, blindness/deafness, darkness, knock, resist energy, web*; 3rd—*blink, fly, haste, hold person, lightning bolt, magic circle against good*; 4th—*beast shape II, dimension door, elemental body I, enervation, fire shield, ice storm*; 5th—*cloudkill, cone of cold, dominate person, dream, wall of stone*; 6th—*antimagic field, chain lightning, circle of death, greater dispel magic, mass suggestion*; 7th—*control undead, finger of death, forcecage, greater teleport, power word blind, spell turning*; 8th—*horrid wilting, incendiary cloud, power word stun, symbol of death, trap the soul*; 9th—*imprisonment, meteor swarm, power word kill, wail of the banshee*

Tactics: Athransma begins combat by casting *greater dispelling* on the PCs. On subsequent rounds he uses *blink*, followed by *chain lightning* on the PCs, targeting either a cleric or mage for the first blast. The following round he attempts to *force cage* on fighters who threaten him followed by *horrid wilting* centered on the most characters he can catch within its area of effect. The following round he casts *spell turning* on himself followed by *wail of the banshee*. Next he uses *mass suggestion*, attempting to force the PCs to drop their weapons and raise their hands as he uses *power word kill* on survivors. If Athransma is notified ahead of time of a hostile threat, he has already put up *spell turning* and *blink*. Against stronger opponents he starts with the *wail of the banshee*, and *chain lightning*, followed by *incendiary cloud* and *horrid wilting*.

Athransma has found through his research with his assistant Tholka Khet and the otherworldly knowledge possessed of their ally Tlip Lopodi and his intellect devourer cohorts that it was the Ancients who bound the mighty Eliphaz within the volcano. It is these same Ancients whose inanimate forms keep Eliphaz deep in his slumber through some unknown combination of arcane and divine power. The great mage Athransma made it his goal during his lifetime to uncover the secrets of the Ancients, knowing that to possess the power to bind a primeval god unmoving for ten thousand years is true power. When age began to wear upon Athransma prepared the proper phylacteries and performed the powerful rituals, transforming into a mighty lich. Now, with an unlimited lifespan to work with he could continue his research of the Ancients and attempt to rouse Eliphaz from his slumber. Failing this Athransma seeks to twist to his will the Ancients, a pair of astral devas locked for an eternity within the pillars of light.

Treasure: 3,400 pp, 2,500 gp in gems, three golden ewers (200 gp each). Several old spell books of Athransma are on a bookshelf along the back wall containing all of Athransma's 1st- through 5th-level spells, a *Letek're stone* bearing the same script as the base of the pillar in **Area 4**, a scroll detailing the ritual for raising Eliphaz, which mentions the *elemental belt*.

His high level spellbooks are hidden within a *secret chest* which requires the use of *legend lore*, or some other such divination spell to uncover the magic words to recover these books. The chest is trapped with a Heightened *bestow curse* which triggers automatically upon the touch of anyone but Athransma. Every page of his high-level spell books is covered in *illusory script* to baffle those thieves who would delve the depths of his knowledge.

HEIGHTENED *BESTOW CURSE* TRAP **CR 10**
XP 9,600
Type magic; **Perception** DC 34; **Disable Device** DC 34

Trigger touch; **Reset** none
Effect spell effect (Heightened *bestow curse* [9th-level]; –6 Charisma; DC 23 Will resists); **Note:** A failed Will save results in the victim suffering boils on his face and body spell out the words: *"I am a thief. I stole from the Mighty Athransma!"*

Final Confrontations (CR 17+)

The following section details the possible ramifications of freeing Eliphaz from his slumber, or dirty dealings with Athransma.

The PCs Slay Athransma, and free Eliphaz

In this scenario, the PCs, having defeated Athransma, use the *Letek're stones* and rituals described in Athransma's personal effects to raise Eliphaz from his prison in the dead volcanic cone. Eliphaz goes into a rage, attacking the PCs with every power and weapon at his disposal. It should be noted that using the *Letek're stones* in this manner destroys the Ancients forever.

PCs Free the Ancients

After the second Ancient is freed from his pillar of light the maze of Ancients begins to rock and sway with the shocks of an earthquake. Every round the PCs remain within the Maze of Ancients, they must succeed on a cumulative Reflex save (starting at DC 10, +1 per round spent within the maze). If the Reflex save rolled is a natural 1, the individual must succeed on a second Reflex save (DC 15, +1 per round spent within the maze) or fall over the side. Success on the second roll means they have caught hold of the edge of the maze. Failure means they fall down the chasm to their doom. Players entering any chamber of the Maze may use *teleport* or *dimension door* to escape the Maze.

Upon escaping the maze the PCs are greeted by the sight of a great rumbling from the volcano upon the Isle of Eliphaz. The Ancients appear within a moment before the PCs, warning them that the slumbering one is awakening. The Ancients reiterate their plan if the PCs are still reluctant to stop Athransma and Eliphaz. The Ancients intend to do their best to draw off Eliphaz, however the PCs must enter the Elemental's bed of stone as soon as he rises and seize the *elemental belt*. With the *elemental belt*, a druid may find it possible to command the elemental to rejoin the earth forever.

The devas offer to fly the characters over to the island of Eliphaz, setting down near the volcano's edge but can only move two players at a time. Ten rounds after the PCs exit the **Maze of Ancients** the top of the volcano collapses. A huge being made of stone rippling with waves of heat rises from the center of the volcanic crater where the tower once stood. Over 25 feet tall and armed with a greatsword glowing hot in his massive fists, Eliphaz roars with rage and exultation at being freed after all these thousands of years. Eliphaz waves his hand and summons a **Huge fire elemental**, a **Huge earth elemental**, and an **efreeti** to guard his resting place. With a rumble that seems as if it could rip the world asunder, the mighty god Eliphaz steps from the crater, his lava-like, glowing eyes seeking the devas. He speaks, his voice a roar like a lava flow:

> "Arisen from my prison in the earth Eliphaz shall slake his thirst, destruction to things green with sap and red with blood, for they do not respect the living stone, and seek to shape it as their own. Eliphaz shall teach them of their insolence!"

Eliphaz moves quickly to do battle with the astral devas, ignoring the PCs unless he is attacked and takes damage from one of them, at which time he unleashes his fury upon the pathetic mortal offenders.

ELIPHAZ **CR 17**
XP 102,400
hp 270 (See **New Monsters** at the end of this adventure for details)

Within the crater where the tower once stood is an island surrounded by a 20-foot wide ring of lava. Three great ward stones lie broken at the bottom where the elemental's hands and feet were bound. Upon an outcropping of rock is a wide belt fashioned out of rare stone. Eliphaz uses his summoning abilities to summon guardians for the *elemental belt*. All three fight as a team and must be overcome before *elemental belt* can be won. See the **New Magic Item** at the end of this adventure for details.

Written upon the stone where *elemental belt* sits is are the following words written in the Druidic Tongue:

> *"Servant of Nature Blessed Be through earthly magic set we free, in turn to do the celestial task. Let the elemental belt set thee on the path for from the earth's great fire he comes at last with Primal Fury and Volcanic Blast, perform the task lest ye sojourn and bind forever the Elemental in his otherworldly home. Speak the words written here:*
>
> *Eliphaz return to that place of fire from whence you came! Your ties to this world are torn asunder! Let the earth open up and swallow you under!*
>
> *Say three times with a commanding voice; he must obey and has no choice."*

Only a druid can use the *elemental belt* to command Eliphaz to return to his home plane, never to bother this world again. The druid must succeed on a DC 20 concentration check and spend one round chanting the above incantation. Eliphaz, of course, attempts to disrupt the druid from her task if he is able. At this point, if the astral devas are still alive, they do their best to distract him as he turns to rush against the one calling the words to send him home.

Once the druid has managed to shout the incantation three times, the earth beneath Eliphaz opens in a fiery abyss. The great elemental god screams in rage and is swallowed whole in a great flash of light.

The PCs Return the *Letek're stones* to Athransma:

Should the PCs return to Athransma with the *Letek're stone* from **Area 7: The Shrine of the Ancients,** Athransma cackles with glee shouting:

> "At last I have them! Now the pillars of the Ancients fall and Eliphaz shall rise again and the world will see Athransma's true mercy! Thank you fools. Take whatever you desire from this treasure trove, for the treasure I now possess is greater than any shining gold or twinkling of gems."

Athransma quickly attempts to depart the chamber via *dimension door*, heading to **Area 9**. As a parting shot he unleashes a *chain lightning* spell centered on the toughest looking player character. Once within his laboratory, he begins the ritual to bring down the pillars of light and destroy the Ancients, taking control of Eliphaz as his personal slave. The ritual takes 10 rounds to complete, and he cannot be interrupted in this time or the ritual fails. If the ritual fails, the Ancients are destroyed and Eliphaz is freed, but Athransma has no control over him. Eliphaz now seeks to destroy him. At the end of the 10 rounds, the roof of **Area 9** disappears. The entire room experiences a *plane shift*; it is now hovering over the volcano as Eliphaz rises from his slumber, completely under the command of Athransma.

Note: When all three *Letek're stones* are placed on their special altars within the laboratory of Athransma, the laboratory gains the abilities of a *carpet of flying* with the following abilities: Size 15 ft. by 15 ft.; Capacity 24,00 lbs.; Speed 80 ft. Only Athransma knows the command words to make his laboratory fly successfully.

All is not Lost

Should this unfortunate series of events take place, remember that the players may still have the box from **Area C3**. Simply getting back to the larger island and turning the key causes the floating laboratory to crash 50 feet to the ground leaving Athransma with only his undead powers to protect him. Of course there is still Eliphaz to deal with, however without the magic of the *Letek're stones* to control him he soon sees Athransma as the villain. Eliphaz waits until the PCs have destroyed the lich. Eliphaz thanks them for his freedom and offers them the *elemental belt* as a token of his respect, quickly departing the world for his true home on a demiplane of fire and earth. He never returns.

New Magic Items

Elemental Belt (Artifact)

Aura strong universal; **CL** 20th
Slot belt; **Weight** 2 lbs.

DESCRIPTION

The elemental belt consists of four very thin plates of jade, malachite, bloodstone and obsidian attached to a wide belt made from various animal pelts. These fine stone plates are ornately carved with symbols of the four elements of Fire, Earth, Water, and Wind.When worn by a druid, the elemental belt grants the following benefits:

• A +4 enhancement bonus to Strength, a +4 enhancement bonus to Wisdom, and a +3 deflection bonus to AC.

• Fire resistance 15.

• The ability to cast stoneskin once per day.

• The elemental belt allows the user to command any elemental of up to Huge size once per day. The targeted elemental must succeed on a DC 20 Will save or come under the complete control of the druid for up to 24 hours or until dismissed by the druid. This power includes elementals summoned by others, which the druid can turn upon their master.

While wearing this belt, the druid may use any of their spells while in animal form as if he possessed the Natural Spell feat.

DESTRUCTION

The belt can be destroyed if heated in a gas-fed forge and beaten by an adamantine hammer upon a cold iron anvil by an iron golem.

Letek're Stone

The Letek're stones are made from a single piece of a solid jade-like stone that is impossible to break. They were carved in ancient times by the first Great Druid and tell the story of the traditional druidic creation epic. Their value as works of art is well over 5,000 gp each. The magic within the Letek're stones is subsumed as soon as either the Ancients are freed, or Eliphaz is deposed.

New Monster: Eliphaz

This massive elemental appears as a nearly perfect humanoid specimen made completely of semi molten stone. Waves of heat pour off of its rocky skin. As it moves cracks appear revealing spider-webs of glowing lava across its surface. It wields within its great fists of stone a greatsword of red glowing iron which its swings with deadly ferocity.

ELIPHAZ **CR 17**
XP 102,400
CN Gargantuan outsider (earth, elemental, extraplanar, fire)
Init +7; **Senses** darkvision 60 ft.; **Perception** +29
Aura heat (30 ft., 1d8 fire, DC 28 Fortitude save resists)

AC 30, touch 9, flat-footed 27 (+3 Dex, +21 natural, –4 size)
hp 270 (20d10+160)
Fort +14; **Ref** +15; **Will** +18
Defensive Abilities melt weapons; **DR** 20/magic; **Immune** elemental traits, fire; **Resist** type amount; **SR** 20

Speed 40 ft.
Melee greatsword +28/+23/+18/+12 (6d6+15/17–20 plus 2d6 burn), 2 slams +26 (2d6+10 plus 2d6 burn)
Space 20 ft.; **Reach** 20 ft.
Special Attacks burn (2d6, DC 28), magmaball (3/day), magma spray
Spell-like Abilities (CL 20th):
At will—*wall of fire*
1/day—*summon elemental* (one elder fire or earth elemental, 1d3 Huge fire or earth elementals, 1d3 efreet or stone giants, 1d6 salamanders or xorns, or 3d6 fire or earth mephits)

Str 30, **Dex** 17, **Con** 26, **Int** 20, **Wis** 23, **Cha** 28
Base Atk +20; **CMB** +34; **CMD** 47
Feats Cleave, Great Cleave, Great Fortitude, Improved Critical (greatsword), Improved Initiative, Iron Will, Lightning Reflexes, Power Attack, Weapon Focus (greatsword), Whirlwind Attack
Skills Bluff +32, Diplomacy +32, Intimidate +32, Knowledge (arcana) +25, Knowledge (history) +28, Knowledge (local) +25, Knowledge (nature) +28, Knowledge (planes) +28, Perception +29, Sense Motive +29, Stealth +14
Languages Common, Draconic, Druidic, Ignan, Sylvan, Terran, Undercommon
Combat Gear masterwork fire-immune greatsword

Environment any land
Organization unique, or troupe (Eliphaz plus 1–4 fire elementals and 1–4 earth elementals)
Treasure triple

Melt Weapons (Ex) Any non-magical slashing or piercing metal weapon that strikes Eliphaz must succeed on a DC 33 a Fortitude save or melt away into slag before it can injure him.
Magmaball (Su) 3/day — 20d6 fire damage, burns for 1d3 rounds for 10d6 fire damage per round. Other than that, the *magmaball* functions as a *fireball* spell cast as a 20th level sorcerer. Targets are allowed a DC 33 Reflex save for half damage
Magma Spray (Ex): If Eliphaz is hit with a slashing or piercing weapon, magma sprays from the wound for one round. The attacker must succeed on a DC 33 Reflex save or take 4d6 points of fire damage. The magma burns for 1d3 rounds and deals 2d6 points of damage per round.

Eliphaz is a wild elemental spirit. In the days when the world was young he felt great anger that things of flesh and blood, sap and leaf were given higher standing on the mortal realm than things of fire and stone. Quietly his rage built until at last he began taking his vengeance out upon all living things. After a great battle in which many demons and celestial beings were destroyed trying to vanquish his indomitable force of elemental will, three Deva finally bound Eliphaz within a volcano. There they too were forced to bind themselves to the mortal world in the event he should ever escape and again make war upon living things.

Eliphaz typically uses his summoning ability, followed by throwing a magmaball into the largest gathering of his enemies, even if they are at his feet, for he is immune to such energies. Should the enemy be foolish enough to gather around him within his reach, Eliphaz gladly makes them pay with his Whirlwind attack.

New Monster: Guardian Familiar

This cat-like creature has sleek golden fur that appears almost metallic with its sheen. Its slitted, yellow eyes glow faintly with a malevolent aura.

GUARDIAN FAMILIAR **CR 1/2**
XP 135
LE Tiny outsider (evil, extraplanar)

Init +2; **Senses** darkvision 60 ft.; **Perception** +5

AC 14, touch 14, flat-footed 12 (+2 Dex, +2 size)
hp 5 (1d10)
Fort +0; **Ref** +4; **Will** +3
DR 5/magic; **Resist** cold 5, fire 5; **SR** 11

Speed 30 ft.
Melee 2 claws +5 (1d2–4), bite +4 (1d3–4)
Space 2 1/2 ft.; **Reach** 0 ft.

Str 3, **Dex** 15, **Con** 10, **Int** 10, **Wis** 12, **Cha** 10
Base Atk +1; **CMB** –5; **CMD** 7 (11 vs. trip)
Feats Weapon Finesse
Skills Acrobatics +6, Climb +10, Perception +5, Sense Motive +5, Stealth +14, Survival +5; **Racial Modifiers** +4 Climb, +4 Stealth
Languages Infernal
SQ nine lives

Environment any
Organization solitary
Treasure none (although it may be guarding a significant treasure)

Nine Lives (Su) The guardian familiar has nine lives. Each time it is slain it is reborn in 1d2 rounds, stronger than it was in its previous incarnation. If slain a ninth time, it remains dead. Each time it is slain and reborn, the guardian familiar increases in power as shown on the table below. When its Strength score equals or surpasses its Dexterity score, it loses the Weapon Finesse feats and gains the Weapon Focus (bite) feats. The damage dice for its claws and bite also increase to the next larger die as it grows in size (from 1d2 to 1d3; from 1d3 to 1d4, etc.). This ability cannot be dispelled or negated except by the following: *disintegrate*, *flesh to stone*, *miracle*, *temporal stasis*, or *wish*. A *dismissal* spell sends the guardian familiar back to its plane of origin.

When awarding XP for defeating a guardian familiar, only award XP for the highest CR at which the PCs defeated it. If the PCs defeat a guardian familiar and return to defeat it again later, award XP equal to the difference between the previous CR and the current one. For example, if the PCs defeat a guardian familiar 4 times, they receive XP for a CR 2 encounter. If they later return and defeat it when it is CR 4, they get XP equal to the difference between a CR 2 and CR 4 encounter.

Guardian familiars resemble fiendish golden cats. They are often summed evil wizards and witches to guard doorways and treasures. Even in Hell, guardian familiars are known for their tenacity, for once given a task they are relentless in the execution of their duty.

Guardian Familiar Nine Lives

Life	Bonus*	AC	Size	DR/ Resistances	Saves**	CR	SR	Str	Dex	Con
1	+1	+0	Tiny	5	+0	1/2	11	+0	+0	+0
2	+2	+1	Tiny	5	+0	1/2	11	+0	+0	+0
3	+3	+2	Small	5	+1	2	13	+4	–2	+2
4	+4	+3	Small	5	+1	2	13	+0	+0	+0
5	+5	+4	Medium	10	+2	4	15	+4	–2	+4
6	+6	+5	Medium	10	+2	4	15	+0	+0	+0
7	+7	+6	Large	10	+3	6	17	+8	–2	+4
8	+8	+7	Large	10	+3	6	17	+0	+0	+0
9	+9	+8	Huge	10	+4	8	19	+8	–2	+4

*This bonus applies to attacks, CMB, CMD, and skill checks.
**This bonus applies to all saving throws.